J.G. BALLARD was born [...] was a businessman. Foll[...] and his family were placed in a civilian prison camp. They returned to England in 1946. After two years at Cambridge, where he read medicine, Ballard worked as a copywriter and Covent Garden porter before going to Canada with the RAF. He started writing short stories in the late 1950s, while working on a scientific journal. His first major novel, *The Drowned World*, was published in 1962. His acclaimed novels include *The Crystal World*, *The Atrocity Exhibition*, *Crash* (filmed by David Cronenberg), *High-Rise*, *The Unlimited Dream Company*, *The Kindness of Women* (the sequel to *Empire of the Sun*), *Cocaine Nights*, *Super-Cannes*, *Millennium People* and, most recently, *Kingdom Come*.

Visit www.AuthorTracker.co.uk for exclusive information on your favourite HarperCollins authors.

From the reviews of *The Complete Short Stories*:

'This marvellous, inexhaustible book is a monument at the end of fertile lands ... Ballard is a superb writer; few could publish a book of this size which is never boring, where the invention never flags. Unfailingly ingenious and perverse'   PHILIP HENSHER, *Daily Telegraph*

'A feast, and not only for those who think – as I do – that Ballard has long been Britain's most original and inventive writer. For anyone bored with the stale conventions of mainstream fiction, his stories of stilled time, desolate beauty and personal fulfilment in extreme situations will be sheer delight'   JOHN GRAY, *New Statesman*

'[J.G. Ballard has] one of the most haunting, cogent and individual imaginations in contemporary literature'
WILLIAM BOYD, *Mail on Sunday*

'Thank God for J.G. Ballard and his short stories in which wonder and awe never fade. It is no exaggeration to say that Ballard's stories are beyond compare. This is a collection of tales and fables to be savoured by admirers and newcomers alike'
ROBERT EDRIC, *Spectator*

'This collection is essential for anyone who cares about contemporary fiction'   *Observer*

By the same author

The Drowned World
The Voices of Time
The Terminal Beach
The Drought
The Crystal World
The Day of Forever
The Venus Hunters
The Disaster Area
The Atrocity Exhibition
Vermilion Sands
Crash
Concrete Island
High-Rise
Low-Flying Aircraft
The Unlimited Dream Company
Hello America
Myths of the Near Future
Empire of the Sun
Running Wild
The Day of Creation
War Fever
The Kindness of Women
Rushing to Paradise
A User's Guide to the Millennium
Cocaine Nights
Super-Cannes
Millennium People
Kingdom Come

J.G. BALLARD

The Complete Short Stories

VOLUME I

HARPER PERENNIAL
London, New York, Toronto and Sydney

Harper Perennial
An imprint of HarperCollins*Publishers*
77–85 Fulham Palace Road
Hammersmith
London W6 8JB

www.harperperennial.co.uk

This edition published by Harper Perennial 2006

4

First published in Great Britain by Flamingo in 2001
First published in paperback by Flamingo in 2002

This collection copyright © J.G. Ballard 2001

Most of the stories in this book appeared in the following smaller collections:

The Voices of Time © J.G. Ballard 1963
The Terminal Beach © J.G. Ballard 1964

J.G. Ballard asserts the moral right to
be identified as the author of this work.

This collection is entirely a work of fiction. The names,
characters and incidents portrayed in it are the work of the
author's imagination. Any resemblance to actual persons,
living or dead, events or localities is entirely coincidental.

A catalogue record for this book is available from the British Library

ISBN-13: 978-0-00-724229-0
ISBN-10: 0-00-724229-8

Typeset in Minion with Helvetica Neue display by
Palimpsest Book Production Limited, Grangemouth, Stirlingshire

Printed and bound in Great Britain by Clays Ltd, St Ives plc

All rights reserved. No part of this publication may be
reproduced, stored in a retrieval system, or transmitted,
in any form or by any means, electronic, mechanical,
photocopying, recording or otherwise, without the prior
permission of the publishers.

This book is sold subject to the condition that it shall not,
by way of trade or otherwise, be lent, re-sold, hired out or
otherwise circulated without the publisher's prior consent
in any form of binding or cover other than that in which it
is published and without a similar condition including this
condition being imposed on the subsequent purchaser.

Contents

Introduction	vii
Prima Belladonna	1
Escapement	16
The Concentration City	30
Venus Smiles	51
Manhole 69	66
Track 12	90
The Waiting Grounds	96
Now: Zero	128
The Sound-Sweep	142
Zone of Terror	184
Chronopolis	202
The Voices of Time	228
The Last World of Mr Goddard	264
Studio 5, The Stars	281
Deep End	317
The Overloaded Man	330
Mr F. is Mr F.	345
Billennium	362
The Gentle Assassin	379
The Insane Ones	393
The Garden of Time	405
The Thousand Dreams of Stellavista	414
Thirteen to Centaurus	436
Passport to Eternity	461

The Cage of Sand	482
The Watch-Towers	507
The Singing Statues	537
The Man on the 99th Floor	550
The Subliminal Man	559
The Reptile Enclosure	578
A Question of Re-Entry	590
The Time-Tombs	623
Now Wakes the Sea	641
The Venus Hunters	652
End-Game	685
Minus One	708
The Sudden Afternoon	721
The Screen Game	736
Time of Passage	761

INTRODUCTION

Short stories are the loose change in the treasury of fiction, easily ignored beside the wealth of novels available, an over-valued currency that often turns out to be counterfeit. At its best, in Borges, Ray Bradbury and Edgar Allan Poe, the short story is coined from precious metal, a glint of gold that will glow for ever in the deep purse of your imagination.

Short stories have always been important to me. I like their snapshot quality, their ability to focus intensely on a single subject. They're also a useful way of trying out the ideas later developed at novel length. Almost all my novels were first hinted at in short stories, and readers of *The Crystal World*, *Crash* and *Empire of the Sun* will find their seeds germinating somewhere in this collection.

When I started writing, fifty years ago, short stories were immensely popular with readers, and some newspapers printed a new short story every day. Sadly, I think that people at present have lost the knack of reading short stories, a response perhaps to the baggy and long-winded narratives of television serials. Young writers, myself included, have always seen their first novels as a kind of virility test, but so many novels published today would have been better if they had been recast as short stories. Curiously, there are many perfect short stories, but no perfect novels.

The short story still survives, especially in science fiction, which makes the most of its closeness to the folk tale and the parable. Many of the stories in this collection were first published in science fiction magazines, though readers at the time loudly complained that they weren't science fiction at all.

But I was interested in the real future that I could see approaching, and less in the invented future that science fiction preferred. The future, needless to say, is a dangerous area to enter, heavily mined and with a tendency to turn and bite your ankles as you stride forward. A correspondent recently pointed out to me that the poetry-writing computers in *Vermilion Sands* are powered by valves. And why don't all those sleek people living in the future have PCs and pagers?

I could only reply that *Vermilion Sands* isn't set in the future at all, but in a kind of visionary present – a description that fits the stories in this book and almost everything else I have written. But oh for a steam-powered computer and a wind-driven television set. Now, there's an idea for a short story ...

J.G. Ballard, 2001

PRIMA BELLADONNA

I first met Jane Ciracylides during the Recess, that world slump of boredom, lethargy and high summer which carried us all so blissfully through ten unforgettable years, and I suppose that may have had a lot to do with what went on between us. Certainly I can't believe I could make myself as ridiculous now, but then again, it might have been just Jane herself.

Whatever else they said about her, everyone had to agree she was a beautiful girl, even if her genetic background was a little mixed. The gossips at Vermilion Sands soon decided there was a good deal of mutant in her, because she had a rich patina-golden skin and what looked like insects for eyes, but that didn't bother either myself or any of my friends, one or two of whom, like Tony Miles and Harry Devine, have never since been quite the same to their wives.

We spent most of our time in those days on the balcony of my apartment off Beach Drive, drinking beer – we always kept a useful supply stacked in the refrigerator of my music shop on the street level – yarning in a desultory way and playing i-Go, a sort of decelerated chess which was popular then. None of the others ever did any work; Harry was an architect and Tony Miles sometimes sold a few ceramics to the tourists, but I usually put a couple of hours in at the shop each morning, getting off the foreign orders and turning the beer.

One particularly hot lazy day I'd just finished wrapping up a delicate soprano mimosa wanted by the Hamburg Oratorio Society when Harry phoned down from the balcony.

'Parker's Choro-Flora?' he said. 'You're guilty of overproduction. Come up here. Tony and I have something beautiful to show you.'

When I went up I found them grinning happily like two dogs who had just discovered an interesting tree.

'Well?' I asked. 'Where is it?'

Tony tilted his head slightly. 'Over there.'

I looked up and down the street, and across the face of the apartment house opposite.

'Careful,' he warned me. 'Don't gape at her.'

I slid into one of the wicker chairs and craned my head round cautiously.

'Fourth floor,' Harry elaborated slowly, out of the side of his mouth. 'One left from the balcony opposite. Happy now?'

'Dreaming,' I told him, taking a long slow focus on her. 'I wonder what else she can do?'

Harry and Tony sighed thankfully. 'Well?' Tony asked.

'She's out of my league,' I said. 'But you two shouldn't have any trouble. Go over and tell her how much she needs you.'

Harry groaned. 'Don't you realize, this one is poetic, emergent, something straight out of the primal apocalyptic sea. She's probably divine.'

The woman was strolling around the lounge, rearranging the furniture, wearing almost nothing except a large metallic hat. Even in shadow the sinuous lines of her thighs and shoulders gleamed gold and burning. She was a walking galaxy of light. Vermilion Sands had never seen anything like her.

'The approach has got to be equivocal,' Harry continued, gazing into his beer. 'Shy, almost mystical. Nothing urgent or grabbing.'

The woman stooped down to unpack a suitcase and the metal vanes of her hat fluttered over her face. She saw us staring at her, looked around for a moment and lowered the blinds.

We sat back and looked thoughtfully at each other, like three triumvirs deciding how to divide an empire, not saying too much, and one eye watching for any chance of a double-deal.

Five minutes later the singing started.

At first I thought it was one of the azalea trios in trouble with an alkaline pH, but the frequencies were too high. They were almost out of the audible range, a thin tremolo quaver which came out of nowhere and rose up the back of the skull.

Harry and Tony frowned at me.

'Your livestock's unhappy about something,' Tony told me. 'Can you quieten it down?'

'It's not the plants,' I told him. 'Can't be.'

The sound mounted in intensity, scraping the edges off my occipital bones. I was about to go down to the shop when Harry and Tony leapt out of their chairs and dived back against the wall.

'Steve, look out!' Tony yelled at me. He pointed wildly at the table I was leaning on, picked up a chair and smashed it down on the glass top.

I stood up and brushed the fragments out of my hair.

'What the hell's the matter?'

Tony was looking down at the tangle of wickerwork tied round the metal struts of the table. Harry came forward and took my arm gingerly.

'That was close. You all right?'

'It's gone,' Tony said flatly. He looked carefully over the balcony floor and down over the rail into the street.

'What was it?' I asked.

Harry peered at me closely. 'Didn't you see it? It was about three inches from you. Emperor scorpion, big as a lobster.' He sat down weakly on a beer crate. 'Must have been a sonic one. The noise has gone now.'

After they'd left I cleared up the mess and had a quiet beer to myself. I could have sworn nothing had got on to the table.

On the balcony opposite, wearing a gown of ionized fibre, the golden woman was watching me.

I found out who she was the next morning. Tony and Harry were down at the beach with their wives, probably enlarging on the scorpion, and I was in the shop tuning up a Khan-Arachnid orchid with the UV lamp. It was a difficult bloom, with a normal full range of twenty-four octaves, but unless it got a lot of exercise it tended to relapse into neurotic minor-key transpositions which were the devil to break. And as the senior bloom in the shop it naturally affected all the others. Invariably when I opened the shop in the mornings, it sounded like a madhouse, but as soon as I'd fed the Arachnid and straightened out one or two pH gradients the rest promptly took their cues from it and dimmed down quietly in their control tanks, two-time, three-four, the multi-tones, all in perfect harmony.

There were only about a dozen true Arachnids in captivity; most of the others were either mutes or grafts from dicot stems, and I was lucky to have mine at all. I'd bought the place five years earlier from an old half-deaf man called Sayers, and the day before he left he moved a lot of rogue stock out to the garbage disposal scoop behind the apartment block. Reclaiming some of the tanks, I'd come across the Arachnid, thriving on a diet of algae and perished rubber tubing.

Why Sayers had wanted to throw it away I had never discovered. Before he came to Vermilion Sands he'd been a curator at the Kew Conservatoire where the first choro-flora had been bred, and had worked under the Director, Dr Mandel. As a young botanist of twenty-five Mandel had discovered the prime Arachnid in the Guiana forest. The orchid took its name from the Khan-Arachnid spider which pollinated the flower, simultaneously laying its own eggs in the fleshy ovule, guided, or as Mandel always insisted, actually mesmerized to it by the vibrations which the orchid's calyx emitted at pollination time. The first Arachnid orchids beamed out only a few random frequencies, but by cross-breeding and maintaining them artificially at the pollination stage Mandel had produced a strain that spanned a maximum of twenty-four octaves.

Not that he had ever been able to hear them. At the climax of his life's work Mandel, like Beethoven, was stone deaf, but apparently by merely looking at a blossom he could listen to its music. Strangely though, after he went deaf he never looked at an Arachnid.

That morning I could almost understand why. The orchid was in a vicious mood. First it refused to feed, and I had to coax it along in a fluoraldehyde flush, and then it started going ultra-sonic, which meant complaints from all the dog owners in the area. Finally it tried to fracture the tank by resonating.

The whole place was in uproar, and I was almost resigned to shutting them down and waking them all by hand individually – a backbreaking job with eighty tanks in the shop – when everything suddenly died away to a murmur.

I looked round and saw the golden-skinned woman walk in.

'Good morning,' I said. 'They must like you.'

She laughed pleasantly. 'Hello. Weren't they behaving?'

Under the black beach robe her skin was a softer, more mellow gold, and it was her eyes that held me. I could just see them under the wide-brimmed hat. Insect legs wavered delicately round two points of purple light.

She walked over to a bank of mixed ferns and stood looking at them. The ferns reached out towards her and trebled eagerly in their liquid fluted voices.

'Aren't they sweet?' she said, stroking the fronds gently. 'They need so much affection.'

Her voice was low in the register, a breath of cool sand pouring, with a lilt that gave it music.

'I've just come to Vermilion Sands,' she said, 'and my apartment seems awfully quiet. Perhaps if I had a flower, one would be enough, I shouldn't feel so lonely.'

I couldn't take my eyes off her.

'Yes,' I agreed, brisk and businesslike. 'What about something colourful? This Sumatra Samphire, say? It's a pedigree mezzo-soprano from the same follicle as the Bayreuth Festival Prima Belladonna.'

'No,' she said. 'It looks rather cruel.'

'Or this Louisiana Lute Lily? If you thin out its SO_2 it'll play some beautiful madrigals. I'll show you how to do it.'

She wasn't listening to me. Slowly, her hands raised in front of her breasts so that she almost seemed to be praying, she moved towards the display counter on which the Arachnid stood.

'How beautiful it is,' she said, gazing at the rich yellow and purple leaves hanging from the scarlet-ribbed vibrocalyx.

* * *

I followed her across the floor and switched on the Arachnid's audio so that she could hear it. Immediately the plant came to life. The leaves stiffened and filled with colour and the calyx inflated, its ribs sprung tautly. A few sharp disconnected notes spat out.

'Beautiful, but evil,' I said.

'Evil?' she repeated. 'No, proud.' She stepped closer to the orchid and looked down into its malevolent head. The Arachnid quivered and the spines on its stem arched and flexed menacingly.

'Careful,' I warned her. 'It's sensitive to the faintest respiratory sounds.'

'Quiet,' she said, waving me back. 'I think it wants to sing.'

'Those are only key fragments,' I told her. 'It doesn't perform. I use it as a frequency –'

'Listen!' She held my arm and squeezed it tightly.

A low, rhythmic fusion of melody had been coming from the plants around the shop, and mounting above them I heard a single stronger voice calling out, at first a thin high-pitched reed of sound that began to pulse and deepen and finally swelled into full baritone, raising the other plants in chorus about itself.

I had never heard the Arachnid sing before. I was listening to it open-eared when I felt a glow of heat burn against my arm. I turned and saw the woman staring intently at the plant, her skin aflame, the insects in her eyes writhing insanely. The Arachnid stretched out towards her, calyx erect, leaves like blood-red sabres.

I stepped round her quickly and switched off the argon feed. The Arachnid sank to a whimper, and around us there was a nightmarish babel of broken notes and voices toppling from high C's and L's into discord. A faint whispering of leaves moved over the silence.

The woman gripped the edge of the tank and gathered herself. Her skin dimmed and the insects in her eyes slowed to a delicate wavering.

'Why did you turn it off?' she asked heavily.

'I'm sorry,' I said. 'But I've got ten thousand dollars' worth of stock here and that sort of twelve-tone emotional storm can blow a lot of valves. Most of these plants aren't equipped for grand opera.'

She watched the Arachnid as the gas drained out of its calyx. One by one its leaves buckled and lost their colour.

'How much is it?' she asked me, opening her bag.

'It's not for sale,' I said. 'Frankly I've no idea how it picked up those bars –'

'Will a thousand dollars be enough?' she asked, her eyes fixed on me steadily.

'I can't,' I told her. 'I'd never be able to tune the others without it. Anyway,' I added, trying to smile, 'that Arachnid would be dead in ten minutes if you took it out of its vivarium. All these cylinders and leads would look a little odd inside your lounge.'

'Yes, of course,' she agreed, suddenly smiling back at me. 'I was stupid.' She gave the orchid a last backward glance and strolled away across the floor to the long Tchaikovsky section popular with the tourists.

'*Pathétique*,' she read off a label at random. 'I'll take this.'

I wrapped up the scabia and slipped the instructional booklet into the crate, keeping my eye on her all the time.

'Don't look so alarmed,' she said with amusement. 'I've never heard anything like that before.'

I wasn't alarmed. It was that thirty years at Vermilion Sands had narrowed my horizons.

'How long are you staying at Vermilion Sands?' I asked her.

'I open at the Casino tonight,' she said. She told me her name was Jane Ciracylides and that she was a speciality singer.

'Why don't you look in?' she asked, her eyes fluttering mischievously. 'I come on at eleven. You may find it interesting.'

I did. The next morning Vermilion Sands hummed. Jane created a sensation. After her performance three hundred people swore they'd seen everything from a choir of angels taking the vocal in the music of the spheres to Alexander's Ragtime Band. As for myself, perhaps I'd listened to too many flowers, but at least I knew where the scorpion on the balcony had come from.

Tony Miles had heard Sophie Tucker singing the 'St Louis Blues', and Harry, the elder Bach conducting the B Minor Mass.

They came round to the shop and argued over their respective performances while I wrestled with the flowers.

'Amazing,' Tony exclaimed. 'How does she do it? Tell me.'

'The Heidelberg score,' Harry ecstased. 'Sublime, absolute.' He looked irritably at the flowers. 'Can't you keep these things quiet? They're making one hell of a row.'

They were, and I had a shrewd idea why. The Arachnid was completely out of control, and by the time I'd clamped it down in a weak saline it had blown out over three hundred dollars' worth of shrubs.

'The performance at the Casino last night was nothing on the one she gave here yesterday,' I told them. '*The Ring of the Niebelungs* played by Stan Kenton. That Arachnid went insane. I'm sure it wanted to kill her.'

Harry watched the plant convulsing its leaves in rigid spasmic movements.

'If you ask me it's in an advanced state of rut. Why should it want to kill her?'

'Her voice must have overtones that irritate its calyx. None of the other plants minded. They cooed like turtle doves when she touched them.'

Tony shivered happily.

Light dazzled in the street outside.

I handed Tony the broom. 'Here, lover, brace yourself on that. Miss Ciracylides is dying to meet you.'

Jane came into the shop, wearing a flame yellow cocktail skirt and another of her hats.

I introduced her to Harry and Tony.

'The flowers seem very quiet this morning,' she said. 'What's the matter with them?'

'I'm cleaning out the tanks,' I told her. 'By the way, we all want to congratulate you on last night. How does it feel to be able to name your fiftieth city?'

She smiled shyly and sauntered away round the shop. As I

knew she would, she stopped by the Arachnid and levelled her eyes at it.

I wanted to see what she'd say, but Harry and Tony were all around her, and soon got her up to my apartment, where they had a hilarious morning playing the fool and raiding my scotch.

'What about coming out with us after the show tonight?' Tony asked her. 'We can go dancing at the Flamingo.'

'But you're both married,' Jane protested. 'Aren't you worried about your reputations?'

'Oh, we'll bring the girls,' Harry said airily. 'And Steve here can come along and hold your coat.'

We played i-Go together. Jane said she'd never played the game before, but she had no difficulty picking up the rules, and when she started sweeping the board with us I knew she was cheating. Admittedly it isn't every day that you get a chance to play i-Go with a golden-skinned woman with insects for eyes, but never the less I was annoyed. Harry and Tony, of course, didn't mind.

'She's charming,' Harry said, after she'd left. 'Who cares? It's a stupid game anyway.'

'I care,' I said. 'She cheats.'

The next three or four days at the shop were an audio-vegetative armageddon. Jane came in every morning to look at the Arachnid, and her presence was more than the flower could bear. Unfortunately I couldn't starve the plants below their thresholds. They needed exercise and they had to have the Arachnid to lead them. But instead of running through its harmonic scales the orchid only screeched and whined. It wasn't the noise, which only a couple of dozen people complained about, but the damage being done to their vibratory chords that worried me. Those in the seventeenth century catalogues stood up well to the strain, and the moderns were immune, but the Romantics burst their calyxes by the score. By the third day after Jane's arrival I'd lost two hundred dollars' worth of Beethoven and more Mendelssohn and Schubert than I could bear to think about.

Jane seemed oblivious to the trouble she was causing me.

'What's wrong with them all?' she asked, surveying the chaos of gas cylinders and drip feeds spread across the floor.

'I don't think they like you,' I told her. 'At least the Arachnid doesn't. Your voice may move men to strange and wonderful visions, but it throws that orchid into acute melancholia.'

'Nonsense,' she said, laughing at me. 'Give it to me and I'll show you how to look after it.'

'Are Tony and Harry keeping you happy?' I asked her. I was annoyed that I couldn't go down to the beach with them and instead had to spend my time draining tanks and titrating up norm solutions, none of which ever worked.

'They're very amusing,' she said. 'We play i-Go and I sing for them. But I wish you could come out more often.'

After another two weeks I had to give up. I decided to close the plants down until Jane had left Vermilion Sands. I knew it would take me three months to rescore the stock, but I had no alternative.

The next day I received a large order for mixed coloratura herbaceous from the Santiago Garden Choir. They wanted delivery in three weeks.

'I'm sorry,' Jane said, when she heard I wouldn't be able to fill the order. 'You must wish that I'd never come to Vermilion Sands.'

She stared thoughtfully into one of the darkened tanks.

'Couldn't I score them for you?' she suggested.

'No thanks,' I said, laughing. 'I've had enough of that already.'

'Don't be silly, of course I could.'

I shook my head.

Tony and Harry told me I was crazy.

'Her voice has a wide enough range,' Tony said. 'You admit it yourself.'

'What have you got against her?' Harry asked. 'That she cheats at i-Go?'

'It's nothing to do with that,' I said. 'And her voice has a wider range than you think.'

We played i-Go at Jane's apartment. Jane won ten dollars from each of us.

'I am lucky,' she said, very pleased with herself. 'I never seem to lose.' She counted up the bills and put them away carefully in her bag, her golden skin glowing.

Then Santiago sent me a repeat query.

I found Jane down among the cafés, holding off a siege of admirers.

'Have you given in yet?' she asked me, smiling at the young men.

'I don't know what you're doing to me,' I said, 'but anything is worth trying.'

Back at the shop I raised a bank of perennials past their thresholds. Jane helped me attach the gas and fluid lines.

'We'll try these first,' I said. 'Frequencies 543–785. Here's the score.'

Jane took off her hat and began to ascend the scale, her voice clear and pure. At first the Columbine hesitated and Jane went down again and drew them along with her. They went up a couple of octaves together and then the plants stumbled and went off at a tangent of stepped chords.

'Try K sharp,' I said. I fed a little chlorous acid into the tank and the Columbine followed her up eagerly, the infra-calyxes warbling delicate variations on the treble clef.

'Perfect,' I said.

It took us only four hours to fill the order.

'You're better than the Arachnid,' I congratulated her. 'How would you like a job? I'll fit you out with a large cool tank and all the chlorine you can breathe.'

'Careful,' she told me. 'I may say yes. Why don't we rescore a few more of them while we're about it?'

'You're tired,' I said. 'Let's go and have a drink.'

'Let me try the Arachnid,' she suggested. 'That would be more of a challenge.'

Her eyes never left the flower. I wondered what they'd do if I left them together. Try to sing each other to death?

'No,' I said. 'Tomorrow perhaps.'

We sat on the balcony together, glasses at our elbows, and talked the afternoon away.

She told me little about herself, but I gathered that her father had been a mining engineer in Peru and her mother a dancer at a Lima vu-tavern. They'd wandered from deposit to deposit, the father digging his concessions, the mother signing on at the nearest bordello to pay the rent.

'She only sang, of course,' Jane added. 'Until my father came.' She blew bubbles into her glass. 'So you think I give them what they want at the Casino. By the way, what do you see?'

'I'm afraid I'm your one failure,' I said. 'Nothing. Except you.'

She dropped her eyes. 'That sometimes happens,' she said. 'I'm glad this time.'

A million suns pounded inside me. Until then I'd been reserving judgment on myself.

Harry and Tony were polite, if disappointed.

'I can't believe it,' Harry said sadly. 'I won't. How did you do it?'

'That mystical left-handed approach, of course,' I told him. 'All ancient seas and dark wells.'

'What's she like?' Tony asked eagerly. 'I mean, does she burn or just tingle?'

Jane sang at the Casino every night from eleven to three, but apart from that I suppose we were always together. Sometimes in the late afternoons we'd drive out along the beach to the Scented Desert and sit alone by one of the pools, watching the sun fall away behind the reefs and hills, lulling ourselves on the rose-sick air. When the wind began to blow cool across the sand we'd slip down into the water, bathe ourselves and drive back to town, filling the streets and café terraces with jasmine and musk-rose and helianthemum.

On other evenings we'd go down to one of the quiet bars at Lagoon West, and have supper out on the flats, and Jane would tease the waiters and sing honeybirds and angelcakes to the children who came in across the sand to watch her.

I realize now that I must have achieved a certain notoriety along the beach, but I didn't mind giving the old women – and beside Jane they all seemed to be old women – something to talk about. During the Recess no one cared very much about anything, and for that reason I never questioned myself too closely over my affair with Jane Ciracylides. As I sat on the balcony with her looking out over the cool early evenings or felt her body glowing beside me in the darkness I allowed myself few anxieties.

Absurdly, the only disagreement I ever had with her was over her cheating.

I remember that I once taxed her with it.

'Do you know you've taken over five hundred dollars from me, Jane? You're still doing it. Even now!'

She laughed impishly. 'Do I cheat? I'll let you win one day.'

'But why do you?' I insisted.

'It's more fun to cheat,' she said. 'Otherwise it's so boring.'

'Where will you go when you leave Vermilion Sands?' I asked her.

She looked at me in surprise. 'Why do you say that? I don't think I shall ever leave.'

'Don't tease me, Jane. You're a child of another world than this.'

'My father came from Peru,' she reminded me.

'But you didn't get your voice from him,' I said. 'I wish I could have heard your mother sing. Had she a better voice than yours, Jane?'

'She thought so. My father couldn't stand either of us.'

That was the evening I last saw Jane. We'd changed, and in the half an hour before she left for the Casino we sat on the balcony and I listened to her voice, like a spectral fountain, pour its luminous notes into the air. The music remained with me even after she'd gone, hanging faintly in the darkness around her chair.

I felt curiously sleepy, almost sick on the air she'd left behind, and at 11.30, when I knew she'd be appearing on stage at the Casino, I went out for a walk along the beach.

As I left the elevator I heard music coming from the shop.

At first I thought I'd left one of the audio switches on, but I knew the voice only too well.

The windows of the shop had been shuttered, so I got in through the passage which led from the garage courtyard round at the back of the apartment house.

The lights had been turned out, but a brilliant glow filled the shop, throwing a golden fire on to the tanks along the counters. Across the ceiling liquid colours danced in reflection.

The music I had heard before, but only in overture.

The Arachnid had grown to three times its size. It towered nine feet high out of the shattered lid of the control tank, leaves tumid and inflamed, its calyx as large as a bucket, raging insanely.

Arched forwards into it, her head thrown back, was Jane.

I ran over to her, my eyes filling with light, and grabbed her arm, trying to pull her away from it.

'Jane!' I shouted over the noise. 'Get down!'

She flung my hand away. In her eyes, fleetingly, was a look of shame.

While I was sitting on the stairs in the entrance Tony and Harry drove up.

'Where's Jane?' Harry asked. 'Has anything happened to her? We were down at the Casino.' They both turned towards the music. 'What the hell's going on?'

Tony peered at me suspiciously. 'Steve, anything wrong?'

Harry dropped the bouquet he was carrying and started towards the rear entrance.

'Harry!' I shouted after him. 'Get back!'

Tony held my shoulder. 'Is Jane in there?'

I caught them as they opened the door into the shop.

'Good God!' Harry yelled. 'Let go of me, you fool!' He struggled to get away from me. 'Steve, it's trying to kill her!'

I jammed the door shut and held them back.

I never saw Jane again. The three of us waited in my apartment. When the music died away we went down and found the shop in darkness. The Arachnid had shrunk to its normal size.

The next day it died.

Where Jane went to I don't know. Not long afterwards the

Recess ended, and the big government schemes came along and started up all the clocks and kept us too busy working off the lost time to worry about a few bruised petals. Harry told me that Jane had been seen on her way through Red Beach, and I heard recently that someone very like her was doing the nightclubs this side out of Pernambuco.

So if any of you around here keep a choro-florist's, and have a Khan-Arachnid orchid, look out for a golden-skinned woman with insects for eyes. Perhaps she'll play i-Go with you, and I'm sorry to have to say it, but she'll always cheat.

1956

ESCAPEMENT

Neither of us was watching the play too closely when I first noticed the slip. I was stretched back in front of the fire with the crossword, braising gently and toying with 17 down ('told by antique clocks? 5, 5.') while Helen was hemming an old petticoat, looking up only when the third lead, a heavy-chinned youth with a 42-inch neck and a base-surge voice, heaved manfully downscreen. The play was 'My Sons, My Sons', one of those Thursday night melodramas Channel 2 put out through the winter months, and had been running for about an hour; we'd reached that ebb somewhere round Act 3 Scene 3 just after the old farmer learns that his sons no longer respect him. The whole play must have been recorded on film, and it sounded extremely funny to switch from the old man's broken mutterings back to the showdown sequence fifteen minutes earlier when the eldest son starts drumming his chest and dragging in the high symbols. Somewhere an engineer was out of a job.

'They've got their reels crossed,' I told Helen. 'This is where we came in.'

'Is it?' she said, looking up. 'I wasn't watching. Tap the set.'

'Just wait and see. In a moment everyone in the studio will start apologizing.'

Helen peered at the screen. 'I don't think we've seen this,' she said. 'I'm sure we haven't. Quiet.'

I shrugged and went back to 17 down, thinking vaguely about sand dials and water clocks. The scene dragged on; the old man stood his ground, ranted over his turnips and thundered desperately for Ma. The studio must have decided to run it straight through again and pretend no one had noticed. Even so they'd be fifteen minutes behind their schedule.

Ten minutes later it happened again.

I sat up. 'That's funny,' I said slowly. 'Haven't they spotted it yet? They can't all be asleep.'

'What's the matter?' Helen asked, looking up from her needle basket. 'Is something wrong with the set?'

'I thought you were watching. I told you we'd seen this before. Now they're playing it back for the third time.'

'They're not,' Helen insisted. 'I'm sure they aren't. You must have read the book.'

'Heaven forbid.' I watched the set closely. Any minute now an announcer spitting on a sandwich would splutter red-faced to the screen. I'm not one of those people who reach for their phones every time someone mispronounces meteorology, but this time I knew there'd be thousands who'd feel it their duty to keep the studio exchanges blocked all night. And for any go-ahead comedian on a rival station the lapse was a god-send.

'Do you mind if I change the programme?' I asked Helen. 'See if anything else is on.'

'Don't. This is the most interesting part of the play. You'll spoil it.'

'Darling, you're not even watching. I'll come back to it in a moment, I promise.'

On Channel 5 a panel of three professors and a chorus girl were staring hard at a Roman pot. The question-master, a suave-voiced Oxford don, kept up a lot of crazy patter about scraping the bottom of the barrow. The professors seemed stumped, but the girl looked as if she knew exactly what went into the pot but didn't dare say it.

On 9 there was a lot of studio laughter and someone was giving a sports-car to an enormous woman in a cartwheel hat. The woman nervously ducked her head away from the camera and stared glumly at the car. The compère opened the door for her and I was wondering whether she'd try to get into it when Helen cut in:

'Harry, don't be mean. You're just playing.'

I turned back to the play on Channel 2. The same scene was on, nearing the end of its run.

'Now watch it,' I told Helen. She usually managed to catch on the third time round. 'Put that sewing away, it's getting on my nerves. God, I know this off by heart.'

'Sh!' Helen told me. 'Can't you stop talking?'

I lit a cigarette and lay back in the sofa, waiting. The apologies, to say the least, would have to be magniloquent. Two ghost runs at £100 a minute totted up to a tidy heap of doubloons.

The scene drew to a close, the old man stared heavily at his boots, the dusk drew down and –

We were back where we started from.

'Fantastic!' I said, standing up and turning some snow off the screen. 'It's incredible.'

'I didn't know you enjoyed this sort of play,' Helen said calmly. 'You never used to.' She glanced over at the screen and then went back to her petticoat.

I watched her warily. A million years earlier I'd probably have run howling out of the cave and flung myself thankfully under the nearest dinosaur. Nothing in the meanwhile had lessened the dangers hemming in the undaunted husband.

'Darling,' I explained patiently, just keeping the edge out of my voice, 'in case you hadn't noticed they are now playing this same scene through for the fourth time.'

'The fourth time?' Helen said doubtfully. 'Are they repeating it?'

I was visualizing a studio full of announcers and engineers slumped unconscious over their mikes and valves, while an automatic camera pumped out the same reel. Eerie but unlikely. There were monitor receivers as well as the critics, agents, sponsors, and, unforgivably, the playwright himself weighing every minute and every word in their private currencies. They'd all have a lot to say under tomorrow's headlines.

'Sit down and stop fidgeting,' Helen said. 'Have you lost your bone?'

I felt round the cushions and ran my hand along the carpet below the sofa.

'My cigarette,' I said. 'I must have thrown it into the fire. I don't think I dropped it.'

I turned back to the set and switched on the give-away programme, noting the time, 9.03, so that I could get back to Channel 2 at 9.15. When the explanation came I just had to hear it.

'I thought you were enjoying the play,' Helen said. 'Why've you turned it off?'

I gave her what sometimes passes in our flat for a withering frown and settled back.

The enormous woman was still at it in front of the cameras, working her way up a pyramid of questions on cookery. The audience was subdued but interest mounted. Eventually she answered the jackpot question and the audience roared and thumped their seats like a lot of madmen. The compère led her across the stage to another sports car.

'She'll have a stable of them soon,' I said aside to Helen.

The woman shook hands and awkwardly dipped the brim of her hat, smiling nervously with embarrassment.

The gesture was oddly familiar.

I jumped up and switched to Channel 5. The panel were still staring hard at their pot.

Then I started to realize what was going on.

All three programmes were repeating themselves.

'Helen,' I said over my shoulder. 'Get me a scotch and soda, will you?'

'What *is* the matter? Have you strained your back?'

'Quickly, quickly!' I snapped my fingers.

'Hold on.' She got up and went into the pantry.

I looked at the time. 9.12. Then I returned to the play and kept my eyes glued to the screen. Helen came back and put something down on the end-table.

'There you are. You all right?'

When it switched I thought I was ready for it, but the surprise must have knocked me flat. I found myself lying out on the sofa. The first thing I did was reach round for the drink.

'Where did you put it?' I asked Helen.

'What?'

'The scotch. You brought it in a couple of minutes ago. It was on the table.'

'You've been dreaming,' she said gently. She leant forward and started watching the play.

I went into the pantry and found the bottle. As I filled a tumbler I noticed the clock over the kitchen sink. 9.07. An hour slow, now that I thought about it. But my wristwatch said 9.05, and always ran perfectly. And the clock on the mantelpiece in the lounge also said 9.05.

Before I really started worrying I had to make sure.

Mullvaney, our neighbour in the flat above, opened his door when I knocked.

'Hello, Bartley. Corkscrew?'

'No, no,' I told him. 'What's the right time? Our clocks are going crazy.'

He glanced at his wrist. 'Nearly ten past.'

'Nine or ten?'

He looked at his watch again. 'Nine, should be. What's up?'

'I don't know whether I'm losing my —' I started to say. Then I stopped.

Mullvaney eyed me curiously. Over his shoulder I heard a wave of studio applause, broken by the creamy, unctuous voice of the giveaway compère.

'How long's that programme been on?' I asked him.

'About twenty minutes. Aren't you watching?'

'No,' I said, adding casually, 'Is anything wrong with your set?'

He shook his head. 'Nothing. Why?'

'Mine's chasing its tail. Anyway, thanks.'

'OK,' he said. He watched me go down the stairs and shrugged as he shut his door.

I went into the hall, picked up the phone and dialled.

'Hello, Tom?' Tom Farnold works the desk next to mine at the office. 'Tom, Harry here. What time do you make it?'

'Time the liberals were back.'

'No, seriously.'

'Let's see. Twelve past nine. By the way, did you find those pickles I left for you in the safe?'

'Yeah, thanks. Listen, Tom,' I went on, 'the goddamdest things are happening here. We were watching Diller's play on Channel 2 when –'

'I'm watching it now. Hurry it up.'

'You are? Well, how do you explain this repetition business? And the way the clocks are stuck between 9 and 9.15?'

Tom laughed. 'I don't know,' he said. 'I suggest you go outside and give the house a shake.'

I reached out for the glass I had with me on the hall table, wondering how to explain to –

The next moment I found myself back on the sofa. I was holding the newspaper and looking at 17 down. A part of my mind was thinking about antique clocks.

I pulled myself out of it and glanced across at Helen. She was sitting quietly with her needle basket. The all too familiar play was repeating itself and by the clock on the mantelpiece it was still just after 9.

I went back into the hall and dialled Tom again, trying not to stampede myself. In some way, I hadn't begun to understand how, a section of time was spinning round in a circle, with myself in the centre.

'Tom,' I asked quickly as soon as he picked up the phone. 'Did I call you five minutes ago?'

'Who's that again?'

'Harry here. Harry Bartley. Sorry, Tom.' I paused and rephrased the question, trying to make it sound intelligible. 'Tom, did you phone me up about five minutes ago? We've had a little trouble with the line here.'

'No,' he told me. 'Wasn't me. By the way, did you get those pickles I left in the safe?'

'Thanks a lot,' I said, beginning to panic. 'Are you watching the play, Tom?'

'Yes. I think I'll get back to it. See you.'

I went into the kitchen and had a long close look at myself in the mirror. A crack across it dropped one side of my face three inches below the other, but apart from that I couldn't see anything that added up to a psychosis. My eyes seemed steady, pulse was in the low seventies, no tics or clammy traumatic sweat. Everything around me seemed much too solid and authentic for a dream.

I waited for a minute and then went back to the lounge and sat down. Helen was watching the play.

I leant forward and turned the knob round. The picture dimmed and swayed off.

'Harry, I'm watching that! Don't switch it off.'

I went over to her. 'Poppet,' I said, holding my voice together. 'Listen to me, please. Very carefully. It's important.'

She frowned, put her sewing down and took my hands.

'For some reason, I don't know why, we seem to be in a sort of circular time trap, just going round and round. You're not aware of it, and I can't find anyone else who is either.'

Helen stared at me in amazement. 'Harry,' she started, 'what are you –'

'Helen!' I insisted, gripping her shoulders. 'Listen! For the last two hours a section of time about 15 minutes long has been repeating itself. The clocks are stuck between 9 and 9.15. That play you're watching has –'

'Harry, darling.' She looked at me and smiled helplessly. 'You are silly. Now turn it on again.'

I gave up.

As I switched the set on I ran through all the other channels just to see if anything had changed.

The panel stared at their pot, the fat woman won her sports car, the old farmer ranted. On Channel 1, the old BBC service which put out a couple of hours on alternate evenings, two newspaper men were interviewing a scientific pundit who appeared on popular educational programmes.

'What effect these dense eruptions of gas will have so far it's impossible to tell. However, there's certainly no cause for any alarm. These billows have mass, and I think we can expect a lot of strange optical effects as the light leaving the sun is deflected by them gravitationally.'

He started playing with a set of coloured celluloid balls running on concentric metal rings, and fiddled with a ripple tank mounted against a mirror on the table.

One of the newsmen asked: 'What about the relationship between light and time? If I remember my relativity they're tied up together pretty closely. Are you sure we won't all need to add another hand to our clocks and watches?'

The pundit smiled. 'I think we'll be able to get along without that. Time is extremely complicated, but I can assure you the clocks won't suddenly start running backwards or sideways.'

I listened to him until Helen began to remonstrate. I switched the play on for her and went off into the hall. The fool didn't know what he was talking about. What I couldn't understand was why I was the only person who realized what was going on. If I could get Tom over I might just be able to convince him.

I picked up the phone and glanced at my watch.

9.13. By the time I got through to Tom the next changeover would be due. Somehow I didn't like the idea of being picked up and flung to the sofa, however painless it might be. I put the phone down and went into the lounge.

The jump-back was smoother than I expected. I wasn't conscious of anything, not even the slightest tremor. A phrase was stuck in my mind: Olden Times.

The newspaper was back on my lap, folded around the crossword. I looked through the clues.

17 down: Told by antique clocks? 5, 5.

I must have solved it subconsciously.

I remembered that I'd intended to phone Tom.

'Hullo, Tom?' I asked when I got through. 'Harry here.'

'Did you get those pickles I left in the safe?'

'Yes, thanks a lot. Tom, could you come round tonight? Sorry to ask you this late, but it's fairly urgent.'

'Yes, of course,' he said. 'What's the trouble?'

'I'll tell you when you get here. As soon as you can?'

'Sure. I'll leave right away. Is Helen all right?'

'Yes, she's fine. Thanks again.'

I went into the dining room and pulled a bottle of gin and a couple of tonics out of the sideboard. He'd need a drink when he heard what I had to say.

Then I realized he'd never make it. From Earls Court it would take him at least half an hour to reach us at Maida Vale and he'd probably get no further than Marble Arch.

I filled my glass out of the virtually bottomless bottle of scotch and tried to work out a plan of action.

The first step was to get hold of someone like myself who retained his awareness of the past switch-backs. Somewhere else there must be others trapped in their little 15-minute cages who were also wondering desperately how to get out. I could start by phoning everyone I knew and then going on at random through the phonebook. But what could we do if we did find each other? In fact there was nothing to do except sit tight and wait for it all to wear off. At least I knew I wasn't looping my loop. Once these billows or whatever they were had burnt themselves out we'd be able to get off the round-about.

Until then I had an unlimited supply of whisky waiting for me in the half-empty bottle standing on the sink, though of course there was one snag: I'd never be able to get drunk.

I was musing round some of the other possibilities available and wondering how to get a permanent record of what was going on when an idea hit me.

I got out the phone-directory and looked up the number of KBC-TV, Channel 9.

A girl at reception answered the phone. After haggling with her for a couple of minutes I persuaded her to put me through to one of the producers.

'Hullo,' I said. 'Is the jackpot question in tonight's programme known to any members of the studio audience?'

'No, of course not.'

'I see. As a matter of interest, do you yourself know it?'

'No,' he said. 'All the questions tonight are known only to our senior programme producer and M. Phillipe Soisson of Savoy Hotels Limited. They're a closely guarded secret.'

'Thanks,' I said. 'If you've got a piece of paper handy I'll give you the jackpot question. "List the complete menu at the Guildhall Coronation Banquet in July 1953."'

There were muttered consultations, and a second voice came through.

'Who's that speaking?'

'Mr H.R. Bartley, 129b Sutton Court Road, N.W. –'

Before I could finish I found myself back in the lounge.

The jump-back had caught me. But instead of being stretched out on the sofa I was standing up, leaning on one elbow against the mantelpiece, looking down at the newspaper.

My eyes were focused clearly on the crossword puzzle, and before I pulled them away and started thinking over my call to the studio I noticed something that nearly dropped me into the grate.

17 down had been filled in.

I picked up the paper and showed it to Helen.

'Did you do this clue? 17 down?'

'No,' she said. 'I never even look at the crossword.'

The clock on the mantelpiece caught my eye, and I forgot about the studio and playing tricks with other people's time.

9.03.

The merry-go-round was closing in. I thought the jump-back had come sooner than I expected. At least two minutes earlier, somewhere around 9.13.

And not only was the repetition interval getting shorter, but as the arc edged inwards on itself it was uncovering the real time stream running below it, the stream in which the other I, unknown to myself here, had solved the clue, stood up, walked over to the mantelpiece and filled in 17 down.

I sat down on the sofa, watching the clock carefully.

For the first time that evening Helen was thumbing over the pages of a magazine. The work basket was tucked away on the bottom shelf of the bookcase.

'Do you want this on any longer?' she asked me. 'It's not very good.'

I turned to the panel game. The three professors and the chorus girl were still playing around with their pot.

On Channel 1 the pundit was sitting at the table with his models.

'. . . alarm. The billows have mass, and I think we can expect a lot of strange optical effects as the light —'

I switched it off.

The next jump-back came at 9.11. Somewhere I'd left the mantelpiece, gone back to the sofa and lit a cigarette.

It was 9.04. Helen had opened the verandah windows and was looking out into the street.

The set was on again so I pulled the plug out at the main. I threw the cigarette into the fire; not having seen myself light it, made it taste like someone else's.

'Harry, like to go out for a stroll?' Helen suggested. 'It'll be rather nice in the park.'

Each successive jump-back gave us a new departure point. If now I bundled her outside and got her down to the end of the road, at the next jump we'd both be back in the lounge again, but probably have decided to drive to the pub instead.

'Harry?'

'What, sorry?'

'Are you asleep, angel? Like to go for a walk? It'll wake you up.'

'All right,' I said. 'Go and get your coat.'

'Will you be warm enough like that?'

She went off into the bedroom

I walked round the lounge and convinced myself that I was awake. The shadows, the solid feel of the chairs, the definition was much too fine for a dream.

It was 9.08. Normally Helen would take ten minutes to put on her coat.

The jump-back came almost immediately.

It was 9.06.

I was still on the sofa and Helen was bending down and picking up her work basket.

This time, at last, the set was off.

'Have you got any money on you?' Helen asked.

I felt in my pocket automatically. 'Yes. How much do you want?'

Helen looked at me. 'Well, what do you usually pay for the drinks? We'll only have a couple.'

'We're going to the pub, are we?'

'Darling, are you all right?' She came over to me. 'You look all strangled. Is that shirt too tight?'

'Helen,' I said, getting up. 'I've got to try to explain something to you. I don't know why it's happening, it's something to do with these billows of gas the sun's releasing.'

Helen was watching me with her mouth open.

'Harry,' she started to say nervously. 'What's the matter?'

'I'm quite all right,' I assured her. 'It's just that everything is happening very rapidly and I don't think there's much time left.'

I kept on glancing at the clock and Helen followed my eyes to it and went over to the mantelpiece. Watching me she moved it round and I heard the pendulum jangle.

'No, no,' I shouted. I grabbed it and pushed it back against the wall.

We jumped back to 9.07.

Helen was in the bedroom. I had exactly a minute left.

'Harry,' she called. 'Darling, do you want to, or don't you?'

I was by the lounge window, muttering something.

I was out of touch with what my real self was doing in the normal time channel. The Helen talking to me now was a phantom.

It was I, not Helen and everybody else, who was riding the merry-go-round.

Jump.

9.07-15.

Helen was standing in the doorway.

'... down to the ... the ...' I was saying.

Helen watched me, frozen. A fraction of a minute left.

I started to walk over to her.

to walk over to her
ver to her
er

I came out of it like a man catapulted from a revolving door. I was stretched out flat on the sofa, a hard aching pain running from the top of my head down past my right ear into my neck.

I looked at the time. 9.45. I could hear Helen moving around in the dining room. I lay there, steadying the room round me, and in a few minutes she came in carrying a tray and a couple of glasses.

'How do you feel?' she asked, making up an alka-seltzer.

I let it fizzle down and drank it.

'What happened?' I asked. 'Did I collapse?'

'Not exactly. You were watching the play. I thought you looked rather seedy so I suggested we go out for a drink. You went into a sort of convulsion.'

I stood up slowly and rubbed my neck. 'God, I didn't dream all that! I couldn't have done.'

'What was it about?'

'A sort of crazy merry-go-round –' The pain grabbed at my neck when I spoke. I went over to the set and switched it on. 'Hard to explain coherently. Time was –' I flinched as the pain bit in again.

'Sit down and rest,' Helen said. 'I'll come and join you. Like a drink?'

'Thanks. A big scotch.'

I looked at the set. On Channel 1 there was a breakdown sign, a cabaret on 2, a flood-lit stadium on 5, and a variety show on 9. No sign anywhere of either Diller's play or the panel game.

Helen brought the drink in and sat down on the sofa with me.

'It started off when we were watching the play,' I explained, massaging my neck.

'Sh, don't bother now. Just relax.'

I put my head on Helen's shoulder and looked up at the ceiling, listening to the sound coming from the variety show. I thought back through each turn of the round-about, wondering whether I could have dreamt it all.

Ten minutes later Helen said, 'Well, I didn't think much of that. And they're doing an encore. Good heavens.'

'Who are?' I asked. I watched the light from the screen flicker across her face.

'That team of acrobats. The something Brothers. One of them even slipped. How do you feel?'

'Fine.' I turned my head round and looked at the screen.

Three or four acrobats with huge v-torsos and skin briefs were doing simple handstands on to each other's arms. They finished the act and went into a more involved routine, throwing around a girl in leopard skin panties. The applause was deafening. I thought they were moderately good.

Two of them began to give what seemed to be a demonstration of dynamic tension, straining against each other like a pair of catatonic bulls, their necks and legs locked, until one of them was levered slowly off the ground.

'Why do they keep on doing that?' Helen said. 'They've done it twice already.'

'I don't think they have,' I said. 'This is a slightly different act.'

The pivot man tremored, one of his huge banks of muscles collapsed, and the whole act toppled and then sprung apart.

'They slipped there the last time,' Helen said.

'No, no,' I pointed out quickly. 'That one was a headstand. Here they were stretched out horizontally.'

'You weren't watching,' Helen told me. She leant forward. 'Well, what are they playing at? They're repeating the whole thing for the third time.'

It was an entirely new act to me, but I didn't try to argue.

I sat up and looked at the clock.

10.05.

'Darling,' I said, putting my arm round her. 'Hold tight.'

'What do you mean?'

'This is the merry-go-round. And you're driving.'

1956

THE CONCENTRATION CITY

Noon talk on Millionth Street:

'Sorry, these are the West Millions. You want 9775335th East.'

'Dollar five a cubic foot? Sell!'

'Take a westbound express to 495th Avenue, cross over to a Redline elevator and go up a thousand levels to Plaza Terminal. Carry on south from there and you'll find it between 568th Avenue and 422nd Street.'

'There's a cave-in down at KEN County! Fifty blocks by twenty by thirty levels.'

'Listen to this – "PYROMANIACS STAGE MASS BREAKOUT! FIRE POLICE CORDON BAY COUNTY!"'

'It's a beautiful counter. Detects up to .005 per cent monoxide. Cost me three hundred dollars.'

'Have you seen those new intercity sleepers? They take only ten minutes to go up 3,000 levels!'

'Ninety cents a foot? Buy!'

'You say the idea came to you in a dream?' the voice snapped. 'You're sure no one else gave it to you.'

'No,' M. said. A couple of feet away from him a spot-lamp threw a cone of dirty yellow light into his face. He dropped his eyes from the glare and waited as the sergeant paced over to his desk, tapped his fingers on the edge and swung round on him again.

'You talked it over with your friends?'

'Only the first theory,' M. explained. 'About the possibility of flight.'

'But you told me the other theory was more important. Why keep it from them?'

M. hesitated. Outside somewhere a trolley shunted and clanged along the elevated. 'I was afraid they wouldn't understand what I meant.'

The sergeant laughed. 'Do you mean they would have thought you really were insane?'

M. shifted uncomfortably on the stool. Its seat was only six inches off the floor and his thighs felt like slabs of inflamed rubber. After three hours of cross-questioning logic had faded. 'The concept was a little abstract. There weren't any words for it.'

The sergeant shook his head. 'I'm glad to hear you say it.' He sat down on the desk, watched M. for a moment and then went over to him.

'Now look,' he said confidentially. 'It's getting late. Do you still think both theories are reasonable?'

M. looked up. 'Aren't they?'

The sergeant turned to the man watching in the shadows by the window. 'We're wasting our time,' he snapped. 'I'll hand him over to Psycho. You've seen enough, haven't you, Doctor?'

The surgeon stared at his hands. He had taken no part in the interrogation, as if bored by the sergeant's method of approach.

'There's something I want to find out,' he said. 'Leave me alone with him for half an hour.'

When the sergeant had gone the surgeon sat down behind the desk and stared out of the window, listening to the dull hum of air through the ventilator shaft which rose out of the street below the station. A few roof lights were still burning and two hundred yards away a single policeman patrolled the iron catwalk running above the street, his boots ringing across the darkness.

M. sat on the stool, elbows between his knees, trying to edge a little life back into his legs.

Eventually the surgeon glanced down at the charge sheet.

```
Name................  Franz M.
Age.................  20.
Occupation..........  Student.
Address.............  3599719 West 783rd St, Level
                      549-7705-45 KNI (Local).
Charge..............  Vagrancy.
```

'Tell me about this dream,' he said, idly flexing a steel rule between his hands as he looked across at M.

'I think you've heard everything, sir,' M. said.

'In detail.'

M. shifted uneasily. 'There wasn't much to it, and what I do remember isn't too clear now.'

The surgeon yawned. M. waited and then started to recite what he had already repeated twenty times.

'I was suspended in the air above a flat stretch of open ground, something like the floor of an enormous arena. My arms were out at my sides, and I was looking down, floating –'

'Hold on,' the surgeon interrupted. 'Are you sure you weren't swimming?'

'No,' M. said. 'I'm certain I wasn't. All around me there was free space. That was the most important part about it. There were no walls. Nothing but emptiness. That's all I remember.'

The surgeon ran his finger along the edge of the rule.

'Go on.'

'Well, the dream gave me the idea of building a flying machine. One of my friends helped me construct it.'

The surgeon nodded. Almost absently he picked up the charge sheet and crushed it with a single motion of his hand.

'Don't be absurd, Franz!' Gregson remonstrated. They took their places in the chemistry cafeteria queue. 'It's against the laws of hydrodynamics. Where would you get your buoyancy?'

'Suppose you had a rigid fabric vane,' Franz explained as they shuffled past the hatchways. 'Say ten feet across, like one of those composition wall sections, with hand grips on the ventral surface. And then you jumped down from the gallery at the Coliseum Stadium. What would happen?'

'You'd make a hole in the floor. Why?'

'No, seriously.'

'If it was large enough and held together you'd swoop down like a paper dart.'

'Glide,' Franz said. 'Right.' Thirty levels above them one of the intercity expresses roared over, rattling the tables and cutlery in the cafeteria. Franz waited until they reached a table and sat forward, his food forgotten.

'And say you attached a propulsive unit, such as a battery-driven ventilator fan, or one of those rockets they use on the Sleepers. With enough thrust to overcome your weight. What then?'

Gregson shrugged. 'If you could control the thing, you'd, you'd . . .' He frowned at Franz. 'What's the word? You're always using it.'

'Fly.'

'Basically, Matheson, the machine is simple,' Sanger, the physics lector, commented as they entered the science library. 'An elementary application of the Venturi Principle. But what's the point of it? A trapeze would serve its purpose equally well, and be far less dangerous. In the first place consider the enormous clearances it would require. I hardly think the traffic authorities will look upon it with any favour.'

'I know it wouldn't be practical here,' Franz admitted. 'But in a large open area it should be.'

'Allowed. I suggest you immediately negotiate with the Arena Garden on Level 347–25,' the lector said whimsically. 'I'm sure they'll be glad to hear about your scheme.'

Franz smiled politely. 'That wouldn't be large enough. I was really thinking of an area of totally free space. In three dimensions, as it were.'

Sanger looked at Franz curiously. 'Free space? Isn't that a contradiction in terms? Space is a dollar a cubic foot.' He scratched his nose. 'Have you begun to construct this machine yet?'

'No,' Franz said.

'In that event I should try to forget all about it. Remember, Matheson, the task of science is to consolidate existing knowledge, to systematize and reinterpret the discoveries of the past, not to chase wild dreams into the future.'

He nodded and disappeared among the dusty shelves.

Gregson was waiting on the steps.

'Well?' he asked.

'Let's try it out this afternoon,' Franz said. 'We'll cut Text 5 Pharmacology. I know those Fleming readings backwards. I'll ask Dr McGhee for a couple of passes.'

They left the library and walked down the narrow, dimly-lit alley which ran behind the huge new civil engineering laboratories. Over seventy-five per cent of the student enrolment was in the architectural and engineering faculties, a meagre two per cent in pure sciences. Consequently the physics and chemistry libraries were housed in the oldest quarter of the university, in two virtually condemned galvanized hutments which once contained the now closed philosophy school.

At the end of the alley they entered the university plaza and started to climb the iron stairway leading to the next level a hundred feet above. Halfway up a white-helmeted F.P. checked them cursorily with his detector and waved them past.

'What did Sanger think?' Gregson asked as they stepped up into 637th Street and walked across to the suburban elevator station.

'He's no use at all,' Franz said. 'He didn't even begin to understand what I was talking about.'

Gregson laughed ruefully. 'I don't know whether I do.'

Franz took a ticket from the automat and mounted the down platform. An elevator dropped slowly towards him, its bell jangling.

'Wait until this afternoon,' he called back. 'You're really going to see something.'

The floor manager at the Coliseum initialled the two passes.

'Students, eh? All right.' He jerked a thumb at the long package Franz and Gregson were carrying. 'What have you got there?'

'It's a device for measuring air velocities,' Franz told him.

The manager grunted and released the stile.

Out in the centre of the empty arena Franz undid the package and they assembled the model. It had a broad fan-like wing of wire and paper, a narrow strutted fuselage and a high curving tail.

Franz picked it up and launched it into the air. The model glided for twenty feet and then slithered to a stop across the sawdust.

'Seems to be stable,' Franz said. 'We'll tow it first.'

He pulled a reel of twine from his pocket and tied one end to the nose. As they ran forward the model lifted gracefully into the air and followed them around the stadium, ten feet off the floor.

'Let's try the rockets now,' Franz said. He adjusted the wing and tail settings and fitted three firework display rockets into a wire bracket mounted above the wing.

The stadium was four hundred feet in diameter and had a roof two hundred and fifty feet high. They carried the model over to one side and Franz lit the tapers.

There was a burst of flame and the model accelerated across the floor, two feet in the air, a bright trail of coloured smoke spitting out behind it. Its wings rocked gently from side to side. Suddenly the tail burst into flames. The model lifted steeply and looped up towards the roof, stalled just before it hit one of the pilot lights and dived down into the sawdust.

They ran across to it and stamped out the glowing cinders. 'Franz!' Gregson shouted. 'It's incredible! It actually works.'

Franz kicked the shattered fuselage. 'Of course it works,' he said impatiently. 'But as Sanger said, what's the point of it?'

'The point? It flies! Isn't that enough?'

'No. I want one big enough to hold me.'

'Franz, slow down. Be reasonable. Where could you fly it?'

'I don't know,' Franz said fiercely. 'But there must be somewhere!'

The floor manager and two assistants, carrying fire extinguishers, ran across the stadium to them.

'Did you hide the matches?' Franz asked quickly. 'They'll lynch us if they think we're Pyros.'

Three afternoons later Franz took the elevator up 150 levels to 677–98, where the Precinct Estate Office had its bureau.

'There's a big development between 493 and 554 in the next sector,' one of the clerks told him. 'I don't know whether that's any good to you. Sixty blocks by twenty by fifteen levels.'

'Nothing bigger?' Franz queried.

The clerk looked up. 'Bigger? No. *What* are you looking for – a slight case of agoraphobia?'

Franz straightened the maps spread across the counter. 'I wanted to find an area of more or less continuous development. Two or three hundred blocks long.'

The clerk shook his head and went back to his ledger. 'Didn't you go to engineering school?' he asked scornfully. 'The City won't take it. One hundred blocks is the maximum.'

Franz thanked him and left.

A south-bound express took him to the development in two hours. He left the car at the detour point and walked the three hundred yards to the end of the level.

The street, a seedy but busy thoroughfare of garment shops and small business premises running through the huge ten-mile-thick B.I.R. Industrial Cube, ended abruptly in a tangle of ripped girders and concrete. A steel rail had been erected along the edge and Franz looked down over it into the cavity, three miles long, a mile wide and twelve hundred feet deep, which thousands of engineers and demolition workers were tearing out of the matrix of the City.

Eight hundred feet below him unending lines of trucks and railcars carried away the rubble and debris, and clouds of dust swirled up into the arc-lights blazing down from the roof. As he watched, a chain of explosions ripped along the wall on his left and the whole face slipped and fell slowly towards the floor, revealing a perfect cross-section through fifteen levels of the City.

Franz had seen big developments before, and his own parents had died in the historic QUA County cave-in ten years earlier, when three master-pillars had sheared and two hundred levels of the City had abruptly sunk ten thousand feet, squashing half a million people like flies in a concertina, but the enormous gulf of emptiness still stunned his imagination.

All around him, standing and sitting on the jutting terraces of girders, a silent throng stared down.

'They say they're going to build gardens and parks for us,' an elderly man at Franz's elbow remarked in a patient voice. 'I even heard they might be able to get a tree. It'll be the only tree in the whole county.'

A man in a frayed sweat-shirt spat over the rail. 'That's what they always say. At a dollar a foot promises are all they can waste space on.'

Below them a woman who had been looking out into the air started to simper nervously. Two bystanders took her by the arms and tried to lead her away. The woman began to thresh about and an F.P. came over and pulled her away roughly.

'Poor fool,' the man in the sweat-shirt commented. 'She probably lived out there somewhere. They gave her ninety cents a foot when they took it away from her. She doesn't know yet she'll have to pay a dollar ten to get it back. Now they're going to start charging five cents an hour just to sit up here and watch.'

Franz looked out over the railing for a couple of hours and then bought a postcard from one of the vendors and walked back to the elevator.

He called in to see Gregson before returning to the student dormitory. The Gregsons lived in the West millions on 985th Avenue, in a top three-room flat right under the roof. Franz had known them since his parents' death, but Gregson's mother still regarded him with a mixture of sympathy and suspicion. As she let him in with her customary smile of welcome he noticed her glancing at the detector mounted in the hall.

Gregson was in his room, happily cutting out frames of paper and pasting them on to a great rickety construction that vaguely resembled Franz's model.

'Hullo, Franz. What was it like?'

Franz shrugged. 'Just a development. Worth seeing.'

Gregson pointed to his construction. 'Do you think we can try it out there?'

'We could do.' Franz sat down on the bed. He picked up a paper dart lying beside him and tossed it out of the window. It swam into the street, lazed down in a wide spiral and vanished into the open mouth of the ventilator shaft.

'When are you going to build another model?' Gregson asked.

'I'm not.'

Gregson looked up. 'Why? You've proved your theory.'

'That's not what I'm after.'

'I don't get you, Franz. What are you after?'

'Free space.'

'Free?' Gregson repeated.

Franz nodded. 'In both senses.'

Gregson shook his head sadly and snipped out another paper panel. 'Franz, you're mad.'

Franz stood up. 'Take this room,' he said. 'It's twenty feet by fifteen by ten. Extend its dimensions infinitely. What do you find?'

'A development.'

'*Infinitely!*'

'Non-functional space.'

'Well?' Franz asked patiently.

'The concept's absurd.'

'Why?'

'Because it couldn't exist.'

Franz pounded his forehead in despair. '*Why* couldn't it?'

Gregson gestured with the scissors. 'It's self-contradictory. Like the statement "I am lying". Just a verbal freak. Interesting theoretically, but it's pointless to press it for meaning.' He tossed the scissors on to the table. 'And anyway, do you know how much free space would cost?'

Franz went over to the bookshelf and pulled out one of the volumes. 'Let's have a look at your street atlas.' He turned to the index. 'This gives a thousand levels. KNI County, one hundred thousand cubic miles, population 30 million.'

Gregson nodded.

Franz closed the atlas. 'Two hundred and fifty counties, including KNI, together form the 493rd Sector, and an association of 1,500 adjacent sectors comprise the 298th Local Union.' He broke off and looked at Gregson. 'As a matter of interest, ever heard of it?'

Gregson shook his head. 'No. How did –'

Franz slapped the atlas on to the table. 'Roughly 4×10^{15} cubic Great-Miles.' He leaned on the window-ledge. 'Now tell me: what lies beyond the 298th Local Union?'

'Other unions, I suppose,' Gregson said. 'I don't see your difficulty.'

'And beyond those?'

'Farther ones. Why not?'

'For ever?' Franz pressed.

'Well, as far as for ever is.'

'The great street directory in the old Treasury Library on 247th Street is the largest in the county,' Franz said. 'I went down there this morning. It occupies three complete levels. Millions of volumes. But it doesn't extend beyond the 598th Local Union. No one there had any idea what lay farther out. Why not?'

'Why should they?' Gregson asked. 'Franz, what are you driving at?'

Franz walked across to the door. 'Come down to the Bio-History Museum. I'll show you.'

The birds perched on humps of rock or waddled about the sandy paths between the water pools.

'"Archaeopteryx",' Franz read off one of the cage indicators. The bird, lean and mildewed, uttered a painful croak when he fed a handful of beans to it.

'Some of these birds have the remnants of a pectoral girdle,' Franz said. 'Minute fragments of bone embedded in the tissues around their rib cages.'

'Wings?'

'Dr McGhee thinks so.'

They walked out between the lines of cages.

'When does he think they were flying?'

'Before the Foundation,' Franz said. 'Three million years ago.'

When they were outside the museum they started down 859th Avenue. Halfway down the street a dense crowd had gathered and people were packed into the windows and balconies above the elevated, watching a squad of Fire Police break their way into a house.

The bulkheads at either end of the block had been closed and heavy steel traps sealed off the stairways from the levels above and below. The ventilator and exhaust shafts were silent and already the air was stale and soupy.

'Pyros,' Gregson murmured. 'We should have brought our masks.'

'It's only a scare,' Franz said. He pointed to the monoxide detectors which were out everywhere, their long snouts sucking at the air. The dial needles stood safely at zero. 'Let's wait in the restaurant opposite.'

They edged their way over to the restaurant, sat down in the window and ordered coffee. This, like everything else on the menu, was cold. All cooking appliances were thermostated to a maximum 95°F., and only in the more expensive restaurants and hotels was it possible to obtain food that was at most tepid.

Below them in the street a lot of shouting went up. The Fire Police seemed unable to penetrate beyond the ground floor of the house and had started to baton back the crowd. An electric winch was wheeled up and bolted to the girders running below the kerb, and half a dozen heavy steel grabs were carried into the house and hooked round the walls.

Gregson laughed. 'The owners are going to be surprised when they get home.'

Franz was watching the house. It was a narrow shabby dwelling sandwiched between a large wholesale furniture store and a new supermarket. An old sign running across the front had been painted over and evidently the ownership had recently changed. The present tenants had made a half-hearted attempt to convert the ground floor room into a cheap stand-up diner. The Fire Police appeared to be doing their best to wreck everything, and pies and smashed crockery were strewn all over the pavement.

The noise died away and everyone waited as the winch began to revolve. The hawsers wound in and tautened, and the front wall of the house staggered outwards in rigid jerky movements.

Suddenly there was a yell from the crowd.

Franz raised his arm. 'Up there! Look!'

On the fourth floor a man and woman had come to the window and were looking down helplessly. The man lifted the woman on to the ledge and she crawled out and clung to one of the waste pipes. Bottles were lobbed up at them and bounced down among the police. A wide crack split the house from top to bottom and the floor on which the man was standing dropped and catapulted him backwards out of sight. Then one of the lintels in the first floor snapped and the entire house tipped over and collapsed.

Franz and Gregson stood up, almost knocking over the table.

The crowd surged forward through the cordon. When the dust had settled there was nothing left but a heap of masonry and twisted beams. Embedded in this was the battered figure of the man. Almost smothered by the dust he moved slowly, trying to free himself with one hand, and the crowd started roaring again as one of the grabs wound in and dragged him down under the rubble.

The manager of the restaurant pushed past Franz and leant out of the window, his eyes fixed on the dial of a portable detector. Its needle, like all the others, pointed to zero.

A dozen hoses were playing on the remains of the house and after a few minutes the crowd shifted and began to thin out.

The manager switched off the detector and left the window, nodding to Franz. 'Damn Pyros. You can relax now, boys.'

Franz pointed at the detector. 'Your dial was dead. There wasn't a trace of monoxide anywhere here. How do you know they were Pyros?'

'Don't worry, we know.' He smiled obliquely. 'We don't want that sort of element in this neighbourhood.'

Franz shrugged and sat down. 'I suppose that's one way of getting rid of them.'

The manager eyed Franz. 'That's right, boy. This is a good dollar five neighbourhood.' He smirked to himself. 'Maybe a dollar six now everybody knows about our safety record.'

'Careful, Franz,' Gregson warned him when the manager had gone. 'He may be right. Pyromaniacs do take over small cafés and food bars.'

Franz stirred his coffee. 'Dr McGhee estimates that at least fifteen per cent of the City's population are submerged Pyros. He's convinced the number's growing and that eventually the whole City will flame-out.'

He pushed away his coffee. 'How much money have you got?'

'On me?'

'Altogether.'

'About thirty dollars.'

'I've saved fifteen,' Franz said. 'Forty-five dollars; that should be enough for three or four weeks.'

'Where?' Gregson asked.

'On a Supersleeper.'

'Super –!' Gregson broke off, alarmed. 'Three or four weeks! What do you mean?'

'There's only one way to find out,' Franz explained calmly. 'I can't just sit here thinking. Somewhere there's free space and I'll ride the Sleeper until I find it. Will you lend me your thirty dollars?'

'But Franz –'

'If I don't find anything within a couple of weeks I'll change tracks and come back.'

'But the ticket will cost ...' Gregson searched '... billions. Forty-five dollars won't even get you out of the Sector.'

'That's just for coffee and sandwiches,' Franz said. 'The ticket will be free.' He looked up from the table. 'You know ...'

Gregson shook his head doubtfully. 'Can you try that on the Supersleepers?'

'Why not? If they query it I'll say I'm going back the long way round. Greg, will you?'

'I don't know if I should.' Gregson played helplessly with his coffee. 'Franz, how can there be free space? How?'

'That's what I'm going to find out,' Franz said. 'Think of it as my first physics practical.'

Passenger distances on the transport system were measured point to point by the application of $a = \sqrt{b^2 + c^2 + d^2}$. The actual itinerary taken was the passenger's responsibility, and as long as he remained within the system he could choose any route he liked. Tickets were checked only at the station exits, where necessary surcharges were collected by an inspector. If the passenger was unable to pay the surcharge – ten cents a mile – he was sent back to his original destination.

Franz and Gregson entered the station on 984th Street and went over to the large console where tickets were automatically dispensed. Franz put in a penny and pressed the destination button marked 984. The machine rumbled, coughed out a ticket, and the change slot gave him back his coin.

'Well, Greg, goodbye,' Franz said as they moved towards the barrier. 'I'll see you in about two weeks. They're covering me down at the dormitory. Tell Sanger I'm on Fire Duty.'

'What if you don't get back, Franz?' Gregson asked. 'Suppose they take you off the Sleeper?'

'How can they? I've got my ticket.'

'And if you do find free space? Will you come back then?'

'If I can.'

Franz patted Gregson on the shoulder reassuringly, waved and disappeared among the commuters.

He took the local Suburban Green to the district junction in the next county. The Green Line train travelled at an interrupted 70 m.p.h. and the ride took two and a half hours.

At the junction he changed to an express elevator which lifted him out of the sector in ninety minutes, at 400 m.p.h. Another fifty minutes in a Through-Sector Special brought him to the Mainline Terminus which served the Union.

There he bought a coffee and gathered his determination together. Supersleepers ran east and west, halting at this and every tenth station. The next arrived in seventy-two hours time, westbound.

The Mainline Terminus was the largest station Franz had seen, a mile-long cavern thirty levels in depth. Hundreds of elevator shafts sank through the station and the maze of platforms, escalators, restaurants, hotels and theatres seemed like an exaggerated replica of the City itself.

Getting his bearings from one of the information booths, Franz made his way up an escalator to Tier 15, where the Supersleepers berthed. Running the length of the station were two steel vacuum tunnels each three hundred feet in diameter, supported at thirty-four intervals by huge concrete buttresses.

Franz walked along the platform and stopped by the telescopic gangway that plunged into one of the airlocks. Two hundred and seventy degrees true, he thought, gazing up at the curving underbelly of the tunnel. It must come out somewhere. He had forty-five dollars in his pocket, sufficient coffee and sandwich money to last him three weeks, six if he needed it, time anyway to find the City's end.

He passed the next three days nursing cups of coffee in any of the thirty cafeterias in the station, reading discarded newspapers and sleeping in the local Red trains which ran four-hour journeys round the nearest sector.

When at last the Supersleeper came in he joined the small group of Fire Police and municipal officials waiting by the gangway, and followed them into the train. There were two cars; a sleeper which no one used, and a day coach.

Franz took an inconspicuous corner seat near one of the indicator panels in the day coach, and pulled out his notebook ready to make his first entry.

1st Day: West 270°. Union 4,350.

'Coming out for a drink?' a Fire Captain across the aisle asked. 'We have a ten-minute break here.'

'No thanks,' Franz said. 'I'll hold your seat for you.'

Dollar five a cubic foot. Free space, he knew, would bring the price down. There was no need to leave the train or make too many inquiries. All he had to do was borrow a paper and watch the market averages.

2nd Day: West 270°. Union 7,550.

'They're slowly cutting down on these Sleepers,' someone told him. 'Everyone sits in the day coach. Look at this one. Seats sixty, and only four people in it. There's no need to move around. People are staying where they are. In a few years there'll be nothing left but the suburban services.'

97 *cents.*

At an average of a dollar a cubic foot, Franz calculated idly, it's so far worth about 4×10^{27}.

'Going on to the next stop, are you? Well, goodbye, young fellow.'

Few of the passengers stayed on the Sleeper for more than three or four hours. By the end of the second day Franz's back and neck ached from the constant acceleration. He managed to take a little exercise walking up and down the narrow corridor in the deserted sleeping coach, but had to spend most of his time strapped to his seat as the train began its long braking runs into the next station.

3rd Day: West 270°. Federation 657.

'Interesting, but how could you demonstrate it?'

'It's just an odd idea of mine,' Franz said, screwing up the sketch and dropping it in the disposal chute. 'Hasn't any real application.'

'Curious, but it rings a bell somewhere.'

Franz sat up. 'Do you mean you've seen machines like this? In a newspaper or a book?'

'No, no. In a dream.'

Every half day's run the pilot signed the log, the crew handed over to their opposites on an Eastbound sleeper, crossed the platform and started back for home.

125 *cents.*

8×10^{28}.

4th Day: West 270°. Federation 1,225.

'Dollar a cubic foot. You in the estate business?'

'Starting up,' Franz said easily. 'I'm hoping to open a new office of my own.'

He played cards, bought coffee and rolls from the dispenser in the washroom, watched the indicator panel and listened to the talk around him.

'Believe me, a time will come when each union, each sector, almost I might say, each street and avenue will have achieved complete local independence. Equipped with its own power services, aerators, reservoirs, farm laboratories ...'

The car bore.

6×10^{75}.

5th Day: West 270°. 17th Greater Federation.

At a kiosk on the station Franz bought a clip of razor blades and glanced at the brochure put out by the local chamber of commerce.

'12,000 levels, 98 cents a foot, unique Elm Drive, fire safety records unequalled ...'

He went back to the train, shaved, and counted the thirty dollars left. He was now ninety-five million Great-Miles from the suburban station on 984th Street and he knew he could not delay his return much longer. Next time he would save up a couple of thousand.

7×10^{127}.

7th Day: West 270°. 212th Metropolitan Empire.

Franz peered at the indicator.

'Aren't we stopping here?' he asked a man three seats away. 'I wanted to find out the market average.'

'Varies. Anything from fifty cents a –'

'Fifty!' Franz shot back, jumping up. 'When's the next stop? I've got to get off!'

'Not here, son.' He put out a restraining hand. 'This is Night Town. You in real estate?'

Franz nodded, holding himself back. 'I thought ...'

'Relax.' He came and sat opposite Franz. 'It's just one big slum. Dead areas. In places it goes as low as five cents. There are no services, no power.'

It took them two days to pass through.

'City Authority are starting to seal it off,' the man told him.

'Huge blocks. It's the only thing they can do. What happens to the people inside I hate to think.' He chewed on a sandwich. 'Strange, but there are a lot of these black areas. You don't hear about them, but they're growing. Starts in a back street in some ordinary dollar neighbourhood; a bottleneck in the sewage disposal system, not enough ash cans, and before you know it – a million cubic miles have gone back to jungle. They try a relief scheme, pump in a little cyanide, and then – brick it up. Once they do that they're closed for good.'

Franz nodded, listening to the dull humming air.

'Eventually there'll be nothing left but these black areas. The City will be one huge cemetery!'

10th Day: East 90°. 755th Greater Metropolitan –

'Wait!' Franz leapt out of his seat and stared at the indicator panel.

'What's the matter?' someone opposite asked.

'East!' Franz shouted. He banged the panel sharply with his hand but the lights held. 'Has this train changed direction?'

'No, it's eastbound,' another of the passengers told him. 'Are you on the wrong train?'

'It should be heading west,' Franz insisted. 'It has been for the last ten days.'

'Ten days!' the man exclaimed. 'Have you been on this sleeper for ten days?'

Franz went forward and found the car attendant. 'Which way is this train going? West?'

The attendant shook his head. 'East, sir. It's always been going east.'

'You're crazy,' Franz snapped. 'I want to see the pilot's log.'

'I'm afraid that isn't possible. May I see your ticket, sir?'

'Listen,' Franz said weakly, all the accumulated frustration of the last twenty years mounting inside him. 'I've been on this . . .'

He stopped and went back to his seat.

The five other passengers watched him carefully.

'Ten days,' one of them was still repeating in an awed voice.

Two minutes later someone came and asked Franz for his ticket.

'And of course it was completely in order,' the police surgeon commented. 'Strangely enough there's no regulation to prevent anyone else doing the same thing. I used to go for free rides myself when I was younger, though I never tried anything like your journey.'

He went back to the desk. 'We'll drop the charge,' he said. 'You're not a vagrant in any indictable sense, and the transport authorities can do nothing against you. How this curvature was built into the system they can't explain, it seems to be some inherent feature of the City itself. Now about yourself. Are you going to continue this search?'

'I want to build a flying machine,' M. said carefully. 'There must be free space somewhere. I don't know . . . perhaps on the lower levels.'

The surgeon stood up. 'I'll see the sergeant and get him to hand you over to one of our psychiatrists. He'll be able to help you with your dreams!'

The surgeon hesitated before opening the door. 'Look,' he began to explain, 'you can't get out of time, can you? Subjectively it's a plastic dimension, but whatever you do to yourself you'll never be able to stop that clock' – he pointed to the one on the desk – 'or make it run backwards. In exactly the same way you can't get out of the City.'

'The analogy doesn't hold,' M. said. He gestured at the walls around them and the lights in the street outside. 'All this was built by us. The question nobody can answer is: what was here before we built it?'

'It's always been here,' the surgeon said. 'Not these particular bricks and girders, but others before them. You accept that time has no beginning and no end. The City is as old as time and continuous with it.'

'The first bricks were laid by someone,' M. insisted. 'There was the Foundation.'

'A myth. Only the scientists believe in that, and even they don't try to make too much of it. Most of them privately admit that the Foundation Stone is nothing more than a superstition. We pay it lip service out of convenience, and because it gives us a sense of tradition. Obviously there can't have been a first brick. If there was, how can you explain who laid it and, even more difficult, where they came from?'

'There must be free space somewhere,' M. said doggedly. 'The City must have bounds.'

'*Why?*' the surgeon asked. 'It can't be floating in the middle of nowhere. Or is that what you're trying to believe?'

M. sank back limply. 'No.'

The surgeon watched M. silently for a few minutes and paced back to the desk. 'This peculiar fixation of yours puzzles me. You're caught between what the psychiatrists call paradoxical faces. I suppose you haven't misinterpreted something you've heard about the Wall?'

M. looked up. 'Which wall?'

The surgeon nodded to himself. 'Some advanced opinion maintains that there's a wall around the City, through which it's impossible to penetrate. I don't pretend to understand the theory myself. It's far too abstract and sophisticated. Anyway I suspect they've confused this Wall with the bricked-up black areas you passed through on the Sleeper. I prefer the accepted view that the City stretches out in all directions without limits.'

He went over to the door. 'Wait here, and I'll see about getting you a probationary release. Don't worry, the psychiatrists will straighten everything out for you.'

When the surgeon had left M. stared at the floor, too exhausted to feel relieved. He stood up and stretched himself, walking unsteadily round the room.

Outside the last pilot lights were going out and the patrolman on the catwalk under the roof was using his torch. A police car roared down one of the avenues crossing the street, its rails screaming. Three lights snapped on along the street and then one by one went off again.

M. wondered why Gregson hadn't come down to the station.

Then the calendar on the desk riveted his attention. The date exposed on the fly leaf was 12 August. That was the day he had started off on his journey – exactly three weeks ago.

Today!

Take a westbound Green to 298th Street, cross over at the intersection and get a Red elevator up to Level 237. Walk down to the station on Route 175, change to a 438 suburban and go down to 795th Street. Take a Blue line to the Plaza, get off at 4th and 275th, turn left at the roundabout and –

You're back where you first started from.

$\$Hell \times 10^n$.

1957

VENUS SMILES

Low notes on a high afternoon.

As we drove away after the unveiling my secretary said, 'Mr Hamilton, I suppose you realize what a fool you've made of yourself?'

'Don't sound so prim,' I told her. 'How was I to know Lorraine Drexel would produce something like that?'

'Five thousand dollars,' she said reflectively. 'It's nothing but a piece of old scrap iron. And the noise! Didn't you look at her sketches? What's the Fine Arts Committee for?'

My secretaries have always talked to me like this, and just then I could understand why. I stopped the car under the trees at the end of the square and looked back. The chairs had been cleared away and already a small crowd had gathered around the statue, staring up at it curiously. A couple of tourists were banging one of the struts, and the thin metal skeleton shuddered weakly. Despite this, a monotonous and high-pitched wailing sounded from the statue across the pleasant morning air, grating the teeth of passers-by.

'Raymond Mayo is having it dismantled this afternoon,' I said. 'If it hasn't already been done for us. I wonder where Miss Drexel is?'

'Don't worry, you won't see her in Vermilion Sands again. I bet she's halfway to Red Beach by now.'

I patted Carol on the shoulder. 'Relax. You looked beautiful in your new skirt. The Medicis probably felt like this about Michelangelo. Who are we to judge?'

'*You* are,' she said. 'You were on the committee, weren't you?'

'Darling,' I explained patiently. 'Sonic sculpture is the thing. You're trying to fight a battle the public lost thirty years ago.'

We drove back to my office in a thin silence. Carol was annoyed because she had been forced to sit beside me on the platform when the audience began to heckle my speech at the unveiling, but even so the morning had been disastrous on every count. What might be perfectly acceptable at Expo 75 or the Venice Biennale was all too obviously passé at Vermilion Sands.

When we had decided to commission a sonic sculpture for the square in the centre of Vermilion Sands, Raymond Mayo and I had agreed that we should patronize a local artist. There were dozens of professional sculptors in Vermilion Sands, but only three had deigned to present themselves before the committee. The first two we saw were large, bearded men with enormous fists and impossible schemes – one for a hundred-foot-high vibrating aluminium pylon, and the other for a vast booming family group that involved over fifteen tons of basalt mounted on a megalithic step-pyramid. Each had taken an hour to be argued out of the committee room.

The third was a woman: Lorraine Drexel. This elegant and autocratic creature in a cartwheel hat, with her eyes like black orchids, was a sometime model and intimate of Giacometti and John Cage. Wearing a blue crêpe de Chine dress ornamented with lace serpents and other art nouveau emblems, she sat before us like some fugitive Salome from the world of Aubrey Beardsley. Her immense eyes regarded us with an almost hypnotic calm, as if she had discovered that very moment some unique quality in these two amiable dilettantes of the Fine Arts Committee.

She had lived in Vermilion Sands for only three months, arriving via Berlin, Calcutta and the Chicago New Arts Centre. Most of her sculpture to date had been scored for various Tantric and Hindu hymns, and I remembered her brief affair with a world-famous pop-singer, later killed in a car crash, who had been an enthusiastic devotee of the sitar. At the time, however, we had given no thought to the whining quarter-tones of this infernal instrument, so grating on the Western ear. She had shown us an album of her sculptures, interesting chromium constructions that compared favourably with the run of illustrations in the latest art magazines. Within half an hour we had drawn up a contract.

* * *

I saw the statue for the first time that afternoon thirty seconds before I started my speech to the specially selected assembly of Vermilion Sands notables. Why none of us had bothered to look at it beforehand I fail to understand. The title printed on the invitation cards – 'Sound and Quantum: Generative Synthesis 3' – had seemed a little odd, and the general shape of the shrouded statue even more suspicious. I was expecting a stylized human figure but the structure under the acoustic drapes had the proportions of a medium-sized radar aerial. However, Lorraine Drexel sat beside me on the stand, her bland eyes surveying the crowd below. A dream-like smile gave her the look of a tamed Mona Lisa.

What we saw after Raymond Mayo pulled the tape I tried not to think about. With its pedestal the statue was twelve feet high. Three spindly metal legs, ornamented with spikes and crosspieces, reached up from the plinth to a triangular apex. Clamped on to this was a jagged structure that at first sight seemed to be an old Buick radiator grille. It had been bent into a rough U five feet across, and the two arms jutted out horizontally, a single row of sonic cores, each about a foot long, poking up like the teeth of an enormous comb. Welded on apparently at random all over the statue were twenty or thirty filigree vanes.

That was all. The whole structure of scratched chromium had a blighted look like a derelict antenna. Startled a little by the first shrill whoops emitted by the statue, I began my speech and was about halfway through when I noticed that Lorraine Drexel had left her seat beside me. People in the audience were beginning to stand up and cover their ears, shouting to Raymond to replace the acoustic drape. A hat sailed through the air over my head and landed neatly on one of the sonic cores. The statue was now giving out an intermittent high-pitched whine, a sitar-like caterwauling that seemed to pull apart the sutures of my skull. Responding to the boos and protests, it suddenly began to whoop erratically, the horn-like sounds confusing the traffic on the far side of the square.

As the audience began to leave their seats *en masse* I stuttered inaudibly to the end of my speech, the wailing of the statue interrupted by shouts and jeers. Then Carol tugged me sharply by the arm, her eyes flashing. Raymond Mayo pointed with a nervous hand.

The three of us were alone on the platform, the rows of overturned chairs reaching across the square. Standing twenty yards from the statue, which had now begun to whimper plaintively, was Lorraine Drexel. I expected to see a look of fury and outrage on her face, but instead her unmoving eyes showed the calm and implacable contempt of a grieving widow insulted at her husband's funeral. As we waited awkwardly, watching the wind carry away the torn programme cards, she turned on a diamond heel and walked across the square.

No one else wanted anything to do with the statue, so I was finally presented with it. Lorraine Drexel left Vermilion Sands the day it was dismantled. Raymond spoke briefly to her on the telephone before she went. I presumed she would be rather unpleasant and didn't bother to listen in on the extension.

'Well?' I asked. 'Does she want it back?'

'No.' Raymond seemed slightly preoccupied. 'She said it belonged to us.'

'You and me?'

'Everybody.' Raymond helped himself to the decanter of scotch on the veranda table. 'Then she started laughing.'

'Good. What at?'

'I don't know. She just said that we'd grow to like it.'

There was nowhere else to put the statue so I planted it out in the garden. Without the stone pedestal it was only six feet high. Shielded by the shrubbery, it had quietened down and now emitted a pleasant melodic harmony, its soft rondos warbling across the afternoon heat. The sitar-like twangs, which the statue had broadcast in the square like some pathetic love-call from Lorraine Drexel to her dead lover, had vanished completely, almost as if the statue had been rescored. I had been so stampeded by the disastrous unveiling that I had had little chance to see it and I thought it looked a lot better in the garden than it had done in Vermilion Sands, the chromium struts and abstract shapes standing out against the desert like something in a vodka advertisement. After a few days I could almost ignore it.

A week or so later we were out on the terrace after lunch, lounging back in the deck chairs. I was nearly asleep when Carol said, 'Mr Hamilton, I think it's moving.'

'What's moving?'

Carol was sitting up, head cocked to one side. 'The statue. It looks different.'

I focused my eyes on the statue twenty feet away. The radiator grille at the top had canted around slightly but the three stems still seemed more or less upright.

'The rain last night must have softened the ground,' I said. I listened to the quiet melodies carried on the warm eddies of air, and then lay back drowsily. I heard Carol light a cigarette with four matches and walk across the veranda.

When I woke in an hour's time she was sitting straight up in the deck chair, a frown creasing her forehead.

'Swallowed a bee?' I asked. 'You look worried.'

Then something caught my eye.

I watched the statue for a moment. 'You're right. It is moving.'

Carol nodded. The statue's shape had altered perceptibly. The grille had spread into an open gondola whose sonic cores seemed to feel at the sky, and the three stem-pieces were wider apart. All the angles seemed different.

'I thought you'd notice it eventually,' Carol said as we walked over to it. 'What's it made of?'

'Wrought iron – I think. There must be a lot of copper or lead in it. The heat is making it sag.'

'Then why is it sagging upwards instead of down?'

I touched one of the shoulder struts. It was springing elastically as the air moved across the vanes and went on vibrating against my palm. I gripped it in both hands and tried to keep it rigid. A low but discernible pulse pumped steadily against me.

I backed away from it, wiping the flaking chrome off my hands. The Mozartian harmonies had gone, and the statue was now producing a series of low Mahler-like chords. As Carol stood there in her bare feet I remembered that the height specification we had given to Lorraine Drexel had been exactly two metres. But the statue was a good three feet higher than Carol, the gondola at least six or seven across. The spars and struts looked thicker and stronger.

'Carol,' I said. 'Get me a file, would you? There are some in the garage.'

She came back with two files and a hacksaw.

'Are you going to cut it down?' she asked hopefully.

'Darling, this is an original Drexel.' I took one of the files. 'I just want to convince myself that I'm going insane.'

I started cutting a series of small notches all over the statue, making sure they were exactly the width of the file apart. The metal was soft and worked easily; on the surface there was a lot of rust but underneath it had a bright sappy glint.

'All right,' I said when I had finished. 'Let's go and have a drink.'

We sat on the veranda and waited. I fixed my eyes on the statue and could have sworn that it didn't move. But when we went back an hour later the gondola had swung right round again, hanging down over us like an immense metal mouth.

There was no need to check the notch intervals against the file. They were all at least double the original distance apart.

'Mr Hamilton,' Carol said. 'Look at this.'

She pointed to one of the spikes. Poking through the outer scale of chrome were a series of sharp little nipples. One or two were already beginning to hollow themselves. Unmistakably they were incipient sonic cores.

Carefully I examined the rest of the statue. All over it new shoots of metal were coming through: arches, barbs, sharp double helixes, twisting the original statue into a thicker and more elaborate construction. A medley of half-familiar sounds, fragments of a dozen overtures and symphonies, murmured all over it. The statue was well over twelve feet high. I felt one of the heavy struts and the pulse was stronger, beating steadily through the metal, as if it was thrusting itself on to the sound of its own music.

Carol was watching me with a pinched and worried look.

'Take it easy,' I said. 'It's only growing.'

We went back to the veranda and watched.

By six o'clock that evening it was the size of a small tree. A spirited simultaneous rendering of Brahms's *Academic Festival Overture* and Rachmaninov's First Piano Concerto trumpeted across the garden.

'The strangest thing about it,' Raymond said the next morning, raising his voice above the din, 'is that it's still a Drexel.'

'Still a piece of sculpture, you mean?'

'More than that. Take any section of it and you'll find the original motifs being repeated. Each vane, each helix has all the authentic Drexel mannerisms, almost as if she herself were shaping it. Admittedly, this penchant for the late Romantic composers is a little out of keeping with all that sitar twanging, but that's rather a good thing, if you ask me. You can probably expect to hear some Beethoven any moment now – the Pastoral Symphony, I would guess.'

'Not to mention all five piano concertos – played at once,' I said sourly. Raymond's loquacious delight in this musical monster out in the garden annoyed me. I closed the veranda windows, wishing that he himself had installed the statue in the living room of his downtown apartment. 'I take it that it won't go on growing for ever?'

Carol handed Raymond another scotch. 'What do you think we ought to do?'

Raymond shrugged. 'Why worry?' he said airily. 'When it starts tearing the house down cut it back. Thank God we had it dismantled. If this had happened in Vermilion Sands . . .'

Carol touched my arm. 'Mr Hamilton, perhaps that's what Lorraine Drexel expected. She wanted it to start spreading all over the town, the music driving everyone crazy –'

'Careful,' I warned her. 'You're running away with yourself. As Raymond says, we can chop it up any time we want to and melt the whole thing down.'

'Why don't you, then?'

'I want to see how far it'll go,' I said. In fact my motives were more mixed. Clearly, before she left, Lorraine Drexel had set some perverse jinx at work within the statue, a bizarre revenge on us all for deriding her handiwork. As Raymond had said, the present babel of symphonic music had no connection with the melancholy cries the statue had first emitted. Had those forlorn chords been intended to be a requiem for her dead lover – or even, conceivably, the beckoning calls of a still unsurrendered heart? Whatever her motives, they had now vanished into this strange travesty lying across my garden.

I watched the statue reaching slowly across the lawn. It had collapsed under its own weight and lay on its side in a huge angular spiral, twenty feet long and about fifteen feet high, like the skeleton of a futuristic whale. Fragments of the *Nutcracker Suite* and Mendelssohn's 'Italian' Symphony sounded from it, overlaid by sudden blaring excerpts from the closing movements of Grieg's Piano Concerto. The selection of these hack classics seemed deliberately designed to get on my nerves.

I had been up with the statue most of the night. After Carol went to bed I drove my car on to the strip of lawn next to the house and turned on the headlamps. The statue stood out almost luminously in the darkness, booming away to itself, more and more of the sonic cores budding out in the yellow glare of the lights. Gradually it lost its original shape; the toothed grille enveloped itself and then put out new struts and barbs that spiralled upwards, each throwing off secondary and tertiary shoots in its turn. Shortly after midnight it began to lean and then suddenly toppled over.

By now its movement was corkscrew. The plinth had been carried into the air and hung somewhere in the middle of the tangle, revolving slowly, and the main foci of activity were at either end. The growth rate was accelerating. We watched a new shoot emerge. As one of the struts curved round a small knob poked through the flaking chrome. Within a minute it grew into a spur an inch long, thickened, began to curve and five minutes later had developed into a full-throated sonic core twelve inches long.

Raymond pointed to two of my neighbours standing on the roofs of their houses a hundred yards away, alerted by the music carried across to them. 'You'll soon have everyone in Vermilion Sands out here. If I were you, I'd throw an acoustic drape over it.'

'If I could find one the size of a tennis court. It's time we did something, anyway. See if you can trace Lorraine Drexel. I'm going to find out what makes this statue go.'

Using the hacksaw, I cut off a two-foot limb and handed it to Dr Blackett, an eccentric but amiable neighbour who sometimes dabbled in sculpture himself. We walked back to the comparative quiet of the veranda. The single sonic core emitted a few random notes, fragments from a quartet by Webern.

'What do you make of it?'

'Remarkable,' Blackett said. He bent the bar between his hands. 'Almost plastic.' He looked back at the statue. 'Definite circumnutation there. Probably phototropic as well. Hmm, almost like a plant.'

'Is it alive?'

Blackett laughed. 'My dear Hamilton, of course not. How can it be?'

'Well, where is it getting its new material? From the ground?'

'From the air. I don't know yet, but I imagine it's rapidly synthesizing an allotropic form of ferrous oxide. In other words, a purely physical rearrangement of the constituents of rust.' Blackett stroked his heavy brush moustache and stared at the statue with a dream-like eye. 'Musically, it's rather curious – an appalling conglomeration of almost every bad note ever composed. Somewhere the statue must have suffered some severe sonic trauma. It's behaving as if it had been left for a week in a railroad shunting yard. Any idea what happened?'

'Not really.' I avoided his glance as we walked back to the statue. It seemed to sense us coming and began to trumpet out the opening bars of Elgar's 'Pomp and Circumstance' march. Deliberately breaking step, I said to Blackett: 'So in fact all I have to do to silence the thing is chop it up into two-foot lengths?'

'If it worries you. However, it would be interesting to leave it, assuming you can stand the noise. There's absolutely no danger of it going on indefinitely.' He reached up and felt one of the spars. 'Still firm, but I'd say it was almost there. It will soon start getting pulpy like an over-ripe fruit and begin to shred off and disintegrate, playing itself out, one hopes, with Mozart's *Requiem* and the finale of the *Götterdämmerung*.' He smiled at me, showing his strange teeth. 'Die, if you prefer it.'

However, he had reckoned completely without Lorraine Drexel.

At six o'clock the next morning I was woken by the noise. The statue was now fifty feet long and crossing the flower beds on either side of the garden. It sounded as if a complete orchestra were performing some Mad Hatter's symphony out in the centre of the lawn. At the far end, by the rockery, the sonic cores were still working their way through the Romantic catalogue, a babel of Mendelssohn, Schubert and Grieg, but near the veranda the cores were beginning to emit the jarring and syncopated rhythms of Stravinsky and Stockhausen.

I woke Carol and we ate a nervous breakfast.

'Mr Hamilton!' she shouted. 'You've got to stop it!' The nearest tendrils were only five feet from the glass doors of the veranda. The largest limbs were over three inches in diameter and the pulse thudded through them like water under pressure in a fire hose.

When the first police cars cruised past down the road I went into the garage and found the hacksaw.

The metal was soft and the blade sank through it quickly. I left the pieces I cut off in a heap to one side, random notes sounding out into the air. Separated from the main body of the statue, the fragments were almost inactive, as Dr Blackett had stated. By two o'clock that afternoon I had cut back about half the statue and got it down to manageable proportions.

'That should hold it,' I said to Carol. I walked round and lopped off a few of the noisier spars. 'Tomorrow I'll finish it off altogether.'

I wasn't in the least surprised when Raymond called and said that there was no trace anywhere of Lorraine Drexel.

* * *

At two o'clock that night I woke as a window burst across the floor of my bedroom. A huge metal helix hovered like a claw through the fractured pane, its sonic core screaming down at me.

A half-moon was up, throwing a thin grey light over the garden. The statue had sprung back and was twice as large as it had been at its peak the previous morning. It lay all over the garden in a tangled mesh, like the skeleton of a crushed building. Already the advance tendrils had reached the bedroom windows, while others had climbed over the garage and were sprouting downwards through the roof, tearing away the galvanized metal sheets.

All over the statue thousands of sonic cores gleamed in the light thrown down from the window. At last in unison, they hymned out the finale of Bruckner's *Apocalyptic Symphony*.

I went into Carol's bedroom, fortunately on the other side of the house, and made her promise to stay in bed. Then I telephoned Raymond Mayo. He came around within an hour, an oxyacetylene torch and cylinders he had begged from a local contractor in the back seat of his car.

The statue was growing almost as fast as we could cut it back, but by the time the first light came up at a quarter to six we had beaten it.

Dr Blackett watched us slice through the last fragments of the statue. 'There's a section down in the rockery that might just be audible. I think it would be worth saving.'

I wiped the rust-stained sweat from my face and shook my head. 'No. I'm sorry, but believe me, once is enough.'

Blackett nodded in sympathy, and stared gloomily across the heaps of scrap iron which were all that remained of the statue.

Carol, looking a little stunned by everything, was pouring coffee and brandy. As we slumped back in two of the deck chairs, arms and faces black with rust and metal filings, I reflected wryly that no one could accuse the Fine Arts Committee of not devoting itself wholeheartedly to its projects.

I went off on a final tour of the garden, collecting the section Blackett had mentioned, then guided in the local contractor who had arrived with his truck. It took him and his two men an hour to load the scrap – an estimated ton and a half – into the vehicle.

'What do I do with it?' he asked as he climbed into the cab. 'Take it to the museum?'

'No!' I almost screamed. 'Get rid of it. Bury it somewhere, or better still, have it melted down. As soon as possible.'

When they had gone Blackett and I walked around the garden together. It looked as if a shrapnel shell had exploded over it. Huge divots were strewn all over the place, and what grass had not been ripped up by the statue had been trampled away by us. Iron filings lay on the lawn like dust, a faint ripple of lost notes carried away on the steepening sunlight.

Blackett bent down and scooped up a handful of grains. 'Dragon's teeth. You'll look out of the window tomorrow and see the B Minor Mass coming up.' He let it run out between his fingers. 'However, I suppose that's the end of it.'

He couldn't have been more wrong.

Lorraine Drexel sued us. She must have come across the newspaper reports and realized her opportunity. I don't know where she had been hiding, but her lawyers materialized quickly enough, waving the original contract and pointing to the clause in which we guaranteed to protect the statue from any damage that might be done to it by vandals, livestock or other public nuisance. Her main accusation concerned the damage we had done to her reputation – if we had decided not to exhibit the statue we should have supervised its removal to some place of safekeeping, not openly dismembered it and then sold off the fragments to a scrap dealer. This deliberate affront had, her lawyers insisted, cost her commissions to a total of at least fifty thousand dollars.

At the preliminary hearings we soon realized that, absurdly, our one big difficulty was going to be proving to anyone who had not been there that the statue had actually started growing. With luck we managed to get several postponements, and Raymond and I tried to trace what we could of the statue. All we found were three small struts, now completely inert, rusting in the sand on the edge of one of the junkyards in Red Beach. Apparently taking me at my word, the contractor had shipped the rest of the statue to a steel mill to be melted down.

Our only case now rested on what amounted to a plea of self-defence. Raymond and myself testified that the statue had started to grow, and then Blackett delivered a long homily to the judge on what he believed to be the musical shortcomings of the statue. The judge, a crusty and short-tempered old man of the hanging school, immediately decided that we were trying to pull his leg. We were finished from the start.

The final judgment was not delivered until ten months after we had first unveiled the statue in the centre of Vermilion Sands, and the verdict, when it came, was no surprise.

Lorraine Drexel was awarded thirty thousand dollars.

'It looks as if we should have taken the pylon after, all,' I said to Carol as we left the courtroom. 'Even the step-pyramid would have been less trouble.'

Raymond joined us and we went out on to the balcony at the end of the corridor for some air.

'Never mind,' Carol said bravely. 'At least it's all over with.'

I looked out over the rooftops of Vermilion Sands, thinking about the thirty thousand dollars and wondering whether we would have to pay it ourselves.

The court building was a new one and by an unpleasant irony ours had been the first case to be heard there. Much of the floor and plasterwork had still to be completed, and the balcony was untiled. I was standing on an exposed steel crossbeam; one or two floors down someone must have been driving a rivet into one of the girders, and the beam under my feet vibrated soothingly.

Then I noticed that there were no sounds of riveting going on anywhere, and that the movement under my feet was not so much a vibration as a low rhythmic pulse.

I bent down and pressed my hands against the beam. Raymond and Carol watched me curiously. 'Mr Hamilton, what is it?' Carol asked when I stood up.

'Raymond,' I said. 'How long ago did they first start on this building? The steel framework, anyway.'

'Four months, I think. Why?'

'Four.' I nodded slowly. 'Tell me, how long would you say it took any random piece of scrap iron to be reprocessed through a steel mill and get back into circulation?'

'Years, if it lay around in the wrong junkyards.'

'But if it had actually arrived at the steel mill?'

'A month or so. Less.'

I started to laugh, pointing to the girder. 'Feel that! Go on, feel it!'

Frowning at me, they knelt down and pressed their hands to the girder. Then Raymond looked up at me sharply.

I stopped laughing. 'Did you feel it?'

'Feel it?' Raymond repeated. 'I can *hear* it. Lorraine Drexel – the statue. It's here!'

Carol was patting the girder and listening to it. 'I think it's humming,' she said, puzzled. 'It sounds like the statue.'

When I started to laugh again Raymond held my arm. 'Snap out of it, the whole building will be singing soon!'

'I know,' I said weakly. 'And it won't be just this building either.' I took Carol by the arm. 'Come on, let's see if it's started.'

We went up to the top floor. The plasterers were about to move in and there were trestles and laths all over the place. The walls were still bare brick, girders at fifteen-foot intervals between them.

We didn't have to look very far.

Jutting out from one of the steel joists below the roof was a long metal helix, hollowing itself slowly into a delicate sonic core. Without moving, we counted a dozen others. A faint twanging sound came from them, like early arrivals at a rehearsal of some vast orchestra of sitar-players, seated on every plain and hilltop of the earth. I remembered when we had last heard the music, as Lorraine Drexel sat beside me at the unveiling in Vermilion Sands. The statue had made its call to her dead lover, and now the refrain was to be taken up again.

'An authentic Drexel,' I said. 'All the mannerisms. Nothing much to look at yet, but wait till it really gets going.'

Raymond wandered round, his mouth open. 'It'll tear the building apart. Just think of the noise.'

Carol was staring up at one of the shoots. 'Mr Hamilton, you said they'd melted it all down.'

'They did, angel. So it got back into circulation, touching off all the other metal it came into contact with. Lorraine Drexel's statue is here, in this building, in a dozen other buildings, in ships and planes and a million new automobiles. Even if it's only one screw or ball-bearing, that'll be enough to trigger the rest off.'

'They'll stop it,' Carol said.

'They might,' I admitted. 'But it'll probably get back again somehow. A few pieces always will.' I put my arm round her waist and began to dance to the strange abstracted music, for some reason as beautiful now as Lorraine Drexel's wistful eyes. 'Did you say it was all over? Carol, it's only just beginning. The whole world will be singing.'

1957

MANHOLE 69

For the first few days all went well.

'Keep away from windows and don't think about it,' Dr Neill told them. 'As far as you're concerned it was just another compulsion. At eleven thirty or twelve go down to the gym and throw a ball around, play some table-tennis. At two they're running a film for you in the Neurology theatre. Read the papers for a couple of hours, put on some records. I'll be down at six. By seven you'll be in a manic swing.'

'Any chance of a sudden blackout, Doctor?' Avery asked.

'Absolutely none,' Neill said. 'If you get tired, rest, of course. That's the one thing you'll probably have a little difficulty getting used to. Remember, you're still using only 3,500 calories, so your kinetic level – and you'll notice this most by day – will be about a third lower. You'll have to take things easier, make allowances. Most of these have been programmed in for you, but start learning to play chess, focus that inner eye.'

Gorrell leaned forward. 'Doctor,' he asked, 'if we want to, can we look out of the windows?'

Dr Neill smiled. 'Don't worry,' he said. 'The wires are cut. You couldn't go to sleep now if you tried.'

Neill waited until the three men had left the lecture room on their way back to the Recreation Wing and then stepped down from the dais and shut the door. He was a short, broad-shouldered man in his fifties, with a sharp, impatient mouth and small features. He swung a chair out of the front row and straddled it deftly.

'Well?' he asked.

Morley was sitting on one of the desks against the back wall, playing aimlessly with a pencil. At thirty he was the youngest member of the team working under Neill at the Clinic, but for some reason Neill liked to talk to him.

He saw Neill was waiting for an answer and shrugged.

'Everything seems to be all right,' he said. 'Surgical convalescence is over. Cardiac rhythms and EEG are normal. I saw the X-rays this morning and everything has sealed beautifully.'

Neill watched him quizzically. 'You don't sound as if you approve.'

Morley laughed and stood up. 'Of course I do.' He walked down the aisle between the desks, white coat unbuttoned, hands sunk deep in his pockets. 'No, so far you've vindicated yourself on every point. The party's only just beginning, but the guests are in damn good shape. No doubt about it. I thought three weeks was a little early to bring them out of hypnosis, but you'll probably be right there as well. Tonight is the first one they take on their own. Let's see how they are tomorrow morning.'

'What are you secretly expecting?' Neill asked wryly. 'Massive feedback from the medulla?'

'No,' Morley said. 'There again the psychometric tests have shown absolutely nothing coming up at all. Not a single trauma.' He stared at the blackboard and then looked round at Neill. 'Yes, as a cautious estimate I'd say you've succeeded.'

Neill leaned forward on his elbows. He flexed his jaw muscles. 'I think I've more than succeeded. Blocking the medullary synapses has eliminated a lot of material I thought would still be there – the minor quirks and complexes, the petty aggressive phobias, the bad change in the psychic bank. Most of them have gone, or at least they don't show in the tests. However, they're the side targets, and thanks to you, John, and to everyone else in the team, we've hit a bull's eye on the main one.'

Morley murmured something, but Neill ran on in his clipped voice. 'None of you realize it yet, but this is as big an advance as the step the first ichthyoid took out of the protozoic sea 300 million years ago. At last we've freed the mind, raised it out of that archaic sump called sleep, its nightly retreat into the medulla.

With virtually one cut of the scalpel we've added twenty years to those men's lives.'

'I only hope they know what to do with them,' Morley commented.

'Come, John,' Neill snapped back. 'That's not an argument. What they do with the time is their responsibility anyway. They'll make the most of it, just as we've always made the most, eventually, of any opportunity given us. It's too early to think about it yet, but visualize the universal application of our technique. For the first time Man will be living a full twenty-four hour day, not spending a third of it as an invalid, snoring his way through an eight-hour peepshow of infantile erotica.'

Tired, Neill broke off and rubbed his eyes. 'What's worrying you?'

Morley made a small, helpless gesture with one hand. 'I'm not sure, it's just that I . . .' He played with the plastic brain mounted on a stand next to the blackboard. Reflected in one of the frontal whorls was a distorted image of Neill, with a twisted chinless face and vast domed cranium. Sitting alone among the desks in the empty lecture room he looked like an insane genius patiently waiting to take an examination no one could set him.

Morley turned the model with his finger, watched the image blur and dissolve. Whatever his doubts, Neill was probably the last person to understand them.

'I know all you've done is close off a few of the loops in the hypothalamus, and I realize the results are going to be spectacular. You'll probably precipitate the greatest social and economic revolution since the Fall. But for some reason I can't get that story of Chekov's out of my mind – the one about the man who accepts a million-rouble bet that he can't shut himself up alone for ten years. He tries to, nothing goes wrong, but one minute before the time is up he deliberately steps out of his room. Of course, he's insane.'

'So?'

'I don't know. I've been thinking about it all week.'

Neill let out a light snort. 'I suppose you're trying to say that sleep is some sort of communal activity and that these three men are now isolated, exiled from the group unconscious, the dark oceanic dream. Is that it?'

'Maybe.'

'Nonsense, John. The further we hold back the unconscious the better. We're reclaiming some of the marshland. Physiologically sleep is nothing more than an inconvenient symptom of cerebral anoxaemia. It's not *that* you're afraid of missing, it's the dream. You want to hold on to your front-row seat at the peepshow.'

'No,' Morley said mildly. Sometimes Neill's aggressiveness surprised him; it was almost as if he regarded sleep itself as secretly discreditable, a concealed vice. 'What I really mean is that for better or worse Lang, Gorrell and Avery are now stuck with themselves. They're never going to be able to get away, not even for a couple of minutes, let alone eight hours. How much of yourself can you stand? Maybe you need eight hours off a day just to get over the shock of being yourself. Remember, you and I aren't always going to be around, feeding them with tests and films. What will happen if they get fed up with themselves?'

'They won't,' Neill said. He stood up, suddenly bored by Morley's questions. 'The total tempo of their lives will be lower than ours, these stresses and tensions won't begin to crystallize. We'll soon seem like a lot of manic-depressives to them, running round like dervishes half the day, then collapsing into a stupor the other half.'

He moved towards the door and reached out to the light switch. 'Well, I'll see you at six o'clock.'

They left the lecture room and started down the corridor together.

'What are you doing now?' Morley asked.

Neill laughed. 'What do you think?' he said. 'I'm going to get a good night's sleep.'

A little after midnight Avery and Gorrell were playing table-tennis in the floodlit gymnasium. They were competent players, and passed the ball backwards and forwards with a minimum of effort. Both felt strong and alert; Avery was sweating slightly, but this was due to the arc-lights blazing down from the roof

– maintaining, for safety's sake, an illusion of continuous day – rather than to any excessive exertion of his own. The oldest of the three volunteers, a tall and somewhat detached figure, with a lean, closed face, he made no attempt to talk to Gorrell and concentrated on adjusting himself to the period ahead. He knew he would find no trace of fatigue, but as he played he carefully checked his respiratory rhythms and muscle tonus, and kept one eye on the clock.

Gorrell, a jaunty, self-composed man, was also subdued. Between strokes he glanced cautiously round the gymnasium, noting the hangar-like walls, the broad, polished floor, the shuttered skylights in the roof. Now and then, without realizing it, he fingered the circular trepan scar at the back of his head.

Out in the centre of the gymnasium a couple of armchairs and a sofa had been drawn up round a gramophone, and here Lang was playing chess with Morley, doing his section of night duty. Lang hunched forward over the chessboard. Wiry-haired and aggressive, with a sharp nose and mouth, he watched the pieces closely. He had played regularly against Morley since he arrived at the Clinic four months earlier, and the two were almost equally matched, with perhaps a slight edge to Morley. But tonight Lang had opened with a new attack and after ten moves had completed his development and begun to split Morley's defence. His mind felt clear and precise, focused sharply on the game in front of him, though only that morning had he finally left the cloudy limbo of post-hypnosis through which he and the two others had drifted for three weeks like lobotomized phantoms.

Behind him, along one wall of the gymnasium, were the offices housing the control unit. Over his shoulder he saw a face peering at him through the circular observation window in one of the doors. Here, at constant alert, a group of orderlies and interns sat around waiting by their emergency trollies. (The end door, into a small ward containing three cots, was kept carefully locked.) After a few moments the face withdrew. Lang smiled at the elaborate machinery watching over him. His transference on to Neill had been positive and he had absolute faith in the success of the experiment. Neill had assured him that, at worst, the sudden accumulation of metabolites in his bloodstream might induce a mild torpor, but his brain would be unimpaired.

'Nerve fibre, Robert,' Neill had told him time and again, 'never fatigues. The brain cannot tire.'

While he waited for Morley to move he checked the time from the clock mounted against the wall. Twelve twenty. Morley yawned, his face drawn under the grey skin. He looked tired and drab. He slumped down into the armchair, face in one hand. Lang reflected how frail and primitive those who slept would soon seem, their minds sinking off each evening under the load of accumulating toxins, the edge of their awareness worn and frayed. Suddenly he realized that at that very moment Neill himself was asleep. A curiously disconcerting vision of Neill, huddled in a rumpled bed two floors above, his blood-sugar low, and his mind drifting, rose before him.

Lang laughed at his own conceit, and Morley retrieved the rook he had just moved.

'I must be going blind. What am I doing?'

'No,' Lang said. He started to laugh again. 'I've just discovered I'm awake.'

Morley smiled. 'We'll have to put that down as one of the sayings of the week.' He replaced the rook, sat up and looked across at the table-tennis pair. Gorrell had hit a fast backhand low over the net and Avery was running after the ball.

'They seem to be okay. How about you?'

'Right on top of myself,' Lang said. His eyes flicked up and down the board and he moved before Morley caught his breath back.

Usually they went right through into the end-game, but tonight Morley had to concede on the twentieth move.

'Good,' he said encouragingly. 'You'll be able to take on Neill soon. Like another?'

'No. Actually the game bores me. I can see that's going to be a problem.'

'You'll face it. Give yourself time to find your legs.'

Lang pulled one of the Bach albums out of its rack in the record cabinet. He put a Brandenburg Concerto on the turntable and lowered the sapphire. As the rich, contrapuntal patterns chimed out he sat back, listening intently to the music.

Morley thought: Absurd. How fast can you run? Three weeks ago you were strictly a hep-cat.

The next few hours passed rapidly.

At one thirty they went up to the Surgery, where Morley and one of the interns gave them a quick physical, checking their renal clearances, heart rate and reflexes.

Dressed again, they went into the empty cafeteria for a snack and sat on the stools, arguing what to call this new fifth meal. Avery suggested 'Midfood', Morley 'Munch'.

At two they took their places in the Neurology theatre, and spent a couple of hours watching films of the hypno-drills of the past three weeks.

When the programme ended they started down for the gymnasium, the night almost over. They were still relaxed and cheerful; Gorrell led the way, playfully teasing Lang over some of the episodes in the films, mimicking his trance-like walk.

'Eyes shut, mouth open,' he demonstrated, swerving into Lang, who jumped nimbly out of his way. 'Look at you; you're doing it even now. Believe me, Lang, you're not awake, you're somnambulating.' He called back to Morley, 'Agreed, Doctor?'

Morley swallowed a yawn. 'Well, if he is, that makes two of us.' He followed them along the corridor, doing his best to stay awake, feeling as if he, and not the three men in front of him, had been without sleep for the last three weeks.

Though the Clinic was quiet, at Neill's orders all lights along the corridors and down the stairway had been left on. Ahead of them two orderlies checked that windows they passed were safely screened and doors were shut. Nowhere was there a single darkened alcove or shadow-trap.

Neill had insisted on this, reluctantly acknowledging a possible reflex association between darkness and sleep: 'Let's admit it. In all but a few organisms the association *is* strong enough to be a reflex. The higher mammals depend for their survival on a highly acute sensory apparatus, combined with a varying ability to store and classify information. Plunge them into darkness, cut off the flow of visual data to the cortex, and they're paralysed. Sleep is a defence reflex. It lowers the metabolic rate, conserves energy, increases the organism's survival-potential by merging it into its habitat...'

On the landing halfway down the staircase was a wide, shuttered window that by day opened out on to the parkscape behind the Clinic. As he passed it Gorrell stopped. He went over, released the blind, then unlatched the shutter.

Still holding it closed, he turned to Morley, watching from the flight above.

'Taboo, Doctor?' he asked.

Morley looked at each of the three men in turn. Gorrell was calm and unperturbed, apparently satisfying nothing more sinister than an idle whim. Lang sat on the rail, watching curiously with an expression of clinical disinterest. Only Avery seemed slightly anxious, his thin face wan and pinched. Morley had an irrelevant thought: four a.m. shadow – they'll need to shave twice a day. Then: why isn't Neill here? He knew they'd make for a window as soon as they got the chance.

He noticed Lang giving him an amused smile and shrugged, trying to disguise his uneasiness.

'Go ahead, if you want to. As Neill said, the wires are cut.'

Gorrell threw back the shutter, and they clustered round the window and stared out into the night. Below, pewter-grey lawns stretched towards the pines and low hills in the distance. A couple of miles away on their left a neon sign winked and beckoned.

Neither Gorrell nor Lang noticed any reaction, and their interest began to flag within a few moments. Avery felt a sudden lift under the heart, then controlled himself. His eyes began to sift the darkness; the sky was clear and cloudless, and through the stars he picked out the narrow, milky traverse of the galactic rim. He watched it silently, letting the wind cool the sweat on his face and neck.

Morley stepped over to the window and leaned his elbows on the sill next to Avery. Out of the corner of his eye he carefully waited for any motor tremor – a fluttering eyelid, accelerated breathing – that would signal a reflex discharging. He remembered Neill's warning: 'In Man sleep is largely volitional, and the reflex is conditioned by habit. But just because we've cut out the hypothalamic loops regulating the flow of consciousness doesn't mean the reflex won't discharge down some other pathway. However, sooner or later we'll have to take the risk and give them a glimpse of the dark side of the sun.'

Morley was musing on this when something nudged his shoulder.

'Doctor,' he heard Lang say. 'Doctor Morley.'

He pulled himself together with a start. He was alone at the window. Gorrell and Avery were halfway down the next flight of stairs.

'What's up?' Morley asked quickly.

'Nothing,' Lang assured him. 'We're just going back to the gym.' He looked closely at Morley. 'Are you all right?'

Morley rubbed his face. 'God, I must have been asleep.' He glanced at his watch. Four twenty. They had been at the window for over fifteen minutes. All he could remember was leaning on the sill. 'And I was worried about *you*.'

Everybody was amused, Gorrell particularly. 'Doctor,' he drawled, 'if you're interested I can recommend you to a good narcotomist.'

After five o'clock they felt a gradual ebb of tonus from their arm and leg muscles. Renal clearances were falling and breakdown products were slowly clogging their tissues. Their palms felt damp and numb, the soles of their feet like pads of sponge rubber. The sensation was vaguely unsettling, allied to no feelings of mental fatigue.

The numbness spread. Avery noticed it stretching the skin over his cheekbones, pulling at his temples and giving him a slight frontal migraine. He doggedly turned the pages of a magazine, his hands like lumps of putty.

Then Neill came down, and they began to revive. Neill looked fresh and spruce, bouncing on the tips of his toes.

'How's the night shift going?' he asked briskly, walking round each one of them in turn, smiling as he sized them up. 'Feel all right?'

'Not too bad, Doctor,' Gorrell told him. 'A slight case of insomnia.'

Neill roared, slapped him on the shoulder and led the way up to the Surgery laboratory.

At nine, shaved and in fresh clothes, they assembled in the lecture room. They felt cool and alert again. The peripheral numbness and slight head torpor had gone as soon as the detoxication drips had been plugged in, and Neill told them that within a week their kidneys would have enlarged sufficiently to cope on their own.

All morning and most of the afternoon they worked on a series of IQ, associative and performance tests. Neill kept them hard at it, steering swerving blips of light around a cathode screen, juggling with intricate numerical and geometric sequences, elaborating word-chains.

He seemed more than satisfied with the results.

'Shorter access times, deeper memory traces,' he pointed out to Morley when the three men had gone off at five for the rest period. 'Barrels of prime psychic marrow.' He gestured at the test cards spread out across the desk in his office. 'And you were worried about the Unconscious. Look at those Rorschachs of Lang's. Believe me, John, I'll soon have him reminiscing about his foetal experiences.'

Morley nodded, his first doubts fading.

Over the next two weeks either he or Neill was with the men continuously, sitting out under the floodlights in the centre of the gymnasium, assessing their assimilation of the eight extra hours, carefully watching for any symptoms of withdrawal. Neill carried everyone along, from one programme phase to the next, through the test periods, across the long hours of the interminable nights, his powerful ego injecting enthusiasm into every member of the unit.

Privately, Morley worried about the increasing emotional overlay apparent in the relationship between Neill and the three men. He was afraid they were becoming conditioned to identify Neill with the experiment. (Ring the meal bell and the subject salivates; but suddenly stop ringing the bell after a long period of conditioning and it temporarily loses the ability to feed itself. The hiatus barely harms a dog, but it might trigger disaster in an already oversensitized psyche.)

Neill was fully alert to this. At the end of the first two weeks, when he caught a bad head cold after sitting up all night and decided to spend the next day in bed, he called Morley into his office.

'The transference is getting much too positive. It needs to be eased off a little.'

'I agree,' Morley said. 'But how?'

'Tell them I'll be asleep for forty-eight hours,' Neill said. He picked up a stack of reports, plates and test cards and bundled them under one arm. 'I've deliberately overdosed myself with sedative to get some rest. I'm worn to a shadow, full fatigue syndrome, load-cells screaming. Lay it on.'

'Couldn't that be rather drastic?' Morley asked. 'They'll hate you for it.'

But Neill only smiled and went off to requisition an office near his bedroom.

That night Morley was on duty in the gymnasium from ten p.m. to six a.m. As usual he first checked that the orderlies were ready with their emergency trolleys, read through the log left by the previous supervisor, one of the senior interns, and then went over to the circle of chairs. He sat back on the sofa next to Lang and leafed through a magazine, watching the three men carefully. In the glare of the arc-lights their lean faces had a sallow, cyanosed look. The senior intern had warned him that Avery and Gorrell might overtire themselves at table-tennis, but by eleven p.m. they stopped playing and settled down in the armchairs. They read desultorily and made two trips up to the cafeteria, escorted each time by one of the orderlies. Morley told them about Neill, but surprisingly none of them made any comment.

Midnight came slowly. Avery read, his long body hunched up in an armchair. Gorrell played chess against himself.

Morley dozed.

Lang felt restless. The gymnasium's silence and absence of movement oppressed him. He switched on the gramophone and played through a Brandenburg, analysing its theme-trains. Then he ran a word-association test on himself, turning the pages of a book and using the top right-hand corner words as the control list.

Morley leaned over. 'Anything come up?' he asked.

'A few interesting responses.' Lang found a note-pad and jotted something down. 'I'll show them to Neill in the morning – or whenever he wakes up.' He gazed up pensively at the arc-lights. 'I was just speculating. What do you think the next step forward will be?'

'Forward where?' Morley asked.

Lang gestured expansively. 'I mean up the evolutionary slope. Three hundred million years ago we became air-breathers and left the seas behind. Now we've taken the next logical step forward and eliminated sleep. What's next?'

Morley shook his head. 'The two steps aren't analogous. Anyway, in point of fact you haven't left the primeval sea behind. You're still carrying a private replica of it around as your bloodstream. All you did was encapsulate a necessary piece of the physical environment in order to escape it.'

Lang nodded. 'I was thinking of something else. Tell me, has it ever occurred to you how completely death-orientated the psyche is?'

Morley smiled. 'Now and then,' he said, wondering where this led.

'It's curious,' Lang went on reflectively. 'The pleasure-pain principle, the whole survival-compulsion apparatus of sex, the Super-Ego's obsession with tomorrow – most of the time the psyche can't see farther than its own tombstone. Now why has it got this strange fixation? For one very obvious reason.' He tapped the air with his forefinger. 'Because every night it's given a pretty convincing reminder of the fate in store for it.'

'You mean the black hole,' Morley suggested wryly. 'Sleep?'

'Exactly. It's simply a pseudo-death. Of course, you're not aware of it, but it must be terrifying.' He frowned. 'I don't think even Neill realizes that, far from being restful, sleep is a genuinely traumatic experience.'

So that's it, Morley thought. The great father analyst has been caught napping on his own couch. He tried to decide which were worse – patients who knew a lot of psychiatry, or those who only knew a little.

'Eliminate sleep,' Lang was saying, 'and you also eliminate all the fear and defence mechanisms erected round it. Then, at last, the psyche has a chance to orientate towards something more valid.'

'Such as . . . ?' Morley asked.

'I don't know. Perhaps . . . Self?'

'Interesting,' Morley commented. It was three ten a.m. He decided to spend the next hour going through Lang's latest test cards.

He waited a discretionary five minutes, then stood up and walked over to the surgery office.

Lang hooked an arm across the back of the sofa and watched the orderly room door.

'What's Morley playing at?' he asked. 'Have either of you seen him anywhere?'

Avery lowered his magazine. 'Didn't he go off into the orderly room?'

'Ten minutes ago,' Lang said. 'He hasn't looked in since. There's supposed to be someone on duty with us continuously. Where is he?'

Gorrell, playing solitaire chess, looked up from his board. 'Perhaps these late nights are getting him down. You'd better wake him before Neill finds out. He's probably fallen asleep over a batch of your test cards.'

Lang laughed and settled down on the sofa. Gorrell reached out to the gramophone, took a record out of the rack and slid it on to the turntable.

As the gramophone began to hum Lang noticed how silent and deserted the gymnasium seemed. The Clinic was always quiet, but even at night a residual ebb and flow of sound – a chair dragging in the orderly room, a generator charging under one of the theatres – eddied through and kept it alive.

Now the air was flat and motionless. Lang listened carefully. The whole place had the dead, echoless feel of an abandoned building.

He stood up and strolled over to the orderly room. He knew Neill discouraged casual conversation with the control crew, but Morley's absence puzzled him.

He reached the door and peered through the window to see if Morley was inside.

The room was empty.

The light was on. Two emergency trolleys stood in their usual place against the wall near the door, a third was in the middle of the floor, a pack of playing cards strewn across its deck, but the group of three or four interns had gone.

Lang hesitated, reached down to open the door, and found it had been locked.

He tried the handle again, then called out over his shoulder:

'Avery. There's nobody in here.'

'Try next door. They're probably being briefed for tomorrow.'

Lang stepped over to the surgery office. The light was off but he could see the white enamelled desk and the big programme charts round the wall. There was no one inside.

Avery and Gorrell were watching him.

'Are they in there?' Avery asked.

'No.' Lang turned the handle. 'The door's locked.'

Gorrell switched off the gramophone and he and Avery came over. They tried the two doors again.

'They're here somewhere,' Avery said. 'There must be at least one person on duty.' He pointed to the end door. 'What about that one?'

'Locked,' Lang said. '69 always has been. I think it leads down to the basement.'

'Let's try Neill's office,' Gorrell suggested. 'If they aren't in there we'll stroll through to Reception and try to leave. This must be some trick of Neill's.'

There was no window in the door to Neill's office. Gorrell knocked, waited, knocked again more loudly.

Lang tried the handle, then knelt down. 'The light's off,' he reported.

Avery turned and looked round at the two remaining doors out of the gymnasium, both in the far wall, one leading up to the cafeteria and the Neurology wing, the other into the car park at the rear of the Clinic.

'Didn't Neill hint that he might try something like this on us?' he asked. 'To see whether we can go through a night on our own.'

'But Neill's asleep,' Lang objected. 'He'll be in bed for a couple of days. Unless . . .'

Gorrell jerked his head in the direction of the chairs. 'Come on. He and Morley are probably watching us now.'

They went back to their seats.

Gorrell dragged the chess stool over to the sofa and set up the pieces. Avery and Lang stretched out in armchairs and opened magazines, turning the pages deliberately. Above them the banks of arc-lights threw their wide cones of light down into the silence.

The only noise was the slow left-right, left-right motion of the clock.

Three fifteen a.m.

The shift was imperceptible. At first a slight change of perspective, a fading and regrouping of outlines. Somewhere a focus slipped, a shadow swung slowly across a wall, its angles breaking and lengthening. The motion was fluid, a procession of infinitesimals, but gradually its total direction emerged.

The gymnasium was shrinking. Inch by inch, the walls were moving inwards, encroaching across the periphery of the floor. As they shrank towards each other their features altered: the rows of skylights below the ceiling blurred and faded, the power cable running along the base of the wall merged into the skirting board, the square baffles of the air vents vanished into the grey distemper.

Above, like the undersurface of an enormous lift, the ceiling sank towards the floor ...

Gorrell leaned his elbows on the chessboard, face sunk in his hands. He had locked himself in a perpetual check, but he continued to shuttle the pieces in and out of one of the corner squares, now and then gazing into the air for inspiration, while his eyes roved up and down the walls around him.

Somewhere, he knew, Neill was watching him.

He moved, looked up and followed the wall opposite him down to the far corner, alert for the telltale signs of a retractable panel. For some while he had been trying to discover Neill's spy-hole, but without any success. The walls were blank and featureless; he had twice covered every square foot of the two facing him, and apart from the three doors there appeared to be no fault or aperture of even the most minute size anywhere on their surface.

After a while his left eye began to throb painfully, and he pushed away the chessboard and lay back. Above him a line of fluorescent tubes hung down from the ceiling, mounted in checkered plastic brackets that diffused the light. He was about to comment on his search for the spy-hole to Avery and Lang when he realized that any one of them could conceal a microphone.

He decided to stretch his legs, stood up and sauntered off across the floor. After sitting over the chessboard for half an hour he felt cramped and restless, and would have enjoyed tossing a ball up and down, or flexing his muscles on a rowing machine. But annoyingly no recreational facilities, apart from the three armchairs and the gramophone, had been provided.

He reached the end wall and wandered round, listening for any sound from the adjacent rooms. He was beginning to resent Neill spying on him and the entire keyhole conspiracy, and he noted with relief that it was a quarter past three: in under three hours it would all be over.

The gymnasium closed in. Now less than half its original size, its walls bare and windowless, it was a vast, shrinking box. The sides slid into each other, merging along an abstract hairline, like planes severing in a multi-dimensional flux. Only the clock and a single door remained ...

Lang had discovered where the microphone was hidden.

He sat forward in his chair, cracking his knuckles until Gorrell returned, then rose and offered him his seat. Avery was in the other armchair, feet up on the gramophone.

'Sit down for a bit,' Lang said. 'I feel like a stroll.'

Gorrell lowered himself into the chair. 'I'll ask Neill if we can have a ping-pong table in here. It should help pass the time and give us some exercise.'

'A good idea,' Lang agreed. 'If we can get the table through the door. I doubt if there's enough room in here, even if we moved the chairs right up against the wall.'

He walked off across the floor, surreptitiously peering through the orderly room window. The light was on, but there was still no one inside.

He ambled over to the gramophone and paced up and down near it for a few moments. Suddenly he swung round and caught his foot under the flex leading to the wall socket.

The plug fell out on to the floor. Lang left it where it lay, went over and sat down on the arm of Gorrell's chair.

'I've just disconnected the microphone,' he confided.

Gorrell looked round carefully. 'Where was it?'

Lang pointed. 'Inside the gramophone.' He laughed softly. 'I thought I'd pull Neill's leg. He'll be wild when he realizes he can't hear us.'

'Why do you think it was in the gramophone?' Gorrell asked.

'What better place? Besides, it couldn't be anywhere else. Apart from in there.' He gestured at the light bowl suspended from the centre of the ceiling. 'It's empty except for the two bulbs. The gramophone is the obvious place. I had a feeling it was there, but I wasn't sure until I noticed we had a gramophone, but no records.'

Gorrell nodded sagely.

Lang moved away, chuckling to himself.

Above the door of Room 69 the clock ticked on at three fifteen.

The motion was accelerating. What had once been the gymnasium was now a small room, seven feet wide, a tight, almost perfect cube. The walls plunged inwards, along colliding diagonals, only a few feet from their final focus . . .

Avery noticed Gorrell and Lang pacing around his chair. 'Either of you want to sit down yet?' he asked.

They shook their heads. Avery rested for a few minutes and then climbed out of the chair and stretched himself.

'Quarter past three,' he remarked, pressing his hands against the ceiling. 'This is getting to be a long night.'

He leaned back to let Gorrell pass him, and then started to follow the others round the narrow space between the armchair and the walls.

'I don't know how Neill expects us to stay awake in this hole for twenty-four hours a day,' he went on. 'Why haven't we got a television set in here? Even a radio would be something.'

They sidled round the chair together, Gorrell, followed by Avery, with Lang completing the circle, their shoulders beginning to hunch, their heads down as they watched the floor, their feet falling into the slow, leaden rhythm of the clock.

This, then, was the manhole: a narrow, vertical cubicle, a few feet wide, six deep. Above, a solitary, dusty bulb gleamed down from a steel grille. As if crumbling under the impetus of their own momentum, the surface of the walls had coarsened, the texture was that of stone, streaked and pitted . . .

Gorrell bent down to loosen one of his shoelaces and Avery bumped into him sharply, knocking his shoulder against the wall.

'All right?' he asked, taking Gorrell's arm. 'This place is a little overcrowded. I can't understand why Neill ever put us in here.'

He leaned against the wall, head bowed to prevent it from touching the ceiling, and gazed about thoughtfully.

Lang stood squeezed into the corner next to him, shifting his weight from one foot to the other.

Gorrell squatted down on his heels below them.

'What's the time?' he asked.

'I'd say about three fifteen,' Lang offered. 'More or less.'

'Lang,' Avery asked, 'where's the ventilator here?'

Lang peered up and down the walls and across the small square of ceiling. 'There must be one somewhere.' Gorrell stood up and they shuffled about, examining the floor between their feet.

'There may be a vent in the light grille,' Gorrell suggested. He reached up and slipped his fingers through the cage, running them behind the bulb.

'Nothing there. Odd. I should have thought we'd use the air in here within half an hour.'

'Easily,' Avery said. 'You know, there's something –'

Just then Lang broke in. He gripped Avery's elbow.

'Avery,' he asked. 'Tell me. How did we get here?'

'What do you mean, get here? We're on Neill's team.'

Lang cut him off. 'I know that.' He pointed at the floor. 'I mean, in here.'

Gorrell shook his head. 'Lang, relax. How do you think? Through the door.'

Lang looked squarely at Gorrell, then at Avery.

'What door?' he asked calmly.

Gorrell and Avery hesitated, then swung round to look at each wall in turn, scanning it from floor to ceiling. Avery ran his hands over the heavy masonry, then knelt down and felt the floor, digging his fingers at the rough stone slabs. Gorrell crouched beside him, scrabbling at the thin seams of dirt.

Lang backed out of their way into a corner, and watched them impassively. His face was calm and motionless, but in his left temple a single vein fluttered insanely.

When they finally stood up, staring at each other unsteadily, he flung himself between them at the opposite wall.

'Neill! Neill!' he shouted. He pounded angrily on the wall with his fists. 'Neill! Neill!'

Above him the light began to fade.

Morley closed the door of the surgery office behind him and went over to the desk. Though it was three fifteen a.m., Neill was probably awake, working on the latest material in the office next to his bedroom. Fortunately that afternoon's test cards, freshly marked by one of the interns, had only just reached his in-tray.

Morley picked out Lang's folder and started to sort through the cards. He suspected that Lang's responses to some of the key words and suggestion triggers lying disguised in the question forms might throw illuminating sidelights on to the real motives behind his equation of sleep and death.

The communicating door to the orderly room opened and an intern looked in.

'Do you want me to take over in the gym, Doctor?'

Morley waved him away. 'Don't bother. I'm going back in a moment.'

He selected the cards he wanted and began to initial his withdrawals. Glad to get away from the glare of the arc-lights, he delayed his return as long as he could, and it was three twenty-five a.m. when he finally left the office and stepped back into the gymnasium.

The men were sitting where he had left them. Lang watched him approach, head propped comfortably on a cushion. Avery was slouched down in his armchair, nose in a magazine, while Gorrell hunched over the chessboard, hidden behind the sofa.

'Anybody feel like coffee?' Morley called out, deciding they needed some exercise.

None of them looked up or answered. Morley felt a flicker of annoyance, particularly at Lang, who was staring past him at the clock.

Then he saw something that made him stop.

Lying on the polished floor ten feet from the sofa was a chess piece. He went over and picked it up. The piece was the black king. He wondered how Gorrell could be playing chess with one of the two essential pieces of the game missing when he noticed three more pieces lying on the floor near by.

His eyes moved to where Gorrell was sitting.

Scattered over the floor below the chair and sofa was the rest of the set. Gorrell was slumped over the stool. One of his elbows had slipped and the arm dangled between his knees, knuckles resting on the floor. The other hand supported his face. Dead eyes peered down at his feet.

Morley ran over to him, shouting: 'Lang! Avery! Get the orderlies!'

He reached Gorrell and pulled him back off the stool.

'Lang!' he called again.

Lang was still staring at the clock, his body in the stiff, unreal posture of a waxworks dummy.

Morley let Gorrell loll back on to the sofa, leaned over and glanced at Lang's face.

He crossed to Avery, stretched out behind the magazine, and jerked his shoulder. Avery's head bobbed stiffly. The magazine slipped and fell from his hands, leaving his fingers curled in front of his face.

Morley stepped over Avery's legs to the gramophone. He switched it on, gripped the volume control and swung it round to full amplitude.

Above the orderly room door an alarm bell shrilled out through the silence.

'Weren't you with them?' Neill asked sharply.

'No,' Morley admitted. They were standing by the door of the emergency ward. Two orderlies had just dismantled the electro-therapy unit and were wheeling the console away on a trolley. Outside in the gymnasium a quiet, urgent traffic of nurses and interns moved past. All but a single bank of arc-lights had been switched off, and the gymnasium seemed like a deserted stage at the end of a performance.

'I slipped into the office to pick up a few test cards,' he explained. 'I wasn't gone more than ten minutes.'

'You were supposed to watch them continuously,' Neill snapped.

'Not wander off by yourself whenever you felt like it. What do you think we had the gym and this entire circus set up for?'

It was a little after five thirty a.m. After working hopelessly on the three men for a couple of hours, he was close to exhaustion. He looked down at them, lying inertly in their cots, canvas sheets buckled up to their chins. They had barely changed, but their eyes were open and unblinking, and their faces had the empty, reflexless look of psychic zero.

An intern bent over Lang, thumbing a hypodermic. Morley stared at the floor. 'I think they would have gone anyway.'

'How can you say that?' Neill clamped his lips together. He felt frustrated and impotent. He knew Morley was probably right – the three men were in terminal withdrawal, unresponsive to either insulin or electrotherapy, and a vice-tight catatonic seizure didn't close in out of nowhere – but as always refused to admit anything without absolute proof.

He led the way into his office and shut the door.

'Sit down.' He pulled a chair out for Morley and prowled off round the room, slamming a fist into his palm.

'All right, John. What is it?'

Morley picked up one of the test cards lying on the desk, balanced it on a corner and spun it between his fingers. Phrases swam through his mind, tentative and uncertain, like blind fish.

'What do you want me to say?' he asked. 'Reactivation of the infantile imago? A regression into the great, slumbering womb? Or to put it more simply still – just a fit of pique?'

'Go on.'

Morley shrugged. 'Continual consciousness is more than the brain can stand. Any signal repeated often enough eventually loses its meaning. Try saying the word "sleep" fifty times. After a point the brain's self-awareness dulls. It's no longer able to grasp who or why it is, and it rides adrift.'

'What do we do then?'

'Nothing. Short of re-scoring all the way down to Lumbar 1. The central nervous system can't stand narcotomy.'

Neill shook his head. 'You're lost,' he said curtly. 'Juggling with generalities isn't going to bring those men back. First, we've got to find out what happened to them, what they actually felt and saw.'

Morley frowned dubiously. 'That jungle is marked "private". Even if you do, is a psychotic's withdrawal drama going to make any sense?'

'Of course it will. However insane it seems to us, it was real enough to them. If we know the ceiling fell in or the whole gym filled with ice-cream or turned into a maze, we've got something to work on.' He sat down on the desk. 'Do you remember that story of Chekov's you told me about?'

'"The Bet"? Yes.'

'I read it last night. Curious. It's a lot nearer what you're really trying to say than you know.' He gazed round the office. 'This room in which the man is penned for ten years symbolizes the mind driven to the furthest limits of self-awareness ... Something very similar happened to Avery, Gorrell and Lang. They must have reached a stage beyond which they could no longer contain the idea of their own identity. But far from being unable to grasp the idea, I'd say that they were conscious of nothing else. Like the man in the spherical mirror, who can only see a single gigantic eye staring back at him.'

'So you think their withdrawal is a straightforward escape from the eye, the overwhelming ego?'

'Not escape,' Neill corrected. 'The psychotic never escapes from anything. He's much more sensible. He merely readjusts reality to suit himself. Quite a trick to learn, too. The room in Chekov's story gives me an idea as to how they might have re-adjusted. Their particular equivalent of this room was the gym. I'm beginning to realize it was a mistake to put them in there – all those lights blazing down, the huge floor, high walls. They merely exaggerate the sensation of overload. In fact the gym might easily have become an external projection of their own egos.'

Neill drummed his fingers on the desk. 'My guess is that at this moment they're either striding around in there the size of hundred-foot giants, or else they've cut it down to their own dimensions. More probably that. They've just pulled the gym in on themselves.'

Morley grinned bleakly. 'So all we've got to do now is pump them full of honey and apomorphine and coax them out. Suppose they refuse?'

'They won't,' Neill said. 'You'll see.'

There was a rap on the door. An intern stuck his head through.

'Lang's coming out of it, Doctor. He's calling for you.'

Neill bounded out.

Morley followed him into the ward.

Lang was lying in his cot, body motionless under the canvas sheet. His lips were parted slightly. No sound came from them but Morley, bending over next to Neill, could see his hyoid bone vibrating in spasms.

'He's very faint,' the intern warned.

Neill pulled up a chair and sat down next to the cot. He made a visible effort of concentration, flexing his shoulders. He bent his head close to Lang's and listened.

Five minutes later it came through again.

Lang's lips quivered. His body arched under the sheet, straining at the buckles, and then subsided.

'Neill . . . Neill,' he whispered. The sounds, thin and strangled, seemed to be coming from the bottom of a well. 'Neill . . . Neill . . . Neill . . .'

Neill stroked his forehead with a small, neat hand.

'Yes, Bobby,' he said gently. His voice was feather-soft, caressing. 'I'm here, Bobby. You can come out now.'

1957

TRACK 12

'Guess again,' Sheringham said.

Maxted clipped on the headphones, carefully settled them over his ears. He concentrated as the disc began to spin, trying to catch some echo of identity.

The sound was a rapid metallic rustling, like iron filings splashing through a funnel. It ran for ten seconds, repeated itself a dozen times, then ended abruptly in a string of blips.

'Well?' Sheringham asked. 'What is it?'

Maxted pulled off his headphones, rubbed one of his ears. He had been listening to the records for hours and his ears felt bruised and numb.

'Could be anything. An ice-cube melting?'

Sheringham shook his head, his little beard wagging.

Maxted shrugged. 'A couple of galaxies colliding?'

'No. Sound waves don't travel through space. I'll give you a clue. It's one of those *proverbial* sounds.' He seemed to be enjoying the catechism.

Maxted lit a cigarette, threw the match onto the laboratory bench. The head melted a tiny pool of wax, froze and left a shallow black scar. He watched it pleasurably, conscious of Sheringham fidgeting beside him.

He pumped his brains for an obscene simile. 'What about a fly –'

'Time's up,' Sheringham cut in. '*A pin dropping.*' He took the 3-inch disc off the player, angled it into its sleeve.

'In actual fall, that is, not impact. We used a fifty-foot shaft and eight microphones. I thought you'd get that one.'

He reached for the last record, a 12-inch LP, but Maxted stood up before he got it to the turntable. Through the french windows he could see the patio, a table, glasses and decanter gleaming in the darkness. Sheringham and his infantile games suddenly irritated him; he felt impatient with himself for tolerating the man so long.

'Let's get some air,' he said brusquely, shouldering past one of the amplifier rigs. 'My ears feel like gongs.'

'By all means,' Sheringham agreed promptly. He placed the record carefully on the turntable and switched off the player. 'I want to save this one until later anyway.'

They went out into the warm evening air. Sheringham turned on the Japanese lanterns and they stretched back in the wicker chairs under the open sky.

'I hope you weren't too bored,' Sheringham said as he handled the decanter. 'Microsonics is a fascinating hobby, but I'm afraid I may have let it become an obsession.'

Maxted grunted non-committally. 'Some of the records are interesting,' he admitted. 'They have a sort of crazy novelty value, like blown-up photographs of moths' faces and razor blades. Despite what you claim, though, I can't believe microsonics will ever become a scientific tool. It's just an elaborate laboratory toy.'

Sheringham shook his head. 'You're completely wrong, of course. Remember the cell division series I played first of all? Amplified 100,000 times animal cell division sounds like a lot of girders and steel sheets being ripped apart – how did you put it? – a car smash in slow motion. On the other hand, plant cell division is an electronic poem, all soft chords and bubbling tones. Now there you have a perfect illustration of how microsonics can reveal the distinction between the animal and plant kingdoms.'

'Seems a damned roundabout way of doing it,' Maxted commented, helping himself to soda. 'You might as well calculate the speed of your car from the apparent motion of the stars. Possible, but it's easier to look at the speedometer.'

Sheringham nodded, watching Maxted closely across the table. His interest in the conversation appeared to have exhausted itself, and the two men sat silently with their glasses. Strangely, the hostility between them, of so many years' standing, now became less veiled, the contrast of personality, manner and physique more pronounced. Maxted, a tall fleshy man with a coarse handsome face, lounged back almost horizontally in his chair, thinking about Susan Sheringham. She was at the Turnbulls' party, and but for the fact that it was no longer discreet of him to be seen at the Turnbulls' – for the all-too-familiar reason – he would have passed the evening with her, rather than with her grotesque little husband.

He surveyed Sheringham with as much detachment as he could muster, wondering whether this prim unattractive man, with his pedantry and in-bred academic humour, had any redeeming qualities whatever. None, certainly, at a casual glance, though it required some courage and pride to have invited him round that evening. His motives, however, would be typically eccentric.

The pretext, Maxted reflected, had been slight enough – Sheringham, professor of biochemistry at the university, maintained a lavish home laboratory; Maxted, a run-down athlete with a bad degree, acted as torpedo-man for a company manufacturing electron microscopes; a visit, Sheringham had suggested over the phone, might be to the profit of both.

Of course, nothing of this had in fact been mentioned. But nor, as yet, had he referred to Susan, the real subject of the evening's charade. Maxted speculated upon the possible routes Sheringham might take towards the inevitable confrontation scene; not for him the nervous circular pacing, the well-thumbed photostat, or the tug at the shoulder. There was a vicious adolescent streak running through Sheringham –

Maxted broke out of his reverie abruptly. The air in the patio had become suddenly cooler, almost as if a powerful refrigerating unit had been switched on. A rash of goose-flesh raced up his thighs and down the back of his neck, and he reached forward and finished what was left of his whisky.

'Cold out here,' he commented.

Sheringham glanced at his watch. 'Is it?' he said. There was a hint of indecision in his voice; for a moment he seemed to be waiting for a signal. Then he pulled himself together and, with an odd half-smile, said: 'Time for the last record.'

'What do you mean?' Maxted asked.

'Don't move,' Sheringham said. He stood up. 'I'll put it on.' He pointed to a loudspeaker screwed to the wall above Maxted's head, grinned and ducked out.

Shivering uncomfortably, Maxted peered up into the silent evening sky, hoping that the vertical current of cold air that had sliced down into the patio would soon dissipate itself.

A low noise crackled from the speaker, multiplied by a circle of other speakers which he noticed for the first time had been slung among the trellis-work around the patio.

Shaking his head sadly at Sheringham's antics, he decided to help himself to more whisky. As he stretched across the table he swayed and rolled back uncontrollably into his chair. His stomach seemed to be full of mercury, ice-cold and enormously heavy. He pushed himself forward again, trying to reach the glass, and knocked it across the table. His brain began to fade, and he leaned his elbows helplessly on the glass edge of the table and felt his head fall onto his wrists.

When he looked up again Sheringham was standing in front of him, smiling sympathetically.

'Not too good, eh?' he said.

Breathing with difficulty, Maxted managed to lean back. He tried to speak to Sheringham, but he could no longer remember any words. His heart switchbacked, and he grimaced at the pain.

'Don't worry,' Sheringham assured him. 'The fibrillation is only a side effect. Disconcerting, perhaps, but it will soon pass.'

He strolled leisurely around the patio, scrutinizing Maxted from several angles. Evidently satisfied, he sat down on the table. He picked up the siphon and swirled the contents about. 'Chromium cyanate. Inhibits the coenzyme system controlling the body's fluid balances, floods hydroxyl ions into the bloodstream. In brief, you drown. Really drown, that is, not merely suffocate as you would if you were immersed in an external bath. However, I mustn't distract you.'

He inclined his head at the speakers. Being fed into the patio was a curiously muffled spongy noise, like elastic waves lapping in a latex sea. The rhythms were huge and ungainly, overlaid by the deep leaden wheezing of a gigantic bellows. Barely audible at first, the sounds rose until they filled the patio and shut out the few traffic noises along the highway.

'Fantastic, isn't it?' Sheringham said. Twirling the siphon by its neck he stepped over Maxted's legs and adjusted the tone control under one of the speaker boxes. He looked blithe and spruce, almost ten years younger. 'These are 30-second repeats, 400 microsens, amplification one thousand. I admit I've edited the track a little, but it's still remarkable how repulsive a beautiful sound can become. You'll never guess what this was.'

Maxted stirred sluggishly. The lake of mercury in his stomach was as cold and bottomless as an oceanic trench, and his arms and legs had become enormous, like the bloated appendages of a drowned giant. He could just see Sheringham bobbing about in front of him, and hear the slow beating of the sea in the distance. Nearer now, it pounded with a dull insistent rhythm, the great waves ballooning and bursting like bubbles in a lava sea.

'I'll tell you, Maxted, it took me a year to get that recording,' Sheringham was saying. He straddled Maxted, gesturing with the siphon. 'A year. Do you know how ugly a year can be?' For a moment he paused, then tore himself from the memory. 'Last Saturday, just after midnight, you and Susan were lying back in this same chair. You know, Maxted, there are audio-probes everywhere here. Slim as pencils, with a six-inch focus. I had four in that headrest alone.' He added, as a footnote: 'The wind is your own breathing, fairly heavy at the time, if I remember; your interlocked pulses produced the thunder effect.'

Maxted drifted in a wash of sound.

Some while later Sheringham's face filled his eyes, beard wagging, mouth working wildly.

'Maxted! You've only two more guesses, so for God's sake concentrate,' he shouted irritably, his voice almost lost among the thunder rolling from the sea. 'Come on, man, what is it? Maxted!'

he bellowed. He leapt for the nearest loudspeaker and drove up the volume. The sound boomed out of the patio, reverberating into the night.

Maxted had almost gone now, his fading identity a small featureless island nearly eroded by the waves beating across it.

Sheringham knelt down and shouted into his ear.

'Maxted, can you hear the sea? Do you know where you're drowning?'

A succession of gigantic flaccid waves, each more lumbering and enveloping than the last, rode down upon them.

'In a kiss!' Sheringham screamed. 'A kiss!'

The island slipped and slid away into the molten shelf of the sea.

1958

THE WAITING GROUNDS

Whether Henry Tallis, my predecessor at Murak Radio Observatory, knew about the Waiting Grounds I can't say. On the whole it seems obvious he must have done, and that the three weeks he spent handing the station over to me – a job which could easily have been done in three days – were merely to give him sufficient time to decide whether or not to tell me about them. Certainly he never did, and the implied judgment against me is one I haven't yet faced up to.

I remember that on the first evening after my arrival at Murak he asked me a question I've been puzzling over ever since.

We were up on the lounge deck of the observatory, looking out at the sand-reefs and fossil cones of the volcano jungle glowing in the false dusk, the great 250-foot steel bowl of the telescope humming faintly in the air above us.

'Tell me, Quaine,' Tallis suddenly asked, 'where would you like to be when the world ends?'

'I haven't really thought about it,' I admitted. 'Is there any urgency?'

'Urgency?' Tallis smiled at me thinly, his eyes amiable but assessing me shrewdly. 'Wait until you've been here a little longer.'

He had almost finished his last tour at the observatory and I assumed he was referring to the desolation around us which he, after fifteen years, was leaving thanklessly to my entire care. Later, of course, I realized how wrong I was, just as I misjudged the whole of Tallis's closed, complex personality.

He was a lean, ascetic-looking man of about fifty, withheld and moody, as I discovered the moment I debarked from the freighter flying me in to Murak – instead of greeting me at the ramp he sat in the half-track a hundred yards away at the edge of the port, watching silently through dark glasses as I heaved my suitcases across the burning, lava-thick sunlight, legs weary after the massive deceleration, stumbling in the unfamiliar gravity.

The gesture seemed characteristic. Tallis's manner was aloof and sardonic; everything he said had the same deliberately ambiguous overtones, that air of private mystery recluses and extreme introjects assume as a defence. Not that Tallis was in any way pathological – no one could spend fifteen years, even with six-monthly leaves, virtually alone on a remote planetary clinker like Murak without developing a few curious mannerisms. In fact, as I all too soon realized, what was really remarkable about Tallis was the degree to which he had preserved his sanity, not surrendered it.

He listened keenly to the latest news from Earth.

'The first pilotless launchings to Proxima Centauri are scheduled for 2250 ... the UN Assembly at Lake Success have just declared themselves a sovereign state ... V-R Day celebrations are to be discontinued – you must have heard it all on the radiocasts.'

'I haven't got a radio here,' Tallis said. 'Apart from the one up there, and that's tuned to the big spiral networks in Andromeda. On Murak we listen only to the important news.'

I nearly retorted that by the time it reached Murak the news, however important, would be a million years old, but on that first evening I was preoccupied with adjusting myself to an unfamiliar planetary environment – notably a denser atmosphere, slightly higher (1.2 E) gravity, vicious temperature swings from $-30°$ to $+160°$ – and programming new routines to fit myself into Murak's 18-hour day.

Above all, there was the prospect of two years of near-absolute isolation.

Ten miles from Murak Reef, the planet's only settlement, the observatory was sited among the first hills marking the northern edge of the inert volcano jungle which spread southward to

Murak's equator. It consisted of the giant telescope and a straggling nexus of twenty or thirty asbestos domes which housed the automatic data processing and tracking units, generator and refrigerating plant, and a miscellany of replacement and vehicle stores, workshops and ancillary equipment.

The observatory was self-sufficient as regards electric power and water. On the near-by slopes farms of solar batteries had been planted out in quarter-mile strips, the thousands of cells winking in the sunlight like a field of diamonds, sucking power from the sun to drive the generator dynamos. On another slope, its huge mouth permanently locked into the rock face, a mobile water synthesizer slowly bored its way through the desert crust, mining out oxygen and hydrogen combined into the surface minerals.

'You'll have plenty of spare time on your hands,' the Deputy Director of the Astrographic Institute on Ceres had warned me when I initialled the contract. 'There's a certain amount of routine maintenance, checking the power feeds to the reflector traverses and the processing units, but otherwise you won't need to touch the telescope. A big digital does the heavy thinking, tapes all the data down in 2000-hour schedules. You fly the cans out with you when you go on leave.'

'So apart from shovelling the sand off the doorstep there's virtually nothing for me to do?' I'd commented.

'That's what you're being paid for. Probably not as much as you deserve. Two years will seem a long time, even with three leave intervals. But don't worry about going crazy. You aren't alone on Murak. You'll just be bored. £2000 worth, to be exact. However, you say you have a thesis to write. And you never know, you may like it there. Tallis, the observer you're taking over from, went out in '03 for two years like yourself, and stayed fifteen. He'll show you the ropes. Pleasant fellow, by all accounts, a little whimsical, probably try to pull your leg.'

Tallis drove me down to the settlement the first morning to collect my heavy vacuum baggage that had travelled spacehold.

'Murak Reef,' he pointed out as the old '95 Chrysler half-track churned through the thick luminous ash silted over the metal road. We crossed a system of ancient lava lakes, flat grey disks half a mile wide, their hard crusts blistered and pocked by the countless meteor showers that had driven into Murak during the past million years. In the distance a group of long flat-roofed sheds and three high ore elevators separated themselves from the landscape.

'I suppose they warned you. One supplies depot, a radio terminal and the minerals concession. Latest reliable estimates put the total population at seven.'

I stared out at the surrounding desert floor, cracked and tiered by the heat swings into what looked like huge plates of rusted iron, and at the massed cones of the volcano jungle yellowing in the sand haze. It was 4 o'clock local time – early morning – but the temperature was already over 80°. We drove with windows shuttered, sun curtain down, refrigerating unit pumping noisily.

'Must be fun on Saturday night,' I commented. 'Isn't there anything else?'

'Just the thermal storms, and a mean noon temperature of 160°.'

'In the shade?'

Tallis laughed. 'Shade? You must have a sense of humour. There isn't any shade on Murak. Don't ever forget it. Half an hour before noon the temperature starts to go up two degrees a minute. If you're caught out in it you'll be putting a match to your own pyre.'

Murak Reef was a dust hole. In the sheds backing onto the depot the huge ore crushers and conveyors of the extraction plants clanked and slammed. Tallis introduced me to the agent, a morose old man called Pickford, and to two young engineers taking the wraps off a new grader. No one made any attempt at small talk. We nodded briefly, loaded my luggage onto the half-track and left.

'A taciturn bunch,' I said. 'What are they mining?'

'Tantalum, Columbium, the Rare Earths. A heartbreaking job, the concentrations are barely workable. They're tempted to Murak by fabulous commission rates, but they're lucky if they can even fill their norms.'

'You can't be sorry you're leaving. What made you stay here fifteen years?'

'It would take me fifteen years to tell you,' Tallis rejoined. 'I like the empty hills and the dead lakes.'

I murmured some comment, and aware that I wasn't satisfied he suddenly scooped a handful of grey sand off the seat, held it up and let it sift away through his fingers. 'Prime archezoic loam. Pure bedrock. Spit on it and anything might happen. Perhaps you'll understand me if I say I've been waiting for it to rain.'

'Will it?'

Tallis nodded. 'In about two million years, so someone who came here told me.'

He said it with complete seriousness.

During the next few days, as we checked the stores and equipment inventories and ran over the installation together, I began to wonder if Tallis had lost his sense of time. Most men left to themselves for an indefinite period develop some occupational interest: chess or an insoluble dream-game or merely a compulsive wood-whittling. But Tallis, as far as I could see, did nothing. The cabin, a three-storey drum built round a central refrigerating column, was spartan and comfortless. Tallis's only recreation seemed to be staring out at the volcano jungle. This was an almost obsessive activity – all evening and most of the afternoon he would sit up on the lounge deck, gazing out at the hundreds of extinct cones visible from the observatory, their colours running the spectrum from red to violet as the day swung round into night.

The first indication of what Tallis was watching for came about a week before he was due to leave. He had crated up his few possessions and we were clearing out one of the small storage domes near the telescope. In the darkness at the back, draped across a pile of old fans, track links and beer coolers, were two pedal-powered refrigerator suits, enormous unwieldy sacks equipped with chest pylons and hand-operated cycle gears.

'Do you ever have to use these?' I asked Tallis, glumly visualizing what a generator failure could mean.

He shook his head. 'They were left behind by a survey team which did some work out in the volcanoes. There's an entire camp lying around in these sheds, in case you ever feel like a weekend on safari.'

Tallis was by the door. I moved my flashlight away and was about to switch it off when something flickered up at me from the floor. I stepped over the debris, searched about and found a small circular aluminium chest, about two feet across by a foot deep. Mounted on the back was a battery pack, thermostat and temperature selector. It was a typical relic of an expensively mounted expedition, probably a cocktail cabinet or hat box. Embossed in heavy gold lettering on the lid were the initials 'C.F.N.'

Tallis came over from the door.

'What's this?' he asked sharply, adding his flash to mine.

I would have left the case where it lay, but there was something in Tallis's voice, a distinct inflection of annoyance, that made me pick it up and shoulder past into the sunlight.

I cleaned off the dust, Tallis at my shoulder. Keying open the vacuum seals I sprung back the lid. Inside was a small tape recorder, spool racks and a telescopic boom mike that cantilevered three feet up into the air, hovering a few inches from my mouth. It was a magnificent piece of equipment, a single-order job hand-made by a specialist, worth at least £500 apart from the case.

'Beautifully tooled,' I remarked to Tallis. I tipped the platform and watched it spring gently. 'The air bath is still intact.'

I ran my fingers over the range indicator and the selective six-channel reading head. It was even fitted with a sonic trip, a useful device which could be set to trigger at anything from a fly's foot-fall to a walking crane's.

The trip had been set; I wondered what might have strayed across it when I saw that someone had anticipated me. The tape between the spools had been ripped out, so roughly that one spool had been torn off its bearings. The rack was empty, and the two frayed tabs hooked to the spool axles were the only pieces of tape left.

'Somebody was in a hurry,' I said aloud. I depressed the lid and polished the initials with my fingertips. 'This must have belonged to one of the members of the survey. *C. F. N.* Do you want to send it on to him?'

Tallis watched me pensively. 'No. I'm afraid the two members of the team died here. Just over a year ago.'

He told me about the incident. Two Cambridge geologists had negotiated through the Institute for Tallis's help in establishing a camp ten miles out in the volcano jungle, where they intended to work for a year, analysing the planet's core materials. The cost of bringing a vehicle to Murak was prohibitive, so Tallis had transported all the equipment to the camp site and set it up for them.

'I arranged to visit them once a month with power packs, water and supplies. The first time everything seemed all right. They were both over sixty, but standing up well to the heat. The camp and laboratory were running smoothly, and they had a small transmitter they could have used in an emergency.

'I saw them three times altogether. On my fourth visit they had vanished. I estimated that they'd been missing for about a week. Nothing was wrong. The transmitter was working, and there was plenty of water and power. I assumed they'd gone out collecting samples, lost themselves and died quickly in the first noon high.'

'You never found the bodies?'

'No. I searched for them, but in the volcano jungle the contours of the valley floors shift from hour to hour. I notified the Institute and two months later an inspector flew in from Ceres and drove out to the site with me. He certified the deaths, told me to dismantle the camp and store it here. There were a few personal things, but I've heard nothing from any friends or relatives.'

'Tragic,' I commented. I closed the tape recorder and carried it into the shed. We walked back to the cabin. It was an hour to noon, and the parabolic sun bumper over the roof was a bowl of liquid fire.

I said to Tallis: 'What on earth were they hoping to catch in the volcano jungle? The sonic trip was set.'

'Was it?' Tallis shrugged. 'What are you suggesting?'

'Nothing. It's just curious. I'm surprised there wasn't more of an investigation.'

'Why? To start with, the fare from Ceres is £800, over £3000 from Earth. They were working privately. Why should anyone waste time and money doubting the obvious?'

I wanted to press Tallis for detail, but his last remark seemed to close the episode. We ate a silent lunch, then went out on a tour of the solar farms, replacing burnt-out thermo-couples. I was left with a vanished tape, two deaths, and a silent teasing suspicion that linked them neatly together.

Over the next days I began to watch Tallis more closely, waiting for another clue to the enigma growing around him.

I did learn one thing that astonished me.

I had asked him about his plans for the future; these were indefinite – he said something vague about a holiday, nothing he anticipated with any eagerness, and sounded as if he had given no thought whatever to his retirement. Over the last few days, as his departure time drew closer, the entire focus of his mind became fixed upon the volcano jungle; from dawn until late into the night he sat quietly in his chair, staring out at the ghostless panorama of disintegrating cones, adrift in some private time sea.

'When are you coming back?' I asked with an attempt at playfulness, curious why he was leaving Murak at all.

He took the question seriously. 'I'm afraid I won't be. Fifteen years is long enough, just about the limit of time one can spend continuously in a single place. After that one gets institutionalized –'

'Continuously?' I broke in. 'You've had your leaves?'

'No, I didn't bother. I was busy here.'

'Fifteen years!' I shouted. 'Good God, why? In this of all places! And what do you mean, "busy"? You're just sitting here, waiting for nothing. What are you supposed to be watching for, anyway?'

Tallis smiled evasively, started to say something and then thought better of it.

The question pressed round him. What *was* he waiting for? Were the geologists still alive? Was he expecting them to return, or make some signal? As I watched him pace about the cabin on his last morning I was convinced there was something he couldn't quite bring himself to tell me. Almost melodramatically he watched out over the desert, delaying his departure until the thirty-minute take-off siren hooted from the port. As we climbed into the half-track I fully expected the glowing spectres of the two geologists to come looming out of the volcano jungle, uttering cries of murder and revenge.

He shook my hand carefully before he went aboard. 'You've got my address all right? You're quite sure?' For some reason, which confused my cruder suspicions, he had made a special point of ensuring that both I and the Institute would be able to contact him.

'Don't worry,' I said. 'I'll let you know if it rains.'

He looked at me sombrely. 'Don't wait too long.' His eyes strayed past my head towards the southern horizon, through the sand-haze to the endless sea of cones. He added: 'Two million years is a long time.'

I took his arm as we walked to the ramp. 'Tallis,' I asked quietly, 'what are you watching for? There's something, isn't there?'

He pulled away from me, collected himself. 'What?' he said shortly, looking at his wristwatch.

'You've been trying to tell me all week,' I insisted. 'Come on, man.'

He shook his head abruptly, muttered something about the heat and stepped quickly through the lock.

I started to shout after him: 'Those two geologists are out there . . . !' but the five-minute siren shattered the air and by the time it stopped Tallis had disappeared down the companionway and crewmen were shackling on the launching gantry and sealing the cargo and passenger locks.

I stood at the edge of the port as the ship cleared its take-off check, annoyed with myself for waiting until the last impossible moment to press Tallis for an explanation. Half an hour later he was gone.

Over the next few days Tallis began to slide slowly into the back of my mind. I gradually settled into the observatory, picked out new routines to keep time continuously on the move. Mayer, the metallurgist down at the mine, came over to the cabin most evenings to play chess and forget his pitifully low extraction rates. He was a big, muscular fellow of thirty-five who loathed Murak's climate, geology and bad company, a little crude but the sort of tonic I needed after an overdose of Tallis.

Mayer had met Tallis only once, and had never heard about the deaths of the two geologists.

'Damned fools, what were they looking for? Nothing to do with geology, Murak hasn't got one.'

Pickford, the old agent down at the depot, was the only person on Murak who remembered the two men, but time had garbled his memories.

'Salesmen, they were,' he told me, blowing into his pipe. 'Tallis did the heavy work for them. Should never have come here, trying to sell all those books.'

'Books?'

'Cases full. Bibles, if I recall.'

'Textbooks,' I suggested. 'Did you see them?'

'Sure I did,' he said, puttering to himself. 'Guinea moroccos.' He jerked his head sharply. 'You won't sell them here, I told them.'

It sounded exactly like a dry piece of academic humour. I could see Tallis and the two scientists pulling Pickford's leg, passing off their reference library as a set of commercial samples.

I suppose the whole episode would eventually have faded, but Tallis's charts kept my interest going. There were about twenty of them, half million aerials of the volcano jungle within a fifteen-mile radius of the observatory. One of them was marked with what I assumed to be the camp site of the geologists and alternative routes to and from the observatory. The camp was just over ten miles away, across terrain that was rough but not over-difficult for a tracked car.

I still suspected I was getting myself wound up over nothing. A meaningless approach arrow on the charts, the faintest suggestion of a cryptic 'X', and I should have been off like a rocket after a geldspar mine or two mysterious graves. I was almost sure that Tallis had not been responsible, either by negligence or design, for the deaths of the two men, but that still left a number of unanswered questions.

The next clear day I checked over the half-track, strapped a flare pistol into my knee holster and set off, warning Pickford to listen out for a mayday call on the Chrysler's transmitter.

It was just after dawn when I gunned the half-track out of the observatory compound and headed up the slope between two battery farms, following the route mapped out on the charts. Behind me the telescope swung slowly on its bogies, tirelessly sweeping its great steel ear through the Cepheid talk. The temperature was in the low seventies, comfortably cool for Murak, the sky a fresh cerise, broken by lanes of indigo that threw vivid violet lights on the drifts of grey ash on the higher slopes of the volcano jungle.

The observatory soon fell behind, obscured by the exhaust dust. I passed the water synthesizer, safely pointed at ten thousand tons of silicon hydrate, and within twenty minutes reached the nearest cone, a white broad-backed giant two hundred feet high, and drove round it into the first valley. Fifty feet across at their summits, the volcanoes jostled together like a herd of enormous elephants, separated by narrow dust-filled valleys, sometimes no more than a hundred yards apart, here and there giving way to the flat mile-long deck of a fossil lava lake. Wherever possible the route took advantage of these, and I soon picked up the tracks left by the Chrysler on its trips a year earlier.

I reached the site in three hours. What was left of the camp stood on a beach overlooking one of the lakes, a dismal collection of fuel cylinders, empty cold stores and water tanks sinking under the tides of dust washed up by the low thermal winds. On the far side of the lake the violet-capped cones of the volcanoes ranged southwards. Behind, a crescent of sharp cliffs cut off half the sky.

I walked round the site, looking for some trace of the two geologists. A battered tin field-desk lay on its side, green paint blistered and scratched. I turned it over and pulled out its drawers, finding nothing except a charred notebook and a telephone, the receiver melted solidly into its cradle.

Tallis had done his job too well.

The temperature was over 100° by the time I climbed back into the half-track and a couple of miles ahead I had to stop as the cooling unit was draining power from the spark plugs and stalling the engine. The outside temperature was 130°, the sky a roaring shield, reflected in the slopes around me so that they seemed to stream with molten wax. I sealed all the shutters and changed into neutral, even then having to race the ancient engine to provide enough current for the cooler. I sat there for over an hour in the dim gloom of the dashboard, ears deadened by the engine roar, right foot cramping, cursing Tallis and the two geologists.

That evening I unfurled some crisp new vellum, flexed my slide rule and determined to start work on my thesis.

One afternoon, two or three months later, as we turned the board between chess games, Mayer remarked: 'I saw Pickford this morning. He told me he had some samples to show you.'

'TV tapes?'

'Bibles, I thought he said.'

I looked in on Pickford the next time I was down at the settlement. He was hovering about in the shadows behind the counter, white suit dirty and unpressed.

He puffed smoke at me. 'Those salesmen,' he explained. 'You were inquiring about. I told you they were selling Bibles.'

I nodded. 'Well?'

'I kept some.'

I put out my cigarette. 'Can I see them?'

He gestured me round the counter with his pipe. 'In the back.'

I followed him between the shelves, loaded with fans, radios and TV-scopes, all outdated models imported years earlier to satisfy the boom planet Murak had never become.

'There it is,' Pickford said. Standing against the back wall of the depot was a three-by-three wooden crate, taped with metal bands. Pickford ferreted about for a wrench. 'Thought you might like to buy some.'

'How long has it been here?'

'About a year. Tallis forgot to collect it. Only found it last week.'

Doubtful, I thought: more likely he was simply waiting for Tallis to be safely out of the way. I watched while he prised off the lid. Inside was a tough brown wrapping paper. Pickford broke the seals and folded the sides back carefully, revealing a layer of black morocco-bound volumes.

I pulled out one of them and held the heavily ribbed spine up to the light.

It was a Bible, as Pickford had promised. Below it were a dozen others.

'You're right,' I said. Pickford pulled up a radiogram and sat down, watching me.

I looked at the Bible again. It was in mint condition, the King James Authorized Version. The marbling inside the endboards was unmarked. A publisher's ticket slipped out onto the floor, and I realized that the copy had hardly come from a private library.

The bindings varied slightly. The next volume I pulled out was a copy of the Vulgate.

'How many crates did they have altogether?' I asked Pickford.

'Bibles? Fourteen, fifteen with this one. They ordered them all after they got here. This was the last one.' He pulled out another volume and handed it to me. 'Good condition, eh?'

It was a Koran.

I started lifting the volumes out and got Pickford to help me sort them on the shelves. When we counted them up there were ninety in all: thirty-five Holy Bibles (twenty-four Authorized Versions and eleven Vulgates), fifteen copies of the Koran, five of the Talmud, ten of the Bhagavat Gita and twenty-five of the Upanishads.

I took one of each and gave Pickford a £10 note.

'Any time you want some more,' he called after me. 'Maybe I can arrange a discount.' He was chuckling to himself, highly pleased with the deal, one up on the salesmen.

When Mayer called round that evening he noticed the six volumes on my desk.

'Pickford's samples,' I explained. I told him how I had found the crate at the depot and that it had been ordered by the geologists after their arrival. 'According to Pickford they ordered a total of fifteen crates. All Bibles.'

'He's senile.'

'No. His memory is good. There were certainly other crates because this one was sealed and he knew it contained Bibles.'

'Damned funny. Maybe they were salesmen.'

'Whatever they were they certainly weren't geologists. Why did Tallis say they were? Anyway, why didn't he ever mention that they had ordered all these Bibles?'

'Perhaps he'd forgotten.'

'Fifteen crates? Fifteen crates of Bibles? Heavens above, what did they do with them?'

Mayer shrugged. He went over to the window. 'Do you want me to radio Ceres?'

'Not yet. It still doesn't add up to anything.'

'There might be a reward. Probably a big one. God, I could go home!'

'Relax. First we've got to find out what these so-called geologists were doing here, why they ordered this fantastic supply of Bibles. One thing: whatever it was, I swear Tallis knew about it. Originally I thought they might have discovered a geldspar mine and been double-crossed by Tallis – that sonic trip was suspicious. Or else that they'd deliberately faked their own deaths so that they could spend a couple of years working the mine, using Tallis as their supply source. But all these Bibles mean we must start thinking in completely different categories.'

Round the clock for three days, with only short breaks for sleep hunched in the Chrysler's driving seat, I systematically swept the volcano jungle, winding slowly through the labyrinth of valleys, climbing to the crest of every cone, carefully checking every exposed quartz vein, every rift or gulley that might hide what I was convinced was waiting for me.

Mayer deputized at the observatory, driving over every afternoon. He helped me recondition an old diesel generator in one of the storage domes and we lashed it on to the back of the half-track to power the cabin heater needed for the $-30°$ nights and the three big spotlights fixed on the roof, providing a $360°$ traverse. I made two trips with a full cargo of fuel out to the camp site, dumped them there and made it my base.

Across the thick glue-like sand of the volcano jungle, we calculated, a man of sixty could walk at a maximum of one mile an hour, and spend at most two hours in $70°$ or above sunlight. That meant that whatever there was to find would be within twelve square miles of the camp site, three square miles if we included a return journey.

I searched the volcanoes as exactingly as I could, marking each cone and the adjacent valleys on the charts as I covered them, at a steady five miles an hour, the great engine of the Chrysler roaring ceaselessly, from noon, when the valleys filled with fire and seemed to run with lava again, round to midnight, when the huge cones became enormous mountains of bone, sombre graveyards presided over by the fantastic colonnades and hanging galleries of the sand reefs, suspended from the lake rims like inverted cathedrals.

I forced the Chrysler on, swinging the bumpers to uproot any suspicious crag or boulder that might hide a mine shaft, ramming through huge drifts of fine white sand that rose in soft clouds around the half-track like the dust of powdered silk.

I found nothing. The reefs and valleys were deserted, the volcano slopes untracked, craters empty, their shallow floors littered with meteor debris, rock sulphur and cosmic dust.

* * *

I decided to give up just before dawn on the fourth morning, after waking from a couple of hours of cramped and restless sleep.

'I'm coming in now,' I reported to Mayer over the transmitter. 'There's nothing out here. I'll collect what fuel there is left from the site and see you for breakfast.'

Dawn had just come up as I reached the site. I loaded the fuel cans back onto the half-track, switched off the spotlights and took what I knew would be my last look round. I sat down at the field desk and watched the sun arching upward through the cones across the lake. Scooping a handful of ash off the desk, I scrutinized it sadly for geldspar.

'Prime archezoic loam,' I said, repeating Tallis's words aloud to the dead lake. I was about to spit on it, more in anger than in hope, when some of the tumblers in my mind started to click.

About five miles from the far edge of the lake, silhouetted against the sunrise over the volcanoes, was a long 100-foot-high escarpment of hard slate-blue rock that lifted out of the desert bed and ran for about two miles in a low clean sweep across the horizon, disappearing among the cones in the south-west. Its outlines were sharp and well defined, suggesting that its materials pre-dated the planet's volcanic period. The escarpment sat squarely across the desert, gaunt and rigid, and looked as if it had been there since Murak's beginning, while the soft ashy cones and grey hillocks around it had known only the planet's end.

It was no more than an uninformed guess, but suddenly I would have bet my entire two years' salary that the rocks of the escarpment were archezoic. It was about three miles outside the area I had been combing, just visible from the observatory.

The vision of a geldspar mine returned sharply!

The lake took me nearly halfway there. I raced the Chrysler across it at forty, wasted thirty minutes picking a route through an elaborate sand reef, and then entered a long steeply walled valley which led directly towards the escarpment.

A mile away I saw that the escarpment was not, as it first seemed, a narrow continuous ridge, but a circular horizontal table. A curious feature was the almost perfect flatness of the table top, as if it had been deliberately levelled by a giant sword. Its sides were unusually symmetrical; they sloped at exactly the same angle, about 35°, and formed a single cliff unbroken by fissures or crevices.

I reached the table in an hour, parked the half-track at its foot and looked up at the great rounded flank of dull blue rock sloping away from me, rising like an island out of the grey sea of the desert floor.

I changed down into bottom gear and floored the accelerator. Steering the Chrysler obliquely across the slope to minimize the angle of ascent, I roared slowly up the side, tracks skating and racing, swinging the half-track around like a frantic pendulum.

Scaling the crest, I levelled off and looked out over a plateau about two miles in diameter, bare except for a light blue carpet of cosmic dust.

In the centre of the plateau, at least a mile across, was an enormous metallic lake, heat ripples spiralling upwards from its dark smooth surface.

I edged the half-track forward, head out of the side window, watching carefully, holding down the speed that picked up too easily. There were no meteorites or rock fragments lying about; presumably the lake surface cooled and set at night, to melt and extend itself as the temperature rose the next day.

Although the roof seemed hard as steel I stopped about 300 yards from the edge, cut the engine and climbed up onto the cabin.

The shift of perspective was slight but sufficient. The lake vanished, and I realized I was looking down at a shallow basin, about half a mile wide, scooped out of the roof.

I swung back into the cab and slammed in the accelerator. The basin, like the table top, was a perfect circle, sloping smoothly to the floor about one hundred feet below its rim, in imitation of a volcanic crater.

I braked the half-track at the edge and jumped out.

Four hundred yards away, in the basin's centre, five gigantic rectangular slabs of stone reared up from a vast pentagonal base.

* * *

This, then, was the secret Tallis had kept from me.

The basin was empty, the air warmer, strangely silent after three days of the Chrysler's engine roaring inside my head.

I lowered myself over the edge and began to walk down the slope towards the great monument in the centre of the basin. For the first time since my arrival on Murak I was unable to see the desert and the brilliant colours of the volcano jungle. I had strayed into a pale blue world, as pure and exact as a geometric equation, composed of the curving floor, the pentagonal base and the five stone rectangles towering up into the sky like the temple of some abstract religion.

It took me nearly three minutes to reach the monument. Behind me, on the sky-line, the half-track's engine steamed faintly. I went up to the base stone, which was a yard thick and must have weighed over a thousand tons, and placed my palms on its surface. It was still cool, the thin blue grain closely packed. Like the megaliths standing on it, the pentagon was unornamented and geometrically perfect.

I heaved myself up and approached the nearest megalith. The shadows around me were enormous parallelograms, their angles shrinking as the sun blazed up into the sky. I walked slowly round into the centre of the group, dimly aware that neither Tallis nor the two geologists could have carved the megaliths and raised them onto the pentagon, when I saw that the entire inner surface of the nearest megalith was covered by row upon row of finely chiselled hieroglyphs.

Swinging round, I ran my hands across its surface. Large patches had crumbled away, leaving a faint indecipherable tracery, but most of the surface was intact, packed solidly with pictographic symbols and intricate cuneiform glyphics that ran down it in narrow columns.

I stepped over to the next megalith. Here again, the inner face was covered with tens of thousands of minute carved symbols, the rows separated by finely cut dividing rules that fell the full fifty-foot height of the megalith.

There were at least a dozen languages, all in alphabets I

had never seen before, strings of meaningless ciphers among which I could pick odd cross-hatched symbols that seemed to be numerals, and peculiar serpentine forms that might have represented human figures in stylized poses.

Suddenly my eye caught:

CYR*RK VII   A*PHA LEP**IS   *D 1317

Below was another, damaged but legible.

AMEN*TEK LC*V   *LPHA LE*ORIS   AD 13**

There were blanks among the letters, where time had flaked away minute grains of the stone.

My eyes raced down the column. There were a score more entries:

PONT*AR*H*CV   ALPH* L*PORIS   A* *318
MYR*K LV*   A**HA LEPORI*   AD 13*6
KYR** XII   ALPH* LEP*RIS   AD 1*19
....
....

The list of names, all from Alpha Leporis, continued down the column. I followed it to the base, where the names ended three inches from the bottom, then moved along the surface, across rows of hieroglyphs, and picked up the list three or four columns later.

M*MARYK XX*V   A*PHA LEPORI*   AD 1389
CYRARK IX   ALPHA *EPORIS   AD 1390
....

I went over to the megalith on my left and began to examine the inscriptions carefully.

Here the entries read:

MINYS-259	DELT* ARGUS	AD 1874
TYLNYS-413	DELTA ARGUS	*D 1874
....	....	....

There were fewer blanks; to the right of the face the entries were more recent, the lettering sharper. In all there were five distinct languages, four of them, including Earth's, translations of the first entry running down the left-hand margin of each column.

The third and fourth megaliths recorded entries from Gamma Grus and Beta Trianguli. They followed the same pattern, their surfaces divided into eighteen-inch-wide columns, each of which contained five rows of entries, the four hieroglyphic languages followed by Earth's, recording the same minimal data in the same terse formula: Name – Place – Date

I had looked at four of the megaliths. The fifth stood with its back to the sun, its inner face hidden.

I walked over to it, crossing the oblique panels of shadow withdrawing to their sources, curious as to what fabulous catalogue of names I should find.

The fifth megalith was blank.

My eyes raced across its huge unbroken surface, marked only by the quarter-inch-deep grooves of the dividing rules some thoughtful master mason from the stars had chiselled to tabulate the entries from Earth that had never come.

I returned to the other megaliths and for half an hour read at random, arms outstretched involuntarily across the great inscription panels, fingertips tracing the convolutions of the hieroglyphs, seeking among the thousands of signatures some clue to the identity and purpose of the four stellar races.

| COPT*C LEAGUE MILV | BETA TRIANGULI | *D 1723 |
| ISARI* LEAGUE *VII | BETA *RIANGULI | AD 1724 |

| MAR-5-GO | GAMMA GRUS | AD 1959 |
| VEN-7-GO | GAMMA GRUS | AD 1960 |

TETRARK XII   ALPHA LEPORIS   AD 2095

Dynasties recurred again and again, Cyrark's, Minys-'s, -Go's, separated by twenty- or thirty-year intervals that appeared to be generations. Before AD 1200 all entries were illegible. This represented something over half the total. The surfaces of the megaliths were almost completely covered, and initially I assumed that the first entries had been made roughly 2200 years earlier, shortly after the birth of Christ. However, the frequency of the entries increased algebraically: in the 15th century there were one or two a year, by the 20th century there were five or six, and by the present year the number varied from twenty entries from Delta Argus to over thirty-five from Alpha Leporis.

The last of these, at the extreme right corner of the megalith, was:

CYRARK CCCXXIV   ALPHA LEPORIS   AD 2218

The letters were freshly incised, perhaps no more than a day old, even a few hours. Below, a free space of two feet reached to the floor.

Breaking off my scrutiny, I jumped down from the base stone and carefully searched the surrounding basin, sweeping the light dust carpet for vehicle or foot marks, the remains of implements or scaffolding.

But the basin was empty, the dust untouched except for the single file of prints leading down from the half-track.

I was sweating uncomfortably, and the thermo-alarm strapped to my wrist rang, warning me that the air temperature was 85°, ninety minutes to noon. I re-set it to 100°, took a last look round the five megaliths, and then made my way back to the half-track.

Heat waves raced and glimmered round the rim of the basin, and the sky was a dark inflamed red, mottled by the thermal pressure fields massing overhead like storm clouds. I jogged along at a half run, in a hurry to contact Mayer. Without his confirmation the authorities on Ceres would treat my report as the fantasy of a sand-happy lunatic. In addition, I wanted him to bring his camera; we could develop the reels within half an hour and radio a dozen stills as indisputable proof.

More important, I wanted someone to share the discovery, provide me with at least some cover in numbers. The frequency of entries on the megaliths, and the virtual absence of any further space – unless the reverse sides were used, which seemed unlikely – suggested a climax was soon to be reached, probably the climax for which Tallis had been waiting. Hundreds of entries had been made during his fifteen years on Murak; watching all day from the observatory he must have seen every landing.

As I swung into the half-track the emergency light on the transceiver above the windscreen was pulsing insistently. I switched to audio and Mayer's voice snapped into my ear.

'Quaine? Is that you? Where the hell are you, man? I nearly put out a mayday for you!'

He was at the camp site. Calling in from the observatory when I failed to arrive, he assumed I had broken down and abandoned the half-track, and had come out searching for me.

I picked him up at the camp site half an hour later, retroversed the tracks in a squealing circle of dust and kicked off again at full throttle. Mayer pressed me all the way back but I told him nothing, driving the Chrysler hard across the lake, paralleling the two previous sets of tracks and throwing up a huge cloud of dust 150 feet into the air. It was now over 95°, and the ash hills in the valley at the end of the lake were beginning to look angry and boiled.

Eager to get Mayer down into the basin, and with my mind spinning like a disintegrating flywheel, it was only as the half-track roared up the table slope that I felt a first chilling pang of fear. Through the windscreen I hesitantly scanned the tilting sky. Soon after reaching the basin we would have to shut down for an hour, two of us crammed together in the fume-filled cabin, deafened by the engine, sitting targets with the periscope blinded by the glare.

The centre of the plateau was a pulsing blur, as the air trapped in the basin throbbed upward into the sun. I drove straight towards it, Mayer stiffening in his seat. A hundred yards from the basin's edge the air suddenly cleared and we could see the tops of the megaliths. Mayer leapt up and swung out of the door onto the running board as I cut the engine and slammed the half-track to a halt by the rim. We jumped down, grabbing flare pistols and shouting to each other, slid into the basin and sprinted through the boiling air to the megaliths looming up in the centre.

I half-expected to find a reception party waiting for us, but the megaliths were deserted. I reached the pentagon fifty yards ahead of Mayer, climbed up and waited for him, gulping in the molten sunlight.

I helped him up and led him over to one of the megaliths, picked a column and began to read out the entries. Then I took him round the others, recapitulating everything I had discovered, pointing out the blank tablet reserved for Earth.

Mayer listened, broke away and wandered off, staring up dully at the megaliths.

'Quaine, you've really found something,' he muttered softly. 'Crazy, must be some sort of temple.'

I followed him round, wiping the sweat off my face and shielding my eyes from the glare reflected off the great slabs.

'Look at them, Mayer! They've been coming here for ten thousand years! Do you know what this means?'

Mayer tentatively reached out and touched one of the megaliths. '"Argive League XXV . . . Beta Tri-"' he read out. 'There are others, then. God Almighty. What do you think they look like?'

'What does it matter? Listen. They must have levelled this plateau themselves, scooped out the basin and cut these tablets from the living rock. Can you even imagine the tools they used?'

We crouched in the narrow rectangle of shadow in the lee of the sunward megalith. The temperature climbed, forty-five minutes to noon, 105°

'What is all this, though?' Mayer asked. 'Their burial ground?'
'Unlikely. Why leave a tablet for Earth? If they've been able

to learn our language they'd know the gesture was pointless. Anyway, elaborate burial customs are a sure sign of decadence, and there's something here that suggests the exact opposite. I'm convinced they expect that some time in the future we'll take an active part in whatever is celebrated here.'

'Maybe, but what? Think in new categories, remember?' Mayer squinted up at the megaliths. 'This could be anything from an ethnological bill of lading to the guest list at an all-time cosmic house party.'

He noticed something, frowned, then suddenly wrenched away from me. He leapt to his feet, pressed his hands against the surface of the slab behind us and ran his eyes carefully over the grain.

'What's worrying you?' I asked.

'Shut up!' he snapped. He scratched his thumbnail at the surface, trying to dislodge a few grains. 'What are you talking about, Quaine, these slabs aren't made of stone!'

He slipped out his jack knife, sprung the blade and stabbed viciously at the megalith, slashing a two-foot-long groove across the inscriptions.

I stood up and tried to restrain him but he shouldered me away and ran his finger down the groove, collecting a few fragments.

He turned on me angrily. 'Do you know what this is? *Tantalum oxide!* Pure ninety-nine per cent paygold. No wonder our extraction rates are fantastically small. I couldn't understand it, but these people –' he jerked his thumb furiously at the megaliths '– have damn well milked the planet dry to build these crazy things!'

It was 115°. The air was beginning to turn yellow and we were breathing in short exhausted pants.

'Let's get back to the truck,' I temporized. Mayer was losing control, carried away by his rage. With his big burly shoulders hunched in anger, staring up blindly at the five great megaliths, face contorted by the heat, he looked like an insane sub-man pinned in the time trophy of a galactic super-hunter.

He was ranting away as we stumbled through the dust towards the half-track.

'What do you want to do?' I shouted. 'Cut them down and put them through your ore crushers?'

Mayer stopped, the blue dust swirling about his legs. The air was humming as the basin floor expanded in the heart. The half-track was only fifty yards away, its refrigerated cabin a cool haven.

Mayer was watching me, nodding slowly. 'It could be done. Ten tons of Hy-Dyne planted round those slabs would crack them into small enough pieces for a tractor to handle. We could store them out at the observatory, then sneak them later into my refining tanks.'

I walked on, shaking my head with a thin grin. The heat was hitting Mayer, welling up all the irrational bitterness of a year's frustration. 'It's an idea. Why don't you get in touch with Gamma Grus? Maybe they'll give you the lease.'

'I'm serious, Quaine,' Mayer called after me. 'In a couple of years we'd be rich men.'

'You're crazy!' I shouted back at him. 'The sun's boiling your brains.'

I began to scale the slope up to the rim. The next hour in the cabin was going to be difficult, cooped up with a maniac eager to tear the stars apart. The butt of the flare pistol swinging on my knee caught my eye; a poor weapon, though, against Mayer's physique.

I had climbed almost up to the rim when I heard his feet thudding through the dust. I started to turn round just as he was on me, swinging a tremendous blow that struck me on the back of the head. I fell, watched him close in and then stood up, my skull exploding, and grappled with him. We stumbled over each other for a moment, the walls of the basin diving around us like a switchback, and then he knocked my hands away and smashed a heavy right cross into my face.

I fell on my back, stunned by the pain; the blow seemed to have loosened my jaw and damaged all the bones on the left side of my face. I managed to sit up and saw Mayer running past. He reached one hand to the rim, pulled himself up and lurched over to the half-track.

I dragged the flare pistol out of its holster, snapped back the bolt and trained it at Mayer. He was thirty yards away, turning the nearside door handle. I held the butt with both hands and fired as he opened the door. He looked round at the sharp detonation and watched the silver shell soar swiftly through the air towards him, ready to duck.

The shell missed him by three feet and exploded against the cabin roof. There was a brilliant flash of light that resolved itself a fraction of a second later into a fireball of incandescent magnesium vapour ten feet in diameter. This slowly faded to reveal the entire driving cabin, bonnet and forward side-panels of the half-track burning strongly with a loud, heavy crackling. Out of this maelstrom suddenly plunged the figure of Mayer, moving with violent speed, blackened arms across his face. He tripped over the rim, catapulted down into the dust and rolled for about twenty yards before he finally lay still, a shapeless bundle of smoking rags.

I looked numbly at my wristwatch. It was ten minutes to noon. The temperature was 130°. I pulled myself to my feet and trudged slowly up the slope towards the half-track, head thudding like a volcano, uncertain whether I would be strong enough to lift myself out of the basin.

When I was ten feet from the rim I could see that the windscreen of the half-track had melted and was dripping like treacle onto the dashboard.

I dropped the flare pistol and turned round.

It was five minutes to noon. Around me, on all sides, enormous sheets of fire were cascading slowly from the sky, passing straight through the floor of the basin, and then rising again in an inverted torrent. The megaliths were no longer visible, screened by curtains of brilliant light, but I groped forward, following the slope, searching for what shade would still be among them.

Twenty yards farther on I saw that the sun was directly overhead. It expanded until the disc was as wide as the basin, and then lowered itself to about ten feet above my head, a thousand rivers of fire streaming across its surface in all directions. There was a terrifying roaring and barking noise, overlaid by a dull, massive pounding as all the volcanoes in the volcano jungle began to erupt again. I walked on, in a dream, shuffling slowly, eyes closed to shut out the furnace around me. Then I discovered that I was sitting on the floor of the basin, which started to spin, setting up a high-pitched screaming.

A strange vision swept like a flame through my mind.

For aeons I plunged, spiralling weightlessly through a thousand whirling vortexes, swirled and buffeted down chasmic eddies, splayed out across the disintegrating matrix of the continuum, a dreamless ghost in flight from the cosmic Now. Then a million motes of light prickled the darkness above me, illuminating enormous curving causeways of time and space veering out past the stars to the rim of the galaxy. My dimensions shrank to a metaphysical extension of astral zero, I was propelled upward to the stars. Aisles of light broke and splintered around me, I passed Aldebaran, soared over Betelgeuse and Vega, zoomed past Antares, finally halted a hundred light years above the crown of Canopus.

Epochs drifted. Time massed on gigantic fronts, colliding like crippled universes. Abruptly, the infinite worlds of tomorrow unfolded before me – ten thousand years, a hundred thousand, unnumbered millennia raced past me in a blur of light, an iridescent cataract of stars and nebulae, interlaced by flashing trajectories of flight and exploration.

I entered deep time.

Deep Time: 1,000,000 mega-years. I saw the Milky Way, a wheeling carousel of fire, and Earth's remote descendants, countless races inhabiting every stellar system in the galaxy. The dark intervals between the stars were a continuously flickering field of light, a gigantic phosphorescent ocean, filled with the vibrating pulses of electromagnetic communication pathways.

To cross the enormous voids between the stars they have progressively slowed their physiological time, first ten, then a hundred-fold, so accelerating stellar and galactic time. Space has become alive with transient swarms of comets and meteors, the constellations have begun to dislocate and shift, the slow majestic rotation of the universe itself is at last visible.

Deep Time: 10,000,000 mega-years. Now they have left the Milky Way, which has started to fragment and dissolve. To reach the island galaxies they have further slowed their time schemes by a factor of 10,000, and can thus communicate with each other across vast inter-galactic distances in a subjective period of only a few years. Continuously expanding into deep space, they have extended their physiological dependence upon electronic memory banks which store the atomic and molecular patterns within their bodies, transmit them outward at the speed of light, and later re-assemble them.

Deep Time: 100,000,000 mega-years. They have spread now to all the neighbouring galaxies, swallowing thousands of nebulae. Their time schemes have decelerated a million-fold, they have become the only permanent forms in an ever-changing world. In a single instant of their lives a star emerges and dies, a sub-universe is born, a score of planetary life-systems evolve and vanish. Around them the universe sparkles and flickers with myriad points of light, as untold numbers of constellations appear and fade.

Now, too, they have finally shed their organic forms and are composed of radiating electromagnetic fields, the primary energy substratum of the universe, complex networks of multiple dimensions, alive with the constant tremor of the sentient messages they carry, bearing the life-ways of the race.

To power these fields, they have harnessed entire galaxies riding the wave-fronts of the stellar explosions out towards the terminal helixes of the universe.

Deep Time: 1,000,000,000 mega-years. They are beginning to dictate the form and dimensions of the universe. To girdle the distances which circumscribe the cosmos they have reduced their time period to 0.00000001 of its previous phase. The great galaxies and spiral nebulae which once seemed to live for eternity are now of such brief duration that they are no longer visible. The universe is now almost filled by the great vibrating mantle of ideation, a vast shimmering harp which has completely translated itself into pure wave form, independent of any generating source.

As the universe pulses slowly, its own energy vortices flexing and dilating, so the force-fields of the ideation mantle flex and dilate in sympathy, growing like an embryo within the womb of the cosmos, a child which will soon fill and consume its parent.

Deep Time: 10,000,000,000 mega-years. The ideation-field has now swallowed the cosmos, substituted its own dynamic, its own spatial and temporal dimensions. All primary time and energy fields have been engulfed. Seeking the final extension of itself within its own bounds the mantle has reduced its time period to an almost infinitesimal 0.00000000 ... n of its previous interval. Time has virtually ceased to exist, the ideation-field is nearly stationary, infinitely slow eddies of sentience undulating outward across its mantles.

Ultimately it achieves the final predicates of time and space, eternity and infinity, and slows to absolute zero. Then with a cataclysmic eruption it disintegrates, no longer able to contain itself. Its vast energy patterns begin to collapse, the whole system twists and thrashes in its mortal agony, thrusting outwards huge cataracts of fragmenting energy. In parallel, time emerges.

Out of this debris the first proto-galactic fields are formed, coalescing to give the galaxies and nebulae, the stars encircled by their planetary bodies. Among these, from the elemental seas, based on the carbon atom, emerge the first living forms.

So the cycle renews itself ...

The stars swam, their patterns shifting through a dozen constellations, novas flooded the darkness like blinding arcs, revealing the familiar profiles of the Milky Way, the constellations Orion, Coma Berenices, Cygnus.

Lowering my eyes from the storm-tossed sky, I saw the five megaliths. I was back on Murak. Around me the basin was filled with a great concourse of silent figures, ranged upward along the darkened slopes, shoulder to shoulder in endless ranks, like spectators in a spectral arena.

Beside me a voice spoke, and it seemed to have told me everything I had witnessed of the great cosmic round.

Just before I sank into unconsciousness for the last time I tried to ask the question ever present in my drifting mind, but it answered before I spoke, the star-littered sky, the five megaliths and the watching multitude spinning and swirling away into a dream as it said

'Meanwhile we wait here, at the threshold of time and space, celebrating the identity and kinship of the particles within our bodies with those of the sun and the stars of our brief private times with the vast periods of the galaxies, with the total unifying time of the cosmos . . .'

I woke lying face downward in the cool evening sand, shadows beginning to fill the basin, the thermal winds blowing a crisp refreshing breeze across my head and back. Below, the megaliths rose up into the thin blue air, their lower halves cut by the shadow-line of the sinking sun. I lay quietly, stirring my legs and arms tentatively, conscious of the gigantic rifts that had driven through my mind. After a few minutes I pulled myself to my feet and gazed round at the slopes curving away from me, the memory of the insane vision vivid in my mind.

The vast concourse that had filled the basin, the dream of the cosmic cycle, the voice of my interlocutor – were still real to me, a world in parallel I had just stepped from, and the door to which hung somewhere in the air around me.

Had I dreamed everything, assembling the entire fantasy in my mind as I lay raving in the noon heat, saved by some thermodynamic freak of the basin's architecture?

I held my thermo-alarm up to the fading light, checking the maximum and minimum levels. The maximum read 162°. Yet I had survived! I felt relaxed, restored, almost rejuvenated. My hands and face were unburnt – a temperature of over 160° would have boiled the flesh off my bones, left my skin a blackened crisp.

Over my shoulder I noticed the half-track standing on the rim. I ran towards it, for the first time remembering Mayer's death. I felt my cheek-bones, testing my jaw muscles. Surprisingly Mayer's heavy punches had left no bruise.

Mayer's body had gone! A single line of footsteps led down from the half-track to the megaliths, but otherwise the carpet of light blue dust was untouched. Mayer's prints, all marks of our scuffle, had vanished.

I quickly scaled the rim and reached the half-track, peering under the chassis and between the tracks. I flung open the cabin door, found the compartment empty.

The windscreen was intact. The paintwork on the door and bonnet was unmarked, the metal trim around the windows unscratched. I dropped to my knees, vainly searched for any flakes of magnesium ash. On my knee the flare pistol lodged securely in its holster, a primed star shell in the breach.

I left the Chrysler, jumped down into the basin and ran over to the megaliths. For an hour I paced round them, trying to resolve the countless questions that jammed my mind.

Just before I left I went over to the fifth tablet. I looked up at the top left corner, wondering whether I should have qualified for its first entry had I died that afternoon.

A single row of letters, filled with shadow by the falling light, stood out clearly.

I stepped back and craned up at them. There were the symbols of the four alien languages, and then, proudly against the stars:

CHARLES FOSTER NELSON EARTH   AD 2217

'Tell me, Quaine, where would you like to be when the world ends?'

In the seven years since Tallis first asked me this question I must have re-examined it a thousand times. Somehow it seems the key to all the extraordinary events that have happened on Murak, with their limitless implications for the people of Earth (to me a satisfactory answer contains an acceptable statement of one's philosophy and beliefs, an adequate discharge of the one moral debt we owe ourselves and the universe).

Not that the world is about to 'end'. The implication is rather that it has already ended and regenerated itself an infinite number of times, and that the only remaining question is what to do with ourselves in the meantime. The four stellar races who built the megaliths chose to come to Murak. What exactly they are waiting for here I can't be certain. A cosmic redeemer, perhaps, the first sight of the vast mantle of ideation I glimpsed in my vision. Recalling the period of two million years Tallis cited for life to appear on Murak it may be that the next cosmic cycle will receive its impetus here, and that we are advance spectators, five kings come to attend the genesis of a super-species which will soon outstrip us.

That there are others here, invisible and sustained by preternatural forces, is without doubt. Apart from the impossibility of surviving a Murak noon, I certainly didn't remove Mayer's body from the basin and arrange to have him electrocuted by one of the data-processing units at the observatory. Nor did I conceive the vision of the cosmic cycle myself.

It looks as if the two geologists stumbled upon the Waiting Grounds, somehow divined their significance, and then let Tallis in on their discovery. Perhaps they disagreed, as Mayer and I did, and Nelson may have been forced to kill his companion, to die himself a year later in the course of his vigil.

Like Tallis I shall wait here if necessary for fifteen years. I go out to the Grounds once a week and watch them from the observatory the rest of the time. So far I have seen nothing, although two or three hundred more names have been added to the tablets. However, I am certain that whatever we are waiting for will soon arrive. When I get tired or impatient, as I sometimes do, I remind myself that they have been coming to Murak and waiting here, generation upon generation, for 10,000 years.

Whatever it is, it must be worth waiting for.

1959

NOW: ZERO

You ask: how did I discover this insane and fantastic power? Like Dr Faust, was it bestowed upon me by the Devil himself, in exchange for the deed to my soul? Did I, perhaps, acquire it with some strange talismanic object – idol's eyepiece or monkey's paw – unearthed in an ancient chest or bequeathed by a dying mariner? Or, again, did I stumble upon it myself while researching into the obscenities of the Eleusinian Mysteries and the Black Mass, suddenly perceiving its full horror and magnitude through clouds of sulphurous smoke and incense?

None of these. In fact, the power revealed itself to me quite accidentally, during the commonplaces of the everyday round, appearing unobtrusively at my fingertips like a talent for embroidery. Indeed, its appearance was so unheralded, so gradual, that at first I failed to recognize it at all.

But again you ask: why should I tell you this, describe the incredible and hitherto unsuspected sources of my power, freely catalogue the names of my victims, the date and exact manner of their quietus? Am I so mad as to be positively eager for justice – arraignment, the black cap, and the hangman leaping on to my shoulders like Quasimodo, ringing the deathbell from my throat?

No, (consummate irony!) it is the strange nature of my power that I have nothing to fear from broadcasting its secret to all who will listen. I am the power's servant, and in describing it now I still serve it, carrying it faithfully, as you shall see, to its final conclusion.

However, to begin.

Rankin, my immediate superior at the Everlasting Insurance

company, became the hapless instrument of the fate which was first to reveal the power to me.

I loathed Rankin. He was bumptious and assertive, innately vulgar, and owed his position solely to an unpleasant cunning and his persistent refusal to recommend me to the directorate for promotion. He had consolidated his position as department manager by marrying a daughter of one of the directors (a dismal harridan, I may add) and was consequently unassailable. Our relationship was based on mutual contempt, but whereas I was prepared to accept my role, confident that my own qualities would ultimately recommend themselves to the directors, Rankin deliberately took advantage of his seniority, seizing every opportunity to offend and denigrate me.

He would systematically undermine my authority over the secretarial staff, who were tacitly under my control, by appointing others at random to the position. He would give me long-term projects of little significance to work on, so segregating me from the rest of the office. Above all, he sought to antagonize me by his personal mannerisms. He would sing, hum, sit uninvited on my desk as he made small talk with the typists, then call me into his office and keep me waiting pointlessly at his shoulder as he read silently through an entire file.

Although I controlled myself, my abomination of Rankin grew remorselessly. I would leave the office seething with anger at his viciousness, sit in the train home with my newspaper opened but my eyes blinded by rage. My evenings and weekends would be ruined, wastelands of anger and futile bitterness.

Inevitably, thoughts of revenge grew, particularly as I suspected that Rankin was passing unfavourable reports of my work to the directors. Satisfactory revenge, however, was hard to achieve. Finally I decided upon a course I despised, driven to it by desperation: the anonymous letter – not to the directors, for the source would have been too easily discovered, but to Rankin and his wife.

My first letters, the familiar indictments of infidelity, I never posted. They seemed naïve, inadequate, too obviously the handiwork of a paranoiac with a grudge. I locked them away in a small steel box, later re-drafted them, striking out the staler crudities and trying to substitute something more subtle, a hint of perversion and obscenity, that would plunge deeper barbs of suspicion into the reader's mind.

It was while composing the letter to Mrs Rankin, itemizing in an old notebook the more despicable of her husband's qualities, that I discovered the curious relief afforded by the exercise of composition, by the formal statement, in the minatory language of the anonymous letter (which is, certainly, a specialized branch of literature, with its own classical rules and permitted devices) of the viciousness and depravity of the letter's subject and the terrifying nemesis awaiting him. Of course, this catharsis is familiar to those regularly able to recount unpleasant experiences to priest, friend or wife, but to me, who lived a solitary, friendless life, its discovery was especially poignant.

Over the next few days I made a point each evening on my return home of writing out a short indictment of Rankin's iniquities, analysing his motives, and even anticipating the slights and abuses of the next day. These I would cast in the form of narrative, allowing myself a fair degree of licence, introducing imaginary situations and dialogues that served to highlight Rankin's atrocious behaviour and my own stoical forbearance.

The compensation was welcome, for simultaneously Rankin's campaign against me increased. He became openly abusive, criticized my work before junior members of the staff, even threatened to report me to the directors. One afternoon he drove me to such a frenzy that I barely restrained myself from assaulting him. I hurried home, unlocked my writing box and sought relief in my diaries. I wrote page after page, re-enacting in my narrative the day's events, then reaching forward to our final collision the following morning, culminating in an accident that intervened to save me from dismissal.

My last lines were:

. . . Shortly after 2 o'clock the next afternoon, spying from his usual position on the 7th floor stairway for any employees returning late

from lunch, Rankin suddenly lost his balance, toppled over the rail and fell to his death in the entrance hall below.

As I wrote this fictitious scene it seemed scant justice, but little did I realize that a weapon of enormous power had been placed gently between my fingers.

Coming back to the office after lunch the next day I was surprised to find a small crowd gathered outside the entrance, a police car and ambulance pulled up by the kerb. As I pushed forward up the steps, several policemen emerged from the building clearing the way for two orderlies carrying a stretcher across which a sheet had been drawn, revealing the outlines of a human form. The face was concealed, and I gathered from conversation around me that someone had died. Two of the directors appeared, their faces shocked and drawn.

'Who is it?' I asked one of the office boys who were hanging around breathlessly.

'Mr Rankin,' he whispered. He pointed up the stairwell. 'He slipped over the railing on the 7th floor, fell straight down, completely smashed one of those big tiles outside the lift . . .'

He gabbled on, but I turned away, numbed and shaken by the sheer physical violence that hung in the air. The ambulance drove off, the crowd dispersed, the directors returned, exchanging expressions of grief and astonishment with other members of the staff, the janitors took away their mops and buckets, leaving behind them a damp red patch and the shattered tile.

Within an hour I had recovered. Sitting in front of Rankin's empty office, watching the typists hover helplessly around his desk, apparently unconvinced that their master would never return, my heart began to warm and sing. I became transformed, a load which had threatened to break me had been removed from my back, my mind relaxed, the tensions and bitterness dissipated. Rankin had gone, finally and irrevocably. The era of injustice had ended.

I contributed generously to the memorial fund which made

the rounds of the office; I attended the funeral, gloating inwardly as the coffin was bundled into the sod, joining fulsomely in the expressions of regret. I readied myself to occupy Rankin's desk, my rightful inheritance.

My surprise a few days later can easily be imagined when Carter, a younger man of far less experience and generally accepted as my junior, was promoted to fill Rankin's place. At first I was merely baffled, quite unable to grasp the tortuous logic that could so offend all laws of precedence and merit. I assumed that Rankin had done his work of denigrating me only too well.

However, I accepted the rebuff, offered Carter my loyalty and assisted his reorganization of the office.

Superficially these changes were minor. But later I realized that they were far more calculating than at first seemed, and transferred the bulk of power within the office to Carter's hands, leaving me with the routine work, the files of which never left the department or passed to the directors. I saw too that over the previous year Carter had been carefully familiarizing himself with all aspects of my job and was taking credit for work I had done during Rankin's tenure of office.

Finally I challenged Carter openly, but far from being evasive he simply emphasized my subordinate role. From then on he ignored my attempts at a rapprochement and did all he could to antagonize me.

The final insult came when Jacobson joined the office to fill Carter's former place and was officially designated Carter's deputy.

That evening I brought down the steel box in which I kept record of Rankin's persecutions and began to describe all that I was beginning to suffer at the hands of Carter.

During a pause the last entry in the Rankin diary caught my eye:

> *... Rankin suddenly lost his balance, toppled over the rail and fell to his death in the entrance hall below.*

The words seemed to be alive, they had strangely vibrant overtones. Not only were they a remarkably accurate forecast of Rankin's fate, but they had a distinctly magnetic and compulsive power that separated them sharply from the rest of the entries. Somewhere within my mind a voice, vast and sombre, slowly intoned them.

On a sudden impulse I turned the page, found a clean sheet and wrote:

The next afternoon Carter died in a street accident outside the office.

What childish game was I playing? I was forced to smile at myself, as primitive and irrational as a Haitian witch doctor transfixing a clay image of his enemy.

I was sitting in the office the following day when the squeal of tyres in the street below riveted me to my chair. Traffic stopped abruptly and there was a sudden hubbub followed by silence. Only Carter's office overlooked the street; he had gone out half an hour earlier so we pressed past his desk and leaned out through the window.

A car had skidded sharply across the pavement and a group of ten or a dozen men were lifting it carefully back on to the roadway. It was undamaged but what appeared to be oil was leaking sluggishly into the gutter. Then we saw the body of a man outstretched beneath the car, his arms and head twisted awkwardly.

The colour of his suit was oddly familiar.

Two minutes later we knew it was Carter.

That night I destroyed my notebook and all records I had made about Rankin's behaviour. Was it coincidence, or in some way had I willed his death, and in the same way Carter's? Impossible – no conceivable connection could exist between the diaries and the two deaths, the pencil marks on the sheets of paper were arbitrary curved lines of graphite, representing ideas which existed only in my mind.

But the solution to my doubts and speculations was too obvious to be avoided.

I locked the door, turned a fresh page of the notebook and cast round for a suitable subject. I picked up my evening paper. A young man had just been reprieved from the death penalty for the murder of an old woman. His face stared from a photograph coarse, glowering, conscienceless.

I wrote:

Frank Taylor died the next day in Pentonville Prison.

The scandal created by Taylor's death almost brought about the resignations of both the Home Secretary and the Prison Commissioners. During the next few days violent charges were levelled in all directions by the newspapers, and it finally transpired that Taylor had been brutally beaten to death by his warders. I carefully read the evidence and findings of the tribunal of enquiry when they were published, hoping that they might throw some light on the extraordinary and malevolent agency which linked the statements in my diaries with the inevitable deaths on the subsequent day.

However, as I feared, they suggested nothing. Meanwhile I sat quietly in my office, automatically carrying out my work, obeying Jacobson's instructions without comment, my mind elsewhere, trying to grasp the identity and import of the power bestowed on me.

Still unconvinced, I decided on a final test, in which I would give precisely detailed instructions, to rule out once and for all any possibility of coincidence.

Conveniently, Jacobson offered himself as my subject.

So, the door locked securely behind me, I wrote with trembling fingers, fearful lest the pencil wrench itself from me and plunge into my heart.

Jacobson died at 2.43 P.M. the next day after slashing his wrists with a razor blade in the second cubicle from the left in the men's washroom on the third floor.

I sealed the notebook into an envelope, locked it into the box and lay awake through a sleepless night, the words echoing in my ears, glowing before my eyes like jewels of Hell.

After Jacobson's death – exactly according to my instructions – the staff of the department were given a week's holiday (in part to keep them away from curious newspapermen, who were beginning to scent a story, and also because the directors believed that Jacobson had been morbidly influenced by the deaths of Rankin and Carter). During those seven days I chafed impatiently to return to work. My whole attitude to the power had undergone a considerable change. Having to my own satisfaction verified its existence, if not its source, my mind turned again towards the future. Gaining confidence, I realized that if I had been bequeathed the power it was my obligation to restrain any fears and make use of it. I reminded myself that I might be merely the tool of some greater force.

Alternatively, was the diary no more than a mirror which revealed the future, was I in some fantastic way twenty-four hours ahead of time when I described the deaths, simply a recorder of events that had already taken place?

These questions exercised my mind ceaselessly.

On my return to work I found that many members of the staff had resigned, their places being filled only with difficulty, news of the three deaths, particularly Jacobson's suicide, having reached the newspapers. The directors' appreciation of those senior members of the staff who remained with the firm I was able to turn to good account in consolidating my position. At last I took over command of the department – but this was no more than my due, and my eyes were now set upon a directorship.

All too literally, I would step into dead men's shoes.

Briefly, my strategy was to precipitate a crisis in the affairs of the firm which would force the board to appoint new executive directors from the ranks of the department managers. I therefore waited until a week before the next meeting of the board, and then wrote out four slips of paper, one for each of the executive directors. Once a director I should be in a position to propel myself rapidly to the chairmanship of the board, by appointing my own candidates to vacancies as they successively appeared. As chairman I should automatically find a seat on the board of the parent company, there to repeat the process, with whatever variations necessary. As soon as real power came within my orbit my rise to absolute national, and ultimately global, supremacy would be swift and irreversible.

If this seems naïvely ambitious, remember that I had as yet failed to appreciate the real dimensions and purpose of the power, and still thought in the categories of my own narrow world and background.

A week later, as the sentences on the four directors simultaneously expired, I sat calmly in my office, reflecting upon the brevity of human life, waiting for the inevitable summons to the board. Understandably, the news of their deaths, in a succession of car accidents, brought general consternation upon the office, of which I was able to take advantage by retaining the only cool head.

To my amazement the next day I, with the rest of the staff, received a month's pay in lieu of notice. Completely flabbergasted – at first I feared that I had been discovered – I protested volubly to the chairman, but was assured that although everything I had done was deeply appreciated, the firm was nonetheless no longer able to support itself as a viable unit and was going into enforced liquidation.

A farce indeed! So a grotesque justice had been done. As I left the office for the last time that morning I realized that in future I must use my power ruthlessly. Hesitation, the exercise of scruple, the calculation of niceties – these merely made me all the more vulnerable to the inconstancies and barbarities of fate. Henceforth I would be brutal, merciless, bold. Also, I must not delay. The power might wane, leave me defenceless, even less fortunately placed than before it revealed itself.

My first task was to establish the power's limits. During the next week I carried out a series of experiments to assess its capacity, working my way progressively up the scale of assassination.

It happened that my lodgings were positioned some two or three hundred feet below one of the principal airlanes into the city. For years I had suffered the nerve-shattering roar of airliners flying in overhead at two-minute intervals, shaking the walls and ceiling, destroying thought. I took down my notebooks. Here was a convenient opportunity to couple research with redress.

You wonder did I feel no qualms of conscience for the 75 victims who hurtled to their deaths across the evening sky twenty-four hours later, no sympathy for their relatives, no doubts as to the wisdom of wielding my power indiscriminately?

I answer: No! Far from being indiscriminate I was carrying out an experiment vital to the furtherance of my power.

I decided on a bolder course. I had been born in Stretchford, a mean industrial slum that had done its best to cripple my spirit and body. At last it could justify itself by testing the efficacy of the power over a wide area.

In my notebook I wrote the short flat statement:

Every inhabitant of Stretchford died at noon the next day.

Early the following morning I went out and bought a radio, sat by it patiently all day, waiting for the inevitable interruption of the afternoon programmes by the first horrified reports of the vast Midland holocaust.

Nothing, however, was reported! I was astonished, the orientations of my mind disrupted, its very sanity threatened. Had my power dissipated itself, vanishing as quickly and unexpectedly as it had appeared?

Or were the authorities deliberately suppressing all mention of the cataclysm, fearful of national hysteria?

I immediately took the train to Stretchford.

At the station I tactfully made inquiries, was assured that the city was firmly in existence. Were my informants, though, part of the government's conspiracy of silence, was it aware that a monstrous agency was at work, and was somehow hoping to trap it?

But the city was inviolate, its streets filled with traffic, the smoke of countless factories drifting across the blackened rooftops.

I returned late that evening, only to find my landlady importuning me for my rent. I managed to postpone her demands for a day, promptly unlocked my diary and passed sentence upon her, praying that the power had not entirely deserted me.

The sweet relief I experienced the next morning when she was discovered at the foot of the basement staircase, claimed by a sudden stroke, can well be imagined.

So my power still existed!

During the succeeding weeks its principal features disclosed themselves. First, I discovered that it operated only within the bounds of feasibility. Theoretically the simultaneous deaths of the entire population of Stretchford might have been effected by the coincident explosions of several hydrogen bombs, but as this event was itself apparently impossible (hollow, indeed, are the boastings of our militarist leaders) the command was never carried out.

Secondly, the power entirely confined itself to the passage of the sentence of death. I attempted to control or forecast the motions of the stock market, the results of horse races, the behaviour of my employers at my new job – all to no avail.

As for the sources of the power, these never revealed themselves. I could only conclude that I was merely the agent, the willing clerk, of some macabre nemesis struck like an arc between the point of my pencil and the vellum of my diaries.

Sometimes it seemed to me that the brief entries I made were cross-sections through the narrative of some vast book of the dead existing in another dimension, and that as I made them my handwriting overlapped that of a greater scribe's along the narrow pencilled line where our respective planes of time crossed each other, instantly drawing from the eternal banks of death a final statement of account on to some victim within the tangible world around me.

The diaries I kept securely sealed within a large steel safe and all entries were made with the utmost care and secrecy, to prevent any suspicion linking me with the mounting catalogue of deaths and disasters. The majority of these were effected solely for purposes of experiment and brought me little or no personal gain.

It was therefore all the more surprising when I discovered that the police had begun to keep me under sporadic observation.

I first noticed this when I saw my landlady's successor in surreptitious conversation with the local constable, pointing up the stairs to my room and making head-tapping motions, presumably to indicate my telepathic and mesmeric talents. Later, a man whom I can now identify as a plainclothes detective stopped me in the street on some flimsy pretext and started a wandering conversation about the weather, obviously designed to elicit information.

No charges were ever laid against me, but subsequently my employers also began to watch me in a curious manner. I therefore assumed that the possession of the power had invested me with a distinct and visible aura, and it was this that stimulated curiosity.

As this aura became detectable by greater and greater numbers of people – it would be noticed in bus queues and cafés – and the first oblique, and for some puzzling reason, amused references to it were made openly by members of the public, I knew that the power's period of utility was ending. No longer would I be able to exercise it without fear of detection. I should have to destroy the diary, sell the safe which so long had held its secret, probably even refrain from ever thinking about the power lest this alone generate the aura.

To be forced to lose the power, when I was only on the threshold of its potential, seemed a cruel turn of fate. For reasons which still remained closed to me, I had managed to penetrate behind the veil of commonplaces and familiarity which masks the inner world of the timeless and the preternatural. Must the power, and the vision it revealed, be lost forever?

This question ran through my mind as I looked for the last time through my diary. It was almost full now, and I reflected that it formed one of the most extraordinary texts, if unpublished, in the history of literature. Here, indeed, was established the primacy of the pen over the sword!

Savouring this thought, I suddenly had an inspiration of remarkable force and brilliance. I had stumbled upon an ingenious but simple method of preserving the power in its most impersonal and lethal form without having to wield it myself and itemize my victims' names.

This was my scheme: I would write and have published an apparently fictional story in conventional narrative in which I would describe, with complete frankness, my discovery of the power and its subsequent history. I would detail precisely the names of my victims, the mode of their deaths, the growth of my diary and the succession of experiments I carried out. I would be scrupulously honest, holding nothing back whatsoever. In conclusion I would tell of my decision to abandon the power and publish a full and dispassionate account of all that had happened.

Accordingly, after a considerable labour, the story was written and published in a magazine of wide circulation.

You show surprise? I agree; as such I should merely have been signing my own death warrant in indelible ink and delivering myself straight to the gallows. However, I omitted a single feature of the story: its denouement, or surprise ending, the twist in its tail. Like all respectable stories, this one too had its twist, indeed one so violent as to throw the earth itself out of its orbit. This was precisely what it was designed to do.

For the twist in this story was that it contained my last command to the power, my final sentence of death.

Upon whom? Who else, but upon the story's reader!

Ingenious, certainly, you willingly admit. As long as issues of the magazine remain in circulation (and their proximity to victims of this extraordinary plague guarantees that) the power will continue its task of annihilation. Its author alone will remain unmolested, for no court will hear evidence at second hand, and who will live to give it at first hand?

But where, you ask, was the story published, fearful that you may inadvertently buy the magazine and read it.

I answer: Here! It is the story that lies before you now. Savour it well, its finish is your own. As you read these last few lines you will be overwhelmed by horror and revulsion, then by fear and panic. Your heart seizes, its pulse falling ... your mind clouds ... your life ebbs ... you are sinking, within a few seconds you will join eternity ... three ... two ... one ...

Now!

Zero.

1959

THE SOUND-SWEEP

ONE

By midnight Madame Gioconda's headache had become intense. All day the derelict walls and ceiling of the sound stage had reverberated with the endless din of traffic accelerating across the mid-town flyover which arched fifty feet above the studio's roof, a frenzied hypermanic babel of jostling horns, shrilling tyres, plunging brakes and engines that hammered down the empty corridors and stairways to the sound stage on the second floor, making the faded air feel leaden and angry.

Exhausting but at least impersonal, these sounds Madame Gioconda could bear. At dusk, however, when the flyover quietened, they were overlaid by the mysterious clapping of her phantoms, the sourceless applause that rustled down on to the stage from the darkness around her. At first a few scattered ripples from the front rows, it soon spread to the entire auditorium, mounting to a tumultuous ovation in which she suddenly detected a note of sarcasm, a single shout of derision that drove a spear of pain through her forehead, followed by an uproar of boos and catcalls that filled the tortured air, driving her away towards her couch where she lay gasping helplessly until Mangon arrived at midnight, hurrying on to the stage with his sonovac.

Understanding her, he first concentrated on sweeping the walls and ceiling clean, draining away the heavy depressing under-layer of traffic noises. Carefully he ran the long snout of the sonovac over the ancient scenic flats (relics of her previous roles at the Metropolitan Opera House) which screened in Madame Gioconda's make-shift home – the great collapsing Byzantine bed (*Othello*) mounted against the microphone turret; the huge framed mirrors with their peeling silver-screen (*Orpheus*) stacked in one corner by the bandstand; the stove (*Trovatore*) set up on the programme director's podium; the gilt-trimmed dressing table and wardrobe (*Figaro*) stuffed with newspaper and magazine cuttings. He swept them methodically, moving the sonovac's nozzle in long strokes, drawing out the dead residues of sound that had accumulated during the day.

By the time he finished the air was clear again, the atmosphere lightened, its overtones of fatigue and irritation dissipated. Gradually Madame Gioconda recovered. Sitting up weakly, she smiled wanly at Mangon. Mangon grinned back encouragingly, slipped the kettle on to the stove for Russian tea, sweetened by the usual phenobarbitone chaser, switched off the sonovac and indicated to her that he was going outside to empty it.

Down in the alley behind the studio he clipped the sonovac on to the intake manifold of the sound truck. The vacuum drained in a few seconds, but he waited a discretionary two or three minutes before returning, keeping up the pretence that Madame Gioconda's phantom audience was real. Of course the cylinder was always empty, containing only the usual daily detritus – the sounds of a door slam, a partition collapsing somewhere or the kettle whistling, a grunt or two, and later, when the headaches began, Madame Gioconda's pitiful moanings. The riotous applause, which would have lifted the roof off the Met, let alone a small radio station, the jeers and hoots of derision were, he knew, quite imaginary, figments of Madame Gioconda's world of fantasy, phantoms from the past of a once great *prima donna* who had been dropped by her public and had retreated into her imagination, each evening conjuring up a blissful dream of being once again applauded by a full house at the Metropolitan, a dream that guilt and resentment turned sour by midnight, inverting it into a nightmare of fiasco and failure.

Why she should torment herself was difficult to understand, but at least the nightmare kept Madame Gioconda just this side of sanity and Mangon, who revered and loved Madame Gioconda, would have been the last person in the world to disillusion her.

Each evening, when he finished his calls for the day, he would drive his sound truck all the way over from the West Side to the abandoned radio station under the flyover at the deserted end of F Street, go through the pretence of sweeping Madame Gioconda's apartment on the stage of studio 2, charging no fee, make tea and listen to her reminiscences and plans for revenge, then see her asleep and tiptoe out, a wry but pleased smile on his youthful face.

He had been calling on Madame Gioconda for nearly a year, but what his precise role was in relation to her he had not yet decided. Oddly enough, although he was more or less indispensable now to the effective operation of her fantasy world she showed little personal interest or affection for Mangon, but he assumed that this indifference was merely part of the autocratic personality of a world-famous *prima donna*, particularly one very conscious of the tradition, now alas meaningless, Melba – Callas – Gioconda. To serve at all was the privilege. In time, perhaps, Madame Gioconda might accord him some sign of favour.

Without him, certainly, her prognosis would have been poor. Lately the headaches had become more menacing, as she insisted that the applause was growing stormier, the boos and catcalls more vicious. Whatever the psychic mechanism generating the fantasy system, Mangon realized that ultimately she would need him at the studio all day, holding back the enveloping tides of nightmare and insanity with sham passes of the sonovac. Then, perhaps, when the dream crumbled, he would regret having helped her to delude herself. With luck though she might achieve her ambition of making a comeback. She had told him something of her scheme – a serpentine mixture of blackmail and bribery – and privately Mangon hoped to launch a plot of his own to return her to popularity. By now she had unfortunately reached the point where success alone could save her from disaster.

She was sitting up when he returned, propped back on an enormous gold *lamé* cushion, the single lamp at the foot of the couch throwing a semicircle of light on to the great flats which divided the sound stage from the auditorium. These were all from her last operatic role – *The Medium* – and represented a complete interior of the old spiritualist's seance chamber, the one coherent feature in Madame Gioconda's present existence. Surrounded by fragments from a dozen roles, even Madame Gioconda herself, Mangon reflected, seemed compounded of several separate identities. A tall regal figure, with full shapely shoulders and massive rib-cage, she had a large handsome face topped by a magnificent coiffure of rich blue-black hair – the exact prototype of the classical diva. She must have been almost fifty, yet her soft creamy complexion and small features were those of a child. The eyes, however, belied her. Large and watchful, slashed with mascara, they regarded the world around her balefully, narrowing even as Mangon approached. Her teeth too were bad, stained by tobacco and cheap cocaine. When she was roused, and her full violet lips curled with rage, revealing the blackened hulks of her dentures and the acid flickering tongue, her mouth looked like a very vent of hell. Altogether she was a formidable woman.

As Mangon brought her tea she heaved herself up and made room for him by her feet among the debris of beads, loose diary pages, horoscopes and jewelled address books that littered the couch. Mangon sat down, surreptitiously noting the time (his first calls were at 9.30 the next morning and loss of sleep deadened his acute hearing), and prepared himself to listen to her for half an hour.

Suddenly she flinched, shrank back into the cushion and gestured agitatedly in the direction of the darkened bandstand.

'They're still clapping!' she shrieked. 'For God's sake sweep them away, they're driving me insane. Oooohh ...' she rasped theatrically, 'over there, quickly ... !'

Mangon leapt to his feet. He hurried over to the bandstand and carefully focused his ears on the tiers of seats and plywood music stands. They were all immaculately clean, well below the threshold at which embedded sounds began to radiate detectable echoes. He turned to the corner walls and ceiling. Listening very carefully he could just hear seven muted pads, the dull echoes of his footsteps across the floor. They faded and vanished, followed by a low threshing noise like blurred radio static – in fact Madame Gioconda's present tantrum. Mangon could almost distinguish the individual words, but repetition muffled them.

Madame Gioconda was still writhing about on the couch, evidently not to be easily placated, so Mangon climbed down off the stage and made his way through the auditorium to where he had left his sonovac by the door. The power lead was outside in the truck but he was sure Madame Gioconda would fail to notice.

For five minutes he worked away industriously, pretending to sweep the bandstand again, then put down the sonovac and returned to the couch.

Madame Gioconda emerged from the cushion, sounded the air carefully with two or three slow turns of the head, and smiled at him.

'Thank you, Mangon,' she said silkily, her eyes watching him thoughtfully. 'You've saved me again from my assassins. They've become so cunning recently, they can even hide from you.'

Mangon smiled ruefully to himself at this last remark. So he had been a little too perfunctory earlier on; Madame Gioconda was keeping him up to the mark.

However, she seemed genuinely grateful. 'Mangon, my dear,' she reflected as she remade her face in the mirror of an enormous compact, painting on magnificent green eyes like a cobra's, 'what would I do without you? How can I ever repay you for looking after me?'

The questions, whatever their sinister undertones (had he detected them, Mangon would have been deeply shocked) were purely rhetorical, and all their conversations for that matter entirely one-sided. For Mangon was a mute. From the age of three, when his mother had savagely punched him in the throat to stop him crying, he had been stone dumb, his vocal cords irreparably damaged. In all their endless exchanges of midnight confidences, Mangon had contributed not a single spoken word.

His muteness, naturally, was part of the attraction he felt for Madame Gioconda. Both of them in a sense had lost their voices, he to a cruel mother, she to a fickle and unfaithful public. This bound them together, gave them a shared sense of life's injustice, though Mangon, like all innocents, viewed his misfortune without rancour. Both, too, were social outcasts. Rescued from his degenerate parents when he was four, Mangon had been brought up in a succession of state institutions, a solitary wounded child. His one talent had been his remarkable auditory powers, and at fourteen he was apprenticed to the Metropolitan Sonic Disposal Service. Regarded as little better than garbage collectors, the sound-sweeps were an outcast group of illiterates, mutes (the city authorities preferred these – their discretion could be relied upon) and social cripples who lived in a chain of isolated shacks on the edge of an old explosives plant in the sand dunes to the north of the city which served as the sonic dump.

Mangon had made no friends among the sound-sweeps, and Madame Gioconda was the first person in his life with whom he had been intimately involved. Apart from the pleasure of being able to help her, a considerable factor in Mangon's devotion was that until her decline she had represented (as to all mutes) the most painful possible reminder of his own voiceless condition, and that now he could at last come to terms with years of unconscious resentment.

This soon done, he devoted himself wholeheartedly to serving Madame Gioconda.

Inhaling moodily on a black cigarette clamped into a long jade holder, she was outlining her plans for a comeback. These had been maturing for several months and involved nothing less than persuading Hector LeGrande, chairman-in-chief of Video City, the huge corporation that transmitted a dozen TV and radio channels, into providing her with a complete series of television spectaculars. Built around Madame Gioconda and lavishly dressed and orchestrated, they would spearhead the international revival of classical opera that was her unfading dream.

'La Scala, Covent Garden, the Met – what are they now?' she demanded angrily. 'Bowling alleys! Can you believe, Mangon, that in those immortal theatres where I created my Tosca, my

Butterfly, my Brünnhilde, they now have –' she spat out a gust of smoke '– beer and skittles!'

Mangon shook his head sympathetically. He pulled a pencil from his breast-pocket and on the wrist-pad stitched to his left sleeve wrote:

Mr LeGrande?

Madame Gioconda read the note, let it fall to the floor.

'Hector? Those lawyers poison him. He's surrounded by them, I think they steal all my telegrams to him. Of course Hector had a complete breakdown on the spectaculars. Imagine, Mangon, what a scoop for him, a sensation! "The great Gioconda will appear on television!" Not just some moronic bubblegum girl, but the Gioconda in person.'

Exhausted by this vision Madame Gioconda sank back into her cushion, blowing smoke limply through the holder.

Mangon wrote:

Contract?

Madame Gioconda frowned at the note, then pierced it with the glowing end of her cigarette.

'I am having a new contract drawn up. Not for the mere 300,000 I was prepared to take at first, not even 500,000. For each show I shall now demand precisely *one million* dollars. Nothing less! Hector will have to pay for ignoring me. Anyway, think of the publicity value of such a figure. Only a star could think of such vulgar extravagance. If he's short of cash he can sack all those lawyers. Or devalue the dollar, I don't mind.'

Madame Gioconda hooted with pleasure at the prospect. Mangon nodded, then scribbled another message.

Be practical.

Madame Gioconda ground out her cigarette. 'You think I'm raving, don't you, Mangon? "Fantastic dreams, million-dollar contracts, poor old fool." But let me assure you that Hector will be only too eager to sign the contract. And I don't intend to rely solely on his good judgement as an impresario.' She smirked archly to herself.

What else?

Madame Gioconda peered round the darkened stage, then lowered her eyes.

'You see, Mangon, Hector and I are very old friends. You know what I mean, of course?' She waited for Mangon, who had swept out a thousand honeymoon hotel suites, to nod and then continued: 'How well I remember that first season at Bayreuth, when Hector and I...'

Mangon stared unhappily at his feet as Madame Gioconda outlined this latest venture into blackmail. Certainly she and LeGrande had been intimate friends – the cuttings scattered around the stage testified frankly to this. In fact, were it not for the small monthly cheque which LeGrande sent Madame Gioconda she would long previously have disintegrated. To turn on him and threaten ancient scandal (LeGrande was shortly to enter politics) was not only grotesque but extremely dangerous, for LeGrande was ruthless and unsentimental. Years earlier he had used Madame Gioconda as a stepping-stone, reaping all the publicity he could from their affair, then abruptly kicking her away.

Mangon fretted. A solution to her predicament was hard to find. Brought about through no fault of her own, Madame Gioconda's decline was all the harder to bear. Since the introduction a few years earlier of ultrasonic music, the human voice – indeed, audible music of any type – had gone completely out of fashion. Ultrasonic music, employing a vastly greater range of octaves, chords and chromatic scales than are audible by the human ear, provided a direct neural link between the sound stream and the auditory lobes, generating an apparently sourceless sensation of harmony, rhythm, cadence and melody uncontaminated by the noise and vibration of audible music.

The re-scoring of the classical repertoire allowed the ultrasonic audience the best of both worlds. The majestic rhythms of Beethoven, the popular melodies of Tchaikovsky, the complex fugal elaborations of Bach, the abstract images of Schoenberg – all these were raised in frequency above the threshold of conscious audibility. Not only did they become inaudible, but the original works were re-scored for the much wider range of the ultrasonic orchestra, became richer in texture, more profound in theme, more sensitive, tender or lyrical as the ultrasonic arranger chose.

The first casualty in this change-over was the human voice. This alone of all instruments could not be re-scored, because its sounds were produced by non-mechanical means which the neurophonic engineer could never hope, or bother, to duplicate.

The earliest ultrasonic recordings had met with resistance, even ridicule. Radio programmes consisting of nothing but silence interrupted at half-hour intervals by commercial breaks seemed absurd. But gradually the public discovered that the silence was golden, that after leaving the radio switched to an ultrasonic channel for an hour or so a pleasant atmosphere of rhythm and melody seemed to generate itself spontaneously around them. When an announcer suddenly stated that an ultrasonic version of Mozart's Jupiter Symphony or Tchaikovsky's Pathétique had just been played the listener identified the real source.

A second advantage of ultrasonic music was that its frequencies were so high they left no resonating residues in solid structures, and consequently there was no need to call in the sound-sweep. After an audible performance of most symphonic music, walls and furniture throbbed for days with disintegrating residues that made the air seem leaden and tumid, an entire room virtually uninhabitable.

An immediate result was the swift collapse of all but a few symphony orchestras and opera companies. Concert halls and opera houses closed overnight. In the age of noise the tranquillizing balms of silence began to be rediscovered.

But the final triumph of ultrasonic music had come with a second development – the short-playing record, spinning at 900 r.p.m., which condensed the 45 minutes of a Beethoven symphony to 20 seconds of playing time, the three hours of a Wagner opera to little more than two minutes. Compact and cheap, SP records sacrificed nothing to brevity. One 30-second SP record delivered as much neurophonic pleasure as a natural length recording, but with deeper penetration, greater total impact.

Ultrasonic SP records swept all others off the market. Sonic LP records became museum pieces – only a crank would choose to listen to an audible full-length version of *Siegfried* or the *Barber of Seville* when he could have both wrapped up inaudibly inside the same five-minute package *and* appreciate their full musical value.

The heyday of Madame Gioconda was over. Unceremoniously left on the shelf, she had managed to survive for a few months vocalizing on radio commercials. Soon these too went ultrasonic. In a despairing act of revenge she bought out the radio station which fired her and made her home on one of the sound stages. Over the years the station became derelict and forgotten, its windows smashed, neon portico collapsing, aerials rusting. The huge eight-lane flyover built across it sealed it conclusively into the past.

Now Madame Gioconda proposed to win her way back at stiletto-point.

Mangon watched her impassively as she ranted on nastily in a cloud of purple cigarette smoke, a large seedy witch. The phenobarbitone was making her drowsy and her threats and ultimatums were becoming disjointed.

'... memoirs too, don't forget, Hector. Frank exposure, no holds barred. I mean ... damn, have to get a ghost. Hotel de Paris at Monte, lots of pictures. Oh yes, I kept the photographs.' She grubbed about on the couch, came up with a crumpled soap coupon and a supermarket pay slip. 'Wait till those lawyers see them. Hector –' Suddenly she broke off, stared glassily at Mangon and sagged back.

Mangon waited until she was finally asleep, stood up and peered closely at her. She looked forlorn and desperate. He watched her reverently for a moment, then tiptoed to the rheostat mounted on the control panel behind the couch, damped down the lamp at Madame Gioconda's feet and left the stage.

He sealed the auditorium doors behind him, made his way down to the foyer and stepped out, sad but at the same time oddly exhilarated, into the cool midnight air. At last he accepted that he would have to act swiftly if he was to save Madame Gioconda.

TWO

Driving his sound truck into the city shortly after nine the next morning, Mangon decided to postpone his first call – the weird Neo-Corbusier Episcopalian Oratory sandwiched among the office blocks in the down-town financial sector – and instead turned west on Mainway and across the park towards the white-faced apartment batteries which reared up above the trees and lakes along the north side.

The Oratory was a difficult and laborious job that would take him three hours of concentrated effort. The Dean had recently imported some rare thirteenth-century pediments from the Church of St Francis at Assisi, beautiful sonic matrices rich with seven centuries of Gregorian chant, overlaid by the timeless tolling of the Angelus. Mounted into the altar they emanated an atmosphere resonant with litany and devotion, a mellow, deeply textured hymn that silently evoked the most sublime images of prayer and meditation.

But at 50,000 dollars each they also represented a terrifying hazard to the clumsy sound-sweep. Only two years earlier the entire north transept of Rheims Cathedral, rose window intact, purchased for a record 1,000,000 dollars and re-erected in the new Cathedral of St Joseph at San Diego, had been drained of its priceless heritage of tonal inlays by a squad of illiterate sound-sweeps who had misread their instructions and accidentally swept the wrong wall.

Even the most conscientious sound-sweep was limited by his skill, and Mangon, with his auditory super-sensitivity, was greatly in demand for his ability to sweep selectively, draining from the walls of the Oratory all extraneous and discordant noises – coughing, crying, the clatter of coins and mumble of prayer – leaving behind the chorales and liturgical chants which enhanced their devotional overtones. His skill alone would lengthen the life of the Assisi pediments by twenty years; without him they would soon become contaminated by the miscellaneous traffic of the congregation. Consequently he had no fears that the Dean would complain if he failed to appear as usual that morning.

Halfway along the north side of the park he swung off into the forecourt of a huge forty-storey apartment block, a glittering white cliff ribbed by jutting balconies. Most of the apartments were Superlux duplexes occupied by showbusiness people. No one was about, but as Mangon entered the hallway, sonovac in one hand, the marble walls and columns buzzed softly with the echoing chatter of guests leaving parties four or five hours earlier.

In the elevator the residues were clearer – confident male tones, the sharp wheedling of querulous wives, soft negatives of amatory blondes, punctuated by countless repetitions of 'dahling'. Mangon ignored the echoes, which were almost inaudible, a dim insect hum. He grinned to himself as he rode up to the penthouse apartment; if Madame Gioconda had known his destination she would have strangled him on the spot.

Ray Alto, doyen of the ultrasonic composers and the man more than any other responsible for Madame Gioconda's decline, was one of Mangon's regular calls. Usually Mangon swept his apartment once a week, calling at three in the afternoon. Today, however, he wanted to make sure of finding Alto before he left for Video City, where he was a director of programme music.

The houseboy let him in. He crossed the hall and made his way down the black glass staircase into the sunken lounge. Wide studio windows revealed an elegant panorama of park and mid-town skyscrapers.

A white-slacked young man sitting on one of the long slab sofas – Paul Merrill, Alto's arranger – waved him back.

'Mangon, hold on to your dive breaks. I'm really on reheat this morning.' He twirled the ultrasonic trumpet he was playing, a tangle of stops and valves from which half a dozen leads trailed off across the cushions to a cathode tube and tone generator at the other end of the sofa.

Mangon sat down quietly and Merrill clamped the mouthpiece to his lips. Watching the ray tube intently, where he could check the shape of the ultrasonic notes, he launched into a brisk allegretto sequence, then quickened and flicked out a series of brilliant arpeggios, stripping off high P and Q notes that danced across the cathode screen like frantic eels, fantastic glissandos that raced up twenty octaves in as many seconds, each note distinct and symmetrically exact, tripping off the tone generator in turn so that escalators of electronic chords interweaved the original scale, a multi-channel melodic stream that crowded the cathode screen with exquisite, flickering patterns. The whole thing was inaudible, but the air around Mangon felt vibrant and accelerated, charged with gaiety and sparkle, and he applauded generously when Merrill threw off a final dashing riff.

'*Flight of the Bumble Bee*,' Merrill told him. He tossed the trumpet aside and switched off the cathode tube. He lay back and savoured the glistening air for a moment. 'Well, how are things?'

Just then the door from one of the bedrooms opened and Ray Alto appeared, a tall, thoughtful man of about forty, with thinning blonde hair, wearing pale sunglasses over cool eyes.

'Hello, Mangon,' he said, running a hand over Mangon's head. 'You're early today. Full programme?' Mangon nodded. 'Don't let it get you down.' Alto picked a dictaphone off one of the end tables, carried it over to an armchair. 'Noise, noise, noise – the greatest single disease-vector of civilization. The whole world's rotting with it, yet all they can afford is a few people like Mangon fooling around with sonovacs. It's hard to believe that only a few years ago people completely failed to realize that sound left any residues.'

'Are we any better?' Merrill asked. 'This month's *Transonics* claims that eventually unswept sonic resonances will build up to a critical point where they'll literally start shaking buildings apart. The entire city will come down like Jericho.'

'Babel,' Alto corrected. 'Okay, now, let's shut up. We'll be gone soon, Mangon. Buy him a drink, would you, Paul.'

Merrill brought Mangon a coke from the bar, then wandered off. Alto flipped on the dictaphone, began to speak steadily into it. 'Memo 7: Betty, when does the copyright on Stravinsky lapse? Memo 8: Betty, file melody for projected nocturne: L, L sharp, BB, Y flat, Q, VT, L, L sharp. Memo 9: Paul, the bottom three octaves of the ultra-tuba are within the audible spectrum of the canine ear – congrats on that SP of the *Anvil Chorus* last night; about three million dogs thought the roof had fallen in on them. Memo 10: Betty –' He broke off, put down the microphone. 'Mangon, you look worried.'

Mangon, who had been lost in reverie, pulled himself together and shook his head.

'Working too hard?' Alto pressed. He scrutinized Mangon suspiciously. 'Are you still sitting up all night with that Gioconda woman?'

Embarrassed, Mangon lowered his eyes. His relationship with Alto was, obliquely, almost as close as that with Madame Gioconda. Although Alto was brusque and often irritable with Mangon, he took a sincere interest in his welfare. Possibly Mangon's muteness reminded him of the misanthropic motives behind his hatred of noise, made him feel indirectly responsible for the act of violence Mangon's mother had committed. Also, one artist to another, he respected Mangon's phenomenal auditory sensitivity.

'She'll exhaust you, Mangon, believe me.' Alto knew how much the personal contact meant to Mangon and hesitated to be over-critical. 'There's nothing you can do for her. Offering her sympathy merely fans her hopes for a come-back. She hasn't a chance.'

Mangon frowned, wrote quickly on his wrist-pad:

She WILL sing again!

Alto read the note pensively. Then, in a harder voice, he said: 'She's using you for her own purposes, Mangon. At present you satisfy one whim of hers – the neurotic headaches and fantasy applause. God forbid what the next whim might be.'

She is a great artist.

'She *was*,' Alto pointed out. 'No more, though, sad as it is. I'm afraid that the times change.'

Annoyed by this, Mangon gritted his teeth and tore off another sheet.

Entertainment, perhaps. Art, No!

Alto accepted the rebuke silently; he reproved himself as much as Mangon did for selling out to Video City. In his four years there his output of original ultrasonic music consisted of little more than one nearly finished symphony – aptly titled *Opus Zero* – shortly to receive its first performance, a few nocturnes and one quartet. Most of his energies went into programme music, prestige numbers for spectaculars and a mass of straight transcriptions of the classical repertoire. The last he particularly despised, fit work for Paul Merrill, but not for a responsible composer.

He added the sheet to the two in his left hand and asked: 'Have you ever heard Madame Gioconda sing?'

Mangon's answer came back scornfully:

No! But you have. Please describe.

Alto laughed shortly, tore up his sheets and walked across to the window.

'All right, Mangon, you've made your point. You're carrying a torch for art, doing your duty to one of the few perfect things the world has ever produced. I hope you're equal to the responsibility. La Gioconda might be quite a handful. Do you know that at one time the doors of Covent Garden, La Scala *and* the Met were closed to her? They said Callas had temperament, but she was a girl guide compared with Gioconda. Tell me, how is she? Eating enough?'

Mangon held up his coke bottle.

'Snow? That's tough. But how does she afford it?' He glanced at his watch. 'Dammit, I've got to leave. Clean this place out thoroughly, will you. It gives me a headache just listening to myself think.'

He started to pick up the dictaphone but Mangon was scribbling rapidly on his pad.

Give Madame Gioconda a job.

Alto read the note, then gave it back to Mangon, puzzled. 'Where? In this apartment?' Mangon shook his head. 'Do you mean at V.C.? *Singing?*' When Mangon began to nod vigorously he looked up at the ceiling with a despairing groan. 'For heaven's sake, Mangon, the last vocalist sang at Video City over ten years ago. No audience would stand for it. If I even suggested such an idea they'd tear my contract into a thousand pieces.' He shuddered, only half-playfully. 'I don't know about you, Mangon, but I've got my ulcer to support.'

He made his way to the staircase, but Mangon intercepted him, pencil flashing across the wrist-pad.

Please. Madame Gioconda will start blackmail soon. She is desperate.

Must sing again. Could arrange make-believe programme in research studios. Closed circuit.

Alto folded the note carefully, left the dictaphone on the staircase and walked slowly back to the window.

'This blackmail. Are you absolutely sure? Who, though, do you know?' Mangon nodded, but looked away. 'Okay, I won't press you. LeGrande, probably, eh?' Mangon turned round in surprise, then gave an elaborate parody of a shrug.

'Hector LeGrande. Obvious guess. But there are no secrets there, it's all on open file. I suppose she's just threatening to make enough of an exhibition of herself to block his governorship.' Alto pursed his lips. He loathed LeGrande, not merely for having bribed him into a way of life he could never renounce, but also because, once having exploited his weakness, LeGrande never hesitated to remind Alto of it, treating him and his music with contempt. If Madame Gioconda's blackmail had the slightest hope of success he would have been only too happy, but he knew LeGrande would destroy her, probably take Mangon too.

Suddenly he felt a paradoxical sense of loyalty for Madame Gioconda. He looked at Mangon, waiting patiently, big spaniel eyes wide with hope.

'The idea of a closed circuit programme is insane. Even if we went to all the trouble of staging it she wouldn't be satisfied. She doesn't want to sing, she wants to be a *star*. It's the trappings of stardom she misses – the cheering galleries, the piles of bouquets, the green room parties. I could arrange a half-hour session on closed circuit with some trainee technicians – a few straight selections from *Tosca* and *Butterfly*, say, with even a sonic piano accompaniment, I'd be glad to play it myself – but I can't provide the gossip columns and theatre reviews. What would happen when she found out?'

She wants to SING.

Alto reached out and patted Mangon on the shoulder. 'Good for you. All right, then, I'll think about it. God knows how we'd arrange it. We'd have to tell her that she'll be making a surprise guest appearance on one of the big shows – that'll explain the absence of any programme announcement and we'll be able to keep her in an isolated studio. Stress the importance of surprise, to prevent her from contacting the newspapers ... Where are you going?'

Mangon reached the staircase, picked up the dictaphone and returned to Alto with it. He grinned happily, his jaw working wildly as he struggled to speak. Strangled sounds quavered in his throat.

Touched, Alto turned away from him and sat down. 'Okay, Mangon,' he snapped brusquely, 'you can get on with your job. Remember, I haven't promised anything.' He flicked on the dictaphone, then began: 'Memo 11: Ray ...'

THREE

It was just after four o'clock when Mangon braked the sound truck in the alley behind the derelict station. Overhead the traffic hammered along the flyover, dinning down on to the cobbled walls. He had been trying to finish his rounds early enough to bring Madame Gioconda the big news before her headaches began. He had swept out the Oratory in an hour, whirled through a couple of movie theatres, the Museum of Abstract Art, and a dozen private calls in half his usual time, driven by his almost overwhelming joy at having won a promise of help from Ray Alto.

He ran through the foyer, already fumbling at his wrist-pad. For the first time in many years he really regretted his muteness, his inability to tell Madame Gioconda orally of his triumph that morning.

Studio 2 was in darkness, the rows of seats and litter of old programmes and ice-cream cartons reflected dimly in the single light masked by the tall flats. His feet slipped in some shattered plaster fallen from the ceiling and he was out of breath when he clambered up on to the stage and swung round the nearest flat.

Madame Gioconda had gone!

The stage was deserted, the couch a rumpled mess, a clutter of cold saucepans on the stove. The wardrobe door was open, dresses wrenched outwards off their hangers.

For a moment Mangon panicked, unable to visualize why she should have left, immediately assuming that she had discovered his plot with Alto.

Then he realized that never before had he visited the studio until midnight at the earliest, and that Madame Gioconda had merely gone out to the supermarket. He smiled at his own stupidity and sat down on the couch to wait for her, sighing with relief.

As vivid as if they had been daubed in letters ten feet deep, the words leapt out from the walls, nearly deafening him with their force.

'You grotesque old witch, you must be insane! You ever threaten me again and I'll have you destroyed! LISTEN, you pathetic –'

Mangon spun round helplessly, trying to screen his ears. The words must have been hurled out in a paroxysm of abuse, they were only an hour old, vicious sonic scars slashed across the immaculately swept walls.

His first thought was to rush out for the sonovac and sweep the walls clear before Madame Gioconda returned. Then it dawned on him that she had already heard the original of the echoes – in the background he could just detect the muffled rhythms and intonations of her voice.

All too exactly, he could identify the man's voice.

He had heard it many times before, raging in the same ruthless tirades, when deputizing for one of the sound-sweeps, he had swept out the main boardroom at Video City.

Hector LeGrande! So Madame Gioconda had been more desperate than he thought.

The bottom drawer of the dressing table lay on the floor, its contents upended. Propped against the mirror was an old silver portrait frame, dull and verdigrised, some cotton wool and a tin of cleansing fluid next to it. The photograph was one of LeGrande, taken twenty years earlier. She must have known LeGrande was coming and had searched out the old portrait, probably regretting the threat of blackmail.

But the sentiment had not been shared.

Mangon walked round the stage, his heart knotting with rage, filling his ears with LeGrande's taunts. He picked up the portrait, pressed it between his palms, and suddenly smashed it across the edge of the dressing table.

'Mangon!'

The cry riveted him to the air. He dropped what was left of the frame, saw Madame Gioconda step quietly from behind one of the flats.

'Mangon, please,' she protested gently. 'You frighten me.' She sidled past him towards the bed, dismantling an enormous purple hat. 'And do clean up all that glass, or I shall cut my feet.'

She spoke drowsily and moved in a relaxed, sluggish way that

Mangon first assumed indicated acute shock. Then she drew from her handbag six white vials and lined them up carefully on the bedside table. These were her favourite confectionery – so LeGrande had sweetened the pill with another cheque. Mangon began to scoop the glass together with his feet, at the same time trying to collect his wits. The sounds of LeGrande's abuse dinned the air, and he broke away and ran off to fetch the sonovac.

Madame Gioconda was sitting on the edge of the bed when he returned, dreamily dusting a small bottle of bourbon which had followed the cocaine vials out of the handbag. She hummed to herself melodically and stroked one of the feathers in her hat.

'Mangon,' she called when he had almost finished. 'Come here.'

Mangon put down the sonovac and went across to her.

She looked up at him, her eyes suddenly very steady. 'Mangon, why did you break Hector's picture?' She held up a piece of the frame. 'Tell me.'

Mangon hesitated, then scribbled on his pad:

I am sorry. I adore you very much. He said such foul things to you.

Madame Gioconda glanced at the note, then gazed back thoughtfully at Mangon. 'Were you hiding here when Hector came?'

Mangon shook his head categorically. He started to write on his pad but Madame Gioconda restrained him.

'That's all right, dear. I thought not.' She looked around the stage for a moment, listening carefully. 'Mangon, when you came in could you hear what Mr LeGrande said?'

Mangon nodded. His eyes flickered to the obscene phrases on the walls and he began to frown. He still felt LeGrande's presence and his attempt to humiliate Madame Gioconda.

Madame Gioconda pointed around them. 'And you can actually hear what he said even now? How remarkable. Mangon, you have a wondrous talent.'

I am sorry you have to suffer so much.

Madame Gioconda smiled at this. 'We all have our crosses to bear. I have a feeling you may be able to lighten mine considerably.' She patted the bed beside her. 'Do sit down, you must be tired.' When he was settled she went on, 'I'm very interested, Mangon. Do you mean you can distinguish entire phrases and sentences in the sounds you sweep? You can hear complete conversations hours after they have taken place?'

Something about Madame Gioconda's curiosity made Mangon hesitate. His talent, so far as he knew, was unique, and he was not so naïve as to fail to appreciate its potentialities. It had developed in his late adolescence and so far he had resisted any temptation to abuse it. He had never revealed the talent to anyone, knowing that if he did his days as a sound-sweeper would be over.

Madame Gioconda was watching him, an expectant smile on her lips. Her thoughts, of course, were solely of revenge. Mangon listened again to the walls, focused on the abuse screaming out into the air.

Not complete conversations. Long fragments, up to twenty syllables. Depending on resonances and matrix. Tell no one. I will help you have revenge on LeGrande.

Madame Gioconda squeezed Mangon's hand. She was about to reach for the bourbon bottle when Mangon suddenly remembered the point of his visit. He leapt off the bed and started frantically scribbling on his wrist-pad.

He tore off the first sheet and pressed it into her startled hands, then filled three more, describing his encounter with the musical director at V.C., the latter's interest in Madame Gioconda and the conditional promise to arrange her guest appearance. In view of LeGrande's hostility he stressed the need for absolute secrecy.

He waited happily while Madame Gioconda read quickly through the notes, tracing out Mangon's child-like script with a long scarlet fingernail. When she finished he nodded his head rapidly and gestured triumphantly in the air.

Bemused, Madame Gioconda gazed uncomprehendingly at the notes. Then she reached out and pulled Mangon to her, taking his big faun-like head in her jewelled hands and pressing it to her lap.

'My dear child, how much I need you. You must never leave me now.'

As she stroked Mangon's hair her eyes roved questingly around the walls.

The miracle happened shortly before eleven o'clock the next morning.

After breakfast, sprawled across Madame Gioconda's bed with her scrapbooks, an old gramophone salvaged by Mangon from one of the studios playing operatic selections, they had decided to drive out to the stockades – the sound-sweeps left for the city at nine and they would be able to examine the sonic dumps unmolested. Having spent so much time with Madame Gioconda and immersed himself so deeply in her world, Mangon was eager now to introduce Madame Gioconda to his. The stockades, bleak though they might be, were all he had to show her.

For Mangon, Madame Gioconda had now become the entire universe, a source of certainty and wonder as potent as the sun. Behind him his past life fell away like the discarded chrysalis of a brilliant butterfly, the grey years of his childhood at the orphanage dissolving into the magical kaleidoscope that revolved around him. As she talked and murmured affectionately to him, the drab flats and props in the studio seemed as brightly coloured and meaningful as the landscape of a mescalin fantasy, the air tingling with a thousand vivid echoes of her voice.

They set off down F Street at ten, soon left behind the dingy warehouses and abandoned tenements that had enclosed Madame Gioconda for so long. Squeezed together in the driving-cab of the sound truck they looked an incongruous pair – the gangling Mangon, in zip-fronted yellow plastic jacket and yellow peaked cap, at the wheel, dwarfed by the vast flamboyant Madame Gioconda, wearing a parrot-green cartwheel hat and veil, her huge creamy breast glittering with pearls, gold stars and jewelled crescents, a small selection of the orders that had showered upon her in her heyday.

She had breakfasted well, on one of the vials and a tooth-glass of bourbon. As they left the city she gazed out amiably at the fields stretching away from the highway, and trilled out a light recitative from *Figaro*.

Mangon listened to her happily, glad to see her in such good form. Determined to spend every possible minute with Madame Gioconda, he had decided to abandon his calls for the day, if not for the next week and month. With her he at last felt completely secure. The pressure of her hand and the warm swell of her shoulder made him feel confident and invigorated, all the more proud that he was able to help her back to fame.

He tapped on the windshield as they swung off the highway on to the narrow dirt track that led towards the stockades. Here and there among the dunes they could see the low ruined outbuildings of the old explosives plant, the white galvanized iron roof of one of the sound-sweep's cabins. Desolate and unfrequented, the dunes ran on for miles. They passed the remains of a gateway that had collapsed to one side of the road; originally a continuous fence ringed the stockade, but no one had any reason for wanting to penetrate it. A place of strange echoes and festering silences, overhung by a gloomy miasma of a million compacted sounds, it remained remote and haunted, the graveyard of countless private babels.

The first of the sonic dumps appeared two or three hundred yards away on their right. This was reserved for aircraft sounds swept from the city's streets and municipal buildings, and was a tightly packed collection of sound-absorbent baffles covering several acres. The baffles were slightly larger than those in the other stockades; twenty feet high and fifteen wide, each supported by heavy wooden props, they faced each other in a random labyrinth of alleyways, like a store lot of advertisement hoardings. Only the top two or three feet were visible above the dunes, but the charged air hit Mangon like a hammer, a pounding niagara of airliners blaring down the glideway, the piercing whistle of jets jockeying at take-off, the ceaseless mind-sapping roar that hangs like a vast umbrella over any metropolitan complex.

All around, odd sounds shaken loose from the stockades were

beginning to reach them. Over the entire area, fed from the dumps below, hung an unbroken phonic high, invisible but nonetheless as tangible and menacing as an enormous black thundercloud. Occasionally, when super-saturation was reached after one of the summer holiday periods, the sonic pressure fields would split and discharge, venting back into the stockades a nightmarish cataract of noise, raining on to the sound-sweeps not only the howling of cats and dogs, but the multi-lunged tumult of cars, express trains, fairgrounds and aircraft, the cacophonic *musique concrète* of civilization.

To Mangon the sounds reaching them, though scaled higher in the register, were still distinct, but Madame Gioconda could hear nothing and felt only an overpowering sense of depression and irritation. The air seemed to grate and rasp. Mangon noticed her beginning to frown and hold her hand to her forehead. He wound up his window and indicated to her to do the same. He switched on the sonovac mounted under the dashboard and let it drain the discordancies out of the sealed cabin.

Madame Gioconda relaxed in the sudden blissful silence. A little further on, when they passed another stockade set closer to the road, she turned to Mangon and began to say something to him.

Suddenly she jerked violently in alarm, her hat toppling. Her voice had frozen! Her mouth and lips moved frantically, but no sounds emerged. For a moment she was paralysed. Clutching her throat desperately, she filled her lungs and screamed.

A faint squeak piped out of her cavernous throat, and Mangon swung round in alarm to see her gibbering apoplectically, pointing helplessly to her throat.

He stared at her bewildered, then doubled over the wheel in a convulsion of silent laughter, slapping his thigh and thumping the dashboard. He pointed to the sonovac, then reached down and turned up the volume.

'. . . aaauuuoooh,' Madame Gioconda heard herself groan. She grasped her hat and secured it. 'Mangon, what a dirty trick, you should have warned me.'

Mangon grinned. The discordant sounds coming from the

stockades began to fill the cabin again, and he turned down the volume. Gleefully, he scribbled on his wrist-pad:

Now you know what it is like!

Madame Gioconda opened her mouth to reply, then stopped in time, hiccuped and took his arm affectionately.

FOUR

Mangon slowed down as they approached a side road. Two hundred yards away on their left a small pink-washed cabin stood on a dune overlooking one of the stockades. They drove up to it, turned into a circular concrete apron below the cabin and backed up against one of the unloading bays, a battery of red-painted hydrants equipped with manifold gauges and release pipes running off into the stockade. This was only twenty feet away at its nearest point, a forest of door-shaped baffles facing each other in winding corridors, like a set from a surrealist film.

As she climbed down from the truck Madame Gioconda expected the same massive wave of depression and overload that she had felt from the stockade of aircraft noises, but instead the air seemed brittle and frenetic, darting with sudden flashes of tension and exhilaration.

As they walked up to the cabin Mangon explained:

Party noises – company for me.

The twenty or thirty baffles nearest the cabin he reserved for those screening him from the miscellaneous chatter that filled the rest of the stockade. When he woke in the mornings he would listen to the laughter and small talk, enjoy the gossip and wisecracks as much as if he had been at the parties himself.

The cabin was a single room with a large window overlooking

the stockade, well insulated from the hubbub below. Madame Gioconda showed only a cursory interest in Mangon's meagre belongings, and after a few general remarks came to the point and went over to the window. She opened it slightly, listened experimentally to the stream of atmospheric shifts that crowded past her.

She pointed to the cabin on the far side of the stockade. 'Mangon, whose is that?'

Gallagher's. My partner. He sweeps City Hall, University, V.C., big mansions on 5th and A. Working now.

Madame Gioconda nodded and surveyed the stockade with interest. 'How fascinating. It's like a zoo. All that talk, talk, talk. And *you* can hear it all.' She snapped back her bracelets with swift decisive flicks of the wrist.

Mangon sat down on the bed. The cabin seemed small and dingy, and he was saddened by Madame Gioconda's disinterest. Having brought her all the way out to the dumps he wondered how he was going to keep her amused. Fortunately the stockade intrigued her. When she suggested a stroll through it he was only too glad to oblige.

Down at the unloading bay he demonstrated how he emptied the tanker, clipping the exhaust leads to the hydrant, regulating the pressure through the manifold and then pumping the sound away into the stockade.

Most of the stockade was in a continuous state of uproar, sounding something like a crowd in a football stadium, and as he led her out among the baffles he picked their way carefully through the quieter aisles. Around them voices chattered and whined fretfully, fragments of conversation drifted aimlessly over the air. Somewhere a woman pleaded in thin nervous tones, a man grumbled to himself, another swore angrily, a baby bellowed. Behind it all was the steady background murmur of countless TV programmes, the easy patter of announcers, the endless monotones of race-track commentators, the shrieking audiences of quiz shows, all pitched an octave up the scale so that they sounded an eerie parody of themselves.

A shot rang out in the next aisle, followed by screams and shouting. Although she heard nothing, the pressure pulse made Madame Gioconda stop.

'Mangon, wait. Don't be in so much of a hurry. Tell me what they're saying.'

Mangon selected a baffle and listened carefully. The sounds appeared to come from an apartment over a launderette. A battery of washing machines chuntered to themselves, a cash register slammed interminably, there was a dim almost sub-threshold echo of 60-cycle hum from an SP record-player.

He shook his head, waved Madame Gioconda on.

'Mangon, what did they *say*?' she pestered him. He stopped again, sharpened his ears and waited. This time he was more lucky, an over-emotional female voice was gasping '... but if he finds you here he'll kill you, he'll kill us both, what shall we do ...' He started to scribble down this outpouring, Madame Gioconda craning breathlessly over his shoulder, then recognized its source and screwed up the note.

'Mangon, for heaven's sake, what was it? Don't throw it away! Tell me!' She tried to climb under the wooden superstructure of the baffle to recover the note, but Mangon restrained her and quickly scribbled another message.

Adam and Eve. Sorry.

'What, the film? Oh, how ridiculous! Well, come on, try again.'

Eager to make amends, Mangon picked the next baffle, one of a group serving the staff married quarters of the University. Always a difficult job to keep clean, he struck paydirt almost at once.

'... my God, there's Bartok all over the place, that damned Steiner woman, I'll swear she's sleeping with her ...'

Mangon took it all down, passing the sheets to Madame Gioconda as soon as he covered them. Squinting hard at his crabbed handwriting, she gobbled them eagerly, disappointed when, after half a dozen, he lost the thread and stopped.

'Go on, Mangon, what's the matter?' She let the notes fall to the ground. 'Difficult, isn't it. We'll have to teach you shorthand.'

They reached the baffles Mangon had just filled from the previous day's rounds. Listening carefully he heard Paul Merrill's voice: '... month's *Transonics* claims that ... the entire city will come down like Jericho.'

He wondered if he could persuade Madame Gioconda to wait for fifteen minutes, when he would be able to repeat a few carefully edited fragments from Alto's promise to arrange her guest appearance, but she seemed eager to move deeper into the stockade.

'You said your friend Gallagher sweeps out Video City, Mangon. Where would that be?'

Hector LeGrande. Of course, Mangon realized, why had he been so obtuse. This was the chance to pay the man back.

He pointed to an area a few aisles away. They climbed between the baffles, Mangon helping Madame Gioconda over the beams and props, steering her full skirt and wide hat brim away from splinters and rusted metalwork.

The task of finding LeGrande was simple. Even before the baffles were in sight Mangon could hear the hard, unyielding bite of the tycoon's voice, dominating every other sound from the Video City area. Gallagher in fact swept only the senior dozen or so executive suites at V.C., chiefly to relieve their occupants of the distasteful echoes of LeGrande's voice.

Mangon steered their way among these, searching for LeGrande's master suite, where anything of a really confidential nature took place.

There were about twenty baffles, throwing off an unending chorus of 'Yes, H.L.', 'Thanks, H.L.', 'Brilliant, H.L.' Two or three seemed strangely quiet, and he drew Madame Gioconda over to them.

This was LeGrande with his personal secretary and PA. He took out his pencil and focused carefully.

'... of Third National Bank, transfer two million to private holding and threaten claim for stock depreciation ... redraft escape clauses, including non-liability purchase benefits ...'

Madame Gioconda tapped his arm but he gestured her away. Most of the baffle appeared to be taken up by dubious financial dealings, but nothing that would really hurt LeGrande if revealed.

Then he heard –

'... Bermuda Hilton. Private Island, with anchorage, have the beach cleaned up, last time the water was full of fish ... I don't care, poison them, hang some nets out ... Imogene will fly in from Idlewild as Mrs Edna Burgess, warn Customs to stay away ...'

'... call Cartiers, something for the Contessa, 17 carats say, ceiling of ten thousand. No, make it eight thousand ...'

'... hat-check girl at the Tropicabana. Usual dossier ...'

Mangon scribbled furiously, but LeGrande was speaking at rapid dictation speed and he could get down only a few fragments. Madame Gioconda barely deciphered his handwriting, and became more and more frustrated as her appetite was whetted. Finally she flung away the notes in a fury of exasperation.

'This is absurd, you're missing everything!' she cried. She pounded on one of the baffles, then broke down and began to sob angrily. 'Oh God, God, *God*, how ridiculous! Help me, I'm going insane ...'

Mangon hurried across to her, put his arms round her shoulders to support her. She pushed him away irritably, railing at herself to discharge her impatience. 'It's useless, Mangon, it's stupid of me, I was a fool –'

'*STOP!*'

The cry split the air like the blade of a guillotine.

They both straightened, stared at each other blankly. Mangon put his fingers slowly to his lips, then reached out tremulously and put his hands in Madame Gioconda's. Somewhere within him a tremendous tension had begun to dissolve.

'Stop,' he said again in a rough but quiet voice. 'Don't cry. I'll help you.'

Madame Gioconda gaped at him with amazement. Then she let out a tremendous whoop of triumph.

'Mangon, you can talk! You've got your voice back! It's absolutely astounding! Say something, quickly, for heaven's sake!'

Mangon felt his mouth again, ran his fingers rapidly over his throat. He began to tremble with excitement, his face brightened, he jumped up and down like a child.

'I can talk,' he repeated wonderingly. His voice was gruff, then seesawed into a treble. 'I can talk,' he said louder, controlling its pitch. 'I can talk, I can talk, *I can talk*!' He flung his head back, let out an ear-shattering shout. 'I CAN TALK! HEAR ME!' He ripped the wrist-pad off his sleeve, hurled it away over the baffles.

Madame Gioconda backed away, laughing agreeably. 'We can hear you, Mangon. Dear me, how sweet.' She watched Mangon thoughtfully as he cavorted happily in the narrow interval between the aisles. 'Now don't tire yourself out or you'll lose it again.'

Mangon danced over to her, seized her shoulders and squeezed them tightly. He suddenly realized that he knew no diminutive or Christian name for her.

'Madame Gioconda,' he said earnestly, stumbling over the syllables, the words that were so simple yet so enormously complex to pronounce. 'You gave me back my voice. Anything you want –' He broke off, stuttering happily, laughing through his tears. Suddenly he buried his head in her shoulder, exhausted by his discovery, and cried gratefully, 'It's a *wonderful* voice.'

Madame Gioconda steadied him maternally. 'Yes, Mangon,' she said, her eyes on the discarded notes lying in the dust. 'You've got a wonderful voice, all right.' *Sotto voce*, she added: 'But your hearing is even more wonderful.'

Paul Merrill switched off the SP player, sat down on the arm of the sofa and watched Mangon quizzically.

'Strange. You know, my guess is that it was psychosomatic.'

Mangon grinned. 'Psychosemantic,' he repeated, garbling the word half-deliberately. 'Clever. You can do amazing things with words. They help to crystallize the truth.'

Merrill groaned playfully. 'God, you sit there, you drink your coke, you philosophize. Don't you realize you're supposed to stand quietly in a corner, positively dumb with gratitude? Now you're even ramming your puns down my throat. Never mind, tell me again how it happened.'

'Once a pun a time –' Mangon ducked the magazine Merrill flung at him, let out a loud 'Olé!'

For the last two weeks he had been *en fête*.

Every day he and Madame Gioconda followed the same routine; after breakfast at the studio they drove out to the stockade, spent two or three hours compiling their confidential file on LeGrande, lunched at the cabin and then drove back to the city, Mangon going off on his rounds while Madame Gioconda slept until he returned shortly before midnight. For Mangon their existence was idyllic; not only was he rediscovering himself in terms of the complex spectra and patterns of speech – a completely new category of existence – but at the same time his relationship with Madame Gioconda revealed areas of sympathy, affection and understanding that he had never previously seen. If he sometimes felt that he was too preoccupied with his side of their relationship and the extraordinary benefits it had brought him, at least Madame Gioconda had been equally well served. Her headaches and mysterious phantoms had gone, she had cleaned up the studio and begun to salvage a little dignity and self-confidence, which made her single-minded sense of ambition seem less obsessive. Psychologically, she needed Mangon less now than he needed her, and he was sensible to restrain his high spirits and give her plenty of attention. During the first week Mangon's incessant chatter had been rather wearing, and once, on their way to the stockade, she had switched on the sonovac in the driving-cab and left Mangon mouthing silently at the air like a stranded fish. He had taken the hint.

'What about the sound-sweeping?' Merrill asked. 'Will you give it up?'

Mangon shrugged. 'It's my talent, but living at the stockade, let in at back doors, cleaning up the verbal garbage – it's a degraded job. I want to help Madame Gioconda. She will need a secretary when she starts to go on tour.'

Merrill shook his head warily. 'You're awfully sure there's going to be a sonic revival, Mangon. Every sign is against it.'

'They have not heard Madame Gioconda sing. Believe me, I know the power and wonder of the human voice. Ultrasonic music is great for atmosphere, but it has no content. It can't express ideas, only emotions.'

'What happened to that closed circuit programme you and Ray were going to put on for her?'

'It – fell through,' Mangon lied. The circuits Madame Gioconda would perform on would be open to the world. He had told them nothing of the visits to the stockade, of his power to read the baffles, of the accumulating file on LeGrande. Soon Madame Gioconda would strike.

Above them in the hallway a door slammed, someone stormed through into the apartment in a tempest, kicking a chair against a wall. It was Alto. He raced down the staircase into the lounge, jaw tense, fingers flexing angrily.

'Paul, don't interrupt me until I've finished,' he snapped, racing past without looking at them. 'You'll be out of a job but I warn you, if you don't back me up one hundred per cent I'll shoot you. That goes for you too, Mangon, I need you in on this.' He whirled over to the window, bolted out the traffic noises below, then swung back and watched them steadily, feet planted firmly in the carpet. For the first time in the three years Mangon had known him he looked aggressive and confident.

'Headline,' he announced. 'The Gioconda is to sing again! Incredible and terrifying though the prospect may seem, exactly two weeks from now the live, uncensored voice of the Gioconda will go out coast to coast on all three V.C. radio channels. Surprised, Mangon? It's no secret, they're printing the bills right now. Eight-thirty to nine-thirty, right up on the peak, even if they have to give the time away.'

Merrill sat forward. 'Bully for her. If LeGrande wants to drive the whole ship into the ground, why worry?'

Alto punched the sofa viciously. 'Because you and I are going to be on board! Didn't you hear me? Eight-thirty, a fortnight today! *We* have a programme on then. Well, guess who our guest star is?'

Merrill struggled to make sense of this. 'Wait a minute, Ray. You mean she's actually going to appear – she's going to *sing* – in the middle of *Opus Zero*?' Alto nodded grimly. Merrill threw up his hands and slumped back. 'It's crazy, she can't. Who says she will?'

'Who do you think? The great LeGrande.' Alto turned to Mangon. 'She must have raked up some real dirt to frighten him into this. I can hardly believe it.'

'But why on *Opus Zero*?' Merrill pressed. 'Let's switch the première to the week after.'

'Paul, you're missing the point. Let me fill you in. Sometime yesterday Madame Gioconda paid a private call on LeGrande. Something she told him persuaded him that it would be absolutely wonderful for her to have a whole hour to herself on one of the feature music programmes, singing a few old-fashioned songs from the old-fashioned shows, with a full-scale ultrasonic backing. Eager to give her a completely free hand he even asked her which of the regular programmes she'd like. Well, as the last show she appeared on ten years ago was cancelled to make way for Ray Alto's *Total Symphony* you can guess which one she picked.'

Merrill nodded. 'It all fits together. We're broadcasting from the concert studio. A single ultrasonic symphony, no station breaks, not even a commentary. Your first world première in three years. There'll be a big invited audience. White tie, something like the old days. Revenge is sweet.' He shook his head sadly. 'Hell, all that work.'

Alto snapped: 'Don't worry, it won't be wasted. Why should we pay the bill for LeGrande? This symphony is the one piece of serious music I've written since I joined V.C. and it isn't going to be ruined.' He went over to Mangon, sat down next to him. 'This afternoon I went down to the rehearsal studios. They'd found an ancient sonic grand somewhere and one of the old-timers was accompanying her. Mangon, it's ten years since she sang last. If she'd practised for two or three hours a day she might have preserved her voice, but you sweep her radio station, you know she hasn't sung a note. She's an old woman now. What time alone hasn't done to her, cocaine and self-pity have.' He paused, watching Mangon searchingly. 'I hate to say it, Mangon, but it sounded like a cat being strangled.'

You lie, Mangon thought icily. *You are simply so ignorant, your taste in music is so debased, that you are unable to recognize real genius when you see it.* He looked at Alto with contempt, sorry for the man, with his absurd silent symphonies. He felt like shouting: *I know what silence is! The voice of the Gioconda is a stream of gold, molten and pure, she will find it again as I found mine.* However, something about Alto's manner warned him to wait.

He said: 'I understand.' Then: 'What do you want me to do?'

Alto patted him on the shoulder. 'Good boy. Believe me, you'll be helping her in the long run. What I propose will save all of us from looking foolish. We've got to stand up to LeGrande, even if it means a one-way ticket out of V.C. Okay, Paul?' Merrill nodded firmly and he went on: 'Orchestra will continue as scheduled. According to the programme Madame Gioconda will be singing to an accompaniment by *Opus Zero*, but that means nothing and there'll be no connection at any point. In fact she won't turn up until the night itself. She'll stand well down-stage on a special platform, and the only microphone will be an aerial about twenty feet diagonally above her. It will be live – *but her voice will never reach it*. Because you, Mangon, will be in the cue-box directly in front of her, with the most powerful sonovac we can lay our hands on. As soon as she opens her mouth you'll let her have it. She'll be at least ten feet away from you so she'll hear herself and won't suspect what is happening.'

'What about the audience?' Merrill asked.

'They'll be listening to my symphony, enjoying a neurophonic experience of sufficient beauty and power, I hope, to distract them from the sight of a blowzy *prima donna* gesturing to herself in a cocaine fog. They'll probably think she's conducting. Remember, they may be expecting her to sing but how many people still know what the word really means? Most of them will assume it's ultrasonic.'

'And LeGrande?'

'He'll be in Bermuda. Business conference.'

FIVE

Madame Gioconda was sitting before her dressing-table mirror, painting on a face like a Hallowe'en mask. Beside her the gramophone played scratchy sonic selections from *Traviata*. The stage was still a disorganized jumble, but there was now an air of purpose about it.

Making his way through the flats, Mangon walked up to her quietly and kissed her bare shoulder. She stood up with a flourish, an enormous monument of a woman in a magnificent black silk dress sparkling with thousands of sequins.

'Thank you, Mangon,' she sang out when he complimented her. She swirled off to a hat-box on the bed, pulled out a huge peacock feather and stabbed it into her hair.

Mangon had come round at six, several hours before usual; over the past two days he had felt increasingly uneasy. He was convinced that Alto was in error, and yet logic was firmly on his side. Could Madame Gioconda's voice have preserved itself? Her spoken voice, unless she was being particularly sweet, was harsh and uneven, recently even more so. He assumed that with only a week to her performance nervousness was making her irritable.

Again she was going out, as she had done almost every night. With whom, she never explained; probably to the theatre restaurants, to renew contacts with agents and managers. He would have liked to go with her, but he felt out of place on this plane of Madame Gioconda's existence.

'Mangon, I won't be back until very late,' she warned him. 'You look rather tired and pasty. You'd better go home and get some sleep.'

Mangon noticed he was still wearing his yellow peaked cap.

Unconsciously he must already have known he would not be spending the night there.

'Do you want to go to the stockade tomorrow?' he asked.

'Hmmmh ... I don't think so. It gives me rather a headache. Let's leave it for a day or two.'

She turned on him with a tremendous smile, her eyes glittering with sudden affection.

'Goodbye, Mangon, it's been wonderful to see you.' She bent down and pressed her cheek maternally to his, engulfing him in a heady wave of powder and perfume. In an instant all his doubts and worries evaporated, he looked forward to seeing her the next day, certain that they would spend the future together.

For half an hour after she had gone he wandered around the deserted sound stage, going through his memories. Then he made his way out to the alley and drove back to the stockade.

As the day of Madame Gioconda's performance drew closer Mangon's anxieties mounted. Twice he had been down to the concert studio at Video City, had rehearsed with Alto his entry beneath the stage to the cue-box, a small compartment off the corridor used by the electronics engineers. They had checked the power points, borrowed a sonovac from the services section – a heavy duty model used for shielding VIPs and commentators at airports – and mounted its nozzle in the cue-hood.

Alto stood on the platform erected for Madame Gioconda, shouted at the top of his voice at Merrill sitting in the third row of the stalls.

'Hear anything?' he called afterwards.

Merrill shook his head. 'Nothing, no vibration at all.'

Down below Mangon flicked the release toggle, vented a long-drawn-out 'Fiivvveeee! ... Foouuurrr! ... Thrreeeee! ... Twooooo! ... Onnneeee ... !'

'Good enough,' Alto decided. Chicago-style, they hid the sonovac in a triple-bass case, stored it in Alto's office.

'Do you want to hear her sing, Mangon?' Alto asked. 'She should be rehearsing now.'

Mangon hesitated, then declined.

'It's tragic that she's unable to realize the truth herself,' Alto commented. 'Her mind must be fixed fifteen or twenty years in the past, when she sang her greatest roles at La Scala. That's the voice she hears, the voice she'll probably always hear.'

Mangon pondered this. Once he tried to ask Madame Gioconda how her practice sessions were going, but she was moving into a different zone and answered with some grandiose remark. He was seeing less and less of her, whenever he visited the station she was either about to go out or else tired and eager to be rid of him. Their trips to the stockade had ceased. All this he accepted as inevitable; after the performance, he assured himself, after her triumph, she would come back to him.

He noticed, however, that he was beginning to stutter.

On the final afternoon, a few hours before the performance that evening, Mangon drove down to F Street for what was to be the last time. He had not seen Madame Gioconda the previous day and he wanted to be with her and give her any encouragement she needed.

As he turned into the alley he was surprised to see two large removal vans parked outside the station entrance. Four or five men were carrying out pieces of furniture and the great scenic flats from the sound stage.

Mangon ran over to them. One of the vans was full; he recognized all Madame Gioconda's possessions – the rococo wardrobe and dressing table, the couch, the huge Desdemona bed, up-ended and wrapped in corrugated paper – as he looked at it he felt that a section of himself had been torn from him and rammed away callously. In the bright daylight the peeling threadbare flats had lost all illusion of reality; with them Mangon's whole relationship with Madame Gioconda seemed to have been dismantled.

The last of the workmen came out with a gold cushion under his arm, tossed it into the second van. The foreman sealed the doors and waved on the driver.

'W ... wh ... where are you going?' Mangon asked him urgently.

The foreman looked him up and down. 'You're the sweeper, are you?' He jerked a thumb towards the station. 'The old girl said there was a message for you in there. Couldn't see one myself.'

Mangon left him and ran into the foyer and up the stairway towards Studio 2. The removers had torn down the blinds and a grey light was flooding into the dusty auditorium. Without the flats the stage looked exposed and derelict.

He raced down the aisle, wondering why Madame Gioconda had decided to leave without telling him.

The stage had been stripped. The music stands had been kicked over, the stove lay on its side with two or three old pans around it, underfoot there was a miscellaneous litter of paper, ash and empty vials.

Mangon searched around for the message, probably pinned to one of the partitions.

Then he heard it screaming at him from the walls, violent and concise.

'GO AWAY YOU UGLY CHILD! NEVER TRY TO SEE ME AGAIN!'

He shrank back, involuntarily tried to shout as the walls seemed to fall in on him, but his throat had frozen.

As he entered the corridor below the stage shortly before eight-twenty, Mangon could hear the sounds of the audience arriving and making their way to their seats. The studio was almost full, a hubbub of well-heeled chatter. Lights flashed on and off in the corridor, and oblique atmospheric shifts cut through the air as the players on the stage tuned their instruments.

Mangon slid past the technicians manning the neurophonic rigs which supplied the orchestra, trying to make the enormous triple-bass case as inconspicuous as possible. They were all busy checking the relays and circuits, and he reached the cue-box and slipped through the door unnoticed.

The box was almost in darkness, a few rays of coloured light filtering through the pink and white petals of the chrysanthemums stacked over the hood. He bolted the door, then opened the case, lifted out the sonovac and clipped the snout into the canister.

Leaning forward, with his hands he pushed a small aperture among the flowers.

Directly in front of him he could see a velvet-lined platform, equipped with a white metal rail to the centre of which a large floral ribbon had been tied. Beyond was the orchestra, disposed in a semicircle, each of the twenty members sitting at a small box-like desk on which rested his instrument, tone generator and cathode tube. They were all present, and the light reflected from the ray screens threw a vivid phosphorescent glow on to the silver wall behind them.

Mangon propped the nozzle of the sonovac into the aperture, bent down, plugged in the lead and switched on.

Just before eight-twenty-five someone stepped across the platform and paused in front of the cue-hood. Mangon crouched back, watching the patent leather shoes and black trousers move near the nozzle.

'Mangon!' he heard Alto snap. He craned forward, saw Alto eyeing him. Mangon waved to him and Alto nodded slowly, at the same time smiling to someone in the audience, then turned on his heel and took his place in the orchestra.

At eight-thirty a sequence of red and green lights signalled the start of the programme. The audience quietened, waiting while an announcer in an off-stage booth introduced the programme.

A compère appeared on stage, standing behind the cue-hood, and addressed the audience. Mangon sat quietly on the small wooden seat fastened to the wall, staring blankly at the canister of the sonovac. There was a round of applause, and a steady green light shone downwards through the flowers. The air in the cue-box began to sweeten, a cool motionless breeze eddied vertically around him as a rhythmic ultrasonic pressure wave pulsed past. It relaxed the confined dimensions of the box, with a strange mesmeric echo that held his attention. Somewhere in his mind he realized that the symphony had started, but he was too distracted to pull himself together and listen to it consciously.

Suddenly, through the gap between the flowers and the sonovac nozzle, he saw a large white mass shifting about on the platform. He slipped off the seat and peered up.

Madame Gioconda had taken her place on the platform. Seen from below she seemed enormous, a towering cataract of glistening white satin that swept down to her feet. Her arms were folded loosely in front of her, fingers flashing with blue and white stones. He could only just glimpse her face, the terrifying witch-like mask turned in profile as she waited for some off-stage signal.

Mangon mobilized himself, slid his hand down to the trigger of the sonovac. He waited, feeling the steady subliminal music of Alto's symphony swell massively within him, its tempo accelerating. Presumably Madame Gioconda's arranger was waiting for a climax at which to introduce her first aria.

Abruptly Madame Gioconda looked forward at the audience and took a short step to the rail. Her hands parted and opened palms upward, her head moved back, her bare shoulders swelled.

The wave front pulsing through the cue-box stopped, then soared off in a continuous unbroken crescendo. At the same time Madame Gioconda thrust her head out, her throat muscles contracted powerfully.

As the sound burst from her throat Mangon's finger locked rigidly against the trigger guard. An instant later, before he could think, a shattering blast of sound ripped through his ears, followed by a slightly higher note that appeared to strike a hidden ridge half-way along its path, wavered slightly, then recovered and sped on, like an express train crossing lines.

Mangon listened to her numbly, hands gripping the barrel of the sonovac. The voice exploded in his brain, flooding every nexus of cells with its violence. It was grotesque, an insane parody of a classical soprano. Harmony, purity, cadence had gone. Rough and cracked, it jerked sharply from one high note to a lower, its breath intervals uncontrolled, sudden precipices of gasping silence which plunged through the volcanic torrent, dividing it into a loosely connected sequence of *bravura* passages.

He barely recognized what she was singing: the Toreador song from *Carmen*. Why she had picked this he could not imagine. Unable to reach its higher notes she fell back on the swinging rhythm of the refrain, hammering out the rolling phrases with tosses of her head. After a dozen bars her pace slackened, she slipped into an extempore humming, then broke out of this into a final climactic assault.

Appalled, Mangon watched as two or three members of the orchestra stood up and disappeared into the wings. The others had stopped playing, were switching off their instruments and conferring with each other. The audience was obviously restive; Mangon could hear individual voices in the intervals when Madame Gioconda refilled her lungs.

Behind him someone hammered on the door. Startled, Mangon nearly tripped across the sonovac. Then he bent down and wrenched the plug out of its socket. Snapping open the two catches beneath the chassis of the sonovac, he pulled off the canister to reveal the valves, amplifier and generator. He slipped his fingers carefully through the leads and coils, seized them as firmly as he could and ripped them out with a single motion. Tearing his nails, he stripped the printed circuit off the bottom of the chassis and crushed it between his hands.

Satisfied, he dropped the sonovac to the floor, listened for a moment to the caterwauling above, which was now being drowned by the mounting vocal opposition of the audience, then unlatched the door.

Paul Merrill, his bow tie askew, burst in. He gaped blankly at Mangon, at the blood dripping from his fingers and the smashed sonovac on the floor.

He seized Mangon by the shoulders, shook him roughly. 'Mangon, are you crazy? What are you trying to do?'

Mangon attempted to say something, but his voice had died. He pulled himself away from Merrill, pushed past into the corridor.

Merrill shouted after him. 'Mangon, help me fix this! Where are you going?' He got down on his knees, started trying to piece the sonovac together.

From the wings Mangon briefly watched the scene on the stage.

Madame Gioconda was still singing, her voice completely

inaudible in the uproar from the auditorium. Half the audience were on their feet, shouting towards the stage and apparently remonstrating with the studio officials. All but a few members of the orchestra had left their instruments, these sitting on their desks and watching Madame Gioconda in amazement.

The programme director, Alto and one of the compères stood in front of her, banging on the rail and trying to attract her attention. But Madame Gioconda failed to notice them. Head back, eyes on the brilliant ceiling lights, hands gesturing majestically, she soared along the private causeways of sound that poured unrelentingly from her throat, a great white angel of discord on her homeward flight.

Mangon watched her sadly, then slipped away through the stage-hands pressing around him. As he left the theatre by the stage door a small crowd was gathering by the main entrance. He flicked away the blood from his fingers, then bound his handkerchief round them.

He walked down the side street to where the sound truck was parked, climbed into the cab and sat still for a few minutes looking out at the bright evening lights in the bars and shopfronts.

Opening the dashboard locker, he hunted through it and pulled out an old wrist-pad, clipped it into his sleeve.

In his ears the sounds of Madame Gioconda singing echoed like an insane banshee.

He switched on the sonovac under the dashboard, turned it full on, then started the engine and drove off into the night.

1960

ZONE OF TERROR

Larsen had been waiting all day for Bayliss, the psychologist who lived in the next chalet, to pay the call he had promised on the previous evening. Characteristically, Bayliss had made no precise arrangements as regards time; a tall, moody man with an off-hand manner, he had merely gestured vaguely with his hypodermic and mumbled something about the following day: he would look in, probably. Larsen knew damned well he would look in, the case was too interesting to miss. In an oblique way it meant as much to Bayliss as it did to himself.

Except that it was Larsen who had to do the worrying – by three that afternoon Bayliss had still not materialized. What was he doing except sitting in his white-walled, air-conditioned lounge, playing Bartok quartets on the stereogram? Meanwhile Larsen had nothing to do but roam around the chalet, slamming impatiently from one room to the next like a tiger with an anxiety neurosis, and cook up a quick lunch (coffee and three amphetamines, from a private cache Bayliss as yet only dimly suspected. God, he needed the stimulants after those massive barbiturate shots Bayliss had pumped into him after the attack). He tried to settle down with Kretschmer's *An Analysis of Psychotic Time*, a heavy tome, full of graphs and tabular material, which Bayliss had insisted he read, asserting that it filled in necessary background to the case. Larsen had spent a couple of hours on it, but so far he had got no further than the preface to the third edition.

Periodically he went over to the window and peered through the plastic blind for any signs of movement in the next chalet. Beyond, the desert lay in the sunlight like an enormous bone, against which the aztec-red fins of Bayliss's Pontiac flared like the tail feathers of a flamboyant phoenix. The remaining three chalets were empty; the complex was operated by the electronics company for which he and Bayliss worked as a sort of 're-creational' centre for senior executives and tired 'think-men'. The desert site had been chosen for its hypotensive virtues, its supposed equivalence to psychic zero. Two or three days of leisurely reading, of watching the motionless horizon, and tension and anxiety thresholds rose to more useful levels.

However, two days there, Larsen reflected, and he had very nearly gone mad. It was lucky Bayliss had been around with his hypodermic. Though the man was certainly casual when it came to supervising his patients; he left them to their own resources. In fact, looking back, he – Larsen – had been responsible for just about all the diagnosis. Bayliss had done little more than thumb his hypo, toss Kretschmer into his lap, and offer some cogitating asides.

Perhaps he was waiting for something?

Larsen tried to decide whether to phone Bayliss on some pretext; his number – O, on the internal system – was almost too inviting. Then he heard a door clatter outside, and saw the tall, angular figure of the psychologist crossing the concrete apron between the chalets, head bowed pensively in the sharp sunlight.

Where's his case, Larsen thought, almost disappointed. Don't tell me he's putting on the barbiturate brakes. Maybe he'll try hypnosis. Masses of post-hypnotic suggestions, in the middle of shaving I'll suddenly stand on my head.

He let Bayliss in, fidgeting around him as they went into the lounge.

'Where the hell have you been?' he asked. 'Do you realize it's nearly four?'

Bayliss sat down at the miniature executive desk in the middle of the lounge and looked round critically, a ploy Larsen resented but never managed to anticipate.

'Of course I realize it. I'm fully wired for time. How have you felt today?' He pointed to the straight-backed chair placed in the interviewee's position. 'Sit down and try to relax.'

Larsen gestured irritably. 'How can I relax while I'm just hanging around here, waiting for the next bomb to go off?' He began his analysis of the past twenty-four hours, a task he enjoyed, larding the case history with liberal doses of speculative commentary.

'Actually, last night was easier. I think I'm entering a new zone. Everything's beginning to stabilize, I'm not looking over my shoulder all the time. I've left the inside doors open, and before I enter a room I deliberately anticipate it, try to extrapolate its depth and dimensions so that it doesn't *surprise* me – before I used to open a door and just dive through like a man stepping into an empty lift shaft.'

Larsen paced up and down, cracking his knuckles. Eyes half closed, Bayliss watched him. 'I'm pretty sure there won't be another attack,' Larsen continued. 'In fact, the best thing is probably for me to get straight back to the plant. After all, there's no point in sitting around here indefinitely. I feel more or less completely okay.'

Bayliss nodded. 'In that case, then, why are you so jumpy?'

Exasperated, Larsen clenched his fists. He could almost hear the artery thudding in his temple. 'I'm *not* jumpy! For God's sake, Bayliss, I thought the advanced view was that psychiatrist and patient shared the illness together, forgot their own identities and took equal responsibility. You're trying to evade –'

'I am not,' Bayliss cut in firmly. 'I accept complete responsibility for you. That's why I want you to stay here until you've come to terms with this thing.'

Larsen snorted. '"Thing"! Now you're trying to make it sound like something out of a horror film. All I had was a simple hallucination. And I'm not even completely convinced it was that.' He pointed through the window. 'Suddenly opening the garage door in that bright sunlight – it might have been a shadow.'

'You described it pretty exactly,' Bayliss commented. 'Colour of the hair, moustache, the clothes he wore.'

'Back projection. The detail in dreams is authentic too.' Larsen moved the chair out of the way and leaned forwards across the desk. 'Another thing. I don't feel you're being entirely frank.'

Their eyes levelled. Bayliss studied Larsen carefully for a moment, noticing his widely dilated pupils.

'Well?' Larsen pressed.

Bayliss buttoned his jacket and walked across to the door. 'I'll call in tomorrow. Meanwhile try to unwind yourself a little. I'm not trying to alarm you, Larsen, but this problem may be rather more complicated than you imagine.' He nodded, then slipped out before Larsen could reply.

Larsen stepped over to the window and through the blind watched the psychologist disappear into his chalet. Disturbed for a moment, the sunlight again settled itself heavily over everything. A few minutes later the sounds of one of the Bartok quartets whined fretfully across the apron.

Larsen went back to the desk and sat down, elbows thrust forward aggressively. Bayliss irritated him, with his neurotic music and inaccurate diagnoses. He felt tempted to climb straight into his car and drive back to the plant. Strictly speaking, though, the psychologist outranked Larsen, and probably had executive authority over him while he was at the chalet, particularly as the five days he had spent there were on the company's time.

He gazed round the silent lounge, tracing the cool horizontal shadows that dappled the walls, listening to the low soothing hum of the air-conditioner. His argument with Bayliss had refreshed him and he felt composed and confident. Yet residues of tension and uneasiness still existed, and he found it difficult to keep his eyes off the open doors to the bedroom and kitchen.

He had arrived at the chalet five days earlier, exhausted and overwrought, on the verge of a total nervous collapse. For three months he had been working without a break on programming the complex circuitry of a huge brain simulator which the company's Advanced Designs Division were building for one of the major psychiatric foundations. This was a complete electronic replica of the central nervous system, each spinal level represented by a single computer, other computers holding memory banks in which sleep, tension, aggression and other psychic functions were coded and stored, building blocks that could be played into the CNS simulator to construct models of dissociation states and withdrawal syndromes – any psychic complex on demand.

The design teams working on the simulator had been watched vigilantly by Bayliss and his assistants, and the weekly tests had revealed the mounting load of fatigue that Larsen was carrying. Finally Bayliss had pulled him off the project and sent him out to the desert for two or three days' recuperation.

Larsen had been glad to get away. For the first two days he had lounged aimlessly around the deserted chalets, pleasantly fuddled by the barbiturates Bayliss prescribed, gazing out across the white deck of the desert floor, going to bed by eight and sleeping until noon. Every morning the caretaker had driven in from the town near by to clean up and leave the groceries and menu slips, but Larsen never saw her. He was only too glad to be alone. Deliberately seeing no one, allowing the natural rhythms of his mind to re-establish themselves, he knew he would soon recover.

In fact, however, the first person he had seen had stepped up to him straight out of a nightmare.

Larsen still looked back on the encounter with a shudder.

After lunch on his third day at the chalet he had decided to drive out into the desert and examine an old quartz mine in one of the canyons. This was a two-hour trip and he had made up a thermos of iced martini. The garage was adjacent to the chalet, set back from the kitchen side entrance, and fitted with a roll steel door that lifted vertically and curved up under the roof.

Larsen had locked the chalet behind him, then raised the garage door and driven his car out on to the apron. Going back for the thermos which he had left on the bench at the rear of the garage, he had noticed a full can of petrol in the shadows against one corner. For a moment he paused, adding up his mileage, and decided to take the can with him. He carried it over to the car, then turned round to close the garage door.

The roll had failed to retreat completely when he had first raised it, and reached down to the level of his chin. Putting his weight on the handle, Larsen managed to move it down a few inches, but the inertia was too much for him. The sunlight reflected in the steel panels was dazzling his eyes. Pressing his palms under the door, he jerked it upwards slightly to gain more momentum on the downward swing.

The space was small, no more than six inches, but it was just enough for him to see into the darkened garage.

Hiding in the shadows against the back wall near the bench was the indistinct but nonetheless unmistakable figure of a man. He stood motionless, arms loosely at his sides, watching Larsen. He wore a light cream suit – covered by patches of shadow that gave him a curious fragmentary look – a neat blue sports-shirt and two-tone shoes. He was stockily built, with a thick brush moustache, a plump face, and eyes that stared steadily at Larsen but somehow seemed to be focused beyond him.

Still holding the door with both hands, Larsen gaped at the man. Not only was there no means by which he could have entered the garage – there were no windows or side doors – but there was something aggressive about his stance.

Larsen was about to call to him when the man moved forward and stepped straight out of the shadows towards him.

Aghast, Larsen backed away. The dark patches across the man's suit were not shadows at all, but the outline of the work bench directly behind him.

The man's body and clothes were transparent.

Galvanized into life, Larsen seized the garage door and hurled it down. He snapped the bolt in and jammed it closed with both hands, knees pressed against it.

Half paralysed by cramp and barely breathing, his suit soaked with sweat, he was still holding the door down when Bayliss drove up thirty minutes later.

Larsen drummed his fingers irritably on the desk, stood up and went into the kitchen. Cut off from the barbiturates they had been intended to counteract, the three amphetamines had begun to make him feel restless and overstimulated. He switched the coffee percolator on and then off, prowled back to the lounge and sat down on the sofa with the copy of Kretschmer.

He read a few pages, increasingly impatient. What light

Kretschmer threw on his problem was hard to see; most of the case histories described deep schizos and irreversible paranoids. His own problem was much more superficial, a momentary aberration due to overloading. Why wouldn't Bayliss see this? For some reason he seemed to be unconsciously wishing for a major crisis, probably because he, the psychologist, secretly wanted to become the patient.

Larsen tossed the book aside and looked out through the window at the desert. Suddenly the chalet seemed dark and cramped, a claustrophobic focus of suppressed aggressions. He stood up, strode over to the door and stepped out into the clear open air.

Grouped in a loose semicircle, the chalets seemed to shrink towards the ground as he strolled to the rim of the concrete apron a hundred yards away. The mountains behind loomed up enormously. It was late afternoon, on the edge of dusk, and the sky was a vivid vibrant blue, the deepening colours of the desert floor overlaid by the huge lanes of shadow that reached from the mountains against the sunline. Larsen looked back at the chalets. There was no sign of movement, other than a faint discordant echo of the atonal music Bayliss was playing. The whole scene seemed suddenly unreal.

Reflecting on this, Larsen felt something shift inside his mind. The sensation was undefined, like an expected cue that had failed to materialize, a forgotten intention. He tried to recall it, unable to remember whether he had switched on the coffee percolator.

He walked back to the chalets, noticing that he had left the kitchen door open. As he passed the lounge window on his way to close it he glanced in.

A man was sitting on the sofa, legs crossed, face hidden by the volume of Kretschmer. For a moment Larsen assumed that Bayliss had called in to see him, and walked on, deciding to make coffee for them both. Then he noticed that the stereogram was still playing in Bayliss's chalet.

Picking his steps carefully, he moved back to the lounge window. The man's face was still hidden, but a single glance confirmed that the visitor was not Bayliss. He was wearing the same cream suit Larsen had seen two days earlier, the same two-tone shoes. But this time the man was no hallucination; his hands and clothes were solid and palpable. He shifted about on the sofa, denting one of the cushions, and turned a page of the book, flexing the spine between his hands.

Pulse thickening, Larsen braced himself against the windowledge. Something about the man, his posture, the way he held his hands, convinced him that he had seen him before their fragmentary encounter in the garage.

Then the man lowered the book and threw it on to the seat beside him. He sat back and looked through the window, his focus only a few inches from Larsen's face.

Mesmerized, Larsen stared back at him. He recognized the man without doubt, the pudgy face, the nervous eyes, the too thick moustache. Now at last he could see him clearly and realized he knew him only too well, better than anyone else on Earth.

The man was himself.

Bayliss clipped the hypodermic into his valise, and placed it on the lid of the stereogram.

'Hallucination is the wrong term altogether,' he told Larsen, who was lying stretched out on Bayliss's sofa, sipping weakly at a glass of hot whisky. 'Stop using it. A psychoretinal image of remarkable strength and duration, but not an hallucination.'

Larsen gestured feebly. He had stumbled into Bayliss's chalet an hour earlier, literally beside himself with fright. Bayliss had calmed him down, then dragged him back across the apron to the lounge window and made him accept that his double was gone. Bayliss was not in the least surprised at the identity of the phantom, and this worried Larsen almost as much as the actual hallucination. What else was Bayliss hiding up his sleeve?

'I'm surprised you didn't realize it sooner yourself,' Bayliss remarked. 'Your description of the man in the garage was so obvious – the same cream suit, the same shoes and shirt, let alone the exact physical similarity, even down to your moustache.'

Recovering a little, Larsen sat up. He smoothed down his cream gabardine suit and brushed the dust off his brown-and-white shoes. 'Thanks for warning me. All you've got to do now is tell me who he is.'

Bayliss sat down in one of the chairs. 'What do you mean, who he is? He's you, of course.'

'I know that, but why, where does he come from? God, I must be going insane.'

Bayliss snapped his fingers. 'No you're not. Pull yourself together. This is a purely functional disorder, like double vision or amnesia; nothing more serious. If it was, I'd have pulled you out of here long ago. Perhaps I should have done that anyway, but I think we can find a safe way out of the maze you're in.'

He took a notebook out of his breast pocket. 'Let's have a look at what we've got. Now, two features stand out. First, the phantom is yourself. There's no doubt about that; he's an exact replica of you. More important, though, he is you as you are now, your exact contemporary in time, unidealized and unmutilated. He isn't the shining hero of the super-ego, or the haggard grey-beard of the death wish. He is simply a photographic double. Displace one eyeball with your finger and you'll see a double of me. Your double is no more unusual, with the exception that the displacement is not in space but in time. You see, the second thing I noticed about your garbled description of this phantom was that, not only was he a photographic double, but he was doing exactly what you yourself had been doing a few minutes previously. The man in the garage was standing by the workbench, just where you stood when you were wondering whether to take the can of petrol. Again, the man reading in the armchair was merely repeating exactly what you had been doing with the same book five minutes earlier. He even stared out of the window as you say you did before going out for a stroll.'

Larsen nodded, sipping his whisky. 'You're suggesting that the hallucination was a mental flashback?'

'Precisely. The stream of retinal images reaching the optic lobe is nothing more than a film strip. Every image is stored away, thousands of reels, a hundred thousand hours of running time. Usually flashbacks are deliberate, when we consciously select a few blurry stills from the film library, a childhood scene, the image of our neighbourhood streets we carry around with us all day near the surface of consciousness. But upset the projector slightly – overstrain could do it – jolt it back a few hundred frames, and you'll superimpose a completely irrelevant strip of already exposed film, in your case a glimpse of yourself sitting on the sofa. It's the apparent irrelevancy that is so frightening.'

Larsen gestured with his glass. 'Wait a minute, though. When I was sitting on the sofa reading Kretschmer I didn't actually see myself, any more than I can see myself now. So where did the superimposed images come from?'

Bayliss put away his notebook. 'Don't take the analogy of the film strip too literally. You may not see yourself sitting on that sofa, but your awareness of being there is just as powerful as any visual corroboration. It's the stream of tactile, positional and psychic images that form the real data store. Very little extrapolation is needed to transpose the observer's eye a few yards to the other side of a room. Purely visual memories are never completely accurate anyway.'

'How do you explain why the man I saw in the garage was transparent?'

'Quite simply. The process was only just beginning, the intensity of the image was weak. The one you saw this afternoon was much stronger. I cut you off barbiturates deliberately, knowing full well that those stimulants you were taking on the sly would set off something if they were allowed to operate unopposed.'

He went over to Larsen, took his glass and refilled it from the decanter. 'But let's think of the future. The most interesting aspect of all this is the light it throws on one of the oldest archetypes of the human psyche – the ghost – and the whole supernatural army of phantoms, witches, demons and so on. Are they all, in fact, nothing more than psychoretinal flashbacks, transposed images of the observer himself, jolted on to the retinal screen by fear, bereavement, religious obsession? The most notable thing about the majority of ghosts is how prosaically equipped they are, compared with the elaborate literary productions of the great mystics and dreamers. The nebulous white sheet is probably the observer's own nightgown. It's an interesting field for speculation.

For example, take the most famous ghost in literature and reflect how much more sense Hamlet makes if you realize that the ghost of his murdered father is really Hamlet himself.'

'All right, all right,' Larsen cut in irritably. 'But how does this help me?'

Bayliss broke off his reflective up-and-down patrol of the floor and fixed an eye on Larsen. 'I'm coming to that. There are two methods of dealing with this disfunction of yours. The classical technique is to pump you full of tranquillizers and confine you to a bed for a year or so. Gradually your mind would knit together. Long job, boring for you and everybody else. The alternative method is, frankly, experimental, but I think it might work. I mentioned the phenomenon of the ghost because it's an interesting fact that although there have been tens of thousands of recorded cases of people being pursued by ghosts, and a few of the ghosts themselves being pursued, there have been no cases of ghost and observer actually meeting of their own volition. Tell me, what would have happened if, when you saw your double this afternoon, you had gone straight into the lounge and spoken to him?'

Larsen shuddered. 'Obviously nothing, if your theory holds. I wouldn't like to test it.'

'That's just what you're going to do. Don't panic. The next time you see a double sitting in a chair reading Kretschmer, go up and speak to him. If he doesn't reply sit down in the chair yourself. That's all you have to do.'

Larsen jumped up, gesticulating. 'For heaven's sake, Bayliss, are you crazy? Do you know what it's like to suddenly see yourself? All you want to do is run.'

'I realize that, but it's the worst thing you can do. Why whenever anyone grapples with a ghost does it always vanish instantly? Because forcibly occupying the same physical co-ordinates as the double jolts the psychic projector on to a single channel again. The two separate streams of retinal images coincide and fuse. You've got to try, Larsen. It may be quite an effort, but you'll cure yourself once and for all.'

Larsen shook his head stubbornly. 'The idea's insane.' To

himself he added: I'd rather shoot the thing. Then he remembered the .38 in his suitcase, and the presence of the weapon gave him a stronger sense of security than all Bayliss's drugs and advice. The revolver was a simple symbol of aggression, and even if the phantom was only an intruder in his own mind, it gave that portion which still remained intact greater confidence, enough possibly to dissipate the double's power.

Eyes half closed with fatigue, he listened to Bayliss. Half an hour later he went back to his chalet, found the revolver and hid it under a magazine in the letterbox outside the front door. It was too conspicuous to carry and anyway might fire accidentally and injure him. Outside the front door it would be safely hidden and yet easily accessible, ready to mete out a little old-fashioned punishment to any double dealer trying to get into the game.

Two days later, with unexpected vengeance, the opportunity came.

Bayliss had driven into town to buy a new stylus for the stereogram, leaving Larsen to prepare lunch for them while he was away. Larsen pretended to resent the chore, but secretly he was glad of something to do. He was tired of hanging around the chalets while Bayliss watched him as if he were an experimental animal, eagerly waiting for the next crisis. With luck this might never come, if only to spite Bayliss, who had been having everything too much his own way.

After laying the table in Bayliss's kitchenette and getting plenty of ice ready for the martinis (alcohol was just the thing, Larsen readily decided, a wonderful CNS depressant) he went back to his chalet and put on a clean shirt. On an impulse he decided to change his shoes and suit as well, and fished out the blue office serge and black oxfords he had worn on his way out to the desert. Not only were the associations of the cream suit and sports shoes unpleasant, but a complete change of costume might well forestall the double's reappearance, provide a fresh psychic image of himself powerful enough to suppress any wandering versions. Looking at himself in the mirror, he decided to carry the principle even farther. He switched on his shaver and cut away his moustache. Then he thinned out his hair and plastered it back smoothly across his scalp.

The transformation was effective. When Bayliss climbed out of his car and walked into the lounge he almost failed to recognize Larsen. He flinched back at the sight of the sleek-haired, dark-suited figure who stepped from behind the kitchen door.

'What the hell are you playing at?' he snapped at Larsen. 'This is no time for practical jokes.' He surveyed Larsen critically. 'You look like a cheap detective.'

Larsen guffawed. The incident put him in high spirits, and after several martinis he began to feel extremely buoyant. He talked away rapidly through the meal. Strangely, though, Bayliss seemed eager to get rid of him; he realized why shortly after he returned to his chalet. His pulse had quickened. He found himself prowling around nervously; his brain felt overactive and accelerated. The martinis had only been partly responsible for his elation. Now that they were wearing off he began to see the real agent – a stimulant Bayliss had given him in the hope of precipitating another crisis.

Larsen stood by the window, staring out angrily at Bayliss's chalet. The psychologist's utter lack of scruple outraged him. His fingers fretted nervously across the blind. Suddenly he felt like kicking the whole place down and speeding off. With its plywood-thin walls and match-box furniture the chalet was nothing more than a cardboard asylum. Everything that had happened there, the breakdowns and his nightmarish phantoms, had probably been schemed up by Bayliss deliberately.

Larsen noticed that the stimulant seemed to be extremely powerful. The take-off was sustained and unbroken. He tried hopelessly to relax, went into the bedroom and kicked his suitcase around, lit two cigarettes without realizing it.

Finally, unable to contain himself any longer, he slammed the front door back and stormed out across the apron, determined to have everything out with Bayliss and demand an immediate sedative.

Bayliss's lounge was empty. Larsen plunged through into the kitchen and bedroom, discovered to his annoyance that Bayliss was having a shower. He hung around in the lounge for a few moments, then decided to wait in his chalet.

Head down, he crossed the bright sunlight at a fast stride, and was only a few steps from the darkened doorway when he noticed that a man in a blue suit was standing there watching him.

Heart leaping, Larsen shrank back, recognizing the double even before he had completely accepted the change of costume, the smooth-shaven face with its altered planes. The man hovered indecisively, flexing his fingers, and appeared to be on the verge of stepping down into the sunlight.

Larsen was about ten feet from him, directly in line with Bayliss's door. He backed away, at the same time swinging to his left to the lee of the garage. There he stopped and pulled himself together. The double was still hesitating in the doorway, longer, he was sure, than he himself had done. Larsen looked at the face, repulsed, not so much by the absolute accuracy of the image, but by a strange, almost luminous pastiness that gave the double's features the waxy sheen of a corpse. It was this unpleasant gloss that held Larsen back – the double was an arm's length from the letterbox holding the .38, and nothing could have induced Larsen to approach it.

He decided to enter the chalet and watch the double from behind. Rather than use the kitchen door, which gave access to the lounge on the double's immediate right, he turned to circle the garage and climb in through the bedroom window on the far side.

He was picking his way through a dump of old mortar and barbed wire behind the garage when he heard a voice call out:

'Larsen, you idiot, what do you think you're doing?'

It was Bayliss, leaning out of his bathroom window. Larsen stumbled, found his balance and waved Bayliss back angrily. Bayliss merely shook his head and leaned farther out, drying his neck with a towel.

Larsen retraced his steps, signalling to Bayliss to keep quiet. He was crossing the space between the garage wall and the near corner of Bayliss's chalet when out of the side of his eye he noticed a dark-suited figure standing with its back to him a few yards from the garage door.

The double had moved! Larsen stopped, Bayliss forgotten, and watched the double warily. He was poised on the balls of his feet, as Larsen had been only a minute or so earlier, elbows up, hands waving defensively. His eyes were hidden, but he appeared to be looking at the front door of Larsen's chalet.

Automatically, Larsen's eyes also moved to the doorway.

The original blue-suited figure still stood there, staring out into the sunlight.

There was not one double now, but two.

For a moment Larsen stared helplessly at the two figures, standing on either side of the apron like half-animated dummies in a waxworks tableau.

The figure with its back to him swung on one heel and began to stalk rapidly towards him. He gazed sightlessly at Larsen, the sunlight exposing his face. With a jolt of horror Larsen recognized for the first time the perfect similarity of the double – the same plump cheeks, the same mole by the right nostril, the white upper lip with the same small razor cut where the moustache had been shaved away. Above all he recognized the man's state of shock, the nervous lips, the tension around the neck and facial muscles, the utter exhaustion just below the surface of the mask.

His voice strangled, Larsen turned and bolted.

He stopped running about two hundred yards out in the desert beyond the edge of the apron. Gasping for breath, he dropped to one knee behind a narrow sandstone outcropping and looked back at the chalets. The second double was making his way around the garage, climbing through the tangle of old wire. The other was crossing the space between the chalets. Oblivious of them both, Bayliss was struggling with the bathroom window, forcing it back so that he could see out into the desert.

Trying to steady himself, Larsen wiped his face on his jacket sleeve. So Bayliss had been right, although he had never anticipated that more than one image could be seen during any single attack. But in fact Larsen had spawned two in close succession, each at a critical phase during the last five minutes. Wondering whether to wait for the images to fade, Larsen remembered the revolver in the letterbox. However irrational, it seemed his only hope. With it he would be able to test the ultimate validity of the doubles.

The outcropping ran diagonally to the edge of the apron. Crouching forwards, he scurried along it, pausing at intervals to follow the scene. The two doubles were still holding their positions, though Bayliss had closed his window and disappeared.

Larsen reached the edge of the apron, which was built on a shallow table about a foot off the desert floor, and moved along its rim to where an old fifty-gallon drum gave him a vantage point. To reach the revolver he decided to go round the far side of Bayliss's chalet, where he would find his own doorway unguarded except for the double watching by the garage.

He was about to step forward when something made him look over his shoulder.

Running straight towards him along the outcropping, head down, hands almost touching the ground, was an enormous ratlike creature. Every ten or fifteen yards it paused for a moment, and looked out at the chalets, and Larsen caught a glimpse of its face, insane and terrified, another replica of his own.

'Larsen! Larsen!'

Bayliss stood by the chalet, waving out at the desert.

Larsen glanced back at the phantom hurtling towards him, now only thirty feet away, then jumped up and lurched helplessly across to Bayliss.

Bayliss caught him firmly with his hands. 'Larsen, what's the matter with you? Are you having an attack?'

Larsen gestured at the figures around him. 'Stop them, Bayliss, for God's sake,' he gasped. 'I can't get away from them.'

Bayliss shook him roughly. 'You can see *more* than one? Where are they? Show me.'

Larsen pointed at the two figures hovering luminously near the chalet, then waved limply in the direction of the desert. 'By the garage, and over there along the wall. There's another hiding along that ridge.'

Bayliss seized him by the arm. 'Come on, man, you've got

to face up to them, it's no use running.' He tried to drag Larsen towards the garage, but Larsen slipped down on to the concrete.

'I can't, Bayliss, believe me. There's a gun in my letterbox. Get it for me. It's the only way.'

Bayliss hesitated, looking down at Larsen. 'All right. Try to hold on.'

Larsen pointed to the far corner of Bayliss's chalet. 'I'll wait over there for you.'

As Bayliss ran off he hobbled towards the corner. Halfway there he tripped across the remains of a ladder lying on the ground and twisted his right ankle between two of the rungs.

Clasping his foot, he sat down just as Bayliss appeared between the chalets, the revolver in his hand. He looked around for Larsen, who cleared his throat to call him.

Before he could open his mouth he saw the double who had followed him along the ridge leap up from behind the drum and stumble up to Bayliss across the concrete floor. He was dishevelled and exhausted, jacket almost off his shoulders, the tie knot under one ear. The image was still pursuing him, dogging his footsteps like an obsessed shadow.

Larsen tried to call to Bayliss again, but something he saw choked the voice in his throat.

Bayliss was looking at his double.

Larsen stood up, feeling a sudden premonition of terror. He tried to wave to Bayliss, but the latter was watching the double intently as it pointed to the figures near by, nodding to it in apparent agreement.

'Bayliss!'

The shot drowned his cry. Bayliss had fired somewhere between the garages, and the echo of the shot bounded among the chalets. The double was still beside him, pointing in all directions. Bayliss raised the revolver and fired again. The sound slammed across the concrete, making Larsen feel stunned and sick.

Now Bayliss too was seeing simultaneous images, not of himself but of Larsen, on whom his mind had been focusing for the past weeks. A repetition of Larsen stumbling over to him and pointing at the phantoms was being repeated in Bayliss's mind, at the exact moment when he had returned with the revolver and was searching for a target.

Larsen started to crawl away, trying to reach the corner. A third shot roared through the air, the flash reflected in the bathroom window.

He had almost reached the corner when he heard Bayliss shout. Leaning one hand against the wall, he looked back.

Mouth open, Bayliss was staring wildly at him, the revolver clenched like a bomb in his hand. Beside him the blue-suited figure stood quietly, straightening its tie. At last Bayliss had realized he could see two images of Larsen, one beside him, the other twenty feet away against the chalet.

But how was he to know which was the real Larsen?

Staring at Larsen, he seemed unable to decide.

Then the double by his shoulder raised one arm and pointed at Larsen, towards the corner wall to which he himself had pointed a minute earlier.

Larsen tried to shout, then hurled himself at the wall and pulled himself along it. Behind him Bayliss's feet came thudding across the concrete.

He heard only the first of the three shots.

1960

CHRONOPOLIS

His trial had been fixed for the next day. Exactly when, of course, neither Newman nor anyone else knew. Probably it would be during the afternoon, when the principals concerned – judge, jury and prosecutor – managed to converge on the same courtroom at the same time. With luck his defence attorney might also appear at the right moment, though the case was such an open and shut one that Newman hardly expected him to bother – besides, transport to and from the old penal complex was notoriously difficult, involved endless waiting in the grimy depot below the prison walls.

Newman had passed the time usefully. Luckily, his cell faced south and sunlight traversed it for most of the day. He divided its arc into ten equal segments, the effective daylight hours, marking the intervals with a wedge of mortar prised from the window ledge. Each segment he further subdivided into twelve smaller units.

Immediately he had a working timepiece, accurate to within virtually a minute (the final subdivision into fifths he made mentally). The sweep of white notches, curving down one wall, across the floor and metal bedstead, and up the other wall, would have been recognizable to anyone who stood with his back to the window, but no one ever did. Anyway, the guards were too stupid to understand, and the sundial had given Newman a tremendous advantage over them. Most of the time, when he wasn't recalibrating the dial, he would press against the grille, keeping an eye on the orderly room.

'Brocken!' he would shout out at 7.15, as the shadow line hit the first interval. 'Morning inspection! On your feet, man!' The sergeant would come stumbling out of his bunk in a sweat, cursing the other warders as the reveille bell split the air.

Later, Newman sang out the other events on the daily roster: roll-call, cell fatigues, breakfast, exercise and so on round to the evening roll just before dusk. Brocken regularly won the block merit for the best-run cell deck and he relied on Newman to programme the day for him, anticipate the next item on the roster and warn him if anything went on for too long – in some of the other blocks fatigues were usually over in three minutes while breakfast or exercise could go on for hours, none of the warders knowing when to stop, the prisoners insisting that they had only just begun.

Brocken never inquired how Newman organized everything so exactly; once or twice a week, when it rained or was overcast, Newman would be strangely silent, and the resulting confusion reminded the sergeant forcefully of the merits of co-operation. Newman was kept in cell privileges and all the cigarettes he needed. It was a shame that a date for the trial had finally been named.

Newman, too, was sorry. Most of his research so far had been inconclusive. Primarily his problem was that, given a northward-facing cell for the bulk of his sentence, the task of estimating the time might become impossible. The inclination of the shadows in the exercise yards or across the towers and walls provided too blunt a reading. Calibration would have to be visual; an optical instrument would soon be discovered.

What he needed was an internal timepiece, an unconsciously operating psychic mechanism regulated, say, by his pulse or respiratory rhythms. He had tried to train his time sense, running an elaborate series of tests to estimate its minimum in-built error, and this had been disappointingly large. The chances of conditioning an accurate reflex seemed slim.

However, unless he could tell the exact time at any given moment, he knew he would go mad.

His obsession, which now faced him with a charge of murder, had revealed itself innocently enough.

As a child, like all children, he had noticed the occasional ancient clock tower, bearing the same white circle with its twelve intervals. In the seedier areas of the city the round characteristic dials often hung over cheap jewellery stores, rusting and derelict.

'Just signs,' his mother explained. 'They don't mean anything, like stars or rings.'

Pointless embellishment, he had thought.

Once, in an old furniture shop, they had seen a clock with hands, upside down in a box full of fire-irons and miscellaneous rubbish.

'Eleven and twelve,' he had pointed out. 'What does it mean?'

His mother had hurried him away, reminding herself never to visit that street again. Time Police were still supposed to be around, watching for any outbreak. 'Nothing,' she told him sharply. 'It's all finished.' To herself she added experimentally: Five and twelve. Five *to* twelve. Yes.

Time unfolded at its usual sluggish, half-confused pace. They lived in a ramshackle house in one of the amorphous suburbs, a zone of endless afternoons. Sometimes he went to school, until he was ten spent most of his time with his mother queueing outside the closed food stores. In the evenings he would play with the neighbourhood gang around the abandoned railway station, punting a home-made flat car along the overgrown tracks, or break into one of the unoccupied houses and set up a temporary command post.

He was in no hurry to grow up; the adult world was unsynchronized and ambitionless. After his mother died he spent long days in the attic, going through her trunks and old clothes, playing with the bric-à-brac of hats and beads, trying to recover something of her personality.

In the bottom compartment of her jewellery case he came across a small flat gold-cased object, equipped with a wrist strap. The dial had no hands but the twelve-numbered face intrigued him and he fastened it to his wrist.

His father choked over his soup when he saw it that evening.

'Conrad, my God! Where in heaven did you get that?'

'In Mamma's bead box. Can't I keep it?'

'No. Conrad, give it to me! Sorry, son.' Thoughtfully: 'Let's see, you're fourteen. Look, Conrad, I'll explain it all in a couple of years.'

With the impetus provided by this new taboo there was no need to wait for his father's revelations. Full knowledge came soon. The older boys knew the whole story, but strangely enough it was disappointingly dull.

'Is that all?' he kept saying. 'I don't get it. Why worry so much about clocks? We have calendars, don't we?'

Suspecting more, he scoured the streets, carefully inspecting every derelict clock for a clue to the real secret. Most of the faces had been mutilated, hands and numerals torn off, the circle of minute intervals stripped away, leaving a shadow of fading rust. Distributed apparently at random all over the city, above stores, banks and public buildings, their real purpose was hard to discover. Sure enough, they measured the progress of time through twelve arbitrary intervals, but this seemed barely adequate grounds for outlawing them. After all, a whole variety of timers were in general use: in kitchens, factories, hospitals, wherever a fixed period of time was needed. His father had one by his bed at night. Sealed into the standard small black box, and driven by miniature batteries, it emitted a high penetrating whistle shortly before breakfast the next morning, woke him if he overslept. A clock was no more than a calibrated timer, in many ways less useful, as it provided you with a steady stream of irrelevant information. What if it was half past three, as the old reckoning put it, if you weren't planning to start or finish anything then?

Making his questions sound as naïve as possible, he conducted a long, careful poll. Under fifty no one appeared to know anything at all about the historical background, and even the older people were beginning to forget. He also noticed that the less educated they were the more they were willing to talk, indicating that manual and lower-class workers had played no part in the revolution and consequently had no guilt-charged memories to repress. Old Mr Crichton, the plumber who lived in the basement apartment; reminisced without any prompting, but nothing he said threw any light on the problem.

'Sure, there were thousands of clocks then, millions of them, everybody had one. Watches we called them, strapped to the wrist, you had to screw them up every day.'

'But what did you *do* with them, Mr Crichton?' Conrad pressed.

'Well, you just – looked at them, and you knew what time it was. One o'clock, or two, or half past seven – that was when I'd go off to work.'

'But you go off to work now when you've had breakfast. And if you're late the timer rings.'

Crichton shook his head. 'I can't explain it to you, lad. You ask your father.'

But Mr Newman was hardly more helpful. The explanation promised for Conrad's sixteenth birthday never materialized. When his questions persisted Mr Newman tired of side-stepping, shut him up with an abrupt: 'Just stop thinking about it, do you understand? You'll get yourself and the rest of us into a lot of trouble.'

Stacey, the young English teacher, had a wry sense of humour, liked to shock the boys by taking up unorthodox positions on marriage or economics. Conrad wrote an essay describing an imaginary society completely preoccupied with elaborate rituals revolving around a minute by minute observance of the passage of time.

Stacey refused to play, however, gave him a non-committal beta plus, after class quietly asked Conrad what had prompted the fantasy. At first Conrad tried to back away, then finally came out with the question that contained the central riddle.

'Why is it against the law to have a clock?'

Stacey tossed a piece of chalk from one hand to the other.

'Is it against the law?'

Conrad nodded. 'There's an old notice in the police station offering a bounty of one hundred pounds for every clock or wristwatch brought in. I saw it yesterday. The sergeant said it was still in force.'

Stacey raised his eyebrows mockingly. 'You'll make a million. Thinking of going into business?'

Conrad ignored this. 'It's against the law to have a gun because you might shoot someone. But how can you hurt anybody with a clock?'

'Isn't it obvious? You can time him, know exactly how long it takes him to do something.'

'Well?'

'Then you can make him do it faster.'

At seventeen, on a sudden impulse, he built his first clock. Already his preoccupation with time was giving him a marked lead over his class-mates. One or two were more intelligent, others more conscientious, but Conrad's ability to organize his leisure and homework periods allowed him to make the most of his talents. When the others were lounging around the railway yard on their way home Conrad had already completed half his prep, allocating his time according to its various demands.

As soon as he finished he would go up to the attic playroom, now his workshop. Here, in the old wardrobes and trunks, he made his first experimental constructions: calibrated candles, crude sundials, sand-glasses, an elaborate clockwork contraption developing about half a horse power that drove its hands progressively faster and faster in an unintentional parody of Conrad's obsession.

His first serious clock was water-powered, a slowly leaking tank holding a wooden float that drove the hands as it sank downwards. Simple but accurate, it satisfied Conrad for several months while he carried out his ever-widening search for a real clock mechanism. He soon discovered that although there were innumerable table clocks, gold pocket watches and timepieces of every variety rusting in junk shops and in the back drawers of most homes, none of them contained their mechanisms. These, together with the hands, and sometimes the digits, had always been removed. His own attempts to build an escapement that would regulate the motion of the ordinary clockwork motor met with no success; everything he had heard about clock movements confirmed that they were precision instruments of exact design and construction. To satisfy his secret ambition – a portable timepiece, if possible an actual wristwatch – he would have to find one, somewhere, in working order.

Finally, from an unexpected source, a watch came to him. One afternoon in a cinema an elderly man sitting next to Conrad had a sudden heart attack. Conrad and two members of the audience carried him out to the manager's office. Holding one of his arms, Conrad noticed in the dim aisle light a glint of metal inside the sleeve. Quickly he felt the wrist with his fingers, identified the unmistakable lens-shaped disc of a wristwatch.

As he carried it home its tick seemed as loud as a death-knell. He clamped his hand around it, expecting everyone in the street to point accusingly at him, the Time Police to swoop down and seize him.

In the attic he took it out and examined it breathlessly, smothering it in a cushion whenever he heard his father shift about in the bedroom below. Later he realized that its noise was almost inaudible. The watch was of the same pattern as his mother's, though with a yellow and not a red face. The gold case was scratched and peeling, but the movement seemed to be in perfect condition. He prised off the rear plate, watched the frenzied flickering world of miniature cogs and wheels for hours, spellbound. Frightened of breaking the main spring, he kept the watch only half wound, packed away carefully in cotton wool.

In taking the watch from its owner he had not, in fact, been motivated by theft; his first impulse had been to hide the watch before the doctor discovered it feeling for the man's pulse. But once the watch was in his possession he abandoned any thought of tracing the owner and returning it.

That others were still wearing watches hardly surprised him. The water clock had demonstrated that a calibrated timepiece added another dimension to life, organized its energies, gave the countless activities of everyday existence a yardstick of significance. Conrad spent hours in the attic gazing at the small yellow dial, watching its minute hand revolve slowly, its hour hand press on imperceptibly, a compass charting his passage through the future. Without it he felt rudderless, adrift in a grey purposeless limbo of timeless events. His father began to seem idle and stupid, sitting around vacantly with no idea when anything was going to happen.

Soon he was wearing the watch all day. He stitched together a slim cotton sleeve, fitted with a narrow flap below which he could see the face. He timed everything – the length of classes, football games, meal breaks, the hours of daylight and darkness, sleep and waking. He amused himself endlessly by baffling his friends with demonstrations of this private sixth sense, anticipating the frequency of their heartbeats, the hourly newscasts on the radio, boiling a series of identically consistent eggs without the aid of a timer.

Then he gave himself away.

Stacey, shrewder than any of the others, discovered that he was wearing a watch. Conrad had noticed that Stacey's English classes lasted exactly forty-five minutes, let himself slide into the habit of tidying his desk a minute before Stacey's timer pipped up. Once or twice he noticed Stacey looking at him curiously, but he could not resist the temptation to impress Stacey by always being the first one to make for the door.

One day he had stacked his books and clipped away his pen when Stacey pointedly asked him to read out a précis he had done. Conrad knew the timer would pip out in less than ten seconds, and decided to sit tight and wait for the usual stampede to save him the trouble.

Stacey stepped down from the dais, waiting patiently. One or two boys turned around and frowned at Conrad, who was counting away the closing seconds.

Then, amazed, he realized that the timer had failed to sound! Panicking, he first thought his watch had broken, just restrained himself in time from looking at it.

'In a hurry, Newman?' Stacey asked dryly. He sauntered down the aisle to Conrad, smiling sardonically. Baffled, and face reddening with embarrassment, Conrad fumbled open his exercise book, read out the précis. A few minutes later, without waiting for the timer, Stacey dismissed the class.

'Newman,' he called out. 'Here a moment.'

He rummaged behind the rostrum as Conrad approached. 'What happened then?' he asked. 'Forget to wind up your watch this morning?'

Conrad said nothing. Stacey took out the timer, switched off the silencer and listened to the pip that buzzed out.

'Where did you get it from? Your parents? Don't worry, the Time Police were disbanded years ago.'

Conrad examined Stacey's face carefully. 'It was my mother's,' he lied. 'I found it among her things.' Stacey held out his hand and Conrad nervously unstrapped the watch and handed it to him.

Stacey slipped it half out of its sleeve, glanced briefly at the yellow face. 'Your mother, you say? Hmh.'

'Are you going to report me?' Conrad asked.

'What, and waste some over-worked psychiatrist's time even further?'

'Isn't it breaking the law to wear a watch?'

'Well, you're not exactly the greatest living menace to public security.' Stacey started for the door, gesturing Conrad with him. He handed the watch back. 'Cancel whatever you're doing on Saturday afternoon. You and I are taking a trip.'

'Where?' Conrad asked.

'Back into the past,' Stacey said lightly. 'To Chronopolis, the Time City.'

Stacey had hired a car, a huge battered mastodon of chromium and fins. He waved jauntily to Conrad as he picked him up outside the public library.

'Climb into the turret,' he called out. He pointed to the bulging briefcase Conrad slung on to the seat between them. 'Have you had a look at those yet?'

Conrad nodded. As they moved off around the deserted square he opened the briefcase and pulled out a thick bundle of road maps. 'I've just worked out that the city covers over 500 square miles. I'd never realized it was so big. Where is everybody?'

Stacey laughed. They crossed the main street, cut down into a long tree-lined avenue of semi-detached houses. Half of them were empty, windows wrecked and roofs sagging. Even the inhabited houses had a makeshift appearance, crude water towers on home-made scaffolding lashed to their chimneys, piles of logs dumped in over-grown front gardens.

'Thirty million people once lived in this city,' Stacey remarked. 'Now the population is little more than two, and still declining. Those of us left hang on in what were once the distal suburbs, so that the city today is effectively an enormous ring, five miles in width, encircling a vast dead centre forty or fifty miles in diameter.'

They wove in and out of various back roads, past a small factory still running although work was supposed to end at noon, finally picked up a long, straight boulevard that carried them steadily westwards. Conrad traced their progress across successive maps. They were nearing the edge of the annulus Stacey had described. On the map it was overprinted in green so that the central interior appeared a flat, uncharted grey, a massive *terra incognita*.

They passed the last of the small shopping thoroughfares he remembered, a frontier post of mean terraced houses, dismal streets spanned by massive steel viaducts. Stacey pointed up at one as they drove below it. 'Part of the elaborate railway system that once existed, an enormous network of stations and junctions that carried fifteen million people into a dozen great terminals every day.'

For half an hour they drove on, Conrad hunched against the window, Stacey watching him in the driving mirror. Gradually, the landscape began to change. The houses were taller, with coloured roofs, the sidewalks were railed off and fitted with pedestrian lights and turnstiles. They had entered the inner suburbs, completely deserted streets with multi-level supermarkets, towering cinemas and department stores.

Chin in one hand, Conrad stared out silently. Lacking any means of transport he had never ventured into the uninhabited interior of the city, like the other children always headed in the opposite direction for the open country. Here the streets had died twenty or thirty years earlier; plate-glass shopfronts had slipped and smashed into the roadway, old neon signs, window frames and overhead wires hung down from every cornice, trailing a ragged webwork of disintegrating metal across the pavements. Stacey drove slowly, avoiding the occasional bus or truck abandoned in the middle of the road, its tyres peeling off their rims.

Conrad craned up at the empty windows, into the narrow alleys and side-streets, but nowhere felt any sensation of fear or anticipation. These streets were merely derelict, as unhaunted as a half-empty dustbin.

One suburban centre gave way to another, to long intervening stretches of congested ribbon developments. Mile by mile, the architecture altered its character; buildings were larger, ten- or fifteen-storey blocks, clad in facing materials of green and blue tiles, glass or copper sheathing. They were moving forward in time rather than, as Conrad had expected, back into the past of a fossil city.

Stacey worked the car through a nexus of side-streets towards a six-lane expressway that rose on tall concrete buttresses above the roof-tops. They found a side road that circled up to it, levelled out and then picked up speed sharply, spinning along one of the clear centre lanes.

Conrad craned forward. In the distance, two or three miles away, the tall rectilinear outlines of enormous apartment blocks reared up thirty or forty storeys high, hundreds of them lined shoulder to shoulder in apparently endless ranks, like giant dominoes.

'We're entering the central dormitories here,' Stacey told him. On either side buildings overtopped the motorway, the congestion mounting so that some of them had been built right up against the concrete palisades.

In a few minutes they passed between the first of the apartment batteries, the thousands of identical living units with their slanting balconies shearing up into the sky, the glass in-falls of the aluminium curtain walling speckling in the sunlight. The smaller houses and shops of the outer suburbs had vanished. There was no room on the ground level. In the narrow intervals between the blocks there were small concrete gardens, shopping complexes, ramps banking down into huge underground car parks.

And on all sides there were the clocks. Conrad noticed them immediately, at every street corner, over every archway, three-quarters of the way up the sides of buildings, covering every conceivable angle of approach. Most of them were too high off the ground to be reached by anything less than a fireman's ladder and still retained their hands. All registered the same time: 12.01.

Conrad looked at his wristwatch, noted that it was just 2.45 p.m.

'They were driven by a master clock,' Stacey told him. 'When that stopped they all seized at the same moment. One minute after midnight, thirty-seven years ago.'

The afternoon had darkened, as the high cliffs cut off the sunlight, the sky a succession of narrow vertical intervals opening and closing around them. Down on the canyon floor it was dismal and oppressive, a wilderness of concrete and frosted glass. The expressway divided and pressed on westwards. After a few more miles the apartment blocks gave way to the first office buildings in the central zone. These were even taller, sixty or seventy storeys high, linked by spiralling ramps and causeways. The expressway was fifty feet off the ground yet the first floors of the office blocks were level with it, mounted on massive stilts that straddled the glass-enclosed entrance bays of lifts and escalators. The streets were wide but featureless. The sidewalks of parallel roadways merged below the buildings, forming a continuous concrete apron. Here and there were the remains of cigarette kiosks, rusting stairways up to restaurants and arcades built on platforms thirty feet in the air.

Conrad, however, was looking only at the clocks. Never had he visualized so many, in places so dense that they obscured each other. Their faces were multi-coloured: red, blue, yellow, green. Most of them carried four or five hands. Although the master hands had stopped at a minute past twelve, the subsidiary hands had halted at varying positions, apparently dictated by their colour.

'What were the extra hands for?' he asked Stacey. 'And the different colours?'

'Time zones. Depending on your professional category and the consumer-shifts allowed. Hold on, though, we're almost there.'

They left the expressway and swung off down a ramp that fed them into the north-east corner of a wide open plaza, eight hundred yards long and half as wide, down the centre of which had once been laid a continuous strip of lawn, now rank and overgrown. The plaza was empty, a sudden block of free space bounded by tall glass-faced cliffs that seemed to carry the sky.

Stacey parked, and he and Conrad climbed out and stretched themselves. Together they strolled across the wide pavement towards the strip of waist-high vegetation. Looking down the vistas receding from the plaza Conrad grasped fully for the first time the vast perspectives of the city, the massive geometric jungle of buildings.

Stacey put one foot up on the balustrade running around the lawn bed, pointed to the far end of the plaza, where Conrad saw a low-lying huddle of buildings of unusual architectural style, nineteenth-century perpendicular, stained by the atmosphere and badly holed by a number of explosions. Again, however, his attention was held by the clock face built into a tall concrete tower just behind the older buildings. This was the largest clock dial he had ever seen, at least a hundred feet across, huge black hands halted at a minute past twelve. The dial was white, the first they had seen, but on wide semicircular shoulders built out off the tower below the main face were a dozen smaller faces, no more than twenty feet in diameter, running the full spectrum of colours. Each had five hands, the inferior three halted at random.

'Fifty years ago,' Stacey explained, gesturing at the ruins below the tower, 'that collection of ancient buildings was one of the world's greatest legislative assemblies.' He gazed at it quietly for a few moments, then turned to Conrad. 'Enjoy the ride?'

Conrad nodded fervently. 'It's impressive, all right. The people who lived here must have been giants. What's really remarkable is that it looks as if they left only yesterday. Why don't we go back?'

'Well, apart from the fact that there aren't enough of us now, even if there were we couldn't control it. In its hey-day this city was a fantastically complex social organism. The communications problems are difficult to imagine merely by looking at these blank façades. It's the tragedy of this city that there appeared to be only one way to solve them.'

'Did they solve them?'

'Oh, yes, certainly. But they left themselves out of the equation. Think of the problems, though. Transporting fifteen million office workers to and from the centre every day, routeing in an endless stream of cars, buses, trains, helicopters, linking every office, almost every desk, with a videophone, every apartment with television, radio, power, water, feeding and entertaining this enormous number of people, guarding them with ancillary services, police, fire squads, medical units – it all hinged on one factor.'

Stacey threw a fist out at the great tower clock. 'Time! Only by synchronizing every activity, every footstep forward or backward, every meal, bus-halt and telephone call, could the organism support itself. Like the cells in your body, which proliferate into mortal cancers if allowed to grow in freedom, every individual here had to subserve the overriding needs of the city or fatal bottlenecks threw it into total chaos. You and I can turn on the tap any hour of the day or night, because we have our own private water cisterns, but what would happen here if everybody washed the breakfast dishes within the same ten minutes?'

They began to walk slowly down the plaza towards the clock tower. 'Fifty years ago, when the population was only ten million, they could just provide for a potential peak capacity, but even then a strike in one essential service paralysed most of the others; it took workers two or three hours to reach their offices, as long again to queue for lunch and get home. As the population climbed the first serious attempts were made to stagger hours; workers in certain areas started the day an hour earlier or later than those in others. Their railway passes and car number plates were coloured accordingly, and if they tried to travel outside the permitted periods they were turned back. Soon the practice spread; you could only switch on your washing machine at a given hour, post a letter or take a bath at a specific period.'

'Sounds feasible,' Conrad commented, his interest mounting. 'But how did they enforce all this?'

'By a system of coloured passes, coloured money, an elaborate set of schedules published every day like the TV or radio programmes. And, of course, by all the thousands of clocks you can see around you here. The subsidiary hands marked out the number of minutes remaining in any activity period for people in the clock's colour category.'

Stacey stopped, pointed to a blue-faced clock mounted on one of the buildings overlooking the plaza. 'Let's say, for example, that a lower-grade executive leaving his office at the allotted time, 12 o'clock, wants to have lunch, change a library book, buy some aspirin, and telephone his wife. Like all executives, his identity zone is blue. He takes out his schedule for the week, or looks down the blue-time columns in the newspaper, and notes that his lunch period for that day is 12.15 to 12.30. He has fifteen minutes to kill. Right, he then checks the library. Time code for today is given as 3, that's the third hand on the clock. He looks at the nearest blue clock, the third hand says 37 minutes past – he has 23 minutes, ample time, to reach the library. He starts down the street, but finds at the first intersection that the pedestrian lights are only shining red and green and he can't get across. The area's been temporarily zoned off for lower-grade women office workers – red, and manuals – greens.'

'What would happen if he ignored the lights?' Conrad asked.

'Nothing immediately, but all blue clocks in the zoned area would have returned to zero, and no shops or the library would serve him, unless he happened to have red or green currency and a forged set of library tickets. Anyway, the penalties were too high to make the risk worthwhile, and the whole system was evolved for his convenience, no one else's. So, unable to reach the library, he decides on the chemist. The time code for the chemist is 5, the fifth, smallest hand. It reads 54 minutes past: he has six minutes to find a chemist and make his purchase. This done, he still has five minutes before lunch, decides to phone his wife. Checking the phone code he sees that no period has been provided for private calls that day – or the next. He'll just have to wait until he sees her that evening.'

'What if he did phone?'

'He wouldn't be able to get his money in the coin box, and even then, his wife, assuming she is a secretary, would be in a red time zone and no longer in her office for that day – hence the prohibition on phone calls. It all meshed perfectly. Your time programme told you when you could switch on your TV set and when to switch off. All electric appliances were fused, and if you strayed outside the programmed periods you'd have a hefty fine and repair bill to meet. The viewer's economic status obviously determined the choice of programme, and vice versa, so there was no question of coercion. Each day's programme listed your permitted activities: you could go to the hairdresser's, cinema, bank, cocktail bar, at stated times, and if you went then you were sure of being served quickly and efficiently.'

They had almost reached the far end of the plaza. Facing them on its tower was the enormous clock face, dominating its constellation of twelve motionless attendants.

'There were a dozen socio-economic categories: blue for executives, gold for professional classes, yellow for military and government officials – incidentally, it's odd your parents ever got hold of that wristwatch, none of your family ever worked for the government – green for manual workers and so on. But, naturally, subtle subdivisions were possible. The lower-grade executive I mentioned left his office at 12, but a senior executive, with exactly the same time codes, would leave at 11.45, have an extra fifteen minutes, would find the streets clear before the lunch-hour rush of clerical workers.'

Stacey pointed up at the tower. 'This was the Big Clock, the master from which all others were regulated. Central Time Control, a sort of Ministry of Time, gradually took over the old parliamentary buildings as their legislative functions diminished. The programmers were, effectively, the city's absolute rulers.'

As Stacey continued Conrad gazed up at the battery of timepieces, poised helplessly at 12.01. Somehow time itself seemed to have been suspended, around him the great office buildings hung in a neutral interval between yesterday and tomorrow. If one could only start the master clock the entire city would probably slide into gear and come to life, in an instant be repeopled with its dynamic jostling millions.

They began to walk back towards the car. Conrad looked over his shoulder at the clock face, its gigantic arms upright on the silent hour.

'Why did it stop?' he asked.

Stacey looked at him curiously. 'Haven't I made it fairly plain?'

'What do you mean?' Conrad pulled his eyes off the scores of clocks lining the plaza, frowned at Stacey.

'Can you imagine what life was like for all but a few of the thirty million people here?'

Conrad shrugged. Blue and yellow clocks, he noticed, outnumbered all others; obviously the major governmental agencies had operated from the plaza area. 'Highly organized but better than the sort of life we lead,' he replied finally, more interested in the sights around him. 'I'd rather have the telephone for one hour a day than not at all. Scarcities are always rationed, aren't they?'

'But this was a way of life in which everything was scarce. Don't you think there's a point beyond which human dignity is surrendered?'

Conrad snorted. 'There seems to be plenty of dignity here. Look at these buildings, they'll stand for a thousand years. Try comparing them with my father. Anyway, think of the beauty of the system, engineered as precisely as a watch.'

'That's all it was,' Stacey commanded dourly. 'The old metaphor of the cog in the wheel was never more true than here. The full sum of your existence was printed for you in the newspaper columns, mailed to you once a month from the Ministry of Time.'

Conrad was looking off in some other direction and Stacey pressed on in a slightly louder voice. 'Eventually, of course, revolt came. It's interesting that in any industrial society there is usually one social revolution each century, and that successive revolutions receive their impetus from progressively higher social levels. In the eighteenth century it was the urban proletariat, in the nineteenth the artisan classes, in this revolt the white collar office worker, living in his tiny so-called modern flat, supporting through credit pyramids an economic system that denied him all freedom of will or personality, chained him to a thousand clocks ...' He broke off. 'What's the matter?'

Conrad was staring down one of the side streets. He hesitated, then asked in a casual voice: 'How were these clocks driven? Electrically?'

'Most of them. A few mechanically. Why?'

'I just wondered ... how they kept them all going.' He dawdled at Stacey's heels, checking the time from his wristwatch and glancing to his left. There were twenty or thirty clocks hanging from the buildings along the side street, indistinguishable from those he had seen all afternoon.

Except for the fact that one of them was working!

It was mounted in the centre of a black glass portico over an entrance-way fifty yards down the right-hand side, about eighteen inches in diameter, with a faded blue face. Unlike the others its hands registered 3.15, the correct time. Conrad had nearly mentioned this apparent coincidence to Stacey when he had suddenly seen the minute hand move on an interval. Without doubt someone had restarted the clock; even if it had been running off an inexhaustible battery, after thirty-seven years it could never have displayed such accuracy.

He hung behind Stacey, who was saying: 'Every revolution has its symbol of oppression ...'

The clock was almost out of view. Conrad was about to bend down and tie his shoelace when he saw the minute hand jerk downwards, tilt slightly from the horizontal.

He followed Stacey towards the car, no longer bothering to listen to him. Ten yards from it he turned and broke away, ran swiftly across the roadway towards the nearest building.

'Newman!' he heard Stacey shout. 'Come back!' He reached the pavement, ran between the great concrete pillars carrying the building. He paused for a moment behind an elevator shaft, saw Stacey climbing hurriedly into the car. The engine coughed and roared out, and Conrad sprinted on below the building into a rear alley that led back to the side-street. Behind him he heard the car accelerating, a door slam as it picked up speed.

When he entered the side-street the car came swinging off the plaza thirty yards behind him. Stacey swerved off the roadway, bumped up on to the pavement and gunned the car towards Conrad, throwing on the brakes in savage lurches, blasting the horn in an attempt to frighten him. Conrad side-stepped out of its way, almost falling over the bonnet, hurled himself up a narrow stairway leading to the first floor and raced up the steps to a short landing that ended in tall glass doors. Through them he could see a wide balcony that ringed the building. A fire-escape crisscrossed upwards to the roof, giving way on the fifth floor to a cafeteria that spanned the street to the office building opposite.

Below he heard Stacey's feet running across the pavement. The glass doors were locked. He pulled a fire-extinguisher from its bracket, tossed the heavy cylinder against the centre of the plate. The glass slipped and crashed to the tiled floor in a sudden cascade, splashing down the steps. Conrad stepped through on to the balcony, began to climb the stairway. He had reached the third floor when he saw Stacey below, craning upwards. Hand over hand, Conrad pulled himself up the next two flights, swung over a bolted metal turnstile into the open court of the cafeteria. Tables and chairs lay about on their sides, mixed up with the splintered remains of desks thrown down from the upper floors.

The doors into the covered restaurant were open, a large pool of water lying across the floor. Conrad splashed through it, went over to a window and peered down past an old plastic plant into the street. Stacey seemed to have given up. Conrad crossed the rear of the restaurant, straddled the counter and climbed through a window on to the open terrace running across the street. Beyond the rail he could see into the plaza, the double line of tyre marks curving into the street below.

He had almost crossed to the opposite balcony when a shot roared out into the air. There was a sharp tinkle of falling glass and the sound of the explosion boomed away among the empty canyons.

For a few seconds he panicked. He flinched back from the exposed rail, his ear drums numbed, looking up at the great rectangular masses towering above him on either side, the endless tiers of windows like the faceted eyes of gigantic insects. So Stacey had been armed, almost certainly was a member of the Time Police!

On his hands and knees Conrad scurried along the terrace, slid through the turnstiles and headed for a half-open window on the balcony.

Climbing through, he quickly lost himself in the building.

He finally took up a position in a corner office on the sixth floor, the cafeteria just below him to the right, the stairway up which he had escaped directly opposite.

All afternoon Stacey drove up and down the adjacent streets, sometimes free-wheeling silently with the engine off, at others blazing through at speed. Twice he fired into the air, stopping the car afterwards to call out, his words lost among the echoes rolling from one street to the next. Often he drove along the pavements, swerved about below the buildings as if he expected to flush Conrad from behind one of the banks of escalators.

Finally he appeared to drive off for good, and Conrad turned his attention to the clock in the portico. It had moved on to 6.45, almost exactly the time given by his own watch. Conrad reset this to what he assumed was the correct time, then sat back and waited for whoever had wound it to appear. Around him the thirty or forty other clocks he could see remained stationary at 12.01.

For five minutes he left his vigil, scooped some water off the pool in the cafeteria, suppressed his hunger and shortly after midnight fell asleep in a corner behind the desk.

He woke the next morning to bright sunlight flooding into the office. Standing up, he dusted his clothes, turned around to find a small grey-haired man in a patched tweed suit surveying him with sharp eyes. Slung in the crook of his arm was a large black-barrelled weapon, its hammers menacingly cocked.

The man put down a steel ruler he had evidently tapped against a cabinet, waited for Conrad to collect himself.

'What are you doing here?' he asked in a testy voice. Conrad noticed his pockets were bulging with angular objects that weighed down the sides of his jacket.

'I . . . er . . .' Conrad searched for something to say. Something about the old man convinced him that this was the clock-winder. Suddenly he decided he had nothing to lose by being frank, and blurted out: 'I saw the clock working. Down there on the left. I want to help wind them all up again.'

The old man watched him shrewdly. He had an alert bird-like face, twin folds under his chin like a cockerel's.

'How do you propose to do that?' he asked.

Stuck by this one, Conrad said lamely: 'I'd find a key somewhere.'

The old man frowned. 'One key? That wouldn't do much good.' He seemed to be relaxing slowly, shook his pockets with a dull chink.

For a few moments neither of them said anything. Then Conrad had an inspiration, bared his wrist. 'I have a watch,' he said. 'It's 7.45.'

'Let me see.' The old man stepped forward, briskly took Conrad's wrist, examined the yellow dial. 'Movado Supermatic,' he said to himself. 'CTC issue.' He stepped back, lowering the shotgun, seemed to be summing Conrad up. 'Good,' he remarked at last. 'Let's see. You probably need some breakfast.'

They made their way out of the building, began to walk quickly down the street.

'People sometimes come here,' the old man said. 'Sightseers and police. I watched your escape yesterday, you were lucky not to be killed.' They swerved left and right across the empty streets, the old man darting between the stairways and buttresses. As he walked he held his hands stiffly to his sides, preventing his pockets from swinging. Glancing into them, Conrad saw that they were full of keys, large and rusty, of every design and combination.

'I presume that was your father's watch,' the old man remarked.

'Grandfather's,' Conrad corrected. He remembered Stacey's lecture, and added: 'He was killed in the plaza.'

The old man frowned sympathetically, for a moment held Conrad's arm.

They stopped below a building, indistinguishable from the others nearby, at one time a bank. The old man looked carefully around him, eyeing the high cliff walls on all sides, then led the way up a stationary escalator.

His quarters were on the second floor, beyond a maze of steel grilles and strongdoors, a stove and a hammock slung in the centre of a large workshop. Lying about on thirty or forty desks in what had once been a typing pool, was an enormous collection of clocks, all being simultaneously repaired. Tall cabinets surrounded them, loaded with thousands of spare parts in neatly labelled correspondence trays – escapements, ratchets, cogwheels, barely recognizable through the rust.

The old man led Conrad over to a wall chart, pointed to the total listed against a column of dates. 'Look at this. There are now 278 running continuously. Believe me, I'm glad you've come. It takes me half my time to keep them wound.'

He made breakfast for Conrad, told him something about himself. His name was Marshall. Once he had worked in Central Time Control as a programmer, had survived the revolt and the Time Police, ten years later returned to the city. At the beginning of each month he cycled out to one of the perimeter towns to cash his pension and collect supplies. The rest of the time he spent winding the steadily increasing number of functioning clocks and searching for others he could dismantle and repair.

'All these years in the rain hasn't done them any good,' he explained, 'and there's nothing I can do with the electrical ones.'

Conrad wandered off among the desks, gingerly feeling the dismembered timepieces that lay around like the nerve cells of some vast unimaginable robot. He felt exhilarated and yet at the same time curiously calm, like a man who has staked his whole life on the turn of a wheel and is waiting for it to spin.

'How can you make sure that they all tell the same time?'

he asked Marshall, wondering why the question seemed so important.

Marshall gestured irritably. 'I can't, but what does it matter? There is no such thing as a perfectly accurate clock. The nearest you can get is one that has stopped. Although you never know when, it *is* absolutely accurate twice a day.'

Conrad went over to the window, pointed to the great clock visible in an interval between the rooftops. 'If only we could start that, and run all the others off it.'

'Impossible. The entire mechanism was dynamited. Only the chimer is intact. Anyway, the wiring of the electrically driven clocks perished years ago. It would take an army of engineers to recondition them.'

Conrad nodded, looked at the scoreboard again. He noticed that Marshall appeared to have lost his way through the years – the completion dates he listed were seven and a half years out. Idly, Conrad reflected on the significance of this irony, but decided not to mention it to Marshall.

For three months Conrad lived with the old man, following him on foot as he cycled about on his rounds, carrying the ladder and the satchel full of keys with which Marshall wound up the clocks, helping him to dismantle recoverable ones and carry them back to the workshop. All day, and often through half the night, they worked together, repairing the movements, restarting the clocks and returning them to their original positions.

All the while, however, Conrad's mind was fixed upon the great clock in its tower dominating the plaza. Once a day he managed to sneak off and make his way into the ruined Time buildings. As Marshall had said, neither the clock nor its twelve satellites would ever run again. The movement house looked like the engine-room of a sunken ship, a rusting tangle of rotors and drive wheels exploded into contorted shapes. Every week he would climb the long stairway up to the topmost platform two hundred feet above, look out through the bell tower at the flat roofs of the office blocks stretching away to the horizon. The hammers rested against their trips in long ranks just below him.

Once he kicked one of the treble trips playfully, sent a dull chime out across the plaza.

The sound drove strange echoes into his mind.

Slowly he began to repair the chimer mechanism, rewiring the hammers and the pulley systems, trailing fresh wire up the great height of the tower, dismantling the winches in the movement room below and renovating their clutches.

He and Marshall never discussed their self-appointed tasks. Like animals obeying an instinct they worked tirelessly, barely aware of their own motives. When Conrad told him one day that he intended to leave and continue the work in another sector of the city, Marshall agreed immediately, gave Conrad as many tools as he could spare and bade him goodbye.

Six months later, almost to the day, the sounds of the great clock chimed out across the rooftops of the city, marking the hours, the half-hours and the quarter-hours, steadily tolling the progress of the day. Thirty miles away, in the towns forming the perimeter of the city, people stopped in the streets and in doorways, listening to the dim haunted echoes reflected through the long aisles of apartment blocks on the far horizon, involuntarily counting the slow final sequences that told the hour. Older people whispered to each other: 'Four o'clock, or was it five? They have started the clock again. It seems strange after these years.'

And all through the day they would pause as the quarter and half hours reached across the miles to them, a voice from their childhoods reminding them of the ordered world of the past. They began to reset their timers by the chimes, at night before they slept they would listen to the long count of midnight, wake to hear them again in the thin clear air of the morning.

Some went down to the police station and asked if they could have their watches and clocks back again.

After sentence, twenty years for the murder of Stacey, five for fourteen offences under the Time Laws, to run concurrently, Newman was led away to the holding cells in the basement of the court. He had expected the sentence and made no comment when invited by the judge. After waiting trial for a year the afternoon in the courtroom was nothing more than a momentary intermission.

He made no attempt to defend himself against the charge of killing Stacey, partly to shield Marshall, who would be able to continue their work unmolested, and partly because he felt indirectly responsible for the policeman's death. Stacey's body, skull fractured by a twenty- or thirty-storey fall, had been discovered in the back seat of his car in a basement garage not far from the plaza. Presumably Marshall had discovered him prowling around and dealt with him single-handed. Newman recalled that one day Marshall had disappeared altogether and had been curiously irritable for the rest of the week.

The last time he had seen the old man had been during the three days before the police arrived. Each morning as the chimes boomed out across the plaza Newman had seen his tiny figure striding briskly down the plaza towards him, waving up energetically at the tower, bareheaded and unafraid.

Now Newman was faced with the problem of how to devise a clock that would chart his way through the coming twenty years. His fears increased when he was taken the next day to the cell block which housed the long-term prisoners – passing his cell on the way to meet the superintendent he noticed that his window looked out on to a small shaft. He pumped his brains desperately as he stood to attention during the superintendent's homilies, wondering how he could retain his sanity. Short of counting the seconds, each one of the 86,400 in every day, he saw no possible means of assessing the time.

Locked into his cell, he sat limply on the narrow bed, too tired to unpack his small bundle of possessions. A moment's inspection confirmed the uselessness of the shaft. A powerful light mounted half-way up masked the sunlight that slipped through a steel grille fifty feet above.

He stretched himself out on the bed and examined the ceiling. A lamp was recessed into its centre, but a second, surprisingly, appeared to have been fitted to the cell. This was on the wall, a few feet above his head. He could see the curving bowl of the protective case, some ten inches in diameter.

He was wondering whether this could be a reading light when he realized that there was no switch.

Swinging round, he sat up and examined it, then leapt to his feet in astonishment.

It was a clock! He pressed his hands against the bowl, reading the circle of numerals, noting the inclination of the hands. 4.53, near enough the present time. Not simply a clock, but one in running order! Was this some sort of macabre joke, or a misguided attempt at rehabilitation?

His pounding on the door brought a warder.

'What's all the noise about? The clock? What's the matter with it?' He unlocked the door and barged in, pushing Newman back.

'Nothing. But why is it here? They're against the law.'

'Oh, is that what's worrying you.' The warder shrugged. 'Well, you see, the rules are a little different in here. You lads have got a lot of time ahead of you, it'd be cruel not to let you know where you stood. You know how to work it, do you? Good.' He slammed the door, bolted it fast, smiled at Newman through the cage. 'It's a long day here, son, as you'll be finding out, that'll help you get through it.'

Gleefully, Newman lay on the bed, his head on a rolled blanket at its foot, staring up at the clock. It appeared to be in perfect order, electrically driven, moving in rigid half-minute jerks. For an hour after the warder left he watched it without a break, then began to tidy up his cell, glancing over his shoulder every few minutes to reassure himself that it was still there, still running efficiently. The irony of the situation, the total inversion of justice, delighted him, even though it would cost him twenty years of his life.

He was still chuckling over the absurdity of it all two weeks later when for the first time he noticed the clock's insanely irritating tick . . .

1960

THE VOICES OF TIME

ONE

Later Powers often thought of Whitby, and the strange grooves the biologist had cut, apparently at random, all over the floor of the empty swimming pool. An inch deep and twenty feet long, interlocking to form an elaborate ideogram like a Chinese character, they had taken him all summer to complete, and he had obviously thought about little else, working away tirelessly through the long desert afternoons. Powers had watched him from his office window at the far end of the Neurology wing, carefully marking out his pegs and string, carrying away the cement chips in a small canvas bucket. After Whitby's suicide no one had bothered about the grooves, but Powers often borrowed the supervisor's key and let himself into the disused pool, and would look down at the labyrinth of mouldering gulleys, half-filled with water leaking in from the chlorinator, an enigma now past any solution.

Initially, however, Powers was too preoccupied with completing his work at the Clinic and planning his own final withdrawal. After the first frantic weeks of panic he had managed to accept an uneasy compromise that allowed him to view his predicament with the detached fatalism he had previously reserved for his patients. Fortunately he was moving down the physical and mental gradients simultaneously – lethargy and inertia blunted his anxieties, a slackening metabolism made it necessary to concentrate to produce a connected thought-train. In fact, the lengthening intervals of dreamless sleep were almost restful. He found himself beginning to look forward to them, and made no effort to wake earlier than was essential.

At first he had kept an alarm clock by his bed, tried to compress as much activity as he could into the narrowing hours of consciousness, sorting out his library, driving over to Whitby's laboratory every morning to examine the latest batch of X-ray plates, every minute and hour rationed like the last drops of water in a canteen.

Anderson, fortunately, had unwittingly made him realize the pointlessness of this course.

After Powers had resigned from the Clinic he still continued to drive in once a week for his check-up, now little more than a formality. On what turned out to be the last occasion Anderson had perfunctorily taken his blood-count, noting Powers' slacker facial muscles, fading pupil reflexes and unshaven cheeks.

He smiled sympathetically at Powers across the desk, wondering what to say to him. Once he had put on a show of encouragement with the more intelligent patients, even tried to provide some sort of explanation. But Powers was too difficult to reach – neurosurgeon extraordinary, a man always out on the periphery, only at ease working with unfamiliar materials. To himself he thought: *I'm sorry, Robert. What can I say – 'Even the sun is growing cooler' –?* He watched Powers drum his fingers restlessly on the enamel desk top, his eyes glancing at the spinal level charts hung around the office. Despite his unkempt appearance – he had been wearing the same unironed shirt and dirty white plimsolls a week ago – Powers looked composed and self-possessed, like a Conradian beachcomber more or less reconciled to his own weaknesses.

'What are you doing with yourself, Robert?' he asked. 'Are you still going over to Whitby's lab?'

'As much as I can. It takes me half an hour to cross the lake, and I keep on sleeping through the alarm clock. I may leave my place and move in there permanently.'

Anderson frowned. 'Is there much point? As far as I could make out Whitby's work was pretty speculative –' He broke off, realizing the implied criticism of Powers' own disastrous work at the Clinic, but Powers seemed to ignore this, was examining the pattern of shadows on the ceiling. 'Anyway, wouldn't it be better to stay where you are, among your own things, read through Toynbee and Spengler again?'

Powers laughed shortly. 'That's the last thing I want to do. I want to *forget* Toynbee and Spengler, not try to remember them. In fact, Paul, I'd like to forget everything. I don't know whether I've got enough time, though. How much can you forget in three months?'

'Everything, I suppose, if you want to. But don't try to race the clock.'

Powers nodded quietly, repeating this last remark to himself. Racing the clock was exactly what he had been doing. As he stood up and said goodbye to Anderson he suddenly decided to throw away his alarm clock, escape from his futile obsession with time. To remind himself he unfastened his wristwatch and scrambled the setting, then slipped it into his pocket. Making his way out to the car park he reflected on the freedom this simple act gave him. He would explore the lateral byways now, the side doors, as it were, in the corridors of time. Three months could be an eternity.

He picked his car out of the line and strolled over to it, shielding his eyes from the heavy sunlight beating down across the parabolic sweep of the lecture theatre roof. He was about to climb in when he saw that someone had traced with a finger across the dust caked over the windshield:

96,688,365,498,721

Looking over his shoulder, he recognized the white Packard parked next to him, peered inside and saw a lean-faced young man with blond sun-bleached hair and a high cerebrotonic forehead watching him behind dark glasses. Sitting beside him at the wheel was a raven-haired girl whom he had often seen around the psychology department. She had intelligent but somehow rather oblique eyes, and Powers remembered that the younger doctors called her 'the girl from Mars'.

'Hello, Kaldren,' Powers said to the young man. 'Still following me around?'

Kaldren nodded. 'Most of the time, doctor.' He sized Powers up shrewdly. 'We haven't seen very much of you recently, as a matter of fact. Anderson said you'd resigned, and we noticed your laboratory was closed.'

Powers shrugged. 'I felt I needed a rest. As you'll understand, there's a good deal that needs re-thinking.'

Kaldren frowned half-mockingly. 'Sorry to hear that, doctor. But don't let these temporary setbacks depress you.' He noticed the girl watching Powers with interest. 'Coma's a fan of yours. I gave her your papers from *American Journal of Psychiatry*, and she's read through the whole file.'

The girl smiled pleasantly at Powers, for a moment dispelling the hostility between the two men. When Powers nodded to her she leaned across Kaldren and said: 'Actually I've just finished Noguchi's autobiography – the great Japanese doctor who discovered the spirochaete. Somehow you remind me of him – there's so much of yourself in all the patients you worked on.'

Powers smiled wanly at her, then his eyes turned and locked involuntarily on Kaldren's. They stared at each other sombrely for a moment, and a small tic in Kaldren's right cheek began to flicker irritatingly. He flexed his facial muscles, after a few seconds mastered it with an effort, obviously annoyed that Powers should have witnessed this brief embarrassment.

'How did the clinic go today?' Powers asked. 'Have you had any more ... headaches?'

Kaldren's mouth snapped shut, he looked suddenly irritable. 'Whose care am I in, doctor? Yours or Anderson's? Is that the sort of question you should be asking now?'

Powers gestured deprecatingly. 'Perhaps not.' He cleared his throat; the heat was ebbing the blood from his head and he felt tired and eager to get away from them. He turned towards his car, then realized that Kaldren would probably follow, either try to crowd him into the ditch or block the road and make Powers sit in his dust all the way back to the lake. Kaldren was capable of any madness.

'Well, I've got to go and collect something,' he said, adding in a firmer voice: 'Get in touch with me, though, if you can't reach Anderson.'

He waved and walked off behind the line of cars. From the reflection in the windows he could see Kaldren looking back and watching him closely.

He entered the Neurology wing, paused thankfully in the cool foyer, nodding to the two nurses and the armed guard at the reception desk. For some reason the terminals sleeping in the adjacent dormitory block attracted hordes of would-be sightseers, most of them cranks with some magical anti-narcoma remedy, or merely the idly curious, but a good number of quite normal people, many of whom had travelled thousands of miles, impelled towards the Clinic by some strange instinct, like animals migrating to a preview of their racial graveyards.

He walked along the corridor to the supervisor's office overlooking the recreation deck, borrowed the key and made his way out through the tennis courts and callisthenics rigs to the enclosed swimming pool at the far end. It had been disused for months, and only Powers' visits kept the lock free. Stepping through, he closed it behind him and walked past the peeling wooden stands to the deep end.

Putting a foot up on the diving board, he looked down at Whitby's ideogram. Damp leaves and bits of paper obscured it, but the outlines were just distinguishable. It covered almost the entire floor of the pool and at first glance appeared to represent a huge solar disc, with four radiating diamond-shaped arms, a crude Jungian mandala.

Wondering what had prompted Whitby to carve the device before his death, Powers noticed something moving through the debris in the centre of the disc. A black, horny-shelled animal about a foot long was nosing about in the slush, heaving itself on tired legs. Its shell was articulated, and vaguely resembled an armadillo's. Reaching the edge of the disc, it stopped and hesitated, then slowly backed away into the centre again, apparently unwilling or unable to cross the narrow groove.

Powers looked around, then stepped into one of the changing stalls and pulled a small wooden clothes locker off its rusty wall bracket. Carrying it under one arm, he climbed down the chromium ladder into the pool and walked carefully across the slithery floor towards the animal. As he approached it sidled away from him, but he trapped it easily, using the lid to lever it into the box.

The animal was heavy, at least the weight of a brick. Powers tapped its massive olive-black carapace with his knuckle, noting the triangular warty head jutting out below its rim like a turtle's, the thickened pads beneath the first digits of the pentadactyl forelimbs.

He watched the three-lidded eyes blinking at him anxiously from the bottom of the box.

'Expecting some really hot weather?' he murmured. 'That lead umbrella you're carrying around should keep you cool.'

He closed the lid, climbed out of the pool and made his way back to the supervisor's office, then carried the box out to his car.

> '... Kaldren continues to reproach me (Powers wrote in his diary). For some reason he seems unwilling to accept his isolation, is elaborating a series of private rituals to replace the missing hours of sleep. Perhaps I should tell him of my own approaching zero, but he'd probably regard this as the final unbearable insult, that I should have in excess what he so desperately yearns for. God knows what might happen. Fortunately the nightmarish visions appear to have receded for the time being...'

Pushing the diary away, Powers leaned forward across the desk and stared out through the window at the white floor of the lake bed stretching towards the hills along the horizon. Three miles away, on the far shore, he could see the circular bowl of the radio-telescope revolving slowly in the clear afternoon air, as Kaldren tirelessly trapped the sky, sluicing in millions of cubic parsecs of sterile ether, like the nomads who trapped the sea along the shores of the Persian Gulf.

Behind him the air-conditioner murmured quietly, cooling the pale blue walls half-hidden in the dim light. Outside the air was bright and oppressive, the heat waves rippling up from the clumps of gold-tinted cacti below the Clinic blurring the sharp terraces of the twenty-storey Neurology block. There, in the silent dormitories behind the sealed shutters, the terminals slept their long dreamless sleep. There were now over 500 of them in the Clinic, the vanguard of a vast somnambulist army massing for its last march. Only five years had elapsed since the first narcoma syndrome had been recognized, but already huge government hospitals in the east were being readied for intakes in the thousands, as more and more cases came to light.

Powers felt suddenly tired, and glanced at his wrist, wondering how long he had to 8 o'clock, his bedtime for the next week or so. Already he missed the dusk, soon would wake to his last dawn.

His watch was in his hip-pocket. He remembered his decision not to use his timepieces, and sat back and stared at the bookshelves beside the desk. There were rows of green-covered AEC publications he had removed from Whitby's library, papers in which the biologist described his work out in the Pacific after the H-tests. Many of them Powers knew almost by heart, read a hundred times in an effort to grasp Whitby's last conclusions. Toynbee would certainly be easier to forget.

His eyes dimmed momentarily, as the tall black wall in the rear of his mind cast its great shadow over his brain. He reached for the diary, thinking of the girl in Kaldren's car – Coma he had called her, another of his insane jokes – and her reference to Noguchi. Actually the comparison should have been made with Whitby, not himself; the monsters in the lab were nothing more than fragmented mirrors of Whitby's mind, like the grotesque radio-shielded frog he had found that morning in the swimming pool.

Thinking of the girl Coma, and the heartening smile she had given him, he wrote:

> Woke 6-33 am. Last session with Anderson. He made it plain he's seen enough of me, and from now on I'm better alone. To sleep 8-00? (these countdowns terrify me.)

He paused, then added:

Goodbye, Eniwetok.

TWO

He saw the girl again the next day at Whitby's laboratory. He had driven over after breakfast with the new specimen, eager to get it into a vivarium before it died. The only previous armoured mutant he had come across had nearly broken his neck. Speeding along the lake road a month or so earlier he had struck it with the offside front wheel, expecting the small creature to flatten instantly. Instead its hard lead-packed shell had remained rigid, even though the organism within it had been pulped, had flung the car heavily into the ditch. He had gone back for the shell, later weighed it at the laboratory, found it contained over 600 grammes of lead.

Quite a number of plants and animals were building up heavy metals as radiological shields. In the hills behind the beach house a couple of old-time prospectors were renovating the derelict gold-panning equipment abandoned over eighty years ago. They had noticed the bright yellow tints of the cacti, run an analysis and found that the plants were assimilating gold in extractable quantities, although the soil concentrations were unworkable. Oak Ridge was at last paying a dividend!!

Waking that morning just after 6-45 – ten minutes later than the previous day (he had switched on the radio, heard one of the regular morning programmes as he climbed out of bed) – he had eaten a light unwanted breakfast, then spent an hour packing away some of the books in his library, crating them up and taping on address labels to his brother.

He reached Whitby's laboratory half an hour later. This was housed in a 100-foot-wide geodesic dome built beside his chalet on the west shore of the lake about a mile from Kaldren's summer house. The chalet had been closed after Whitby's suicide, and many of the experimental plants and animals had died before Powers had managed to receive permission to use the laboratory.

As he turned into the driveway he saw the girl standing on the apex of the yellow-ribbed dome, her slim figure silhouetted against the sky. She waved to him, then began to step down across the glass polyhedrons and jumped nimbly into the driveway beside the car.

'Hello,' she said, giving him a welcoming smile. 'I came over to see your zoo. Kaldren said you wouldn't let me in if he came so I made him stay behind.'

She waited for Powers to say something while he searched for his keys, then volunteered: 'If you like, I can wash your shirt.'

Powers grinned at her, peered down ruefully at his dust-stained sleeves. 'Not a bad idea. I thought I was beginning to look a little uncared-for.' He unlocked the door, took Coma's arm. 'I don't know why Kaldren told you that – he's welcome here any time he likes.'

'What have you got in there?' Coma asked, pointing at the wooden box he was carrying as they walked between the gear-laden benches.

'A distant cousin of ours I found. Interesting little chap. I'll introduce you in a moment.'

Sliding partitions divided the dome into four chambers. Two of them were storerooms, filled with spare tanks, apparatus, cartons of animal food and test rigs. They crossed the third section, almost filled by a powerful X-ray projector, a giant 250 amp G.E. Maxitron, angled on to a revolving table, concrete shielding blocks lying around ready for use like huge building bricks.

The fourth chamber contained Powers' zoo, the vivaria jammed together along the benches and in the sinks, big coloured cardboard charts and memos pinned on to the draught hoods above them, a tangle of rubber tubing and power leads trailing across the floor. As they walked past the lines of tanks dim forms shifted behind the frosted glass, and at the far end of the aisle there was a sudden scurrying in a large cage by Powers' desk.

Putting the box down on his chair, he picked a packet of peanuts off the desk and went over to the cage. A small black-haired chimpanzee wearing a dented jet pilot's helmet swarmed deftly up the bars to him, chirped happily and then jumped down to a miniature control panel against the rear wall of the cage. Rapidly it flicked a series of buttons and toggles, and a succession of coloured lights lit up like a juke box and jangled out a two-second blast of music.

'Good boy,' Powers said encouragingly, patting the chimp's back and shovelling the peanuts into its hands. 'You're getting much too clever for that one, aren't you?'

The chimp tossed the peanuts into the back of its throat with the smooth, easy motions of a conjuror, jabbering at Powers in a sing-song voice.

Coma laughed and took some of the nuts from Powers. 'He's sweet. I think he's talking to you.'

Powers nodded. 'Quite right, he is. Actually he's got a two-hundred-word vocabulary, but his voice box scrambles it all up.' He opened a small refrigerator by the desk, took out half a packet of sliced bread and passed a couple of pieces to the chimp. It picked an electric toaster off the floor and placed it in the middle of a low wobbling table in the centre of the cage, whipped the pieces into the slots. Powers pressed a tab on the switchboard beside the cage and the toaster began to crackle softly.

'He's one of the brightest we've had here, about as intelligent as a five-year-old child, though much more self-sufficient in a lot of ways.' The two pieces of toast jumped out of their slots and the chimp caught them neatly, nonchalantly patting its helmet each time, then ambled off into a small ramshackle kennel and relaxed back with one arm out of a window, sliding the toast into its mouth.

'He built that house himself,' Powers went on, switching off the toaster. 'Not a bad effort, really.' He pointed to a yellow polythene bucket by the front door of the kennel, from which a battered-looking geranium protruded. 'Tends that plant, cleans up the cage, pours out an endless stream of wisecracks. Pleasant fellow all round.'

Coma was smiling broadly to herself. 'Why the space helmet, though?'

Powers hesitated. 'Oh, it – er – it's for his own protection. Sometimes he gets rather bad headaches. His predecessors all –' He broke off and turned away. 'Let's have a look at some of the other inmates.'

He moved down the line of tanks, beckoning Coma with him. 'We'll start at the beginning.' He lifted the glass lid off one of the tanks, and Coma peered down into a shallow bath of water, where a small round organism with slender tendrils was nestling in a rockery of shells and pebbles.

'Sea anemone. Or was. Simple coelenterate with an open-ended body cavity.' He pointed down to a thickened ridge of tissue around the base. 'It's sealed up the cavity, converted the channel into a rudimentary notochord, first plant ever to develop a nervous system. Later the tendrils will knot themselves into a ganglion, but already they're sensitive to colour. Look.' He borrowed the violet handkerchief in Coma's breast-pocket, spread it across the tank. The tendrils flexed and stiffened, began to weave slowly, as if they were trying to focus.

'The strange thing is that they're completely insensitive to white light. Normally the tendrils register shifting pressure gradients, like the tympanic diaphragms in your ears. Now it's almost as if they can *hear* primary colours, suggests it's re-adapting itself for a non-aquatic existence in a static world of violent colour contrasts.'

Coma shook her head, puzzled. 'Why, though?'

'Hold on a moment. Let me put you in the picture first.' They moved along the bench to a series of drum-shaped cages made of wire mosquito netting. Above the first was a large white cardboard screen bearing a blown-up microphoto of a tall pagoda-like chain, topped by the legend: 'Drosophila: 15 röntgens/min.'

Powers tapped a small perspex window in the drum. 'Fruitfly. Its huge chromosomes make it a useful test vehicle.' He bent down, pointed to a grey V-shaped honeycomb suspended from the roof. A few flies emerged from entrances, moving about busily. 'Usually it's solitary, a nomadic scavenger. Now it forms itself into well-knit social groups, has begun to secrete a thin sweet lymph something like honey.'

'What's this?' Coma asked, touching the screen.

'Diagram of a key gene in the operation.' He traced a spray of arrows leading from a link in the chain. The arrows were labelled: 'Lymph gland' and subdivided 'sphincter muscles, epithelium, templates.'

'It's rather like the perforated sheet music of a player-piano,' Powers commented, 'or a computer punch tape. Knock out one link with an X-ray beam, lose a characteristic, change the score.'

Coma was peering through the window of the next cage and pulling an unpleasant face. Over her shoulder Powers saw she was watching an enormous spider-like insect, as big as a hand, its dark hairy legs as thick as fingers. The compound eyes had been built up so that they resembled giant rubies.

'He looks unfriendly,' she said. 'What's that sort of rope ladder he's spinning?' As she moved a finger to her mouth the spider came to life, retreated into the cage and began spewing out a complex skein of interlinked grey thread which it slung in long loops from the roof of the cage.

'A web,' Powers told her. 'Except that it consists of nervous tissue. The ladders form an external neural plexus, an inflatable brain as it were, that he can pump up to whatever size the situation calls for. A sensible arrangement, really, far better than our own.'

Coma backed away. 'Gruesome. I wouldn't like to go into his parlour.'

'Oh, he's not as frightening as he looks. Those huge eyes staring at you are blind. Or, rather, their optical sensitivity has shifted down the band, the retinas will only register gamma radiation. Your wristwatch has luminous hands. When you moved it across the window he started thinking. World War IV should really bring him into his element.'

They strolled back to Powers' desk. He put a coffee pan over a bunsen and pushed a chair across to Coma. Then he opened the box, lifted out the armoured frog and put it down on a sheet of blotting paper.

'Recognize him? Your old childhood friend, the common frog. He's built himself quite a solid little air-raid shelter.' He carried the animal across to a sink, turned on the tap and let the water play softly over its shell. Wiping his hands on his shirt, he came back to the desk.

Coma brushed her long hair off her forehead, watched him curiously.

'Well, what's the secret?'

Powers lit a cigarette. 'There's no secret. Teratologists have been breeding monsters for years. Have you ever heard of the "silent pair"?'

She shook her head.

Powers stared moodily at the cigarette for a moment, riding the kick the first one of the day always gave him. 'The so-called "silent pair" is one of modern genetics' oldest problems, the apparently baffling mystery of the two inactive genes which occur in a small percentage of all living organisms, and appear to have no intelligible role in their structure or development. For a long while now biologists have been trying to activate them, but the difficulty is partly in identifying the silent genes in the fertilized germ cells of parents known to contain them, and partly in focusing a narrow enough X-ray beam which will do no damage to the remainder of the chromosome. However, after about ten years' work Dr Whitby successfully developed a whole-body irradiation technique based on his observation of radiobiological damage at Eniwetok.'

Powers paused for a moment. 'He had noticed that there appeared to be more biological damage after the tests – that is, a greater transport of energy – than could be accounted for by direct radiation. What was happening was that the protein lattices in the genes were building up energy in the way that any vibrating membrane accumulates energy when it resonates – you remember the analogy of the bridge collapsing under the soldiers marching in step – and it occurred to him that if he could first identify the critical resonance frequency of the lattices in any particular silent gene he could then radiate the entire living organism, and not simply its germ cells, with a low field that would act selectively on the silent gene and cause no damage to the remainder of the chromosomes, whose lattices would resonate critically only at other specific frequencies.'

Powers gestured around the laboratory with his cigarette. 'You see some of the fruits of this "resonance transfer" technique around you.'

Coma nodded. 'They've had their silent genes activated?'

'Yes, all of them. These are only a few of the thousands of specimens who have passed through here, and as you've seen, the results are pretty dramatic.'

He reached up and pulled across a section of the sun curtain. They were sitting just under the lip of the dome, and the mounting sunlight had begun to irritate him.

In the comparative darkness Coma noticed a stroboscope winking slowly in one of the tanks at the end of the bench behind her. She stood up and went over to it, examining a tall sunflower with a thickened stem and greatly enlarged receptacle. Packed around the flower, so that only its head protruded, was a chimney of grey-white stones, neatly cemented together and labelled:

Cretaceous Chalk: 60,000,000 years

Beside it on the bench were three other chimneys, these labelled 'Devonian Sandstone: 290,000,000 years', 'Asphalt: 20 years', 'Polyvinylchloride: 6 months'.

'Can you see those moist white discs on the sepals,' Powers pointed out. 'In some way they regulate the plant's metabolism. It literally *sees* time. The older the surrounding environment, the more sluggish its metabolism. With the asphalt chimney it will complete its annual cycle in a week, with the PVC one in a couple of hours.'

'Sees time,' Coma repeated, wonderingly. She looked up at Powers, chewing her lower lip reflectively. 'It's fantastic. Are these the creatures of the future, doctor?'

'I don't know,' Powers admitted. 'But if they are their world must be a monstrous surrealist one.'

THREE

He went back to the desk, pulled two cups from a drawer and poured out the coffee, switching off the bunsen. 'Some people have speculated that organisms possessing the silent pair of genes are the forerunners of a massive move up the evolutionary slope, that the silent genes are a sort of code, a divine message that we inferior organisms are carrying for our more highly developed descendants. It may well be true – perhaps we've broken the code too soon.'

'Why do you say that?'

'Well, as Whitby's death indicates, the experiments in this laboratory have all come to a rather unhappy conclusion. Without exception the organisms we've irradiated have entered a final phase of totally disorganized growth, producing dozens of specialized sensory organs whose function we can't even guess. The results are catastrophic – the anemone will literally explode, the Drosophila cannibalize themselves, and so on. Whether the future implicit in these plants and animals is ever intended to take place, or whether we're merely extrapolating – I don't know. Sometimes I think, though, that the new sensory organs developed are parodies of their real intentions. The specimens you've seen today are all in an early stage of their secondary growth cycles. Later on they begin to look distinctly bizarre.'

Coma nodded. 'A zoo isn't complete without its keeper,' she commented. 'What about Man?'

Powers shrugged. 'About one in every 100,000 – the usual average – contain the silent pair. You might have them – or I. No one has volunteered yet to undergo whole-body irradiation. Apart from the fact that it would be classified as suicide, if the experiments here are any guide the experience would be savage and violent.'

He sipped at the thin coffee, feeling tired and somehow bored. Recapitulating the laboratory's work had exhausted him.

The girl leaned forward. 'You look awfully pale,' she said solicitously. 'Don't you sleep well?'

Powers managed a brief smile. 'Too well,' he admitted. 'It's no longer a problem with me.'

'I wish I could say that about Kaldren. I don't think he sleeps anywhere near enough. I hear him pacing around all night.' She added: 'Still, I suppose it's better than being a terminal. Tell me, doctor, wouldn't it be worth trying this radiation technique on the sleepers at the Clinic? It might wake them up before the end. A few of them must possess the silent genes.'

'They *all* do,' Powers told her. 'The two phenomena are very closely linked, as a matter of fact.' He stopped, fatigue dulling his brain, and wondered whether to ask the girl to leave. Then he climbed off the desk and reached behind it, picked up a tape-recorder.

Switching it on, he zeroed the tape and adjusted the speaker volume.

'Whitby and I often talked this over. Towards the end I took it all down. He was a great biologist, so let's hear it in his own words. It's absolutely the heart of the matter.'

He flipped the table on, adding: 'I've played it over to myself a thousand times, so I'm afraid the quality is poor.'

An older man's voice, sharp and slightly irritable, sounded out above a low buzz of distortion, but Coma could hear it clearly.

WHITBY: . . . for heaven's sake, Robert, look at those FAO statistics. Despite an annual increase of five per cent in acreage sown over the past fifteen years, world wheat crops have continued to decline by a factor of about two per cent. The same story repeats itself *ad nauseam*. Cereals and root crops, dairy yields, ruminant fertility – are all down. Couple these with a mass of parallel symptoms, anything you care to pick from altered migratory routes to longer hibernation periods, and the overall pattern is incontrovertible.

POWERS: Population figures for Europe and North America show no decline, though.

WHITBY: Of course not, as I keep pointing out. It will take a century for such a fractional drop in fertility to have any effect in areas where extensive birth control provides an artificial reservoir. One must look at the countries of the Far East, and particularly at those where infant mortality has remained at a steady level. The population of Sumatra, for example, has declined by over fifteen per cent in the last twenty years. A fabulous decline! Do you realize that only two or three decades ago the Neo-Malthusians were talking about a 'world population explosion'? In fact, it's an implosion. Another factor is –

Here the tape had been cut and edited, and Whitby's voice, less querulous this time, picked up again.

... just as a matter of interest, tell me something: how long do you sleep each night?

POWERS: I don't know exactly; about eight hours, I suppose.

WHITBY: The proverbial eight hours. Ask anyone and they say automatically 'eight hours'. As a matter of fact you sleep about ten and a half hours, like the majority of people. I've timed you on a number of occasions. I myself sleep eleven. Yet thirty years ago people did indeed sleep eight hours, and a century before that they slept six or seven. In Vasari's *Lives* one reads of Michelangelo sleeping for only four or five hours, painting all day at the age of eighty and then working through the night over his anatomy table with a candle strapped to his forehead. Now he's regarded as a prodigy, but it was unremarkable then. How do you think the ancients, from Plato to Shakespeare, Aristotle to Aquinas, were able to cram so much work into their lives? Simply because they had an extra six or seven hours every day. Of course, a second disadvantage under which we labour is a lowered basal metabolic rate – another factor no one will explain.

POWERS: I suppose you could take the view that the lengthened sleep interval is a compensation device, a sort of mass neurotic attempt to escape from the terrifying pressures of urban life in the late twentieth century.

WHITBY: You could, but you'd be wrong. It's simply a matter of biochemistry. The ribonucleic acid templates which unravel the protein chains in all living organisms are wearing out, the dies inscribing the protoplasmic signature have become blunted. After all, they've been running now for over a thousand million years. It's time to re-tool. Just as an individual organism's life span is finite, or the life of a yeast colony or a given species, so the life of an entire biological kingdom is of fixed duration. It's always been assumed that the evolutionary slope reaches forever upwards, but in fact the peak has already been reached, and the pathway now leads downwards to the common biological grave. It's a despairing and at present unacceptable vision of the future, but it's the only one. Five thousand centuries from now our descendants, instead of being multi-brained star-men, will probably be naked prognathous idiots with hair on their foreheads, grunting their way through the remains of this Clinic like Neolithic men caught in a macabre inversion of time. Believe me, I pity them, as I pity myself. My total failure, my absolute lack of any moral or biological right to existence, is implicit in every cell of my body ...

The tape ended, the spool ran free and stopped. Powers closed the machine, then massaged his face. Coma sat quietly, watching him and listening to the chimp playing with a box of puzzle dice.

'As far as Whitby could tell,' Powers said, 'the silent genes represent a last desperate effort of the biological kingdom to keep its head above the rising waters. Its total life period is determined by the amount of radiation emitted by the sun, and once this reaches a certain point the sure-death line has been passed and extinction is inevitable. To compensate for this, alarms have been built in which alter the form of the organism and adapt it to living in a hotter radiological climate. Soft-skinned organisms develop hard shells, these contain heavy metals as radiation screens. New organs of perception are developed too. According to Whitby, though, it's all wasted effort in the long run – but sometimes I wonder.'

He smiled at Coma and shrugged. 'Well, let's talk about something else. How long have you known Kaldren?'

'About three weeks. Feels like ten thousand years.'

'How do you find him now? We've been rather out of touch lately.'

Coma grinned. 'I don't seem to see very much of him either. He makes me sleep all the time. Kaldren has many strange talents, but he lives just for himself. You mean a lot to him, doctor. In fact, you're my one serious rival.'

'I thought he couldn't stand the sight of me.'

'Oh, that's just a sort of surface symptom. He really thinks of you continually. That's why we spend all our time following you around.' She eyed Powers shrewdly. 'I think he feels guilty about something.'

'Guilty?' Powers exclaimed. '*He* does? I thought I was supposed to be the guilty one.'

'Why?' she pressed. She hesitated, then said: 'You carried out some experimental surgical technique on him, didn't you?'

'Yes,' Powers admitted. 'It wasn't altogether a success, like so much of what I seem to be involved with. If Kaldren feels guilty, I suppose it's because he feels he must take some of the responsibility.'

He looked down at the girl, her intelligent eyes watching him closely. 'For one or two reasons it may be necessary for you to know. You said Kaldren paced around all night and didn't get enough sleep. Actually he doesn't get any sleep at all.'

The girl nodded. 'You . . .' She made a snapping gesture with her fingers.

'. . . narcotomized him,' Powers completed. 'Surgically speaking, it was a great success, one might well share a Nobel for it. Normally the hypothalamus regulates the period of sleep, raising the threshold of consciousness in order to relax the venous capillaries in the brain and drain them of accumulating toxins. However, by sealing off some of the control loops the subject is unable to receive the sleep cue, and the capillaries drain while he remains conscious. All he feels is a temporary lethargy, but this passes within three or four hours. Physically speaking, Kaldren has had another twenty years added to his life. But the psyche seems to need sleep for its own private reasons, and consequently Kaldren has periodic storms that tear him apart. The whole thing was a tragic blunder.'

Coma frowned pensively. 'I guessed as much. Your papers in the neurosurgery journals referred to the patient as K. A touch of pure Kafka that came all too true.'

'I may leave here for good, Coma,' Powers said. 'Make sure that Kaldren goes to his clinics. Some of the deep scar tissue will need to be cleaned away.'

'I'll try. Sometimes I feel I'm just another of his insane terminal documents.'

'What are those?'

'Haven't you heard? Kaldren's collection of final statements about *homo sapiens*. The complete works of Freud, Beethoven's blind quartets, transcripts of the Nuremberg trials, an automatic novel, and so on.' She broke off. 'What's that you're drawing?'

'Where?'

She pointed to the desk blotter, and Powers looked down and realized he had been unconsciously sketching an elaborate doodle, Whitby's four-armed sun. 'It's nothing,' he said. Somehow, though, it had a strangely compelling force.

Coma stood up to leave. 'You must come and see us, doctor. Kaldren has so much he wants to show you. He's just got hold of an old copy of the last signals sent back by the Mercury Seven twenty years ago when they reached the moon, and can't think about anything else. You remember the strange messages they recorded before they died, full of poetic ramblings about the white gardens. Now that I think about it they behaved rather like the plants in your zoo here.'

She put her hands in her pockets, then pulled something out. 'By the way, Kaldren asked me to give you this.'

It was an old index card from the observatory library. In the centre had been typed the number:

96,688,365,498,720

'It's going to take a long time to reach zero at this rate,' Powers remarked dryly. 'I'll have quite a collection when we're finished.'

After she had left he chucked the card into the waste bin and sat down at the desk, staring for an hour at the ideogram on the blotter.

Halfway back to his beach house the lake road forked to the left through a narrow saddle that ran between the hills to an abandoned Air Force weapons range on one of the remoter salt lakes. At the nearer end were a number of small bunkers and camera towers, one or two metal shacks and a low-roofed storage hangar. The white hills encircled the whole area, shutting it off from the world outside, and Powers liked to wander on foot down the gunnery aisles that had been marked down the two-mile length of the lake towards the concrete sight-screens at the far end. The abstract patterns made him feel like an ant on a bone-white chess-board, the rectangular screens at one end and the towers and bunkers at the other like opposing pieces.

His session with Coma had made Powers feel suddenly dissatisfied with the way he was spending his last months. *Goodbye, Eniwetok*, he had written, but in fact systematically forgetting everything was exactly the same as remembering it, a cataloguing in reverse, sorting out all the books in the mental library and putting them back in their right places upside down.

Powers climbed one of the camera towers, leaned on the rail and looked out along the aisles towards the sight-screens. Ricocheting shells and rockets had chipped away large pieces of the circular concrete bands that ringed the target bulls, but the outlines of the huge 100-yard-wide discs, alternately painted blue and red, were still visible.

For half an hour he stared quietly at them, formless ideas shifting through his mind. Then, without thinking, he abruptly left the rail and climbed down the companionway. The storage hangar was fifty yards away. He walked quickly across to it, stepped into the cool shadows and peered around the rusting electric trolleys and empty flare drums. At the far end, behind a pile of lumber and bales of wire, were a stack of unopened cement bags, a mound of dirty sand and an old mixer.

Half an hour later he had backed the Buick into the hangar and hooked the cement mixer, charged with sand, cement and water scavenged from the drums lying around outside, on to the rear bumper, then loaded a dozen more bags into the car's trunk and rear seat. Finally he selected a few straight lengths of timber, jammed them through the window and set off across the lake towards the central target bull.

For the next two hours he worked away steadily in the centre of the great blue disc, mixing up the cement by hand, carrying it across to the crude wooden forms he had lashed together from the timber, smoothing it down so that it formed a six-inch high wall around the perimeter of the bull. He worked without pause, stirring the cement with a tyre lever, scooping it out with a hub-cap prised off one of the wheels.

By the time he finished and drove off, leaving his equipment where it stood, he had completed a thirty-foot-long section of wall.

FOUR

June 7: Conscious, for the first time, of the brevity of each day. As long as I was awake for over twelve hours I still orientated my time around the meridian, morning and afternoon set their old rhythms. Now, with just over eleven hours of consciousness left, they form a continuous interval, like a length of tape-measure. I can see exactly how much is left on the spool and can do little to affect the rate at which it unwinds. Spend the time slowly packing away the library; the crates are too heavy to move and lie where they are filled.
Cell count down to 400,000.
Woke 8-10. To sleep 7-15. (Appear to have lost my watch without realizing it, had to drive into town to buy another.)

June 14: 9½ *hours. Time races, flashing past like an expressway. However, the last week of a holiday always goes faster than the first. At the present rate there should be about 4–5 weeks left. This morning I tried to visualize what the last week or so – the final, 3, 2, 1, out – would be like, had a sudden chilling attack of pure fear, unlike anything I've ever felt before. Took me half an hour to steady myself for an intravenous.*
Kaldren pursues me like my luminescent shadow, chalked up on the gateway '96,688,365,498,702'. Should confuse the mail man.
Woke 9-05. To sleep 6-36.

June 19: 8¾ *hours. Anderson rang up this morning. I nearly put the phone down on him, but managed to go through the pretence of making the final arrangements. He congratulated me on my stoicism, even used the word 'heroic'. Don't feel it. Despair erodes everything – courage, hope, self-discipline, all the better qualities. It's so damned difficult to sustain that impersonal attitude of passive acceptance implicit in the scientific tradition. I try to think of Galileo before the Inquisition, Freud surmounting the endless pain of his jaw cancer surgery.*

Met Kaldren down town, had a long discussion about the Mercury Seven. He's convinced that they refused to leave the moon deliberately, after the 'reception party' waiting for them had put them in the cosmic picture. They were told by the mysterious emissaries from Orion that the exploration of deep space was pointless, that they were too late as the life of the universe is now virtually over!!! According to K. there are Air Force generals who take this nonsense seriously, but I suspect it's simply an obscure attempt on K.'s part to console me.
Must have the phone disconnected. Some contractor keeps calling me up about payment for 50 bags of cement he claims I collected ten days ago. Says he helped me load them on to a truck himself. I did drive Whitby's pick-up into town but only to get some lead screening. What does he think I'd do with all that cement? Just the sort of irritating thing you don't expect to hang over your final exit. (Moral: don't try too hard to forget Eniwetok.)
Woke 9-40. To sleep 4-15.

June 25: 7½ hours. Kaldren was snooping around the lab again today. Phoned me there, when I answered a recorded voice he'd rigged up rambled out a long string of numbers, like an insane super-Tim. These practical jokes of his get rather wearing. Fairly soon I'll have to go over and come to terms with him, much as I hate the prospect. Anyway, Miss Mars is a pleasure to look at.
One meal is enough now, topped up with a glucose shot. Sleep is still 'black', completely unrefreshing. Last night I took a 16 mm. film of the first three hours, screened it this morning at the lab. The first true horror movie, I looked like a half-animated corpse.
Woke 10-25. To sleep 3-45.

July 3: 5¾ hours. Little done today. Deepening lethargy, dragged myself over to the lab, nearly left the road twice. Concentrated enough to feed the zoo and get the log up to date. Read through the operating manuals Whitby left for the last time, decided on a delivery rate of 40 röntgens/min., target distance of 350 cm. Everything is ready now.
Woke 11-05. To sleep 3-15.

Powers stretched, shifted his head slowly across the pillow, focusing on the shadows cast on to the ceiling by the blind. Then he looked down at his feet, saw Kaldren sitting on the end of the bed, watching him quietly.

'Hello, doctor,' he said, putting out his cigarette. 'Late night? You look tired.'

Powers heaved himself on to one elbow, glanced at his watch. It was just after eleven. For a moment his brain blurred, and he swung his legs around and sat on the edge of the bed, elbows on his knees, massaging some life into his face.

He noticed that the room was full of smoke. 'What are you doing here?' he asked Kaldren.

'I came over to invite you to lunch.' He indicated the bedside phone. 'Your line was dead so I drove round. Hope you don't mind me climbing in. Rang the bell for about half an hour. I'm surprised you didn't hear it.'

Powers nodded, then stood up and tried to smooth the creases out of his cotton slacks. He had gone to sleep without changing for over a week, and they were damp and stale.

As he started for the bathroom door Kaldren pointed to the camera tripod on the other side of the bed. 'What's this? Going into the blue movie business, doctor?'

Powers surveyed him dimly for a moment, glanced at the tripod without replying and then noticed his open diary on the bedside table. Wondering whether Kaldren had read the last entries, he went back and picked it up, then stepped into the bathroom and closed the door behind him.

From the mirror cabinet he took out a syringe and an ampoule, after the shot leaned against the door waiting for the stimulant to pick up.

Kaldren was in the lounge when he returned to him, reading the labels on the crates lying about in the centre of the floor.

'Okay, then,' Powers told him, 'I'll join you for lunch.' He examined Kaldren carefully. He looked more subdued than usual, there was an air almost of deference about him.

'Good,' Kaldren said. 'By the way, are you leaving?'

'Does it matter?' Powers asked curtly. 'I thought you were in Anderson's care?'

Kaldren shrugged. 'Please yourself. Come round at about twelve,' he suggested, adding pointedly: 'That'll give you time to clean up and change. What's that all over your shirt? Looks like lime.'

Powers peered down, brushed at the white streaks. After Kaldren had left he threw the clothes away, took a shower and unpacked a clean suit from one of the trunks.

Until his liaison with Coma, Kaldren lived alone in the old abstract summer house on the north shore of the lake. This was a seven-storey folly originally built by an eccentric millionaire mathematician in the form of a spiralling concrete ribbon that wound around itself like an insane serpent, serving walls, floors and ceilings. Only Kaldren had solved the building, a geometric model of $\sqrt{-1}$, and consequently he had been able to take it off the agents' hands at a comparatively low rent. In the evenings Powers had often watched him from the laboratory, striding restlessly from one level to the next, swinging through the labyrinth of inclines and terraces to the roof-top, where his lean angular figure stood out like a gallows against the sky, his lonely eyes sifting out radio lanes for the next day's trapping.

Powers noticed him there when he drove up at noon, poised on a ledge 150 feet above, head raised theatrically to the sky.

'Kaldren!' he shouted up suddenly into the silent air, half-hoping he might be jolted into losing his footing.

Kaldren broke out of his reverie and glanced down into the court. Grinning obliquely, he waved his right arm in a slow semi-circle.

'Come up,' he called, then turned back to the sky.

Powers leaned against the car. Once, a few months previously, he had accepted the same invitation, stepped through the entrance and within three minutes lost himself helplessly in a second-floor cul-de-sac. Kaldren had taken half an hour to find him.

Powers waited while Kaldren swung down from his eyrie, vaulting through the wells and stairways, then rode up in the elevator with him to the penthouse suite.

They carried their cocktails through into a wide glass-roofed studio, the huge white ribbon of concrete uncoiling around them like toothpaste squeezed from an enormous tube. On the staged levels running parallel and across them rested pieces of grey abstract furniture, giant photographs on angled screens, carefully labelled exhibits laid out on low tables, all dominated by twenty-foot-high black letters on the rear wall which spelt out the single vast word:

YOU

Kaldren pointed to it. 'What you might call the supraliminal approach.' He gestured Powers in conspiratorially, finishing his drink in a gulp. 'This is *my* laboratory, doctor,' he said with a note of pride. 'Much more significant than yours, believe me.'

Powers smiled wryly to himself and examined the first exhibit, an old EEG tape traversed by a series of faded inky wriggles. It was labelled: 'Einstein, A.; Alpha Waves, 1922.'

He followed Kaldren around, sipping slowly at his drink, enjoying the brief feeling of alertness the amphetamine provided. Within two hours it would fade, leave his brain feeling like a block of blotting paper.

Kaldren chattered away, explaining the significance of the so-called Terminal Documents 'They're end-prints, Powers, final statements, the products of total fragmentation. When I've got enough together I'll build a new world for myself out of them.' He picked a thick paper-bound volume off one of the tables, riffled through its pages. 'Association tests of the Nuremberg Twelve. I have to include these . . .'

Powers strolled on absently without listening. Over in the corner were what appeared to be three ticker-tape machines, lengths of tape hanging from their mouths. He wondered whether Kaldren was misguided enough to be playing the stock market, which had been declining slowly for twenty years.

'Powers,' he heard Kaldren say. 'I was telling you about the Mercury Seven.' He pointed to a collection of typewritten sheets tacked to a screen. 'These are transcripts of their final signals radioed back from the recording monitors.'

Powers examined the sheets cursorily, read a line at random.

'. . . BLUE . . . PEOPLE . . . RE-CYCLE . . . ORION . . . TELEMETERS . . .'

Powers nodded noncommittally. 'Interesting. What are the ticker tapes for over there?'

Kaldren grinned. 'I've been waiting for months for you to ask me that. Have a look.'

Powers went over and picked up one of the tapes. The machine was labelled: 'Auriga 225-G. Interval: 69 hours.'

The tape read:

96,688,365,498,695
96,688,365,498,694
96,688,365,498,693
96,688,365,498,692

THE VOICES OF TIME

Powers dropped the tape. 'Looks rather familiar. What does the sequence represent?'

Kaldren shrugged. 'No one knows.'

'What do you mean? It must replicate something.'

'Yes, it does. A diminishing mathematical progression. A countdown, if you like.'

Powers picked up the tape on the right, tabbed: 'Aries 44R951. Interval: 49 days.'

Here the sequence ran:

$$876,567,988,347,779,877,654,434$$
$$876,567,988,347,779,877,654,433$$
$$876,567,988,347,779,877,654,432$$

Powers looked round. 'How long does it take each signal to come through?'

'Only a few seconds. They're tremendously compressed laterally, of course. A computer at the observatory breaks them down. They were first picked up at Jodrell Bank about twenty years ago. Nobody bothers to listen to them now.'

Powers turned to the last tape.

$$6,554$$
$$6,553$$
$$6,552$$
$$6,551$$

'Nearing the end of its run,' he commented. He glanced at the label on the hood, which read: 'Unidentified radio source, Canes Venatici. Interval: 97 weeks.'

He showed the tape to Kaldren. 'Soon be over.'

Kaldren shook his head. He lifted a heavy directory-sized volume off a table, cradled it in his hands. His face had suddenly become sombre and haunted. 'I doubt it,' he said. 'Those are only the last four digits. The whole number contains over 50 million.'

He handed the volume to Powers, who turned to the title

page. 'Master Sequence of Serial Signal received by Jodrell Bank Radio-Observatory, University of Manchester, England, 0012-59 hours, 21-5-72. Source: NGC 9743, Canes Venatici.' He thumbed the thick stack of closely printed pages, millions of numerals, as Kaldren had said, running up and down across a thousand consecutive pages.

Powers shook his head, picked up the tape again and stared at it thoughtfully.

'The computer only breaks down the last four digits,' Kaldren explained. 'The whole series comes over in each 15-second-long package, but it took IBM more than two years to unscramble one of them.'

'Amazing,' Powers commented. 'But what is it?'

'A countdown, as you can see. NGC 9743, somewhere in Canes Venatici. The big spirals there are breaking up, and they're saying goodbye. God knows who they think we are but they're letting us know all the same, beaming it out on the hydrogen line for everyone in the universe to hear.' He paused. 'Some people have put other interpretations on them, but there's one piece of evidence that rules out everything else.'

'Which is?'

Kaldren pointed to the last tape from Canes Venatici. 'Simply that it's been estimated that by the time this series reaches zero the universe will have just ended.'

Powers fingered the tape reflectively. 'Thoughtful of them to let us know what the real time is,' he remarked.

'I agree, it is,' Kaldren said quietly. 'Applying the inverse square law that signal source is broadcasting at a strength of about three million megawatts raised to the hundredth power. About the size of the entire Local Group. Thoughtful is the word.'

Suddenly he gripped Powers' arm, held it tightly and peered into his eyes closely, his throat working with emotion.

'You're not alone, Powers, don't think you are. These are the voices of time, and they're all saying goodbye to you. Think of yourself in a wider context. Every particle in your body, every grain of sand, every galaxy carries the same signature. As you've just said, you know what the time is now, so what does the rest matter? There's no need to go on looking at the clock.'

Powers took his hand, squeezed it firmly. 'Thanks, Kaldren. I'm glad you understand.' He walked over to the window, looked down across the white lake. The tension between himself and Kaldren had dissipated, he felt that all his obligations to him had at last been met. Now he wanted to leave as quickly as possible, forget him as he had forgotten the faces of the countless other patients whose exposed brains had passed between his fingers.

He went back to the ticker machines, tore the tapes from their slots and stuffed them into his pockets. 'I'll take these along to remind myself. Say goodbye to Coma for me, will you.'

He moved towards the door, when he reached it looked back to see Kaldren standing in the shadow of the three giant letters on the far wall, his eyes staring listlessly at his feet.

As Powers drove away he noticed that Kaldren had gone up on to the roof, watched him in the driving mirror waving slowly until the car disappeared around a bend.

FIVE

The outer circle was now almost complete. A narrow segment, an arc about ten feet long, was missing, but otherwise the low perimeter wall ran continuously six inches off the concrete floor around the outer lane of the target bull, enclosing the huge rebus within it. Three concentric circles, the largest a hundred yards in diameter, separated from each other by ten-foot intervals, formed the rim of the device, divided into four segments by the arms of an enormous cross radiating from its centre, where a small round platform had been built a foot above the ground.

Powers worked swiftly, pouring sand and cement into the mixer, tipping in water until a rough paste formed, then carried it across to the wooden forms and tamped the mixture down into the narrow channel.

Within ten minutes he had finished, quickly dismantled the forms before the cement had set and slung the timbers into the back seat of the car. Dusting his hands on his trousers, he went over to the mixer and pushed it fifty yards away into the long shadow of the surrounding hills.

Without pausing to survey the gigantic cipher on which he had laboured patiently for so many afternoons, he climbed into the car and drove off on a wake of bone-white dust, splitting the pools of indigo shadow.

He reached the laboratory at three o'clock, jumped from the car as it lurched back on its brakes. Inside the entrance he first switched on the lights, then hurried round, pulling the sun curtains down and shackling them to the floor slots, effectively turning the dome into a steel tent.

In their tanks behind him the plants and animals stirred quietly, responding to the sudden flood of cold fluorescent light. Only the chimpanzee ignored him. It sat on the floor of its cage, neurotically jamming the puzzle dice into the polythene bucket, exploding in bursts of sudden rage when the pieces refused to fit.

Powers went over to it, noticing the shattered glass fibre reinforcing panels bursting from the dented helmet. Already the chimp's face and forehead were bleeding from self-inflicted blows. Powers picked up the remains of the geranium that had been hurled through the bars, attracted the chimp's attention with it, then tossed a black pellet he had taken from a capsule in the desk drawer. The chimp caught it with a quick flick of the wrist, for a few seconds juggled the pellet with a couple of dice as it concentrated on the puzzle, then pulled it out of the air and swallowed it in a gulp.

Without waiting, Powers slipped off his jacket and stepped towards the X-ray theatre. He pulled back the high sliding doors to reveal the long glassy metallic snout of the Maxitron, then started to stack the lead screening shields against the rear wall.

A few minutes later the generator hummed into life.

The anemone stirred. Basking in the warm subliminal sea of radiation rising around it, prompted by countless pelagic memories, it reached tentatively across the tank, groping blindly towards the dim uterine sun. Its tendrils flexed, the thousands of dormant neural cells in their tips regrouping and multiplying, each harnessing the unlocked energies of its nucleus. Chains forged themselves, lattices tiered upwards into multi-faceted lenses, focused slowly on the vivid spectral outlines of the sounds dancing like phosphorescent waves around the darkened chamber of the dome.

Gradually an image formed, revealing an enormous black fountain that poured an endless stream of brilliant light over the circle of benches and tanks. Beside it a figure moved, adjusting the flow through its mouth. As it stepped across the floor its feet threw off vivid bursts of colour, its hands racing along the benches conjured up a dazzling chiaroscuro, balls of blue and violet light that exploded fleetingly in the darkness like miniature star-shells.

Photons murmured. Steadily, as it watched the glimmering screen of sounds around it, the anemone continued to expand. Its ganglia linked, heeding a new source of stimuli from the delicate diaphragms in the crown of its notochord. The silent outlines of the laboratory began to echo softly, waves of muted sound fell from the arc lights and echoed off the benches and furniture below. Etched in sound, their angular forms resonated with sharp persistent overtones. The plastic-ribbed chairs were a buzz of staccato discords, the square-sided desk a continuous double-featured tone.

Ignoring these sounds once they had been perceived, the anemone turned to the ceiling, which reverberated like a shield in the sounds pouring steadily from the fluorescent tubes. Streaming through a narrow skylight, its voice clear and strong, interweaved by numberless overtones, the sun sang . . .

It was a few minutes before dawn when Powers left the laboratory and stepped into his car. Behind him the great dome lay silently in the darkness, the thin shadows of the white moonlit hills falling across its surface. Powers freewheeled the car down the long curving drive to the lake road below, listening to the tyres cutting across the blue gravel, then let out the clutch and accelerated the engine.

As he drove along, the limestone hills half hidden in the

darkness on his left, he gradually became aware that, although no longer looking at the hills, he was still in some oblique way conscious of their forms and outlines in the back of his mind. The sensation was undefined but none the less certain, a strange almost visual impression that emanated most strongly from the deep clefts and ravines dividing one cliff face from the next. For a few minutes Powers let it play upon him, without trying to identify it, a dozen strange images moving across his brain.

The road swung up around a group of chalets built on to the lake shore, taking the car right under the lee of the hills, and Powers suddenly felt the massive weight of the escarpment rising up into the dark sky like a cliff of luminous chalk, and realized the identity of the impression now registering powerfully within his mind. Not only could he see the escarpment, but he was aware of its enormous age, felt distinctly the countless millions of years since it had first reared out of the magma of the earth's crust. The ragged crests three hundred feet above him, the dark gulleys and fissures, the smooth boulders by the roadside at the foot of the cliff, all carried a distinct image of themselves across to him, a thousand voices that together told of the total time that had elapsed in the life of the escarpment, a psychic picture defined and clear as the visual image brought to him by his eyes.

Involuntarily, Powers had slowed the car, and turning his eyes away from the hill face he felt a second wave of time sweep across the first. The image was broader but of shorter perspectives, radiating from the wide disc of the salt lake, breaking over the ancient limestone cliffs like shallow rollers dashing against a towering headland.

Closing his eyes, Powers lay back and steered the car along the interval between the two time fronts, feeling the images deepen and strengthen within his mind. The vast age of the landscape, the inaudible chorus of voices resonating from the lake and from the white hills, seemed to carry him back through time, down endless corridors to the first thresholds of the world.

He turned the car off the road along the track leading towards the target range. On either side of the culvert the cliff faces boomed and echoed with vast impenetrable time fields, like enormous opposed magnets. As he finally emerged between them on to the flat surface of the lake it seemed to Powers that he could feel the separate identity of each sand-grain and salt crystal calling to him from the surrounding ring of hills.

He parked the car beside the mandala and walked slowly towards the outer concrete rim curving away into the shadows. Above him he could hear the stars, a million cosmic voices that crowded the sky from one horizon to the next, a true canopy of time. Like jostling radio beacons, their long aisles interlocking at countless angles, they plunged into the sky from the narrowest recesses of space. He saw the dim red disc of Sirius, heard its ancient voice, untold millions of years old, dwarfed by the huge spiral nebulae in Andromeda, a gigantic carousel of vanished universes, their voices almost as old as the cosmos itself. To Powers the sky seemed an endless babel, the time-song of a thousand galaxies overlaying each other in his mind. As he moved slowly towards the centre of the mandala he craned up at the glittering traverse of the Milky Way, searching the confusion of clamouring nebulae and constellations.

Stepping into the inner circle of the mandala, a few yards from the platform at its centre, he realized that the tumult was beginning to fade, and that a single stronger voice had emerged and was dominating the others. He climbed on to the platform, raised his eyes to the darkened sky, moving through the constellations to the island galaxies beyond them, hearing the thin archaic voices reaching to him across the millennia. In his pockets he felt the paper tapes, and turned to find the distant diadem of Canes Venatici, heard its great voice mounting in his mind.

Like an endless river, so broad that its banks were below the horizons, it flowed steadily towards him, a vast course of time that spread outwards to fill the sky and the universe, enveloping everything within them. Moving slowly, the forward direction of its majestic current almost imperceptible, Powers knew that its source was the source of the cosmos itself. As it passed him, he felt its massive magnetic pull, let himself be drawn into it, borne gently on its powerful back. Quietly it carried him away, and he rotated slowly, facing the direction of the tide. Around him the outlines of the hills and the lake had faded, but the image of the mandala, like a cosmic clock, remained fixed before his eyes, illuminating the broad surface of the stream. Watching it constantly, he felt his body gradually dissolving, its physical dimensions melting into the vast continuum of the current, which bore him out into the centre of the great channel, sweeping him onward, beyond hope but at last at rest, down the broadening reaches of the river of eternity.

As the shadows faded, retreating into the hill slopes, Kaldren stepped out of his car, walked hesitantly towards the concrete rim of the outer circle. Fifty yards away, at the centre, Coma knelt beside Powers' body, her small hands pressed to his dead face. A gust of wind stirred the sand, dislodging a strip of tape that drifted towards Kaldren's feet. He bent down and picked it up, then rolled it carefully in his hands and slipped it into his pocket. The dawn air was cold, and he turned up the collar of his jacket, watching Coma impassively.

'It's six o'clock,' he told her after a few minutes. 'I'll go and get the police. You stay with him.' He paused and then added: 'Don't let them break the clock.'

Coma turned and looked at him. 'Aren't you coming back?'

'I don't know.' Nodding to her, Kaldren swung on his heel.

He reached the lake road, five minutes later parked the car in the drive outside Whitby's laboratory.

The dome was in darkness, all its windows shuttered, but the generator still hummed in the X-ray theatre. Kaldren stepped through the entrance and switched on the lights. In the theatre he touched the grilles of the generator, felt the warm cylinder of the beryllium end-window. The circular target table was revolving slowly, its setting at 1 r.p.m., a steel restraining chair shackled to it hastily. Grouped in a semicircle a few feet away were most of the tanks and cages, piled on top of each other haphazardly. In one of them an enormous squid-like plant had almost managed to climb from its vivarium. Its long translucent tendrils clung to the edges of the tank, but its body had burst into a jellified pool of globular mucilage. In another an enormous spider had trapped itself in its own web, hung helplessly in the centre of a huge three-dimensional maze of phosphorescing thread, twitching spasmodically.

All the experimental plants and animals had died. The chimp lay on its back among the remains of the hutch, the helmet forward over its eyes. Kaldren watched it for a moment, then sat down on the desk and picked up the phone.

While he dialled the number he noticed a film reel lying on the blotter. For a moment he stared at the label, then slid the reel into his pocket beside the tape.

After he had spoken to the police he turned off the lights and went out to the car, drove off slowly down the drive.

When he reached the summer house the early sunlight was breaking across the ribbon-like balconies and terraces. He took the lift to the penthouse, made his way through into the museum. One by one he opened the shutters and let the sunlight play over the exhibits. Then he pulled a chair over to a side window, sat back and stared up at the light pouring through into the room.

Two or three hours later he heard Coma outside, calling up to him. After half an hour she went away, but a little later a second voice appeared and shouted up at Kaldren. He left his chair and closed all the shutters overlooking the front courtyard, and eventually he was left undisturbed.

Kaldren returned to his seat and lay back quietly, his eyes gazing across the lines of exhibits. Half-asleep, periodically he leaned up and adjusted the flow of light through the shutter, thinking to himself, as he would do through the coming months, of Powers and his strange mandala, and of the seven and their journey to the white gardens of the moon, and the blue people who had come from Orion and spoken in poetry to them of ancient beautiful worlds beneath golden suns in the island galaxies, vanished for ever now in the myriad deaths of the cosmos.

1960

THE LAST WORLD OF MR GODDARD

For no apparent reason, the thunder particularly irritated Mr Goddard. All day, as he moved about his duties as ground floor supervisor, he listened to it booming and rolling in the distance, almost lost amid the noise and traffic of the department store. Twice, on some pretext, he took the lift up to the roof-top cafeteria and carefully scanned the sky, searching the horizons for any sign of storm-cloud or turbulence. As usual, however, the sky was a bland, impassive blue, mottled by a few clumps of leisurely cumuli.

This was what worried Mr Goddard. Leaning on the cafeteria railing he could hear the thunder distinctly, cleaving the air only a thousand feet above his head, the huge claps lumbering past like the colliding wing streams of enormous birds. Intermittently the sounds would stop, to re-start a few minutes later.

Mr Goddard was not the only one to notice them – the people at the tables on the terrace were craning up at the sourceless din, as perplexed as himself. Normally Mr Goddard would have exchanged some pleasantry with them – his elderly grey-haired figure in its old-world herringbone suit had been a byword for kindly concern for over twenty years – but today he hurried past without even looking at them. Down on the ground floor he felt less uneasy, but throughout the afternoon, while he roved among the busy counters, patting the children on the head, he listened to the thunder sounding faintly in the distance, inexplicable and strangely threatening.

At six o'clock he took up his position in the time-keeper's booth, waited impatiently until the final time card had been stamped, then handed over to the night watchman, and the last of the staff had left for home. As he made his way out, pulling on his ancient overcoat and deerstalker, the clear evening air was still stirred by occasional rumblings.

Mr Goddard's house was less than half a mile away, a small two-storey villa surrounded by tall hedges. Superficially dilapidated though still sound, at first glance it was indistinguishable from any other bachelor residence, although anyone entering the short drive would have noticed one unusual feature – all the windows, both upstairs and down, were securely shuttered. Indeed, they had remained shuttered for so long that the ivy growing across the front of the house had matted itself through the wooden slats, here and there pulling apart the rotting wood.

Closer inspection at these points would have revealed, behind the dusty panes, the interlocking diagonals of steel grilles.

Collecting a bottle of milk off the doorstep, Mr Goddard let himself into the kitchen. This was furnished with an armchair and a small couch, and served him as his living room. He busied himself preparing an evening meal. Halfway through, a neighbouring cat, a regular visitor, scratched at the door and was allowed in. They sat at the table together, the cat on its customary cushion up on one of the chairs, watching Mr Goddard with its small, hard eyes.

Shortly before eight o'clock Mr Goddard began his invariable evening routine. Opening the kitchen door, he glanced up and down the side entrance, then locked it behind him, securing both windows and door with a heavy drop bar. He next entered the hall, ushering the cat before him, and began his inspection of the house.

This was done with great care, using the cat as his sixth sense. Mr Goddard watched it carefully, noting its reactions as it wandered softly through the deserted rooms, singing remotely to itself.

The house was completely empty. Upstairs the floorboards were bare, the windows without curtains, lamp bulbs shadeless. Dust gathered in the corners and stained the fraying Victorian wallpaper. All the fireplaces had been bricked up, and the bare stonework above the mantels showed that the chimneys had been solidly filled in.

Once or twice Mr Goddard tested the grilles, which effectively turned the room into a succession of steel cages. Satisfied, he made his way downstairs and went into the front room, noting that nothing was amiss. He steered the cat into the kitchen, poured it a bowl of milk as a reward and slipped back into the hallway, latching the door behind him.

One room he had still not entered – the real lounge. Taking a key from his pocket, Mr Goddard turned the lock and let himself through.

Like the other rooms, this was bare and unfurnished, except for a wooden chair and a large black safe that stood with its back to one wall. The other distinctive feature was a single light bulb of considerable power suspended on an intricate pulley system from the centre of the ceiling.

Buttoning his jacket, Mr Goddard went over to the safe. Massive and ancient, it was approximately three feet wide and deep. Once it had been painted a dark bottle green, but by now most of the paint had peeled, revealing a dull black steel. A huge door, the full width and depth of the safe, was recessed into its face.

Beside the safe was the chair, a celluloid visor slung over its back. Mr Goddard pulled this on, giving himself the look of a refined elderly counterfeiter about to settle down to a hard evening's work. From his key chain he selected a small silver key, and fitted it into the lock. Turning the handle full circle, he drew the caissons back into the door, then pulled steadily with both hands and swung it open.

The safe was without shelves, a single continuous vault. Occupying the entire cavity, separated from the three-inch-thick walls by a narrow interval, was a large black tin document box.

Pausing to regain his breath, Mr Goddard heard a dull rumble of thunder sound through the darkness beyond the shuttered windows. Frowning involuntarily, he suddenly noticed a feathery thudding noise coming from inside the safe. He bent down and was just in time to see a large white moth emerge from the space above the document box, ricocheting erratically off the roof, at each impact sending a dull echo reverberating through the tin walls.

Mr Goddard smiled broadly to himself, as if divining something that had puzzled him all day. Leaning on the safe, he watched the moth circle the light, frantically shaking to pieces its damaged wings. Finally it plunged into one of the walls and fell stunned to the floor. Mr Goddard went over and swept it through the door with his foot, then returned to the safe. Reaching inside, with great care he lifted the document box out by the handles fastened to the centre of the lid.

The box was heavy. It required all Mr Goddard's efforts to steer it out without banging it against the safe, but with long practice he withdrew it in a single motion. He placed it gently on the floor, pulled up the chair and lowered the light until it was a few inches above his head. Releasing a catch below the lid, he tilted it back on its hinges.

Below him, brightly reflected in the light, was what appeared to be an elaborate doll's house. In fact, however, it was a whole complex of miniature buildings, perfectly constructed models with carefully detailed roof-tops and cornices, walls and brickwork so exactly duplicating the original that but for the penumbral figure of Mr Goddard looming out of the darkness they might have passed for real buildings and houses. The doors and windows were exquisitely worked, fitted with minute lattices and panes, each the size of a soap flake. The paving stones, the street furniture, the camber of the roadways, were perfect scale reductions.

The tallest building in the box was about fourteen inches high, containing six storeys. It stood at one corner of a crossroads that traversed the centre of the box, and was obviously a replica of the department store at which Mr Goddard worked. Its interior had been furnished and decorated with as much care as its external façade; through the windows could be seen the successive floors laid out with their miniature merchandise, rolls of carpet on the first, lingerie and women's fashions on the second, furniture on the third. The roof-top cafeteria had been equipped with small metal chairs and tables, set with plates, cutlery and bowls of tiny flowers.

On the corners to the left and right of the store were the bank and supermarket, with the town hall diagonally opposite. Again, these were perfect replicas of their originals: in the drawers behind the counters in the bank were bundles of minuscule banknotes, a glitter of coins like heaps of silver dust. The interior of the supermarket was an exercise in a thousand virtuosities. The stalls were stacked with pyramids of tins and coloured packets almost too small for the eye to distinguish.

Beyond the buildings dominating the crossroads were the lesser shops and premises lining the side-streets – the drapers, a public house, shoeshops and tobacconists. Looking around, the entire town seemed to stretch away into the distance. The walls of the box had been painted so skilfully, with such clever control of perspective, that it was almost impossible to tell where the models ended and the walls intervened. The micro-cosmic world was so perfect in its own right, the illusion of reality so absolute that it appeared to be the town itself, its very dimensions those of reality.

Suddenly, through the warm early morning sunlight, a shadow moved. The glass door of one of the shoeshops opened, a figure stepped out for a moment onto the pavement, glanced up and down the still deserted street, then retreated into the dark recesses of the shop's interior. A middle-aged man in a grey suit and white collar, it was presumably the manager opening the shop in the morning. In agreement with this, a second doorway opened farther down the street; and this time a woman came out of a hairdresser's, and began to wind down the blind. She wore a black skirt and pink plastic smock. As she went back into the salon she waved to someone walking down the street towards the town hall.

More figures emerged from the doorways, strolled along the pavements talking to each other, starting the day's business. Soon the streets were full; the offices over the shops came to life, typists moving in among the desks and filing cabinets. Signs were put up or taken down; calendars moved on. The first customers arrived at the department store and supermarket, ambled past the fresh counter displays. At the town hall clerks sat at their ledgers, in their private offices behind the oak panelling the senior officials had their first cups of tea. Like a well-ordered hive, the town came to life.

High above it all, his gigantic face hidden in the shadows, Mr Goddard quietly watched his lilliputian scene like a discreet aged Gulliver. He sat forward, the green shade shielding his eyes, hands clasped lightly in his lap. Occasionally he would lean over a few inches to catch a closer glimpse of the figures below him, or tilt his head to see into one of the shops or offices. His face showed no emotion, he seemed content to be simply a spectator. Two feet away the hundreds of tiny figures moved about their lives, and a low murmur of street noises crept out into the room.

The tallest of the figures were no more than an inch and a half in height, yet their perfectly formed faces were completely furnished with character and expression. Most of them Mr Goddard knew by sight, many by name. He saw Mrs Hamilton, the lingerie buyer, late for work, hurrying down the alleyway to the staff entrance. Through a window he could see the managing director's office, where Mr Sellings was delivering his usual weekly pep-talk to a trio of department heads. In the streets outside were scores of regular customers Mr Goddard had known intimately for years, buying their groceries, posting their letters, exchanging gossip.

As the scene below him unfolded, Mr Goddard gradually edged nearer the box, taking a particular interest in two or three of the score of separate tableaux. An interesting feature of his vantage point was that by some freak of architecture or perspective it afforded him a multiplicity of perfect angles by which to observe almost every one of the diminutive figures. The high windows of the bank provided him with a view of each of the clerks at their counters; a transom beyond exposed the strongroom, the rows of deposit boxes on their shelves behind the grille, one of the junior cashiers amusing himself by reading the labels. The department store, with its wide floors, he could cover merely by inclining his head. The smaller shops along the streets were just as exposed. Rarely more than two rooms deep, their rear windows and fanlights provided him all the access he needed. Nothing escaped Mr Goddard's scrutiny. In the back alleys he could see the stacked bicycles, the charwomen's mops in their buckets by the basement doors, the dustbins half-filled with refuse.

The first scene to attract Mr Goddard's attention was one involving the stockroom supervisor at the store, Mr Durrant. Casting his eye at random through the bank, Mr Goddard noticed him in the manager's office, leaning across the latter's desk and explaining something earnestly. Usually Durrant would have been a member of the group being harangued by Mr Sellings, and only urgent business could have taken him to the bank. The manager, however, appeared to be doing what he could to get rid of Durrant, avoiding his face and fiddling with some papers. Suddenly Durrant lost his temper. Tie askew, he began to shout angrily. The manager accepted this silently, shaking his head slowly with a bleak smile. Finally Durrant strode to the door, hesitated with a look of bitter reproach, and stalked out.

Leaving the bank, and apparently oblivious of his duties at the store, he walked briskly down the High Street. Stopping at the hairdresser's, he went in and made his way through to a private booth at the back where a large man in a check suit, still wearing a green trilby, was being shaved. Mr Goddard watched their conversation through a skylight above them. The man in the chair, the local bookmaker, lay back silently behind his lather until Durrant finished talking, then with a casual flip of one hand waved him to a seat.

Putting two and two together, Mr Goddard waited with interest for their conversation to be resumed. What he had just seen confirmed suspicions recently prompted by Durrant's distracted manner.

However, just as the bookmaker pulled off the towel and stood up, something more important caught Mr Goddard's eye.

Directly behind the department store was a small cul-de-sac sealed off from the alleyway leading in from the street by high wooden doors. It was piled with old packing cases and miscellaneous refuse, and its far side was formed by the rear wall of the box, a sheer cliff that rose straight up into the distant glare above. The glazed windows of a service lift shaft overlooked the yard, topped on the fifth floor by a small balcony.

It was this balcony that had attracted Mr Goddard's attention. Two men were crouched on it, manipulating a long wooden contraption that Mr Goddard identified as a telescopic ladder. Together they hoisted it into the air, and by pulling on a system of ropes extended it against the wall to a point about fifteen feet above their heads. Satisfied, they lashed the lower end securely to the balcony railings; then one of them mounted the ladder and climbed up to its topmost rung, arms outstretched across the wall, high over the yard below.

They were trying to escape from the box! Mr Goddard hunched forward, watching them with astonishment. The top of the ladder was still seven or eight inches from the overhanging rim of the box, thirty or forty feet away from the men on the balcony, but their industry was impressive. He watched them motionlessly while they tightened the guyropes.

Dimly, in the distance, midnight chimed. Mr Goddard looked at his watch, then without a further glance into the box pushed the lamp towards the ceiling and lowered the lid. He stood up and carried the box carefully to the safe, stowed it away, and sealed the door. Switching off the light, he let himself noiselessly out of the room.

The next day at the store Mr Goddard made his usual rounds, dispensing his invariable prescription of friendly chatter and *bonhomie* to sales assistants and customers alike, making full use of the countless trivial insights he had been provided with the previous evening. All the while he kept a constant lookout for Mr Durrant; reluctant to interfere, he was nevertheless afraid that without some drastic re-direction of the man's fortunes his entanglement with the bookmaker would soon end in tragedy.

No one in the stockrooms had seen Durrant all morning, but shortly after 12 o'clock Mr Goddard spotted him hurrying down the street past the main entrance. Durrant stopped, glanced around indecisively, then began to wander through the showcases as he pondered something.

Mr Goddard made his way out, and casually sidled up to Durrant.

'Fine day, isn't it?' he remarked. 'Everybody's starting to think about their holidays.'

Durrant nodded absently, examining a display of alpine equipment in the sports-goods window. 'Are they? Good.'

'You going away, Mr Durrant? South of France again, I suppose.'

'What? No, I don't think we will be this year.' Durrant began to move off, but Mr Goddard caught up with him.

'Sorry to hear that, Mr Durrant. I thought you deserved a good holiday abroad. Nothing the trouble, I hope.' He looked searchingly into Durrant's face. 'If I can help at all, do let me know. I'd be glad to make you a small loan. An old man like me hasn't much use for it.'

Durrant stopped and peered thoughtfully at Mr Goddard. 'That's kind of you, Goddard,' he said at last. 'Very kind.'

Mr Goddard smiled deprecatingly. 'Don't give it a thought. I like to stand by the firm, you know. Forgive me mentioning it, but would fifty be any use to you?'

Durrant's eyes narrowed slightly. 'Yes, it would be a lot of use.' — He paused, then asked quietly: 'Are you doing this off your own bat, or did Sellings put you up to it?'

'Put me up to it –?'

Durrant closed the interval between them, and in a harder voice rapped out: 'You must have been following me around for days. You know just about everything about everybody, don't you, Goddard? I've a damn good mind to report you.'

Mr Goddard backed away, wondering how to retrieve the

situation. Just then he noticed that they were alone at the showcases. The groups of people who usually milled around the windows were pressing into the alleyway beside the store; there was a lot of shouting in the distance.

'What the hell's going on?' Durrant snapped. He joined the crowd in the alleyway and peered over the heads.

Mr Goddard hurried back into the store. All the assistants were craning over their shoulders and whispering to each other; some had left the counters and were gathering around the service doors at the rear.

Mr Goddard pushed his way through, someone was calling for the police and a woman from the personnel department came down in the freight lift carrying a pair of blankets.

The commissionaire holding the throng back let Mr Goddard past. In the yard outside was a group of fifteen or twenty people, all looking up at the fifth-floor balcony. Tied to the railings was the lower half of a home-made ladder, jutting up into the air at an angle of 45 degrees. The top section, a limb about twelve feet long, had been lashed to the upper end, but the joint had failed, and the section now hung down vertically, swinging slowly from side to side above the heads of the people in the yard.

With an effort Mr Goddard controlled his voice. Someone had covered the two bodies with the blankets, and a man kneeling beside them – presumably a doctor – was shaking his head slowly.

'What I can't understand,' one of the assistant managers was whispering to the commissionaire, 'is where they were trying to climb to. The ladder must have pointed straight up into the air.'

The commissionaire nodded. 'Mr Masterman and Mr Streatfield, too. What would they be building a ladder for, senior men like that?'

Mr Goddard followed the line of the ladder up towards the sky. The rear wall of the yard was only seven or eight feet high, beyond it lay the galvanized iron roof of a bicycle shed and an open car park. The ladder had pointed nowhere, but the compulsion driving the two men had been blind and irresistible.

* * *

That evening Mr Goddard made the rounds of his house more perfunctorily than usual, glanced briefly into the empty rooms, closing the doors before the cat had a chance to do more than test the air. He shut it into the kitchen, then hurried off to unlock the safe.

Carrying the box out into the centre of the floor, he unlatched the lid.

As the town came to life below him he scrutinized it carefully, moving up and down the miniature streets, peering through all the windows in turn, fixing the identity and role of as many as possible of the tiny inhabitants. Like a thousand shuttles weaving an infinitely intricate pattern, they threaded through the shops and offices, in and out of countless doorways, every one of them touching a score of others somewhere among the pavements and arcades, adding another stitch to the tapestry of incident and motive ravelling their lives together. Mr Goddard traced each thread, trying to detect any shift in direction, and untoward interlocking of behaviour.

The pattern, he realized, was changing. As yet it was undefined, but slight variations were apparent, subtle shifts in the relationships between the people in the box: rival storekeepers seemed to be on intimate terms, strangers had begun to talk to each other, there was a great deal of unnecessary and purposeless activity.

Mr Goddard searched for a focus, an incident that would unmask the sources of the new pattern. He examined the balcony behind the lift shaft, watching for any further attempts to escape. The ladder had been removed but nothing had been done to replace it. Other potential escape routes – the roof of the cinema, the clock tower of the town hall – revealed no further clues.

One incident alone stood out, puzzling him even more. This was the unique spectacle, in a quiet alcove of the billiards saloon, of Mr Durrant introducing his bank manager to the bookmaker. The trio were still in earnest conversation when he closed the box reluctantly at two o'clock the next morning.

* * *

Over the following days Mr Goddard watched the crowds passing through the store, waiting to detect, as it were in the macrocosm, some of the tendencies he had observed in the box. His sixty-fifth birthday, soon due to fall, was a handy topic which provided ready conversational access to the senior members of the staff. Curiously, however, the friendly responses he expected were missing; the exchanges were brief, sometimes almost to the point of rudeness. This he put down to the changed atmosphere in the store since the deaths of the two ladder climbers. At the inquest there had been a confused hysterical outburst by one of the saleswomen, and the coroner had cryptically remarked that it appeared that information was being deliberately withheld. A murmur of agreement had spontaneously swept the entire room, but what exactly he meant no one seemed to know.

Another symptom of this uneasiness was the rash of notices that were handed in. Almost a third of the staff were due to leave, most of them for reasons that were patently little more than excuses. When Mr Goddard probed for the real reasons he discovered that few people were aware of them. The motivation was purely unconscious.

As if to emphasize this intrusion of the irrational, one evening as Mr Goddard was leaving the store he saw the bank manager standing high above the street on the clock tower of the town hall, gazing up into the sky.

During the next week little occurred within the box to clarify the situation. The shifting and regrouping of relationships continued. He saw the bank manager more and more in the company of the bookmaker, and realized that he had been completely mistaken in assuming that Durrant was under pressure of his gambling debts – in fact, his role seemed to be that of intermediary between the bookmaker and bank manager, who had at last been persuaded to join them in their scheme.

That some sort of conspiracy was afoot he was sure. At first he assumed that a mass break-out from the box was being planned, but nothing confirmed this. Rather he felt that some obscure compulsion, as yet unidentified to itself, was generating within the minds of those in the box, reflected in the bizarre and unpredictable behaviour of their counterparts in the outside world. Unconscious of their own motives and only half aware of themselves, his fellow employees at the store had begun to resemble the pieces of some enormous puzzle, like disjointed images fixed in the fragments of a shattered mirror. In conclusion he decided on a policy of *laissez-faire*. A few more weeks would certainly reveal the sources of the conspiracy.

Unfortunately, sooner than Mr Goddard anticipated, events moved forward rapidly to a spectacular crisis.

The day of his sixty-fifth birthday, he made his way to the store half an hour later than usual, and on arrival was told that Mr Sellings wished to see him.

Sellings first offered his congratulations, then launched into a recapitulation of Mr Goddard's years of service to the store, and concluded by wishing him as many years again of contented retirement.

It took Mr Goddard several moments to grasp the real significance of this. Nothing had ever been said to him about his retirement, and he had always assumed that he would stay on until, like many members of the staff, he was well into his seventies.

Collecting himself, he said as much to Sellings. 'I haven't exactly been expecting retirement, Mr Sellings. I think there must have been some mistake.'

Sellings stood up, shaking his head with a quick smile. 'No mistake at all, Mr Goddard, I assure you. As a matter of fact the board carefully considered your case yesterday, and we agreed that you well deserve an uninterrupted rest after all these years.'

Mr Goddard frowned. 'But I don't wish to retire, sir. I've made no plans.'

'Well, now's the time to start.' Sellings was on his way to the door, handshake ready. 'Comfortable pension, little house of your own, the world's your oyster.'

Mr Goddard sat tight, thinking quickly. 'Mr Sellings, I'm afraid I can't accept the board's decision. I'm sure, for the sake of the business, I should stay on in my present post.' The smile had gone from Sellings' face; he looked impatient and irritable. 'If you were to ask the floor managers and assistants, not to speak of the customers, they would all insist that I stay on. They would be very shocked at the suggestion of retirement.'

'Would they?' Sellings asked curtly. 'My information is to the contrary. Believe me, your retirement has come at a very lucky time for you, Mr Goddard. I've had a great number of complaints recently that otherwise I should have been obliged to act upon. Promptly and drastically.'

As he left the accounts department for the last time Mr Goddard numbly repeated these words to himself. He found them almost impossible to believe. And yet Sellings was a responsible man who would never take a single opinion on such an important matter. Somehow, though, he was colossally in error.

Or was he? As he made his farewell rounds, half-hoping that the news of his sudden retirement would rally support to him, Mr Goddard realized that Sellings was right. Floor by floor, department by department, counter by counter, he recognized the same inner expression, the same attitude of tacit approval. *They were all glad he was going.* Not one of them showed real regret; a good number slipped away before he could shake hands with them, others merely grunted briefly. Several of the older hands, who had known Mr Goddard for twenty or thirty years, seemed slightly embarrassed, but none of them offered a word of sympathy.

Finally, when one group in the furniture department deliberately turned their backs to avoid speaking to him, Mr Goddard cut short his tour. Stunned and humiliated, he collected his few possessions from his locker and made his way out.

It seemed to take him all day to reach his house. Head down, he walked slowly along the quiet side-streets, oblivious of the passers-by, pathetically trying to absorb this blow to all he had assumed about himself for so many years. His interest in other people was sincere and unaffected, he knew without doubt. Countless times he had gone out of his way to be of help to others, had put endless thought into arriving at the best solutions to their problems. But with what result? He had aroused only contempt, envy and distrust.

On his doorstep the cat waited patiently. Surprised to see him so early it ran forward, purring and rubbing itself against his legs as he latched the gate. But Mr Goddard failed to notice it. Fumbling, he unlocked the kitchen door, closed it automatically behind him. Taking off his coat, he made himself some tea, and without thinking poured a saucer of milk for the cat. He watched it drink, still trying helplessly to understand the antagonism he had aroused in so many people.

Suddenly he pushed his tea away and went to the door. Without bothering to go upstairs he made his way straight into the lounge. Switching on the light, he stared heavily at the safe. Somewhere here, he knew, was the reason for his dismissal that morning. If only his eyes were sharp enough, he would discover it.

Unlocking the safe, he unclasped the door and pulled it back abruptly, wrenching himself slightly against its great inertia. Impatient to open the box he ignored the twinge in his shoulder, reached down and seized the butterfly handles.

As he swung the box out of the safe he realized that its weight was, momentarily, too much for him. Trying to brace himself, he edged one knee under the box and leaned his elbows on the lid, his shoulder against the safe.

The position was awkward, and he could only support it for a few seconds. Heaving again at the box, in an effort to replace it in the safe, he suddenly began to feel dizzy. A small spiral revolved before his eyes, gradually thickening into a deep black whirlpool that filled his head.

Before he could restrain it, the box tore itself from his hands and plunged to the floor with a violent metallic clatter.

Kneeling beside the safe, Mr Goddard slumped back limply against the wall, head lolling onto his chest.

The box lay on its side, just within the circle of light. The impact had forced the catches on the lid, and this was now open; a single narrow beam reflected off the under-surface into the interior of the box.

For a few minutes the room was quiet, except for the laboured uneven sounds of Mr Goddard's breathing. Then, almost imperceptibly, something moved in the interval between the lid and the floor. A small figure stepped tentatively out of the shadow, peered around itself in the full glare of the light, and disappeared again. Ten seconds later three more figures emerged, followed by others. In small groups they spread out across the floor, their tiny legs and arms rippling in the light. Behind them a score more appeared, pressing out in a solid stream, pushing past each other to escape from the box. Soon the circle of light was alive with swarms of the tiny figures, flickering like minnows in a floodlit pool.

In the darkness by the corner, the door creaked sharply. Together, the hundreds of figures froze. Eyes glinting suspiciously, the head of Mr Goddard's cat swung round into the room. For a moment it paused, assessing the scene before it.

A sharp cry hissed through its teeth. With vicious speed, it bounded forward.

It was several hours later that Mr Goddard pulled himself slowly to his feet. Leaning weakly against the safe, he looked down at the upended safe beneath the bright cone of light. Carefully collecting himself, he rubbed his cheekbones and painfully massaged his chest and shoulders. Then he limped across to the box and steered it back onto its base. Gingerly, he lifted the lid and peered inside.

Abruptly he dropped the lid, glanced around the floor, swinging the light so that it swept the far corners. Then he turned and hurried out into the hall, switched on the light and examined the floor carefully, along the skirting boards and behind the grilles.

Over his shoulder he noticed that the kitchen door was open. He crossed to it and stepped in on tiptoe, eyes ranging between the table and chair legs, behind the broom and coal bucket.

'Sinbad!' Mr Goddard shouted.

Startled, the cat dropped the tiny object between its paws and backed away below the couch.

Mr Goddard bent down. He stared hard at the object for a few seconds, then stood up and leaned against the cupboard, his eyes closing involuntarily.

The cat pounced, its teeth flickering at its paws. It gulped noisily.

'Sinbad,' Mr Goddard said in a quieter voice. He gazed listlessly at the cat, finally stepped over to the door.

'Come outside,' he called to it.

The cat followed him, its tail whipping slowly from side to side. They walked down the pathway to the gate. Mr Goddard looked at his watch. It was 2.45, early afternoon. The houses around him were silent, the sky a distant, pacific blue. Here and there sunlight was reflected off one of the upstairs bay windows, but the street was motionless, its stillness absolute and unbroken.

Mr Goddard gestured the cat onto the pavement and closed the gate behind it.

Together they walked out into an empty world.

1960

STUDIO 5, THE STARS

Every evening during the summer at Vermilion Sands the insane poems of my beautiful neighbour drifted across the desert to me from Studio 5, The Stars, the broken skeins of coloured tape unravelling in the sand like the threads of a dismembered web. All night they would flutter around the buttresses below the terrace, entwining themselves through the balcony railings, and by morning, before I swept them away, they would hang across the south face of the villa like a vivid cerise bougainvillaea.

Once, after I had been to Red Beach for three days, I returned to find the entire terrace filled by an enormous cloud of coloured tissues, which burst through the french windows as I opened them and pushed into the lounge, spreading across the furniture and bookcases like the delicate tendrils of some vast and gentle plant. For days afterwards I found fragments of the poems everywhere.

I complained several times, walking the three hundred yards across the dunes to deliver a letter of protest, but no one ever answered the bell. I had only once seen my neighbour, on the day she arrived, driving down the Stars in a huge El Dorado convertible, her long hair swept behind her like the head-dress of a goddess. She had vanished in a glimmer of speed, leaving me with a fleeting image of sudden eyes in an ice-white face.

Why she refused to answer her bell I could never understand, but I noticed that each time I walked across to Studio 5 the sky was full of sand-rays, wheeling and screeching like anguished bats. On the last occasion, as I stood by her black glass front door, deliberately pressing the bell into its socket, a giant sand-ray had fallen out of the sky at my feet.

But this, as I realized later, was the crazy season at Vermilion

Sands, when Tony Sapphire heard a sand-ray singing, and I saw the god Pan drive by in a Cadillac.

Who was Aurora Day, I often ask myself now. Sweeping across the placid out-of-season sky like a summer comet, she seems to have appeared in a different role to each of us at the colony along the Stars. To me, at first, she was a beautiful neurotic disguised as a *femme fatale*, but Raymond Mayo saw her as one of Salvador Dali's exploding madonnas, an enigma serenely riding out the apocalypse. To Tony Sapphire and the rest of her followers along the beach she was a reincarnation of Astarte herself, a diamond-eyed time-child thirty centuries old.

I can remember clearly how I found the first of her poems. After dinner one evening I was resting on the terrace – something I did most of the time at Vermilion Sands – when I noticed a streamer lying on the sand below the railing. A few yards away were several others, and for half an hour I watched them being blown lightly across the dunes. A car's headlamps shone in the drive at Studio 5, and I assumed that a new tenant had moved into the villa, which had stood empty for several months.

Finally, out of curiosity, I straddled the rail, jumped down on to the sand and picked up one of the ribbons of pink tissue. It was a fragment about three feet long, the texture of rose petal, so light that it began to flake and dissolve in my fingers.

Holding it up I read: ... COMPARE THEE TO A SUMMER'S DAY, THOU ART MORE LOVELY ...

I let it flutter away into the darkness below the balcony, then bent down and carefully picked up another, disentangling it from one of the buttresses.

Printed along it in the same ornate neo-classical type was: ... SET KEEL TO BREAKERS, FORTH ON THAT GODLY SEA ...

I looked over my shoulder. The light over the desert had gone now, and three hundred yards away my neighbour's villa was lit like a spectral crown. The exposed quartz veins in the sand reefs along the Stars rippled like necklaces in the sweeping headlights of the cars driving into Red Beach.

I glanced at the tape again.

Shakespeare and Ezra Pound? My neighbour had the most curious tastes. My interest fading, I returned to the terrace.

Over the next few days the streamers continued to blow across the dunes, for some reason always starting in the evening, when the lights of the traffic illuminated the lengths of coloured gauze. But to begin with I hardly noticed them – I was then editing *Wave IX*, an avant-garde poetry review, and the studio was full of auto-tapes and old galley proofs. Nor was I particularly surprised to find I had a poetess for my neighbour. Almost all the studios along the Stars are occupied by painters and poets – the majority abstract and non-productive. Most of us were suffering from various degrees of beach fatigue, that chronic malaise which exiles the victim to a limbo of endless sunbathing, dark glasses and afternoon terraces.

Later, however, the streamers drifting across the sand became rather more of a nuisance. When the protest notes achieved nothing I went over to my neighbour's villa with a view to seeing her in person. On this last occasion, after a dying ray had plummeted out of the sky and nearly stung me in its final spasm, I realized that there was little chance of reaching her.

A hunchbacked chauffeur with a club foot and a twisted face like a senile faun's was cleaning the cerise Cadillac in the drive. I went over to him and pointed to the strands of tissue trailing through the first-floor windows and falling on to the desert below.

'These tapes are blowing all over my villa,' I told him. 'Your mistress must have one of her VT sets on open sequence.'

He eyed me across the broad hood of the El Dorado, sat down in the driving seat and took a small flute from the dashboard.

As I walked round to him he began to play some high, irritating chords. I waited until he had finished and asked in a louder voice: 'Do you mind telling her to close the windows?'

He ignored me, his lips pressed moodily to the flute. I bent down and was about to shout into his ear when a gust of wind swirled across one of the dunes just beyond the drive, in an instant whirled over the gravel, flinging up a miniature tornado of dust and ash. This miniature tornado completely enclosed us, blinding my eyes and filling my mouth with grit. Arms shielding my face, I moved away towards the drive, the long streamers whipping around me.

As suddenly as it had started, the squall vanished. The dust stilled and faded, leaving the air as motionless as it had been a few moments previously. I saw that I had backed about thirty yards down the drive, and to my astonishment realized that the Cadillac and chauffeur had disappeared, although the garage door was still open.

My head rang strangely, and I felt irritable and short of breath. I was about to approach the house again, annoyed at having been refused entry and left to suffer the full filthy impact of the dust squall, when I heard the thin piping refrain sound again into the air.

Low, but clear and strangely menacing, it sang in my ears, the planes of sound shifting about me in the air. Looking around for its source, I noticed the dust flicking across the surface of the dunes on either side of the drive.

Without waiting, I turned on my heel and hurried back to my villa.

Angry with myself for having been made such a fool of, and resolved to press some formal complaint, I first went around the terrace, picking up all the strands of tissue and stuffing them into the disposal chute. I climbed below the villa and cut away the tangled masses of streamers.

Cursorily, I read a few of the tapes at random. All printed the same erratic fragments, intact phrases from Shakespeare, Wordsworth, Keats and Eliot. My neighbour's VT set appeared to have a drastic memory fault, and instead of producing a variant on the classical model the selector head was simply regurgitating a dismembered version of the model itself. For a moment I thought seriously of telephoning the IBM agency in Red Beach and asking them to send a repair man round.

*   *   *

That evening, however, I finally spoke to my neighbour in person.

I had gone to sleep at about eleven, and an hour or so later something woke me. A bright moon was at apogee, moving behind strands of pale green cloud that cast a thin light over the desert and the Stars. I stepped out on to the veranda and immediately noticed a curiously luminescent glow moving between the dunes. Like the strange music I had heard from the chauffeur's flute, the glow appeared to be sourceless, but I assumed it was cast by the moon shining through a narrow interval between the clouds.

Then I saw her, appearing for a moment among the dunes, strolling across the midnight sand. She wore a long white gown that billowed out behind her, against which her blue hair drifted loosely in the wind like the tail-fan of a paradise bird. Streamers floated about her feet, and overhead two or three purple rays circled endlessly. She walked on, apparently unaware of them, a single light behind her shining through an upstairs window of her villa.

Belting my dressing gown, I leaned against a pillar and watched her quietly, for the moment forgiving her the streamers and her ill-trained chauffeur. Occasionally she disappeared behind one of the green-shadowed dunes, her head raised slightly, moving from the boulevard towards the sand reefs on the edge of the fossil lake.

She was about a hundred yards from the nearest sand reef, a long inverted gallery of winding groynes and over-hanging grottoes, when something about her straight path and regular unvarying pace made me wonder whether she might in fact be sleepwalking.

I hesitated briefly, watching the rays circling around her head, then jumped over the rail and ran across the sand towards her.

The quartz flints stung at my bare feet, but I managed to reach her just as she neared the edge of the reef. I broke into a walk beside her and touched her elbow.

Three feet above my head the rays spat and whirled in the

darkness. The strange luminosity that I had assumed came from the moon seemed rather to emanate from her white gown.

My neighbour was not somnambulating, as I thought, but lost in some deep reverie or dream. Her black eyes stared opaquely in front of her, her slim white-skinned face like a marble mask, motionless and without expression. She looked round at me sightlessly, one hand gesturing me away. Suddenly she stopped and glanced down at her feet, abruptly becoming aware of herself and her midnight walk. Her eyes cleared and she saw the mouth of the sand reef. She stepped back involuntarily, the light radiating from her gown increasing with her alarm.

Overhead the rays soared upwards into the air, their arcs wider now that she was awake.

'Sorry to startle you,' I apologized. 'But you were getting too close to the reef.'

She pulled away from me, her long black eyebrows arching.

'What?' she said uncertainly. 'Who are you?' To herself, as if completing her dream, she murmured *sotto voce*: 'Oh God, Paris, choose me, not Minerva –' She broke off and stared at me wildly, her carmine lips fretting. She strode off across the sand, the rays swinging like pendulums through the dim air above her, taking with her the pool of amber light.

I waited until she reached her villa and turned away. Glancing at the ground, I noticed something glitter in the small depression formed by one of her footprints. I bent down, picked up a small jewel, a perfectly cut diamond of a single carat, then saw another in the next footprint. Hurrying forwards, I picked up half-a-dozen of the jewels, and was about to call out after her disappearing figure when I felt something wet in my hand.

Where I had held the jewels in the hollow of my palm now swam a pool of ice-cold dew.

I found out who she was the next day.

After breakfast I was in the bar when I saw the El Dorado turn into the drive. The club-footed chauffeur jumped from the car and hobbled over in his curious swinging gait to the front door. In his black-gloved hand he carried a pink envelope. I let him wait a few minutes, then opened the letter on the step as he went back to the car and sat waiting for me, his engine running.

I'm sorry to have been so rude last night. You stepped right into my dream and startled me. Could I make amends by offering you a cocktail? My chauffeur will collect you at noon.

AURORA DAY

I looked at my watch. It was 11:55. The five minutes, presumably, gave me time to compose myself.

The chauffeur was studying his driving wheel, apparently indifferent to my reaction. Leaving the door open, I stepped inside and put on my beach-jacket. On the way out I slipped a proof copy of *Wave IX* into one of the pockets.

The chauffeur barely waited for me to climb in before moving the big car rapidly down the drive.

'How long are you staying in Vermilion Sands?' I asked, addressing the band of curly russet hair between the peaked cap and black collar.

He said nothing. As we drove along the Stars he suddenly cut out into the oncoming lane and gunned the Cadillac forward in a tremendous burst of speed to overtake a car ahead.

Settling myself, I put the question again and waited for him to reply, then smartly tapped his black serge shoulder.

'Are you deaf, or just rude?'

For a second he took his eyes off the road and glanced back at me. I had a momentary impression of bright red pupils, ribald eyes that regarded me with a mixture of contempt and unconcealed savagery. Out of the side of his mouth came a sudden cackling stream of violent imprecations, a short filthy blast that sent me back into my seat.

He jumped out when we reached Studio 5 and opened the door for me, beckoning me up the black marble steps like an attendant spider ushering a very small fly into a particularly large web.

Once inside the doorway he seemed to disappear. I walked through the softly lit hall towards an interior pool where a fountain played and white carp circled tirelessly. Beyond it, in the lounge, I could see my neighbour reclining on a chaise longue, her white gown spread around her like a fan, the jewels embroidered into it glittering in the fountain light.

As I sat down she regarded me curiously, putting away a slender volume bound in yellow calf which appeared to be a private edition of poems. Scattered across the floor beside her was a miscellaneous array of other volumes, many of which I could identify as recently printed collections and anthologies.

I noticed a few coloured streamers trailing through the curtains by the window, and glanced around to see where she kept her VT set, helping myself to a cocktail off the low table between us.

'Do you read a lot of poetry?' I asked, indicating the volumes around her.

She nodded. 'As much as I can bear to.'

I laughed. 'I know what you mean. I have to read rather more than I want.' I took a copy of *Wave IX* from my pocket and passed it to her. 'Have you come across this one?'

She glanced at the title page, her manner moody and autocratic. I wondered why she had bothered to ask me over. 'Yes, I have. Appalling, isn't it? "Paul Ransom",' she noted. 'Is that you? You're the editor? How interesting.'

She said it with a peculiar inflection, apparently considering some possible course of action. For a moment she watched me reflectively. Her personality seemed totally dissociated, her awareness of me varying abruptly from one level to another, like light-changes in a bad motion picture. However, although her mask-like face remained motionless, I none the less detected a quickening of interest.

'Well, tell me about your work. You must know so much about what is wrong with modern poetry. Why is it all so bad?'

I shrugged. 'I suppose it's principally a matter of inspiration. I used to write a fair amount myself years ago, but the impulse faded as soon as I could afford a VT set. In the old days a poet had to sacrifice himself in order to master his medium. Now that technical mastery is simply a question of pushing a button, selecting metre, rhyme, assonance on a dial, there's no need for sacrifice, no ideal to invent to make the sacrifice worthwhile –'

I broke off. She was watching me in a remarkably alert way, almost as if she were going to swallow me.

Changing the tempo, I said: 'I've read quite a lot of your poetry, too. Forgive me mentioning it, but I think there's something wrong with your Verse-Transcriber.'

Her face snapped and she looked away from me irritably. 'I haven't got one of those dreadful machines. Heavens above, you don't think *I* would use one?'

'Then where do the tapes come from?' I asked. 'The streamers that drift across every evening. They're covered with fragments of verse.'

Off-handedly, she said: 'Are they? Oh, I didn't know.' She looked down at the volumes scattered about on the floor. 'Although I should be the last person to write verse, I have been forced to recently. Through sheer necessity, you see, to preserve a dying art.'

She had baffled me completely. As far as I could remember, most of the poems on the tapes had already been written.

She glanced up and gave me a vivid smile.

'I'll send you some.'

The first ones arrived the next morning. They were delivered by the chauffeur in the pink Cadillac, neatly printed on quarto vellum and sealed by a floral ribbon. Most of the poems submitted to me come through the post on computer punch-tape, rolled up like automat tickets, and it was certainly a pleasure to receive such elegant manuscripts.

The poems, however, were impossibly bad. There were six in all, two Petrarchan sonnets, an ode and three free-form longer pieces. All were written in the same hectoring tone, at once minatory and obscure, like the oracular deliriums of an insane witch. Their overall import was strangely disturbing, not so much for the content of the poems as for the deranged mind behind them. Aurora Day was obviously living in a private world which she took very seriously indeed. I decided that she was a wealthy neurotic able to over-indulge her private fantasies.

I flipped through the sheets, smelling the musk-like scent that misted up from them. Where had she unearthed this curious style, these archaic mannerisms, the 'arise, earthly seers, and to thy ancient courses pen now thy truest vows'? Mixed up in some of the metaphors were odd echoes of Milton and Virgil. In fact, the whole tone reminded me of the archpriestess in the Aeneid who lets off blistering tirades whenever Aeneas sits down for a moment to relax.

I was still wondering what exactly to do with the poems – promptly on nine the next morning the chauffeur had delivered a second batch – when Tony Sapphire called to help me with the make-up of the next issue. Most of the time he spent at his beach-chalet at Lagoon West, programming an automatic novel, but he put in a day or two each week on *Wave IX*.

I was checking the internal rhyme chains in an IBM sonnet sequence of Xero Paris's as he arrived. While I held the code chart over the sonnets, checking the rhyme lattices, he picked up the sheets of pink quarto on which Aurora's poems were printed.

'Delicious scent,' he commented, fanning the sheets through the air. 'One way to get round an editor.' He started to read the first of the poems, then frowned and put it down.

'Extraordinary. What are they?'

'I'm not altogether sure,' I admitted. 'Echoes in a stone garden.'

Tony read the signature at the bottom of the sheets. '"Aurora Day." A new subscriber, I suppose. She probably thinks *Wave IX* is the *VT Times*. But what is all this – "nor psalms, nor canticles, nor hollow register to praise the queen of night –"?' He shook his head. 'What are they supposed to be?'

I smiled at him. Like most other writers and poets, he had spent so long sitting in front of his VT set that he had forgotten the period when poetry was actually handspun.

'They're poems, of a sort, obviously.'

'Do you mean she wrote these herself?'

I nodded. 'It has been done that way. In fact the method

enjoyed quite a vogue for twenty or thirty centuries. Shakespeare tried it, Milton, Keats and Shelley – it worked reasonably well then.'

'But not now,' Tony said. 'Not since the VT set. How can you compete with an IBM heavy-duty logomatic analogue? Look at this one, for heaven's sake. It sounds like T.S. Eliot. She can't be serious.'

'You may be right. Perhaps the girl's pulling my leg.'

'Girl. She's probably sixty and tipples her eau de cologne. Sad. In some insane way they may mean something.'

'Hold on,' I told him. I was pasting down one of the Xero's satirical pastiches of Rupert Brooke and was six lines short. I handed Tony the master tape and he played it into the IBM, set the metre, rhyme scheme, verbal pairs, and then switched on, waited for the tape to chunter out of the delivery head, tore off six lines and passed them back to me. I didn't even need to read them.

For the next two hours we worked hard. At dusk we had completed over one thousand lines and broke off for a well-earned drink. We moved on to the terrace and sat, in the cool evening light, watching the colours melting across the desert, listening to the sand-rays cry in the darkness by Aurora's villa.

'What are all these streamers lying around under here?' Tony asked. He pulled one towards him, caught the strands as they broke in his hand and steered them on to the glass-topped table.

'"– nor canticles, nor hollow register –"' He read the line out, then released the tissue and let it blow away on the wind.

He peered across the shadow-covered dunes at Studio 5. As usual a single light was burning in one of the upper rooms, illuminating the threads unravelling in the sand as they moved towards us.

Tony nodded. 'So that's where she lives.' He picked up another of the streamers that had coiled itself through the railing and was fluttering instantly at his elbow.

'You know, old sport, you're quite literally under siege.'

*   *   *

I was. During the next days a ceaseless bombardment of ever more obscure and bizarre poems reached me, always in two instalments, the first brought by the chauffeur promptly at nine o'clock each morning, the second that evening when the streamers began to blow across the dusk to me. The fragments of Shakespeare and Pound had gone now, and the streamers carried fragmented versions of the poems delivered earlier in the day, almost as if they represented her working drafts. Examining the tapes carefully I realized that, as Aurora Day had said, they were not produced by a VT set. The strands were too delicate to have passed through the spools and high-speed cams of a computer mechanism, and the lettering along them had not been printed but embossed by some process I was unable to identify.

Each day I read the latest offerings, carefully filed them away in the centre drawer of my desk. Finally, when I had a week's production stacked together, I placed them in a return envelope, addressed it 'Aurora Day, Studio 5, The Stars, Vermilion Sands', and penned a tactful rejection note, suggesting that she would feel ultimately more satisfied if her work appeared in another of the wide range of poetry reviews.

That night I had the first of what was to be a series of highly unpleasant dreams.

Making myself some strong coffee the next morning, I waited blearily for my mind to clear. I went on to the terrace, wondering what had prompted the savage nightmare that had plagued me through the night. The dream had been the first of any kind I had had for several years – one of the pleasant features of beach fatigue is a heavy dreamless sleep, and the sudden irruption of a dream-filled night made me wonder whether Aurora Day, and more particularly her insane poems, were beginning to prey on my mind more than I realized.

My headache took a long time to dissipate. I lay back, watching the Day villa, its windows closed and shuttered, awnings retracted, like a sealed crown. Who was she anyway, I asked myself, and what did she really want?

Five minutes later, I saw the Cadillac swing out of the drive and coast down the Stars towards me.

Not another delivery! The woman was tireless. I waited by the front door, met the driver halfway down the steps and took from him a wax-sealed envelope.

'Look,' I said to him confidentially. 'I'd hate to discourage an emerging talent, but I think you might well use any influence you have on your mistress and, you know, generally ...' I let the idea hang in front of him, and added: 'By the way, all these streamers that keep blowing across here are getting to be a damn nuisance.'

The chauffeur regarded me out of his red-rimmed foxy eyes, his beaked face contorted in a monstrous grin. Shaking his head sadly, he hobbled back to the car.

As he drove off I opened the letter. Inside was a single sheet of paper.

Mr Ransom,
Your rejection of my poems astounds me. I seriously advise you to reconsider your decision. This is no trifling matter. I expect to see the poems printed in your next issue.

AURORA DAY

That night I had another insane dream.

The next selection of poems arrived when I was still in bed, trying to massage a little sanity back into my mind. I climbed out of bed and made myself a large Martini, ignoring the envelope jutting through the door like the blade of a paper spear.

When I had steadied myself I slit it open, and scanned the three short poems included.

They were dreadful. Dimly I wondered how to persuade Aurora that the requisite talent was missing. Holding the Martini in one hand and peering at the poems in the other, I ambled on to the terrace and slumped down in one of the chairs.

With a shout I sprang into the air, knocking the glass out of my hand. I had sat down on something large and spongy, the size of a cushion but with uneven bony contours.

Looking down, I saw an enormous dead sand-ray lying in the centre of the seat, its white-tipped sting, still viable, projecting a full inch from its sheath above the cranial crest.

Jaw clamped angrily, I went straight into my study, slapped the three poems into an envelope with a rejection slip and scrawled across it: 'Sorry, entirely unsuitable. Please try other publications.'

Half an hour later I drove down to Vermilion Sands and mailed it myself. As I came back I felt quietly pleased with myself.

That afternoon a colossal boil developed on my right cheek.

Tony Sapphire and Raymond Mayo came round the next morning to commiserate. Both thought I was being pigheaded and pedantic.

'Print one,' Tony told me, sitting down on the foot of the bed.

'I'm damned if I will,' I said. I stared out across the desert at Studio 5. Occasionally a window moved and caught the sunlight but otherwise I had seen nothing of my neighbour.

Tony shrugged. 'All you've got to do is accept one and she'll be satisfied.'

'Are you sure?' I asked cynically. 'This may be only the beginning. For all we know she may have a dozen epics in the bottom of her suitcase.'

Raymond Mayo wandered over to the window beside me, slipped on his dark glasses and scrutinized the villa. I noticed that he looked even more dapper than usual, dark hair smoothed back, profile adjusted for maximum impact.

'I saw her at the "psycho i" last night,' he mused. 'She had a private balcony upon the mezzanine. Quite extraordinary. They had to stop the floor show twice.' He nodded to himself. 'There's something formless and unstated there, reminded me of Dali's "Cosmogonic Venus". Made me realize how absolutely terrifying all women really are. If I were you I'd do whatever I was told.'

I set my jaw, as far as I could, and shook my head dogmatically.

'Go away. You writers are always pouring scorn on editors, but when things get tough who's the first to break? This is the sort of situation I'm prepared to handle, my whole training and discipline tell me instinctively what to do. That crazy neurotic over there is trying to bewitch me. She thinks she can call down a plague of dead rays, boils and nightmares and I'll surrender my conscience.'

Shaking their heads sadly over my obduracy, Tony and Raymond left me to myself.

Two hours later the boil had subsided as mysteriously as it had appeared. I was beginning to wonder why when a pick-up from The Graphis Press in Vermilion Sands delivered the advance five-hundred of the next issue of *Wave IX*.

I carried the cartons into the lounge, then slit off the wrapping, thinking pleasurably of Aurora Day's promise that she would have her poems published in the next issue. She had failed to realize that I had passed the final pages two days beforehand, and that I could hardly have printed her poems even if I had wanted to.

Opening the pages, I turned to the editorial, another in my series of examinations of the present malaise affecting poetry.

However, in place of the usual half-dozen paragraphs of 10-point type I was astounded to see a single line of 24-point, announcing in italic caps:

A CALL TO GREATNESS!

I broke off, hurriedly peered at the cover to make sure Graphis had sent me advance copies of the right journal, then raced rapidly through the pages.

The first poem I recognized immediately. I had rejected it only two days earlier. The next three I had also seen and rejected, then came a series that were new to me, all signed 'Aurora Day' and taking the place of the poems I had passed in page proof.

The entire issue had been pirated! Not a single one of the original poems remained, and a completely new make-up had been substituted. I ran back into the lounge and opened a dozen copies. They were all the same.

Ten minutes later I had carried the three cartons out to the incinerator, tipped them in and soaked the copies with petrol, then tossed a match into the centre of the pyre. Simultaneously, a few miles away Graphis Press were doing the same to the remainder of the 5,000 imprint. How the misprinting had occurred they could not explain. They searched out the copy, all on Aurora's typed notepaper, but with editorial markings in my handwriting! My own copy had disappeared, and they soon denied they had ever received it.

As the heavy flames beat into the hot sunlight I thought that through the thick brown smoke I could see a sudden burst of activity coming from my neighbour's house. Windows were opening under the awnings, and the hunchbacked figure of the chauffeur was scurrying along the terrace.

Standing on the roof, her white gown billowing around her like an enormous silver fleece, Aurora Day looked down at me.

Whether it was the large quantity of Martini I had drunk that morning, the recent boil on my cheek or the fumes from the burning petrol, I'm not sure, but as I walked back into the house I felt unsteady, and sat down hazily on the top step, closing my eyes as my brain swam.

After a few seconds my head cleared again. Leaning on my knees, I focused my eyes on the blue glass step between my feet. Cut into the surface in neat letters was:

Why so pale and wan, fond lover?
Prithee, why so pale?

Still too weak to more than register an automatic protest against this act of vandalism, I pulled myself to my feet, taking the door key out of my dressing-gown pocket. As I inserted it into the lock I noticed, inscribed into the brass seat of the lock:

Turn the key deftly in the oiled wards.

There were other inscriptions all over the black leather panelling of the door, cut in the same neat script, the lines crossing each other at random, like filigree decoration around a baroque salver.

Closing the door behind me, I walked into the lounge. The walls seemed darker than usual, and I realized that their entire surface was covered with row upon row of finely cut lettering, endless fragments of verse stretching from ceiling to floor.

I picked my glass off the table and raised it to my lips. The blue crystal bowl had been embossed with the same copperplate lines, spiralling down the stem to the base.

> *Drink to me only with thine eyes.*

Everything in the lounge was covered with the same fragments – the desk, lampstands and shades, the bookshelves, the keys of the baby grand, even the lip of the record on the stereogram turntable.

Dazed, I raised my hand to my face, in horror saw that the surface of my skin was interlaced by a thousand tattoos, writhing and coiling across my hands and arms like insane serpents.

Dropping my glass, I ran to the mirror over the fireplace, saw my face covered with the same tattooing, a living manuscript in which the ink still ran, the letters running and changing as if the pen still cast them.

> *You spotted snakes with double tongue . . .*
> *Weaving spiders, come not here.*

I flung myself away from the mirror, ran out on to the terrace, my feet slipping in the piles of coloured streamers which the evening wind was carrying over the balcony, then vaulted down over the railing on to the ground below.

I covered the distance between our villas in a few moments, raced up the darkening drive to the black front door. It opened as my hand reached for the bell, and I plunged through into the crystal hallway.

Aurora Day was waiting for me on the chaise longue by the fountain pool, feeding the ancient white fish that clustered around her. As I stepped across to her she smiled quietly to the fish and whispered to them.

'Aurora!' I cried. 'For heaven's sake, I give in! Take anything you want, anything, but leave me alone!'

For a moment she ignored me and went on quietly feeding the fish. Suddenly a thought of terror plunged through my mind. Were the huge white carp now nestling at her fingers once her lovers?

We sat together in the luminescent dusk, the long shadows playing across the purple landscape of Dali's 'Persistence of Memory' on the wall behind Aurora, the fish circling slowly in the fountain beside us.

She had stated her terms: nothing less than absolute control of the magazine, freedom to impose her own policy, to make her own selection of material. Nothing would be printed without her first approval.

'Don't worry,' she had said lightly. 'Our agreement will apply to one issue only.' Amazingly she showed no wish to publish her own poems – the pirated issue had merely been a device to bring me finally to surrender.

'Do you think one issue will be enough?' I asked, wondering what really she would do with it now.

She looked up at me idly, tracing patterns across the surface of the pool with a green-tipped finger. 'It all depends on you and your companions. When will you come to your senses and become poets again?'

I watched the patterns in the pool. In some miraculous way they remained etched across the surface.

In the hours, like millennia, we had sat together I seemed to have told her everything about myself, yet learned almost nothing about Aurora. One thing alone was clear – her obsession with the art of poetry. In some curious way she regarded herself as personally responsible for the present ebb at which it found itself, but her only remedy seemed completely retrogressive.

'You must come and meet my friends at the colony,' I suggested.

'I will,' she said. 'I hope I can help them. They all have so much to learn.'

I smiled at this. 'I'm afraid you won't find them very sympathetic to that view. Most of them regard themselves as virtuosos. For them the quest for the perfect sonnet ended years ago. The computer produces nothing else.'

Aurora scoffed. 'They're not poets but mere mechanics. Look at these collections of so-called verse. Three poems and sixty pages of operating instructions. Nothing but volts and amps. When I say they have everything to learn, I mean about their own hearts, not about technique; about the soul of music, not its form.'

She paused to stretch herself, her beautiful body uncoiling like a python. She leaned forward and began to speak earnestly. 'Poetry is dead today, not because of these machines, but because poets no longer search for their true inspiration.'

'Which is?'

Aurora shook her head sadly. 'You call yourself a poet and yet you ask me that?'

She stared down at the pool, her eyes listless. For a moment an expression of profound sadness passed across her face, and I realized that she felt some deep sense of guilt or inadequacy, that some failing of her own was responsible for the present malaise. Perhaps it was this sense of inadequacy that made me unafraid of her.

'Have you ever heard the legend of Melander and Corydon?' she asked.

'Vaguely,' I said, casting my mind back. 'Melander was the Muse of Poetry, if I remember. Wasn't Corydon a court poet who killed himself for her?'

'Good,' Aurora told me. 'You're not completely illiterate, after all. Yes, the court poets found that they had lost their inspiration and that their ladies were spurning them for the company of the knights, so they sought out Melander, the Muse, who told them that she had brought this spell upon them because they had taken their art for granted, forgetting the source from whom it really came. They protested that of course they thought of her always – a blatant lie – but she refused to believe them and told them that they would not recover their power until one of them sacrificed his life for her. Naturally none of them would do so, with the exception of a young poet of great talent called Corydon, who loved the goddess and was the only one to retain his power. For the other poets' sake he killed himself...'

'... to Melander's undying sorrow,' I concluded. 'She was not expecting him to give his life for his art. A beautiful myth,' I agreed. 'But I'm afraid you'll find no Corydons here.'

'I wonder,' Aurora said softly. She stirred the water in the pool, the broken surface throwing a ripple of light across the walls and ceiling. Then I saw that a long series of friezes ran around the lounge depicting the very legend Aurora had been describing. The first panel, on my extreme left, showed the poets and troubadours gathered around the goddess, a tall white-gowned figure whose face bore a remarkable resemblance to Aurora's. As I traced the story through the successive panels the likeness became even more marked, and I assumed that she had sat as Melander for the artist. Had she, in some way, identified herself with the goddess in the myth? In which case, who was her Corydon? – perhaps the artist himself. I searched the panels for the suicidal poet, a slim blond-maned youth whose face, although slightly familiar, I could not identify. However, behind the principal figures in all the scenes I certainly recognized another, her faun-faced chauffeur, here with ass's legs and wild woodwind, representing none other than the attendant Pan.

I had almost detected another likeness among the figures in the friezes when Aurora noticed me searching the panels. She stopped stirring the pool. As the ripples subsided the panels sank again into darkness. For a few seconds Aurora stared at me as if she had forgotten who I was. She appeared to have become tired and withdrawn, as if recapitulating the myth had evoked private memories of pain and fatigue. Simultaneously the hallway and glass-enclosed portico seemed to grow dark and sombre, reflecting her own darkening mood, so dominant was her presence that the air itself paled as she did. Again I felt that her world, into which I had stepped, was completely compounded of illusion.

She was asleep. Around her the room was almost in darkness. The pool lights had faded, the crystal columns that had shone around us were dull and extinguished, like trunks of opaque glass. The only light came from the flower-like jewel between her sleeping breasts.

I stood up and walked softly across to her, looked down at her strange face, its skin smooth and grey, like some pharaonic bride in a basalt dream. Then, beside me at the door I noticed the hunched figure of the chauffeur. His peaked cap hid his face, but the two watchful eyes were fixed on me like small coals.

As we left, hundreds of sleeping sand-rays were dotted about the moonlit floor of the desert. We stepped between them and moved away silently in the Cadillac.

When I reached the villa I went straight into the study, ready to start work on assembling the next issue. During the return ride I had quickly decided on the principal cue-themes and key-images which I would play into the VT sets. All programmed for maximum repetition, within twenty-four hours I would have a folio of moon-sick, muse-mad dithyrambs which would stagger Aurora Day by their heartfelt simplicity and inspiration.

As I entered the study my shoe caught on something sharp. I bent down in the darkness, and found a torn strip of computer circuitry embedded in the white leather flooring.

When I switched on the light I saw that someone had smashed the three VT sets, pounding them to a twisted pulp in a savage excess of violence.

Mine had not been the only targets. Next morning, as I sat at my desk contemplating the three wrecked computers, the telephone rang with news of similar outrages all the way down the Stars. Tony Sapphire's 50-watt IBM had been hammered to pieces, and Raymond Mayo's four new Philco Versomatics had been smashed beyond hope of repair. As far as I could gather, not a single VT set had been left untouched. The previous evening, between the hours of six and midnight, someone had moved rapidly down the Stars, slipped into the studios and apartments and singlemindedly wrecked every VT set.

I had a good idea who. As I climbed out of the Cadillac on my return from Aurora I had noticed two heavy wrenches on the seat beside the chauffeur. However, I decided not to call the police and prefer charges. For one thing, the problem of filling *Wave IX* now looked almost insoluble. When I telephoned Graphis Press I found, more or less as expected, that all Aurora's copy had been mysteriously mislaid.

The problem remained – what would I put in the issue? I couldn't afford to miss an edition or my subscribers would fade away like ghosts.

I telephoned Aurora and pointed this out.

'We should go to press again within a week, otherwise our contract expires and I'll never get another. And reimbursing a year's advance subscriptions would bankrupt me. We've simply got to find some copy. As the new managing editor have you any suggestions?'

Aurora chuckled. 'I suppose you're thinking that I might mysteriously reassemble all those smashed machines?'

'It's an idea,' I agreed, waving at Tony Sapphire who had just called in. 'Otherwise I'm afraid we're never going to get any copy.'

'I can't understand you,' Aurora replied: 'Surely there's one very simple method.'

'Is there? What's that?'

'Write some yourself!'

Before I could protest she burst into a peal of high laughter. 'I gather there are some twenty-three able-bodied versifiers and so-called poets in Vermilion Sands' – this was exactly the number of places broken into the previous evening – 'well, let's see some of them versify.'

'Aurora!' I snapped. 'You can't be serious. Listen, for heaven's sake, this is no joking –'

But she had put the phone down. I turned to Tony Sapphire, then sat back limply and contemplated an intact tape spool I had recovered from one of the sets. 'It looks as if I've had it. Did you hear that – "Write some yourself"?'

'She must be insane,' Tony agreed.

'It's all part of this tragic obsession of hers,' I explained, lowering my voice. 'She genuinely believes she's the Muse of Poetry, returned to earth to re-inspire the dying race of poets. Last night she referred to the myth of Melander and Corydon. I think she's seriously waiting for some young poet to give his life for her.'

Tony nodded. 'She's missing the point, though. Fifty years ago a few people wrote poetry, but no one read it. Now no one writes it either. The VT set merely simplifies the whole process.'

I agreed with him, but of course Tony was somewhat prejudiced there, being one of those people who believed that literature was in essence both unreadable and unwritable. The automatic novel he had been 'writing' was over ten million words long, intended to be one of those gigantic grotesques that tower over the highways of literary history, terrifying the unwary traveller. Unfortunately he had never bothered to get it printed, and the memory drum which carried the electronic coding had been wrecked in the previous night's pogrom.

I was equally annoyed. One of my VT sets had been steadily producing a transliteration of James Joyce's *Ulysses* in terms of a Hellenic Greek setting, a pleasant academic exercise which would have provided an objective test of Joyce's masterpiece by the degree of exactness with which the transliteration matched the original Odyssey. This too had been destroyed.

We watched Studio 5 in the bright morning light. The cerise Cadillac had disappeared somewhere, so presumably Aurora was driving around Vermilion Sands, astounding the café crowds.

I picked up the terrace telephone and sat on the rail. 'I suppose I might as well call everyone up and see what they can do.'

I dialled the first number.

Raymond Mayo said: 'Write some myself? Paul, you're insane.'

Xero Paris said: 'Myself? Of course, Paul, with my toes.'

Fairchild de Mille said: 'It would be rather chic, but . . .'

Kurt Butterworth said, sourly: 'Ever tried to? How?'

Marlene McClintic said: 'Darling, I wouldn't dare. It might develop the wrong muscles or something.'

Sigismund Lutitsch said. 'No, no. Siggy now in new zone. Electronic sculpture, plasma in super-cosmic collisions. Listen –'

Robin Saunders, Macmillan Freebody and Angel Petit said: 'No.'

Tony brought me a drink and I pressed on down the list. 'It's no good,' I said at last. 'No one writes verse any more. Let's face it. After all, do you or I?'

Tony pointed to the notebook. 'There's one name left – we might as well sweep the decks clean before we take off for Red Beach.'

'Tristram Caldwell,' I read. 'That's the shy young fellow with the footballer's build. Something is always wrong with his set. Might as well try him.'

A soft honey-voiced girl answered the phone.

'Tristram?' she purred. 'Er, yes, I think he's here.'

There were sounds of wrestling around on a bed, during which the telephone bounced on the floor a few times, and then Caldwell answered.

'Hello, Ransom, what can I do for you?'

'Tristram,' I said, 'I take it you were paid the usual surprise call last night. Or didn't you notice? How's your VT set?'

'VT set?' he repeated. 'It's fine, just fine.'

'What?' I shouted. 'You mean yours is undamaged? Tristram, pull yourself together and listen to me!' Quickly I explained our problem, but Tristram suddenly began to laugh.

'Well, I think that's just damn funny, don't you? Really rich. I think she's right. Let's get back to the old crafts –'

'Never mind the old crafts,' I told him irritably. 'All I'm interested in is getting some copy together for the next issue. If your set is working we're saved.'

'Well there, wait a minute, Paul. I've been slightly preoccupied recently, haven't had a chance to see the set.'

I waited while he wandered off. From the sounds of his

footsteps and an impatient shout of the girl's, to which he replied distantly, it seemed he had gone outside into the yard. A door slammed open somewhere and there was a vague rummaging. A curious place to keep a VT set, I thought. Then there was a loud hammering noise.

Finally Tristram picked up the phone again. 'Sorry, Paul, but it looks as if she paid me a visit too. The set's a total wreck.' He paused while I cursed the air, then said: 'Look, though, is she really serious about the hand-made material? I take it that's what you were calling about?'

'Yes,' I told him. 'Believe me, I'll print anything. It has to get past Aurora, though. Have you got any old copy lying around?'

Tristram chuckled again. 'You know, Paul, old boy, I believe I have. Rather despaired of ever getting it into print but I'm glad now I held on to it. Tell you what, I'll tidy it up and let you have it tomorrow. Few sonnets, a ballad or two, you should find it interesting.'

He was right. Five minutes after I opened his parcel the next morning I knew he was trying to fool us.

'This is the same old thing,' I explained to Tony. 'That cunning Adonis. Look at these assonances and feminine rhymes, the drifting caesura – the unmistakable Caldwell signature, worn tapes on the rectifier circuits and a leaking condenser. I've been having to re-tread these for years to smooth them out. He's got his set there working away after all.'

'What are you going to do?' Tony asked. 'He'll just deny it.'

'Obviously. Anyway, I can use the material. Who cares if the whole issue is by Tristram Caldwell.'

I started to slip the pages into an envelope before taking them round to Aurora, when an idea occurred to me.

'Tony, I've just had another of my brilliancies. The perfect method of curing this witch of her obsession and exacting sweet revenge at the same time. Suppose we play along with Tristram and tell Aurora that these poems were hand-written by him. His style is thoroughly retrograde and his themes are everything Aurora could ask for – listen to these – "Homage to Cleo", "Minerva 231", "Silence becomes Electra". She'll pass them for press, we'll print this weekend and then, lo and behold, we reveal that these poems apparently born out of the burning breast of Tristram Caldwell are nothing more than a collection of cliché-ridden transcripts from a derelict VT set, the worst possible automatic maunderings.'

Tony whooped. 'Tremendous! She'd never live it down. But do you think she'll be taken in?'

'Why not? Haven't you realized that she sincerely expects us all to sit down and produce a series of model classical exercises on "Night and Day", "Summer and Winter", and so on. When only Caldwell produces anything she'll be only too glad to give him her imprimatur. Remember, our agreement only refers to this issue, and the onus is on her. She's got to find material somewhere.'

So we launched our scheme. All afternoon I pestered Tristram, telling him that Aurora had adored his first consignment and was eager to see more. Duly the next day a second batch arrived, all, as luck would have it, in longhand, although remarkably faded for material fresh from his VT set the previous day. However, I was only too glad for anything that would reinforce the illusion. Aurora was more and more pleased, and showed no suspicions whatever. Here and there she made a minor criticism but refused to have anything altered or rewritten.

'But we always rewrite, Aurora,' I told her. 'One can't expect an infallible selection of images. The number of synonyms is too great.' Wondering whether I had gone too far, I added hastily: 'It doesn't matter whether the author is man or robot, the principle is the same.'

'Really?' Aurora said archly. 'However, I think we'll leave these just as Mr Caldwell wrote them.'

I didn't bother to point out the hopeless fallacy in her attitude, and merely collected the initialled manuscripts and hurried home with them. Tony was at my desk, deep in the phone, pumping Tristram for more copy.

He capped the mouthpiece and gestured to me. 'He's playing coy, probably trying to raise us to two cents a thousand. Pretends he's out of material. Is it worth calling his bluff?'

I shook my head. 'Dangerous. If Aurora discovers we're involved in this fraud of Tristram's she might do anything. Let me talk to him.' I took the phone. 'What's the matter, Tristram, production's way down. We need more material, old boy. Shorten the line, why are you wasting tapes with all these alexandrines?'

'Ransom, what the hell are you talking about? I'm not a damned factory, I'm a poet, I write when I have something to say in the only suitable way to say it.'

'Yes, yes,' I rejoined, 'but I have fifty pages to fill and only a few days in which to do it. You've given me about ten so you've just got to keep up the flow. What have you produced today?'

'Well, I'm working on another sonnet, some nice things in it – to Aurora herself, as a matter of fact.'

'Great,' I told him, 'but careful with those vocabulary selectors. Remember the golden rule: the ideal sentence is one word long. What else have you got?'

'What else? Nothing. This is likely to take all week, perhaps all year.'

I nearly swallowed the phone. 'Tristram, what's the matter? For heaven's sake, haven't you paid the power bill or something? Have they cut you off?'

Before I could find out, however, he had rung off.

'One sonnet a day,' I said to Tony. 'Good God, he must be on manual. Crazy idiot, he probably doesn't realize how complicated those circuits are.'

We sat tight and waited. Nothing came the next morning, and nothing the morning after that. Luckily, however, Aurora wasn't in the least surprised; in fact, if anything she was pleased that Tristram's rate of progress was slowing.

'One poem is enough,' she told me, 'a complete statement. Nothing more needs to be said, an interval of eternity closes for ever.'

Reflectively, she straightened the petals of a hyacinth. 'Perhaps he needs a little encouragement,' she decided.

I could see she wanted to meet him.

'Why don't you ask him over for dinner?' I suggested.

She brightened immediately. 'I will.' She picked up the telephone and handed it to me.

As I dialled Tristram's number I felt a sudden pang of envy and disappointment. Around me the friezes told the story of Melander and Corydon, but I was too preoccupied to anticipate the tragedy the next week would bring.

During the days that followed Tristram and Aurora Day were always together. In the morning they would usually drive out to the film sets at Lagoon West, the chauffeur at the wheel of the huge Cadillac. In the evenings, as I sat out alone on the terrace, watching the lights of Studio 5 shine out into the warm darkness, I could hear their fragmented voices carried across the sand, the faint sounds of crystal music.

I would like to think that I resented their relationship, but to be truthful I cared very little after the initial disappointment had worn off. The beach fatigue from which I suffered numbed the senses insidiously, blunting despair and hope alike.

When, three days after their first meeting, Aurora and Tristram suggested that we all go ray-fishing at Lagoon West, I accepted gladly, eager to observe their affair at closer quarters.

As we set off down the Stars there was no hint of what was to come. Tristram and Aurora were together in the Cadillac while Tony Sapphire, Raymond Mayo and I brought up the rear in Tony's Chevrolet. We could see them through the blue rear window of the Cadillac, Tristram reading the sonnet to Aurora which he had just completed. When we climbed out of the cars at Lagoon West and made our way over to the old abstract film sets near the sand reefs, they were walking hand in hand. Tristram in his white beach shoes and suit looked very much like an Edwardian dandy at a boating party.

The chauffeur carried the picnic hampers, and Raymond Mayo and Tony the spear-guns and nets. Down the reefs below we could see the rays nesting by the thousands, scores of double mambas sleek with off-season hibernation.

After we had settled ourselves under the awnings Raymond and Tristram decided on the course and then gathered everyone together. Strung out in a loose line we began to make our way down into one of the reefs, Aurora on Tristram's arm.

'Ever done any ray-fishing?' Tristram asked me as we entered one of the lower galleries.

'Never,' I said. 'I'll just watch this time. I hear you're quite an expert.'

'Well, with luck I won't be killed.' He pointed to the rays clinging to the cornices above us, wheeling up into the sky as we approached, whistling and screeching. In the dim light the white tips of their stings flexed in their sheaths. 'Unless they're really frightened they'll stay well away from you,' he told us. 'The art is to prevent them from becoming frightened, select one and approach it so slowly that it sits staring at you until you're close enough to shoot it.'

Raymond Mayo had found a large purple mamba resting in a narrow crevice about ten yards on our right. He moved up to it quietly, watching the sting protrude from its sheath and weave menacingly, waiting just long enough for it to retract, lulling the ray with a low humming sound. Finally, when he was five feet away, he raised the gun and took careful aim.

'There may seem little to it,' Tristram whispered to Aurora and me, 'but in fact he's completely at the ray's mercy now. If it chose to attack he'd be defenceless.' The bolt snapped from Raymond's gun and struck the ray on its spinal crest, stunning it instantly. Quickly he stepped over and scooped it into the net, where it revived after a few seconds, threshed its black triangular wings helplessly and then lay inertly.

We moved through the groynes and galleries, the sky a narrow winding interval overhead, following the pathways that curved down into the bed of the reef. Now and then the wheeling rays rising out of our way would brush against the reef and drifts of fine sand would cascade over us. Raymond and Tristram shot several more rays, leaving the chauffeur to carry the nets. Gradually our party split into two, Tony and Raymond taking one pathway with the chauffeur, while I stayed with Aurora and Tristram.

As we moved along I noticed that Aurora's face had become less relaxed, her movements slightly more deliberate and controlled. I had the impression she was watching Tristram carefully, glancing sideways at him as she held his arm.

We entered the terminal fornix of the reef, a deep cathedral-like chamber from which a score of galleries spiralled off to surface like the arms of a galaxy. In the darkness around us the thousands of rays hung motionlessly, their phosphorescing stings flexing and retracting like winking stars.

Two hundred feet away, on the far side of the chamber, Raymond Mayo and the chauffeur emerged from one of the galleries. They waited there for a few moments. Suddenly I heard Tony shouting out. Raymond dropped his spear-gun and disappeared into the gallery.

Excusing myself, I ran across the chamber. I found them in the narrow corridor, peering around in the darkness.

'I tell you,' Tony was insisting. 'I heard the damn thing singing.'

'Impossible,' Raymond told him. They argued with each other, then gave up the search for the mysterious song-ray and stepped down into the chamber. As we went I thought I saw the chauffeur replace something in his pocket. With his beaked face and insane eyes, his hunched figure hung about with the nets of writhing rays, he looked like a figure from Hieronymus Bosch.

After exchanging a few words with Raymond and Tony I turned to make my way back to the others, but they had left the chamber. Wondering which of the galleries they had chosen, I stepped a few yards into the mouth of each one, finally saw them on one of the ramps curving away above me.

I was about to retrace my steps and join them when I caught a glimpse of Aurora's face in profile, saw once again her expression of watchful intent. Changing my mind, I moved quietly along the spiral, just below them, the falls of sand masking my footsteps, keeping them in view through the intervals between the overhanging columns.

At one point I was only a few yards from them, and heard Aurora say clearly: 'Isn't there a theory that you can trap rays by singing to them?'

'By mesmerizing them?' Tristram asked. 'Let's try.'

They moved farther away, and Aurora's voice sounded out softly, a low crooning tone. Gradually the sound rose, echoing and re-echoing through the high vaults, the rays stirring in the darkness.

As we neared the surface their numbers grew, and Aurora stopped and guided Tristram towards a narrow sun-filled arena, bounded by hundred-foot walls, open to the sky above.

Unable to see them now, I retreated into the gallery and climbed the inner slope on to the next level, and from there on to the stage above. I made my way to the edge of the gallery, from which I could now easily observe the arena below. As I did so, however, I was aware of an eerie and penetrating noise, at once toneless and all-pervading, which filled the entire reef, like the high-pitched sounds perceived by epileptics before a seizure. Down in the arena Tristram was searching the walls, trying to identify the source of the noise, hands raised to his head. He had taken his eyes off Aurora, who was standing behind him, arms motionless at her sides, palms slightly raised, like an entranced medium.

Fascinated by this curious stance, I was abruptly distracted by a terrified screeching that came from the lower levels of the reef. It was accompanied by a confused leathery flapping, and almost immediately a cloud of flying rays, frantically trying to escape from the reef, burst from the galleries below.

As they turned into the arena, sweeping low over the heads of Tristram and Aurora, they seemed to lose their sense of direction, and within a moment the arena was packed by a swarm of circling rays, all diving about uncertainly.

Screaming in terror at the rays whipping past her face, Aurora emerged from her trance. Tristram had taken off his straw hat and was striking furiously at them, shielding Aurora with his other arm. Together they backed towards a narrow fault in the rear wall of the arena, which provided an escape route into the galleries on the far side. Following this route to the edge of the cliffs above, I was surprised to see the squat figure of the chauffeur, now divested of his nets and gear, peering down at the couple below.

By now the hundreds of rays jostling within the arena almost obscured Tristram and Aurora. She reappeared from the narrow fault, shaking her head desperately. Their escape route was sealed! Quickly Tristram motioned her to her knees, then leapt into the middle of the arena, slapping wildly at the rays with his hat, trying to drive them away from Aurora.

For a few seconds he was successful. Like a cloud of giant hornets the rays wheeled off in disorder. Horrified, I watched them descend upon him again. Before I could shout Tristram had fallen. The rays swooped and hovered over his outstretched body, then swirled away, soaring into the sky, apparently released from the vortex.

Tristram lay face downwards, his blond hair spilled across the sand, arms twisted loosely. I stared at his body, amazed by the swiftness with which he had died, and looked across to Aurora.

She too was watching the body, but with an expression that showed neither pity nor terror. Gathering her skirt in one hand, she turned and slipped away through the fault –

The escape route had been open after all! Astonished, I realized that Aurora had deliberately told Tristram that the route was closed, virtually forcing him to attack the rays.

A minute later she emerged from the mouth of the gallery above. Briefly she peered down into the arena, the black-uniformed chauffeur at her elbow, watching the motionless body of Tristram. Then they hurried away.

Racing after them, I began to shout at the top of my voice, hoping to attract Tony and Raymond Mayo. As I reached the mouth of the reef my voice boomed and echoed into the galleries below. A hundred yards away Aurora and the chauffeur were stepping into the Cadillac. With a roar of exhaust it swung away among the sets, sending up clouds of dust that obscured the enormous abstract patterns.

I ran towards Tony's car. By the time I reached it the Cadillac was half a mile away, burning across the desert like an escaping dragon.

That was the last I saw of Aurora Day. I managed to follow them as far as the highway to Lagoon West, but there, on the open road, the big car left me behind, and ten miles farther on, by the time I reached Lagoon West, I had lost them completely. At one of the gas stations where the highway forks to Vermilion Sands and Red Beach I asked if anyone had seen a cerise Cadillac go by. Two attendants said they had, on the road *towards* me, and although they both swore this, I suppose Aurora's magic must have confused them.

I decided to try her villa and took the fork back to Vermilion Sands, cursing myself for not anticipating what had happened. I, ostensibly a poet, had failed to take another poet's dreams seriously. Aurora had explicitly forecast Tristram's death.

Studio 5, The Stars, was silent and empty. The rays had gone from the drive, and the black glass door was wide open, the remains of a few streamers drifting across the dust that gathered on the floor. The hallway and lounge were in darkness, and only the white carp in the pool provided a glimmer of light. The air was still and unbroken, as if the house had been empty for centuries.

Cursorily I ran my eye round the friezes in the lounge, then saw that I knew all the faces of the figures in the panels. The likenesses were almost photographic. Tristram was Corydon, Aurora Melander, the chauffeur the god Pan. And I saw myself, Tony Sapphire, Raymond Mayo, Fairchild de Mille and the other members of the colony.

Leaving the friezes, I made my way past the pool. It was now evening, and through the open doorway were the distant lights of Vermilion Sands, the headlights sweeping along the Stars reflected in the glass roof-tiles of my villa. A light wind had risen, stirring the streamers, and as I went down the steps a gust of air moved through the house and caught the door, slamming it behind me. The loud report boomed through the house, a concluding statement upon the whole sequence of fantasy and disaster, a final notice of the departure of the enchantress.

As I walked back across the desert and last streamers were moving over the dark sand, I strode firmly through them, trying to reassemble my own reality again. The fragments of Aurora Day's insane poems caught the dying desert light as they dissolved about my feet, the fading debris of a dream.

Reaching the villa, I saw that the lights were on. I raced inside and to my astonishment discovered the blond figure of Tristram stretched out lazily in a chair on the terrace, an ice-filled glass in one hand.

He eyed me genially, winked broadly before I could speak and put a forefinger to his lips.

I stepped over to him. 'Tristram,' I whispered hoarsely. 'I thought you were dead. What on earth happened down there?'

He smiled at me. 'Sorry, Paul, I had a hunch you were watching. Aurora got away, didn't she?'

I nodded. 'Their car was too fast for the Chevrolet. But weren't you hit by one of the rays? I saw you fall, I thought you'd been killed outright.'

'So did Aurora. Neither of you know much about rays, do you? Their stings are passive in the on season, old chap, or nobody would be allowed in there.' He grinned at me. 'Ever hear of the myth of Melander and Corydon?'

I sat down weakly on the seat next to him. In two minutes he explained what had happened. Aurora had told him of the myth, and partly out of sympathy for her, and partly for amusement, he had decided to play out his role. All the while he had been describing the danger and viciousness of the rays he had been egging Aurora on deliberately, and had provided her with a perfect opportunity to stage his sacrificial murder.

'It *was* murder, of course,' I told him. 'Believe me, I saw the glint in her eye. She really wanted you killed.'

Tristram shrugged. 'Don't look so shocked, old boy. After all, poetry is a serious business.'

Raymond and Tony Sapphire knew nothing of what had happened. Tristram had put together a story of how Aurora had suffered a sudden attack of claustrophobia, and rushed off in a frenzy.

'I wonder what Aurora will do now,' Tristram mused. 'Her prophecy's been fulfilled. Perhaps she'll feel more confident of her own beauty. You know, she had a colossal sense of physical inadequacy. Like the original Melander, who was surprised when Corydon killed himself, Aurora confused her art with her own person.'

I nodded. 'I hope she isn't too disappointed when she finds poetry is still being written in the bad old way. That reminds me, I've got twenty-five pages to fill. How's your VT set running?'

'No longer have one. Wrecked it the morning you phoned up. Haven't used the thing for years.'

I sat up. 'Do you mean that those sonnets you've been sending in are all hand-written?'

'Absolutely, old boy. Every single one a soul-grafted gem.'

I lay back groaning. 'God, I was relying on your set to save me. What the hell am I going to do?'

Tristram grinned. 'Start writing it yourself. Remember the prophecy. Perhaps it will come true. After all, Aurora thinks I'm dead.'

I cursed him roundly. 'If it's any help, I wish you were. Do you know what this is going to cost me?'

After he had gone I went into the study and added up what copy I had left, found that there were exactly twenty-three pages to fill. Oddly enough that represented one page for each of the registered poets at Vermilion Sands. Except that none of them, apart from Tristram, was capable of producing a single line.

It was midnight, but the problems facing the magazine would take every minute of the next twenty-four hours, when the final deadline expired. I had almost decided to write something myself

when the telephone rang. At first I thought it was Aurora Day
– the voice was high and feminine – but it was only Fairchild
de Mille.

'What are you doing up so late?' I growled at him. 'Shouldn't
you be getting your beauty sleep?'

'Well, I suppose I should, Paul, but do you know a rather
incredible thing happened to me this evening. Tell me, are you
still looking for original hand-written verse? I started writing
something a couple of hours ago, it's not bad really. About
Aurora Day, as a matter of fact. I think you'll like it.'

Sitting up, I congratulated him fulsomely, noting down the
linage.

Five minutes later the telephone rang again. This time it was
Angel Petit. He too had a few hand-written verses I might be
interested in. Again, dedicated to Aurora Day.

Within the next half hour the telephone rang a score of times.
Every poet in Vermilion Sands seemed to be awake. I heard from
Macmillan Freebody, Robin Saunders and the rest of them. All,
mysteriously that evening, had suddenly felt the urge to write
something original, and in a few minutes had tossed off a couple
of stanzas to the memory of Aurora Day.

I was musing over it when I stood up after the last call. It was
12.45, and I should have been tired out, but my brain felt keen
and alive, a thousand ideas running through it. A phrase formed
itself in my mind. I picked up my pad and wrote it down.

Time seemed to dissolve. Within five minutes I had produced
the first piece of verse I had written for over ten years. Behind it a
dozen more poems lay just below the surface of my mind, waiting
like gold in a loaded vein to be brought out into daylight.

Sleep would wait. I reached for another sheet of paper and
then noticed a letter on the desk to the IBM agency in Red Beach,
enclosing an order for three new VT sets.

Smiling to myself, I tore it into a dozen pieces.

1961

DEEP END

They always slept during the day. By dawn the last of the townsfolk had gone indoors and the houses would be silent, heat curtains locked across the windows, as the sun rose over the deliquescing salt banks. Most of them were elderly and fell asleep quickly in their darkened chalets, but Granger, with his restless mind and his one lung, often lay awake through the afternoons, while the metal outer walls of the cabin creaked and hummed, trying pointlessly to read through the old log books Holliday had salvaged for him from the crashed space platforms.

By six o'clock the thermal fronts would begin to recede southwards across the kelp flats, and one by one the air-conditioners in the bedrooms switched themselves off. While the town slowly came to life, its windows opening to the cool dusk air, Granger strode down to breakfast at the Neptune Bar, gallantly doffing his sunglasses to left and right at the old couples settling themselves out on their porches, staring at each other across the shadow-filled streets.

Five miles to the north, in the empty hotel at Idle End, Holliday usually rested quietly for another hour, and listened to the coral towers, gleaming in the distance like white pagodas, sing and whistle as the temperature gradients cut through them. Twenty miles away he could see the symmetrical peak of Hamilton, nearest of the Bermuda Islands, rising off the dry ocean floor like a flat-topped mountain, the narrow ring of white beach still visible in the sunset, a scum-line left by the sinking ocean.

That evening he felt even more reluctant than usual to drive down into the town. Not only would Granger be in his private booth at the Neptune, dispensing the same mixture of humour and homily – he was virtually the only person Holliday could talk to, and inevitably he had come to resent his dependence on the older man – but Holliday would have his final interview with the migration officer and make the decision which would determine his entire future.

In a sense the decision had already been made, as Bullen, the migration officer, realized on his trip a month earlier. He did not bother to press Holliday, who had no special skills to offer, no qualities of character or leadership which would be of use on the new worlds. However, Bullen pointed out one small but relevant fact, which Holliday duly noted and thought over in the intervening month.

'Remember, Holliday,' he warned him at the end of the interview in the requisitioned office at the rear of the sheriff's cabin, 'the average age of the settlement is over sixty. In ten years' time you and Granger may well be the only two left here, and if that lung of his goes you'll be on your own.'

He paused to let this prospect sink in, then added quietly: 'All the kids are leaving on the next trip – the Merryweathers' two boys, Tom Juranda (*that lout, good riddance*, Holliday thought to himself, *look out Mars*) – do you realize you'll literally be the only one here under the age of fifty?'

'Katy Summers is staying,' Holliday pointed out quickly, the sudden vision of a white organdy dress and long straw hair giving him courage.

The migration officer had glanced at his application list and nodded grudgingly. 'Yes, but she's just looking after her grandmother. As soon as the old girl dies Katy will be off like a flash. After all, there's nothing to keep her here, is there?'

'No,' Holliday had agreed automatically.

There wasn't now. For a long while he mistakenly believed there was. Katy was his own age, twenty-two, the only person, apart from Granger, who seemed to understand his determination to stay behind and keep watch over a forgotten Earth. But the grandmother died three days after the migration officer left, and the next day Katy had begun to pack. In some insane way Holliday had assumed that she would stay behind, and what worried him was that all his assumptions about himself might be based on equally false premises.

Climbing off the hammock, he went on to the terrace and looked out at the phosphorescent glitter of the trace minerals in the salt banks stretching away from the hotel. His quarters were in the penthouse suite on the tenth floor, the only heat-sealed unit in the building, but its steady settlement into the ocean bed had opened wide cracks in the load walls which would soon reach up to the roof. The ground floor had already disappeared. By the time the next floor went – six months at the outside – he would have been forced to leave the old pleasure resort and return to the town. Inevitably, that would mean sharing a chalet with Granger.

A mile away, an engine droned. Through the dusk Holliday saw the migration officer's helicopter whirling along towards the hotel, the only local landmark, then veer off once Bullen identified the town and circle slowly towards the landing strip.

Eight o'clock, Holliday noted. His interview was at 8.30 the next morning. Bullen would rest the night with the Sheriff, carry out his other duties as graves commissioner and justice of the peace, and then set off after seeing Holliday on the next leg of his journey. For twelve hours Holliday was free, still able to make absolute decisions (or, more accurately, not to make them) but after that he would have committed himself. This was the migration officer's last trip, his final circuit from the deserted cities near St Helena up through the Azores and Bermudas and on to the main Atlantic ferry site at the Canaries. Only two of the big launching platforms were still in navigable orbit – hundreds of others were continuously falling out of the sky – and once they came down Earth was, to all intents, abandoned. From then on the only people likely to be picked up would be a few military communications personnel.

Twice on his way into the town Holliday had to lower the salt-plough fastened to the front bumper of the jeep and ram back the drifts which had melted across the wire roadway during the afternoon. Mutating kelp, their genetic shifts accelerated by the radio-phosphors, reared up into the air on either side of the road like enormous cacti, turning the dark salt-banks into a white lunar garden. But this evidence of the encroaching wilderness only served to strengthen Holliday's need to stay behind on Earth. Most of the nights, when he wasn't arguing with Granger at the Neptune, he would drive around the ocean floor, climbing over the crashed launching platforms, or wander with Katy Summers through the kelp forests. Sometimes he would persuade Granger to come with them, hoping that the older man's expertise – he had originally been a marine biologist – would help to sharpen his own awareness of the bathypelagic flora, but the original sea bed was buried under the endless salt hills and they might as well have been driving about the Sahara.

As he entered the Neptune – a low cream and chromium saloon which abutted the landing strip and had formerly served as a passenger lounge when thousands of migrants from the Southern Hemisphere were being shipped up to the Canaries – Granger called to him and rattled his cane against the window, pointing to the dark outline of the migration officer's helicopter parked on the apron fifty yards away.

'I know,' Holliday said in a bored voice as he went over with his drink. 'Relax, I saw him coming.'

Granger grinned at him. Holliday, with his intent serious face under an unruly thatch of blond hair, and his absolute sense of personal responsibility, always amused him.

'*You* relax,' Granger said, adjusting the shoulder pad under his Hawaiian shirt which disguised his sunken lung. (He had lost it skin-diving thirty years earlier.) '*I'm* not going to fly to Mars next week.'

Holliday stared sombrely into his glass. 'I'm not either.' He looked up at Granger's wry saturnine face, then added sardonically. 'Or didn't you know?'

Granger roared, tapping the window with his cane as if to dismiss the helicopter. 'Seriously, you're not going? You've made up your mind?'

'Wrong. And right. I haven't made up my mind yet – but at the same time I'm not going. You appreciate the distinction?'

'Perfectly, Dr Schopenhauer.' Granger began to grin again. He pushed away his glass. 'You know, Holliday, your trouble is that you take yourself too seriously. You don't realize how ludicrous you are.'

'Ludicrous? Why?' Holliday asked guardedly.

'What does it matter whether you've made up your mind or not? The only thing that counts now is to get together enough courage to head straight for the Canaries and take off into the wide blue yonder. For heaven's sake, what are you staying for? Earth is dead and buried. Past, present and future no longer exist here. Don't you feel any responsibility to your own biological destiny?'

'Spare me that.' Holliday pulled a ration card from his shirt pocket, passed it across to Granger, who was responsible for the stores allocations. 'I need a new pump on the lounge refrigerator. 30-watt Frigidaire. Any left?'

Granger groaned, took the card with a snort of exasperation. 'Good God, man, you're just a Robinson Crusoe in reverse, tinkering about with all these bits of old junk, trying to fit them together. You're the last man on the beach who decides to stay behind after everyone else has left. Maybe you are a poet and dreamer, but don't you realize that those two species are extinct now?'

Holliday stared out at the helicopter on the apron, at the lights of the settlement reflected against the salt hills that encircled the town. Each day they moved a little nearer, already it was difficult to get together a weekly squad to push them back. In ten years' time his position might well be that of a Crusoe. Luckily the big water and kerosene tanks – giant cylinders, the size of gasometers – held enough for fifty years. Without them, of course, he would have had no choice.

'Let's give me a rest,' he said to Granger. 'You're merely trying to find in me a justification for your own enforced stay. Perhaps I am extinct, but I'd rather cling to life here than vanish completely. Anyway, I have a hunch that one day they'll be coming back. Someone's got to stay behind and keep alive a sense of what life here has meant. This isn't an old husk we can throw away when we've finished with it. We were born here. It's the only place we really remember.'

Granger nodded slowly. He was about to speak when a brilliant white arc crossed the darkened window, then soared out of sight, its point of impact with the ground lost behind one of the storage tanks.

Holliday stood up and craned out of the window.

'Must be a launching platform. Looked like a big one, probably one of the Russians'.' A long rolling crump reverberated through the night air, echoing away among the coral towers. Flashes of light flared up briefly. There was a series of smaller explosions, and then a wide diffuse pall of steam fanned out across the north-west.

'Lake Atlantic,' Granger commented. 'Let's drive out there and have a look. It may have uncovered something interesting.'

Half an hour later, a set of Granger's old sample beakers, slides and mounting equipment in the back seat, they set off in the jeep towards the southern tip of Lake Atlantic ten miles away.

It was here that Holliday discovered the fish.

Lake Atlantic, a narrow ribbon of stagnant brine ten miles in length by a mile wide, to the north of the Bermuda Islands, was all that remained of the former Atlantic Ocean, and was, in fact, the sole remnant of the oceans which had once covered two-thirds of the Earth's surface. The frantic mining of the oceans in the previous century to provide oxygen for the atmospheres of the new planets had made their decline swift and irreversible, and with their death had come climatic and other geophysical changes which ensured the extinction of Earth itself. As the oxygen extracted electrolytically from sea-water was compressed and shipped away, the hydrogen released was discharged into the atmosphere. Eventually only a narrow layer of denser, oxygen-containing air was left, little more than a mile in depth, and those people remaining on Earth were forced to retreat into the ocean beds, abandoning the poisoned continental tables.

At the hotel at Idle End, Holliday spent uncounted hours going through the library he had accumulated of magazines and books about the cities of the old Earth, and Granger often described to him his own youth when the seas had been half-full and he had worked as a marine biologist at the University of Miami, a fabulous laboratory unfolding itself for him on the lengthening beaches.

'The seas are our corporate memory,' he often said to Holliday. 'In draining them we deliberately obliterated our own pasts, to a large extent our own self-identities. That's another reason why you should leave. Without the sea, life is insupportable. We become nothing more than the ghosts of memories, blind and homeless, flitting through the dry chambers of a gutted skull.'

They reached the lake within half an hour, worked their way through the swamps which formed its banks. In the dim light the grey salt dunes ran on for miles, their hollows cracked into hexagonal plates, a dense cloud of vapour obscuring the surface of the water. They parked on a low promontory by the edge of the lake and looked up at the great circular shell of the launching platform. This was one of the larger vehicles, almost three hundred yards in diameter, lying upside down in the shallow water, its hull dented and burnt, riven by huge punctures where the power plants had torn themselves loose on impact and exploded off across the lake. A quarter of a mile away, hidden by the blur, they could just see a cluster of rotors pointing up into the sky.

Walking along the bank, the main body of the lake on their right, they moved nearer the platform, tracing out its riveted CCCP markings along the rim. The giant vehicle had cut enormous grooves through the nexus of pools just beyond the tip of the lake, and Granger waded through the warm water, searching for specimens. Here and there were small anemones and starfish, stunted bodies twisted by cancers. Web-like algae draped themselves over his rubber boots, their nuclei beading like jewels in the phosphorescent light. They paused by one of the largest pools, a circular basin 300 feet across, draining slowly as the water poured out through a breach in its side. Granger moved carefully down the deepening bank, forking specimens into the rack of beakers, while Holliday stood on the narrow causeway between the pool and the lake, looking up at the dark overhang of the space platform as it loomed into the darkness above him like the stern of a ship.

He was examining the shattered air-lock of one of the crew domes when he suddenly saw something move across the surface of the deck. For a moment he imagined that he had seen a passenger who had somehow survived the vehicle's crash, then realized that it was merely the reflection in the aluminized skin of a ripple in the pool behind him.

He turned around to see Granger, ten feet below him, up to his knees in the water, staring out carefully across the pool.

'Did you throw something?' Granger asked.

Holliday shook his head. 'No.' Without thinking, he added: 'It must have been a fish jumping.'

'Fish? There isn't a single fish alive on the entire planet. The whole zoological class died out ten years ago. Strange, though.'

Just then the fish jumped again.

For a few moments, standing motionless in the half-light, they watched it together, as its slim silver body leapt frantically out of the tepid shallow water, its short glistening arcs carrying it to and fro across the pool.

'Dog-fish,' Granger muttered. 'Shark family. Highly adaptable – need to be, to have survived here. Damn it, it may well be the only fish still living.'

Holliday moved down the bank, his feet sinking in the oozing mud. 'Isn't the water too salty?'

Granger bent down and scooped up some of the water, sipped it tentatively. 'Saline, but comparatively dilute.' He glanced over his shoulder at the lake. 'Perhaps there's continuous evaporation off the lake surface and local condensation here. A freak distillation couple.' He slapped Holliday on the shoulder. 'Holliday, this should be interesting.'

The dog-fish was leaping frantically towards them, its two-foot body twisting and flicking. Low mud banks were emerging all over the surface of the pool; in only a few places towards the centre was the water more than a foot deep.

Holliday pointed to the breach in the bank fifty yards away, gestured Granger after him and began to run towards it.

Five minutes later they had effectively dammed up the breach. Holliday returned for the jeep and drove it carefully through the winding saddles between the pools. He lowered the ramp and began to force the sides of the fish-pool in towards each other. After two or three hours he had narrowed the diameter from a hundred yards to under sixty, and the depth of the water had increased to over two feet. The dog-fish had ceased to jump and swam smoothly just below the surface, snapping at the countless small plants which had been tumbled into the water by the jeep's ramp. Its slim white body seemed white and unmarked, the small fins trim and powerful.

Granger sat on the bonnet of the jeep, his back against the windshield, watching Holliday with admiration.

'You obviously have hidden reserves,' he said ungrudgingly. 'I didn't think you had it in you.'

Holliday washed his hands in the water, then stepped over the churned mud which formed the boundary of the pool. A few feet behind him the dog-fish veered and lunged.

'I want to keep it alive,' Holliday said matter-of-factly. 'Don't you see, Granger, the fishes stayed behind when the first amphibians emerged from the seas two hundred million years ago, just as you and I, in turn, are staying behind now. In a sense all fish are images of ourselves seen in the sea's mirror.'

He slumped down on the running board. His clothes were soaked and streaked with salt, and he gasped at the damp air. To the west, just above the long bulk of the Florida coastline, rising from the ocean floor like an enormous aircraft carrier, were the first dawn thermal fronts. 'Will it be all right to leave it until this evening?'

Granger climbed into the driving seat. 'Don't worry. Come on, you need a rest.' He pointed up at the overhanging rim of the launching platform. 'That should shade it for a few hours, help to keep the temperature down.'

As they neared the town Granger slowed to wave to the old

people retreating from their porches, fixing the shutters on the steel cabins.

'What about your interview with Bullen?' he asked Holliday soberly. 'He'll be waiting for you.'

'Leave here? After last night? It's out of the question.'

Granger shook his head as he parked the car outside the Neptune. 'Aren't you rather over-estimating the importance of one dog-fish? There were millions of them once, the vermin of the sea.'

'You're missing the point,' Holliday said, sinking back into the seat, trying to wipe the salt out of his eyes. 'That fish means that there's still something to be done here. Earth isn't dead and exhausted after all. We can breed new forms of life, a completely new biological kingdom.'

Eyes fixed on this private vision, Holliday sat holding the steering wheel while Granger went into the bar to collect a crate of beer. On his return the migration officer was with him.

Bullen put a foot on the running board, looked into the car. 'Well, how about it, Holliday? I'd like to make an early start. If you're not interested I'll be off. There's a rich new life out there, first step to the stars. Tom Juranda and the Merryweather boys are leaving next week. Do you want to be with them?'

'Sorry,' Holliday said curtly. He pulled the crate of beer into the car and let out the clutch, gunned the jeep away down the empty street in a roar of dust.

Half an hour later, as he stepped out on to the terrace at Idle End, cool and refreshed after his shower, he watched the helicopter roar overhead, its black propeller scudding, then disappear over the kelp flats towards the hull of the wrecked space platform.

'Come on, let's go! What's the matter?'

'Hold it,' Granger said. 'You're getting over-eager. Don't interfere too much, you'll kill the damn thing with kindness. What have you got there?' He pointed to the can Holliday had placed in the dashboard compartment.

'Breadcrumbs.'

Granger sighed, then gently closed the door. 'I'm impressed. I really am. I wish you'd look after me this way. I'm gasping for air too.'

They were five miles from the lake when Holliday leaned forward over the wheel and pointed to the crisp tyre-prints in the soft salt flowing over the road ahead.

'Someone's there already.'

Granger shrugged. 'What of it? They've probably gone to look at the platform.' He chuckled quietly. 'Don't you want to share the New Eden with anyone else? Or just you alone, and a consultant biologist?'

Holliday peered through the windshield. 'Those platforms annoy me, the way they're hurled down as if Earth were a garbage dump. Still, if it wasn't for this one I wouldn't have found the fish.'

They reached the lake and made their way towards the pool, the erratic track of the car ahead winding in and out of the pools. Two hundred yards from the platform it had been parked, blocking the route for Holliday and Granger.

'That's the Merryweathers' car,' Holliday said as they walked around the big stripped-down Buick, slashed with yellow paint and fitted with sirens and pennants. 'The two boys must have come out here.'

Granger pointed. 'One of them's up on the platform.'

The younger brother had climbed on to the rim, was shouting down like an umpire at the antics of two other boys, one his brother, the other Tom Juranda, a tall broad-shouldered youth in a space cadet's jerkin. They were standing at the edge of the fish-pool, stones and salt blocks in their hands, hurling them into the pool.

Leaving Granger, Holliday sprinted on ahead, shouting at the top of his voice. Too preoccupied to hear him, the boys continued to throw their missiles into the pool, while the younger Merryweather egged them on from the platform above. Just before Holliday reached them Tom Juranda ran a few yards along the bank and began to kick the mud-wall into the air, then resumed his target throwing.

'Juranda! Get away from there!' Holliday bellowed. 'Put those stones down!'

He reached Juranda as the youth was about to hurl a brick-sized lump of salt into the pool, seized him by the shoulder and flung him round, knocking the salt out of his hand into a shower of damp crystals, then lunged at the elder Merryweather boy, kicking him away.

The pool had been drained. A deep breach had been cut through the bank and the water had poured out into the surrounding gulleys and pools. Down in the centre of the basin, in a litter of stones and spattered salt, was the crushed but still wriggling body of the dog-fish, twisting itself helplessly in the bare inch of water that remained. Dark red blood poured from wounds in its body, staining the salt.

Holliday hurled himself at Juranda, shook the youth savagely by the shoulders.

'Juranda! Do you realize what you've done, you –' Exhausted, Holliday released him and staggered down into the centre of the pool, kicked away the stones and stood looking at the fish twitching at his feet.

'Sorry, Holliday,' the older Merryweather boy said tentatively behind him. 'We didn't know it was your fish.'

Holliday waved him away, then let his arms fall limply to his sides. He felt numbed and baffled, unable to resolve his anger and frustration.

Tom Juranda began to laugh, and shouted something derisively. Their tension broken, the boys turned and ran off together across the dunes towards their car, yelling and playing catch with each other, mimicking Holliday's outrage.

Granger let them go by, then walked across to the pool, wincing when he saw the empty basin.

'Holliday,' he called. 'Come on.'

Holliday shook his head, staring at the beaten body of the fish.

Granger stepped down the bank to him. Sirens hooted in the distance as the Buick roared off. 'Those damn children.' He took Holliday gently by the arm. 'I'm sorry,' he said quietly. 'But it's not the end of the world.'

Bending down, Holliday reached towards the fish, lying still now, the mud around it slick with blood. His hands hesitated, then retreated.

'Nothing we can do, is there?' he said impersonally.

Granger examined the fish. Apart from the large wound in its side and the flattened skull the skin was intact. 'Why not have it stuffed?' he suggested seriously.

Holliday stared at him incredulously, his face contorting. For a moment he said nothing. Then, almost berserk, he shouted: 'Have it stuffed? Are you crazy? Do you think I want to make a dummy of myself, fill my own head with straw?'

Turning on his heel, he shouldered past Granger and swung himself roughly out of the pool.

1961

THE OVERLOADED MAN

Faulkner was slowly going insane.

After breakfast he waited impatiently in the lounge while his wife tidied up in the kitchen. She would be gone within two or three minutes, but for some reason he always found the short wait each morning almost unbearable. As he drew the Venetian blinds and readied the reclining chair on the veranda he listened to Julia moving about efficiently. In the same strict sequence she stacked the cups and plates in the dishwasher, slid the pot roast for that evening's dinner into the auto-cooker and selected the alarm, lowered the air-conditioner, refrigerator and immersion heater settings, switched open the oil storage manifolds for the delivery tanker that afternoon, and retracted her section of the garage door.

Faulkner followed the sequence with admiration, counting off each successive step as the dials clicked and snapped.

You ought to be in B-52's, he thought, or in the control house of a petrochemicals plant. In fact Julia worked in the personnel section at the Clinic, and no doubt spent all day in the same whirl of efficiency, stabbing buttons marked 'Jones', 'Smith', and 'Brown', shunting paraplegics to the left, paranoids to the right.

She stepped into the lounge and came over to him, the standard executive product in brisk black suit and white blouse.

'Aren't you going to the school today?' she asked.

Faulkner shook his head, played with some papers on the desk. 'No, I'm still on creative reflection. Just for this week. Professor Harman thought I'd been taking too many classes and getting stale.'

She nodded, looking at him doubtfully. For three weeks now he had been lying around at home, dozing on the veranda, and she was beginning to get suspicious. Sooner or later, Faulkner realized, she would find out, but by then he hoped to be out of reach. He longed to tell her the truth, that two months ago he had resigned from his job as a lecturer at the Business School and had no intention of ever going back. She'd get a damn big surprise when she discovered they had almost expended his last pay cheque, might even have to put up with only one car. Let her work, he thought, she earns more than I did anyway.

With an effort Faulkner smiled at her. *Get out!* his mind screamed, but she still hovered around him indecisively.

'What about your lunch? There's no –'

'Don't worry about me,' Faulkner cut in quickly, watching the clock. 'I gave up eating six months ago. You have lunch at the Clinic.'

Even talking to her had become an effort. He wished they could communicate by means of notes; had even bought two scribble pads for this purpose. However, he had never quite been able to suggest that she use hers, although he did leave messages around for her, on the pretext that his mind was so intellectually engaged that talking would break up his thought trains.

Oddly enough, the idea of leaving her never seriously occurred to him. Such an escape would prove nothing. Besides, he had an alternative plan.

'You'll be all right?' she asked, still watching him warily.

'Absolutely,' Faulkner told her, maintaining the smile. It felt like a full day's work.

Her kiss was quick and functional, like the automatic peck of some huge bottle-topping machine. The smile was still on his face as she reached the door. When she had gone he let it fade slowly, then found himself breathing again and gradually relaxed, letting the tension drain down through his arms and legs. For a few minutes he wandered blankly around the empty house, then made his way into the lounge again, ready to begin his serious work.

His programme usually followed the same course. First, from

the centre drawer of his desk he took a small alarm clock, fitted with a battery and wrist strap. Sitting down on the veranda, he fastened the strap to his wrist, wound and set the clock and placed it on the table next to him, binding his arm to the chair so that there was no danger of dragging the clock onto the floor.

Ready now, he lay back and surveyed the scene in front of him.

Menninger Village, or the 'Bin' as it was known locally, had been built about ten years earlier as a self-contained housing unit for the graduate staff of the Clinic and their families. In all there were some sixty houses in the development, each designed to fit into a particular architectonic niche, preserving its own identity from within and at the same time merging into the organic unity of the whole development. The object of the architects, faced with the task of compressing a great number of small houses into a four-acre site, had been, firstly, to avoid producing a collection of identical hutches, as in most housing estates, and secondly, to provide a showpiece for a major psychiatric foundation which would serve as a model for the corporate living units of the future.

However, as everyone there had found out, living in the Bin was hell on earth. The architects had employed the so-called psycho-modular system – a basic L-design – and this meant that everything under- or overlapped everything else. The whole development was a sprawl of interlocking frosted glass, white rectangles and curves, at first glance exciting and abstract (*Life* magazine had done several glossy photographic treatments of the new 'living trends' suggested by the Village) but to the people within formless and visually exhausting. Most of the Clinic's senior staff had soon taken off, and the Village was now rented to anyone who could be persuaded to live there.

Faulkner gazed out across the veranda, separating from the clutter of white geometric shapes the eight other houses he could see without moving his head. On his left, immediately adjacent, were the Penzils, with the McPhersons on the right; the other six houses were directly ahead, on the far side of a muddle of interlocking garden areas, abstract rat-runs divided by waist-high white panelling, glass angle-pieces and slatted screens.

In the Penzils' garden was a collection of huge alphabet blocks, each three high, which their two children played with. Often they left messages out on the grass for Faulkner to read, sometimes obscene, at others merely gnomic and obscure. This morning's came into the latter category. The blocks spelled out:

STOP AND GO

Speculating on the total significance of this statement, Faulkner let his mind relax, his eyes staring blankly at the houses. Gradually their already obscured outlines began to merge and fade, and the long balconies and ramps partly hidden by the intervening trees became disembodied forms, like gigantic geometric units.

Breathing slowly, Faulkner steadily closed his mind, then without any effort erased his awareness of the identity of the house opposite.

He was now looking at a cubist landscape, a collection of random white forms below a blue backdrop, across which several powdery green blurs moved slowly backwards and forwards. Idly, he wondered what these geometric forms really represented – he knew that only a few seconds earlier they had constituted an immediately familiar part of his everyday existence – but however he rearranged them spatially in his mind, or sought their associations, they still remained a random assembly of geometric forms.

He had discovered this talent only about three weeks ago. Balefully eyeing the silent television set in the lounge one Sunday morning, he had suddenly realized that he had so completely accepted and assimilated the physical form of the plastic cabinet that he could no longer remember its function. It had required a considerable mental effort to recover himself and re-identify it. Out of interest he had tried out the new talent on other objects, found that it was particularly successful with over-associated ones such as washing machines, cars and other consumer goods. Stripped of their accretions of sales slogans and status imperatives, their real claim to reality was so tenuous that it needed little mental effort to obliterate them altogether.

The effect was similar to that of mescaline and other hallucinogens, under whose influence the dents in a cushion became as vivid as the craters of the moon, the folds in a curtain the ripples in the waves of eternity.

During the following weeks Faulkner had experimented carefully, training his ability to operate the cut-out switches. The process was slow, but gradually he found himself able to eliminate larger and larger groups of objects, the mass-produced furniture in the lounge, the over-enamelled gadgets in the kitchen, his car in the garage – de-identified, it sat in the half-light like an enormous vegetable marrow, flaccid and gleaming; trying to identify it had driven him almost out of his mind. 'What on earth could it *possibly* be?' he had asked himself helplessly, splitting his sides with laughter – and as the facility developed he had dimly perceived that here was an escape route from the intolerable world in which he found himself at the Village.

He had described the facility to Ross Hendricks, who lived a few houses away, also a lecturer at the Business School and Faulkner's only close friend.

'I may actually be stepping out of time,' Faulkner speculated. 'Without a time sense consciousness is difficult to visualize. That is, eliminating the vector of time from the de-identified object frees it from all its everyday cognitive associations. Alternatively, I may have stumbled on a means of repressing the photo-associative centres that normally identify visual objects, in the same way that you can so listen to someone speaking your own language that none of the sounds has any meaning. Everyone's tried this at some time.'

Hendricks had nodded. 'But don't make a career out of it, though.' He eyed Faulkner carefully. 'You can't simply turn a blind eye to the world. The subject-object relationship is not as polar as Descartes' "Cogito ergo sum" suggests. By any degree to which you devalue the external world so you devalue yourself. It seems to me that your real problem is to reverse the process.'

But Hendricks, however sympathetic, was beyond helping Faulkner. Besides, it was pleasant to see the world afresh again, to wallow in an endless panorama of brilliantly coloured images. What did it matter if there was form but no content?

A sharp click woke him abruptly. He sat up with a jolt, fumbling with the alarm clock, which had been set to wake him at 11 o'clock. Looking at it, he saw that it was only 10.55. The alarm had not rung, nor had he received a shock from the battery. Yet the click had been distinct. However, there were so many servos and robots around the house that it could have been anything.

A dark shape moved across the frosted glass panel which formed the side wall of the lounge. Through it, into the narrow drive separating his house from the Penzils', he saw a car draw to a halt and park, a young woman in a blue smock climb out and walk across the gravel. This was Penzil's sister-in-law, a girl of about twenty who had been staying with them for a couple of months. As she disappeared into the house Faulkner quickly unstrapped his wrist and stood up. Opening the veranda doors, he sauntered down into the garden, glancing back over his shoulder.

The girl, Louise (he had never spoken to her), went to sculpture classes in the morning, and on her return regularly took a leisurely shower before going out onto the roof to sunbathe.

Faulkner hung around the bottom of the garden, flipping stones into the pond and pretending to straighten some of the pergola slats, then noticed that the McPhersons' 15-year-old son Harvey was approaching along the other garden.

'Why aren't you at school?' he asked Harvey, a gangling youth with an intelligent ferretlike face under a mop of brown hair.

'I should be,' Harvey told him easily. 'But I convinced Mother I was overtense, and Morrison' – his father – 'said I was ratiocinating too much.' He shrugged. 'Patients here are overpermissive.'

'For once you're right,' Faulkner agreed, watching the shower stall over his shoulder. A pink form moved about, adjusting taps, and there was the sound of water jetting.

'Tell me, Mr Faulkner,' Harvey asked. 'Do you realize that since the death of Einstein in 1955 there hasn't been a single living genius? From Michelangelo, through Shakespeare, Newton, Beethoven, Goethe, Darwin, Freud and Einstein there's always been a living genius. Now for the first time in 500 years we're on our own.'

Faulkner nodded, his eyes engaged. 'I know,' he said. 'I feel damned lonely about it too.'

When the shower was over he grunted to Harvey, wandered back to the veranda, and took up his position again in the chair, the battery lead strapped to his wrist.

Steadily, object by object, he began to switch off the world around him. The houses opposite went first. The white masses of the roofs and balconies he resolved quickly into flat rectangles, the lines of windows into small squares of colour like the grids in a Mondrian abstract. The sky was a blank field of blue. In the distance an aircraft moved across it, engines hammering. Carefully Faulkner repressed the identity of the image, then watched the slim silver dart move slowly away like a vanishing fragment from a cartoon dream.

As he waited for the engines to fade he was conscious of the sourceless click he had heard earlier that morning. It sounded only a few feet away, near the French window on his right, but he was too immersed in the unfolding kaleidoscope to rouse himself.

When the plane had gone he turned his attention to the garden, quickly blotted out the white fencing, the fake pergola, the elliptical disc of the ornamental pool. The pathway reached out to encircle the pool, and when he blanked out his memories of the countless times he had wandered up and down its length it reared up into the air like a terracotta arm holding an enormous silver jewel.

Satisfied that he had obliterated the Village and the garden, Faulkner then began to demolish the house. Here the objects around him were more familiar, highly personalized extensions of himself. He began with the veranda furniture, transforming the tubular chairs and glass-topped table into a trio of involuted green coils, then swung his head slightly and selected the TV set inside the lounge on his right. It clung limply to its identity. Easily he unfocused his mind and reduced the brown plastic box, with its fake wooden veining, to an amorphous blur.

One by one he cleared the bookcase and desk of all associations, the standard lamps and picture frames. Like lumber in some psychological warehouse, they were suspended behind him *in vacuo*, the white armchairs and sofas like blunted rectangular clouds.

Anchored to reality only by the alarm mechanism clamped to his wrist, Faulkner craned his head from left to right, systematically obliterating all traces of meaning from the world around him, reducing everything to its formal visual values.

Gradually these too began to lose their meaning, the abstract masses of colour dissolving, drawing Faulkner after them into a world of pure psychic sensation, where blocks of ideation hung like magnetic fields in a cloud chamber ...

With a shattering blast, the alarm rang out, the battery driving sharp spurs of pain into Faulkner's forearm. Scalp tingling, he pulled himself back into reality and clawed away the wrist strap, massaging his arm rapidly, then slapped off the alarm.

For a few minutes he sat kneading his wrist, re-identifying all the objects around him, the houses opposite, the gardens, his home, aware that a glass wall had been inserted between them and his own psyche. However carefully he focused his mind on the world outside, a screen still separated them, its opacity thickening imperceptibly.

On other levels as well, bulkheads were shifting into place.

His wife reached home at 6.00, tired out after a busy intake day, annoyed to find Faulkner ambling about in a semistupor, the veranda littered with dirty glasses.

'Well, clean it up!' she snapped when Faulkner vacated his chair for her and prepared to take off upstairs. 'Don't leave the place like this. What's the matter with you? Come on, *connect*!'

Cramming a handful of glasses together, Faulkner mumbled to himself and started for the kitchen, found Julia blocking the way out when he tried to leave. Something was on her mind. She sipped quickly at her martini, then began to throw out probes about the school. He assumed she had rung there on some pretext and had found her suspicions reinforced when she referred in passing to himself.

'Liaison is terrible,' Faulkner told her. 'Take two days off and no one remembers you work there.' By a massive effort of concentration he had managed to avoid looking his wife in the face since she arrived. In fact, they had not exchanged a direct glance for over a week. Hopefully he wondered if this might be getting her down.

Supper was slow agony. The smells of the auto-cooked pot roast had permeated the house all afternoon. Unable to eat more than a few mouthfuls, he had nothing on which to focus his attention. Luckily Julia had a brisk appetite and he could stare at the top of her head as she ate, let his eyes wander around the room when she looked up.

After supper, thankfully, there was television. Dusk blanked out the other houses in the Village, and they sat in the darkness around the set, Julia grumbling at the programmes.

'Why do we watch *every* night?' she asked. 'It's a total time waster.'

Faulkner gestured airily. 'It's an interesting social document.' Slumped down into the wing chair, hands apparently behind his neck, he could press his fingers into his ears, at will blot out the sounds of the programme. 'Don't pay any attention to what they're saying,' he told his wife. 'It makes more sense.' He watched the characters mouthing silently like demented fish. The close-ups in melodramas were particularly hilarious; the more intense the situation the broader was the farce.

Something kicked his knee sharply. He looked up to see his wife bending over him, eyebrows knotted together, mouth working furiously. Fingers still pressed to his ears, Faulkner examined her face with detachment, for a moment speculated whether to complete the process and switch her off as he had switched off the rest of the world earlier that day. When he did he wouldn't bother to set the alarm . . .

'Harry!' he heard his wife bellow.

He sat up with a start, the row from the set backing up his wife's voice.

'What's the matter? I was asleep.'

'You were in a trance, you mean. For God's sake answer when I talk to you. I was saying that I saw Harriet Tizzard this afternoon.' Faulkner groaned and his wife swerved on him. 'I know you can't stand the Tizzards but I've decided we ought to see more of them . . .'

As his wife rattled on, Faulkner eased himself down behind the wings. When she was settled back in her chair he moved his hands up behind his neck. After a few discretionary grunts, he slid his fingers into his ears and blotted out her voice, then lay quietly watching the silent screen.

By 10 o'clock the next morning he was out on the veranda again, alarm strapped to his wrist. For the next hour he lay back enjoying the disembodied forms suspended around him, his mind free of its anxieties. When the alarm woke him at 11.00 he felt refreshed and relaxed. For a few moments he was able to survey the nearby houses with the visual curiosity their architects had intended. Gradually, however, everything began to secrete its poison again, its overlay of nagging associations, and within ten minutes he was looking fretfully at his wristwatch.

When Louise Penzil's car pulled into the drive he disconnected the alarm and sauntered out into the garden, head down to shut out as many of the surrounding houses as possible. As he was idling around the pergola, replacing the slats torn loose by the roses, Harvey McPherson suddenly popped his head over the fence.

'Harvey, are you still around? Don't you ever go to school?'

'Well, I'm on this relaxation course of Mother's,' Harvey explained. 'I find the competitive context of the classroom is –'

'I'm trying to relax too,' Faulkner cut in. 'Let's leave it at that. Why don't you beat it?'

Unruffled, Harvey pressed on. 'Mr Faulkner, I've got a sort of problem in metaphysics that's been bothering me. Maybe you could help. The only absolute in space-time is supposed to be the speed of light. But as a matter of fact any estimate of the speed of light involves the component of time, which is subjectively variable – so, bam, what's left?'

'Girls,' Faulkner said. He glanced over his shoulder at the Penzil house and then turned back moodily to Harvey.

Harvey frowned, trying to straighten his hair. 'What are you talking about?'

'Girls,' Faulkner repeated. 'You know, the weaker sex, the distaff side.'

'Oh, for Pete's sake.' Shaking his head, Harvey walked back to his house, muttering to himself.

That'll shut you up, Faulkner thought. He started to scan the Penzils' house through the slats of the pergola, then suddenly spotted Harry Penzil standing in the centre of his veranda window, frowning out at him.

Quickly Faulkner turned his back and pretended to trim the roses. By the time he managed to work his way indoors he was sweating heavily. Harry Penzil was the sort of man liable to straddle fences and come out leading with a right swing.

Mixing himself a drink in the kitchen, Faulkner brought it out onto the veranda and sat down waiting for his embarrassment to subside before setting the alarm mechanism.

He was listening carefully for any sounds from the Penzils' when he heard a familiar soft metallic click from the house on his right.

Faulkner sat forward, examining the veranda wall. This was a slab of heavy frosted glass, completely opaque, carrying white roof timbers, clipped onto which were slabs of corrugated polythene sheeting. Just beyond the veranda, screening the proximal portions of the adjacent gardens, was a ten-foot-high metal lattice extending about twenty feet down the garden fence and strung with japonica.

Inspecting the lattice carefully, Faulkner suddenly noticed the outline of a square black object on a slender tripod propped up behind the first vertical support just three feet from the open veranda window, the disc of a small glass eye staring at him unblinkingly through one of the horizontal slots.

A camera! Faulkner leapt out of his chair, gaping incredulously at the instrument. For days it had been clicking away at him. God alone knew what glimpses into his private life Harvey had recorded for his own amusement.

Anger boiling, Faulkner strode across to the lattice, prised one of the metal members off the support beam and seized the camera. As he dragged it through the space the tripod fell away with a clatter and he heard someone on the McPhersons' veranda start up out of a chair.

Faulkner wrestled the camera through, snapping off the remote control cord attached to the shutter lever. Opening the camera, he ripped out the film, then put it down on the floor and stamped its face in with the heel of his shoe. Then, ramming the pieces together, he stepped forward and hurled them over the fence towards the far end of the McPhersons' garden.

As he returned to finish his drink the phone rang in the hall.

'Yes, what is it?' he snapped into the receiver.

'Is that you, Harry? Julia here.'

'Who?' Faulkner said, not thinking. 'Oh, yes. Well, how are things?'

'Not too good, by the sound of it.' His wife's voice had become harder. 'I've just had a long talk with Professor Harman. He told me that you resigned from the school two months ago. Harry, what are you playing at? I can hardly believe it.'

'I can hardly believe it either,' Faulkner retorted jocularly. 'It's the best news I've had for years. Thanks for confirming it.'

'Harry!' His wife was shouting now. 'Pull yourself together! If you think I'm going to support you you're very much mistaken. Professor Harman said –'

'That idiot Harman!' Faulkner interrupted. 'Don't you realize he was trying to drive me insane?' As his wife's voice rose to an hysterical squawk he held the receiver away from him, then quietly replaced it in the cradle. After a pause he took it off again and laid it down on the stack of directories.

Outside, the spring morning hung over the Village like a curtain of silence. Here and there a tree stirred in the warm air, or a window opened and caught the sunlight, but otherwise the quiet and stillness were unbroken.

Lying on the veranda, the alarm mechanism discarded on the floor below his chair, Faulkner sank deeper and deeper into his private reverie, into the demolished world of form and colour which hung motionlessly around him. The houses opposite had vanished, their places taken by long white rectangular bands. The garden was a green ramp at the end of which poised the silver ellipse of the pond. The veranda was a transparent cube, in the centre of which he felt himself suspended like an image floating on a sea of ideation. He had obliterated not only the world around him, but his own body, and his limbs and trunk seemed an extension of his mind, disembodied forms whose physical dimensions pressed upon it like a dream's awareness of its own identity.

Some hours later, as he rotated slowly through his reverie, he was aware of a sudden intrusion into his field of vision. Focusing his eyes, with surprise he saw the dark-suited figure of his wife standing in front of him, shouting angrily and gesturing with her handbag.

For a few minutes Faulkner examined the discrete entity she familiarly presented, the proportions of her legs and arms, the planes of her face. Then, without moving, he began to dismantle her mentally, obliterating her literally limb by limb. First he forgot her hands, forever snapping and twisting like frenzied birds, then her arms and shoulders, erasing all his memories of their energy and motion. Finally, as it pressed closer to him, mouth working wildly, he forgot her face, so that it presented nothing more than a blunted wedge of pink-grey dough, deformed by various ridges and grooves, split by apertures that opened and closed like the vents of some curious bellows.

Turning back to the silent dreamscape, he was aware of her jostling insistently behind him. Her presence seemed ugly and formless, a bundle of obtrusive angles.

Then at last they came into brief physical contact. Gesturing her away, he felt her fasten like a dog upon his arm. He tried to shake her off but she clung to him, jerking about in an outpouring of anger.

Her rhythms were sharp and ungainly. To begin with he tried to ignore them; then he began to restrain and smooth her, moulding her angular form into a softer and rounder one.

As he worked away, kneading her like a sculptor shaping clay, he noticed a series of crackling noises, over which a persistent scream was just barely audible. When he finished he let her fall to the floor, a softly squeaking lump of spongy rubber.

Faulkner returned to his reverie, re-assimilating the unaltered landscape. His brush with his wife had reminded him of the one encumbrance that still remained – his own body. Although he had forgotten its identity it none the less felt heavy and warm, vaguely uncomfortable, like a badly made bed to a restless sleeper. What he sought was pure ideation, the undisturbed sensation of psychic being untransmuted by any physical medium. Only thus could he escape the nausea of the external world.

Somewhere in his mind an idea suggested itself. Rising from his chair, he walked out across the veranda, unaware of the physical movements involved, but propelling himself towards the far end of the garden.

Hidden by the rose pergola, he stood for five minutes at the edge of the pond, then stepped into the water. Trousers billowing around his knees, he waded out slowly. When he reached the centre he sat down, pushing the weeds apart, and lay back in the shallow water.

Slowly he felt the puttylike mass of his body dissolving, its temperature growing cooler and less oppressive. Looking out through the surface of the water six inches above his face, he watched the blue disc of the sky, cloudless and undisturbed, expanding to fill his consciousness. At last he had found the perfect background, the only possible field of ideation, an absolute continuum of existence uncontaminated by material excrescences.

Steadily watching it, he waited for the world to dissolve and set him free.

1961

MR F. IS MR F.

And baby makes three.

... Eleven o'clock. Hanson should have reached here by now. Elizabeth! Damn, why does she always move so quietly?

Climbing down from the window overlooking the road, Freeman ran back to his bed and jumped in, smoothing the blankets over his knees. As his wife poked her head around the door he smiled up at her guilelessly, pretending to read a magazine.

'Everything all right?' she asked, eyeing him shrewdly. She moved her matronly bulk towards him and began to straighten the bed. Freeman fidgeted irritably, pushing her away when she tried to lift him off the pillow on which he was sitting.

'For heaven's sake, Elizabeth, I'm not a child!' he remonstrated, controlling his sing-song voice with difficulty.

'What's happened to Hanson? He was supposed to be here half an hour ago.'

His wife shook her large handsome head and went over to the window. The loose cotton dress disguised her figure, but as she reached up to the bolt Freeman could see the incipient swell of her pregnancy.

'He must have missed his train.' With a single twist of her forearm she securely fastened the upper bolt, which had taken Freeman ten minutes to unlatch.

'I thought I could hear it banging,' she said pointedly. 'We don't want you to catch a cold, do we?'

Freeman waited impatiently for her to leave, glancing at his watch. When his wife paused at the foot of the bed, surveying him carefully, he could barely restrain himself from shouting at her.

'I'm getting the baby's clothes together,' she said, adding aloud to herself, 'which reminds me, you need a new dressing gown. That old one of yours is losing its shape.'

Freeman pulled the lapels of the dressing gown across each other, as much to hide his bare chest as to fill out the gown.

'Elizabeth, I've had this for years and it's perfectly good. You're getting an obsession about renewing everything.' He hesitated, realizing the tactlessness of this remark – he should be flattered that she was identifying him with the expected baby. If the strength of the identification was sometimes alarming, this was probably because she was having her first child at a comparatively late age, in her early forties. Besides, he had been ill and bed-ridden during the past month (and what were *his* unconscious motives?) which only served to reinforce the confusion.

'Elizabeth. I'm sorry. It's been good of you to look after me. Perhaps we should call a doctor.'

No! something screamed inside him.

As if hearing this, his wife shook her head in agreement.

'You'll be all right soon. Let nature take its proper course. I don't think you need to see the doctor yet.'

Yet?

Freeman listened to her feet disappearing down the carpeted staircase. A few minutes later the sound of the washing machine drummed out from the kitchen.

Yet!

Freeman slipped quickly out of bed and went into the bathroom.

The cupboard beside the wash-basin was crammed with drying baby clothes, which Elizabeth had either bought or knitted, then carefully washed and sterilized. On each of the five shelves a large square of gauze covered the neat piles, but he could see that most of the clothes were blue, a few white and none pink.

I hope Elizabeth is right, he thought. *If she is it's certainly going to be the world's best-dressed baby. We're supporting an industry single-handed.*

He bent down to the bottom compartment, and from below

the tank pulled out a small set of scales. On the shelf immediately above he noticed a large brown garment, a six-year-old's one-piece romper suit. Next to it was a set of vests, outsize, almost big enough to fit Freeman himself. He stripped off his dressing gown and stepped on to the platform. In the mirror behind the door he examined his small hairless body, with its thin shoulders and narrow hips, long coltish legs.

Six stone nine pounds yesterday. Averting his eyes from the dial, he listened to the washing machine below, then waited for the pointer to steady.

'*Six stone two pounds!*'

Fumbling with his dressing gown, Freeman pushed the scales under the tank.

Six stone two pounds! A drop of seven pounds in twenty-four hours!

He hurried back into bed, and sat there trembling nervously, fingering for his vanished moustache.

Yet only two months ago he had weighed over eleven stone. Seven pounds in a single day, at this rate –

His mind baulked at the conclusion. Trying to steady his knees, he reached for one of the magazines, turned the pages blindly.

And baby makes two.

He had first become aware of the transformation six weeks earlier, almost immediately after Elizabeth's pregnancy had been confirmed.

Shaving the next morning in the bathroom before going to the office, he discovered that his moustache was thinning. The usually stiff black bristles were soft and flexible, taking on their former ruddy-brown colouring.

His beard, too, was lighter; normally dark and heavy after only a few hours, it yielded before the first few strokes of the razor, leaving his face pink and soft.

Freeman had credited this apparent rejuvenation to the appearance of the baby. He was forty when he married Elizabeth, two or three years her junior, and had assumed unconsciously that he was too old to become a parent, particularly as he had deliberately selected Elizabeth as an ideal mother-substitute, and saw himself as her child rather than as her parental partner. However, now that a child had actually materialized he felt no resentment towards it. Complimenting himself, he decided that he had entered a new phase of maturity and could whole-heartedly throw himself into the role of young parent.

Hence the disappearing moustache, the fading beard, the youthful spring in his step. He crooned:

> 'Just Lizzie and me,
> And baby makes three.'

Behind him, in the mirror, he watched Elizabeth still asleep, her large hips filling the bed. He was glad to see her rest. Contrary to what he had expected, she was even more concerned with him than with the baby, refusing to allow him to prepare his own breakfast. As he brushed his hair, a rich blond growth, sweeping back off his forehead to cover his bald dome, he reflected wryly on the time-honoured saws in the maternity books about the hypersensitivity of expectant fathers – evidently Elizabeth took these counsels seriously.

He tiptoed back into the bedroom and stood by the open window, basking in the crisp early morning air. Downstairs, while he waited for breakfast, he pulled his old tennis racquet out of the hall cupboard, finally woke Elizabeth when one of his practice strokes cracked the glass in the barometer.

To begin with Freeman had revelled in his new-found energy. He took Elizabeth boating, rowing her furiously up and down the river, rediscovering all the physical pleasures he had been too preoccupied to enjoy in his early twenties. He would go shopping with Elizabeth, steering her smoothly along the pavement, carrying all her baby purchases, shoulders back, feeling ten feet tall.

However, it was here that he had his first inkling of what was really happening.

Elizabeth was a large woman, attractive in her way, with broad shoulders and strong hips, and accustomed to wearing high heels. Freeman, a stocky man of medium height, had always been slightly shorter than her, but this had never worried him.

When he found that he barely reached above her shoulder he began to examine himself more closely.

On one of their shopping expeditions (Elizabeth always took Freeman with her, unselfishly asked his opinions, what he preferred, almost as if *he* would be wearing the tiny matinee coats and dresses) a saleswoman unwittingly referred to Elizabeth as his 'mother'. Jolted, Freeman had recognized the obvious disparity between them – the pregnancy was making Elizabeth's face puffy, filling out her neck and shoulders, while his own features were smooth and unlined.

When they reached home he wandered around the lounge and dining room, realized that the furniture and bookshelves seemed larger and more bulky. Upstairs in the bathroom he climbed on the scales for the first time, found that he had lost one stone six pounds in weight.

Undressing that night, he made another curious discovery.

Elizabeth was taking in the seams of his jackets and trousers. She had said nothing to him about this, and when he saw her sewing away over her needle basket he had assumed she was preparing something for the baby.

During the next days his first flush of spring vigour faded. Strange changes were taking place in his body – his skin and hair, his entire musculature, seemed transformed. The planes of his face had altered, the jaw was trimmer, the nose less prominent, cheeks smooth and unblemished.

Examining his mouth in the mirror, he found that most of his old metal fillings had vanished, firm white enamel taking their place.

He continued to go to the office, conscious of the stares of his colleagues around him. The day after he found he could no longer reach the reference books on the shelf behind his desk he stayed at home, feigning an attack of influenza.

Elizabeth seemed to understand completely. Freeman had said nothing to her, afraid that she might be terrified into a miscarriage if she learned the truth. Swathed in his old dressing gown, a woollen scarf around his neck and chest to make his slim figure appear more bulky, he sat on the sofa in the lounge, blankets piled across him, a firm cushion raising him higher off the seat.

Carefully he tried to avoid standing whenever Elizabeth was in the room, and when absolutely necessary circled behind the furniture on tiptoe.

A week later, however, when his feet no longer touched the floor below the dining-room table, he decided to remain in his bed upstairs.

Elizabeth agreed readily. All the while she watched her husband with her bland impassive eyes, quietly readying herself for the baby.

Damn Hanson, Freeman thought. At eleven forty-five he had still not appeared. Freeman flipped through the magazine without looking at it, glancing irritably at his watch every few seconds. The strap was now too large for his wrist and twice he had prised additional holes for the clasp.

How to describe his metamorphosis to Hanson he had not decided, plagued as he was by curious doubts. He was not even sure what *was* happening. Certainly he had lost a remarkable amount of weight – up to eight or nine pounds each day – and almost a foot in height, but without any accompanying loss of health. He had, in fact, reverted to the age and physique of a fourteen-year-old schoolboy.

But what was the real explanation? Freeman asked himself. Was the rejuvenation some sort of psychosomatic excess? Although he felt no conscious animosity towards the expected baby, was he in the grip of an insane attempt at retaliation?

It was this possibility, with its logical prospect of padded cells and white-coated guards, that had frightened Freeman into silence. Elizabeth's doctor was brusque and unsympathetic, and almost certainly would regard Freeman as a neurotic malingerer, perpetrating an elaborate charade designed to substitute himself for his own child in his wife's affections.

Also, Freeman knew, there were other motives, obscure and

intangible. Frightened of examining them, he began to read the magazine.

It was a schoolchild's comic. Annoyed, Freeman stared at the cover, then looked at the stack of magazines which Elizabeth had ordered from the newsagent that morning. They were all the same.

His wife entered her bedroom on the other side of the landing. Freeman slept alone now in what would eventually be the baby's nursery, partly to give himself enough privacy to think, and also to save him the embarrassment of revealing his shrinking body to his wife.

She came in, carrying a small tray on which were a glass of warm milk and two biscuits. Although he was losing weight, Freeman had the eager appetite of a child. He took the biscuits and ate them hurriedly.

Elizabeth sat on the bed, producing a brochure from the pocket of her apron.

'I want to order the baby's cot,' she told him. 'Would you like to choose one of the designs?'

Freeman waved airily. 'Any of them will do. Pick one that's strong and heavy, something he won't be able to climb out of too easily.'

His wife nodded, watching him pensively. All afternoon she spent ironing and cleaning, moving the piles of dry linen into the cupboards on the landing, disinfecting pails and buckets.

They had decided she would have the baby at home.

Four and a half stone!

Freeman gasped at the dial below his feet. During the previous two days he had lost over one stone six pounds, had barely been able to reach up to the handle of the cupboard and open the door. Trying not to look at himself in the mirror, he realized he was now the size of a six-year-old, with a slim chest, slender neck and face. The skirt of the dressing gown trailed across the floor behind him, and only with difficulty could he keep his arms through the voluminous sleeves.

When Elizabeth came up with his breakfast she examined him

critically, put the tray down and went out to one of the landing cupboards. She returned with a small sports-shirt and a pair of corduroy shorts.

'Would you like to wear these, dear?' she asked. 'You'll find them more comfortable.'

Reluctant to use his voice, which had degenerated into a piping treble, Freeman shook his head. After she had gone, however, he pulled off the heavy dressing gown and put on the garments.

Suppressing his doubts, he wondered how to reach the doctor without having to go downstairs to the telephone. So far he had managed to avoid raising his wife's suspicions, but now there was no hope of continuing to do so. He barely reached up to her waist. If she saw him standing upright she might well die of shock on the spot.

Fortunately, Elizabeth left him alone. Once, just after lunch, two men arrived in a van from the department store and delivered a blue cot and play-pen, but he pretended to be asleep until they had gone. Despite his anxiety, Freeman easily fell asleep – he had begun to feel tired after lunch – and woke two hours later to find that Elizabeth had made the bed in the cot, swathing the blue blankets and pillow in a plastic sheet.

Below this, shackled to the wooden sides, he could see the white leather straps of a restraining harness.

The next morning Freeman decided to escape. His weight was down to only three stone one pound, and the clothes Elizabeth had given him the previous day were already three sizes too large, the trousers supporting themselves precariously around his slender waist. In the bathroom mirror Freeman stared at the small boy, watching him with wide eyes. Dimly he remembered snapshots of his own childhood.

After breakfast, when Elizabeth was out in the garden, he crept downstairs. Through the window he saw her open the dustbin and push inside his business suit and black leather shoes.

Freeman waited helplessly for a moment, and then hurried back to his room. Striding up the huge steps required more effort than he imagined, and by the time he reached the top flight he was too exhausted to climb on to the bed. Panting, he leaned against it for a few minutes. Even if he reached the hospital, how could he convince anyone there of what had happened without having to call Elizabeth along to identify him?

Fortunately, his intelligence was still intact. Given a pencil and paper he would soon demonstrate his adult mind, a circumstantial knowledge of social affairs that no infant prodigy could ever possess.

His first task was to reach the hospital or, failing that, the local police station. Luckily, all he needed to do was walk along the nearest main thoroughfare – a four-year-old child wandering about on his own would soon be picked up by a constable on duty.

Below, he heard Elizabeth come slowly up the stairs, the laundry basket creaking under her arm. Freeman tried to lift himself on to the bed, but only succeeded in disarranging the sheets. As Elizabeth opened the door he ran around to the far side of the bed and hid his tiny body behind it, resting his chin on the bedspread.

Elizabeth paused, watching his small plump face. For a moment they gazed at each other, Freeman's heart pounding, wondering how she could fail to realize what had happened to him. But she merely smiled and walked through into the bathroom.

Supporting himself on the bedside table, he climbed in, his face away from the bathroom door. On her way out Elizabeth bent down and tucked him up, then slipped out of the room, shutting the door behind her.

The rest of the day Freeman waited for an opportunity to escape, but his wife was busy upstairs, and early that evening, before he could prevent himself, he fell into a deep dreamless sleep.

He woke in a vast white room. Blue light dappled the high walls, along which a line of giant animal figures danced and gambolled. Looking around, he realized that he was still in the nursery. He was wearing a small pair of polka-dot pyjamas (had Elizabeth changed him while he slept?) but they were almost too large for his shrunken arms and legs.

A miniature dressing gown had been laid out across the foot of the bed, a pair of slippers on the floor. Freeman climbed down from the bed and put them on, his balance unsteady. The door was closed, but he pulled a chair over and stood on it, turning the handle with his two small fists.

On the landing he paused, listening carefully. Elizabeth was in the kitchen, humming to herself. One step at a time, Freeman moved down the staircase, watching his wife through the rail. She was standing over the cooker, her broad back almost hiding the machine, warming some milk gruel. Freeman waited until she turned to the sink, then ran across the hall into the lounge and out through the french windows.

The thick soles of his carpet slippers muffled his footsteps, and he broke into a run once he reached the shelter of the front garden. The gate was almost too stiff for him to open, and as he fumbled with the latch a middle-aged woman stopped and peered down at him, frowning at the windows.

Freeman pretended to run back into the house, hoping that Elizabeth had not yet discovered his disappearance. When the woman moved off, he opened the gate, and hurried down the street towards the shopping centre.

He had entered an enormous world. The two-storey houses loomed like canyon walls, the end of the street one hundred yards away below the horizon. The paving stones were massive and uneven, the tall sycamores as distant as the sky. A car came towards him, daylight between its wheels, hesitated and sped on.

He was still fifty yards from the corner when he tripped over one of the pavement stones and was forced to stop. Out of breath, he leaned against a tree, his legs exhausted.

He heard a gate open, and over his shoulder saw Elizabeth glance up and down the street. Quickly he stepped behind the tree, waited until she returned to the house, and then set off again.

Suddenly, sweeping down from the sky, a vast arm lifted him off his feet. Gasping with surprise, he looked up into the face of Mr Symonds, his bank manager.

'You're out early, young man,' Symonds said. He put Freeman down, holding him tightly by one hand. His car was parked in the drive next to them. Leaving the engine running, he began to walk Freeman back down the street. 'Now, let's see, where do you live?'

Freeman tried to pull himself away, jerking his arm furiously, but Symonds hardly noticed his efforts. Elizabeth stepped out of the gate, an apron around her waist, and hurried towards them. Freeman tried to hide between Symonds' legs, felt himself picked up in the bank manager's strong arms and handed to Elizabeth. She held him firmly, his head over her broad shoulder, thanked Symonds and carried him back into the house.

As they crossed the pathway Freeman hung limply, trying to will himself out of existence.

In the nursery he waited for his feet to touch the bed, ready to dive below the blankets, but instead Elizabeth lowered him carefully to the floor, and he discovered he had been placed in the baby's play-pen. He held the rail uncertainly, while Elizabeth bent over and straightened his dressing gown. Then, to Freeman's relief, she turned away.

For five minutes Freeman stood numbly by the rail, outwardly recovering his breath, but at the same time gradually realizing something of which he had been dimly afraid for several days – by an extraordinary inversion of logic, Elizabeth identified him with the baby inside her womb! Far from showing surprise at Freeman's transformation into a three-year-old child, his wife merely accepted this as a natural concomitant of her own pregnancy. In her mind she had externalized the child within her. As Freeman shrank progressively smaller, mirroring the growth of her child, her eyes were fixed on their common focus, and all she could see was the image of her baby.

Still searching for a means of escape, Freeman discovered that he was unable to climb out of the play-pen. The light wooden bars were too strong for his small arms to break, the whole cage too heavy to lift. Exhausting himself, he sat down on the floor, and fiddled nervously with a large coloured ball.

Instead of trying to evade Elizabeth and hide his transformation from her, he realized that he must now attract her attention and force her to recognize his real identity.

Standing up, he began to rock the play-pen from side to side, edging it across to the wall where the sharp corner set up a steady battering.

Elizabeth came out of her bedroom.

'Now, darling, what's all the noise for?' she asked, smiling at him. 'How about a biscuit?' She knelt down by the pen, her face only a few inches from Freeman's.

Screwing up his courage, Freeman looked straight at her, searching the large, unblinking eyes. He took the biscuit, cleared his throat and said carefully: 'I'd nod blor aby.'

Elizabeth ruffled his long blond hair. 'Aren't you, darling? What a sad shame.'

Freeman stamped his foot, then flexed his lips. 'I'd nod blor aby!' he shouted. 'I'd blor usban!'

Laughing to herself, Elizabeth began to empty the wardrobe beside the bed. As Freeman remonstrated with her, struggling helplessly with the strings of consonants, she took out his dinner jacket and overcoat. Then she emptied the chest of drawers, lifting out his shirts and socks, and wrapped them away inside a sheet.

After she had carried everything out she returned and stripped the bed, pushed it back against the wall, putting the baby cot in its place.

Clutching the rail of the play-pen, Freeman watched dumbfounded as the last remnants of his former existence were dispatched below.

'Lisbeg, lep me, I'd –!'

He gave up, searched the floor of the play-pen for something to write with. Summoning his energies, he rocked the cot over to the wall, and in large letters, using the spit which flowed amply from his mouth, wrote:

ELIZABETH HELP ME! I AM NOT A BABY

Banging on the door with his fists, he finally attracted Elizabeth's attention, but when he pointed to the wall the marks had dried.

Weeping with frustration, Freeman toddled across the cage and began to retrace the message. Before he had completed more than two or three letters Elizabeth put her arms around his waist and lifted him out.

A single place had been set at the head of the dining-room table, a new high chair beside it. Still trying to form a coherent sentence, Freeman felt himself rammed into the seat, a large bib tied around his neck.

During the meal he watched Elizabeth carefully, hoping to detect in her motionless face some inkling of recognition, even a fleeting awareness that the two-year-old child sitting in front of her was her husband. Freeman played with his food, smearing crude messages on the tray around his dish, but when he pointed at them Elizabeth clapped her hands, apparently joining in his little triumphs, and then wiped the tray clean. Worn out, Freeman let himself be carried upstairs, lay strapped in the cot under the miniature blankets.

Time was against him. By now, he found, he was asleep for the greater portion of each day. For the first hours he felt fresh and alert, but his energy faded rapidly and after each meal an overwhelming lethargy closed his eyes like a sleeping draught. Dimly he was aware that his metamorphosis continued unchecked – when he woke he could sit up only with difficulty. The effort of standing upright on his buckling legs tired him after a few minutes.

His power of speech had vanished. All he could produce were a few grotesque grunts, or an inarticulate babble. Lying on his back with a bottle of hot milk in his mouth, he knew that his one hope was Hanson. Sooner or later he would call in and discover that Freeman had disappeared and all traces of him had been carefully removed.

Propped against a cushion on the carpet in the lounge, Freeman noted that Elizabeth had emptied his desk and taken down his books from the shelves beside the fireplace. To all intents she was now the widowed mother of a twelve-month-old son, parted from her husband since their honeymoon.

Unconsciously she had begun to assume this role. When they

went out for their morning walks, Freeman strapped back into the pram, a celluloid rabbit rattling a few inches from his nose and almost driving him insane, they passed many people he had known by sight, and all took it for granted that he was Elizabeth's son. As they bent over the pram, poking him in the stomach and complimenting Elizabeth on his size and precosity, several of them referred to her husband, and Elizabeth replied that he was away on an extended trip. In her mind, obviously, she had already dismissed Freeman, forgetting that he had ever existed.

He realized how wrong he was when they returned from what was to be his last outing.

As they neared home Elizabeth hesitated slightly, jolting the pram, apparently uncertain whether to retrace her steps. Someone shouted at them from the distance, and as Freeman tried to identify the familiar voice Elizabeth bent forwards and pulled the hood over his head.

Struggling to free himself, Freeman recognized the tall figure of Hanson towering over the pram, doffing his hat.

'Mrs Freeman, I've been trying to ring you all week. How are you?'

'Very well, Mr Hanson.' She jerked the pram around, trying to keep it between herself and Hanson. Freeman could see that she was momentarily confused. 'I'm afraid our telephone is out of order.'

Hanson side-stepped around the pram, watching Elizabeth with interest. 'What happened to Charles on Saturday? Have to go off on business?'

Elizabeth nodded. 'He was very sorry, Mr Hanson, but something important came up. He'll be away for some time.'

She knew, Freeman said automatically to himself.

Hanson peered under the hood at Freeman. 'Out for a morning stroll, little chap?' To Elizabeth he commented: 'Fine baby there. I always like the angry-looking ones. Your neighbour's?'

Elizabeth shook her head. 'The son of a friend of Charles's. We must be getting along, Mr Hanson.'

'Do call me Robert. See you again soon, eh?'

Elizabeth smiled, her face composed again. 'I'm sure we will, Robert.'

'Good show.' With a roguish grin, Hanson walked off.

She knew!

Astounded, Freeman pushed the blankets back as far as he could, watching Hanson's retreating figure. He turned once to wave to Elizabeth, who raised her hand and then steered the pram through the gate.

Freeman tried to sit up, his eyes fixed on Elizabeth, hoping she would see the anger in his face. But she wheeled the pram swiftly into the passageway, unfastened the straps and lifted Freeman out.

As they went up the staircase he looked down over her shoulder at the telephone, saw that the receiver was off its cradle. All along she had known what was happening, had deliberately pretended not to notice his metamorphosis. She had anticipated each stage of the transformation, the comprehensive wardrobe had been purchased well in advance, the succession of smaller and smaller garments, the play-pen and cot, had been ordered for him, not for the baby.

For a moment Freeman wondered whether she was pregnant at all. The facial puffiness, the broadening figure, might well have been illusory. When she told him she was expecting a baby he had never imagined that *he* would be the baby.

Handling him roughly, she bundled Freeman into his cot and secured him under the blankets. Downstairs he could hear her moving about rapidly, apparently preparing for some emergency. Propelled by an uncharacteristic urgency, she was closing the windows and doors. As he listened to her, Freeman noticed how cold he felt. His small body was swaddled like a new-born infant in a mass of shawls, but his bones were like sticks of ice. A curious drowsiness was coming over him, draining away his anger and fear, and the centre of his awareness was shifting from his eyes to his skin. The thin afternoon light stung his eyes, and as they closed he slipped off into a blurring limbo of shallow sleep, the tender surface of his body aching for relief.

Some while later he felt Elizabeth's hands pull away the

blankets, and was aware of her carrying him across the hallway. Gradually his memory of the house and his own identity began to fade, and his shrinking body clung helplessly to Elizabeth as she lay on her broad bed.

Hating the naked hair that rasped across his face, he now felt clearly for the first time what he had for so long repressed. Before the end he cried out suddenly with joy and wonder, as he remembered the drowned world of his first childhood.

As the child within her quietened, stirring for the last time, Elizabeth sank back on to the pillow, the birth pains slowly receding. Gradually she felt her strength return, the vast world within her settling and annealing itself. Staring at the darkened ceiling, she lay resting for several hours, now and then adjusting her large figure to fit the unfamiliar contours of the bed.

The next morning she rose for half an hour. The child already seemed less burdensome, and three days later she was able to leave her bed completely, a loose smock hiding what remained of her pregnancy. Immediately she began the last task, clearing away all that remained of the baby's clothing, dismantling the cot and play-pen. The clothing she tied into large parcels, then telephoned a local charity which came and collected them. The pram and cot she sold to the second-hand dealer who drove down the street. Within two days she had erased every trace of her husband, stripping the coloured illustrations from the nursery walls and replacing the spare bed in the centre of the floor.

All that remained was the diminishing knot within her, a small clenching fist. When she could almost no longer feel it Elizabeth went to her jewel box and took off her wedding ring.

On her return from the shopping centre the next morning, Elizabeth noticed someone hailing her from a car parked outside her gate.

'Mrs Freeman!' Hanson jumped out of the car and accosted her gaily. 'It's wonderful to see you looking so well.'

Elizabeth gave him a wide heart-warming smile, her handsome face made more sensual by the tumescence of her features. She was wearing a bright silk dress and all visible traces of the pregnancy had vanished.

'Where's Charles?' Hanson asked. 'Still away?'

Elizabeth's smile broadened, her lips parted across her strong white teeth. Her face was curiously expressionless, her eyes momentarily fixed on some horizon far beyond Hanson's face.

Hanson waited uncertainly for Elizabeth to reply. Then, taking the hint, he leaned back into his car and switched off the engine. He rejoined Elizabeth, holding the gate open for her.

So Elizabeth met her husband. Three hours later the metamorphosis of Charles Freeman reached its climax. In that last second Freeman came to his true beginning, the moment of his conception coinciding with the moment of his extinction, the end of his last birth with the beginning of his first death.

And baby makes one.

1961

BILLENNIUM

All day long, and often into the early hours of the morning, the tramp of feet sounded up and down the stairs outside Ward's cubicle. Built into a narrow alcove in a bend of the staircase between the fourth and fifth floors, its plywood walls flexed and creaked with every footstep like the timbers of a rotting windmill. Over a hundred people lived in the top three floors of the old rooming house, and sometimes Ward would lie awake on his narrow bunk until 2 or 3 a.m., mechanically counting the last residents returning from the all-night movies in the stadium half a mile away. Through the window he could hear giant fragments of the amplified dialogue booming among the rooftops. The stadium was never empty. During the day the huge four-sided screen was raised on its davit and athletics meetings or football matches ran continuously. For the people in the houses abutting the stadium the noise must have been unbearable.

Ward, at least, had a certain degree of privacy. Two months earlier, before he came to live on the staircase, he had shared a room with seven others on the ground floor of a house in 755th Street, and the ceaseless press of people jostling past the window had reduced him to a state of exhaustion. The street was always full, an endless clamour of voices and shuffling feet. By 6.30, when he woke, hurrying to take his place in the bathroom queue, the crowds already jammed it from sidewalk to sidewalk, the din punctuated every half minute by the roar of the elevated trains running over the shops on the opposite side of the road. As soon as he saw the advertisement describing the staircase cubicle he had left (like everyone else, he spent most of his spare time scanning the classifieds in the newspapers, moving his lodgings an average of once every two months) despite the higher rental. A cubicle on a staircase would almost certainly be on its own.

However, this had its drawbacks. Most evenings his friends from the library would call in, eager to rest their elbows after the bruising crush of the public reading room. The cubicle was slightly more than four and a half square metres in floor area, half a square metre over the statutory maximum for a single person, the carpenters having taken advantage, illegally, of a recess beside a nearby chimney breast. Consequently Ward had been able to fit a small straight-backed chair into the interval between the bed and the door, so that only one person at a time needed to sit on the bed – in most single cubicles host and guest had to sit side by side on the bed, conversing over their shoulders and changing places periodically to avoid neck-strain.

'You were lucky to find this place,' Rossiter, the most regular visitor, never tired of telling him. He reclined back on the bed, gesturing at the cubicle. 'It's enormous, the perspectives really zoom. I'd be surprised if you haven't got at least five metres here, perhaps six.'

Ward shook his head categorically. Rossiter was his closest friend, but the quest for living space had forged powerful reflexes. 'Just over four and a half, I've measured it carefully. There's no doubt about it.'

Rossiter lifted one eyebrow. 'I'm amazed. It must be the ceiling then.'

Manipulating the ceiling was a favourite trick of unscrupulous landlords – most assessments of area were made upon the ceiling, out of convenience, and by tilting back the plywood partitions the rated area of a cubicle could be either increased, for the benefit of a prospective tenant (many married couples were thus bamboozled into taking a single cubicle), or decreased temporarily on the visits of the housing inspectors. Ceilings were criss-crossed with pencil marks staking out the rival claims of tenants on opposite sides of a party wall. Someone timid of his rights could be literally squeezed out of existence – in fact, the advertisement 'quiet clientele' was usually a tacit invitation to this sort of piracy.

'The wall does tilt a little,' Ward admitted. 'Actually, it's about four degrees out – I used a plumb-line. But there's still plenty of room on the stairs for people to get by.'

Rossiter grinned. 'Of course, John. I'm just envious, that's all. My room is driving me crazy.' Like everyone, he used the term 'room' to describe his tiny cubicle, a hangover from the days fifty years earlier when people had indeed lived one to a room, sometimes, unbelievably, one to an apartment or house. The microfilms in the architecture catalogues at the library showed scenes of museums, concert halls and other public buildings in what appeared to be everyday settings, often virtually empty, two or three people wandering down an enormous gallery or staircase. Traffic moved freely along the centre of streets, and in the quieter districts sections of sidewalk would be deserted for fifty yards or more.

Now, of course, the older buildings had been torn down and replaced by housing batteries, or converted into apartment blocks. The great banqueting room in the former City Hall had been split horizontally into four decks, each of these cut up into hundreds of cubicles.

As for the streets, traffic had long since ceased to move about them. Apart from a few hours before dawn when only the sidewalks were crowded, every thoroughfare was always packed with a shuffling mob of pedestrians, perforce ignoring the countless 'Keep Left' signs suspended over their heads, wrestling past each other on their way to home and office, their clothes dusty and shapeless. Often 'locks' would occur when a huge crowd at a street junction became immovably jammed. Sometimes these locks would last for days. Two years earlier Ward had been caught in one outside the stadium, for over forty-eight hours was trapped in a gigantic pedestrian jam containing over 20,000 people, fed by the crowds leaving the stadium on one side and those approaching it on the other. An entire square mile of the local neighbourhood had been paralysed, and he vividly remembered the nightmare of swaying helplessly on his feet as the jam shifted and heaved, terrified of losing his balance and being trampled underfoot. When the police had finally sealed off the stadium and dispersed the jam he had gone back to his cubicle and slept for a week, his body blue with bruises.

'I hear they may reduce the allocation to three and a half metres,' Rossiter remarked.

Ward paused to allow a party of tenants from the sixth floor to pass down the staircase, holding the door to prevent it jumping off its latch. 'So they're always saying,' he commented. 'I can remember that rumour ten years ago.'

'It's no rumour,' Rossiter warned him. 'It may well be necessary soon. Thirty million people are packed into this city now, a million increase in just one year. There's been some pretty serious talk at the Housing Department.'

Ward shook his head. 'A drastic revaluation like that is almost impossible to carry out. Every single partition would have to be dismantled and nailed up again, the administrative job alone is so vast it's difficult to visualize. Millions of cubicles to be redesigned and certified, licences to be issued, plus the complete resettlement of every tenant. Most of the buildings put up since the last revaluation are designed around a four-metre modulus – you can't simply take half a metre off the end of each cubicle and then say that makes so many new cubicles. They may be only six inches wide.' He laughed. 'Besides, how can you live in just three and a half metres?'

Rossiter smiled. 'That's the ultimate argument, isn't it? They used it twenty-five years ago at the last revaluation, when the minimum was cut from five to four. It couldn't be done they all said, no one could stand living in only four square metres, it was enough room for a bed and suitcase, but you couldn't open the door to get in.' Rossiter chuckled softly. 'They were all wrong. It was merely decided that from then on all doors would open outwards. Four square metres was here to stay.'

Ward looked at his watch. It was 7.30. 'Time to eat. Let's see if we can get into the food-bar across the road.'

Grumbling at the prospect, Rossiter pulled himself off the bed. They left the cubicle and made their way down the staircase. This was crammed with luggage and packing cases so that only a narrow interval remained around the banister. On the floors below the congestion was worse. Corridors were wide enough to be chopped up into single cubicles, and the air was stale and dead, cardboard walls hung with damp laundry and makeshift larders. Each of the five rooms on the floors contained a dozen tenants, their voices reverberating through the partitions.

People were sitting on the steps above the second floor, using the staircase as an informal lounge, although this was against the fire regulations, women talking to the men queueing in their shirtsleeves outside the washroom, children diving around them. By the time they reached the entrance Ward and Rossiter were having to force their way through the tenants packed together on every landing, loitering around the notice boards or pushing in from the street below.

Taking a breath at the top of the steps, Ward pointed to the food-bar on the other side of the road. It was only thirty yards away, but the throng moving down the street swept past like a river at full tide, crossing them from right to left. The first picture show at the stadium started at 9 o'clock, and people were setting off already to make sure of getting in.

'Can't we go somewhere else?' Rossiter asked, screwing his face up at the prospect of the food-bar. Not only was it packed and take them half an hour to be served, but the food was flat and unappetizing. The journey from the library four blocks away had given him an appetite.

Ward shrugged. 'There's a place on the corner, but I doubt if we can make it.' This was two hundred yards upstream; they would be fighting the crowd all the way.

'Maybe you're right.' Rossiter put his hand on Ward's shoulder. 'You know, John, your trouble is that you never go anywhere, you're too disengaged, you just don't realize how bad everything is getting.'

Ward nodded. Rossiter was right. In the morning, when he set off for the library, the pedestrian traffic was moving with him towards the down-town offices; in the evening, when he came back, it was flowing in the opposite direction. By and large he never altered his routine. Brought up from the age of ten in a municipal hostel, he had gradually lost touch with his father and mother, who lived on the east side of the city and had been unable, or unwilling, to make the journey to see him. Having surrendered his initiative to the dynamics of the city he was reluctant to try to win it back merely for a better cup of coffee. Fortunately his job at the library brought him into contact with a wide range of young people of similar interests. Sooner or later he would marry, find a double cubicle near the library and settle down. If they had enough children (three was the required minimum) they might even one day own a small room of their own.

They stepped out into the pedestrian stream, carried along by it for ten or twenty yards, then quickened their pace and sidestepped through the crowd, slowly tacking across to the other side of the road. There they found the shelter of the shop-fronts, slowly worked their way back to the food-bar, shoulders braced against the countless minor collisions.

'What are the latest population estimates?' Ward asked as they circled a cigarette kiosk, stepping forward whenever a gap presented itself.

Rossiter smiled. 'Sorry, John, I'd like to tell you but you might start a stampede. Besides, you wouldn't believe me.'

Rossiter worked in the Insurance Department at the City Hall, had informal access to the census statistics. For the last ten years these had been classified information, partly because they were felt to be inaccurate, but chiefly because it was feared they might set off a mass attack of claustrophobia. Minor outbreaks had taken place already, and the official line was that world population had reached a plateau, levelling off at 20,000 million. No one believed this for a moment, and Ward assumed that the 3 per cent annual increase maintained since the 1960s was continuing.

How long it could continue was impossible to estimate. Despite the gloomiest prophecies of the Neo-Malthusians, world agriculture had managed to keep pace with the population growth, although intensive cultivation meant that 95 per cent of the population was permanently trapped in vast urban conurbations. The outward growth of cities had at last been checked; in fact, all over the world former suburban areas were being reclaimed for agriculture and population additions were confined within the existing urban ghettos. The countryside, as such, no longer existed. Every single square foot of ground sprouted a crop of one type or other. The one-time fields and meadows of the world were now, in effect, factory floors, as highly mechanized and closed to the public as any industrial area. Economic and ideological rivalries had long since faded before one over-riding quest – the internal colonization of the city.

Reaching the food-bar, they pushed themselves into the entrance and joined the scrum of customers pressing six deep against the counter.

'What is really wrong with the population problem,' Ward confided to Rossiter, 'is that no one has ever tried to tackle it. Fifty years ago short-sighted nationalism and industrial expansion put a premium on a rising population curve, and even now the hidden incentive is to have a large family so that you can gain a little privacy. Single people are penalized simply because there are more of them and they don't fit neatly into double or triple cubicles. But it's the large family with its compact, space-saving logistic that is the real villain.'

Rossiter nodded, edging nearer the counter, ready to shout his order. 'Too true. We all look forward to getting married just so that we can have our six square metres.'

Directly in front of them, two girls turned around and smiled. 'Six square metres,' one of them, a dark-haired girl with a pretty oval face, repeated. 'You sound like the sort of young man I ought to get to know. Going into the real estate business, Henry?'

Rossiter grinned and squeezed her arm. 'Hello, Judith. I'm thinking about it actively. Like to join me in a private venture?'

The girl leaned against him as they reached the counter. 'Well, I might. It would have to be legal, though.'

The other girl, Helen Waring, an assistant at the library, pulled Ward's sleeve. 'Have you heard the latest, John? Judith and I have been kicked out of our room. We're on the street right at this minute.'

'What?' Rossiter cried. They collected their soups and coffee and edged back to the rear of the bar. 'What on earth happened?'

Helen explained: 'You know that little broom cupboard outside our cubicle? Judith and I have been using it as a sort of study hole, going in there to read. It's quiet and restful, if you can get used to not breathing. Well, the old girl found out and kicked up a big fuss, said we were breaking the law and so on. In short, out.' Helen paused. 'Now we've heard she's going to let it as a single.'

Rossiter pounded the counter ledge. 'A broom cupboard? Someone's going to live there? But she'll never get a licence.'

Judith shook her head. 'She's got it already. Her brother works in the Housing Department.'

Ward laughed into his soup. 'But how can she let it? No one will live in a broom cupboard.'

Judith stared at him sombrely. 'You really believe that, John?'

Ward dropped his spoon. 'No, I suppose you're right. People will live anywhere. God, I don't know who I feel more sorry for – you two, or the poor devil who'll be living in that cupboard. What are you going to do?'

'A couple in a place two blocks west are sub-letting half their cubicle to us. They've hung a sheet down the middle and Helen and I'll take turns sleeping on a camp bed. I'm not joking, our room's about two feet wide. I said to Helen that we ought to split up again and sublet one half at twice our rent.'

They had a good laugh over all this. Then Ward said good night to the others and went back to his rooming house.

There he found himself with similar problems.

The manager leaned against the flimsy door, a damp cigar butt revolving around his mouth, an expression of morose boredom on his unshaven face.

'You got four point seven two metres,' he told Ward, who was standing out on the staircase, unable to get into his room. Other tenants pressed by on to the landing, where two women in curlers and dressing gowns were arguing with each other, tugging angrily at the wall of trunks and cases. Occasionally the manager glanced at them irritably. 'Four seven two. I worked it out twice.' He said this as if it ended all possibility of argument.

'Ceiling or floor?' Ward asked.

'Ceiling, whaddya think? How can I measure the floor with all this junk?' He kicked at a crate of books protruding from under the bed.

Ward let this pass. 'There's quite a tilt on the wall,' he pointed out. 'As much as three or four degrees.'

The manager nodded vaguely. 'You're definitely over the four. Way over.' He turned to Ward, who had moved down several steps to allow a man and woman to get past. 'I can rent this as a double.'

'What, only four and a half?' Ward said incredulously. 'How?'

The man who had just passed him leaned over the manager's shoulder and sniffed at the room, taking in every detail in a one-second glance. 'You renting a double here, Louie?'

The manager waved him away and then beckoned Ward into the room, closing the door after him.

'It's a nominal five,' he told Ward. 'New regulation, just came out. Anything over four five is a double now.' He eyed Ward shrewdly. 'Well, whaddya want? It's a good room, there's a lot of space here, feels more like a triple. You got access to the staircase, window slit –' He broke off as Ward slumped down on the bed and started to laugh. 'Whatsa matter? Look, if you want a big room like this you gotta pay for it. I want an extra half rental or you get out.'

Ward wiped his eyes, then stood up wearily and reached for the shelves. 'Relax, I'm on my way. I'm going to live in a broom cupboard. "Access to the staircase" – that's really rich. Tell me, Louie, is there life on Uranus?'

Temporarily, he and Rossiter teamed up to rent a double cubicle in a semi-derelict house a hundred yards from the library. The neighbourhood was seedy and faded, the rooming houses crammed with tenants. Most of them were owned by absentee landlords or by the city corporation, and the managers employed were of the lowest type, mere rent-collectors who cared nothing about the way their tenants divided up the living space, and never ventured beyond the first floors. Bottles and empty cans littered the corridors, and the washrooms looked like sumps. Many of the tenants were old and infirm, sitting about listlessly in their narrow cubicles, wheedling at each other back to back through the thin partitions.

Their double cubicle was on the third floor, at the end of a corridor that ringed the building. Its architecture was impossible to follow, rooms letting off at all angles, and luckily the corridor was a cul de sac. The mounds of cases ended four feet from the end wall and a partition divided off the cubicle, just wide enough for two beds. A high window overlooked the area ways of the buildings opposite.

Possessions loaded on to the shelf above his head, Ward lay back on his bed and moodily surveyed the roof of the library through the afternoon haze.

'It's not bad here,' Rossiter told him, unpacking his case. 'I know there's no real privacy and we'll drive each other insane within a week, but at least we haven't got six other people breathing into our ears two feet away.'

The nearest cubicle, a single, was built into the banks of cases half a dozen steps along the corridor, but the occupant, a man of seventy, was deaf and bed-ridden.

'It's not bad,' Ward echoed reluctantly. 'Now tell me what the latest growth figures are. They might console me.'

Rossiter paused, lowering his voice. 'Four per cent. *Eight hundred million extra people in one year* – just less than half the earth's total population in 1950.'

Ward whistled slowly. 'So they will revalue. What to? Three and a half?'

'Three. From the first of next year.'

'Three square metres!' Ward sat up and looked around him. 'It's unbelievable! The world's going insane, Rossiter. For God's sake, when are they going to do something about it? Do you realize there soon won't be room enough to sit down, let alone lie down?'

Exasperated, he punched the wall beside him, on the second blow knocked in one of the small wooden panels that had been lightly papered over.

'Hey!' Rossiter yelled. 'You're breaking the place down.' He dived across the bed to retrieve the panel, which hung downwards supported by a strip of paper. Ward slipped his hand into the dark interval, carefully drew the panel back on to the bed.

'Who's on the other side?' Rossiter whispered. 'Did they hear?'

Ward peered through the interval, eyes searching the dim light. Suddenly he dropped the panel and seized Rossiter's shoulder, pulled him down on to the bed.

'Henry! Look!'

Directly in front of them, faintly illuminated by a grimy skylight, was a medium-sized room some fifteen feet square, empty except for the dust silted up against the skirting boards. The floor was bare, a few strips of frayed linoleum running across it, the walls covered with a drab floral design. Here and there patches of the paper peeled off and segments of the picture rail had rotted away, but otherwise the room was in habitable condition.

Breathing slowly, Ward closed the open door of the cubicle with his foot, then turned to Rossiter.

'Henry, do you realize what we've found? Do you realize it, man?'

'Shut up. For Pete's sake keep your voice down.' Rossiter examined the room carefully. 'It's fantastic. I'm trying to see whether anyone's used it recently.'

'Of course they haven't,' Ward pointed out. 'It's obvious. There's no door into the room. We're looking through it now. They must have panelled over this door years ago and forgotten about it. Look at that filth everywhere.'

Rossiter was staring into the room, his mind staggered by its vastness.

'You're right,' he murmured. 'Now, when do we move in?'

Panel by panel, they prised away the lower half of the door and nailed it on to a wooden frame, so that the dummy section could be replaced instantly.

Then, picking an afternoon when the house was half empty and the manager asleep in his basement office, they made their first foray into the room, Ward going in alone while Rossiter kept guard in the cubicle.

For an hour they exchanged places, wandering silently around the dusty room, stretching their arms out to feel its unconfined emptiness, grasping at the sensation of absolute spatial freedom. Although smaller than many of the sub-divided rooms in which they had lived, this room seemed infinitely larger, its walls huge cliffs that soared upward to the skylight.

Finally, two or three days later, they moved in.

For the first week Rossiter slept alone in the room, Ward in the cubicle outside, both there together during the day. Gradually they smuggled in a few items of furniture: two armchairs, a table, a lamp fed from the socket in the cubicle. The furniture was heavy and Victorian; the cheapest available, its size emphasized the emptiness of the room. Pride of place was taken by an enormous mahogany wardrobe, fitted with carved angels and castellated mirrors, which they were forced to dismantle and carry into the house in their suitcases. Towering over them, it reminded Ward of the micro-films of gothic cathedrals, with their massive organ lofts crossing vast naves.

After three weeks they both slept in the room, finding the cubicle unbearably cramped. An imitation Japanese screen divided the room adequately and did nothing to diminish its size. Sitting there in the evenings, surrounded by his books and albums, Ward steadily forgot the city outside. Luckily he reached the library by a back alley and avoided the crowded streets. Rossiter and himself began to seem the only real inhabitants of the world, everyone else a meaningless by-product of their own existence, a random replication of identity which had run out of control.

It was Rossiter who suggested that they ask the two girls to share the room with them.

'They've been kicked out again and may have to split up,' he told Ward, obviously worried that Judith might fall into bad company. 'There's always a rent freeze after a revaluation but all the landlords know about it so they're not re-letting. It's damned difficult to find anywhere.'

Ward nodded, relaxing back around the circular red-wood

table. He played with the tassel of the arsenic-green lamp shade, for a moment felt like a Victorian man of letters, leading a spacious, leisurely life among overstuffed furnishings.

'I'm all for it,' he agreed, indicating the empty corners. 'There's plenty of room here. But we'll have to make sure they don't gossip about it.'

After due precautions, they let the two girls into the secret, enjoying their astonishment at finding this private universe.

'We'll put a partition across the middle,' Rossiter explained, 'then take it down each morning. You'll be able to move in within a couple of days. How do you feel?'

'Wonderful!' They goggled at the wardrobe, squinting at the endless reflections in the mirrors.

There was no difficulty getting them in and out of the house. The turnover of tenants was continuous and bills were placed in the mail rack. No one cared who the girls were or noticed their regular calls at the cubicle.

However, half an hour after they arrived neither of them had unpacked her suitcase.

'What's up, Judith?' Ward asked, edging past the girls' beds into the narrow interval between the table and wardrobe.

Judith hesitated, looking from Ward to Rossiter, who sat on the bed, finishing off the plywood partition. 'John, it's just that . . .'

Helen Waring, more matter-of-fact, took over, her fingers straightening the bed-spread. 'What Judith's trying to say is that our position here is a little embarrassing. The partition is –'

Rossiter stood up. 'For heaven's sake, don't worry, Helen,' he assured her, speaking in the loud whisper they had all involuntarily cultivated. 'No funny business, you can trust us. This partition is as solid as a rock.'

The two girls nodded. 'It's not that,' Helen explained, 'but it isn't up all the time. We thought that if an older person were here, say Judith's aunt – she wouldn't take up much room and be no trouble, she's really awfully sweet – we wouldn't need to bother about the partition – except at night,' she added quickly.

Ward glanced at Rossiter, who shrugged and began to scan the floor.

'Well, it's an idea,' Rossiter said. 'John and I know how you feel. Why not?'

'Sure,' Ward agreed. He pointed to the space between the girls' beds and the table. 'One more won't make any difference.'

The girls broke into whoops. Judith went over to Rossiter and kissed him on the cheek. 'Sorry to be a nuisance, Henry.' She smiled at him. 'That's a wonderful partition you've made. You couldn't do another one for Auntie – just a little one? She's very sweet but she is getting on.'

'Of course,' Rossiter said. 'I understand. I've got plenty of wood left over.'

Ward looked at his watch. 'It's seven-thirty, Judith. You'd better get in touch with your aunt. She may not be able to make it tonight.'

Judith buttoned her coat. 'Oh she will,' she assured Ward. 'I'll be back in a jiffy.'

The aunt arrived within five minutes, three heavy suitcases soundly packed.

'It's amazing,' Ward remarked to Rossiter three months later. 'The size of this room still staggers me. It almost gets larger every day.'

Rossiter agreed readily, averting his eyes from one of the girls changing behind the central partition. This they now left in place as dismantling it daily had become tiresome. Besides, the aunt's subsidiary partition was attached to it and she resented the continuous upsets. Ensuring she followed the entrance and exit drills through the camouflaged door and cubicle was difficult enough.

Despite this, detection seemed unlikely. The room had obviously been built as an afterthought into the central well of the house and any noise was masked by the luggage stacked in the surrounding corridor. Directly below was a small dormitory occupied by several elderly women, and Judith's aunt, who visited them socially, swore that no sounds came through the heavy ceiling. Above, the fanlight let out through a dormer window, its lights indistinguishable from the hundred other bulbs in the windows of the house.

Rossiter finished off the new partition he was building and held it upright, fitting it into the slots nailed to the wall between his bed and Ward's. They had agreed that this would provide a little extra privacy.

'No doubt I'll have to do one for Judith and Helen,' he confided to Ward.

Ward adjusted his pillow. They had smuggled the two armchairs back to the furniture shop as they took up too much space. The bed, anyway, was more comfortable. He had never become completely used to the soft upholstery.

'Not a bad idea. What about some shelving around the wall? I've got nowhere to put anything.'

The shelving tidied the room considerably, freeing large areas of the floor. Divided by their partitions, the five beds were in line along the rear wall, facing the mahogany wardrobe. In between was an open space of three or four feet, a further six feet on either side of the wardrobe.

The sight of so much spare space fascinated Ward. When Rossiter mentioned that Helen's mother was ill and badly needed personal care he immediately knew where her cubicle could be placed – at the foot of his bed, between the wardrobe and the side wall.

Helen was overjoyed. 'It's awfully good of you, John,' she told him, 'but would you mind if Mother slept beside me? There's enough space to fit an extra bed in.'

So Rossiter dismantled the partitions and moved them closer together, six beds now in line along the wall. This gave each of them an interval two and a half feet wide, just enough room to squeeze down the side of their beds. Lying back on the extreme right, the shelves two feet above his head, Ward could barely see the wardrobe, but the space in front of him, a clear six feet to the wall ahead, was uninterrupted.

Then Helen's father arrived.

*   *   *

Knocking on the door of the cubicle, Ward smiled at Judith's aunt as she let him in. He helped her swing out the made-up bed which guarded the entrance, then rapped on the wooden panel. A moment later Helen's father, a small, grey-haired man in an undershirt, braces tied to his trousers with string, pulled back the panel.

Ward nodded to him and stepped over the luggage piled around the floor at the foot of the beds. Helen was in her mother's cubicle, helping the old woman to drink her evening broth. Rossiter, perspiring heavily, was on his knees by the mahogany wardrobe, wrenching apart the frame of the central mirror with a jemmy. Pieces of the wardrobe lay on his bed and across the floor.

'We'll have to start taking these out tomorrow,' Rossiter told him. Ward waited for Helen's father to shuffle past and enter his cubicle. He had rigged up a small cardboard door, and locked it behind him with a crude hook of bent wire.

Rossiter watched him, frowning irritably. 'Some people are happy. This wardrobe's a hell of a job. How did we ever decide to buy it?'

Ward sat down on his bed. The partition pressed against his knees and he could hardly move. He looked up when Rossiter was engaged and saw that the dividing line he had marked in pencil was hidden by the encroaching partition. Leaning against the wall, he tried to ease it back again, but Rossiter had apparently nailed the lower edge to the floor.

There was a sharp tap on the outside cubicle door – Judith returning from her office. Ward started to get up and then sat back. 'Mr Waring,' he called softly. It was the old man's duty night.

Waring shuffled to the door of his cubicle and unlocked it fussily, clucking to himself.

'Up and down, up and down,' he muttered. He stumbled over Rossiter's tool-bag and swore loudly, then added meaningly over his shoulder: 'If you ask me there's too many people in here. Down below they've only got six to our seven, and it's the same size room.'

Ward nodded vaguely and stretched back on his narrow bed, trying not to bang his head on the shelving. Waring was not the first to hint that he move out. Judith's aunt had made a similar suggestion two days earlier. Since he had left his job at the library (the small rental he charged the others paid for the little food he needed) he spent most of his time in the room, seeing rather more of the old man than he wanted to, but he had learned to tolerate him.

Settling himself, he noticed that the right-hand spire of the wardrobe, all he had been able to see of it for the past two months, was now dismantled.

It had been a beautiful piece of furniture, in a way symbolizing this whole private world, and the salesman at the store told him there were few like it left. For a moment Ward felt a sudden pang of regret, as he had done as a child when his father, in a moment of exasperation, had taken something away from him and he had known he would never see it again.

Then he pulled himself together. It was a beautiful wardrobe, without doubt, but when it was gone it would make the room seem even larger.

1961

THE GENTLE ASSASSIN

By noon, when Dr Jamieson arrived in London, all entrances into the city had been sealed since six o'clock that morning. The Cornonation Day crowds had waited in their places along the procession route for almost twenty-four hours, and Green Park was deserted as Dr Jamieson slowly made his way up the sloping grass towards the Underground station below the Ritz. Abandoned haversacks and sleeping bags lay about among the litter under the trees, and twice Dr Jamieson stumbled slightly. By the time he reached the station entrance he was perspiring freely, and sat down on a bench, resting his heavy gun-metal suitcase on the grass.

Directly in front of him was one of the high wooden stands. He could see the backs of the top row of spectators, women in bright summer dresses, men in shirtsleeves, newspapers shielding their heads from the hot sunlight, parties of children singing and waving their Union Jacks. All the way down Piccadilly the office blocks were crammed with people leaning out of windows, and the street was a mass of colour and noise. Now and then bands played in the distance, or an officer in charge of the troops lining the route bellowed an order and re-formed his men.

Dr Jamieson listened with interest to all these sounds, savouring the sun-filled excitement. In his middle sixties, he was a small neat figure with greying hair and alert sensitive eyes. His forehead was broad, with a marked slope, which made his somewhat professorial manner appear more youthful. This was helped by the rakish cut of his grey silk suit, its ultra-narrow lapels fastened by a single embroidered button, heavy braided seams on the sleeves and trousers. As someone emerged from the first-aid marquee at the far end of the stand and walked towards him Dr Jamieson sensed the discrepancy between their attire – the man was wearing a baggy blue suit with huge flapping lapels – and frowned to himself in annoyance. Glancing at his watch, he picked up the suitcase and hurried into the Underground station.

The Coronation procession was expected to leave Westminster Abbey at three o'clock, and the streets through which the cortège would pass had been closed to traffic by the police. As he emerged from the station exit on the north side of Piccadilly, Dr Jamieson looked around carefully at the tall office blocks and hotels, here and there repeating a name to himself as he identified a once-familiar landmark. Edging along behind the crowds packed on to the pavement, the metal suitcase bumping painfully against his knees, he reached the entrance to Bond Street, there deliberated carefully and began to walk to the taxi rank fifty yards away. The people pressing down towards Piccadilly glanced at him curiously, and he was relieved when he climbed into the taxi.

'Hotel Westland,' he told the driver, refusing help with the suitcase.

The man cocked one ear. 'Hotel *where*?'

'Westland,' Dr Jamieson repeated, trying to match the modulations of his voice to the driver's. Everyone around him seemed to speak in the same guttural tones. 'It's in Oxford Street, one hundred and fifty yards east of Marble Arch. I think you'll find there's a temporary entrance in Grosvenor Place.'

The driver nodded, eyeing his elderly passenger warily. As they moved off he leaned back. 'Come to see the Coronation?'

'No,' Dr Jamieson said matter-of-factly. 'I'm here on business. Just for the day.'

'I thought maybe you came to watch the procession. You get a wonderful view from the Westland.'

'So I believe. Of course, I'll watch if I get a chance.'

They swung into Grosvenor Square and Dr Jamieson steered the suitcase back onto the seat, examining the intricate metal clasps to make sure the lid held securely. He peered up at the buildings around him, trying not to let his heart become excited as the memories rolled back. Everything, however, differed completely from his recollections, the overlay of the intervening years distorting the original images without his realizing it. The perspectives of the street, the muddle of unrelated buildings and tangle of overhead wires, the signs that sprouted in profuse variety at the slightest opportunity, all seemed entirely new. The whole city was incredibly antiquated and confused, and he found it hard to believe that he had once lived there.

Were his other memories equally false?

He sat forward with surprise, pointing through the open window at the graceful beehive curtain-wall of the American Embassy, answering his question.

The driver noticed his interest, flicked away his cigarette. 'Funny style of place,' he commented. 'Can't understand the Yanks putting up a dump like that.'

'Do you think so?' Dr Jamieson asked. 'Not many people would agree with you.'

The driver laughed. 'You're wrong there, mister. I never heard a good word for it yet.' He shrugged, deciding not to offend his passenger. 'Still, maybe it's just ahead of its time.'

Dr Jamieson smiled thinly at this. 'That's about it,' he said, more to himself than to the driver. 'Let's say about thirty-five years ahead. They'll think very highly of it then.'

His voice had involuntarily become more nasal, and the driver asked: 'You from abroad, sir? New Zealand, maybe?'

'No,' Dr Jamieson said, noticing that the traffic was moving down the left-hand side of the road. 'Not exactly. I haven't been to London for some time, though. But I seem to have picked a good day to come back.'

'You have that, sir. A great day for the young Prince. Or King I should say, rather. King James III, sounds a bit peculiar. But good luck to him, and the new Jack-a-what's-a-name Age.'

'The New Jacobean Age,' Dr Jamieson corrected, laughter softening his face for the first time that day. 'Oh yes, that was it.' Fervently, his hands straying to the metal suitcase, he added *sotto voce*: 'As you say, good luck to it.'

Stepping out at the hotel, he went in through the temporary

entrance, pushed among the throng of people in the small rear foyer, the noise from Oxford Street dinning in his ears. After a five-minute wait, he reached the desk, the suitcase pulling wearily at his arm.

'Dr Roger Jamieson,' he told the clerk. 'I have a room reserved on the first floor.' He leaned against the counter as the clerk hunted through the register, listening to the hubbub in the foyer. Most of the people were stout middle-aged women in floral dresses, conversing excitedly on their way to the TV lounge, where the Abbey ceremony would be on at two o'clock. Dr Jamieson ignored them, examining the others in the foyer, telegraph messenger boys, off-duty waiters, members of the catering staff organizing the parties held in the rooms above. Each of their faces he scrutinized carefully, as if expecting to see someone he knew.

The clerk peered shortsightedly at the ledger. 'Was the reservation in your name, sir?'

'Certainly. Room 17, the corner room on the first floor.'

The clerk shook his head doubtfully. 'There must have been some mistake, sir, we have no record of any reservation. You aren't with one of the parties upstairs?'

Controlling his impatience, Dr Jamieson rested the suitcase on the floor, securing it against the desk with his foot. 'I assure you, I made the reservation myself. Explicitly for Room 17. It was some time ago but the manager told me it was completely in order and would not be cancelled whatever happened.'

Leafing through the entries, the clerk ran carefully through the entries marked off that day. Suddenly he pointed to a faded entry at the top of the first page.

'Here we are, sir. I apologize, but the booking had been brought forward from the previous register. "Dr Roger Jamieson, Room 17."' Putting his finger on the date with surprise, he smiled at Dr Jamieson. 'A lucky choice of day, Doctor, your booking was made over two years ago.'

Finally locking the door of his room, Dr Jamieson sat down thankfully on one of the beds, his hands still resting on the metal case. For a few minutes he slowly recovered his breath, kneading the numbed muscles in his right forearm. Then he pulled himself to his feet and began a careful inspection of the room.

One of the larger rooms in the hotel, the two corner windows gave it a unique view over the crowded street below. Venetian blinds screened the windows from the hot sunlight and the hundreds of people in the balconies of the department store opposite. Dr Jamieson first peered into the built-in cupboards, then tested the bathroom window onto the interior well. Satisfied that they were secure, he moved an armchair over to the side window which faced the procession's direction of approach. His view was uninterrupted for several hundred yards, each one of the soldiers and policemen lining the route plainly visible.

A large piece of red bunting, part of a massive floral tribute, ran diagonally across the window, hiding him from the people in the building adjacent, and he could see down clearly into the pavement, where a crowd ten or twelve deep was pressed against the wooden palisades. Lowering the blind so that the bottom vane was only six inches from the ledge, Dr Jamieson sat forward and quietly scanned them.

None seemed to hold his interest, and he glanced fretfully at his watch. It was just before two o'clock, and the young king would have left Buckingham Palace on his way to the Abbey. Many members of the crowd were carrying portable radios, and the din outside slackened off as the commentary from the Abbey began.

Dr Jamieson went over to the bed and pulled out his key-chain. Both locks on the case were combination devices. He switched the key left and right a set number of times, pressed home and lifted the lid.

Lying inside the case, on the lower half of the divided velvet mould, were the dismantled members of a powerful sporting rifle, and a magazine of six shells. The metal butt had been shortened by six inches and canted so that when raised to the shoulder in the firing position the breach and barrel pointed downwards at an angle of $45°$, both the sights in line with the eye.

Unclipping the sections, Dr Jamieson expertly assembled the weapon, screwing in the butt and adjusting it to the most comfortable angle. Fitting on the magazine, he snapped back the bolt, then pressed it forward and drove the top shell into the breach.

His back to the window, he stared down at the loaded weapon lying on the bedspread in the dim light, listening to the roistering from the parties farther along the corridor, the uninterrupted roar from the street outside. He seemed suddenly very tired, for once the firmness and resolution in his face faded and he looked like an old weary man, friendless in a hotel room in a strange city where everyone but himself was celebrating. He sat down on the bed beside the rifle, wiping the gun-grease off his hands with his handkerchief, his thoughts apparently far away. When he rose he moved stiffly and looked uncertainly around the room, as if wondering why he was there.

Then he pulled himself together. Quickly he dismantled the rifle, clipped the sections into their hasps and lowered the lid, then placed the case in the bottom drawer of the bureau, adding the key to his chain ring. Locking the door behind him, he made his way out of the hotel, a determined spring in his step.

Two hundred yards down Grosvenor Place, he turned into Hallam Street, a small thoroughfare interspersed with minor art galleries and restaurants. Sunlight played on the striped awnings and the deserted street might have been miles from the crowds along the Coronation route. Dr Jamieson felt his confidence return. Every dozen yards or so he stopped under the awnings and surveyed the empty pavements, listening to the distant TV commentaries from the flats above the shops.

Halfway down the street was a small café with three tables outside. Sitting with his back to the window, Dr Jamieson took out a pair of sunglasses and relaxed in the shade, ordering an iced orange juice from the waitress. He sipped it quietly, his face masked by the dark lenses with their heavy frames. Periodically, prolonged cheers drifted across the roof-tops from Oxford Street, marking the progress of the Abbey ceremony, but otherwise the street was quiet.

Shortly after three o'clock, when the deep droning of an organ on the TV sets announced that the Coronation service had ended, Dr Jamieson heard the sounds of feet approaching on his left. Leaning back under the awning, he saw a young man and girl in a white dress walking hand in hand. As they drew nearer Dr Jamieson removed his glasses to inspect the couple more closely, then quickly replaced them and rested one elbow on the table, masking his face with his hand.

The couple were too immersed in each other to notice Dr Jamieson watching them, although to anyone else his intense nervous excitement would have been obvious. The man was about twenty-eight, dressed in the baggy unpressed clothes Dr Jamieson had found everyone wearing in London, an old tie casually hand-knotted around a soft collar. Two fountain pens protruded from his breast pocket, a concert programme from another, and he had the pleasantly informal appearance of a young university lecturer. His handsome introspective face was topped by a sharply sloping forehead, thinning brown hair brushed back with his fingers. He gazed into the girl's face with patent affection, listening to her light chatter with occasional amused interjections.

Dr Jamieson was also looking at the girl. At first he had stared fixedly at the young man, watching his movements and facial expressions with the oblique wariness of a man seeing himself in a mirror, but his attention soon turned to the girl. A feeling of enormous relief surged through him, and he had to restrain himself from leaping out of his seat. He had been frightened of his memories, but the girl was more, not less beautiful than he had remembered.

Barely nineteen or twenty, she strolled along with her head thrown back, long straw-coloured hair drifting lightly across her softly tanned shoulders. Her mouth was full and alive, her wild eyes watching the young man mischievously.

As they passed the café she was in full flight about something, and the young man cut in: 'Hold on, June, I need a rest. Let's sit down and have a drink, the procession won't reach Marble Arch for half an hour.'

'Poor old chap, am I wearing you out?' They sat at the table next to Dr Jamieson, the girl's bare arm only a few inches away, the fresh scent of her body adding itself to his other recollections. Already a whirlwind of memories reeled in his mind, her neat mobile hands, the way she held her chin and spread her flared white skirt across her thighs. 'Still, I don't really care if I miss the procession. This is *my* day, not his.'

The young man grinned, pretending to get up. 'Really? They've all been misinformed. Just wait here, I'll get the procession diverted.' He held her hand across the table, peered critically at the small diamond on her finger. 'Pretty feeble effort. Who bought that for you?'

The girl kissed it fondly. 'It's as big as the Ritz.' She gave a playful growl. 'H'm, what a man, I'll have to marry him one of these days. Roger, isn't it wonderful about the Prize? Three hundred pounds! You're really rich. A pity the Royal Society don't let you spend it on anything, like the Nobel Prizes. Wait till you get one of those.'

The young man smiled modestly. 'Easy darling, don't build your hopes on that.'

'But of course you will. I'm absolutely sure. After all, you've more or less discovered time travel.'

The young man drummed on the table. 'June, for heaven's sake, get this straight, I have *not* discovered time travel.' He lowered his voice, conscious of Dr Jamieson sitting at the next table, the only other person in the deserted street. 'People will think I'm insane if you go around saying that.'

The girl screwed up her pert nose. 'You have, though, let's face it. I know you don't like the phrase, but once you take away the algebra that's what it boils down to, doesn't it?'

The young man gazed reflectively at the table top, his face, as it grew serious, assuming massive intellectual strength. 'In so far as mathematical concepts have their analogies in the physical universe, yes – but that's an enormous caveat. And even then it's not time travel in the usual sense, though I realize the popular press won't agree when my paper in *Nature* comes out. Anyway,

I'm not particularly interested in the time aspect. If I had thirty years to spare it might be worth pursuing, but I've got more important things to do.'

He smiled at the girl, but she leaned forward thoughtfully, taking his hands. 'Roger, I'm not so sure you're right. You say it hasn't any applications in everyday life, but scientists always think that. It's really fantastic, to be able to go backward in time. I mean –'

'Why? We're able to go *forward* in time now, and no one's throwing their hats in the air. The universe itself is just a time machine that from our end of the show seems to be running one way. Or mostly one way. I happened to have noticed that particles in a cyclotron sometimes move in the opposite direction, that's all, arrive at the end of their infinitesimal trips before they've started. That doesn't mean that next week we'll all be able to go back and murder our own grandfathers.'

'What would happen if you did? Seriously?'

The young man laughed. 'I don't know. Frankly, I don't like to think about it. Maybe that's the real reason why I want to keep the work on a theoretical basis. If you extend the problem to its logical conclusion my observations at Harwell must be faulty, because events in the universe obviously take place independently of time, which is just the perspective we put on them. Years from now the problem will probably be known as the Jamieson Paradox, and aspiring mathematicians will be bumping off their grandparents wholesale in the hope of disproving it. We'll have to make sure that all our grandchildren are admirals or archbishops.'

As he spoke Dr Jamieson was watching the girl, every fibre in his body strained to prevent himself from touching her on the arm and speaking to her. The pattern of freckles on her slim forearm, the creases in her dress below her shoulder blades, her minute toenails with their chipped varnish, was each an absolute revelation of his own existence.

He took off his sunglasses and for a moment he and the young man stared straight at each other. The latter seemed embarrassed, realizing the remarkable physiognomical similarity between them, the identical bone structure of their faces, and angled sweep of their foreheads. Fleetingly, Dr Jamieson smiled at him, a feeling of deep, almost paternal affection for the young man coming over him. His naïve earnestness and honesty, his relaxed, gawky charm, were suddenly more important than his intellectual qualities, and Dr Jamieson knew that he felt no jealousy towards him.

He put on his glasses and looked away down the street, his resolve to carry through the next stages of his plan strengthened.

The noise from the streets beyond rose sharply, and the couple leapt to their feet.

'Come on, it's three-thirty!' the young man cried. 'They must be almost here.'

As they ran off the girl paused to straighten her sandal, looking back at the old man in dark glasses who had sat behind her. Dr Jamieson leaned forward, waiting for her to speak, one hand outstretched, but the girl merely looked away and he sank into his chair.

When they reached the first intersection he stood up and hurried back to his hotel.

Locking the door of his room, Dr Jamieson quickly pulled the case from the bureau, assembled the rifle and sat down with it in front of the window. The Coronation procession was already passing, the advance files of marching soldiers and guardsmen, in their ceremonial uniforms, each led by a brass band drumming out martial airs. The crowd roared and cheered, tossing confetti and streamers into the hot sunlight.

Dr Jamieson ignored them and peered below the blind onto the pavement. Carefully he searched the throng, soon picked out the girl in the white dress tip-toeing at the back. She smiled at the people around her and wormed her way towards the front, pulling the young man by the hand. For a few minutes Dr Jamieson followed the girl's every movement, then as the first landaus of the diplomatic corps appeared he began to search the remainder of the crowd, scrutinizing each face carefully, line upon line. From his pocket he withdrew a small plastic envelope; he held it away from his face and broke the seal. There was a hiss of greenish gas and he drew out a large newspaper cutting, yellowed with age, folded to reveal a man's portrait.

Dr Jamieson propped it against the window ledge. The cutting showed a dark-jowled man of about thirty with a thin weasel-like face, obviously a criminal photographed by the police. Under it was the caption: *Anton Remmers.*

Dr Jamieson sat forward intently. The diplomatic corps passed in their carriages, followed by members of the government riding in open cars, waving their silk hats at the crowd. Then came more Horse Guards, and there was a tremendous roar farther down the street as the spectators near Oxford Circus saw the royal coach approaching.

Anxiously, Dr Jamieson looked at his watch. It was three forty-five, and the royal coach was due to pass the hotel in only seven minutes. Around him a tumult of noise made it difficult to concentrate, and the TV sets in the near-by rooms seemed to be at full volume.

Suddenly he clenched the window ledge.

'Remmers!' Directly below, in the entrance to a cigarette kiosk, was a sallow-faced man in a wide-brimmed green hat. He stared at the procession impassively, hands deep in the pockets of a cheap raincoat. Fumbling, Dr Jamieson raised the rifle, resting the barrel on the ledge, watching the man. He made no attempt to press forward into the crowd, and waited by the kiosk, only a few feet from a small arcade that ran back into a side street.

Dr Jamieson began to search the crowd again, the effort draining his face. A gigantic bellow from the crowd deafened him as the gold-plated royal coach hove into view behind a bobbing escort of household cavalry. He tried to see if Remmers looked around at an accomplice, but the man was motionless, hands deep in his pockets.

'Damn you!' Dr Jamieson snarled. 'Where's the other one?' Frantically he pushed away the blind, every ounce of his shrewdness and experience expended as he carried out a dozen split-second character analyses of the people below.

'There were two of them!' he shouted hoarsely to himself. 'There were *two*!'

Fifty yards away, the young king sat back in the golden coach, his robes a blaze of colour in the sunlight. Distracted, Dr Jamieson watched him, then realized abruptly that Remmers had moved. The man was now stepping swiftly around the edge of the crowd, darting about on his lean legs like a distraught tiger. As the crowd surged forward, he pulled a blue thermos flask from his raincoat pocket, with a quick motion unscrewed the cap. The royal coach drew abreast and Remmers transferred the thermos to his right hand, a metal plunger clearly visible in the mouth of the flask.

'*Remmers* had the bomb!' Dr Jamieson gasped, completely disconcerted. Remmers stepped back, extended his right hand low to the ground behind him like a grenadier and then began to throw the bomb forward with a carefully timed swing.

The rifle had been pointed at the man automatically and Dr Jamieson trained the sights on his chest and fired, just before the bomb left his hand. The discharge jolted Dr Jamieson off his feet, the impact tearing at his shoulder, the rifle jangling up into the venetian blind. Remmers slammed back crookedly into the cigarette kiosk, legs lolling, his face like a skull's. The bomb had been knocked out of his hand and was spinning straight up into the air as if tossed by a juggler. It landed on the pavement a few yards away, kicked underfoot as the crowd surged sideways after the royal coach.

Then it exploded.

There was a blinding pulse of expanding air, followed by a tremendous eruption of smoke and hurtling particles. The window facing the street dropped in a single piece and shattered on the floor at Dr Jamieson's feet, driving him back in a blast of glass and torn plastic. He fell across the chair, recovered himself as the shouts outside turned to screams, then dragged himself over to the window and stared out through the stinging air. The crowd was fanning out across the road, people running in all directions, horses rearing under their helmetless riders. Below the window twenty or thirty people lay or sat on the pavement. The royal coach, one wheel missing but otherwise intact, was being dragged away by its team of horses, guardsmen and troops encircling it. Police were swarming down the road towards the hotel, and Dr Jamieson saw someone point up to him and shout.

He looked down at the edge of the pavement, where a girl in a white dress was stretched on her back, her legs twisted strangely. The young man kneeling beside her, his jacket split down the centre of his back, had covered her face with his handkerchief, and a dark stain spread slowly across the tissue.

Voices rose in the corridor outside. He turned away from the window, the rifle still in his hand. On the floor at his feet, unfurled by the blast of the explosion, was the faded newspaper cutting. Numbly, his mouth slack, Dr Jamieson picked it up.

ASSASSINS ATTEMPT TO MURDER KING JAMES
Bomb Kills 27 in Oxford Street
Two men shot dead by police

A sentence had been ringed: '... one was Anton Remmers, a professional killer believed to have been hired by the second assassin, an older man whose bullet-ridden body the police are unable to identify ...'

Fists pounded on the door. A voice shouted, then kicked at the handle. Dr Jamieson dropped the cutting, and looked down at the young man kneeling over the girl, holding her dead hands.

As the door ripped back off its hinges he knew who the second unknown assassin was, the man he had returned to kill after thirty-five years. So his attempt to alter past events had been fruitless, by coming back he had merely implicated himself in the original crime, doomed since he first analysed the cyclotron freaks to return and help to kill his young bride. If he had not shot Remmers the assassin would have lobbed the bomb into the centre of the road, and June would have lived. His whole stratagem selflessly devised for the young man's benefit, a free gift to his own younger self, had defeated itself, destroying the very person it had been intended to save.

Hoping to see her again for the last time, and warn the young man to forget her, he ran forward into the roaring police guns.

1961

THE INSANE ONES

Ten miles outside Alexandria he picked up the coast road that ran across the top of the continent through Tunis and Algiers to the transatlantic tunnel at Casablanca, gunned the Jaguar up to 120 and burned along through the cool night air, letting the brine-filled slipstream cut into his six-day tan. Lolling back against the headrest as the palms flicked by, he almost missed the girl in the white raincoat waving from the steps of the hotel at El Alamein, had only three hundred yards to plunge the car to a halt below the rusting neon sign.

'Tunis?' the girl called out, belting the man's raincoat around her trim waist, long black hair in a Left Bank cut over one shoulder.

'Tunis – Casablanca – Atlantic City,' Gregory shouted back, reaching across to the passenger door. She swung a yellow briefcase behind the seat, settling herself among the magazines and newspapers as they roared off. The headlamps picked out a United World cruiser parked under the palms in the entrance to the war cemetery, and involuntarily Gregory winced and floored the accelerator, eyes clamped to the rear mirror until the road was safely empty.

At 90 he slacked off and looked at the girl, abruptly felt a warning signal sound again. She seemed like any demi-beatnik, with a long melancholy face and grey skin, but something about her rhythms, the slack facial tone and dead eyes and mouth, made him uneasy. Under a flap of the raincoat was a blue-striped gingham skirt, obviously part of a nurse's uniform, out of character, like the rest of her strange gear. As she slid the magazines into the dashboard locker he saw the home-made bandage around the left wrist.

She noticed him watching her and flashed a too-bright smile, then made an effort at small talk.

'Paris *Vogue*, *Neue Frankfurter*, Tel Aviv *Express* – you've really been moving.' She pulled a pack of Del Montes from the breast pocket of the coat, fumbled unfamiliarly with a large brass lighter. 'First Europe, then Asia, now Africa. You'll run out of continents soon.' Hesitating, she volunteered: 'Carole Sturgeon. Thanks for the lift.'

Gregory nodded, watching the bandage slide around her slim wrist. He wondered which hospital she had sneaked away from. Probably Cairo General, the old-style English uniforms were still worn there. Ten to one the briefcase was packed with some careless salesman's pharmaceutical samples. 'Can I ask where you're going? This is the back end of nowhere.'

The girl shrugged. 'Just following the road. Cairo, Alex, you know –' She added: 'I went to see the pyramids.' She lay back, rolling slightly against his shoulder. 'That was wonderful. They're the oldest things on earth. Remember their boast: "*Before Abraham, I was*"?'

They hit a dip in the road and Gregory's licence swung out under the steering column. The girl peered down and read it. 'Do you mind? It's a long ride to Tunis. "Charles Gregory, MD –"' She stopped, repeating his name to herself uncertainly.

Suddenly she remembered. '*Gregory!* Dr Charles Gregory! Weren't you – Muriel Bortman, the President's daughter, she drowned herself at Key West, you were sentenced –' She broke off, staring nervously at the windshield.

'You've got a long memory,' Gregory said quietly. 'I didn't think anyone remembered.'

'Of course I remember.' She spoke in a whisper. 'They were mad what they did to you.' For the next few minutes she gushed out a long farrago of sympathy, interspersed with disjointed details from her own life. Gregory tried not to listen, clenching the wheel until his knuckles whitened, deliberately forgetting everything as fast as she reminded him.

There was a pause, as he felt it coming, the way it invariably did. 'Tell me, doctor, I hope you forgive me asking, but since the Mental Freedom laws it's difficult to get help, one's got to be so careful – you too, of course ...' She laughed uneasily. 'What I really mean is –'

Her edginess drained power from Gregory. '– you need psychiatric assistance,' he cut in, pushing the Jaguar up to 95, eyes swinging to the rear mirror again. The road was dead, palms receding endlessly into the night.

The girl choked on her cigarette, the stub between her fingers a damp mess. 'Well, not me,' she said lamely. 'A close friend of mine. She really needs help, believe me, doctor. Her whole feeling for life is gone, nothing seems to mean anything to her any more.'

Brutally, he said: 'Tell her to look at the pyramids.'

But the girl missed the irony, said quickly: 'Oh, she has. I just left her in Cairo. I promised I'd try to find someone for her.' She turned to examine Gregory, put a hand up to her hair. In the blue desert light she reminded him of the madonnas he had seen in the Louvre two days after his release, when he had run from the filthy prison searching for the most beautiful things in the world, the solemn-faced more-than-beautiful 13-year-olds who had posed for Leonardo and the Bellini brothers. 'I thought perhaps you might know someone –?'

He gripped himself and shook his head. 'I don't. For the last three years I've been out of touch. Anyway, it's against the MF laws. Do you know what would happen if they caught me giving psychiatric treatment?'

Numbly the girl stared ahead at the road. Gregory flipped away his cigarette, pressing down on the accelerator as the last three years crowded back, memories he had hoped to repress on his 10,000-mile drive ... three years at the prison farm near Marseilles, treating scrofulous farm-workers and sailors in the dispensary, even squeezing in a little illicit depth analysis for the corporal of police who couldn't satisfy his wife, three embittered years to accept that he would never practise again the one craft in which he was fully himself. Trick-cyclist or assuager of discontents, whatever his title, the psychiatrist had now passed into history, joining the necromancers, sorcerers and other practitioners of the black sciences.

The Mental Freedom legislation enacted ten years earlier by the ultra-conservative UW government had banned the profession outright and enshrined the individual's freedom to be insane if he wanted to, provided he paid the full civil consequences for any infringements of the law. That was the catch, the hidden object of the MF laws. What had begun as a popular reaction against 'subliminal living' and the uncontrolled extension of techniques of mass manipulation for political and economic ends had quickly developed into a systematic attack on the psychological sciences. Over-permissive courts of law with their condoning of delinquency, pseudo-enlightened penal reformers, 'Victims of society', the psychologist and his patient all came under fierce attack. Discharging their self-hate and anxiety onto a convenient scapegoat, the new rulers, and the great majority electing them, outlawed all forms of psychic control, from the innocent market survey to lobotomy. The mentally ill were on their own, spared pity and consideration, made to pay to the hilt for their failings. The sacred cow of the community was the psychotic, free to wander where he wanted, drooling on the doorsteps, sleeping on sidewalks, and woe betide anyone who tried to help him.

Gregory had made that mistake. Escaping to Europe, first home of psychiatry, in the hope of finding a more tolerant climate, he set up a secret clinic in Paris with six other émigré analysts. For five years they worked undetected, until one of Gregory's patients, a tall ungainly girl with a psychogenic stutter, was revealed to be Muriel Bortman, daughter of the UW President-General. The analysis had failed tragically when the clinic was raided; after her death a lavish show trial (making endless play of electric shock apparatus, movies of insulin coma and the testimony of countless paranoids rounded up in the alleyways) had concluded in a three-year sentence.

Now at last he was out, his savings invested in the Jaguar,

fleeing Europe and his memories of the prison for the empty highways of North Africa. He didn't want any more trouble.

'I'd like to help,' he told the girl. 'But the risks are too high. All your friend can do is try to come to terms with herself.'

The girl chewed her lip fretfully. 'I don't think she can. Thanks, anyway, doctor.'

For three hours they sat back silently in the speeding car, until the lights of Tobruk came up ahead, the long curve of the harbour.

'It's 2 A.M.,' Gregory said. 'There's a motel here. I'll pick you up in the morning.'

After they had gone to their rooms he sneaked back to the registry, booked himself into a new chalet. He fell asleep as Carole Sturgeon wandered forlornly up and down the verandas, whispering out his name.

After breakfast he came back from the sea, found a big United World cruiser in the court, orderlies carrying a stretcher out to an ambulance.

A tall Libyan police colonel was leaning against the Jaguar, drumming his leather baton on the windscreen.

'Ah, Dr Gregory. Good morning.' He pointed his baton at the ambulance. 'A profound tragedy, such a beautiful American girl.'

Gregory rooted his feet in the grey sand, with an effort restrained himself from running over to the ambulance and pulling back the sheet. Fortunately the colonel's uniform and thousands of morning and evening cell inspections kept him safely to attention.

'I'm Gregory, yes.' The dust thickened in his throat. 'Is she dead?'

The colonel stroked his neck with the baton. 'Ear to ear. She must have found an old razor blade in the bathroom. About 3 o'clock this morning.' He headed towards Gregory's chalet, gesturing with the baton. Gregory followed him into the half light, stood tentatively by the bed.

'I was asleep then. The clerk will vouch for that.'

'Naturally.' The colonel gazed down at Gregory's possessions spread out across the bedcover, idly poked the black medical bag.

'She asked you for assistance, doctor? With her personal problems?'

'Not directly. She hinted at it, though. She sounded a little mixed up.'

'Poor child.' The colonel lowered his head sympathetically. 'Her father is a first secretary at the Cairo Embassy, something of an autocrat. You Americans are very stern with your children, doctor. A firm hand, yes, but understanding costs nothing. Don't you agree? She was frightened of him, escaped from the American Hospital. My task is to provide an explanation for the authorities. If I had an idea of what was really worrying her ... no doubt you helped her as best you could?'

Gregory shook his head. 'I gave her no help at all, colonel. In fact, I refused to discuss her problems altogether.' He smiled flatly at the colonel. 'I wouldn't make the same mistake twice, would I?'

The colonel studied Gregory thoughtfully. 'Sensible of you, doctor. But you surprise me. Surely the members of your profession regard themselves as a special calling, answerable to a higher authority. Are these ideals so easy to cast off?'

'I've had a lot of practice.' Gregory began to pack away his things on the bed, bowed to the colonel as he saluted and made his way out into the court.

Half an hour later he was on the Benghasi road, holding the Jaguar at 100, working off his tension and anger in a savage burst of speed. Free for only ten days, already he had got himself involved again, gone through all the agony of having to refuse help to someone desperately needing it, his hands itching to administer relief to the child but held back by the insane penalties. It wasn't only the lunatic legislation but the people enforcing it who ought to be swept away – Bortman and his fellow oligarchs.

He grimaced at the thought of the cold dead-faced Bortman, addressing the World Senate at Lake Success, arguing for increased penalties for the criminal psychopath. The man had stepped straight out of the 14th-century Inquisition, his bureaucratic puritanism masking two real obsessions: dirt and death. Any sane society would have locked Bortman up for ever, or given him a complete brain-lift. Indirectly Bortman was as responsible for the death of Carole Sturgeon as he would have been had he personally handed the razor blade to her.

After Libya, Tunis. He blazed steadily along the coast road, the sea like a molten mirror on the right, avoiding the big towns where possible. Fortunately they weren't so bad as the European cities, psychotics loitering like stray dogs in the uptown parks, wise enough not to shop-lift or cause trouble, but a petty nuisance on the café terraces, knocking on hotel doors at all hours of the night.

At Algiers he spent three days at the Hilton, having a new engine fitted to the car, and hunted up Philip Kalundborg, an old Toronto colleague now working in a WHO children's hospital.

Over their third carafe of burgundy Gregory told him about Carole Sturgeon.

'It's absurd, but I feel guilty about her. Suicide is a highly suggestive act, I reminded her of Muriel Bortman's death. Damn it, Philip, I could have given her the sort of general advice any sensible layman would have offered.'

'Dangerous. Of course you were right,' Philip assured him. 'After the last three years who could argue otherwise?'

Gregory looked out across the terrace at the traffic whirling over the neon-lit cobbles. Beggars sat at their pitches along the sidewalk, whining for sous.

'Philip, you don't know what it's like in Europe now. At least 5 per cent are probably in need of institutional care. Believe me, I'm frightened to go to America. In New York alone they're jumping from the roofs at the rate of ten a day. The world's turning into a madhouse, one half of society gloating righteously over the torments of the other. Most people don't realize which side of the bars they are. It's easier for you. Here the traditions are different.'

Kalundborg nodded. 'True. In the villages up-country it's been standard practice for centuries to blind schizophrenics and exhibit them in a cage. Injustice is so widespread that you build up an indiscriminate tolerance to every form.'

A tall dark-bearded youth in faded cotton slacks and rope sandals stepped across the terrace and put his hands on their table. His eyes were sunk deep below his forehead, around his lips the brown staining of narcotic poisoning.

'Christian!' Kalundborg snapped angrily. He shrugged hopelessly at Gregory, then turned to the young man with quiet exasperation. 'My dear fellow, this has gone on for too long. I can't help you, there's no point in asking.'

The young man nodded patiently. 'It's Marie,' he explained in a slow roughened voice. 'I can't control her. I'm frightened what she may do to the baby. Postnatal withdrawal, you know —'

'Nonsense! I'm not an idiot, Christian. The baby is nearly three. If Marie is a nervous wreck you've made her so. Believe me, I wouldn't help you if I was allowed to. You must cure yourself or you are finished. Already you have chronic barbiturism. Dr Gregory here will agree with me.'

Gregory nodded. The young man stared blackly at Kalundborg, glanced at Gregory and then shambled off through the tables.

Kalundborg filled his glass. 'They have it all wrong today. They think our job was to further addiction, not cure it. In their pantheon the father-figure is always benevolent.'

'That's invariably been Bortman's line. Psychiatry is ultimately self-indulgent, an encouragement to weakness and lack of will. Admittedly there's no one more single-minded than an obsessional neurotic. Bortman himself is a good example.'

As he entered the tenth-floor bedroom the young man was going through his valise on the bed. For a moment Gregory wondered whether he was a UW spy, perhaps the meeting on the terrace had been an elaborate trap.

'Find what you want?'

Christian finished whipping through the bag, then tossed it irritably onto the floor. He edged restlessly away from Gregory around the bed, his eyes hungrily searching the wardrobe top and lamp brackets.

'Kalundborg was right,' Gregory told him quietly. 'You're wasting your time.'

'The hell with Kalundborg,' Christian snarled softly. 'He's working the wrong levels. Do you think I'm looking for a jazz heaven, doctor? With a wife and child? I'm not that irresponsible. I took a Master's degree in law at Heidelberg.' He wandered off around the room, then stopped to survey Gregory closely.

Gregory began to slide in the drawers. 'Well, get back to your jurisprudence. There are enough ills to weigh in this world.'

'Doctor, I've made a start. Didn't Kalundborg tell you I sued Bortman for murder?' When Gregory seemed puzzled he explained: 'A private civil action, not criminal proceedings. My father killed himself five years ago after Bortman had him thrown out of the Bar Association.'

Gregory picked up his valise off the floor. 'I'm sorry,' he said noncommittally. 'What happened to your suit against Bortman?'

Christian stared out through the window into the dark air. 'It was never entered. Some World Bureau investigators saw me after I started to be a nuisance and suggested I leave the States for ever. So I came to Europe to get my degree. I'm on my way back now. I need the barbiturates to stop myself trying to toss a bomb at Bortman.'

Suddenly he propelled himself across the room, before Gregory could stop him was out on the balcony, jack-knifed over the edge. Gregory dived after him, kicked away his feet and tried to pull him off the ledge. Christian clung to it, shouting into the darkness, the lights from the cars racing in the damp street below. On the sidewalk people looked up.

Christian was doubled up with laughter as they fell back into the room, slumped down on the bed, pointing his finger at Gregory, who was leaning against the wardrobe, gasping in exhausted spasms.

'Big mistake there, doctor. You better get out fast before I tip off the Police Prefect. Stopping a suicide! God, with your record you'd get ten years for that. What a joke!'

Gregory shook him by the shoulders, temper flaring. 'Listen, what are you playing at? What do you want?'

Christian pushed Gregory's hands away and lay back weakly. 'Help me, doctor. I want to kill Bortman, it's all I think about. If I'm not careful I'll really try. Show me how to forget him.' His voice rose desperately. 'Damn, I *hated* my father, I was glad when Bortman threw him out.'

Gregory eyed him thoughtfully, then went over to the window and bolted out the night.

Two months later, at the motel outside Casablanca, Gregory finally burned the last of the analysis notes. Christian, clean-shaven and wearing a neat white tropical suit, a neutral tie, watched from the door as the stack of coded entries gutted out in the ashtray, then carried them into the bathroom and flushed them away.

When Christian had loaded his suitcases into the car Gregory said: 'One thing before we go. A complete analysis can't be effected in two months, let alone two years. It's something you work at all your life. If you have a relapse, come to me, even if I'm in Tahiti, or Shanghai or Archangel.' Gregory paused. 'If they ever find out, you know what will happen?' When Christian nodded quietly he sat down in the chair by the writing table, gazing out through the date palms at the huge domed mouth of the transatlantic tunnel a mile away. For a long time he knew he would be unable to relax. In a curious way he felt that the three years at Marseilles had been wasted, that he was starting a suspended sentence of indefinite length. There had been no satisfaction at the successful treatment, perhaps because he had given in to Christian partly for fear of being incriminated in an attack on Bortman.

'With luck, you should be able to live with yourself now.

Try to remember that whatever evils Bortman may perpetrate in the future he's irrelevant to *your* problem. It was the stroke your mother suffered after your father's death that made you realize the guilt you felt subconsciously for hating him, but you conveniently shifted the blame onto Bortman, and by eliminating him you thought you could free yourself. The temptation may occur again.'

Christian nodded, standing motionlessly by the doorway. His face had filled out, his eyes were a placid grey. He looked like any well-groomed UW bureaucrat.

Gregory picked up a newspaper. 'I see Bortman is attacking the American Bar Association as a subversive body, probably planning to have it proscribed. If it succeeds it'll be an irreparable blow to civil liberty.' He looked up thoughtfully at Christian, who showed no reaction. 'Right, let's go. Are you still fixed on getting back to the States?'

'Of course.' Christian climbed into the car, then shook Gregory's hand. Gregory had decided to stay in Africa, find a hospital where he could work and had given Christian the car. 'Marie will wait for me in Algiers until I finish my business.'

'What's that?'

Christian pressed the starter, sent a roar of dust and exhaust across the compound.

'I'm going to kill Bortman,' he said quietly.

Gregory gripped the windscreen. 'You're not serious.'

'You cured me, doctor, and give or take the usual margins I'm completely sane, more than I probably ever will be again. Damn few people in this world are now, so that makes the obligation on me to act rationally even greater. Well, every ounce of logic tells me that someone's got to make the effort to get rid of the grim menagerie running things now, and Bortman looks like a pretty good start. I intend to drive up to Lake Success and take a shot at him.' He shunted the gear change into second, and added, 'Don't try to have me stopped, doctor, because they'll only dig out our long weekend here.'

As he started to take his foot off the clutch Gregory shouted:

'Christian! You'll never get away with it! They'll catch you anyway!' but the car wrenched forward out of his hand.

Gregory ran through the dust after it, stumbling over half-buried stones, realizing helplessly that when they caught Christian and probed down into the past few months they would soon find the real assassin, an exiled doctor with a three-year-grudge.

'Christian!' he yelled, choking on the white ash. 'Christian, you're insane!'

1962

THE GARDEN OF TIME

Towards evening, when the great shadow of the Palladian villa filled the terrace, Count Axel left his library and walked down the wide marble steps among the time flowers. A tall, imperious figure in a black velvet jacket, a gold tie-pin glinting below his George V beard, cane held stiffly in a white-gloved hand, he surveyed the exquisite crystal flowers without emotion, listening to the sounds of his wife's harpsichord, as she played a Mozart rondo in the music room, echo and vibrate through the translucent petals.

The garden of the villa extended for some two hundred yards below the terrace, sloping down to a miniature lake spanned by a white bridge, a slender pavilion on the opposite bank. Axel rarely ventured as far as the lake; most of the time flowers grew in a small grove just below the terrace, sheltered by the high wall which encircled the estate. From the terrace he could see over the wall to the plain beyond, a continuous expanse of open ground that rolled in great swells to the horizon, where it rose slightly before finally dipping from sight. The plain surrounded the house on all sides, its drab emptiness emphasizing the seclusion and mellowed magnificence of the villa. Here, in the garden, the air seemed brighter, the sun warmer, while the plain was always dull and remote.

As was his custom before beginning his evening stroll, Count Axel looked out across the plain to the final rise, where the horizon was illuminated like a distant stage by the fading sun. As the Mozart chimed delicately around him, flowing from his wife's graceful hands, he saw that the advance column of an enormous army was moving slowly over the horizon. At first glance, the long ranks seemed to be progressing in orderly lines, but on closer inspection, it was apparent that, like the obscured detail of a Goya landscape, the army was composed of a vast throng of people, men and women, interspersed with a few soldiers in ragged uniforms, pressing forward in a disorganized tide. Some laboured under heavy loads suspended from crude yokes around their necks, others struggled with cumbersome wooden carts, their hands wrenching at the wheel spokes, a few trudged on alone, but all moved on at the same pace, bowed backs illuminated in the fleeting sun.

The advancing throng was almost too far away to be visible, but even as Axel watched, his expression aloof yet observant, it came perceptibly nearer, the vanguard of an immense rabble appearing from below the horizon. At last, as the daylight began to fade, the front edge of the throng reached the crest of the first swell below the horizon, and Axel turned from the terrace and walked down among the time flowers.

The flowers grew to a height of about six feet, their slender stems, like rods of glass, bearing a dozen leaves, the once transparent fronds frosted by the fossilized veins. At the peak of each stem was the time flower, the size of a goblet, the opaque outer petals enclosing the crystal heart. Their diamond brilliance contained a thousand faces, the crystal seeming to drain the air of its light and motion. As the flowers swayed slightly in the evening air, they glowed like flame-tipped spears.

Many of the stems no longer bore flowers, and Axel examined them all carefully, a note of hope now and then crossing his eyes as he searched for any further buds. Finally he selected a large flower on the stem nearest the wall, removed his gloves and with his strong fingers snapped it off.

As he carried the flower back on to the terrace, it began to sparkle and deliquesce, the light trapped within the core at last released. Gradually the crystal dissolved, only the outer petals remaining intact, and the air around Axel became bright and vivid, charged with slanting rays that flared away into the waning sunlight. Strange shifts momentarily transformed the evening, subtly altering its dimensions of time and space. The darkened portico of the house, its patina of age stripped away, loomed with a curious spectral whiteness as if suddenly remembered in a dream.

Raising his head, Axel peered over the wall again. Only the farthest rim of the horizon was lit by the sun, and the great throng, which before had stretched almost a quarter of the way across the plain, had now receded to the horizon, the entire concourse abruptly flung back in a reversal of time, and appeared to be stationary.

The flower in Axel's hand had shrunk to the size of a glass thimble, the petals contracting around the vanishing core. A faint sparkle flickered from the centre and extinguished itself, and Axel felt the flower melt like an ice-cold bead of dew in his hand.

Dusk closed across the house, sweeping its long shadows over the plain, the horizon merging into the sky. The harpsichord was silent, and the time flowers, no longer reflecting its music, stood motionlessly, like an embalmed forest.

For a few minutes Axel looked down at them, counting the flowers which remained, then greeted his wife as she crossed the terrace, her brocade evening dress rustling over the ornamental tiles.

'What a beautiful evening, Axel.' She spoke feelingly, as if she were thanking her husband personally for the great ornate shadow across the lawn and the dark brilliant air. Her face was serene and intelligent, her hair, swept back behind her head into a jewelled clasp, touched with silver. She wore her dress low across her breast, revealing a long slender neck and high chin. Axel surveyed her with fond pride. He gave her his arm and together they walked down the steps into the garden.

'One of the longest evenings this summer,' Axel confirmed, adding: 'I picked a perfect flower, my dear, a jewel. With luck it should last us for several days.' A frown touched his brow, and he glanced involuntarily at the wall. 'Each time now they seem to come nearer.'

His wife smiled at him encouragingly and held his arm more tightly.

Both of them knew that the time garden was dying.

* * *

Three evenings later, as he had estimated (though sooner than he secretly hoped), Count Axel plucked another flower from the time garden.

When he first looked over the wall the approaching rabble filled the distant half of the plain, stretching across the horizon in an unbroken mass. He thought he could hear the low, fragmentary sounds of voices carried across the empty air, a sullen murmur punctuated by cries and shouts, but quickly told himself that he had imagined them. Luckily, his wife was at the harpsichord, and the rich contrapuntal patterns of a Bach fugue cascaded lightly across the terrace, masking any other noises.

Between the house and the horizon the plain was divided into four huge swells, the crest of each one clearly visible in the slanting light. Axel had promised himself that he would never count them, but the number was too small to remain unobserved, particularly when it so obviously marked the progress of the advancing army. By now the forward line had passed the first crest and was well on its way to the second; the main bulk of the throng pressed behind it, hiding the crest and the even vaster concourse spreading from the horizon. Looking to left and right of the central body, Axel could see the apparently limitless extent of the army. What had seemed at first to be the central mass was no more than a minor advance guard, one of many similar arms reaching across the plain. The true centre had not yet emerged, but from the rate of extension Axel estimated that when it finally reached the plain it would completely cover every foot of ground.

Axel searched for any large vehicles or machines, but all was amorphous and uncoordinated as ever. There were no banners or flags, no mascots or pike-bearers. Heads bowed, the multitude pressed on, unaware of the sky.

Suddenly, just before Axel turned away, the forward edge of the throng appeared on top of the second crest, and swarmed down across the plain. What astounded Axel was the incredible distance it had covered while out of sight. The figures were now twice the size, each one clearly within sight.

Quickly, Axel stepped from the terrace, selected a time flower from the garden and tore it from the stem. As it released its compacted light, he returned to the terrace. When the flower had shrunk to a frozen pearl in his palm he looked out at the plain, with relief saw that the army had retreated to the horizon again.

Then he realized that the horizon was much nearer than previously, and that what he assumed to be the horizon was the first crest.

When he joined the Countess on their evening walk he told her nothing of this, but she could see behind his casual unconcern and did what she could to dispel his worry.

Walking down the steps, she pointed to the time garden. 'What a wonderful display, Axel. There are so many flowers still.'

Axel nodded, smiling to himself at his wife's attempt to reassure him. Her use of 'still' had revealed her own unconscious anticipation of the end. In fact a mere dozen flowers remained of the many hundred that had grown in the garden, and several of these were little more than buds – only three or four were fully grown. As they walked down to the lake, the Countess's dress rustling across the cool turf, he tried to decide whether to pick the larger flowers first or leave them to the end. Strictly, it would be better to give the smaller flowers additional time to grow and mature, and this advantage would be lost if he retained the larger flowers to the end, as he wished to do, for the final repulse. However, he realized that it mattered little either way; the garden would soon die and the smaller flowers required far longer than he could give them to accumulate their compressed cores of time. During his entire lifetime he had failed to notice a single evidence of growth among the flowers. The larger blooms had always been mature, and none of the buds had shown the slightest development.

Crossing the lake, he and his wife looked down at their reflections in the still black water. Shielded by the pavilion on one side and the high garden wall on the other, the villa in the distance, Axel felt composed and secure, the plain with its encroaching multitude a nightmare from which he had safely awakened. He put one arm around his wife's smooth waist and pressed her affectionately to his shoulder, realizing that he had not embraced her for several years, though their lives together had been timeless and he could remember as if yesterday when he first brought her to live in the villa.

'Axel,' his wife asked with sudden seriousness, 'before the garden dies ... may I pick the last flower?'

Understanding her request, he nodded slowly.

One by one over the succeeding evenings, he picked the remaining flowers, leaving a single small bud which grew just below the terrace for his wife. He took the flowers at random, refusing to count or ration them, plucking two or three of the smaller buds at the same time when necessary. The approaching horde had now reached the second and third crests, a vast concourse of labouring humanity that blotted out the horizon. From the terrace Axel could see clearly the shuffling, straining ranks moving down into the hollow towards the final crest, and occasionally the sounds of their voices carried across to him, interspersed with cries of anger and the cracking of whips. The wooden carts lurched from side to side on tilting wheels, their drivers struggling to control them. As far as Axel could tell, not a single member of the throng was aware of its overall direction. Rather, each one blindly moved forward across the ground directly below the heels of the person in front of him, and the only unity was that of the cumulative compass. Pointlessly, Axel hoped that the true centre, far below the horizon, might be moving in a different direction, and that gradually the multitude would alter course, swing away from the villa and recede from the plain like a turning tide.

On the last evening but one, as he plucked the time flower, the forward edge of the rabble had reached the third crest, and was swarming past it. While he waited for the Countess, Axel looked at the two flowers left, both small buds which would carry them back through only a few minutes of the next evening. The glass stems of the dead flowers reared up stiffly into the air, but the whole garden had lost its bloom.

* * *

Axel passed the next morning quietly in his library, sealing the rarer of his manuscripts into the glass-topped cases between the galleries. He walked slowly down the portrait corridor, polishing each of the pictures carefully, then tidied his desk and locked the door behind him. During the afternoon he busied himself in the drawing rooms, unobtrusively assisting his wife as she cleaned their ornaments and straightened the vases and busts.

By evening, as the sun fell behind the house, they were both tired and dusty, and neither had spoken to the other all day. When his wife moved towards the music-room, Axel called her back.

'Tonight we'll pick the flowers together, my dear,' he said to her evenly. 'One for each of us.'

He peered only briefly over the wall. They could hear, less than half a mile away, the great dull roar of the ragged army, the ring of iron and lash, pressing on towards the house.

Quickly, Axel plucked his flower, a bud no bigger than a sapphire. As it flickered softly, the tumult outside momentarily receded, then began to gather again.

Shutting his ears to the clamour, Axel looked around at the villa, counting the six columns in the portico, then gazed out across the lawn at the silver disc of the lake, its bowl reflecting the last evening light, and at the shadows moving between the tall trees, lengthening across the crisp turf. He lingered over the bridge where he and his wife had stood arm in arm for so many summers –

'*Axel!*'

The tumult outside roared into the air, a thousand voices bellowed only twenty or thirty yards away. A stone flew over the wall and landed among the time flowers, snapping several of the brittle stems. The Countess ran towards him as a further barrage rattled along the wall. Then a heavy tile whirled through the air over their heads and crashed into one of the conservatory windows.

'Axel!' He put his arms around her, straightening his silk cravat when her shoulder brushed it between his lapels.

'Quickly, my dear, the last flower!' He led her down the steps and through the garden. Taking the stem between her jewelled fingers, she snapped it cleanly, then cradled it within her palms.

For a moment the tumult lessened slightly and Axel collected himself. In the vivid light sparkling from the flower he saw his wife's white, frightened eyes. 'Hold it as long as you can, my dear, until the last grain dies.'

Together they stood on the terrace, the Countess clasping the brilliant dying jewel, the air closing in upon them as the voices outside mounted again. The mob was battering at the heavy iron gates, and the whole villa shook with the impact.

While the final glimmer of light sped away, the Countess raised her palms to the air, as if releasing an invisible bird, then in a final access of courage put her hands in her husband's, her smile as radiant as the vanished flower.

'Oh, Axel!' she cried.

Like a sword, the darkness swooped down across them.

Heaving and swearing, the outer edges of the mob reached the knee-high remains of the wall enclosing the ruined estate, hauled their carts over it and along the dry ruts of what once had been an ornate drive. The ruin, formerly a spacious villa, barely interrupted the ceaseless tide of humanity. The lake was empty, fallen trees rotting at its bottom, an old bridge rusting into it. Weeds flourished among the long grass in the lawn, overrunning the ornamental pathways and carved stone screens.

Much of the terrace had crumbled, and the main section of the mob cut straight across the lawn, by-passing the gutted villa, but one or two of the more curious climbed up and searched among the shell. The doors had rotted from their hinges and the floors had fallen through. In the music-room an ancient harpsichord had been chopped into firewood, but a few keys still lay among the dust. All the books had been toppled from the shelves in the library, the canvases had been slashed, and gilt frames littered the floor.

As the main body of the mob reached the house, it began to cross the wall at all points along its length. Jostled together, the people stumbled into the dry lake, swarmed over the terrace and pressed through the house towards the open doors on the north side.

One area alone withstood the endless wave. Just below the

terrace, between the wrecked balcony and the wall, was a dense, six-foot-high growth of heavy thorn-bushes. The barbed foliage formed an impenetrable mass, and the people passing stepped around it carefully, noticing the belladonna entwined among the branches. Most of them were too busy finding their footing among the upturned flagstones to look up into the centre of the thornbushes, where two stone statues stood side by side, gazing out over the grounds from their protected vantage point. The larger of the figures was the effigy of a bearded man in a high-collared jacket, a cane under one arm. Beside him was a woman in an elaborate full-skirted dress, her slim, serene face unmarked by the wind and rain. In her left hand she lightly clasped a single rose, the delicately formed petals so thin as to be almost transparent.

As the sun died away behind the house a single ray of light glanced through a shattered cornice and struck the rose, reflected off the whorl of petals on to the statues, lighting up the grey stone so that for a fleeting moment it was indistinguishable from the long-vanished flesh of the statues' originals.

1962

THE THOUSAND DREAMS OF STELLAVISTA

No one ever comes to Vermilion Sands now, and I suppose there are few people who have ever heard of it. But ten years ago, when Fay and I first went to live at 99 Stellavista, just before our marriage broke up, the colony was still remembered as the one-time playground of movie stars, delinquent heiresses and eccentric cosmopolites in those fabulous years before the Recess. Admittedly most of the abstract villas and fake palazzos were empty, their huge gardens overgrown, two-level swimming pools long drained, and the whole place was degenerating like an abandoned amusement park, but there was enough bizarre extravagance in the air to make one realize that the giants had only just departed.

I remember the day we first drove down Stellavista in the property agent's car, and how exhilarated Fay and I were, despite our bogus front of bourgeois respectability. Fay, I think, was even a little awed – one or two of the big names were living on behind the shuttered terraces – and we must have been the easiest prospects the young agent had seen for months.

Presumably this was why he tried to work off the really weird places first. The half dozen we saw to begin with were obviously the old regulars, faithfully paraded in the hope that some unwary client might be staggered into buying one of them, or failing that, temporarily lose all standards of comparison and take the first tolerably conventional pile to come along.

One, just off Stellavista and M, would have shaken even an old-guard surrealist on a heroin swing. Screened from the road by a mass of dusty rhododendrons, it consisted of six aluminium-shelled spheres suspended like the elements of a mobile from an enormous concrete davit. The largest sphere contained the lounge, the others, successively smaller and spiralling upwards into the air, the bedrooms and kitchen. Many of the hull plates had been holed, and the entire slightly tarnished structure hung down into the weeds poking through the cracked concrete court like a collection of forgotten spaceships in a vacant lot.

Stamers, the agent, left us sitting in the car, partly shielded by the rhododendrons. He ran across to the entrance and switched the place on (all the houses in Vermilion Sands, it goes without saying, were psychotropic). There was a dim whirring, and the spheres tipped and began to rotate, brushing against the undergrowth.

Fay sat in the car, staring up in amazement at this awful, beautiful thing, but out of curiosity I got out and walked over to the entrance, the main sphere slowing as I approached, uncertainly steering a course towards me, the smaller ones following.

According to the descriptive brochure, the house had been built eight years earlier for a TV mogul as a weekend retreat. The pedigree was a long one, through two movie starlets, a psychiatrist, an ultrasonic composer (the late Dmitri Shochmann – a notorious madman. I remembered that he had invited a score of guests to his suicide party, but no one had turned up to watch. Chagrined, he bungled the attempt.) and an automobile stylist. With such an overlay of more or less blue-chip responses built into it, the house should have been snapped up within a week, even in Vermilion Sands. To have been on the market for several months, if not years, indicated that the previous tenants had been none too happy there.

Ten feet from me, the main sphere hovered uncertainly, the entrance extending downwards. Stamers stood in the open doorway, smiling encouragingly, but the house seemed nervous of something. As I stepped forward it suddenly jerked away, almost in alarm, the entrance retracting and sending a low shudder through the rest of the spheres.

It's always interesting to watch a psychotropic house try to adjust itself to strangers, particularly those at all guarded or suspicious. The responses vary, a blend of past reactions to negative emotions, the hostility of the previous tenants, a traumatic encounter with a bailiff or burglar (though both these usually stay well away from PT houses; the dangers of an inverting balcony or the sudden deflatus of a corridor are too great). The initial reaction can be a surer indication of a house's true condition than any amount of sales talk about horsepower and moduli of elasticity.

This one was definitely on the defensive. When I climbed on to the entrance Stamers was fiddling desperately with the control console recessed into the wall behind the door, damping the volume down as low as possible. Usually a property agent will select medium/full, trying to heighten the PT responses.

He smiled thinly at me. 'Circuits are a little worn. Nothing serious, we'll replace them on contract. Some of the previous owners were showbusiness people, had an over-simplified view of the full life.

I nodded, walking on to the balcony which ringed the wide sunken lounge. It was a beautiful room all right, with opaque plastex walls and white fluo-glass ceiling, but something terrible had happened there. As it responded to me, the ceiling lifted slightly and the walls grew less opaque, reflecting my perspective-seeking eye. I noticed that curious mottled knots were forming where the room had been strained and healed faultily. Hidden rifts began to distort the sphere, ballooning out one of the alcoves like a bubble of over-extended gum.

Stamers tapped my elbow.

'Lively responses, aren't they, Mr Talbot?' He put his hand on the wall behind us. The plastex swam and whirled like boiling toothpaste, then extruded itself into a small ledge. Stamers sat down on the lip, which quickly expanded to match the contours of his body, providing back and arm rests. 'Sit down and relax, Mr Talbot, let yourself feel at home here.'

The seat cushioned up around me like an enormous white hand, and immediately the walls and ceiling quietened – obviously Stamers's first job was to get his clients off their feet before their restless shuffling could do any damage. Someone living there must have put in a lot of anguished pacing and knuckle-cracking.

'Of course, you're getting nothing but custom-built units here,' Stamers said. 'The vinyl chains in this plastex were hand-crafted literally molecule by molecule.'

I felt the room shift around me. The ceiling was dilating and contracting in steady pulses, an absurdly exaggerated response to our own respiratory rhythms, but the motions were overlayed by sharp transverse spasms, feed-back from some cardiac ailment.

The house was not only frightened of us, it was seriously ill. Somebody, Dmitri Shochmann perhaps, overflowing with self-hate, had committed an appalling injury to himself, and the house was recapitulating its previous response. I was about to ask Stamers if the suicide party had been staged here when he sat up and looked around fretfully.

At the same time my ears started to sing. Mysteriously, the air pressure inside the lounge was building up, gusts of old grit whirling out into the hallway towards the exit.

Stamers was on his feet, the seat telescoping back into the wall.

'Er, Mr Talbot, let's stroll around the garden, give you the feel of –'

He broke off, face creased in alarm. The ceiling was only five feet above our heads, contracting like a huge white bladder.

'– explosive decompression,' Stamers finished automatically, taking my arm. 'I don't understand this,' he muttered as we ran out into the hallway, the air whooshing past us.

I had a shrewd idea what was happening, and sure enough we found Fay peering into the control console, swinging the volume tabs.

Stamers dived past her. We were almost dragged back into the lounge as the ceiling began its outward leg and sucked the air in through the doorway. He reached the emergency panel and switched the house off.

Wide-eyed, he buttoned his shirt. 'That was close, Mrs Talbot, really close.' He gave a light hysterical laugh.

As we walked back to the car, the giant spheres resting among the weeds, he said: 'Well, Mr Talbot, it's a fine property. A remarkable pedigree for a house only eight years old. An exciting challenge, you know, a new dimension in living.'

I gave him a weak smile. 'Maybe, but it's not exactly *us*, is it?'

We had come to Vermilion Sands for two years, while I opened a law office in downtown Red Beach twenty miles away. Apart from the dust, smog and inflationary prices of real estate in Red Beach, a strong motive for coming out to Vermilion Sands was that any number of potential clients were mouldering away there in the old mansions – forgotten movie queens, lonely impresarios and the like, some of the most litigious people in the world. Once installed, I could make my rounds of the bridge tables and dinner parties, tactfully stimulating a little righteous will-paring and contract-breaking.

However, as we drove down Stellavista on our inspection tour I wondered if we'd find anywhere suitable. Rapidly we went through a mock Assyrian ziggurat (the last owner had suffered from St Vitus's Dance, and the whole structure still jittered like a galvanized Tower of Pisa), and a converted submarine pen (here the problem had been alcoholism, we could *feel* the gloom and helplessness come down off those huge damp walls).

Finally Stamers gave up and brought us back to earth. Unfortunately his more conventional properties were little better. The real trouble was that most of Vermilion Sands is composed of early, or primitive-fantastic psychotropic, when the possibilities offered by the new bio-plastic medium rather went to architects' heads. It was some years before a compromise was reached between the one hundred per cent responsive structive and the rigid non-responsive houses of the past. The first PT houses had so many senso-cells distributed over them, echoing every shift of mood and position of the occupants, that living in one was like inhabiting someone else's brain.

Unluckily bioplastics need a lot of exercise or they grow rigid and crack, and many people believe that PT buildings are still given unnecessarily subtle memories and are far too sensitive – there's the apocryphal story of the millionaire of plebian origins who was literally frozen out of a million-dollar mansion he had bought from an aristocratic family. The place had been trained to respond to their habitual rudeness and bad temper, and reacted discordantly when readjusting itself to the millionaire, unintentionally parodying his soft-spoken politeness.

But although the echoes of previous tenants can be intrusive, this naturally has its advantages. Many medium-priced PT homes resonate with the bygone laughter of happy families, the relaxed harmony of a successful marriage. It was something like this that I wanted for Fay and myself. In the previous year our relationship had begun to fade a little, and a really well-integrated house with a healthy set of reflexes – say, those of a prosperous bank president and his devoted spouse – would go a long way towards healing the rifts between us.

Leafing through the brochures when we reached the end of Stellavista I could see that domesticated bank presidents had been in short supply at Vermilion Sands. The pedigrees were either packed with ulcer-ridden, quadri-divorced TV executives, or discreetly blank.

99 Stellavista was in the latter category. As we climbed out of the car and walked up the short drive I searched the pedigree for data on the past tenants, but only the original owner was given: a Miss Emma Slack, psychic orientation unstated.

That it was a woman's house was obvious. Shaped like an enormous orchid, it was set back on a low concrete dais in the centre of a blue gravel court. The white plastex wings, which carried the lounge on one side and the master bedroom on the other, spanned out across the magnolias on the far side of the drive. Between the two wings, on the first floor, was an open terrace around a heart-shaped swimming pool. The terrace ran back to the central bulb, a three-storey segment containing the chauffeur's apartment and a vast two-decker kitchen.

The house seemed to be in good condition. The plastex was unscarred, its thin seams running smoothly to the far rim like the veins of a giant leaf.

Curiously, Stamers was in no hurry to switch on. He pointed to left and right as we made our way up the glass staircase to the terrace, underlining various attractive features, but made no effort to find the control console, and suspected that the house might be a static conversion – a fair number of PT houses are frozen in one or other position at the end of their working lives, and make tolerable static homes.

'It's not bad,' I admitted, looking across the powder-blue water as Stamers piled on the superlatives. Through the glass bottom of the pool the car parked below loomed like a coloured whale asleep on the ocean bed. 'This is the sort of thing, all right. But what about switching it on?'

Stamers stepped around me and headed after Fay. 'You'll want to see the kitchen first, Mr Talbot. There's no hurry, let yourself feel at home here.'

The kitchen was fabulous, banks of gleaming control panels and auto units. Everything was recessed and stylized, blending into the overall colour scheme, complex gadgets folding back into self-sealing cabinets. Boiling an egg there would have taken me a couple of days.

'Quite a plant,' I commented. Fay wandered around in a daze of delight, automatically fingering the chrome. 'Looks as if it's tooled up to produce penicillin.' I tapped the brochure. 'But why so cheap? At twenty-five thousand it's damn nearly being given away.'

Stamers's eyes brightened. He flashed me a broad conspiratorial smile which indicated that this was *my* year, *my* day. Taking me off on a tour of the rumpus room and library, he began to hammer home the merits of the house, extolling his company's thirty-five-year, easy-purchase plan (they wanted anything except cash – there was no money in that) and the beauty and simplicity of the garden (mostly flexible polyurethane perennials).

Finally, apparently convinced that I was sold, he switched the house on.

I didn't know then what it was, but something strange had taken place in that house. Emma Slack had certainly been a woman with a powerful and oblique personality. As I walked slowly around the empty lounge, feeling the walls angle and edge away, doorways widen when I approached, curious echoes stirred through the memories embedded in the house. The responses were undefined, but somehow eerie and unsettling, like being continually watched over one's shoulder, each room adjusting itself to my soft, random footsteps as if they contained the possibility of some explosive burst of passion or temperament.

Inclining my head, I seemed to hear other echoes, delicate and feminine, a graceful swirl of movement reflected in a brief, fluid sweep in one corner, the decorous unfolding of an archway or recess.

Then, abruptly, the mood would invert, and the hollow eeriness return.

Fay touched my arm. 'Howard, it's strange.'

I shrugged. 'Interesting, though. Remember, our own responses will overlay these within a few days.'

Fay shook her head. 'I couldn't stand it, Howard. Mr Stamers must have something normal.'

'Darling, Vermilion Sands is Vermilion Sands. Don't expect to find the suburban norms. People here were individualists.'

I looked down at Fay. Her small oval face, with its childlike mouth and chin, the fringe of blonde hair and pert nose, seemed lost and anxious.

I put my arm around her shoulder. 'Okay, sweetie, you're quite right. Let's find somewhere we can put our feet up and relax. Now, what are we going to say to Stamers?'

Surprisingly, Stamers didn't seem all that disappointed. When I shook my head he put up a token protest but soon gave in and switched off the house.

'I know how Mrs Talbot feels,' he conceded as we went down

the staircase. 'Some of these places have got too much personality built into them. Living with someone like Gloria Tremayne isn't too easy.'

I stopped, two steps from the bottom, a curious ripple of recognition running through my mind.

'Gloria Tremayne? I thought the only owner was a Miss Emma Slack.'

Stamers nodded. 'Yes. Gloria Tremayne. Emma Slack was her real name. Don't say I told you, though everybody living around here knows it. We keep it quiet as long as we can. If we said Gloria Tremayne no one would even look at the place.'

'Gloria Tremayne,' Fay repeated, puzzled. 'She was the movie star who shot her husband, wasn't she? He was a famous architect – Howard, weren't you on that case?'

As Fay's voice chattered on I turned and looked up the staircase towards the sun-lounge, my mind casting itself back ten years to one of the most famous trials of the decade, whose course and verdict were as much as anything else to mark the end of a whole generation, and show up the irresponsibilities of the world before the Recess. Even though Gloria Tremayne had been acquitted, everyone knew that she had cold-bloodedly murdered her husband, the architect Miles Vanden Starr. Only the silver-tongued pleading of Daniel Hammett, her defence attorney, assisted by a young man called Howard Talbot, had saved her. I said to Fay, 'Yes, I helped to defend her. It seems a long time ago. Angel, wait in the car. I want to check something.'

Before she could follow me I ran up the staircase on to the terrace and closed the glass double doors behind me. Inert and unresponsive now, the white walls rose into the sky on either side of the pool. The water was motionless, a transparent block of condensed time, through which I could see the drowned images of Fay and Stamers sitting in the car, like an embalmed fragment of my future.

For three weeks, during her trial ten years earlier, I sat only a few feet from Gloria Tremayne, and like everyone else in that crowded courtroom I would never forget her mask-like face, the composed eyes that examined each of the witnesses as they gave their testimony – chauffeur, police surgeon, neighbours who heard the shots – like a brilliant spider arraigned by its victims, never once showing any emotion or response. As they dismembered her web, skein by skein, she sat impassively at its centre, giving Hammett no encouragement, content to repose in the image of herself ('The Ice Face') projected across the globe for the previous fifteen years.

Perhaps in the end this saved her. The jury were unable to outstare the enigma. To be honest, by the last week of the trial I had lost all interest in it. As I steered Hammett through his brief, opening and shutting his red wooden suitcase (the Hammett hallmark, it was an excellent jury distractor) whenever he indicated, my attention was fixed completely on Gloria Tremayne, trying to find some flaw in the mask through which I could glimpse her personality. I suppose that I was just another naive young man who had fallen in love with a myth manufactured by a thousand publicity agents, but for me the sensation was the real thing, and when she was acquitted the world began to revolve again.

That justice had been flouted mattered nothing. Hammett, curiously, believed her innocent. Like many successful lawyers he had based his career on the principle of prosecuting the guilty and defending the innocent – this way he was sure of a sufficiently high proportion of successes to give him a reputation for being brilliant and unbeatable. When he defended Gloria Tremayne most lawyers thought he had been tempted to depart from principle by a fat bribe from her studio, but in fact he volunteered to take the case. Perhaps he, too, was working off a secret infatuation.

Of course, I never saw her again. As soon as her next picture had been safely released her studio dropped her. Later she briefly reappeared on a narcotics charge after a car smash, and then disappeared into a limbo of alcoholics hospitals and psychiatric wards. When she died five years afterwards few newspapers gave her more than a couple of lines.

* * *

Below, Stamers sounded the horn. Leisurely I retraced my way through the lounge and bedrooms, scanning the empty floors, running my hands over the smooth plastex walls, bracing myself to feel again the impact of Gloria Tremayne's personality. Blissfully, her presence would be everywhere in the house, a thousand echoes of her distilled into every matrix and senso-cell, each moment of emotion blended into a replica more intimate than anyone, apart from her dead husband, could ever know. The Gloria Tremayne with whom I had become infatuated had ceased to exist, but this house was the shrine that entombed the very signatures of her soul.

To begin with everything went quietly. Fay remonstrated with me, but I promised her a new mink wrap out of the savings we made on the house. Secondly, I was careful to keep the volume down for the first few weeks, so that there would be no clash of feminine wills. A major problem of psychotropic houses is that after several months one has to increase the volume to get the same image of the last owner, and this increases the sensitivity of the memory cells and their rate of contamination. At the same time, magnifying the psychic underlay emphasizes the cruder emotional ground-base. One begins to taste the lees rather than the distilled cream of the previous tenancy. I wanted to savour the quintessence of Gloria Tremayne as long as possible so I deliberately rationed myself, turning the volume down during the day while I was out, then switching on only those rooms in which I sat in the evenings.

Right from the outset I was neglecting Fay. Not only were we both preoccupied with the usual problems of adjustment faced by every married couple moving into a new house – undressing in the master bedroom that first night was a positive honeymoon debut all over again – but I was completely immersed in the exhilarating persona of Gloria Tremayne, exploring every alcove and niche in search of her.

In the evenings I sat in the library, feeling her around me in the stirring walls, hovering nearby as I emptied the packing cases like an attendant succubus. Sipping my scotch while night closed over the dark blue pool, I carefully analysed her personality, deliberately varying my moods to evoke as wide a range of responses. The memory cells in the house were perfectly bonded, never revealing any flaws of character, always reposed and self-controlled. If I leapt out of my chair and switched the stereogram abruptly from Stravinsky to Stan Kenton to the MJQ, the room adjusted its mood and tempo without effort.

And yet how long was it before I discovered that there was another personality present in that house, and began to feel the curious eeriness Fay and I had noticed as soon as Stamers switched the house on? Not for a few weeks, when the house was still responding to my star-struck idealism. While my devotion to the departed spirit of Gloria Tremayne was the dominant mood, the house played itself back accordingly, recapitulating only the more serene aspects of Gloria Tremayne's character.

Soon, however, the mirror was to darken.

It was Fay who broke the spell. She quickly realized that the initial responses were being overlaid by others from a more mellow and, from her point of view, more dangerous quarter of the past. After doing her best to put up with them she made a few guarded attempts to freeze Gloria out, switching the volume controls up and down, selecting the maximum of bass lift – which stressed the masculine responses – and the minimum of alto lift.

One morning I caught her on her knees by the console, poking a screwdriver at the memory drum, apparently in an effort to erase the entire store.

Taking it from her, I locked the unit and hooked the key on to my chain.

'Darling, the mortgage company could sue us for destroying the pedigree. Without it this house would be valueless. What are you trying to do?'

Fay dusted her hands on her skirt and stared me straight in the eye, chin jutting.

'I'm trying to restore a little sanity here and if possible, find my own marriage again. I thought it might be in there somewhere.'

I put my arm around her and steered her back towards the kitchen. 'Darling, you're getting over-intuitive again. Just relax, don't try to upset everything.'

'Upset –? Howard, what are you talking about? Haven't I a right to my own husband? I'm sick of sharing him with a homicidal neurotic who died five years ago. It's positively ghoulish!'

I winced as she snapped this out, feeling the walls in the hallway darken and retreat defensively. The air became clouded and frenetic, like a dull storm-filled day.

'Fay, you know your talent for exaggeration . . .' I searched around for the kitchen, momentarily disoriented as the corridor walls shifted and backed. 'You don't know how lucky you –'

I didn't get any further before she interrupted. Within five seconds we were in the middle of a blistering row. Fay threw all caution to the winds, deliberately, I think, in the hope of damaging the house permanently, while I stupidly let a lot of my unconscious resentment towards her come out. Finally she stormed away into her bedroom and I stamped into the shattered lounge and slumped down angrily on the sofa.

Above me the ceiling flexed and quivered, the colour of roof slates, here and there mottled by angry veins that bunched the walls in on each other. The air pressure mounted but I felt too tired to open a window and sat stewing in a pit of black anger.

It must have been then that I recognized the presence of Miles Vanden Starr. All echoes of Gloria Tremayne's personality had vanished, and for the first time since moving in I had recovered my normal perspectives. The mood of anger and resentment in the lounge was remarkably persistent, far longer than expected from what had been little more than a tiff. The walls continued to pulse and knot for over half an hour, long after my own irritation had faded and I was sitting up and examining the room clear-headedly.

The anger, deep and frustrated, was obviously masculine. I assumed, correctly, that the original source had been Vanden Starr, who had designed the house for Gloria Tremayne and lived there for over a year before his death. To have so grooved the memory drum meant that this atmosphere of blind, neurotic hostility had been maintained for most of that time.

As the resentment slowly dispersed I could see that for the time being Fay had succeeded in her object. The serene persona of Gloria Tremayne had vanished. The feminine motif was still there, in a higher and shriller key, but the dominant presence was distinctly Vanden Starr's. This new mood of the house reminded me of the courtroom photographs of him; glowering out of 1950-ish groups with Le Corbusier and Lloyd Wright, stalking about some housing project in Chicago or Tokyo like a petty dictator, heavy-jowled, thyroidal, with large lustreless eyes, and then the Vermilion Sands: 1970 shots of him, fitting into the movie colony like a shark into a goldfish bowl.

However, there was power behind those baleful drives. Cued in by our tantrum, the presence of Vanden Starr had descended upon 99 Stellavista like a thundercloud. At first I tried to recapture the earlier halcyon mood, but this had disappeared and my irritation at losing it only served to inflate the thundercloud. An unfortunate aspect of psychotropic houses is the factor of resonance – diametrically opposed personalities soon stabilize their relationship, the echo inevitably yielding to the new source. But where the personalities are of similar frequency and amplitude they mutually reinforce themselves, each adapting itself for comfort to the personality of the other. All too soon I began to assume the character of Vanden Starr, and my increased exasperation with Fay merely drew from the house a harder front of antagonism.

Later I knew that I was, in fact, treating Fay in exactly the way that Vanden Starr had treated Gloria Tremayne, recapitulating the steps of their tragedy with consequences that were equally disastrous.

Fay recognized the changed mood of the house immediately. 'What's happened to our lodger?' she gibed at dinner the next evening. 'Our beautiful ghost seems to be spurning you. Is the spirit unwilling although the flesh is weak?'

'God knows,' I growled testily. 'I think you've really messed the place up.' I glanced around the dining room for any echo of Gloria Tremayne, but she had gone. Fay went out to the kitchen and I sat over my half-eaten hors d'oeuvres, staring at it blankly, when I felt a curious ripple in the wall behind me, a silver dart of movement that vanished as soon as I looked up. I tried to focus it without success, the first echo of Gloria since our row, but later that evening, when I went into Fay's bedroom after I heard her crying, I noticed it again.

Fay had gone into the bathroom. As I was about to find her I felt the same echo of feminine anguish. It had been prompted by Fay's tears, but like Vanden Starr's mood set off by my own anger, it persisted long after the original cue. I followed it into the corridor as it faded out of the room but it diffused outwards into the ceiling and hung there motionlessly.

Starting to walk down to the lounge, I realized that the house was watching me like a wounded animal.

Two days later came the attack on Fay.

I had just returned home from the office, childishly annoyed with Fay for parking her car on my side of the garage. In the cloakroom I tried to check my anger; the senso-cells had picked up the cue and began to suck the irritation out of me, pouring it back into the air until the walls of the cloakroom darkened and seethed.

I shouted some gratuitous insult at Fay, who was in the lounge. A second later she screamed: 'Howard! Quickly!'

Running towards the lounge, I flung myself at the door, expecting it to retract. Instead, it remained rigid, frame locked in the archway. The entire house seemed grey and strained, the pool outside like a tank of cold lead.

Fay shouted again. I seized the metal handle of the manual control and wrenched the door back.

Fay was almost out of sight, on one of the slab sofas in the centre of the room, buried beneath the sagging canopy of the ceiling which had collapsed on to her. The heavy plastex had flowed together directly above her head, forming a blob a yard in diameter.

Raising the flaccid plastex with my hands, I managed to lift it off Fay, who was spread-eagled into the cushions with only her feet protruding. She wriggled out and flung her arms around me, sobbing noiselessly.

'Howard, this house is insane, I think it's trying to kill me!'

'For heaven's sake, Fay, don't be silly. It was simply a freak accumulation of senso-cells. Your breathing probably set it off.' I patted her shoulder, remembering the child I had married a few years earlier. Smiling to myself, I watched the ceiling retract slowly, the walls grow lighter in tone.

'Howard, can't we leave here?' Fay babbled. 'Let's go and live in a static house. I know it's dull, but what does it matter –?'

'Well,' I said, 'it's not just dull, it's dead. Don't worry, angel, you'll learn to like it here.'

Fay twisted away from me. 'Howard, I can't stay in this house any more. You've been so preoccupied recently, you're completely changed.' She started to cry again, and pointed at the ceiling. 'If I hadn't been lying down, do you realize it would have killed me?'

I dusted the end of the sofa. 'Yes, I can see your heel marks.' Irritation welled up like bile before I could stop it. 'I thought I told you not to stretch out here. This isn't a beach, Fay. You know it annoys me.'

Around us the walls began to mottle and cloud again.

Why did Fay anger me so easily? Was it, as I assumed at the time, unconscious resentment that egged me on, or was I merely a vehicle for the antagonism which had accumulated during Vanden Starr's marriage to Gloria Tremayne and was now venting itself on the hapless couple who followed them to 99 Stellavista? Perhaps I'm over-charitable to myself in assuming the latter, but Fay and I had been tolerably happy during our five years of marriage, and I am sure my nostalgic infatuation for Gloria Tremayne couldn't have so swept me off my feet.

Either way, however, Fay didn't wait for a second attempt. Two days later I came home to find a fresh tape on the kitchen memophone. I switched it on to hear her tell me that she could no longer put up with me, my nagging or 99 Stellavista and was going back east to stay with her sister.

Callously, my first reaction, after the initial twinge of indignation, was sheer relief. I still believed that Fay was responsible for Gloria Tremayne's eclipse and the emergence of Vanden Starr, and that with her gone I would recapture the early days of idyll and romance.

I was only partly right. Gloria Tremayne did return, but not in the role expected. I, who had helped to defend her at her trial, should have known better.

A few days after Fay left I became aware that the house had taken on a separate existence, its coded memories discharging themselves independently of my own behaviour. Often when I returned in the evening, eager to relax over half a decanter of scotch, I would find the ghosts of Miles Vanden Starr and Gloria Tremayne in full flight. Starr's black and menacing personality crowded after the tenuous but increasingly resilient quintessence of his wife. This rapier-like resistance could be observed literally – the walls of the lounge would stiffen and darken in a vortex of anger that converged upon a small zone of lightness hiding in one of the alcoves, as if to obliterate its presence, but at the last moment Gloria's persona would flit nimbly away, leaving the room to seethe and writhe.

Fay had set off this spirit of resistance, and I visualized Gloria Tremayne going through a similar period of living hell. As her personality re-emerged in its new role I watched it carefully, volume at maximum despite the damage the house might do to itself. Once Stamers stopped by and offered to get the circuits checked for me. He had seen the house from the road, flexing and changing colour like an anguished squid. Thanking him, I made up some excuse and declined. Later he told me that I had kicked him out unceremoniously – apparently he hardly recognized me; I was striding around the dark quaking house like a madman in an Elizabethan horror tragedy, oblivious of everything.

Although submerged by the personality of Miles Vanden Starr,

I gradually realized that Gloria Tremayne had been deliberately driven out of her mind by him. What had prompted his implacable hostility I can only hazard – perhaps he resented her success, perhaps she had been unfaithful to him. When she finally retaliated and shot him it was, I'm sure, an act of self-defence.

Two months after she went east Fay filed a divorce suit against me. Frantically I telephoned her, explaining that I would be grateful if she postponed the action as the publicity would probably kill my new law office. However, Fay was adamant. What annoyed me most was that she sounded better than she had done for years, really happy again. When I pleaded with her she said she needed the divorce in order to marry again, and then, as a last straw, refused to tell me who the man was.

By the time I slammed the phone down my temper was taking off like a lunar probe. I left the office early and began a tour of the bars in Red Beach, working my way slowly back to Vermilion Sands. I hit 99 Stellavista like a one-man task force, mowing down most of the magnolias in the drive, ramming the car into the garage on the third pass after wrecking both auto-doors.

My keys jammed in the door lock and I finally had to kick my way through one of the glass panels. Raging upstairs on to the darkened terrace I flung my hat and coat into the pool and slammed into the lounge. By 2 a.m., as I mixed myself a nightcap at the bar and put the last act of *Götterdämmerung* on the stereogram, the whole place was really warming up.

On the way to bed I lurched into Fay's room to see what damage I could do to the memories I still retained of her, kicked in a wardrobe and booted the mattress on to the floor, turning the walls literally blue with a salvo of epithets.

Shortly after three o'clock I fell asleep, the house revolving around me like an enormous turntable.

It must have been only four o'clock when I woke, conscious of a curious silence in the darkened room. I was stretched across the bed, one hand around the neck of the decanter, the other holding a dead cigar stub. The walls were motionless, unstirred by even the residual eddies which drift through a psychotropic house when the occupants are asleep.

Something had altered the normal perspectives of the room. Trying to focus on the grey underswell of the ceiling, I listened for footsteps outside. Sure enough, the corridor wall began to retract. The archway, usually a six-inch wide slit, rose to admit someone. Nothing came through, but the room expanded to accommodate an additional presence, the ceiling ballooning upwards. Astounded, I tried not to move my head, watching the unoccupied pressure zone move quickly across the room towards the bed, its motion shadowed by a small dome in the ceiling.

The pressure zone paused at the foot of the bed and hesitated for a few seconds. But instead of stabilizing, the walls began to vibrate rapidly, quivering with strange uncertain tremors, radiating a sensation of acute urgency and indecision.

Then, abruptly, the room stilled. A second later, as I lifted myself up on one elbow, a violent spasm convulsed the room, buckling the walls and lifting the bed off the floor. The entire house started to shake and writhe. Gripped by this seizure, the bedroom contracted and expanded like the chamber of a dying heart, the ceiling rising and falling.

I steadied myself on the swinging bed and gradually the convulsion died away, the walls realigning. I stood up, wondering what insane crisis this psychotropic *grand mal* duplicated.

The room was in darkness, thin moonlight coming through the trio of small circular vents behind the bed. These were contracting as the walls closed in on each other. Pressing my hands against the ceiling, I felt it push downwards strongly. The edges of the floor were blending into the walls as the room converted itself into a sphere.

The air pressure mounted. I tumbled over to the vents, reached them as they clamped around my fists, air whistling through my fingers. Face against the openings, I gulped in the cool night air, and tried to force apart the locking plastex.

The safety cut-out switch was above the door on the other side of the room. I dived across to it, clambering over the tilting bed, but the flowing plastex had submerged the whole unit.

Head bent to avoid the ceiling, I pulled off my tie, gasping at the thudding air. Trapped in the room, I was suffocating as it duplicated the expiring breaths of Vanden Starr after he had been shot. The tremendous spasm had been his convulsive reaction as the bullet from Gloria Tremayne's gun crashed into his chest.

I fumbled in my pockets for a knife, felt my cigarette lighter, pulled it out and flicked it on. The room was now a grey sphere ten feet in diameter. Thick veins, as broad as my arm, were knotting across its surface, crushing the endboards of the bedstead.

I raised the lighter to the surface of the ceiling, and let it play across the opaque fluoglass. Immediately it began to fizz and bubble. It flared alight and split apart, the two burning lips unzipping in a brilliant discharge of heat.

As the cocoon bisected itself, I could see the twisted mouth of the corridor bending into the room below the sagging outline of the dining room ceiling. Feet skating in the molten plastex, I pulled myself up on to the corridor. The whole house seemed to have been ruptured. Walls were buckled, floors furling at their edges. Water was pouring out of the pool as the unit tipped forwards on the weakened foundations. The glass slabs of the staircase had been shattered, the razor-like teeth jutting from the wall.

I ran into Fay's bedroom, found the cut-out switch and stabbed the sprinkler alarm.

The house was still throbbing, but a moment later it locked and became rigid. I leaned against the dented wall and let the spray pour across my face from the sprinkler jets.

Around me, its wings torn and disarrayed, the house reared up like a tortured flower.

Standing in the trampled flower beds, Stamers gazed at the house, an expression of awe and bewilderment on his face. It was just after six o'clock. The last of the three police cars had driven away, the lieutenant in charge finally conceding defeat. 'Dammit, I can't arrest a house for attempted homicide, can I?'

he'd asked me somewhat belligerently. I roared with laughter at this, my initial feelings of shock having given way to an almost hysterical sense of fun.

Stamers found me equally difficult to understand.

'What on earth were you doing in there?' he asked, voice down to a whisper.

'Nothing. I tell you I was fast asleep. And relax. The house can't hear you. It's switched off.'

We wandered across the churned gravel and waded through the water which lay like a black mirror. Stamers shook his head.

'The place must have been insane. If you ask me it needs a psychiatrist to straighten it out.'

'You're right,' I told him. 'In fact, that was exactly my role – to reconstruct the original traumatic situation and release the repressed material.'

'Why joke about it? It tried to kill you.'

'Don't be absurd. The real culprit is Vanden Starr. But as the lieutenant implied, you can't arrest a man who's been dead for ten years. It was the pent-up memory of his death which tried to kill me. Even if Gloria Tremayne was driven to pulling the trigger, Starr pointed the gun. Believe me, I lived out his role for a couple of months. What worries me is that if Fay hadn't had enough good sense to leave she might have been hypnotized by the persona of Gloria Tremayne into killing *me*.'

Much to Stamers's surprise, I decided to stay on at 99 Stellavista. Apart from the fact that I hadn't enough cash to buy another place, the house had certain undeniable memories for me that I didn't want to forsake. Gloria Tremayne was still there, and I was sure that Vanden Starr had at last gone. The kitchen and service units were still functional, and apart from their contorted shapes most of the rooms were habitable. In addition I needed a rest, and nothing is so quiet as a static house.

Of course, in its present form 99 Stellavista can hardly be regarded as a typical static dwelling. Yet, the deformed rooms and twisted corridors have as much personality as any psychotropic house. The PT unit is still working and one day I shall switch it on again. But one thing worries me. The violent spasms which ruptured the house may in some way have damaged Gloria Tremayne's personality. To live with it might well be madness for me, as there's a subtle charm about the house even in its distorted form, like the ambiguous smile of a beautiful but insane woman.

Often I unlock the control console and examine the memory drum. Her personality, whatever it may be, is there. Nothing would be simpler than to erase it. But I can't.

One day soon, whatever the outcome, I know that I shall have to switch the house on again.

1962

THIRTEEN TO CENTAURUS

Abel knew.

Three months earlier, just after his sixteenth birthday, he had guessed, but had been too unsure of himself, too overwhelmed by the logic of his discovery, to mention it to his parents. At times, lying back half asleep in his bunk while his mother crooned one of the old lays to herself, he would deliberately repress the knowledge, but always it came back, nagging at him insistently, forcing him to jettison most of what he had long regarded as the real world.

None of the other children at the Station could help. They were immersed in their games in Playroom, or chewing pencils over their tests and homework.

'Abel, what's the matter?' Zenna Peters called after him as he wandered off to the empty store-room on D-Deck. 'You're looking sad again.'

Abel hesitated, watching Zenna's warm, puzzled smile, then slipped his hands into his pockets and made off, springing down the metal stairway to make sure she didn't follow him. Once she sneaked into the store-room uninvited and he had pulled the light-bulb out of the socket, shattered about three weeks of conditioning. Dr Francis had been furious.

As he hurried along the D-Deck corridor he listened carefully for the doctor, who had recently been keeping an eye on Abel, watching him shrewdly from behind the plastic models in Playroom. Perhaps Abel's mother had told him about the nightmare, when he would wake from a vice of sweating terror, an image of a dull burning disc fixed before his eyes.

If only Dr Francis could cure him of that dream.

Every six yards down the corridor he stepped through a bulkhead, and idly touched the heavy control boxes on either side of the doorway. Deliberately unfocusing his mind, Abel identified some of the letters above the switches

M–T—R SC—N

but they scrambled into a blur as soon as he tried to read the entire phrase. Conditioning was too strong. After he trapped her in the store-room Zenna had been able to read a few of the notices, but Dr Francis whisked her away before she could repeat them. Hours later, when she came back, she remembered nothing.

As usual when he entered the store-room, he waited a few seconds before switching on the light, seeing in front of him the small disc of burning light that in his dreams expanded until it filled his brain like a thousand arc lights. It seemed endlessly distant, yet somehow mysteriously potent and magnetic, arousing dormant areas of his mind close to those which responded to his mother's presence.

As the disc began to expand he pressed the switch tab.

To his surprise, the room remained in darkness. He fumbled for the switch, a short cry slipping involuntarily through his lips.

Abruptly, the light went on.

'Hello, Abel,' Dr Francis said easily, right hand pressing the bulb into its socket. 'Quite a shock, that one.' He leaned against a metal crate. 'I thought we'd have a talk together about your essay.' He took an exercise book out of his white plastic suit as Abel sat down stiffly. Despite his dry smile and warm eyes there was something about Dr Francis that always put Abel on his guard.

Perhaps Dr Francis knew too?

'The Closed Community,' Dr Francis read out. 'A strange subject for an essay, Abel.'

Abel shrugged. 'It was a free choice. Aren't we really expected to choose something unusual?'

Dr Francis grinned. 'A good answer. But seriously, Abel, why pick a subject like that?'

Abel fingered the seals on his suit. These served no useful purpose, but by blowing through them it was possible to inflate the suit. 'Well, it's a sort of study of life at the Station, how we all get on with each other. What else is there to write about? I don't see that it's so strange.'

'Perhaps not. No reason why you shouldn't write about the Station. All four of the others did too. But you called yours "The Closed Community". The Station isn't closed, Abel, is it?'

'It's closed in the sense that we can't go outside,' Abel explained slowly. 'That's all I meant.'

'Outside,' Dr Francis repeated. 'It's an interesting concept. You must have given the whole subject a lot of thought. When did you first start thinking along these lines?'

'After the dream,' Abel said. Dr Francis had deliberately sidestepped his use of the word 'outside' and he searched for some means of getting to the point. In his pocket he felt the small plumbline he carried around. 'Dr Francis, perhaps you can explain something to me. Why is the Station revolving?'

'Is it?' Dr Francis looked up with interest. 'How do you know?'

Abel reached up and fastened the plumbline to the ceiling stanchion. 'The interval between the ball and the wall is about an eighth of an inch greater at the bottom than at the top. Centrifugal forces are driving it outwards. I calculated that the Station is revolving at about two feet per second.'

Dr Francis nodded thoughtfully. 'That's just about right,' he said matter-of-factly. He stood up. 'Let's take a trip to my office. It looks as if it's time you and I had a serious talk.'

The Station was on four levels. The lower two contained the crew's quarters, two circular decks of cabins which housed the 14 people on board the Station. The senior clan was the Peters, led by Captain Theodore, a big stern man of taciturn disposition who rarely strayed from Control. Abel had never been allowed there, but the Captain's son, Matthew, often described the hushed dome-like cabin filled with luminous dials and flickering lights, the strange humming music.

All the male members of the Peters clan worked in Control – grandfather Peters, a white-haired old man with humorous eyes, had been Captain before Abel was born – and with the Captain's wife and Zenna they constituted the elite of the Station.

However, the Grangers, the clan to which Abel belonged, was in many respects more important, as he had begun to realize. The day-to-day running of the Station, the detailed programming of emergency drills, duty rosters and commissary menus, was the responsibility of Abel's father, Matthias, and without his firm but flexible hand the Bakers, who cleaned the cabins and ran the commissary, would never have known what to do. And it was only the deliberate intermingling in Recreation which his father devised that brought the Peters and Bakers together, or each family would have stayed indefinitely in its own cabins.

Lastly, there was Dr Francis. He didn't belong to any of the three clans. Sometimes Abel asked himself where Dr Francis had come from, but his mind always fogged at a question like that, as the conditioning blocks fell like bulkheads across his thought trains (logic was a dangerous tool at the Station). Dr Francis' energy and vitality, his relaxed good humour – in a way, he was the only person in the Station who ever made any jokes – were out of character with everyone else. Much as he sometimes disliked Dr Francis for snooping around and being a know-all, Abel realized how dreary life in the Station would seem without him.

Dr Francis closed the door of his cabin and gestured Abel into a seat. All the furniture in the Station was bolted to the floor, but Abel noticed that Dr Francis had unscrewed his chair so that he could tilt it backwards. The huge vacuum-proof cylinder of the doctor's sleeping tank jutted from the wall, its massive metal body able to withstand any accident the Station might suffer. Abel hated the thought of sleeping in the cylinder – luckily the entire crew quarters were accident-secure – and wondered why Dr Francis chose to live alone up on A-Deck.

'Tell me, Abel,' Dr Francis began, 'has it ever occurred to you to ask why the Station is here?'

Abel shrugged. 'Well, it's designed to keep us alive, it's our home.'

'Yes, that's true, but obviously it has some other object than just our own survival. Who do you think built the Station in the first place?'

'Our fathers, I suppose, or grandfathers. Or *their* grandfathers.'

'Fair enough. And where were they before they built it?'

Abel struggled with the *reductio ad absurdum*. 'I don't know, they must have been floating around in mid-air!'

Dr Francis joined in the laughter. 'Wonderful thought. Actually it's not that far from the truth. But we can't accept that as it stands.'

The doctor's self-contained office gave Abel an idea. 'Perhaps they came from another Station? An even bigger one?'

Dr Francis nodded encouragingly. 'Brilliant, Abel. A first-class piece of deduction. All right, then, let's assume that. Somewhere away from us, a huge Station exists, perhaps a hundred times bigger than this one, maybe even a thousand. Why not?'

'It's possible,' Abel admitted, accepting the idea with surprising ease.

'Right. Now you remember your course in advanced mechanics – the imaginary planetary system, with the orbiting bodies held together by mutual gravitational attraction? Let's assume further that such a system actually exists. Okay?'

'Here?' Abel said quickly. 'In your cabin?' Then he added 'In your sleeping cylinder?'

Dr Francis sat back. 'Abel, you do come up with some amazing things. An interesting association of ideas. No, it would be too big for that. Try to imagine a planetary system orbiting around a central body of absolutely enormous size, each of the planets a million times larger than the Station.' When Abel nodded, he went on. 'And suppose that the big Station, the one a thousand times larger than this, were attached to one of the planets, and that the people in it decided to go to another planet. So they build a smaller Station, about the size of this one, and send it off through the air. Make sense?'

'In a way.' Strangely, the completely abstract concepts were less remote than he would have expected. Deep in his mind dim memories stirred, interlocking with what he had already guessed about the Station. He gazed steadily at Dr Francis. 'You're saying that's what the Station is doing? That the planetary system exists?'

Dr Francis nodded. 'You'd more or less guessed before I told you. Unconsciously, you've known all about it for several years. A few minutes from now I'm going to remove some of the conditioning blocks, and when you wake up in a couple of hours you'll understand everything. You'll know then that in fact the Station is a space ship, flying from our home planet, Earth, where our grandfathers were born, to another planet millions of miles away, in a distant orbiting system. Our grandfathers always lived on Earth, and we are the first people ever to undertake such a journey. You can be proud that you're here. Your grandfather, who volunteered to come, was a great man, and we've got to do everything to make sure that the Station keeps running.'

Abel nodded quickly. 'When do we get there – the planet we're flying to?'

Dr Francis looked down at his hands, his face growing sombre. 'We'll never get there, Abel. The journey takes too long. This is a multi-generation space vehicle, only our children will land and they'll be old by the time they do. But don't worry, you'll go on thinking of the Station as your only home, and that's deliberate, so that you and your children will be happy here.'

He went over to the TV monitor screen by which he kept in touch with Captain Peters, his fingers playing across the control tabs. Suddenly the screen lit up, a blaze of fierce points of light flared into the cabin, throwing a brilliant phosphorescent glitter across the walls, dappling Abel's hands and suit. He gaped at the huge balls of fire, apparently frozen in the middle of a giant explosion, hanging in vast patterns.

* * *

'This is the celestial sphere,' Dr Francis explained. 'The starfield into which the Station is moving.' He touched a bright speck of light in the lower half of the screen. 'Alpha Centauri, the star around which revolves the planet the Station will one day land upon.' He turned to Abel. 'You remember all these terms I'm using, don't you, Abel? None of them seems strange.'

Abel nodded, the wells of his unconscious memory flooding into his mind as Dr Francis spoke. The TV screen blanked and then revealed a new picture. They appeared to be looking down at an enormous top-like structure, the flanks of a metal pylon sloping towards its centre. In the background the starfield rotated slowly in a clockwise direction. 'This is the Station,' Dr Francis explained, 'seen from a camera mounted in the nose boom. All visual checks have to be made indirectly, as the stellar radiation would blind us. Just below the ship you can see a single star, the Sun, from which we set out 50 years ago. It's now almost too distant to be visible, but a deep inherited memory of it is the burning disc you see in your dreams. We've done what we can to erase it, but unconsciously all of us see it too.'

He switched off the set and the brilliant pattern of light swayed and fell back. 'The social engineering built into the ship is far more intricate than the mechanical, Abel. It's three generations since the Station set off, and birth, marriage and birth again have followed exactly as they were designed to. As your father's heir great demands are going to be made on your patience and understanding. Any disunity here would bring disaster. The conditioning programmes are not equipped to give you more than a general outline of the course to follow. Most of it will be left to you.'

'Will you always be here?'

Dr Francis stood up. 'No, Abel, I won't. No one here lives forever. Your father will die, and Captain Peters and myself.' He moved to the door. 'We'll go now to Conditioning. In three hours' time, when you wake up, you'll find yourself a new man.'

Letting himself back into his cabin, Francis leaned wearily against the bulkhead, feeling the heavy rivets with his fingers, here and there flaking away as the metal slowly rusted. When he switched on the TV set he looked tired and dispirited, and gazed absently at the last scene he had shown Abel, the boom camera's view of the ship. He was just about to select another frame when he noticed a dark shadow swing across the surface of the hull.

He leaned forward to examine it, frowning in annoyance as the shadow moved away and faded among the stars. He pressed another tab, and the screen divided into a large chessboard, five frames wide by five deep. The top line showed Control, the main pilot and navigation deck lit by the dim glow of the instrument panels, Captain Peters sitting impassively before the compass screen.

Next, he watched Matthias Granger begin his afternoon inspection of the ship. Most of the passengers seemed reasonably happy, but their faces lacked any lustre. All spent at least 2–3 hours each day bathing in the UV light flooding through the recreation lounge, but the pallor continued, perhaps an unconscious realization that they had been born and were living in what would also be their own tomb. Without the continuous conditioning sessions, and the hypnotic reassurance of the sub-sonic voices, they would long ago have become will-less automatons.

Switching off the set, he prepared to climb into the sleeping cylinder. The airlock was three feet in diameter, waist-high off the floor. The time seal rested at zero, and he moved it forward 12 hours, then set it so that the seal could only be broken from within. He swung the lock out and crawled in over the moulded foam mattress, snapping the door shut behind him.

Lying back in the thin yellow light, he slipped his fingers through the ventilator grille in the rear wall, pressed the unit into its socket and turned it sharply. Somewhere an electric motor throbbed briefly, the end wall of the cylinder swung back slowly like a vault door and bright daylight poured in.

Quickly, Francis climbed out onto a small metal platform that jutted from the upper slope of a huge white asbestos-covered dome. Fifty feet above was the roof of a large hangar. A maze of pipes and cables traversed the surface of the dome, interlacing like the vessels of a giant bloodshot eye, and a narrow stairway led down to the floor below. The entire dome, some 150 feet wide, was revolving slowly. A line of five trucks was drawn up by the stores depot on the far side of the hangar, and a man in a brown uniform waved to him from one of the glass-walled offices.

At the bottom of the ladder he jumped down on to the hangar floor, ignoring the curious stares from the soldiers unloading the stores. Halfway across he craned up at the revolving bulk of the dome. A black perforated sail, 50 feet square, like a fragment of a planetarium, was suspended from the roof over the apex of the dome, a TV camera directly below it, a large metal sphere mounted about five feet from the lens. One of the guy-ropes had snapped and the sail tilted slightly to reveal the catwalk along the centre of the roof.

He pointed this out to a maintenance sergeant warming his hands in one of the ventilator outlets from the dome. 'You'll have to string that back. Some fool was wandering along the catwalk and throwing his shadow straight on to the model. I could see it clearly on the TV screen. Luckily no one spotted it.'

'Okay, Doctor, I'll get it fixed.' He chuckled sourly. 'That would have been a laugh, though. Really give them something to worry about.'

The man's tone annoyed Francis. 'They've got plenty to worry about as it is.'

'I don't know about that, Doctor. Some people here think they have it all ways. Quiet and warm in there, nothing to do except sit back and listen to those hypno-drills.' He looked out bleakly at the abandoned airfield stretching away to the cold tundra beyond the perimeter, and turned up his collar. 'We're the boys back here on Mother Earth who do the work, out in this Godforsaken dump. If you need any more spacecadets, Doctor, remember me.'

Francis managed a smile and stepped into the control office, made his way through the clerks sitting at trestle tables in front of the progress charts. Each carried the name of one of the dome passengers and a tabulated breakdown of progress through the psychometric tests and conditioning programmes. Other charts listed the day's rosters, copies of those posted that morning by Matthias Granger.

Inside Colonel Chalmers' office Francis relaxed back gratefully in the warmth, describing the salient features of his day's observation. 'I wish you could go in there and move around them, Paul,' he concluded. 'It's not the same spying through the TV cameras. You've got to talk to them, measure yourself against people like Granger and Peters.'

'You're right, they're fine men, like all the others. It's a pity they're wasted there.'

'They're not wasted,' Francis insisted. 'Every piece of data will be immensely valuable when the first space ships set out.' He ignored Chalmers' muttered 'If they do' and went on: 'Zenna and Abel worry me a little. It may be necessary to bring forward the date of their marriage. I know it will raise eyebrows, but the girl is as fully mature at 15 as she will be four years from now, and she'll be a settling influence on Abel, stop him from thinking too much.'

Chalmers shook his head doubtfully. 'Sounds a good idea, but a girl of 15 and a boy of 16 –? You'd raise a storm, Roger. Technically they're wards of court, every decency league would be up in arms.'

Francis gestured irritably. 'Need they know? We've really got a problem with Abel, the boy's too clever. He'd more or less worked out for himself that the Station was a space ship, he merely lacked the vocabulary to describe it. Now that we're starting to lift the conditioning blocks he'll want to know everything. It will be a big job to prevent him from smelling a rat, particularly with the slack way this place is being run. Did you see the shadow on the TV screen? We're damn lucky Peters didn't have a heart attack.'

Chalmers nodded. 'I'm getting that tightened up. A few mistakes are bound to happen, Roger. It's damn cold for the control crew working around the dome. Try to remember that the people outside are just as important as those inside.'

'Of course. The real trouble is that the budget is ludicrously out of date. It's only been revised once in 50 years. Perhaps General

Short can generate some official interest, get a new deal for us. He sounds like a pretty brisk new broom.' Chalmers pursed his lips doubtfully, but Francis continued 'I don't know whether the tapes are wearing out, but the negative conditioning doesn't hold as well as it used to. We'll probably have to tighten up the programmes. I've made a start by pushing Abel's graduation forward.'

'Yes, I watched you on the screen here. The control boys became quite worked up next door. One or two of them are as keen as you, Roger, they'd been programming ahead for three months. It meant a lot of time wasted for them. I think you ought to check with me before you make a decision like that. The dome isn't your private laboratory.'

Francis accepted the reproof. Lamely, he said 'It was one of those spot decisions, I'm sorry. There was nothing else to do.'

Chalmers gently pressed home his point. 'I'm not so sure. I thought you rather overdid the long-term aspects of the journey. Why go out of your way to tell him he would never reach planet-fall? It only heightens his sense of isolation, makes it that much more difficult if we decide to shorten the journey.'

Francis looked up. 'There's no chance of that, is there?'

Chalmers paused thoughtfully. 'Roger, I really advise you not to get too involved with the project. Keep saying to yourself they're-not-going-to-Alpha-Centauri. They're here on Earth, and if the government decided it they'd be let out tomorrow. I know the courts would have to sanction it but that's a formality. It's 50 years since this project was started and a good number of influential people feel that it's gone on for too long. Ever since the Mars and Moon colonies failed, space programmes have been cut right back. They think the money here is being poured away for the amusement of a few sadistic psychologists.'

'You know that isn't true,' Francis retorted. 'I may have been over-hasty, but on the whole this project has been scrupulously conducted. Without exaggeration, if you did send a dozen people on a multi-generation ship to Alpha Centauri you couldn't do better than duplicate everything that's taken place here, down to the last cough and sneeze. If the information we've obtained had been available the Mars and Moon colonies never would have failed!'

'True. But irrelevant. Don't you understand, when everyone was eager to get into space they were prepared to accept the idea of a small group being sealed into a tank for 100 years, particularly when the original team volunteered. Now, when interest has evaporated, people are beginning to feel that there's something obscene about this human zoo; what began as a grand adventure of the spirit of Columbus, has become a grisly joke. In one sense we've learned too much – the social stratification of the three families is the sort of unwelcome datum that doesn't do the project much good. Another is the complete ease with which we've manipulated them, made them believe anything we've wanted.' Chalmers leaned forward across the desk. 'Confidentially, Roger, General Short has been put in command for one reason only – to close this place down. It may take years, but it's going to be done, I warn you. The important job now is to get those people out of there, not keep them in.'

Francis stared bleakly at Chalmers. 'Do you really believe that?'

'Frankly, Roger, yes. This project should never have been launched. You can't manipulate people the way we're doing – the endless hypno-drills, the forced pairing of children – look at yourself, five minutes ago you were seriously thinking of marrying two teenage children just to stop them using their minds. The whole thing degrades human dignity, all the taboos, the increasing degree of introspection – sometimes Peters and Granger don't speak to anyone for two or three weeks – the way life in the dome has become tenable only by accepting the insane situation as the normal one. I think the reaction against the project is healthy.'

Francis stared out at the dome. A gang of men were loading the so-called 'compressed food' (actually frozen foods with the brand names removed) into the commissary hatchway. Next morning, when Baker and his wife dialled the pre-arranged menu, the supplies would be promptly delivered, apparently from the space-hold. To some people, Francis knew, the project might well seem a complete fraud.

Quietly he said: 'The people who volunteered accepted the sacrifice, and all it involved. How's Short going to get them out? Just open the door and whistle?'

Chalmers smiled, a little wearily. 'He's not a fool, Roger. He's as sincerely concerned about their welfare as you are. Half the crew, particularly the older ones, would go mad within five minutes. But don't be disappointed, the project has more than proved its worth.'

'It won't do that until they "land". If the project ends it will be we who have failed, not them. We can't rationalize by saying it's cruel or unpleasant. We owe it to the 14 people in the dome to keep it going.'

Chalmers watched him shrewdly. '14? You mean 13, don't you, Doctor? Or are you inside the dome too?'

This ship had stopped rotating. Sitting at his desk in Command, planning the next day's fire drill, Abel noticed the sudden absence of movement. All morning, as he walked around the ship – he no longer used the term Station – he had been aware of an inward drag that pulled him towards the wall, as if one leg were shorter than the other.

When he mentioned this to his father the older man merely said: 'Captain Peters is in charge of Control. Always let him worry where the navigation of the ship is concerned.'

This sort of advice now meant nothing to Abel. In the previous two months his mind had attacked everything around him voraciously, probing and analysing, examining every facet of life in the Station. An enormous, once-suppressed vocabulary of abstract terms and relationships lay latent below the surface of his mind, and nothing would stop him applying it.

Over their meal trays in the commissary he grilled Matthew Peters about the ship's flight path, the great parabola which would carry it to Alpha Centauri.

'What about the currents built into the ship?' he asked. 'The rotation was designed to eliminate the magnetic poles set up when the ship was originally constructed. How are you compensating for that?'

Matthew looked puzzled. 'I'm not sure, exactly. Probably the instruments are automatically compensated.' When Abel smiled sceptically he shrugged. 'Anyway, Father knows all about it. There's no doubt we're right on course.'

'We hope,' Abel murmured *sotto voce*. The more Abel asked Matthew about the navigational devices he and his father operated in Control the more obvious it became that they were merely carrying out low-level instrument checks, and that their role was limited to replacing burnt-out pilot lights. Most of the instruments operated automatically, and they might as well have been staring at cabinets full of mattress flock.

What a joke if they were!

Smiling to himself, Abel realized that he had probably stated no more than the truth. It would be unlikely for the navigation to be entrusted to the crew when the slightest human error could throw the space ship irretrievably out of control, send it hurtling into a passing star. The designers of the ship would have sealed the automatic pilots well out of reach, given the crew light supervisory duties that created an illusion of control.

That was the real clue to life aboard the ship. None of their roles could be taken at face value. The day-to-day, minute-to-minute programming carried out by himself and his father was merely a set of variations on a pattern already laid down; the permutations possible were endless, but the fact that he could send Matthew Peters to the commissary at 12 o'clock rather than 12.30 didn't give him any real power over Matthew's life. The master programmes printed by the computers selected the day's menus, safety drills and recreation periods, and a list of names to choose from, but the slight leeway allowed, the extra two or three names supplied, were here in case of illness, not to give Abel any true freedom of choice.

One day, Abel promised himself, he would programme himself out of the conditioning sessions. Shrewdly he guessed that the conditioning still blocked out a great deal of interesting material, that half his mind remained submerged. Something about the ship suggested that there might be more to it than –

'Hello, Abel, you look far away.' Dr Francis sat down next to him. 'What's worrying you?'

'I was just calculating something,' Abel explained quickly. 'Tell me, assuming that each member of the crew consumes about three pounds of non-circulated food each day, roughly half a ton per year, the total cargo must be about 800 tons, and that's not allowing for any supplies after planet-fall. There should be at least 1,500 tons aboard. Quite a weight.'

'Not in absolute terms, Abel. The Station is only a small fraction of the ship. The main reactors, fuel tanks and space holds together weigh over 30,000 tons. They provide the gravitational pull that holds you to the floor.'

Abel shook his head slowly. 'Hardly, Doctor. The attraction must come from the stellar gravitational fields, or the weight of the ship would have to be about 6×10^{20} tons.'

Dr Francis watched Abel reflectively, aware that the young man had led him into a simple trap. The figure he had quoted was near enough the Earth's mass. 'These are complex problems, Abel. I wouldn't worry too much about stellar mechanics. Captain Peters has that responsibility.'

'I'm not trying to usurp it,' Abel assured him. 'Merely to extend my own knowledge. Don't you think it might be worth departing from the rules a little? For example, it would be interesting to test the effects of continued isolation. We could select a small group, subject them to artificial stimuli, even seal them off from the rest of the crew and condition them to believe they were back on Earth. It could be a really valuable experiment, Doctor.'

As he waited in the conference room for General Short to finish his opening harangue, Francis repeated the last sentence to himself, wondering idly what Abel, with his limitless enthusiasm, would have made of the circle of defeated faces around the table.

'... regret as much as you do, gentlemen, the need to discontinue the project. However, now that a decision has been made by the Space Department, it is our duty to implement it. Of course, the task won't be an easy one. What we need is a phased withdrawal, a gradual readjustment of the world around the crew that will bring them down to Earth as gently as a parachute.' The General was a brisk, sharp-faced man in his fifties, with burly shoulders but sensitive eyes. He turned to Dr Kersh, who was responsible for the dietary and biometric controls aboard the dome. 'From what you tell me, Doctor, we might not have as much time as we'd like. This boy Abel sounds something of a problem.'

Kersh smiled. 'I was looking in at the commissary, overheard him tell Dr Francis that he wanted to run an experiment on a small group of the crew. An isolation drill, would you believe it. He's estimated that the tractor crews may be isolated for up to two years when the first foraging trips are made.'

Captain Sanger, the engineering officer, added: 'He's also trying to duck his conditioning sessions. He's wearing a couple of foam pads under his earphones, missing about 90 per cent of the subsonics. We spotted it when the EEG tape we record showed no alpha waves. At first we thought it was a break in the cable, but when we checked visually on the screen we saw that he had his eyes open. He wasn't listening.'

Francis drummed on the table. 'It wouldn't have mattered. The sub-sonic was a maths instruction sequence – the four-figure antilog system.'

'A good thing he did miss them,' Kersh said with a laugh. 'Sooner or later he'll work out that the dome is travelling in an elliptical orbit 93 million miles from a dwarf star of the G_0 spectral class.'

'What are you doing about this attempt to evade conditioning, Dr Francis?' Short asked. When Francis shrugged vaguely he added: 'I think we ought to regard the matter fairly seriously. From now on we'll be relying on the programming.'

Flatly, Francis said: 'Abel will resume the conditioning. There's no need to do anything. Without the regular daily contact he'll soon feel lost. The sub-sonic voice is composed of his mother's vocal tones; when he no longer hears it he'll lose his orientations, feel completely deserted.'

Short nodded slowly. 'Well, let's hope so.' He addressed Dr Kersh. 'At a rough estimate, Doctor, how long will it take to bring them back? Bearing in mind they'll have to be given complete freedom and that every TV and newspaper network in the world will interview each one a hundred times.'

Kersh chose his words carefully. 'Obviously a matter of years, General. All the conditioning drills will have to be gradually rescored; as a stop-gap measure we may need to introduce a meteor collision ... guessing, I'd say three to five years. Possibly longer.'

'Fair enough. What would you estimate, Dr Francis?'

Francis fiddled with his blotter, trying to view the question seriously. 'I've no idea. *Bring them back*. What do you really mean, General? Bring what back?' Irritated, he snapped: 'A hundred years.'

Laughter crossed the table, and Short smiled at him, not unamiably. 'That's fifty years more than the original project, Doctor. You can't have been doing a very good job here.'

Francis shook his head. 'You're wrong, General. The original project was to get them to Alpha Centauri. Nothing was said about bringing them *back*.' When the laughter fell away Francis cursed himself for his foolishness; antagonizing the General wouldn't help the people in the dome.

But Short seemed unruffled. 'All right, then, it's obviously going to take some time.' Pointedly, with a glance at Francis he added: 'It's the men and women in the ship we're thinking of, not ourselves; if we need a hundred years we'll take them, not one less. You may be interested to hear that the Space Department chiefs feel about fifteen years will be necessary. At least.' There was a quickening of interest around the table. Francis watched Short with surprise. In fifteen years a lot could happen, there might be another spaceward swing of public opinion.

'The Department recommends that the project continue as before, with whatever budgetary parings we can make – stopping the dome is just a start – and that we condition the crew to believe that a round trip is in progress, that their mission is merely one of reconnaissance, and that they are bringing vital information back to Earth. When they step out of the spaceship they'll be treated as heroes and accept the strangeness of the world around them.'

Short looked across the table, waiting for someone to reply. Kersh stared doubtfully at his hands, and Sanger and Chalmers played mechanically with their blotters.

Just before Short continued Francis pulled himself together, realizing that he was faced with his last opportunity to save the project. However much they disagreed with Short, none of the others would try to argue with him.

'I'm afraid that won't do, General,' he said, 'though I appreciate the Department's foresight and your own sympathetic approach. The scheme you've outlined sounds plausible, but it just won't work.' He sat forward, his voice controlled and precise. 'General, ever since they were children these people have been trained to accept that they were a closed group, and would never have contact with anyone else. On the unconscious level, on the level of their functional nervous systems, no one else in the world exists, for them the neuronic basis of reality is isolation. You'll never train them to invert their whole universe, any more than you can train a fish to fly. If you start to tamper with the fundamental patterns of their psyches you'll produce the sort of complete mental block you see when you try to teach a left-handed person to use his right.'

Francis glanced at Dr Kersh, who was nodding in agreement. 'Believe me, General, contrary to what you and the Space Department naturally assume, the people in the dome do *not* want to come out. Given the choice they would prefer to stay there, just as the goldfish prefers to stay in its bowl.'

Short paused before replying, evidently re-assessing Francis. 'You may be right, Doctor,' he admitted. 'But where does that get us? We've got 15 years, perhaps 25 at the outside.'

'There's only one way to do it,' Francis told him. 'Let the project continue, exactly as before, but with one difference. Prevent them from marrying and having children. In 25 years only the present younger generation will still be alive, and a further five years from then they'll all be dead. A life span in the dome is little more than

45 years. At the age of 30 Abel will probably be an old man. When they start to die off no one will care about them any longer.'

There was a full half minute's silence, and then Kersh said: 'It's the best suggestion, General. Humane, and yet faithful both to the original project and the Department's instructions. The absence of children would be only a slight deviation from the conditioned pathway. The basic isolation of the group would be strengthened, rather than diminished, also their realization that they themselves will never see planet-fall. If we drop the pedagogical drills and play down the space flight they will soon become a small close community, little different from any other out-group on the road to extinction.'

Chalmers cut in: 'Another point, General. It would be far easier – and cheaper – to stage, and as the members died off we could progressively close down the ship until finally there might be only a single deck left, perhaps even a few cabins.'

Short stood up and paced over to the window, looking out through the clear glass over the frosted panes at the great dome in the hangar.

'It sounds a dreadful prospect,' he commented. 'Completely insane. As you say, though, it may be the only way out.'

Moving quietly among the trucks parked in the darkened hangar, Francis paused for a moment to look back at the lighted windows of the control deck. Two or three of the night staff sat watch over the line of TV screens, half asleep themselves as they observed the sleeping occupants of the dome.

He ducked out of the shadows and ran across to the dome, climbed the stairway to the entrance point thirty feet above. Opening the external lock, he crawled in and closed it behind him, then unfastened the internal entry hatch and pulled himself out of the sleeping cylinder into the silent cabin.

A single dim light glowed over the TV monitor screen as it revealed the three orderlies in the control deck, lounging back in a haze of cigarette smoke six feet from the camera.

Francis turned up the speaker volume, then tapped the mouthpiece sharply with his knuckle.

Tunic unbuttoned, sleep still shadowing his eyes, Colonel Chalmers leaned forward intently into the screen, the orderlies at his shoulder.

'Believe me, Roger, you're proving nothing. General Short and the Space Department won't withdraw their decision now that a special bill of enactment has been passed.' When Francis still looked sceptical he added: 'If anything, you're more likely to jeopardize them.'

'I'll take a chance,' Francis said. 'Too many guarantees have been broken in the past. Here I'll be able to keep an eye on things.' He tried to sound cool and unemotional; the cine-cameras would be recording the scene and it was important to establish the right impression. General Short would be only too keen to avoid a scandal. If he decided Francis was unlikely to sabotage the project he would probably leave him in the dome.

Chalmers pulled up a chair, his face earnest, 'Roger, give yourself time to reconsider everything. You may be more of a discordant element than you realize. Remember, nothing would be easier than getting you out – a child could cut his way through the rusty hull with a blunt can-opener.'

'Don't try it,' Francis warned him quietly. 'I'll be moving down to C-Deck, so if you come in after me they'll all know. Believe me, I won't try to interfere with the withdrawal programmes. And I won't arrange any teen-age marriages. But I think the people inside may need me now for more than eight hours a day.'

'Francis!' Chalmers shouted. 'Once you go down there you'll never come out! Don't you realize you're entombing yourself in a situation that's totally unreal? You're deliberately withdrawing into a nightmare, sending yourself off on a non-stop journey to *nowhere*!'

Curtly, before he switched the set off for the last time, Francis replied: 'Not nowhere, Colonel: Alpha Centauri.'

Sitting down thankfully in the narrow bunk in his cabin, Francis rested briefly before setting off for the commissary. All day he had been busy coding the computer punch tapes for Abel, and his eyes ached with the strain of manually stamping each of the thousands of minuscule holes. For eight hours he had sat without a break in the small isolation cell, electrodes clamped to his chest, knees and elbows while Abel measured his cardiac and respiratory rhythms.

The tests bore no relation to the daily programmes Abel now worked out for his father, and Francis was finding it difficult to maintain his patience. Initially Abel had tested his ability to follow a prescribed set of instructions, producing an endless exponential function, then a digital representation of *pi* to a thousand places. Finally Abel had persuaded Francis to cooperate in a more difficult test – the task of producing a totally random sequence. Whenever he unconsciously repeated a simple progression, as he did if he was tired or bored, or a fragment of a larger possible progression, the computer scanning his progress sounded an alarm on the desk and he would have to start afresh. After a few hours the buzzer rasped out every ten seconds, snapping at him like a bad-tempered insect. Francis had finally hobbled over to the door that afternoon, entangling himself in the electrode leads, found to his annoyance that the door was locked (ostensibly to prevent any interruption by a fire patrol), then saw through the small porthole that the computer in the cubicle outside was running unattended.

But when Francis' pounding roused Abel from the far end of the next laboratory he had been almost irritable with the doctor for wanting to discontinue the experiment.

'Damn it, Abel, I've been punching away at these things for three weeks now.' He winced as Abel disconnected him, brusquely tearing off the adhesive tape. 'Trying to produce random sequences isn't all that easy – my sense of reality is beginning to fog.' (Sometimes he wondered if Abel was secretly waiting for this.) 'I think I'm entitled to a vote of thanks.'

'But we arranged for the trial to last three days, Doctor,' Abel pointed out. 'It's only later that the valuable results begin to appear. It's the errors you make that are interesting. The whole experiment is pointless now.'

'Well, it's probably pointless anyway. Some mathematicians

used to maintain that a random sequence was impossible to define.'

'But we can assume that it *is* possible,' Abel insisted. 'I was just giving you some practice before we started on the trans-finite numbers.'

Francis baulked here. 'I'm sorry, Abel. Maybe I'm not so fit as I used to be. Anyway, I've got other duties to attend to.'

'But they don't take long, Doctor. There's really nothing for you to do now.'

He was right, as Francis was forced to admit. In the year he had spent in the dome Abel had remarkably streamlined the daily routines, provided himself and Francis with an excess of leisure time, particularly as the latter never went to conditioning (Francis was frightened of the sub-sonic voices – Chalmers and Short would be subtle in their attempts to extricate him, perhaps too subtle).

Life aboard the dome had been more of a drain on him than he anticipated. Chained to the routines of the ship, limited in his recreations and with few intellectual pastimes – there were no books aboard the ship – he found it increasingly difficult to sustain his former good humour, was beginning to sink into the deadening lethargy that had overcome most of the other crew members. Matthias Granger had retreated to his cabin, content to leave the programming to Abel, spent his time playing with a damaged clock, while the two Peters rarely strayed from Control. The three wives were almost completely inert, satisfied to knit and murmur to each other. The days passed indistinguishably. Sometimes Francis told himself wryly he nearly *did* believe that they were en route for Alpha Centauri. That would have been a joke for General Short!

At 6.30 when he went to the commissary for his evening meal, he found that he was a quarter of an hour late.

'Your meal time was changed this afternoon,' Baker told him, lowering the hatchway. 'I got nothing ready for you.'

Francis began to remonstrate but the man was adamant. 'I can't make a special dip into space-hold just because you didn't look at Routine Orders can I, Doctor?'

On the way out Francis met Abel, tried to persuade him to countermand the order. 'You could have warned me, Abel. Damnation, I've been sitting inside your test rig all afternoon.'

'But you went back to your cabin, Doctor,' Abel pointed out smoothly. 'You pass three SRO bulletins on your way from the laboratory. Always look at them at every opportunity, remember. Last-minute changes are liable at any time. I'm afraid you'll have to wait until 10.30 now.'

Francis went back to his cabin, suspecting that the sudden change had been Abel's revenge on him for discontinuing the test. He would have to be more conciliatory with Abel, or the young man could make his life a hell, literally starve him to death. Escape from the dome was impossible now – there was a mandatory 20 year sentence on anyone making an unauthorized entry into the space simulator.

After resting for an hour or so, he left his cabin at 8 o'clock to carry out his duty checks of the pressure seals by the B-Deck Meteor Screen. He always went through the pretence of reading them, enjoying the sense of participation in the space flight which the exercise gave him, deliberately accepting the illusion.

The seals were mounted in the control point set at ten yard intervals along the perimeter corridor, a narrow circular passageway around the main corridor. Alone there, the servos clicking and snapping, he felt at peace within the space vehicle. 'Earth itself is in orbit around the Sun,' he mused as he checked the seals, 'and the whole solar system is travelling at 40 miles a second towards the constellation Lyra. The degree of illusion that exists is a complex question.'

Something cut through his reverie.

The pressure indicator was flickering slightly. The needle wavered between 0.001 and 0.0015 psi. The pressure inside the dome was fractionally above atmospheric, in order that dust might be expelled through untoward cracks (though the main object of the pressure seals was to get the crew safely into the vacuum-proof emergency cylinders in case the dome was damaged and required internal repairs).

For a moment Francis panicked, wondering whether Short had

decided to come in after him – the reading, although meaningless, indicated that a breach had opened in the hull. Then the hand moved back to zero, and footsteps sounded along the radial corridor at right angles past the next bulkhead.

Quickly Francis stepped into its shadow. Before his death old Peters had spent a lot of time mysteriously pottering around the corridor, probably secreting a private food cache behind one of the rusting panels.

He leaned forward as the footsteps crossed the corridor.

Abel?

He watched the young man disappear down a stairway, then made his way into the radial corridor, searching the steel-grey sheeting for a retractable panel. Immediately adjacent to the end wall of the corridor, against the outer skin of the dome, was a small fire control booth.

A tuft of slate-white hairs lay on the floor of the booth.

Asbestos fibres!

Francis stepped into the booth, within a few seconds located a loosened panel that had rusted off its rivets. About ten inches by six, it slid back easily. Beyond it was the outer wall of the dome, a hand's breadth away. Here too was a loose plate, held in position by a crudely fashioned hook.

Francis hesitated, then lifted the hook and drew back the panel.

He was looking straight down into the hangar!

Below, a line of trucks was disgorging supplies on to the concrete floor under a couple of spotlights, a sergeant shouting orders at the labour squad. To the right was the control deck, Chalmers in his office on the evening shift.

The spy-hole was directly below the stairway, and the overhanging metal steps shielded it from the men in the hangar. The asbestos had been carefully frayed so that it concealed the retractable plate. The wire hook was as badly rusted as the rest of the hull, and Francis estimated that the window had been in use for over 30 or 40 years.

So almost certainly old Peters had regularly looked out through the window, and knew perfectly well that the space ship was a myth. None the less he had stayed aboard, perhaps realizing that the truth would destroy the others, or preferring to be captain of an artificial ship rather than a self-exposed curiosity in the world outside.

Presumably he had passed on the secret. Not to his bleak taciturn son, but to the one other lively mind, one who would keep the secret and make the most of it. For his own reasons he too had decided to stay in the dome, realizing that he would soon be the effective captain, free to pursue his experiments in applied psychology. He might even have failed to grasp that Francis was not a true member of the crew. His confident mastery of the programming, his lapse of interest in Control, his casualness over the safety devices, all meant one thing –

Abel knew!

1962

PASSPORT TO ETERNITY

It was half past love on New Day in Zenith and the clocks were striking heaven. All over the city the sounds of revelry echoed upwards into the dazzling Martian night, but high on Sunset Ridge, among the mansions of the rich, Margot and Clifford Gorrell faced each other in glum silence.

Frowning, Margot flipped impatiently through the vacation brochure on her lap, then tossed it away with an elaborate gesture of despair.

'But Clifford, why do we have to go to the same place every summer? I'd like to do something interesting for a change. This year the Lovatts are going to the Venus Fashion Festival, and Bobo and Peter Anders have just booked into the fire beaches at Saturn. They'll all have a wonderful time, while we're quietly taking the last boat to nowhere.'

Clifford Gorrell nodded impassively, one hand cupped over the sound control in the arm of his chair. They had been arguing all evening, and Margot's voice threw vivid sparks of irritation across the walls and ceiling. Grey and mottled, they would take days to drain.

'I'm sorry you feel like that, Margot. Where would you like to go?'

Margot shrugged scornfully, staring out at the corona of a million neon signs that illuminated the city below. 'Does it matter?'

'Of course. You arrange the vacation this time.'

Margot hesitated, one eye keenly on her husband. Then she sat forward happily, turning up her fluorescent violet dress until she glowed like an Algolian rayfish.

*   *   *

'Clifford, I've got a wonderful idea! Yesterday I was down in the Colonial Bazaar, thinking about our holiday, when I found a small dream bureau that's just been opened. Something like the Dream Dromes in Neptune City everyone was crazy about two or three years ago, but instead of having to plug into whatever programme happens to be going you have your own dream plays specially designed for you.'

Clifford continued to nod, carefully increasing the volume of the sound-sweeper.

'They have their own studios and send along a team of analysts and writers to interview us and afterwards book a sanatorium anywhere we like for the convalescence. Eve Corbusier and I decided a small party of five or six would be best.'

'Eve Corbusier,' Clifford repeated. He smiled thinly to himself and switched on the book he had been reading. 'I wondered when that Gorgon was going to appear.'

'Eve isn't too bad when you get to know her, darling,' Margot told him. 'Don't start reading yet. She'll think up all sorts of weird ideas for the play.' Her voice trailed off. 'What's the matter?'

'Nothing,' Clifford said wearily. 'It's just that I sometimes wonder if you have any sense of responsibility at all.' As Margot's eyes darkened he went on. 'Do you really think that I, a supreme court justice, could take that sort of vacation, even if I wanted to? Those dream plays are packed with advertising commercials and all sorts of corrupt material.' He shook his head sadly. 'And I told you not to go into the Colonial Bazaar.'

'What are we going to do then?' Margot asked coldly. 'Another honeyMoon?'

'I'll reserve a couple of singles tomorrow. Don't worry, you'll enjoy it.' He clipped the hand microphone into his book and began to scan the pages with it, listening to the small metallic voice.

Margot stood up, the vanes in her hat quivering furiously. 'Clifford!' she snapped, her voice dead and menacing. 'I warn you, I'm not going on another honeyMoon!'

Absently, Clifford said: 'Of course, dear,' his fingers racing over the volume control.

'Clifford!'

Her shout sank to an angry squeak. She stepped over to him, her dress blazing like a dragon, jabbering at him noiselessly, the sounds sucked away through the vents over her head and pumped out across the echoing rooftops of the midnight city.

As he sat back quietly in his private vacuum, the ceiling shaking occasionally when Margot slammed a door upstairs, Clifford looked out over the brilliant diadem of down-town Zenith. In the distance, by the space-port, the ascending arcs of hyperliners flared across the sky while below the countless phosphorescent trajectories of hop-cabs enclosed the bowl of rooflight in a dome of glistening hoops.

Of all the cities of the galaxy, few offered such a wealth of pleasures as Zenith, but to Clifford Gorrell it was as distant and unknown as the first Gomorrah. At 35 he was a thin-faced, prematurely ageing man with receding hair and a remote abstracted expression, and in the dark sombre suit and stiff white dog-collar which were the traditional uniform of the Probate Department's senior administrators he looked like a man who had never taken a holiday in his life.

At that moment Clifford wished he hadn't. He and Margot had never been able to agree about their vacations. Clifford's associates and superiors at the Department, all of them ten or twenty years older than himself, took their pleasures conservatively and expected a young but responsible justice to do the same. Margot grudgingly acknowledged this, but her friends who frequented the chic playtime clinics along the beach at Mira Mira considered the so-called honeyMoon trips back to Earth derisively old-fashioned, a last desperate resort of the aged and infirm.

And to tell the truth, Clifford realized, they were right. He had never dared to admit to Margot that he too was bored because it would have been more than his peace of mind was worth, but a change might do them good.

He resolved – next year.

Margot lay back among the cushions on the terrace divan, listening to the flamingo trees singing to each other in the morning sunlight. Twenty feet below, in the high-walled garden, a tall muscular young man was playing with a jet-ball. He had a dark olive complexion and swarthy good looks, and oil gleamed across his bare chest and arms. Margot watched with malicious amusement his efforts to entertain her. This was Trantino, Margot's play-boy, who chaperoned her during Clifford's long absences at the Probate Department.

'Hey, Margot! Catch!' He gestured with the jet-ball but Margot turned away, feeling her swim-suit slide pleasantly across her smooth tanned skin. The suit was made of one of the newer bioplastic materials, and its living tissues were still growing, softly adapting themselves to the contours of her body, repairing themselves as the fibres became worn or grimy. Upstairs in her wardrobes the gowns and dresses purred on their hangers like the drowsing inmates of some exquisite arboreal zoo. Sometimes she thought of commissioning her little Mercurian tailor to run up a bioplastic suit for Clifford – a specially designed suit that would begin to constrict one night as he stood on the terrace, the lapels growing tighter and tighter around his neck, the sleeves pinning his arms to his sides, the waist contracting to pitch him over –

'Margot!' Trantino interrupted her reverie, sailed the jet-ball expertly through the air towards her. Annoyed, Margot caught it with one hand and pointed it away, watched it sail over the wall and the roofs beyond.

Trantino came up to her. 'What's the matter?' he asked anxiously. For his part he felt his inability to soothe Margot a reflection on his professional skill. The privileges of his caste had to be guarded jealously. For several centuries now the managerial and technocratic elite had been so preoccupied with the work of government that they relied on the Templars of Aphrodite not merely to guard their wives from any marauding suitors but also to keep them amused and contented. By definition, of course, their relationship was platonic, a pleasant revival of the old chivalrous ideals, but sometimes Trantino regretted that the only tools in his armoury were a handful of poems and empty romantic gestures. The Guild of which he was a novitiate member was an ancient and honoured one, and it wouldn't do if Margot began to pine and Mr Gorrell reported him to the Masters of the Guild.

'Why are you always arguing with Mr Gorrell?' Trantino asked her. One of the Guild's axioms was 'The husband *is always* right.' Any discord between him and his wife was the responsibility of the play-boy.

Margot ignored Trantino's question. 'Those trees are getting on my nerves,' she complained fractiously. 'Why can't they keep quiet?'

'They're mating,' Trantino told her. He added thoughtfully: 'You should sing to Mr Gorrell.'

Margot stirred lazily as the shoulder straps of the sun-suit unclasped themselves behind her back. 'Tino,' she asked, 'what's the most unpleasant thing I could do to Mr Gorrell?'

'Margot!' Trantino gasped, utterly shocked. He decided that an appeal to sentiment, a method of reconciliation despised by the more proficient members of the Guild, was his only hope. 'Remember, Margot, you will always have me.'

He was about to permit himself a melancholy smile when Margot sat up abruptly.

'Don't look so frightened, you fool! I've just got an idea that should make Mr Gorrell sing to me.'

She straightened the vanes in her hat, waited for the sun-suit to clasp itself discreetly around her, then pushed Trantino aside and stalked off the terrace.

Clifford was browsing among the spools in the library, quietly listening to an old 22nd Century abstract on systems of land tenure in the Trianguli.

'Hello, Margot, feel better now?'

Margot smiled at him coyly. 'Clifford, I'm ashamed of myself. Do forgive me.' She bent down and nuzzled his ear. 'Sometimes I'm very selfish. Have you booked our tickets yet?'

Clifford disengaged her arm and straightened his collar. 'I called the agency, but their bookings have been pretty heavy. They've got a double but no singles. We'll have to wait a few days.'

'No, we won't,' Margot exclaimed brightly. 'Clifford, why don't you and I take the double? Then we can really be together, forget all that ship-board nonsense about never having met before.'

Puzzled, Clifford switched off the player. 'What do you mean?'

Margot explained. 'Look, Clifford, I've been thinking that I ought to spend more time with you than I do at present, really share your work and hobbies. I'm tired of all these play-boys.' She drooped languidly against Clifford, her voice silky and reassuring. 'I want to be with you, Clifford. *Always.*'

Clifford pushed her away. 'Don't be silly, Margot,' he said with an anxious laugh. 'You're being absurd.'

'No, I'm not. After all, Harold Kharkov and his wife haven't got a play-boy and she's very happy.'

Maybe she is, Clifford thought, beginning to panic. Kharkov had once been the powerful and ruthless director of the Department of Justice, now was a third-rate attorney hopelessly trying to eke out a meagre living on the open market, dominated by his wife and forced to spend virtually 24 hours a day with her. For a moment Clifford thought of the days when he had courted Margot, of the long dreadful hours listening to her inane chatter. Trantino's real role was not to chaperone Margot while Clifford was away but while he was at home.

'Margot, be sensible,' he started to say, but she cut him short. 'I've made up my mind, I'm going to tell Trantino to pack his suitcase and go back to the Guild.' She switched on the spool player, selecting the wrong speed, smiling ecstatically as the reading head grated loudly and stripped the coding off the record. 'It's going to be wonderful to share everything with you. Why don't we forget about the vacation this year?'

A facial tic from which Clifford had last suffered at the age of ten began to twitch ominously.

Tony Harcourt, Clifford's personal assistant, came over to the Gorrells' villa immediately after lunch. He was a brisk, polished young man, barely controlling his annoyance at being called back to work on the first day of his vacation. He had carefully booked a sleeper next to Dolores Costane, the most beautiful of the Jovian Heresiarch's vestals, on board a leisure-liner leaving that afternoon for Venus, but instead of enjoying the fruits of weeks of blackmail and intrigue he was having to take part in what seemed a quite uncharacteristic piece of Gorrell whimsy.

He listened in growing bewilderment as Clifford explained.

'We were going to one of our usual resorts on Luna, Tony, but we've decided we need a change. Margot wants a vacation that's different. Something new, exciting, original. So go round all the agencies and bring me their suggestions.'

'All the agencies?' Tony queried. 'Don't you mean just the registered ones?'

'All of them,' Margot told him smugly, relishing every moment of her triumph.

Clifford nodded, and smiled at Margot benignly.

'But there must be 50 or 60 agencies organizing vacations,' Tony protested. 'Only about a dozen of them are accredited. Outside Empyrean Tours and Union-Galactic there'll be absolutely nothing suitable for you.'

'Never mind,' Clifford said blandly. 'We only want an idea of the field. I'm sorry, Tony, but I don't want this all over the Department and I know you'll be discreet.'

Tony groaned. 'It'll take me weeks.'

'Three days,' Clifford told him. 'Margot and I want to leave here by the end of the week.' He looked longingly over his shoulder for the absent Trantino. 'Believe me, Tony, we really need a holiday.'

Fifty-six travel and vacation agencies were listed in the Commercial Directory, Tony discovered when he returned to his office in the top floor of the Justice building in downtown Zenith, all but eight of them alien. The Department had initiated legal proceedings against five, three had closed down, and eight more were fronts for other enterprises.

That left him with forty to visit, spread all over the Upper and Lower Cities and in the Colonial Bazaar, attached to various mercantile, religious and paramilitary organizations, some of them huge concerns with their own police and ecclesiastical forces, others sharing a one-room office and transceiver with a couple of other shoestring firms.

Tony mapped out an itinerary, slipped a flask of Five-Anchor Neptunian Rum into his hip pocket and dialled a helicab.

The first was ARCO PRODUCTIONS INC., a large establishment occupying three levels and a bunker on the fashionable west side of the Upper City. According to the Directory they specialized in hunting and shooting expeditions.

The helicab put him down on the apron outside the entrance. Massive steel columns reached up to a reinforced concrete portico, and the whole place looked less like a travel agency than the last redoubt of some interstellar Seigfried. As he went in a smart jackbooted guard of janissaries in black and silver uniforms snapped to attention and presented arms.

Everyone inside the building was wearing a uniform, moving about busily at standby alert. A huge broad-shouldered woman with sergeant's stripes handed Tony over to a hard-faced Martian colonel.

'I'm making some inquiries on behalf of a wealthy Terran and his wife,' Tony explained. 'They thought they'd do a little big-game hunting on their vacation this year. I believe you organize expeditions.'

The colonel nodded curtly and led Tony over to a broad map-table. 'Certainly. What exactly have they in mind?'

'Well, nothing really. They hoped you'd make some suggestions.'

'Of course.' The colonel pulled out a memo-tape. 'Have they their own air and land forces?'

Tony shook his head. 'I'm afraid not.'

'I see. Can you tell me whether they will require a single army corps, a combined task force or —'

'No,' Tony said. 'Nothing as big as that.'

'An assault party of brigade strength? I understand. Quieter and less elaborate. All the fashion today.' He switched on the star-map and spread his hands across the glimmering screen of stars and nebulae. 'Now the question of the particular theatre. At present only three of the game reserves have open seasons. Firstly the Procyon system; this includes about 20 different races, some of them still with only atomic technologies. Unfortunately there's been a good deal of dispute recently about declaring Procyon a game reserve, and the Resident of Alschain is trying to have it admitted to the Pan-Galactic Conference. A pity, I feel,' the colonel added, reflectively stroking his steel-grey moustache. 'Procyon always put up a great fight against us and an expedition there was invariably lively.'

Tony nodded sympathetically. 'I hadn't realized they objected.'

The colonel glanced at him sharply. 'Naturally,' he said. He cleared his throat. 'That leaves only the Ketab tribes of Ursa Major, who are having their Millennial Wars, and the Sudor Martines of Orion. They are an entirely new reserve, and your best choice without doubt. The ruling dynasty died out recently, and a war of succession could be conveniently arranged.'

Tony was no longer following the colonel, but he smiled intelligently.

'Now,' the colonel asked, 'what political or spiritual creeds do your friends wish to have invoked?'

Tony frowned. 'I don't think they want any. Are they absolutely necessary?'

The colonel regarded Tony carefully. 'No,' he said slowly. 'It's a question of taste. A purely military operation is perfectly feasible. However, we always advise our clients to invoke some doctrine as a *casus belli*, not only to avoid adverse publicity and any feelings of guilt or remorse, but to lend colour and purpose to the campaign. Each of our field commanders specializes in a particular ideological pogrom, with the exception of General Westerling. Perhaps your friends would prefer him?'

Tony's mind started to work again. 'Schapiro Westerling? The former Director-General of Graves Commission?'

The colonel nodded. 'You know him?'

Tony laughed. 'Know him? I thought I was prosecuting him at the current Nova Trials. I can see that we're well behind with the times.' He pushed back his chair. 'To tell the truth I don't think you've anything suitable for my friends. Thanks all the same.'

The colonel stiffened. One of his hands moved below the desk and a buzzer sounded along the wall.

'However,' Tony added, 'I'd be grateful if you'd send them further details.'

The colonel sat impassively in his chair. Three enormous guards appeared at Tony's elbow, idly swinging energy truncheons.

'Clifford Gorrell, Stellar Probate Division, Department of Justice,' Tony said quickly.

He gave the colonel a brief smile and made his way out, cursing Clifford and walking warily across the thickly piled carpet in case it had been mined.

The next one on his list was the A-Z JOLLY JUBILEE COMPANY, alien and unregistered, head office somewhere out of Betelgeuse. According to the Directory they specialized in 'all-in cultural parties and guaranteed somatic weekends.' Their premises occupied the top two tiers of a hanging garden in the Colonial Bazaar. They sounded harmless enough but Tony was ready for them.

'No,' he said firmly to a lovely Antarean wraith-fern who shyly raised a frond to him as he crossed the terrace. 'Not today.'

Behind the bar a fat man in an asbestos suit was feeding sand to a siliconic fire-fish swimming round in a pressure brazier.

'Damn things,' he grumbled, wiping the sweat off his chin and fiddling aimlessly with the thermostat. 'They gave me a booklet when I got it, but it doesn't say anything about it eating a whole beach every day.' He spaded in another couple of shovels from a low dune of sand heaped on the floor behind him. 'You have to keep them at exactly $5750°K$. or they start getting nervous. Can I help you?'

'I thought there was a vacation agency here,' Tony said.

'Sure. I'll call the girls for you.' He pressed a bell.

'Wait a minute,' Tony cut in. 'You advertise something about cultural parties. What exactly are they?'

The fat man chuckled. 'That must be my partner. He's a professor at Vega Tech. Likes to keep the tone up.' He winked at Tony.

Tony sat on one of the stools, looking out over the crazy spiral roof-tops of the Bazaar. A mile away the police patrols circled over the big apartment batteries which marked the perimeter of the Bazaar, keeping their distance.

A tall slim woman appeared from behind the foliage and sauntered across the terrace to him. She was a Canopan slave, hot-housed out of imported germ, a slender green-skinned beauty with moth-like fluttering gills.

The fat man introduced Tony. 'Lucille, take him up to the arbour and give him a run through.'

Tony tried to protest but the pressure brazier was hissing fiercely. The fat man started feeding sand in furiously, the exhaust flames flaring across the terrace.

Quickly, Tony turned and backed up the stairway to the arbour. 'Lucille,' he reminded her firmly, 'this is strictly cultural, remember.'

Half an hour later a dull boom reverberated up from the terrace.

'Poor Jumbo,' Lucille said sadly as a fine rain of sand came down over them.

'Poor Jumbo,' Tony agreed, sitting back and playing with a coil of her hair. Like a soft sinuous snake, it circled around his arm, sleek with blue oil. He drained the flask of Five-Anchor and tossed it lightly over the balustrade. 'Now tell me more about these Canopan prayerbeds ...'

When, after two days, Tony reported back to the Gorrells he looked hollow-eyed and exhausted, like a man who had been brain-washed by the Wardens.

'What happened to you?' Margot asked anxiously, 'we thought you'd been going round the agencies.'

'Exactly,' Tony said. He slumped down in a sofa and tossed a thick folder across to Clifford. 'Take your pick. You've got about 250 schemes there in complete detail, but I've written out a synopsis which gives one or two principal suggestions from each agency. Most of them are out of the question.'

Clifford unclipped the synopsis and started to read through it.

(1) ARCO PRODUCTIONS INC. Unregistered. Private subsidiary of Sagittarius Security Police.
Hunting and shooting. Your own war to order. Raiding parties, revolutions, religious crusades. In anything from a small commando squad to a 3,000-ship armada. ARCO provide publicity, mock War Crimes Tribunal, etc. Samples:

(a) Operation Torquemada. 23-day expedition to Bellatrix IV. 20 ship assault corps under Admiral Storm Wengen. Mission: liberation of (imaginary) Terran hostages. Cost: 300,000 credits.

(b) Operation Klingsor. 15-year crusade against Ursa Major. Combined task force of 2,500 ships. Mission: recovery of runic memory dials stolen from client's shrine.

Cost: 500 billion credits (ARCO will arrange lend-lease but this is dabbling in realpolitik).

(2) ARENA FEATURES INC. Unregistered. Organizers of the Pan-Galactic Tournament held tri-millennially at the Sun Bowl 2-Heliopolis, NGC 3599.
Every conceivable game in the Cosmos is played at the tournament and so formidable is the opposition that a winning contestant can virtually choose his own apotheosis. The challenge round of the Solar Megathlon Group 3 (that is, for any being whose function can be described, however loosely, as living) involves Quantum Jumping, 7-dimensional Maze Ball and Psychokinetic Bridge (pretty tricky against a telepathic Ketos D'Oma). The only Terran ever to win an event was the redoubtable Chippy Yerkes of Altair 5 The Clowns, who introduced the unplayable blank Round Dice. Being a spectator is as exhausting as being a contestant, and you're well advised to substitute.

Cost: 100,000 credits/day.

(3) AGENCE GENERALE DE TOURISME. Registered. Venus.
Concessionaires for the Colony Beatific on Lake Virgo, the Mandrake Casino Circuit and the Miramar-Trauma Senso-channels. Dream-baths, vu-dromes, endocrine-galas. Darleen Costello is

the current Aphrodite and Laurence Mandell makes a versatile Lothario. Plug into these two from 30:30 VST. Room and non-denominational bath at the Gomorrah-Plaza on Mount Venus comes to 1,000 credits a day, but remember to keep out of the Zone. It's just too erotogenous for a Terran.

(4) TERMINAL TOURS LTD. Unregistered. Earth.

For those who want to get away from it all the *Dream of Osiris*, an astral-rigged, 1,000-foot leisure-liner is now fitting out for the Grand Tour. Round-cosmos cruise, visiting every known race and galaxy.

Cost: Doubles at a flat billion, but it's cheap when you realize that the cruise lasts for ever and you'll never be back.

(5) SLEEP TRADERS. Unregistered.

A somewhat shadowy group who handle all dealings on the Blue Market, acting as a general clearing house and buying and selling dreams all through the Galaxy.

Sample: Like to try a really new sort of dream? The Set Corrani Priests of Theta Piscium will link you up with the sacred electronic thought-pools in the Desert of Kish. These mercury lakes are their ancestral memory banks. Surgery is necessary but be careful. Too much cortical damage and the archetypes may get restive. In return one of the Set Corrani (polysexual delta-humanoids about the size of a walking dragline) will take over your cerebral functions for a long weekend. All these transactions are done on an exchange basis and SLEEP TRADERS charge nothing for the service. But they obviously get a rake-off, and may pump advertising into the lower medullary centres. Whatever they're selling I wouldn't advise anybody to buy.

(6) THE AGENCY. Registered. M33 in Andromeda.

The executive authority of the consortium of banking trusts floating Schedule D, the fourth draw of the gigantic PK pyramid lottery sweeping all through the continuum from Sol III out to the island universes. Trance-cells everywhere are now recruiting dream-readers and ESPerceptionists, and there's still time to buy a ticket. There's only one number on all the tickets – the winning one – but don't think that means you'll get away with the kitty. THE AGENCY has just launched UNILIV, the emergency relief fund for victims of Schedule C who lost their deposits and are now committed to paying off impossible debts, some monetary, some moral (if you're unlucky in the draw you may find yourself landed with a guilt complex that would make even a Colonus Rex look sad).

Cost: 1 credit – but with an evaluation in the billions if you have to forfeit.

(7) ARCTURIAN EXPRESS. Unregistered.

Controls all important track events. The racing calendar this year is a causal and not a temporal one and seems a little obscure, but most of the established classics are taking place.

(a) The Rhinosaur Derby. Held this year at Betelgeuse Springs under the rules of the Federation of Amorphs. First to the light horizon. There's always quite a line-up for this one and any form of vehicle is allowed – rockets, beams, racial migrations, ES thought patterns – but frankly it's a waste of effort. It's not just that by the time you're out of your own sight you're usually out of your mind as well, but the Nils of Rigel, who always enter a strong team, are capable of instantaneous transmission.

(b) The Paraplegic Handicap. Recently instituted by the Protists of Lambda Scorpio. The course measures only 0.00015 mm, but that's a long way to urge an Aldebaran Torpid. They are giant viruses embedded in bauxite mountains, and by varying their pressure differentials it's sometimes possible to tickle them into a little life. K 2 on Regulus IX is holding the big bets, but even so the race is estimated to take about 50,000 years to run.

(8) NEW FUTURES INC. Unregistered.

Tired of the same dull round? NEW FUTURES will take you right out of this world. In the island universes the continuum is extra-dimensional, and the time channels are controlled by rival cartels. The element of chance apparently plays the time role, and it's all even more confused by the fact that you may be moving around in someone else's extrapolation.

In the tourist translation manual 185 basic tenses are given, and of these 125 are future conditional. No verb conjugates in the present tense, and you can invent and copyright your own irregulars. This may explain why I got the impression at the bureau that they were only half there.

Cost: simultaneously 3,270 and 2,000,000 credits. They refuse to quibble.

(9) SEVEN SIRENS. Registered. Venus.
A subsidiary of the fashion trust controlling senso-channel Astral Eve.

Ladies, like to win your own beauty contest? Twenty-five of the most beautiful creatures in the Galaxy are waiting to pit their charms against yours, but however divine they may be – and two or three of them, such as the Flamen Zilla Quel-Queen (75–9–25) and the Orthodox Virgin of Altair (76–953–?) certainly will be – they'll stand no chance against you. Your specifications will be defined as the ideal ones.

(10) GENERAL ENTERPRISES. Registered.
Specialists in culture cycles, world struggles, ethnic trends. Organize vacations as a sideline. A vast undertaking for whom ultimately we all work. Their next venture, epoch-making by all accounts, is starting now, and everybody will be coming along. I was politely but firmly informed that it was no use worrying about the cost. When I asked –

Before Clifford could finish one of the houseboys came up to him.

'Priority Call for you, sir.'

Clifford handed the synopsis to Margot. 'Tell me if you find anything. It looks to me as if we've been wasting Tony's time.'

He left them and went through to his study.

'Ah, Gorrell, there you are.' It was Thornwall Harrison, the attorney who had taken over Clifford's office. 'Who the hell are all these people trailing in to see you night and day? The place looks like Colonial Night at the Arena Circus. I can't get rid of them.'

'Which people?' Clifford asked. 'What do they want?'

'You apparently,' Thornwall told him. 'Most of them thought I was you. They've been trying to sell me all sorts of crazy vacation schemes. I said you'd already gone on your vacation and I myself never took one. Then one of them pulled a hypodermic on me. There's even an Anti-Cartel agent sleuthing around, wants to see you about block bookings. Thinks you're a racketeer.'

Back in the lounge Margot and Tony were looking out through the terrace windows into the boulevard which ran from the Gorrells' villa to the level below.

A long column of vehicles had pulled up under the trees: trucks, half-tracks, huge Telesenso studio location vans and several sleek white ambulances. The drivers and crew-men were standing about in little groups in the shadows, quietly watching the villa. Two or three radar scanners on the vans were rotating, and as Clifford looked down a convoy of trucks drove up and joined the tail of the column.

'Looks like there's going to be quite a party,' Tony said. 'What are they waiting for?'

'Perhaps they've come for us?' Margot suggested excitedly.

'They're wasting their time if they have,' Clifford told her. He swung round on Tony. 'Did you give our names to any of the agencies?'

Tony hesitated, then nodded. 'I couldn't help it. Some of those outfits wouldn't take no for an answer.'

Clifford clamped his lips and picked the synopsis off the floor. 'Well, Margot, have you decided where you want to go?'

Margot fiddled with the synopsis. 'There are so many to choose from.'

Tony started for the door. 'Well, I'll leave you to it.' He waved a hand at them. 'Have fun.'

'Hold on,' Clifford told him. 'Margot hasn't made up her mind yet.'

'What's the hurry?' Tony asked. He indicated the line of vehicles outside, their crews now climbing into their driving cabs and turrets. 'Take your time. You may bite off more than you can chew.'

'Exactly. So as soon as Margot decides where we're going you can make the final arrangements for us and get rid of that menagerie.'

'But Clifford, give me a chance.'

'Sorry. Now Margot, hurry up.'

Margot flipped through the synopsis, screwing up her mouth. 'It's so difficult, Clifford, I don't really like any of these. I still think the best agency was the little one I found in the Bazaar.'

'No,' Tony groaned, sinking down on a sofa. 'Margot, please, after all the trouble I've gone to.'

'Yes, definitely that one. The dream bureau. What was it called –'

Before she could finish there was a roar of engines starting up in the boulevard. Startled, Clifford saw the column of cars and trucks churn across the gravel towards the villa. Music, throbbing heavily, came down from the room above, and a sick musky odour seeped through the air.

Tony pulled himself off the sofa. 'They must have had this place wired,' he said quickly. 'You'd better call the police. Believe me, some of these people don't waste time arguing.'

Outside three helmeted men in brown uniforms ran past the terrace, unwinding a coil of fuse wire. The sharp hissing sound of para-rays sucked through the air from the drive.

Margot hid back in her slumber seat. 'Trantino!' she wailed.

Clifford went back into his study. He switched the transceiver to the emergency channel.

Instead of the police signal a thin automatic voice beeped through. 'Remain seated, remain seated. Take-off in zero two minutes, Purser's office on G Deck now –'

Clifford switched to another channel. There was a blare of studio applause and a loud unctuous voice called out:

'And now over to brilliant young Clifford Gorrell and his charming wife Margot about to enter their dream-pool at the fabulous Riviera-Neptune. Are you there, Cliff?'

Angrily, Clifford turned to a third. Static and morse chattered, and then someone rapped out in a hard iron tone: 'Colonel

Sapt is dug in behind the swimming pool. Enfilade along the garage roof –'

Clifford gave up. He went back to the lounge. The music was deafening. Margot was prostrate in her slumber-seat, Tony down on the floor by the window, watching a pitched battle raging in the drive. Heavy black palls of smoke drifted across the terrace, and two tanks with stylized archers emblazoned on their turrets were moving up past the burning wrecks of the studio location vans.

'They must be Arco's!' Tony shouted. 'The police will look after them, but wait until the extra-sensory gang take over!'

Crouching behind a low stone parapet running off the terrace was a group of waiters in dishevelled evening dress, lab technicians in scorched white overalls and musicians clutching their instrument cases. A bolt of flame from one of the tanks flickered over their heads and crashed into the grove of flamingo trees, sending up a shower of sparks and broken notes.

Clifford pulled Tony to his feet. 'Come on, we've got to get out of here. We'll try the library windows into the garden. You'd better take Margot.'

Her yellow beach robe had apparently died of shock, and was beginning to blacken like a dried-out banana skin. Discreetly averting his eyes, Tony picked her up and followed Clifford out into the hall.

Three croupiers in gold uniforms were arguing hotly with two men in white surgeons' coats. Behind them a couple of mechanics were struggling a huge vibrobath up the stairs.

The foreman came over to Clifford. 'Gorrell?' he asked, consulting an invoice. 'Trans-Ocean.' He jerked a thumb at the bath. 'Where do you want it?'

A surgeon elbowed him aside. 'Mr Gorrell?' he asked suavely. 'We are from Cerebro-Tonic Travel. Please allow me to give you a sedative. All this noise –'

Clifford pushed past him and started to walk down the corridor to the library, but the floor began to slide and weave.

He stopped and looked around unsteadily.

Tony was down on his knees, Margot flopped out of his arms across the floor.

Someone swayed up to Clifford and held out a tray.

On it were three tickets.

Around him the walls whirled.

He woke in his bedroom, lying comfortably on his back, gently breathing a cool amber air. The noise had died away, but he could still hear a vortex of sound spinning violently in the back of his mind. It spiralled away, vanished, and he moved his head and looked around.

Margot was lying asleep beside him, and for a moment he thought that the attack on the house had been a dream. Then he noticed the skull-plate clamped over his head, and the cables leading off from a boom to a large console at the foot of the bed. Massive spools loaded with magnetic tape waited in the projector ready to be played.

The real nightmare was still to come! He struggled to get up, found himself clamped in a twilight sleep, unable to move more than a few centimetres.

He lay there powerlessly for ten minutes, tongue clogging his mouth like a wad of cotton-wool when he tried to shout. Eventually a small neatly featured alien in a pink silk suit opened the door and padded quietly over to them. He peered down at their faces and then turned a couple of knobs on the console.

Clifford's consciousness began to clear. Beside him Margot stirred and woke.

The alien beamed down pleasantly. 'Good evening,' he greeted them in a smooth creamy voice. 'Please allow me to apologize for any discomfort you have suffered. However, the first day of a vacation is often a little confused.'

Margot sat up. 'I remember you. You're from the little bureau in the Bazaar.' She jumped round happily. 'Clifford!'

The alien bowed. 'Of course, Mrs Gorrell. I am Dr Terence Sotal-2 Burlington, Professor – Emeritus,' he added to himself as an afterthought, '– of Applied Drama at the University of Alpha

Leporis, and the director of the play you and your husband are to perform during your vacation.'

Clifford cut in: 'Would you release me from this machine immediately? And then get out of my house! I've had –'

'Clifford!' Margot snapped. 'What's the matter with you?'

Clifford dragged at the skull plate and Dr Burlington quietly moved a control on the console. Part of Clifford's brain clouded and he sank back helplessly.

'Everything is all right, Mr Gorrell,' Dr Burlington said.

'Clifford,' Margot warned him. 'Remember your promise.' She smiled at Dr Burlington. 'Don't pay any attention to him, Doctor. Please go on.'

'Thank you, Mrs Gorrell.' Dr Burlington bowed again, as Clifford lay half-asleep, groaning impotently.

'The play we have designed for you,' Dr Burlington explained, 'is an adaptation of a classic masterpiece in the Diphenyl 2-4-6 Cyclopropane canon, and though based on the oldest of human situations, is nonetheless fascinating. It was recently declared the outright winner at the Mira Nuptial Contest, and will always have a proud place in the private repertoires. To you, I believe, it is known as "The Taming of the Shrew".'

Margot giggled and then looked surprised. Dr Burlington smiled urbanely. 'However, allow me to show you the script.' He excused himself and slipped out.

Margot fretted anxiously, while Clifford pulled weakly at the skull-plate.

'Clifford, I'm not sure that I like this altogether. And Dr Burlington does seem rather strange. But I suppose it's only for three weeks.'

Just then the door opened and a stout bearded figure, erect in a stiff blue uniform, white yachting cap jauntily on his head, stepped in.

'Good evening, Mrs Gorrell.' He saluted Margot smartly, 'Captain Linstrom.' He looked down at Clifford. 'Good to have you aboard, sir.'

'Aboard?' Clifford repeated weakly. He looked around at the

familiar furniture in the room, the curtains drawn neatly over the windows. 'What are you raving about? Get out of my house!'

The Captain chuckled. 'Your husband has a sense of humour, Mrs Gorrell. A useful asset on these long trips. Your friend Mr Harcourt in the next cabin seems sadly lacking in one.'

'Tony?' Margot exclaimed. 'Is he still here?'

Captain Linstrom laughed. 'I quite understand you. He seems very worried, quite over-eager to return to Mars. We shall be passing there one day, of course, though not I fear for some time. However, time is no longer a consideration to you. I believe you are to spend the entire voyage in sleep. But a very pleasantly coloured sleep nonetheless.' He smiled roguishly at Margot.

As he reached the door Clifford managed to gasp out: 'Where are we? For heaven's sake, call the police!'

Captain Linstrom paused in surprise. 'But surely you know, Mr Gorrell?' He strode to the window and flung back the curtains. In place of the large square casement were three small portholes. Outside a blaze of incandescent light flashed by, a rush of stars and nebulae.

Captain Linstrom gestured theatrically. 'This is the *Dream of Osiris*, under charter to Terminal Tours, three hours out from Zenith City on the non-stop run. May I wish you sweet dreams!'

1962

THE CAGE OF SAND

At sunset, when the vermilion glow reflected from the dunes along the horizon fitfully illuminated the white faces of the abandoned hotels, Bridgman stepped on to his balcony and looked out over the long stretches of cooling sand as the tides of purple shadow seeped across them. Slowly, extending their slender fingers through the shallow saddles and depressions, the shadows massed together like gigantic combs, a few phosphorescing spurs of obsidian isolated for a moment between the tines, and then finally coalesced and flooded in a solid wave across the half-submerged hotels. Behind the silent façades, in the tilting sand-filled streets which had once glittered with cocktail bars and restaurants, it was already night. Haloes of moonlight beaded the lamp-standards with silver dew, and draped the shuttered windows and slipping cornices like a frost of frozen gas.

As Bridgman watched, his lean bronzed arms propped against the rusting rail, the last whorls of light sank away into the cerise funnel withdrawing below the horizon, and the first wind stirred across the dead Martian sand. Here and there miniature cyclones whirled about a sand-spur, drawing off swirling feathers of moon-washed spray, and a nimbus of white dust swept across the dunes and settled in the dips and hollows. Gradually the drifts accumulated, edging towards the former shoreline below the hotels. Already the first four floors had been inundated, and the sand now reached up to within two feet of Bridgman's balcony. After the next sandstorm he would be forced yet again to move to the floor above.

'Bridgman!'

The voice cleft the darkness like a spear. Fifty yards to his right, at the edge of the derelict sand-break he had once attempted to build below the hotel, a square stocky figure wearing a pair of frayed cotton shorts waved up at him. The moonlight etched the broad sinewy muscles of his chest, the powerful bowed legs sinking almost to their calves in the soft Martian sand. He was about forty-five years old, his thinning hair close-cropped so that he seemed almost bald. In his right hand he carried a large canvas hold-all.

Bridgman smiled to himself. Standing there patiently in the moonlight below the derelict hotel, Travis reminded him of some long-delayed tourist arriving at a ghost resort years after its extinction.

'Bridgman, are you coming?' When the latter still leaned on his balcony rail, Travis added: 'The next conjunction is tomorrow.'

Bridgman shook his head, a rictus of annoyance twisting his mouth. He hated the bi-monthly conjunctions, when all seven of the derelict satellite capsules still orbiting the Earth crossed the sky together. Invariably on these nights he remained in his room, playing over the old memo-tapes he had salvaged from the submerged chalets and motels further along the beach (the hysterical 'This is Mamie Goldberg, 62955 Cocoa Boulevard, I really wanna protest against this crazy evacuation...' or resigned 'Sam Snade here, the Pontiac convertible in the back garage belongs to anyone who can dig it out'). Travis and Louise Woodward always came to the hotel on the conjunction nights – it was the highest building in the resort, with an unrestricted view from horizon to horizon – and would follow the seven converging stars as they pursued their endless courses around the globe. Both would be oblivious of everything else, which the wardens knew only too well, and they reserved their most careful searches of the sand-sea for these bi-monthly occasions. Invariably Bridgman found himself forced to act as look-out for the other two.

'I was out last night,' he called down to Travis. 'Keep away from the north-east perimeter fence by the Cape. They'll be busy repairing the track.'

Most nights Bridgman divided his time between excavating the buried motels for caches of supplies (the former inhabitants of the resort area had assumed the government would soon rescind its evacuation order) and disconnecting the sections of metal roadway laid across the desert for the wardens' jeeps. Each of the squares of wire mesh was about five yards wide and weighed over three hundred pounds. After he had snapped the lines of rivets, dragged the sections away and buried them among the dunes he would be exhausted, and spend most of the next day nursing his strained hands and shoulders. Some sections of the track were now permanently anchored with heavy steel stakes, and he knew that sooner or later they would be unable to delay the wardens by sabotaging the roadway.

Travis hesitated, and with a noncommittal shrug disappeared among the dunes, the heavy tool-bag swinging easily from one powerful arm. Despite the meagre diet which sustained him, his energy and determination seemed undiminished – in a single night Bridgman had watched him dismantle twenty sections of track and then loop together the adjacent limbs of a crossroad, sending an entire convoy of six vehicles off into the wastelands to the south.

Bridgman turned from the balcony, then stopped when a faint tang of brine touched the cool air. Ten miles away, hidden by the lines of dunes, was the sea, the long green rollers of the middle Atlantic breaking against the red Martian strand. When he had first come to the beach five years earlier there had never been the faintest scent of brine across the intervening miles of sand. Slowly, however, the Atlantic was driving the shore back to its former margins. The tireless shoulder of the Gulf Stream drummed against the soft Martian dust and piled the dunes into grotesque rococo reefs which the wind carried away into the sand-sea. Gradually the ocean was returning, reclaiming its great smooth basin, sifting out the black quartz and Martian obsidian which would never be wind-borne and drawing these down into its deeps. More and more often the stain of brine would hang on the evening air, reminding Bridgman why he had first come to the beach and removing any inclination to leave.

Three years earlier he had attempted to measure the rate of approach, by driving a series of stakes into the sand at the water's edge, but the shifting contours of the dunes carried away the coloured poles. Later, using the promontory at Cape Canaveral, where the old launching gantries and landing ramps reared up into the sky like derelict pieces of giant sculpture, he had calculated by triangulation that the advance was little more than thirty yards per year. At this rate – without wanting to, he had automatically made the calculation – it would be well over five hundred years before the Atlantic reached its former littoral at Cocoa Beach. Though discouragingly slow, the movement was nonetheless in a forward direction, and Bridgman was happy to remain in his hotel ten miles away across the dunes, conceding towards its time of arrival the few years he had at his disposal.

Later, shortly after Louise Woodward's arrival, he had thought of dismantling one of the motel cabins and building himself a small chalet by the water's edge. But the shoreline had been too dismal and forbidding. The great red dunes rolled on for miles, cutting off half the sky, dissolving slowly under the impact of the slate-green water. There was no formal tide-line, but only a steep shelf littered with nodes of quartz and rusting fragments of Mars rockets brought back with the ballast. He spent a few days in a cave below a towering sand-reef, watching the long galleries of compacted red dust crumble and dissolve as the cold Atlantic stream sluiced through them, collapsing like the decorated colonnades of a baroque cathedral. In the summer the heat reverberated from the hot sand as from the slag of some molten sun, burning the rubber soles from his boots, and the light from the scattered flints of washed quartz flickered with diamond hardness. Bridgman had returned to the hotel grateful for his room overlooking the silent dunes.

Leaving the balcony, the sweet smell of brine still in his nostrils, he went over to the desk. A small cone of shielded light shone down over the tape-recorder and rack of spools. The rumble of the wardens' unsilenced engines always gave him at least five minutes' warning of their arrival, and it would have been safe to install another lamp in the room – there were no roadways between the hotel and the sea, and from a distance any light reflected on to the balcony was indistinguishable from the corona of glimmering phosphors which hung over the sand like myriads of fire-flies. However, Bridgman preferred to sit in the darkened suite, enclosed by the circle of books on the makeshift shelves, the shadow-filled air playing over his shoulders through the long night as he toyed with the memo-tapes, fragments of a vanished and unregretted past. By day he always drew the blinds, immolating himself in a world of perpetual twilight.

Bridgman had easily adapted himself to his self-isolation, soon evolved a system of daily routines that gave him the maximum of time to spend on his private reveries. Pinned to the walls around him were a series of huge white-prints and architectural drawings, depicting various elevations of a fantastic Martian city he had once designed, its glass spires and curtain walls rising like heliotropic jewels from the vermilion desert. In fact, the whole city was a vast piece of jewellery, each elevation brilliantly visualized but as symmetrical, and ultimately as lifeless, as a crown. Bridgman continually retouched the drawings, inserting more and more details, so that they almost seemed to be photographs of an original.

Most of the hotels in the town – one of a dozen similar resorts buried by the sand which had once formed an unbroken strip of motels, chalets and five-star hotels thirty miles to the south of Cape Canaveral – were well stocked with supplies of canned food abandoned when the area was evacuated and wired off. There were ample reservoirs and cisterns filled with water, apart from a thousand intact cocktail bars six feet below the surface of the sand. Travis had excavated a dozen of these in search of his favourite vintage bourbon. Walking out across the desert behind the town one would suddenly find a short flight of steps cut into the annealed sand and crawl below an occluded sign announcing 'The Satellite Bar' or 'The Orbit Room' into the inner sanctum, where the jutting deck of a chromium bar had been cleared as far as the diamond-paned mirror freighted with its rows of bottles and figurines. Bridgman would have been glad to see them left undisturbed.

The whole trash of amusement arcades and cheap bars on the outskirts of the beach resorts were a depressing commentary on the original space-flights, reducing them to the level of monster side-shows at a carnival.

Outside his room, steps sounded along the corridor, then slowly climbed the stairway, pausing for a few seconds at every landing. Bridgman lowered the memo-tape in his hand, listening to the familiar tired footsteps. This was Louise Woodward, making her invariable evening ascent to the roof ten storeys above. Bridgman glanced at the timetable pinned to the wall. Only two of the satellites would be visible, between 12.25 and 12.35 a.m., at an elevation of 62 degrees in the south-west, passing through Cetus and Eridanus, neither of them containing her husband. Although the siting was two hours away, she was already taking up her position, and would remain there until dawn.

Bridgman listened wanly to the feet recede slowly up the stairwell. All through the night the slim, pale-faced woman would sit out under the moon-lit sky, as the soft Martian sand her husband had given his life to reach sifted around her in the dark wind, stroking her faded hair like some mourning mariner's wife waiting for the sea to surrender her husband's body. Travis usually joined her later, and the two of them sat side by side against the elevator house, the frosted letters of the hotel's neon sign strewn around their feet like the fragments of a dismembered zodiac, then at dawn made their way down into the shadow-filled streets to their eyries in the nearby hotels.

Initially Bridgman often joined their nocturnal vigil, but after a few nights he began to feel something repellent, if not actually ghoulish, about their mindless contemplation of the stars. This was not so much because of the macabre spectacle of the dead astronauts orbiting the planet in their capsules, but because of the curious sense of unspoken communion between Travis and Louise Woodward, almost as if they were celebrating a private rite to which Bridgman could never be initiated. Whatever their original motives, Bridgman sometimes suspected that these had been overlaid by other, more personal ones.

Ostensibly, Louise Woodward was watching her husband's satellite in order to keep alive his memory, but Bridgman guessed that the memories she unconsciously wished to perpetuate were those of herself twenty years earlier, when her husband had been a celebrity and she herself courted by magazine columnists and TV reporters. For fifteen years after his death – Woodward had been killed testing a new lightweight launching platform – she had lived a nomadic existence, driving restlessly in her cheap car from motel to motel across the continent, following her husband's star as it disappeared into the eastern night, and had at last made her home at Cocoa Beach in sight of the rusting gantries across the bay.

Travis's real motives were probably more complex. To Bridgman, after they had known each other for a couple of years, he had confided that he felt himself bound by a debt of honour to maintain a watch over the dead astronauts for the example of courage and sacrifice they had set him as a child (although most of them had been piloting their wrecked capsules for fifty years before Travis's birth), and that now they were virtually forgotten he must singlehandedly keep alive the fading flame of their memory. Bridgman was convinced of his sincerity.

Yet later, going through a pile of old news magazines in the trunk of a car he excavated from a motel port, he came across a picture of Travis wearing an aluminium pressure suit and learned something more of his story. Apparently Travis had at one time himself been an astronaut – or rather, a would-be astronaut. A test pilot for one of the civilian agencies setting up orbital relay stations, his nerve had failed him a few seconds before the last 'hold' of his countdown, a moment of pure unexpected funk that cost the company some five million dollars.

Obviously it was his inability to come to terms with this failure of character, unfortunately discovered lying flat on his back on a contour couch two hundred feet above the launching pad, which had brought Travis to Canaveral, the abandoned Mecca of the first heroes of astronautics.

Tactfully Bridgman had tried to explain that no one would blame him for this failure of nerve – less his responsibility than that of the selectors who had picked him for the flight, or at least the result of an unhappy concatenation of ambiguously worded multiple-choice questions (crosses in the wrong boxes, some heavier to bear and harder to open than others! Bridgman had joked sardonically to himself). But Travis seemed to have reached his own decision about himself. Night after night, he watched the brilliant funerary convoy weave its gilded pathway towards the dawn sun, salving his own failure by identifying it with the greater, but blameless, failure of the seven astronauts. Travis still wore his hair in the regulation 'mohican' cut of the space-man, still kept himself in perfect physical trim by the vigorous routines he had practised before his abortive flight. Sustained by the personal myth he had created, he was now more or less unreachable.

'Dear Harry, I've taken the car and deposit box. Sorry it should end like –'

Irritably, Bridgman switched off the memo-tape and its recapitulation of some thirty-year-old private triviality. For some reason he seemed unable to accept Travis and Louise Woodward for what they were. He disliked this failure of compassion, a nagging compulsion to expose other people's motives and strip away the insulating sheaths around their naked nerve strings, particularly as his own motives for being at Cape Canaveral were so suspect. Why was *he* there, what failure was *he* trying to expiate? And why choose Cocoa Beach as his penitential shore? For three years he had asked himself these questions so often that they had ceased to have any meaning, like a fossilized catechism or the blunted self-recrimination of a paranoiac.

He had resigned his job as the chief architect of a big space development company after the large government contract on which the firm depended, for the design of the first Martian city-settlement, was awarded to a rival consortium. Secretly, however, he realized that his resignation had marked his unconscious acceptance that despite his great imaginative gifts he was unequal to the specialized and more prosaic tasks of designing the settlement. On the drawing board, as elsewhere, he would always remain earth-bound.

His dreams of building a new Gothic architecture of launching ports and control gantries, of being the Frank Lloyd Wright and Le Corbusier of the first city to be raised outside Earth, faded for ever, but leaving him unable to accept the alternative of turning out endless plans for low-cost hospitals in Ecuador and housing estates in Tokyo. For a year he had drifted aimlessly, but a few colour photographs of the vermilion sunsets at Cocoa Beach and a news story about the recluses living on in the submerged motels had provided a powerful compass.

He dropped the memo-tape into a drawer, making an effort to accept Louise Woodward and Travis on their own terms, a wife keeping watch over her dead husband and an old astronaut maintaining a solitary vigil over the memories of his lost comrades-in-arms.

The wind gusted against the balcony window, and a light spray of sand rained across the floor. At night dust-storms churned along the beach. Thermal pools isolated by the cooling desert would suddenly accrete like beads of quicksilver and erupt across the fluffy sand in miniature tornadoes.

Only fifty yards away, the dying cough of a heavy diesel cut through the shadows. Quickly Bridgman turned off the small desk light, grateful for his meanness over the battery packs plugged into the circuit, then stepped to the window.

At the leftward edge of the sand-break, half hidden in the long shadows cast by the hotel, was a large tracked vehicle with a low camouflaged hull. A narrow observation bridge had been built over the bumpers directly in front of the squat snout of the engine housing, and two of the beach wardens were craning up through the plexiglass windows at the balconies of the hotel, shifting their binoculars from room to room. Behind them, under the glass dome of the extended driving cabin, were three more wardens, controlling an outboard spotlight. In the centre of the bowl a thin mote of light pulsed with the rhythm of the engine, ready to throw its powerful beam into any of the open rooms.

Bridgman hid back behind the shutters as the binoculars focused upon the adjacent balcony, moved to his own, hesitated, and passed to the next. Exasperated by the sabotaging of the roadways, the wardens had evidently decided on a new type of vehicle. With their four broad tracks, the huge squat sand-cars would be free of the mesh roadways and able to rove at will through the dunes and sand-hills.

Bridgman watched the vehicle reverse slowly, its engine barely varying its deep bass growl, then move off along the line of hotels, almost indistinguishable in profile among the shifting dunes and hillocks. A hundred yards away, at the first intersection, it turned towards the main boulevard, wisps of dust streaming from the metal cleats like thin spumes of steam. The men in the observation bridge were still watching the hotel. Bridgman was certain that they had seen a reflected glimmer of light, or perhaps some movement of Louise Woodward's on the roof. However reluctant to leave the car and be contaminated by the poisonous dust, the wardens would not hesitate if the capture of one of the beachcombers warranted it.

Racing up the staircase, Bridgman made his way to the roof, crouching below the windows that overlooked the boulevard. Like a huge crab, the sand-car had parked under the jutting overhang of the big department store opposite. Once fifty feet from the ground, the concrete lip was now separated from it by little more than six or seven feet, and the sand-car was hidden in the shadows below it, engine silent. A single movement in a window, or the unexpected return of Travis, and the wardens would spring from the hatchways, their long-handled nets and lassos pinioning them around the necks and ankles. Bridgman remembered one beachcomber he had seen flushed from his motel hideout and carried off like a huge twitching spider at the centre of a black rubber web, the wardens with their averted faces and masked mouths like devils in an abstract ballet.

Reaching the roof, Bridgman stepped out into the opaque white moonlight. Louise Woodward was leaning on the balcony, looking out towards the distant, unseen sea. At the faint sound of the door creaking she turned and began to walk listlessly around the roof, her pale face floating like a nimbus. She wore a freshly ironed print dress she had found in a rusty spin drier in one of the launderettes, and her streaked blonde hair floated out lightly behind her on the wind.

'Louise!'

Involuntarily she started, tripping over a fragment of the neon sign, then moved backwards towards the balcony overlooking the boulevard.

'Mrs Woodward!' Bridgman held her by the elbow, raised a hand to her mouth before she could cry out. 'The wardens are down below. They're watching the hotel. We must find Travis before he returns.'

Louise hesitated, apparently recognizing Bridgman only by an effort, and her eyes turned up to the black marble sky. Bridgman looked at his watch; it was almost 12.25. He searched the stars in the south-west.

Louise murmured: 'They're nearly here now, I must see them. Where is Travis, he should be here?'

Bridgman pulled at her arm. 'Perhaps he saw the sand-car. Mrs Woodward, we should leave.'

Suddenly she pointed up at the sky, then wrenched away from him and ran to the rail. 'There they are!'

Fretting, Bridgman waited until she had filled her eyes with the two companion points of light speeding from the western horizon. These were Merril and Pokrovski – like every schoolboy he knew the sequences perfectly, a second system of constellations with a more complex but far more tangible periodicity and precession – the Castor and Pollux of the orbiting zodiac, whose appearance always heralded a full conjunction the following night.

Louise Woodward gazed up at them from the rail, the rising wind lifting her hair off her shoulders and entraining it horizontally behind her head. Around her feet the red Martian dust swirled and rustled, silting over the fragments of the old neon sign, a brilliant pink spume streaming from her long fingers as they moved along the balcony ledge. When the satellites finally disappeared among the stars along the horizon, she leaned forwards, her face raised to the milk-blue moon as if to delay their departure, then turned back to Bridgman, a bright smile on her face.

His earlier suspicions vanishing, Bridgman smiled back at her encouragingly. 'Roger will be here tomorrow night, Louise. We must be careful the wardens don't catch us before we see him.'

He felt a sudden admiration for her, at the stoical way she had sustained herself during her long vigil. Perhaps she thought of Woodward as still alive, and in some way was patiently waiting for him to return? He remembered her saying once: 'Roger was only a boy when he took off, you know, I feel more like his mother now,' as if frightened how Woodward would react to her dry skin and fading hair, fearing that he might even have forgotten her. No doubt the death she visualized for him was of a different order from the mortal kind.

Hand in hand, they tiptoed carefully down the flaking steps, jumped down from a terrace window into the soft sand below the wind-break. Bridgman sank to his knees in the fine silver moon-dust, then waded up to the firmer ground, pulling Louise after him. They climbed through a breach in the tilting palisades, then ran away from the line of dead hotels looming like skulls in the empty light.

'Paul, wait!' Her head still raised to the sky, Louise Woodward fell to her knees in a hollow between two dunes, with a laugh stumbled after Bridgman as he raced through the dips and saddles. The wind was now whipping the sand off the higher crests, flurries of dust spurting like excited wavelets. A hundred yards away, the town was a fading film set, projected by the camera obscura of the sinking moon. They were standing where the long Atlantic seas had once been ten fathoms deep, and Bridgman could scent again the tang of brine among the flickering white-caps of dust, phosphorescing like shoals of animalcula. He waited for any sign of Travis.

'Louise, we'll have to go back to the town. The sand-storms are blowing up, we'll never see Travis here.'

They moved back through the dunes, then worked their way among the narrow alleyways between the hotels to the northern gateway to the town. Bridgman found a vantage point in a small apartment block, and they lay down looking out below a window lintel into the sloping street, the warm sand forming a pleasant cushion. At the intersections the dust blew across the roadway in white clouds, obscuring the warden's beach-car parked a hundred yards down the boulevard.

Half an hour later an engine surged, and Bridgman began to pile sand into the interval in front of them. 'They're going. Thank God!'

Louise Woodward held his arm. 'Look!'

Fifty feet away, his white vinyl suit half hidden in the dust clouds, one of the wardens was advancing slowly towards them, his lasso twirling lightly in his hand. A few feet behind was a second warden, craning up at the windows of the apartment block with his binoculars.

Bridgman and Louise crawled back below the ceiling, then dug their way under a transom into the kitchen at the rear. A window opened on to a sand-filled yard, and they darted away through the lifting dust that whirled between the buildings.

Suddenly, around a corner, they saw the line of wardens moving down a side-street, the sand-car edging along behind them. Before Bridgman could steady himself a spasm of pain seized his right calf, contorting the gastrocnemius muscle, and he fell to one knee. Louise Woodward pulled him back against the wall, then pointed at a squat, bow-legged figure trudging towards them along the curving road into town.

'Travis –'

The tool-bag swung from his right hand, and his feet rang faintly on the wire-mesh roadway. Head down, he seemed unaware of the wardens hidden by a bend in the road.

'Come on!' Disregarding the negligible margin of safety, Bridgman clambered to his feet and impetuously ran out into the centre of the street. Louise tried to stop him, and they had covered only ten yards before the wardens saw them. There was a warning shout, and the spotlight flung its giant cone down the street. The sand-car surged forward, like a massive dust-covered bull, its tracks clawing at the sand.

'Travis!' As Bridgman reached the bend, Louise Woodward ten yards behind, Travis looked up from his reverie, then flung the tool-bag over one shoulder and raced ahead of them towards the clutter of motel roofs protruding from the other side of the street. Lagging behind the others, Bridgman again felt the cramp attack his leg, broke off into a painful shuffle. When Travis came back for him Bridgman tried to wave him away, but Travis pinioned his elbow and propelled him forward like an attendant straight-arming a patient.

The dust swirling around them, they disappeared through the fading streets and out into the desert, the shouts of the beach-wardens lost in the roar and clamour of the baying engine. Around them, like the strange metallic flora of some extraterrestrial garden, the old neon signs jutted from the red Martian sand – 'Satellite Motel', 'Planet Bar', 'Mercury Motel'. Hiding behind them, they reached the scrub-covered dunes on the edge of the town, then picked up one of the trails that led away among the sand-reefs. There, in the deep grottoes of compacted sand which hung like inverted palaces, they waited until the storm subsided. Shortly before dawn the wardens abandoned their search, unable to bring the heavy sand-car on to the disintegrating reef.

Contemptuous of the wardens, Travis lit a small fire with his cigarette lighter, burning splinters of driftwood that had gathered in the gullies. Bridgman crouched beside it, warming his hands.

'This is the first time they've been prepared to leave the sand-car,' he remarked to Travis. 'It means they're under orders to catch us.'

Travis shrugged. 'Maybe. They're extending the fence along the beach. They probably intend to seal us in for ever.'

'What?' Bridgman stood up with a sudden feeling of uneasiness. 'Why should they? Are you sure? I mean, what would be the point?'

Travis looked up at him, a flicker of dry amusement on his bleached face. Wisps of smoke wreathed his head, curled up past the serpentine columns of the grotto to the winding interval of sky a hundred feet above. 'Bridgman, forgive me saying so, but if you want to leave here, you should leave now. In a month's time you won't be able to.'

Bridgman ignored this, and searched the cleft of dark sky overhead, which framed the constellation Scorpio, as if hoping to see a reflection of the distant sea. 'They must be crazy. How much of this fence did you see?'

'About eight hundred yards. It won't take them long to complete. The sections are prefabricated, about forty feet high.' He smiled ironically at Bridgman's discomfort. 'Relax, Bridgman. If you do want to get out, you'll always be able to tunnel underneath it.'

'I don't want to get out,' Bridgman said coldly. 'Damn them, Travis, they're turning the place into a zoo. You know it won't be the same with a fence all the way around it.'

'A corner of Earth that is forever Mars.' Under the high forehead, Travis's eyes were sharp and watchful. 'I see their point. There hasn't been a fatal casualty now' – he glanced at Louise Woodward, who was strolling about in the colonnades – 'for nearly twenty years, and passenger rockets are supposed to be as safe as commuters' trains. They're quietly sealing off the past, Louise and I and you with it. I suppose it's pretty considerate of them not to burn the place down with flame-throwers. The virus would be a sufficient excuse. After all, we three are probably the only reservoirs left on the planet.' He picked up a handful of red dust and examined the fine crystals with a sombre eye. 'Well, Bridgman, what are you going to do?'

His thoughts discharging themselves through his mind like frantic signal flares, Bridgman walked away without answering.

Behind them, Louise Woodward wandered among the deep galleries of the grotto, crooning to herself in a low voice to the sighing rhythms of the whirling sand.

The next morning they returned to the town, wading through the deep drifts of sand that lay like a fresh fall of red snow between the hotels and stores, coruscating in the brilliant sunlight. Travis and Louise Woodward made their way towards their quarters in the motels further down the beach. Bridgman searched the still, crystal air for any signs of the wardens, but the sand-car had gone, its tracks obliterated by the storm.

In his room he found their calling-card.

A huge tide of dust had flowed through the french windows and submerged the desk and bed, three feet deep against the rear wall. Outside the sand-break had been inundated, and the contours of the desert had completely altered, a few spires of obsidian marking its former perspectives like buoys on a shifting sea. Bridgman spent the morning digging out his books and equipment, dismantled the electrical system and its batteries and carried everything to the room above. He would have moved to the penthouse on the top floor, but his lights would have been visible for miles.

Settling into his new quarters, he switched on the tape-recorder, heard a short, clipped message in the brisk voice which had shouted orders at the wardens the previous evening. 'Bridgman, this is Major Webster, deputy commandant of Cocoa Beach Reservation. On the instructions of the Anti-Viral Sub-committee of the UN General Assembly we are now building a continuous fence around the beach area. On completion no further egress will be allowed, and anyone escaping will be immediately returned to the reservation. Give yourself up now, Bridgman, before –'

Bridgman stopped the tape, then reversed the spool and erased the message, staring angrily at the instrument. Unable to settle down to the task of rewiring the room's circuits, he paced about, fiddling with the architectural drawings propped against the wall. He felt restless and hyper-excited, perhaps because he had been trying to repress, not very successfully, precisely those doubts of which Webster had now reminded him.

He stepped on to the balcony and looked out over the desert, at the red dunes rolling to the windows directly below. For the fourth time he had moved up a floor, and the sequence of identical rooms he had occupied were like displaced images of himself seen through a prism. Their common focus, that elusive final definition of himself which he had sought for so long, still remained to be found. Timelessly the sand swept towards him, its shifting contours, approximating more closely than any other landscape he had found to complete psychic zero, enveloping his past failures and uncertainties, masking them in its enigmatic canopy.

Bridgman watched the red sand flicker and fluoresce in the steepening sunlight. He would never see Mars now, and redress the implicit failure of talent, but a workable replica of the planet was contained within the beach area.

Several million tons of the Martian top-soil had been ferried in as ballast some fifty years earlier, when it was feared that the continuous firing of planetary probes and space vehicles, and the transportation of bulk stores and equipment to Mars would fractionally lower the gravitational mass of the Earth and bring it into tighter orbit around the Sun. Although the distance involved would be little more than a few millimetres, and barely raise the temperature of the atmosphere, its cumulative effects over an extended period might have resulted in a loss into space of the tenuous layers of the outer atmosphere, and of the radiological veil which alone made the biosphere habitable.

Over a twenty-year period a fleet of large freighters had shuttled to and from Mars, dumping the ballast into the sea near the landing grounds of Cape Canaveral. Simultaneously the Russians were filling in a small section of the Caspian Sea. The intention had been that the ballast should be swallowed by the Atlantic and Caspian waters, but all too soon it was found that the microbiological analysis of the sand had been inadequate.

At the Martian polar caps, where the original water vapour in the atmosphere had condensed, a residue of ancient organic matter formed the top-soil, a fine sandy loess containing the fossilized spores of the giant lichens and mosses which had been the last living organisms on the planet millions of years earlier. Embedded in these spores were the crystal lattices of the viruses which had once preyed on the plants, and traces of these were carried back to Earth with the Canaveral and Caspian ballast.

A few years afterwards a drastic increase in a wide range of plant diseases was noticed in the southern states of America and in the Kazakhstan and Turkmenistan republics of the Soviet Union. All over Florida there were outbreaks of blight and mosaic disease, orange plantations withered and died, stunted palms split by the roadside like dried banana skins, saw grass stiffened into paper spears in the summer heat. Within a few years the entire peninsula was transformed into a desert. The swampy jungles of the Everglades became bleached and dry, the rivers cracked husks strewn with the gleaming skeletons of crocodiles and birds, the forests petrified.

The former launching-ground at Canaveral was closed, and shortly afterwards the Cocoa Beach resorts were sealed off and evacuated, billions of dollars of real estate were abandoned to the virus. Fortunately never virulent to animal hosts, its influence was confined to within a small radius of the original loess which had borne it, unless ingested by the human organism, when it symbioted with the bacteria in the gut flora, benign and unknown to the host, but devastating to vegetation thousands of miles from Canaveral if returned to the soil.

Unable to rest despite his sleepless night, Bridgman played irritably with the tape-recorder. During their close escape from the wardens he had more than half hoped they would catch him. The mysterious leg cramp was obviously psychogenic. Although unable to accept consciously the logic of Webster's argument, he would willingly have conceded to the *fait accompli* of physical capture, gratefully submitted to a year's quarantine at the Parasitological Cleansing Unit at Tampa, and then returned to his career as an architect, chastened but accepting his failure.

As yet, however, the opportunity for surrender had failed to offer itself. Travis appeared to be aware of his ambivalent motives; Bridgman noticed that he and Louise Woodward had made no arrangements to meet him that evening for the conjunction.

In the early afternoon he went down into the streets, ploughed through the drifts of red sand, following the footprints of Travis and Louise as they wound in and out of the side-streets, finally saw them disappear into the coarser, flint-like dunes among the submerged motels to the south of the town. Giving up, he returned through the empty, shadowless streets, now and then shouted up into the hot air, listening to the echoes boom away among the dunes.

Later that afternoon he walked out towards the north-east, picking his way carefully through the dips and hollows, crouching in the pools of shadow whenever the distant sounds of the construction gangs along the perimeter were carried across to him by the wind. Around him, in the great dust basins, the grains of red sand glittered like diamonds. Barbs of rusting metal protruded from the slopes, remnants of Mars satellites and launching stages which had fallen on to the Martian deserts and then been carried back again to Earth. One fragment which he passed, a complete section of hull plate like a concave shield, still carried part of an identification numeral, and stood upright in the dissolving sand like a door into nowhere.

Just before dusk he reached a tall spur of obsidian that reared up into the tinted cerise sky like the spire of a ruined church, climbed up among its jutting cornices and looked out across the intervening two or three miles of dunes to the perimeter. Illuminated by the last light, the metal grilles shone with a roseate glow like fairy portcullises on the edge of an enchanted sea. At least half a mile of the fence had been completed, and as he watched another of the giant prefabricated sections was cantilevered into the air and staked to the ground. Already the eastern horizon was cut off by the encroaching fence, the enclosed Martian sand like the gravel scattered at the bottom of a cage.

Perched on the spur, Bridgman felt a warning tremor of pain in his calf. He leapt down in a flurry of dust, without looking back made off among the dunes and reefs.

Later, as the last baroque whorls of the sunset faded below the horizon, he waited on the roof for Travis and Louise Woodward, peering impatiently into the empty moon-filled streets.

Shortly after midnight, at an elevation of 35 degrees in the south-west, between Aquila and Ophiuchus, the conjunction began. Bridgman continued to search the streets, and ignored the seven points of speeding light as they raced towards him from the horizon like an invasion from deep space. There was no indication of their convergent orbital pathways, which would soon scatter them thousands of miles apart, and the satellites moved as if they were always together, in the tight configuration Bridgman had known since childhood, like a lost zodiacal emblem, a constellation detached from the celestial sphere and forever frantically searching to return to its place.

'Travis! Confound you!' With a snarl, Bridgman swung away

from the balcony and moved along to the exposed section of rail behind the elevator head. To be avoided like a pariah by Travis and Louise Woodward forced him to accept that he was no longer a true resident of the beach and now existed in a no-man's-land between them and the wardens.

The seven satellites drew nearer, and Bridgman glanced up at them cursorily. They were disposed in a distinctive but unusual pattern resembling the Greek letter x, a limp cross, a straight lateral member containing four capsules more or less in line ahead – Connolly, Tkachev, Merril and Maiakovski – bisected by three others forming with Tkachev an elongated Z – Pokrovski, Woodward and Brodisnek. The pattern had been variously identified as a hammer and sickle, an eagle, a swastika, and a dove, as well as a variety of religious and runic emblems, but all these were being defeated by the advancing tendency of the older capsules to vaporize.

It was this slow disintegration of the aluminium shells that made them visible – it had often been pointed out that the observer on the ground was looking, not at the actual capsule, but at a local field of vaporized aluminium and ionized hydrogen peroxide gas from the ruptured attitude jets now distributed within half a mile of each of the capsules. Woodward's, the most recently in orbit, was a barely perceptible point of light. The hulks of the capsules, with their perfectly preserved human cargoes, were continually dissolving, and a wide fan of silver spray opened out in a phantom wake behind Merril and Pokrovski (1998 and 1999), like a double star transforming itself into a nova in the centre of a constellation. As the mass of the capsules diminished they sank into a closer orbit around the earth, would soon touch the denser layers of the atmosphere and plummet to the ground.

Bridgman watched the satellites as they moved towards him, his irritation with Travis forgotten. As always, he felt himself moved by the eerie but strangely serene spectacle of the ghostly convoy endlessly circling the dark sea of the midnight sky, the long-dead astronauts converging for the ten-thousandth time upon their brief rendezvous and then setting off upon their lonely flight-paths around the perimeter of the ionosphere, the tidal edge of the beachway into space which had reclaimed them.

How Louise Woodward could bear to look up at her husband he had never been able to understand. After her arrival he once invited her to the hotel, remarking that there was an excellent view of the beautiful sunsets, and she had snapped back bitterly: 'Beautiful? Can you imagine what it's like looking up at a sunset when your husband's spinning through it in his coffin?'

This reaction had been a common one when the first astronauts had died after failing to make contact with the launching platforms in fixed orbit. When these new stars rose in the west an attempt had been made to shoot them down – there was the unsettling prospect of the skies a thousand years hence, littered with orbiting refuse – but later they were left in this natural graveyard, forming their own monument.

Obscured by the clouds of dust carried up into the air by the sand-storm, the satellites shone with little more than the intensity of second-magnitude stars, winking as the reflected light was interrupted by the lanes of strato-cirrus. The wake of diffusing light behind Merril and Pokrovski which usually screened the other capsules seemed to have diminished in size, and he could see both Maiakovski and Brodisnek clearly for the first time in several months. Wondering whether Merril or Pokrovski would be the first to fall from orbit, he looked towards the centre of the cross as it passed overhead.

With a sharp intake of breath, he tilted his head back. In surprise he noticed that one of the familiar points of light was missing from the centre of the group. What he had assumed to be an occlusion of the conjoint vapour trails by dust clouds was simply due to the fact that one of the capsules – Merril's, he decided, the third of the line ahead – had fallen from its orbit.

Head raised, he sidestepped slowly across the roof, avoiding the pieces of rusting neon sign, following the convoy as it passed overhead and moved towards the eastern horizon. No longer overlaid by the wake of Merril's capsule, Woodward's shone with far greater clarity, and almost appeared to have taken the former's place, although he was not due to fall from orbit for at least a century.

In the distance somewhere an engine growled. A moment later, from a different quarter, a woman's voice cried out faintly. Bridgman moved to the rail, over the intervening roof-tops saw two figures silhouetted against the sky on the elevator head of an apartment block, then heard Louise Woodward call out again. She was pointing up at the sky with both hands, her long hair blown about her face, Travis trying to restrain her. Bridgman realized that she had misconstrued Merril's descent, assuming that the fallen astronaut was her husband. He climbed on to the edge of the balcony, watching the pathetic tableau on the distant roof.

Again, somewhere among the dunes, an engine moaned. Before Bridgman could turn around, a brilliant blade of light cleft the sky in the south-west. Like a speeding comet, an immense train of vaporizing particles stretching behind it to the horizon, it soared towards them, the downward curve of its pathway clearly visible. Detached from the rest of the capsules, which were now disappearing among the stars along the eastern horizon, it was little more than a few miles off the ground.

Bridgman watched it approach, apparently on a collision course with the hotel. The expanding corona of white light, like a gigantic signal flare, illuminated the roof-tops, etching the letters of the neon signs over the submerged motels on the outskirts of the town. He ran for the doorway, as he raced down the stairs saw the glow of the descending capsule fill the sombre streets like a hundred moons. When he reached his room, sheltered by the massive weight of the hotel, he watched the dunes in front of the hotel light up like a stage set. Three hundred yards away the low camouflaged hull of the wardens' beach-car was revealed poised on a crest, its feeble spotlight drowned by the glare.

With a deep metallic sigh, the burning catafalque of the dead astronaut soared overhead, a cascade of vaporizing metal pouring from its hull, filling the sky with incandescent light. Reflected below it, like an expressway illuminated by an aircraft's spotlights, a long lane of light several hundred yards in width raced out into the desert towards the sea. As Bridgman shielded his eyes, it suddenly erupted in a tremendous explosion of detonating sand. A huge curtain of white dust lifted into the air and fell slowly to the ground. The sounds of the impact rolled against the hotel, mounting in a sustained crescendo that drummed against the windows. A series of smaller explosions flared up like opalescent fountains. All over the desert fires flickered briefly where fragments of the capsule had been scattered. Then the noise subsided, and an immense glistening pall of phosphorescing gas hung in the air like a silver veil, particles within it beading and winking.

Two hundred yards away across the sand was the running figure of Louise Woodward, Travis twenty paces behind her. Bridgman watched them dart in and out of the dunes, then abruptly felt the cold spotlight of the beach-car hit his face and flood the room behind him. The vehicle was moving straight towards him, two of the wardens, nets and lassos in hand, riding the outboard.

Quickly Bridgman straddled the balcony, jumped down into the sand and raced towards the crest of the first dune. He crouched and ran on through the darkness as the beam probed the air. Above, the glistening pall was slowly fading, the particles of vaporized metal sifting towards the dark Martian sand. In the distance the last echoes of the impact were still reverberating among the hotels of the beach colonies farther down the coast.

Five minutes later he caught up with Louise Woodward and Travis. The capsule's impact had flattened a number of the dunes, forming a shallow basin some quarter of a mile in diameter, and the surrounding slopes were scattered with the still glowing particles, sparkling like fading eyes. The beach-car growled somewhere four or five hundred yards behind him, and Bridgman broke off into an exhausted walk. He stopped beside Travis, who was kneeling on the ground, breath pumping into his lungs. Fifty yards away Louise Woodward was running up and down, distraughtly gazing at the fragments of smouldering metal. For a moment the spotlight of the approaching beach-car illuminated her, and she ran away among the dunes. Bridgman caught a glimpse of the inconsolable anguish in her face.

Travis was still on his knees. He had picked up a piece of the oxidized metal and was pressing it together in his hands.

'Travis, for God's sake tell her! This was Merril's capsule, there's no doubt about it! Woodward's still up there.'

Travis looked up at him silently, his eyes searching Bridgman's face. A spasm of pain tore his mouth, and Bridgman realized that the barb of steel he clasped reverently in his hands was still glowing with heat.

'Travis!' He tried to pull the man's hands apart, the pungent stench of burning flesh gusting into his face, but Travis wrenched away from him. 'Leave her alone, Bridgman! Go back with the wardens!'

Bridgman retreated from the approaching beach-car. Only thirty yards away, its spotlight filled the basin. Louise Woodward was still searching the dunes. Travis held his ground as the wardens jumped down from the car and advanced towards him with their nets, his bloodied hands raised at his sides, the steel barb flashing like a dagger. At the head of the wardens, the only one unmasked was a trim, neat-featured man with an intent, serious face. Bridgman guessed that this was Major Webster, and that the wardens had known of the impending impact and hoped to capture them, and Louise in particular, before it occurred.

Bridgman stumbled back towards the dunes at the edge of the basin. As he neared the crest he trapped his foot in a semicircular plate of metal, sat down and freed his heel. Unmistakably it was part of a control panel, the circular instrument housings still intact.

Overhead the pall of glistening vapour had moved off to the north-east, and the reflected light was directly over the rusting gantries of the former launching site at Cape Canaveral. For a few fleeting seconds the gantries seemed to be enveloped in a sheen of silver, transfigured by the vaporized body of the dead astronaut, diffusing over them in a farewell gesture, his final return to the site from which he had set off to his death a century earlier. Then the gantries sank again into their craggy shadows, and the pall moved off like an immense wraith towards the sea, barely distinguishable from the star glow.

Down below Travis was sitting on the ground surrounded by the wardens. He scuttled about on his hands like a frantic crab, scooping handfuls of the virus-laden sand at them. Holding tight to their masks, the wardens manoeuvred around him, their nets and lassos at the ready. Another group moved slowly towards Bridgman.

Bridgman picked up a handful of the dark Martian sand beside the instrument panel, felt the soft glowing crystals warm his palm. In his mind he could still see the silver-sheathed gantries of the launching site across the bay, by a curious illusion almost identical with the Martian city he had designed years earlier. He watched the pall disappear over the sea, then looked around at the other remnants of Merril's capsule scattered over the slopes. High in the western night, between Pegasus and Cygnus, shone the distant disc of the planet Mars, which for both himself and the dead astronaut had served for so long as a symbol of unattained ambition. The wind stirred softly through the sand, cooling this replica of the planet which lay passively around him, and at last he understood why he had come to the beach and been unable to leave it.

Twenty yards away Travis was being dragged off like a wild dog, his thrashing body pinioned in the centre of a web of lassos. Louise Woodward had run away among the dunes towards the sea, following the vanished gas cloud.

In a sudden access of refound confidence, Bridgman drove his fist into the dark sand, buried his forearm like a foundation pillar. A flange of hot metal from Merril's capsule burned his wrist, bonding him to the spirit of the dead astronaut. Scattered around him on the Martian sand, in a sense Merril had reached Mars after all.

'Damn it!' he cried exultantly to himself as the wardens' lassos stung his neck and shoulders. 'We made it!'

1962

THE WATCH-TOWERS

The next day, for some reason, there was a sudden increase of activity in the watch-towers. This began during the latter half of the morning, and by noon, when Renthall left the hotel on his way to see Mrs Osmond, seemed to have reached its peak. People were standing at their windows and balconies along both sides of the street, whispering agitatedly to each other behind the curtains and pointing up into the sky.

Renthall usually tried to ignore the watch-towers, resenting even the smallest concession to the fact of their existence, but at the bottom of the street, where he was hidden in the shadow thrown by one of the houses, he stopped and craned his head up at the nearest tower.

A hundred feet away from him, it hung over the Public Library, its tip poised no more than twenty feet above the roof. The glass-enclosed cabin in the lowest tier appeared to be full of observers, opening and shutting the windows and shifting about what Renthall assumed were huge pieces of optical equipment. He looked around at the further towers, suspended from the sky at three hundred foot intervals in every direction, noticing an occasional flash of light as a window turned and caught the sun.

An elderly man wearing a shabby black suit and wing collar, who usually loitered outside the library, came across the street to Renthall and backed into the shadows beside him.

'They're up to something all right.' He cupped his hands over his eyes and peered up anxiously at the watch-towers. 'I've never seen them like this as long as I can remember.'

Renthall studied his face. However alarmed, he was obviously relieved by the signs of activity. 'I shouldn't worry unduly,' Renthall told him. 'It's a change to see something going on at all.'

Before the other could reply he turned on his heel and strode away along the pavement. It took him ten minutes to reach the street in which Mrs Osmond lived, and he fixed his eyes firmly on the ground, ignoring the few passers-by. Although dominated by the watch-towers – four of them hung in a line exactly down its centre – the street was almost deserted. Half the houses were untenanted and falling into what would soon be an irreversible state of disrepair. Usually Renthall assessed each property carefully, trying to decide whether to leave his hotel and take one of them, but the movement in the watch-towers had caused him more anxiety than he was prepared to admit, and the terrace of houses passed unnoticed.

Mrs Osmond's house stood halfway down the street, its gate swinging loosely on its rusty hinges. Renthall hesitated under the plane tree growing by the edge of the pavement, and then crossed the narrow garden and quickly let himself through the door.

Mrs Osmond invariably spent the afternoon sitting out on the veranda in the sun, gazing at the weeds in the back garden, but today she had retreated to a corner of the sitting room. She was sorting a suitcase full of old papers when Renthall came in.

Renthall made no attempt to embrace her and wandered over to the window. Mrs Osmond had half drawn the curtains and he pulled them back. There was a watch-tower ninety feet away, almost directly ahead, hanging over the parallel terrace of empty houses. The lines of towers receded diagonally from left to right towards the horizon, partly obscured by the bright haze.

'Do you think you should have come today?' Mrs Osmond asked, shifting her plump hips nervously in the chair.

'Why not?' Renthall said, scanning the towers, hands loosely in his pockets.

'But if they're going to keep a closer watch on us now they'll notice you coming here.'

'I shouldn't believe all the rumours you hear,' Renthall told her calmly.

'What do you think it means then?'

'I've absolutely no idea. Their movements may be as random and meaningless as our own.' Renthall shrugged. 'Perhaps they *are* going to keep a closer watch on us. What does it matter if all they do is stare?'

'Then you mustn't come here any more!' Mrs Osmond protested.

'Why? I hardly believe they can see through walls.'

'They're not that stupid,' Mrs Osmond said irritably. 'They'll soon put two and two together, if they haven't already.'

Renthall took his eyes off the tower and looked down at Mrs Osmond patiently. 'My dear, this house isn't tapped. For all they know we may be darning our prayer rugs or discussing the endocrine system of the tapeworm.'

'Not you, Charles,' Mrs Osmond said with a short laugh. 'Not if they know you.' Evidently pleased by this sally, she relaxed and took a cigarette out of the box on the table.

'Perhaps they don't know me,' Renthall said dryly. 'In fact, I'm quite sure they don't. If they did I can't believe I should still be here.'

He noticed himself stooping, a reliable sign that he was worrying, and went over to the sofa.

'Is the school going to start tomorrow?' Mrs Osmond asked when he had disposed his long, thin legs around the table.

'It should do,' Renthall said. 'Hanson went down to the Town Hall this morning, but as usual they had little idea of what was going on.'

He opened his jacket and pulled out of the inner pocket an old but neatly folded copy of a woman's magazine.

'Charles!' Mrs Osmond exclaimed. 'Where did you get this?'

She took it from Renthall and started leafing through the soiled pages.

'One of my sources,' Renthall said. From the sofa he could still see the watch-tower over the houses opposite. 'Georgina Simons. She has a library of them.'

He rose, went over to the window and drew the curtains across.

'Charles, don't. I can't see.'

'Read it later,' Renthall told her. He lay back on the sofa again. 'Are you coming to the recital this afternoon?'

'Hasn't it been cancelled?' Mrs Osmond asked, putting the magazine down reluctantly.

'No, of course not.'

'Charles, I don't think I want to go.' Mrs Osmond frowned. 'What records is Hanson going to play?'

'Some Tchaikovsky. And Grieg.' He tried to make it sound interesting. 'You must come. We can't just sit about subsiding into this state of boredom and uselessness.'

'I know,' Mrs Osmond said fractiously. 'But I don't feel like it. Not today. All those records bore me. I've heard them so often.'

'They bore me too. But at least it's something to do.' He put an arm around Mrs Osmond's shoulders and began to play with the darker unbleached hair behind her ears, tapping the large nickel ear-rings she wore and listening to them tinkle.

When he put his hand on to her knee Mrs Osmond stood up and prowled aimlessly around the room, straightening her skirt.

'Julia, what is the matter with you?' Renthall asked irritably. 'Have you got a headache?'

Mrs Osmond was by the window, gazing up at the watch-towers. 'Do you think they're going to come down?'

'Of course not!' Renthall snapped. 'Where on earth did you get that idea?'

Suddenly he felt unbearably exasperated. The confined dimensions of the dusty sitting-room seemed to suffocate reason. He stood up and buttoned his jacket. 'I'll see you this afternoon at the Institute, Julia. The recital starts at three.'

Mrs Osmond nodded vaguely, unfastened the french windows and ambled forwards across the veranda into full view of the watch-towers, the glassy expression on her face like a supplicant nun's.

As Renthall had expected, the school did not open the next day. When they tired of hanging around the hotel after breakfast he and Hanson went down to the Town Hall. The building was almost empty and the only official they were able to find was unhelpful.

'We have no instructions at present,' he told them, 'but as soon as the term starts you will be notified. Though from what I hear the postponement is to be indefinite.'

'Is that the committee's decision?' Renthall asked. 'Or just another of the town clerk's brilliant extemporizings?'

'The school committee is no longer meeting,' the official said. 'I'm afraid the town clerk isn't here today.' Before Renthall could speak he added: 'You will, of course, continue to draw your salaries. Perhaps you would care to call in at the treasurer's department on your way out?'

Renthall and Hanson left and looked about for a café. Finally they found one that was open and sat under the awning, staring vacantly at the watch-towers hanging over the roof-tops around them. Their activity had lessened considerably since the previous day. The nearest tower was only fifty feet away, immediately above a disused office building on the other side of the street. The windows in the observation tier remained shut, but every few minutes Renthall noticed a shadow moving behind the panes.

Eventually a waitress came out to them, and Renthall ordered coffee.

'I think I shall have to give a few lessons,' Hanson remarked. 'All this leisure is becoming too much of a good thing.'

'It's an idea,' Renthall agreed. 'If you can find anyone interested. I'm sorry the recital yesterday was such a flop.'

Hanson shrugged. 'I'll see if I can get hold of some new records. By the way, I thought Julia looked very handsome yesterday.'

Renthall acknowledged the compliment with a slight bow of his head. 'I'd like to take her out more often.'

'Do you think that's wise?'

'Why on earth not?'

'Well, just at present, you know.' Hanson inclined a finger at the watch-towers.

'I don't see that it matters particularly,' Renthall said. He disliked personal confidences and was about to change the subject when Hanson leaned forward across the table.

'Perhaps not, but I gather there was some mention of you at the last Council meeting. One or two members were rather critical of your little *ménage à deux*.' He smiled thinly at Renthall, who was frowning into his coffee. 'Sheer spite, no doubt, but your behaviour is a little idiosyncratic.'

Controlling himself, Renthall pushed away the coffee cup. 'Do you mind telling me what damned business it is of theirs?'

Hanson laughed. 'None, really, except that they are the executive authority, and I suppose we should take our cue from them.' Renthall snorted at this, and Hanson went on: 'As a matter of interest, you may receive an official directive over the next few days.'

'A *what*?' Renthall exploded. He sat back, shaking his head incredulously. 'Are you serious?' When Hanson nodded he began to laugh harshly. 'Those idiots! I don't know why we put up with them. Sometimes their stupidity positively staggers me.'

'Steady on,' Hanson demurred. 'I do see their point. Bearing in mind the big commotion in the watch-towers yesterday the Council probably feel we shouldn't do anything that might antagonize them. You never know, they may even be acting on official instructions.'

Renthall glanced contemptuously at Hanson. 'Do you *really* believe that nonsense about the Council being in touch with the watch-towers? It may give a few simpletons a sense of security, but for heaven's sake don't try it on me. My patience is just about exhausted.' He watched Hanson carefully, wondering which of the Council members had provided him with his information. The lack of subtlety depressed him painfully. 'However, thanks for warning me. I suppose it means there'll be an overpowering air of embarrassment when Julia and I go to the cinema tomorrow.'

Hanson shook his head. 'No. Actually the performance has been cancelled. In view of yesterday's disturbances.'

'But why –?' Renthall slumped back. 'Haven't they got the intelligence to realize that it's just at this sort of time that we need every social get-together we can organize? People are hiding away in their back bedrooms like a lot of frightened ghosts. We've got to bring them out, give them something that will pull them together.'

He gazed up thoughtfully at the watch-tower across the street. Shadows circulated behind the frosted panes of the observation windows. 'Some sort of gala, say, or a garden fête. Who could organize it, though?'

Hanson pushed back his chair. 'Careful, Charles. I don't know whether the Council would altogether approve.'

'I'm sure they wouldn't.' After Hanson had left he remained at the table and returned to his solitary contemplation of the watch-towers.

For half an hour Renthall sat at the table, playing absently with his empty coffee cup and watching the few people who passed along the street. No one else visited the café, and he was glad to be able to pursue his thoughts alone, in this miniature urban vacuum, with nothing to intervene between himself and the lines of watch-towers stretching into the haze beyond the roof-tops.

With the exception of Mrs Osmond, Renthall had virtually no close friends in whom to confide. With his sharp intelligence and impatience with trivialities, Renthall was one of those men with whom others find it difficult to relax. A certain innate condescension, a reserved but unmistakable attitude of superiority held them away from him, though few people regarded him as anything but a shabby pedagogue. At the hotel he kept to himself. There was little social contact between the guests; in the lounge and dining room they sat immersed in their old newspapers and magazines, occasionally murmuring quietly to each other. The only thing which could mobilize the simultaneous communion of the guests was some untoward activity in the watch-towers, and at such times Renthall always maintained an absolute silence.

Just before he stood up a square thick-set figure approached down the street. Renthall recognized the man and was about to turn his seat to avoid having to greet him, but something about his expression made him lean forward. Fleshy and dark-jowled, the man walked with an easy, rolling gait, his double-breasted check overcoat open to reveal a well-tended midriff. This was

Victor Boardman, owner of the local flea-pit cinema, sometime bootlegger and procurer at large.

Renthall had never spoken to him, but he was aware that Boardman shared with him the distinction of bearing the stigma of the Council's disapproval. Hanson claimed that the Council had successfully stamped out Boardman's illicit activities, but the latter's permanent expression of smug contempt for the rest of the world seemed to belie this.

As he passed they exchanged glances, and Boardman's face broke momentarily into a knowing smirk. It was obviously directed at Renthall, and implied a pre-judgement of some event about which Renthall as yet knew nothing, presumably his coming collision with the Council. Obviously Boardman expected him to capitulate to the Council without a murmur.

Annoyed, Renthall turned his back on Boardman, then watched him over his shoulder as he padded off down the street, his easy relaxed shoulders swaying from side to side.

The following day the activity in the watch-towers had subsided entirely. The blue haze from which they extended was brighter than it had been for several months, and the air in the streets seemed to sparkle with the light reflected off the observation windows. There was no sign of movement among them, and the sky had a rigid, uniform appearance that indicated an indefinite lull.

For some reason, however, Renthall found himself more nervous than he had been for some time. The school had not yet opened, but he felt strangely reluctant to visit Mrs Osmond and remained indoors all morning, shunning the streets as if avoiding some invisible shadow of guilt.

The long lines of watch-towers stretching endlessly from one horizon to the other reminded him that he could soon expect to receive the Council's 'directive' – Hanson would not have mentioned it by accident – and it was always during the lulls that the Council was most active in consolidating its position, issuing a stream of petty regulations and amendments.

Renthall would have liked to challenge the Council's authority on some formal matter unconnected with himself – the validity, for example, of one of the byelaws prohibiting public assemblies in the street – but the prospect of all the intrigue involved in canvassing the necessary support bored him utterly. Although none of them individually would challenge the Council, most people would have been glad to see it toppled, but there seemed to be no likely focus for their opposition. Apart from the fear that the Council was in touch with the watch-towers, no one would stand up for Renthall's right to carry on his affair with Mrs Osmond.

Curiously enough, she seemed unaware of these cross-currents when he went to see her that afternoon. She had cleaned the house and was in high humour, the windows wide open to the brilliant air.

'Charles, what's the matter with you?' she chided him when he slumped inertly into a chair. 'You look like a broody hen.'

'I felt rather tired this morning. It's probably the hot weather.' When she sat down on the arm of the chair he put one hand listlessly on her hip, trying to summon together his energies. 'Recently I've been developing an *idée fixe* about the Council, I must be going through a crisis of confidence. I need some method of reasserting myself.'

Mrs Osmond stroked his hair soothingly with her cool fingers, her eyes watching him silkily. 'What *you* need, Charles, is a little mother love. You're so isolated at that hotel, among all those old people. Why don't you rent one of the houses in this road? I'd be able to look after you then.'

Renthall glanced up at her sardonically. 'Perhaps I could move in here?' he asked, but she tossed her head back with a derisive snort and went over to the window.

She gazed up at the nearest watch-tower a hundred feet away, its windows closed and silent, the great shaft disappearing into the haze. 'What do you suppose they're thinking about?'

Renthall snapped his fingers off-handedly. 'They're probably not thinking about anything. Sometimes I wonder whether there's anyone there at all. The movements we see may be just optical illusions. Although the windows appear to open no one's ever actually *seen* any of them. For all we know this place may well be nothing more than an abandoned zoo.'

Mrs Osmond regarded him with rueful amusement. 'Charles, you do pick some extraordinary metaphors. I often doubt if you're like the rest of us, I wouldn't dare say the sort of things you do in case –' She broke off, glancing up involuntarily at the watch-towers hanging from the sky.

Idly, Renthall asked: 'In case what?'

'Well, in case –' Irritably, she said: 'Don't be absurd, Charles, doesn't the thought of those towers hanging down over us frighten you at all?'

Renthall turned his head slowly and stared up at the watch-towers. Once he had tried to count them, but there seemed little point. 'Yes, they frighten me,' he said noncommittally. 'In the same way that Hanson and the old people at the hotel and everyone else here does. But not in the sense that the boys at school are frightened of *me*.'

Mrs Osmond nodded, misinterpreting this last remark. 'Children are very perceptive, Charles. They probably know you're not interested in them. Unfortunately they're not old enough to understand what the watch-towers mean.'

She gave a slight shiver, and pulled her cardigan around her shoulders. 'You know, on the days when they're busy behind their windows I can hardly move around, it's terrible. I feel so listless, all I want to do is sit and stare at the wall. Perhaps I'm more sensitive to their, er, radiations than most people.'

Renthall smiled. 'You must be. Don't let them depress you. Next time why don't you put on a paper hat and do a pirouette?'

'What? Oh, Charles, stop being cynical.'

'I'm not. Seriously, Julia, do you think it would make any difference?'

Mrs Osmond shook her head sadly. 'You try, Charles, and then tell me. Where are you going?'

Renthall paused at the window. 'Back to the hotel to rest. By the way, do you know Victor Boardman?'

'I used to, once. Why, what are you getting up to with him?'

'Does he own the garden next to the cinema car park?'

'I think so.' Mrs Osmond laughed. 'Are you going to take up gardening?'

'In a sense.' With a wave, Renthall left.

He began with Dr Clifton, whose room was directly below his own. Clifton's duties at his surgery occupied him for little more than an hour a day – there were virtually no deaths or illnesses – but he still retained sufficient initiative to cultivate a hobby. He had turned one end of his room into a small aviary, containing a dozen canaries, and spent much of his time trying to teach them tricks. His acerbic, matter-of-fact manner always tired Renthall, but he respected the doctor for not sliding into total lethargy like everyone else.

Clifton considered his suggestion carefully. 'I agree with you, something of the sort is probably necessary. A good idea, Renthall. Properly conducted, it might well provide just the lift people need.'

'The main question, Doctor, is one of organization. The only suitable place is the Town Hall.'

Clifton nodded. 'Yes, there's your problem. I'm afraid I've no influence with the Council, if that's what you're suggesting. I don't know what you can do. You'll have to get their permission of course, and in the past they haven't shown themselves to be very radical or original. They prefer to maintain the *status quo*.'

Renthall nodded, then added casually: 'They're only interested in maintaining their own power. At times I become rather tired of our Council.'

Clifton glanced at him and then turned back to his cages. 'You're preaching revolution, Renthall,' he said quietly, a forefinger stroking the beak of one of the canaries. Pointedly, he refrained from seeing Renthall to the door.

Writing the doctor off, Renthall rested for a few minutes in his room, pacing up and down the strip of faded carpet, then went down to the basement to see the manager, Mulvaney.

'I'm only making some initial inquiries. As yet I haven't applied for permission, but Dr Clifton thinks the idea is excellent, and there's no doubt we'll get it. Are you up to looking after the catering?'

Mulvaney's sallow face watched Renthall sceptically. 'Of course I'm up to it, but how serious are you?' He leaned against his roll-top desk. 'You think you'll get permission? You're wrong, Mr Renthall, the Council wouldn't stand for the idea. They even closed the cinema, so they're not likely to allow a public party. Before you know what you'd have people dancing.'

'I hardly think so, but does the idea appal you so much?'

Mulvaney shook his head, already bored with Renthall. 'You get a permit, Mr Renthall, and then we can talk seriously.'

Tightening his voice, Renthall asked: 'Is it necessary to get the Council's permission? Couldn't we go ahead without?'

Without looking up, Mulvaney sat down at his desk. 'Keep trying, Mr Renthall, it's a great idea.'

During the next few days Renthall pursued his inquiries, in all approaching some half-dozen people. In general he met with the same negative response, but as he intended he soon noticed a subtle but nonetheless distinct quickening of interest around him. The usual fragmentary murmur of conversation would fade away abruptly as he passed the tables in the dining room, and the service was fractionally more prompt. Hanson no longer took coffee with him in the mornings, and once Renthall saw him in guarded conversation with the town clerk's secretary, a young man called Barnes. This, he assumed, was Hanson's contact.

In the meantime the activity in the watch-towers remained at zero. The endless lines of towers hung down from the bright, hazy sky, the observation windows closed, and the people in the streets below sank slowly into their usual mindless torpor, wandering from hotel to library to café. Determined on his course of action, Renthall felt his confidence return.

Allowing an interval of a week to elapse, he finally called upon Victor Boardman.

The bootlegger received him in his office above the cinema, greeting him with a wry smile.

'Well, Mr Renthall, I hear you're going into the entertainment business. Drunken gambols and all that. I'm surprised at you.'

'A fête,' Renthall corrected. The seat Boardman had offered him faced towards the window – deliberately, he guessed – and provided an uninterrupted view of the watch-tower over the roof of the adjacent furniture store. Only forty feet away, it blocked off half the sky. The metal plates which formed its rectangular sides were annealed together by some process Renthall was unable to identify, neither welded nor riveted, almost as if the entire tower had been cast *in situ*. He moved to another chair so that his back was to the window.

'The school is still closed, so I thought I'd try to make myself useful. That's what I'm paid for. I've come to you because you've had a good deal of experience.'

'Yes, I've had a lot of experience, Mr Renthall. Very varied. As one of the Council's employees, I take it you have its permission?'

Renthall evaded this. 'The Council is naturally a conservative body, Mr Boardman. Obviously at this stage I'm acting on my own initiative. I shall consult the Council at the appropriate moment later, when I can offer them a practicable proposition.'

Boardman nodded sagely. 'That's sensible, Mr Renthall. Now what exactly do you want me to do? Organize the whole thing for you?'

'No, but naturally I'd be very grateful if you would. For the present I merely want to ask permission to hold the fête on a piece of your property.'

'The cinema? I'm not going to take all those seats out, if that's what you're after.'

'Not the cinema. Though we could use the bar and cloakrooms,' Renthall extemporized, hoping the scheme did not sound too grandiose. 'Is the old beer-garden next to the car park your property?'

For a moment Boardman was silent. He watched Renthall shrewdly, picking his nails with his cigar-cutter, a faint suggestion of admiration in his eyes. 'So you want to hold the fête in the open, Mr Renthall? Is that it?'

Renthall nodded, smiling back at Boardman. 'I'm glad to see

you living up to your reputation for getting quickly to the point. Are you prepared to lend the garden? Of course, you'll have a big share of the profits. In fact, if it's any inducement, you can have all the profits.'

Boardman put out his cigar. 'Mr Renthall, you're obviously a man of many parts. I underestimated you. I thought you merely had a grievance against the Council. I hope you know what you're doing.'

'Mr Boardman, will you lend the garden?' Renthall repeated.

There was an amused but thoughtful smile on Boardman's lips as he regarded the watch-tower framed by the window. 'There are two watch-towers directly over the beer-garden, Mr Renthall.'

'I'm fully aware of that. It's obviously the chief attraction of the property. Now, can you give me an answer?'

The two men regarded each other silently, and then Boardman gave an almost imperceptible nod. Renthall realized that his scheme was being taken seriously by Boardman. He was obviously using Renthall for his own purposes, for once having flaunted the Council's authority he would be able to resume all his other, more profitable activities. Of course, the fête would never be held, but in answer to Boardman's questions he outlined a provisional programme. They fixed the date of the fête at a month ahead, and arranged to meet again at the beginning of the next week.

Two days later, as he expected, the first emissaries of the Council came to see him.

He was waiting at his usual table on the café terrace, the silent watch-towers suspended from the air around him, when he saw Hanson hurrying along the street.

'Do join me.' Renthall drew a chair back. 'What's the news?'

'Nothing – though you should know, Charles.' He gave Renthall a dry smile, as if admonishing a favourite pupil, then gazed about the empty terrace for the waitress. 'Service is appallingly bad here. Tell me, Charles, what's all this talk about you and Victor Boardman. I could hardly believe my ears.'

Renthall leaned back in his chair. 'I don't know, you tell me.'

'We – er, I was wondering if Boardman was taking advantage

of some perfectly innocent remark he might have overheard. This business of a garden party you're supposed to be organizing with him – it sounds absolutely fantastic.'

'Why?'

'But Charles.' Hanson leaned forward to examine Renthall carefully, trying to make sense of his unruffled pose. 'Surely you aren't serious?'

'But why not? If I want to, why shouldn't I organize a garden party – fête, to be more accurate?'

'It doesn't make an iota of difference,' Hanson said tartly. 'Apart from any other reason' – here he glanced skyward – 'the fact remains that you are an employee of the Council.'

Hands in his trouser-pockets, Renthall tipped back his chair. 'But that gives them no mandate to interfere in my private life. You seem to be forgetting, but the terms of my contract specifically exclude any such authority. I am not on the established grade, as my salary differential shows. If the Council disapprove, the only sanction they can apply is to give me the sack.'

'They will, Charles, don't sound so smug.'

Renthall let this pass. 'Fair enough, if they can find anyone else to take on the job. Frankly I doubt it. They've managed to swallow their moral scruples in the past.'

'Charles, this is different. As long as you're discreet no one gives a hoot about your private affairs, but this garden party is a public matter, and well within the Council's province.'

Renthall yawned. 'I'm rather bored with the subject of the Council. Technically, the fête will be a private affair, by invitation only. They've no statutory right to be consulted at all. If a breach of the peace takes place the Chief Constable can take action. Why all the fuss, anyway? I'm merely trying to provide a little harmless festivity.'

Hanson shook his head. 'Charles, you're deliberately evading the point. According to Boardman this fête will take place out of doors – directly under two of the watch-towers. Have you realized what the repercussions would be?'

'Yes.' Renthall formed the word carefully in his mouth. 'Nothing. Absolutely nothing.'

'Charles!' Hanson lowered his head at this apparent blasphemy, glanced up at the watch-towers over the street as if expecting instant retribution to descend from them. 'Look, my dear fellow, take my advice. Drop the whole idea. You don't stand a chance anyway of ever holding this mad jape, so why deliberately court trouble with the Council? Who knows what their real power would be if they were provoked?'

Renthall rose from his seat. He looked up at the watch-tower hanging from the air on the other side of the road, controlling himself when a slight pang of anxiety stirred his heart. 'I'll send you an invitation,' he called back, then walked away to his hotel.

The next afternoon the town clerk's secretary called upon him in his room. During the interval, no doubt intended as a salutary pause for reflection, Renthall had remained at the hotel, reading quietly in his armchair. He paid one brief visit to Mrs Osmond, but she seemed nervous and irritable, evidently aware of the imminent clash. The strain of maintaining an appearance of unconcern had begun to tire Renthall, and he avoided the open streets whenever possible. Fortunately the school had still not opened.

Barnes, the dapper dark-haired secretary, came straight to the point. Refusing Renthall's offer of an armchair, he held a sheet of pink duplicated paper in his hand, apparently a minute of the last Council meeting.

'Mr Renthall, the Council has been informed of your intention to hold a garden fête in some three weeks' time. I have been asked by the chairman of the Watch Committee to express the committee's grave misgivings, and to request you accordingly to terminate all arrangements and cancel the fête immediately, pending an inquiry.'

'I'm sorry, Barnes, but I'm afraid our preparations are too far advanced. We're about to issue invitations.'

Barnes hesitated, casting his eye around Renthall's faded room and few shabby books as if hoping to find some ulterior motive for Renthall's behaviour.

'Mr Renthall, perhaps I could explain that this request is tantamount to a direct order from the Council.'

'So I'm aware.' Renthall sat down on his window-sill and gazed out at the watch-towers. 'Hanson and I went over all this, as you probably know. The Council have no more right to order me to cancel this fête than they have to stop me walking down the street.'

Barnes smiled his thin bureaucratic smirk. 'Mr Renthall, this is not a matter of the Council's statutory jurisdiction. This order is issued by virtue of the authority vested in it by its superiors. If you prefer, you can assume that the Council is merely passing on a direct instruction it has received.' He inclined his head towards the watch-towers.

Renthall stood up. 'Now we're at last getting down to business.' He gathered himself together. 'Perhaps you could tell the Council to convey to its superiors, as you call them, my polite but firm refusal. Do you get *my* point?'

Barnes retreated fractionally. He summed Renthall up carefully, then nodded. 'I think so, Mr Renthall. No doubt you understand what you're doing.'

After he had gone Renthall drew the blinds over the window and lay down on his bed; for the next hour he made an effort to relax.

His final showdown with the Council was to take place the following day. Summoned to an emergency meeting of the Watch Committee, he accepted the invitation with alacrity, certain that with every member of the committee present the main council chamber would be used. This would give him a perfect opportunity to humiliate the Council by publicly calling their bluff.

Both Hanson and Mrs Osmond assumed that he would capitulate without argument.

'Well, Charles, you brought it upon yourself,' Hanson told him. 'Still, I expect they'll be lenient with you. It's a matter of face now.'

'More than that, I hope,' Renthall replied. 'They claim they were passing on a direct instruction from the watch-towers.'

'Well, yes . . .' Hanson gestured vaguely. 'Of course. Obviously the towers wouldn't intervene in such a trivial matter. They rely on the Council to keep a watching brief for them, as long as the Council's authority is respected they're prepared to remain aloof.'

'It sounds an ideally simple arrangement. How do you think the communication between the Council and the watch-towers takes place?' Renthall pointed to the watch-tower across the street from the cabin. The shuttered observation tier hung emptily in the air like an out-of-season gondola. 'By telephone? Or do they semaphore?'

But Hanson merely laughed and changed the subject.

Julia Osmond was equally vague, but equally convinced of the Council's infallibility.

'Of course they receive instructions from the towers, Charles. But don't worry, they obviously have a sense of proportion – they've been letting you come here all this time.' She turned a monitory finger at Renthall, her broad-hipped bulk obscuring the towers from him. 'That's your chief fault, Charles. You think you're more important than you are. Look at you now, sitting there all hunched up with your face like an old shoe. You think the Council and the watch-towers are going to give you some terrible punishment. But they won't, because you're not worth it.'

Renthall picked uneagerly at his lunch at the hotel, conscious of the guests watching from the tables around him. Many had brought visitors with them, and he guessed that there would be a full attendance at the meeting that afternoon.

After lunch he retired to his room, made a desultory attempt to read until the meeting at half past two. Outside, the watch-towers hung in their long lines from the bright haze. There was no sign of movement in the observation windows, and Renthall studied them openly, hands in pockets, like a general surveying the dispositions of his enemy's forces. The haze was lower than usual, filling the interstices between the towers, so that in the distance, where the free space below their tips was hidden by the intervening roof-tops, the towers seemed to rise upwards into the air like rectangular chimneys over an industrial landscape, wreathed in white smoke.

The nearest tower was about seventy-five feet away, diagonally to his left, over the eastern end of the open garden shared by the other hotels in the crescent. Just as Renthall turned away, one of the windows in the observation deck appeared to open, the opaque glass pane throwing a spear of sharp sunlight directly towards him. Renthall flinched back, heart suddenly surging, then leaned forward again. The activity in the tower had subsided as instantly as it had arisen. The windows were sealed, no signs of movement behind them. Renthall listened to the sounds from the rooms above and below him. So conspicuous a motion of the window, the first sign of activity for many days, and a certain indication of more to come, should have brought a concerted rush to the balconies. But the hotel was silent, and below he could hear Dr Clifton at his cages by the window, humming absently to himself.

Renthall scanned the windows on the other side of the garden but the lines of craning faces he expected were absent. He examined the watch-tower carefully, assuming that he had seen a window open in a hotel near by. Yet the explanation dissatisfied him. The ray of sunlight had cleft the air like a silver blade, with a curious luminous intensity that only the windows of the watch-towers seemed able to reflect, aimed unerringly at his head.

He broke off to glance at his watch, cursed when he saw that it was after a quarter past two. The Town Hall was a good half-mile away, and he would arrive dishevelled and perspiring.

There was a knock on his door. He opened it to find Mulvaney. 'What is it? I'm busy now.'

'Sorry, Mr Renthall. A man called Barnes from the Council asked me to give you an urgent message. He said the meeting this afternoon has been postponed.'

'Ha!' Leaving the door open, Renthall snapped his fingers contemptuously at the air. 'So they've had second thoughts after all. Discretion is the better part of valour.' Smiling broadly, he called Mulvaney back into his room. 'Mr Mulvaney! Just a moment!'

'Good news, Mr Renthall?'

'Excellent. I've got them on the run.' He added: 'You wait and see, the next meeting of the Watch Committee will be held in private.'

'You might be right, Mr Renthall. Some people think they have over-reached themselves a bit.'

'Really? That's rather interesting. Good.' Renthall noted this mentally, then gestured Mulvaney over to the window. 'Tell me, Mr Mulvaney, just now while you were coming up the stairs, did you notice any activity out there?'

He gestured briefly towards the tower, not wanting to draw attention to himself by pointing at it. Mulvaney gazed out over the garden, shaking his head slowly. 'Can't say I did, not more than usual. What sort of activity?'

'You know, a window opening . . .' When Mulvaney continued to shake his head, Renthall said: 'Good. Let me know if that fellow Barnes calls again.'

When Mulvaney had gone he strode up and down the room, whistling a Mozart rondo.

Over the next three days, however, the mood of elation gradually faded. To Renthall's annoyance no further date was fixed for the cancelled committee meeting. He had assumed that it would be held *in camera*, but the members must have realized that it would make little difference. Everyone would soon know that Renthall had successfully challenged their claim to be in communication with the watch-towers.

Renthall chafed at the possibility that the meeting had been postponed indefinitely. By avoiding a direct clash with Renthall the Council had cleverly side-stepped the danger before them.

Alternatively, Renthall speculated whether he had underestimated them. Perhaps they realized that the real target of his defiance was not the Council, but the watch-towers. The faint possibility — however hard he tried to dismiss it as childish fantasy the fear still persisted — that there *was* some mysterious collusion between the towers and the Council now began to grow in his mind. The fête had been cleverly conceived as an innocent gesture of defiance towards the towers, and it would be difficult to find something to take its place that would not be blatantly outrageous and stain him indelibly with the sin of hubris.

Besides, as he carefully reminded himself, he was not out to launch open rebellion. Originally he had reacted from a momentary feeling of pique, exasperated by the spectacle of the boredom and lethargy around him and the sullen fear with which everyone viewed the towers. There was no question of challenging their absolute authority – at least, not at this stage. He merely wanted to define the existential margins of their world – if they *were* caught in a trap, let them at least eat the cheese. Also, he calculated that it would take an affront of truly heroic scale to provoke any reaction from the watch-towers, and that a certain freedom by default was theirs, a small but valuable credit to their account built into the system.

In practical, existential terms this might well be considerable, so that the effective boundary between black and white, between good and evil, was drawn some distance from the theoretical boundary. This watershed was the penumbral zone where the majority of the quickening pleasures of life were to be found, and where Renthall was most at home. Mrs Osmond's villa lay well within its territory, and Renthall would have liked to move himself over its margins. First, though, he would have to assess the extent of this 'blue' shift, or moral parallax, but by cancelling the committee meeting the Council had effectively forestalled him.

As he waited for Barnes to call again a growing sense of frustration came over him. The watch-towers seemed to fill the sky, and he drew the blinds irritably. On the flat roof, two floors above, a continuous light hammering sounded all day, but he shunned the streets and no longer went to the café for his morning coffee.

Finally he climbed the stairs to the roof, through the doorway saw two carpenters working under Mulvaney's supervision. They were laying a rough board floor over the tarred cement. As he shielded his eyes from the bright glare a third man came up the stairs behind him, carrying two sections of wooden railing.

'Sorry about the noise, Mr Renthall,' Mulvaney apologized. 'We should be finished by tomorrow.'

'What's going on?' Renthall asked. 'Surely you're not putting a sun garden here.'

'That's the idea.' Mulvaney pointed to the railings. 'A few chairs and umbrellas, be pleasant for the old folk. Dr Clifton suggested it.' He peered down at Renthall, who was still hiding in the doorway. 'You'll have to bring a chair up here yourself, you look as if you could use a little sunshine.'

Renthall raised his eyes to the watch-tower almost directly over their heads. A pebble tossed underhand would easily have rebounded off the corrugated metal underside. The roof was completely exposed to the score of watch-towers hanging in the air around them, and he wondered whether Mulvaney was out of his mind – none of the old people would sit there for more than a second.

Mulvaney pointed to a roof-top on the other side of the garden, where similar activity was taking place. A bright yellow awning was being unfurled, and two seats were already occupied.

Renthall hesitated, lowering his voice. 'But what about the watch-towers?'

'The what –?' Distracted by one of the carpenters, Mulvaney turned away for a moment, then rejoined him. 'Yes, you'll be able to watch everything going on from up here, Mr Renthall.'

Puzzled, Renthall made his way back to his room. Had Mulvaney misheard his question, or was this a fatuous attempt to provoke the towers? Renthall grimly visualized his responsibility if a whole series of petty acts of defiance took place. Perhaps he had accidentally tapped all the repressed resentment that had been accumulating for years?

To Renthall's amazement, a succession of creaking ascents of the staircase the next morning announced the first party of residents to use the sun deck. Just before lunch Renthall went up to the roof, found a group of at least a dozen of the older guests sitting out below the watch-tower, placidly inhaling the cool air. None of them seemed in the least perturbed by the tower. At two or three points around the crescent sun-bathers had emerged, as if answering some deep latent call. People sat on makeshift porches or leaned from the sills, calling to each other.

Equally surprising was the failure of this upsurge of activity to be followed by any reaction from the watch-towers. Half-hidden behind his blinds, Renthall scrutinized the towers carefully, once caught what seemed to be a distant flicker of movement from an observation window half a mile away, but otherwise the towers remained silent, their long ranks receding to the horizon in all directions, motionless and enigmatic. The haze had thinned slightly, and the long shafts protruded further from the sky, their outlines darker and more vibrant.

Shortly before lunch Hanson interrupted his scrutiny. 'Hello, Charles. Great news! The school opens tomorrow. Thank heaven for that, I was getting so bored I could hardly stand up straight.'

Renthall nodded. 'Good. What's galvanized them into life so suddenly?'

'Oh, I don't know. I suppose they had to reopen some time. Aren't you pleased?'

'Of course. Am I still on the staff?'

'Naturally. The Council doesn't bear childish grudges. They might have sacked you a week ago, but things are different now.'

'What do you mean?'

Hanson scrutinized Renthall carefully. 'I mean the school's opened. What is the matter, Charles?'

Renthall went over to the window, his eyes roving along the lines of sun-bathers on the roofs. He waited a few seconds in case there was some sign of activity from the watch-towers.

'When's the Watch Committee going to hear my case?'

Hanson shrugged. 'They won't bother now. They know you're a tougher proposition than some of the people they've been pushing around. Forget the whole thing.'

'But I don't want to forget it. I want the hearing to take place. Damn it, I deliberately invented the whole business of the fête to force them to show their hand. Now they're furiously back-pedalling.'

'Well, what of it? Relax, they have their difficulties too.' He gave a laugh. 'You never know, they'd probably be only too glad of an invitation now.'

'They won't get one. You know, I almost feel they've outwitted me. When the fête doesn't take place everyone will assume I've given in to them.'

'But it will take place. Haven't you seen Boardman recently? He's going great guns, obviously it'll be a tremendous show. Be careful he doesn't cut you out.'

Puzzled, Renthall turned from the window. 'Do you mean Boardman's going ahead with it?'

'Of course. It looks like it anyway. He's got a big marquee over the car park, dozens of stalls, bunting everywhere.'

Renthall drove a fist into his palm. 'The man's insane!' He turned to Hanson. 'We've got to be careful, something's going on. I'm convinced the Council are just biding their time, they're deliberately letting the reins go so we'll over-reach ourselves. Have you seen all these people on the roof-tops? Sun-bathing!'

'Good idea. Isn't that what you've wanted all along?'

'Not so blatantly as this.' Renthall pointed to the nearest watch-tower. The windows were sealed, but the light reflected off them was far brighter than usual. 'Sooner or later there'll be a short, sharp reaction. That's what the Council are waiting for.'

'It's nothing to do with the Council. If people want to sit on the roof whose business is it but their own? Are you coming to lunch?'

'In a moment.' Renthall stood quietly by the window, watching Hanson closely. A possibility he had not previously envisaged crossed his mind. He searched for some method of testing it. 'Has the gong gone yet? My watch has stopped.'

Hanson glanced at his wristwatch. 'It's twelve-thirty.' He looked out through the window towards the clock tower in the distance over the Town Hall. One of Renthall's long-standing grievances against his room was that the tip of the nearby watch-tower hung directly over the clock-face, neatly obscuring it. Hanson nodded, re-setting his watch. 'Twelve-thirty-one. I'll see you in a few minutes.'

After Hanson had gone Renthall sat on the bed, his courage ebbing slowly, trying to rationalize this unforeseen development.

The next day he came across his second case.

Boardman surveyed the dingy room distastefully, puzzled by the spectacle of Renthall hunched up in his chair by the window.

'Mr Renthall, there's absolutely no question of cancelling it now. The fair's as good as started already. Anyway, what would be the point?'

'Our arrangement was that it should be a fête,' Renthall pointed out. 'You've turned it into a fun-fair, with a lot of stalls and hurdy-gurdies.'

Unruffled by Renthall's schoolmasterly manner, Boardman scoffed. 'Well, what's the difference? Anyway, my real idea is to roof it over and turn it into a permanent amusement park. The Council won't interfere. They're playing it quiet now.'

'Are they? I doubt it.' Renthall looked down into the garden. People sat about in their shirt sleeves, the women in floral dresses, evidently oblivious of the watch-towers filling the sky a hundred feet above their heads. The haze had receded still further, and at least two hundred yards of shaft were now visible. There were no signs of activity from the towers, but Renthall was convinced that this would soon begin.

'Tell me,' he asked Boardman in a clear voice. 'Aren't you frightened of the watch-towers?'

Boardman seemed puzzled. 'The what towers?' He made a spiral motion with his cigar. 'You mean the big slide? Don't worry, I'm not having one of those, nobody's got the energy to climb all those steps.'

He stuck his cigar in his mouth and ambled to the door. 'Well, so long, Mr Renthall. I'll send you an invite.'

Later that afternoon Renthall went to see Dr Clifton in his room below.

'Excuse me, Doctor,' he apologized, 'but would you mind seeing me on a professional matter?'

'Well, not here, Renthall, I'm supposed to be off-duty.' He turned from his canary cages by the window with a testy frown, then relented when he saw Renthall's intent expression. 'All right, what's the trouble?'

While Clifton washed his hands Renthall explained. 'Tell me, Doctor, is there any mechanism known to you by which the simultaneous hypnosis of large groups of people could occur? We're all familiar with theatrical displays of the hypnotist's art, but I'm thinking of a situation in which the members of an entire small community – such as the residents of the hotels around this crescent – could be induced to accept a given proposition completely conflicting with reality.'

Clifton stopped washing his hands. 'I thought you wanted to see me professionally. I'm a doctor, not a witch doctor. What are you planning now, Renthall? Last week it was a fête, now you want to hypnotize an entire neighbourhood, you'd better be careful.'

Renthall shook his head. 'It's not I who want to carry out the hypnosis, Doctor. In fact I'm afraid the operation has already taken place. I don't know whether you've noticed anything strange about your patients?'

'Nothing more than usual,' Clifton remarked dryly. He watched Renthall with increased interest. 'Who's responsible for this mass hypnosis?' When Renthall paused and then pointed a forefinger at the ceiling Clifton nodded sagely. 'I see. How sinister.'

'Exactly. I'm glad you understand, Doctor.' Renthall went over to the window, looking out at the sunshades below. He pointed to the watch-towers. 'Just to clarify a small point, Doctor. You do see the watch-towers?'

Clifton hesitated fractionally, moving imperceptibly towards his valise on the desk. Then he nodded: 'Of course.'

'Good. I'm relieved to hear it.' Renthall laughed. 'For a while I was beginning to think that I was the only one in step. Do you realize that both Hanson and Boardman can no longer see the towers? And I'm fairly certain that none of the people down there can or they wouldn't be sitting in the open. I'm convinced that this is the Council's doing, but it seems unlikely that they would have enough power –' He broke off, aware that Clifton was watching him fixedly. 'What's the matter? *Doctor!*'

Clifton quickly took his prescription pad from his valise. 'Renthall, caution is the essence of all strategy. It's important that we beware of over-hastiness. I suggest that we both rest this afternoon. Now, these will give you some sleep –'

For the first time in several days he ventured out into the street. Head down, angry for being caught out by the doctor, he drove himself along the pavement towards Mrs Osmond, determined to find at least one person who could still see the towers. The streets were more crowded than he could remember for a long time and he was forced to look upward as he swerved in and out of the ambling pedestrians. Overhead, like the assault craft from which some apocalyptic air-raid would be launched, the watch-towers hung down from the sky, framed between the twin spires of the church, blocking off a vista down the principal boulevard, yet unperceived by the afternoon strollers.

Renthall passed the café, surprised to see the terrace packed with coffee-drinkers, then saw Boardman's marquee in the cinema car park. Music was coming from a creaking wurlitzer, and the gay ribbons of the bunting fluttered in the air.

Twenty yards from Mrs Osmond's he saw her come through her front door, a large straw hat on her head.

'Charles! What are you doing here? I haven't seen you for days, I wondered what was the matter.'

Renthall took the key from her fingers and pushed it back into the lock. Closing the door behind them, he paused in the darkened hall, regaining his breath.

'Charles, what on earth is going on? Is someone after you? You look terrible, my dear. Your face –'

'Never mind my face.' Renthall collected himself, and led the way into the living room. 'Come in here, quickly.' He went over to the window and drew back the blinds, ascertained that the watch-tower over the row of houses opposite was still there.

'Sit down and relax. I'm sorry to rush in like this but you'll understand in a minute.' He waited until Mrs Osmond settled herself reluctantly on the sofa, then rested his palms on the mantelpiece, organizing his thoughts.

'The last few days have been fantastic, you wouldn't believe it, and to cap everything I've just made myself look the biggest possible fool in front of Clifton. God, I could –'

'Charles –!'

'*Listen!* Don't start interrupting me before I've begun, I've got enough to contend with. Something absolutely insane is going on everywhere, by some freak I seem to be the only one who's still *compos mentis*. I know that sounds as if I'm completely mad, but in fact it's true. Why, I don't know; though I'm frightened it may be some sort of reprisal directed at me. However.' He went over to the window. 'Julia, what can you see out of that window?'

Mrs Osmond dismantled her hat and squinted at the panes. She fidgeted uncomfortably. 'Charles, what is going on? – I'll have to get my glasses.' She subsided helplessly.

'Julia! You've never needed your glasses before to see these. Now tell me, what can you see?'

'Well, the row of houses, and the gardens ...'

'Yes, what else?'

'The windows, of course, and there's a tree ...'

'What about the sky?'

She nodded. 'Yes, I can see that, there's a sort of haze, isn't there? Or is that my eyes?'

'No.' Wearily, Renthall turned away from the window. For the first time a feeling of unassuageable fatigue had come over him. 'Julia,' he asked quietly. 'Don't you remember the watch-towers?'

She shook her head slowly. 'No, I don't. Where were they?' A look of concern came over her face. She took his arm gently. 'Dear, what is going on?'

Renthall forced himself to stand upright. 'I don't know.' He drummed his forehead with his free hand. 'You can't remember the towers at all, or the observation windows?' He pointed to the watch-tower hanging down the centre of the window. 'There –

used to be one over those houses. We were always looking at it. Do you remember how we used to draw the curtains upstairs?'

'Charles! Be careful, people will hear. Where are you going?'

Numbly, Renthall pulled back the door. 'Outside,' he said in a flat voice. 'There's little point now in staying indoors.'

He let himself through the front door, fifty yards from the house heard her call after him, turned quickly into a side road and hurried towards the first intersection.

Above him he was conscious of the watch-towers hanging in the bright air, but he kept his eyes level with the gates and hedges, scanning the empty houses. Now and then he passed one that was occupied, the family sitting out on the lawn, and once someone called his name, reminding him that the school had started without him. The air was fresh and crisp, the light glimmering off the pavements with an unusual intensity.

Within ten minutes he realized that he had wandered into an unfamiliar part of the town and completely lost himself, with only the aerial lines of watch-towers to guide him, but he still refused to look up at them.

He had entered a poorer quarter of the town, where the narrow empty streets were separated by large waste dumps, and tilting wooden fences sagged between ruined houses. Many of the dwellings were only a single storey high, and the sky seemed even wider and more open, the distant watch-towers along the horizon like a continuous palisade.

He twisted his foot on a ledge of stone, and hobbled painfully towards a strip of broken fencing that straddled a small rise in the centre of the waste dump. He was perspiring heavily, and loosened his tie, then searched the surrounding straggle of houses for a way back into the streets through which he had come.

Overhead, something moved and caught his eye. Forcing himself to ignore it, Renthall regained his breath, trying to master the curious dizziness that touched his brain. An immense sudden silence hung over the waste ground, so absolute that it was as if some inaudible piercing music was being played at full volume.

To his right, at the edge of the waste ground, he heard feet shuffle slowly across the rubble, and saw the elderly man in the shabby black suit and wing collar who usually loitered outside the Public Library. He hobbled along, hands in pockets, an almost Chaplinesque figure, his weak eyes now and then feebly scanning the sky as if he were searching for something he had lost or forgotten.

Renthall watched him cross the waste ground, but before he could shout the decrepit figure tottered away behind a ruined wall.

Again something moved above him, followed by a third sharp angular motion, and then a succession of rapid shuttles. The stony rubbish at his feet flickered with the reflected light, and abruptly the whole sky sparkled as if the air was opening and shutting.

Then, as suddenly, everything was motionless again.

Composing himself, Renthall waited for a last moment. Then he raised his face to the nearest watch-tower fifty feet above him, and gazed across at the hundreds of towers that hung from the clear sky like giant pillars. The haze had vanished and the shafts of the towers were defined with unprecedented clarity.

As far as he could see, all the observation windows were open. Silently, without moving, the watchers stared down at him.

1962

THE SINGING STATUES

Again last night, as the dusk air began to move across the desert from Lagoon West, I heard fragments of music coming in on the thermal rollers, remote and fleeting, echoes of the love-song of Lunora Goalen. Walking out over the copper sand to the reefs where the sonic sculptures grow, I wandered through the darkness among the metal gardens, searching for Lunora's voice. No one tends the sculptures now and most of them have gone to seed, but on an impulse I cut away a helix and carried it back to my villa, planting it in the quartz bed below the balcony. All night it sang to me, telling me of Lunora and the strange music she played to herself ...

It must be just over three years ago that I first saw Lunora Goalen, in Georg Nevers's gallery on Beach Drive. Every summer at the height of the season at Vermilion Sands, Georg staged a special exhibition of sonic sculpture for the tourists. Shortly after we opened one morning I was sitting inside my large statue, *Zero Orbit*, plugging in the stereo amplifiers, when Georg suddenly gasped into the skin mike and a boom like a thunderclap nearly deafened me.

Head ringing like a gong, I climbed out of the sculpture ready to crown Georg with a nearby maquette. Putting an elegant fingertip to his lips, he gave me that look which between artist and dealer signals one thing: *Rich client.*

The sculptures in the gallery entrance had begun to hum as someone came in, but the sunlight reflected off the bonnet of a white Rolls-Royce outside obscured the doorway.

Then I saw her, hovering over the stand of art journals,

followed by her secretary, a tall purse-mouthed Frenchwoman almost as famous from the news magazines as her mistress.

Lunora Goalen, I thought, can *all* our dreams come true? She wore an ice-cool sliver of blue silk that shimmered as she moved towards the first statue, a toque hat of black violets and bulky dark glasses that hid her face and were a nightmare to cameramen. While she paused by the statue, one of Arch Penko's frenetic tangles that looked like a rimless bicycle wheel, listening to its arms vibrate and howl, Nevers and I involuntarily steadied ourselves against the wing-piece of my sculpture.

In general it's probably true that the most maligned species on Earth is the wealthy patron of modern art. Laughed at by the public, exploited by dealers, even the artists regard them simply as meal tickets. Lunora Goalen's superb collection of sonic sculpture on the roof of her Venice palazzo, and the million dollars' worth of generous purchases spread around her apartments in Paris, London and New York, represented freedom and life to a score of sculptors, but few felt any gratitude towards Miss Goalen.

Nevers was hesitating, apparently suffering from a sudden intention tremor, so I nudged his elbow.

'Come on,' I murmured. 'This is the apocalypse. Let's go.'

Nevers turned on me icily, noticing, apparently for the first time, my rust-stained slacks and three-day stubble.

'Milton!' he snapped. 'For God's sake, vanish! Sneak out through the freight exit.' He jerked his head at my sculpture. 'And switch that insane thing off! How did I ever let it in here?'

Lunora's secretary, Mme Charcot, spotted us at the rear of the gallery. Georg shot out four inches of immaculate cuff and swayed forward, the smile on his face as wide as a bulldozer. I backed away behind my sculpture, with no intention of leaving and letting Nevers cut my price just for the cachet of making a sale to Lunora Goalen.

Georg was bowing all over the gallery, oblivious of Mme Charcot's contemptuous sneer. He led Lunora over to one of the exhibits and fumbled with the control panel, selecting the alto lift which would resonate most flatteringly with her own body tones. Unfortunately the statue was Sigismund Lubitsch's *Big End*, a squat bull-necked drum like an enormous toad that at its sweetest emitted a rasping grunt. An old-style railroad tycoon might have elicited a sympathetic chord from it, but its response to Lunora was like a bull's to a butterfly.

They moved on to another sculpture, and Mme Charcot gestured to the white-gloved chauffeur standing by the Rolls. He climbed in and moved the car down the street, taking with it the beach crowds beginning to gather outside the gallery. Able now to see Lunora clearly against the hard white walls, I stepped into *Orbit* and watched her closely through the helixes.

Of course I already knew everything about Lunora Goalen. A thousand magazine exposés had catalogued *ad nauseam* her strange flawed beauty, her fits of melancholy and compulsive roving around the world's capitals. Her brief career as a film actress had faltered at first, less as a consequence of her modest, though always interesting, talents than of her simple failure to register photogenically. By a macabre twist of fate, after a major car accident had severely injured her face she had become an extraordinary success. That strangely marred profile and nervous gaze had filled cinemas from Paris to Pernambuco. Unable to bear this tribute to her plastic surgeons, Lunora had abruptly abandoned her career and become a leading patron of the fine arts. Like Garbo in the '40s and '50s, she flitted elusively through the gossip columns and society pages in unending flight from herself.

Her face was the clue. As she took off her sunglasses I could see the curious shadow that fell across it, numbing the smooth white skin. There was a dead glaze in her slate-blue eyes, an uneasy tension around the mouth. Altogether I had a vague impression of something unhealthy, of a Venus with a secret vice.

Nevers was switching on sculptures right and left like a lunatic magician, and the noise was a babel of competing senso-cells, some of the statues responding to Lunora's enigmatic presence, others to Nevers and the secretary.

*   *   *

Lunora shook her head slowly, mouth hardening as the noise irritated her. 'Yes, Mr Nevers,' she said in her slightly husky voice, 'it's all very clever, but a bit of a headache. I *live* with my sculpture, I want something intimate and personal.'

'Of course, Miss Goalen,' Nevers agreed hurriedly, looking around desperately. As he knew only too well, sonic sculpture was now nearing the apogee of its abstract phase; twelve-tone blips and zooms were all that most statues emitted. No purely representational sound, responding to Lunora, for example, with a Mozart rondo or (better) a Webern quartet, had been built for ten years. I guessed that her early purchases were wearing out and that she was hunting the cheaper galleries in tourist haunts like Vermilion Sands in the hope of finding something designed for middle-brow consumption.

Lunora looked up pensively at *Zero Orbit*, towering at the rear of the gallery next to Nevers's desk, apparently unaware that I was hiding inside it. Suddenly realizing that the possibility of selling the statue had miraculously arisen, I crouched inside the trunk and started to breathe heavily, activating the senso-circuits.

Immediately the statue came to life. About twelve feet high, it was shaped like an enormous metal totem topped by two heraldic wings. The microphones in the wing-tips were powerful enough to pick up respiratory noises at a distance of twenty feet. There were four people well within focus, and the statue began to emit a series of low rhythmic pulses.

Seeing the statue respond to her, Lunora came forwards with interest. Nevers backed away discreetly, taking Mme Charcot with him, leaving Lunora and I together, separated by a thin metal skin and three feet of vibrating air. Fumbling for some way of widening the responses, I eased up the control slides that lifted the volume. Neurophonics has never been my strong suit – I regard myself, in an old-fashioned way, as a sculptor, not an electrician – and the statue was only equipped to play back a simple sequence of chord variations on the sonic profile in focus.

Knowing that Lunora would soon realize that the statue's repertory was too limited for her, I picked up the hand-mike used for testing the circuits and on the spur of the moment began to croon the refrain from Creole Love Call. Reinterpreted by the sonic cores, and then relayed through the loudspeakers, the lulling rise and fall was pleasantly soothing, the electronic overtones disguising my voice and amplifying the tremors of emotion as I screwed up my courage (the statue was priced at five thousand dollars – even subtracting Nevers's 90 per cent commission left me with enough for the bus fare home).

Stepping up to the statue, Lunora listened to it motionlessly, eyes wide with astonishment, apparently assuming that it was reflecting, like a mirror, its subjective impressions of herself. Rapidly running out of breath, my speeding pulse lifting the tempo, I repeated the refrain over and over again, varying the bass lift to simulate a climax.

Suddenly I saw Nevers's black patent shoes through the hatch. Pretending to slip his hand into the control panel, he rapped sharply on the statue. I switched off.

'Don't please!' Lunora cried as the sounds fell away. She looked around uncertainly. Mme Charcot was stepping nearer with a curiously watchful expression.

Nevers hesitated. 'Of course, Miss Goalen, it still requires tuning, you –'

'I'll take it,' Lunora said. She pushed on her sunglasses, turned and hurried from the gallery, her face hidden.

Nevers watched her go. 'What happened, for heaven's sake? Is Miss Goalen all right?'

Mme Charcot took a cheque-book out of her blue crocodile handbag. A sardonic smirk played over her lips, and through the helix I had a brief but penetrating glimpse into her relationship with Lunora Goalen. It was then, I think, that I realized Lunora might be something more than a bored dilettante.

Mme Charcot glanced at her watch, a gold pea strung on her scrawny wrist. 'You will have it delivered today. By three o'clock sharp. Now, please, the price?'

Smoothly, Nevers said: 'Ten thousand dollars.'

Choking, I pulled myself out of the statue, and spluttered helplessly at Nevers.

Mme Charcot regarded me with astonishment, frowning at my filthy togs. Nevers trod savagely on my foot. 'Naturally, Mademoiselle, our prices are modest, but as you can see, M. Milton is an inexperienced artist.'

Mme Charcot nodded sagely. 'This is the sculptor? I am relieved. For a moment I feared that he lived in it.'

When she had gone Nevers closed the gallery for the day. He took off his jacket and pulled a bottle of absinthe from the desk. Sitting back in his silk waistcoat, he trembled slightly with nervous exhaustion.

'Tell me, Milton, how can you ever be sufficiently grateful to me?'

I patted him on the back. 'Georg, you were brilliant! She's another Catherine the Great, you handled her like a diplomat. When you go to Paris you'll be a great success. Ten thousand dollars!' I did a quick jig around the statue. 'That's the sort of redistribution of wealth I like to see. How about an advance on my cut?'

Nevers examined me moodily. He was already in the Rue de Rivoli, over-bidding for Leonardos with a languid flicker of a pomaded eyebrow. He glanced at the statue and shuddered. 'An extraordinary woman. Completely without taste. Which reminds me, I see you rescored the memory drum. The aria from *Tosca* cued in beautifully. I didn't realize the statue contained that.'

'It doesn't,' I told him, sitting on the desk. 'That was me. Not exactly Caruso, I admit, but then he wasn't much of a sculptor –'

'What?' Nevers leapt out of his chair. 'Do you mean you were using the hand microphone? You *fool!*'

'What does it matter? She won't know.' Nevers was groaning against the wall, drumming his forehead on his fist. 'Relax, you'll hear nothing.'

Promptly at 9.01 the next morning the telephone rang.

As I drove the pick-up out to Lagoon West Nevers's warnings rang in my ears – '... six international blacklists, sue me for misrepresentation ...' He apologized effusively to Mme Charcot, and assured her that the monotonous booming the statue emitted was most certainly not its natural response. Obviously a circuit had been damaged in transit, the sculptor himself was driving out to correct it.

Taking the beach road around the lagoon, I looked across at the Goalen mansion, an abstract summer palace that reminded me of a Frank Lloyd Wright design for an experimental department store. Terraces jutted out at all angles, and here and there were huge metal sculptures, Brancusi's and Calder mobiles, revolving in the crisp desert light. Occasionally one of the sonic statues hooted mournfully like a distant hoodoo.

Mme Charcot collected me in the vestibule, led me up a sweeping glass stairway. The walls were heavy with Dali and Picasso, but my statue had been given the place of honour at the far end of the south terrace. The size of a tennis court, without rails (or safety net), this jutted out over the lagoon against the skyline of Vermilion Sands, low furniture grouped in a square at its centre.

Dropping the tool-bag, I made a pretence of dismantling the control panel, and played with the amplifier so that the statue let out a series of staccato blips. These put it into the same category as the rest of Lunora Goalen's sculpture. A dozen pieces stood about on the terrace, most of them early period sonic dating back to the '70s, when sculptors produced an incredible sequence of grunting, clanking, barking and twanging statues, and galleries and public squares all over the world echoed night and day with minatory booms and thuds.

'Any luck?'

I turned to see Lunora Goalen. Unheard, she had crossed the terrace, now stood with hands on hips, watching me with interest. In her black slacks and shirt, blonde hair around her shoulders, she looked more relaxed, but sunglasses still masked her face.

'Just a loose valve. It won't take me a couple of minutes.' I gave her a reassuring smile and she stretched out on the chaise longue in front of the statue. Lurking by the french windows at the far end of the terrace was Mme Charcot, eyeing us with a beady smirk. Irritated, I switched on the statue to full volume and coughed loudly into the hand-mike.

The sound boomed across the open terrace like an artillery blank. The old crone backed away quickly.

Lunora smiled as the echoes rolled over the desert, the statues on the lower terraces responding with muted pulses. 'Years ago, when Father was away, I used to go on to the roof and shout at the top of my voice, set off the most wonderful echo trains. The whole place would boom for hours, drive the servants mad.' She laughed pleasantly to herself at the recollection, as if it had been a long time ago.

'Try it now,' I suggested. 'Or is Mme Charcot mad already?'

Lunora put a green-tipped finger to her lips. 'Carefully, you'll get me into trouble. Anyway, Mme Charcot is not my servant.'

'No? What is she then, your jailer?' We spoke mockingly, but I put a curve on the question; something about the Frenchwoman had made me suspect that she might have more than a small part in maintaining Lunora's illusions about herself.

I waited for Lunora to reply, but she ignored me and stared out across the lagoon. Within a few seconds her personality had changed levels, once again she was the remote autocratic princess.

Unobserved, I slipped my hand into the tool-bag and drew out a tape spool. Clipping it into the player deck, I switched on the table. The statue vibrated slightly, and a low melodious chant murmured out into the still air.

Standing behind the statue, I watched Lunora respond to the music. The sounds mounted, steadily swelling as Lunora moved into the statue's focus. Gradually its rhythms quickened, its mood urgent and plaintive, unmistakably a lover's passion-song. A musicologist would have quickly identified the sounds as a transcription of the balcony duet from *Romeo and Juliet*, but to Lunora its only source was the statue. I had recorded the tape that morning, realizing it was the only method of saving the statue. Nevers's confusion of *Tosca* and 'Creole Love Call' reminded me that I had the whole of classical opera in reserve.

For ten thousand dollars I would gladly call once a day and feed in every aria from *Figaro* to *Moses and Aaron*.

Abruptly, the music fell away. Lunora had backed out of the statue's focus, and was standing twenty feet from me. Behind her, in the doorway, was Mme Charcot.

Lunora smiled briefly. 'It seems to be in perfect order,' she said. Without doubt she was gesturing me towards the door.

I hesitated, suddenly wondering whether to tell her the truth, my eyes searching her beautiful secret face. Then Mme Charcot came between us, smiling like a skull.

Did Lunora Goalen really believe that the sculpture was singing to her? For a fortnight, until the tape expired, it didn't matter. By then Nevers would have cashed the cheque and he and I would be on our way to Paris.

Within two or three days, though, I realized that I wanted to see Lunora again. Rationalizing, I told myself that the statue needed to be checked, that Lunora might discover the fraud. Twice during the next week I drove out to the summer-house on the pretext of tuning the sculpture, but Mme Charcot held me off. Once I telephoned, but again she intercepted me. When I saw Lunora she was driving at speed through Vermilion Sands in the Rolls-Royce, a dim glimmer of gold and jade in the back seat.

Finally I searched through my record albums, selected Toscanini conducting *Tristan and Isolde*, in the scene where Tristan mourns his parted lover, and carefully transcribed another tape.

That night I drove down to Lagoon West, parked my car by the beach on the south shore and walked out on to the surface of the lake. In the moonlight the summer-house half a mile away looked like an abstract movie set, a single light on the upper terrace illuminating the outlines of my statue. Stepping carefully across the fused silica, I made my way slowly towards it, fragments of the statue's song drifting by on the low breeze. Two hundred yards from the house I lay down on the warm sand, watching the lights of Vermilion Sands fade one by one like the melting jewels of a necklace.

Above, the statue sang into the blue night, its song never

wavering. Lunora must have been sitting only a few feet above it, the music enveloping her like an overflowing fountain. Shortly after two o'clock it died down and I saw her at the rail, the white ermine wrap around her shoulders stirring in the wind as she stared at the brilliant moon.

Half an hour later I climbed the lake wall and walked along it to the spiral fire escape. The bougainvillaea wreathed through the railings muffled the sounds of my feet on the metal steps. I reached the upper terrace unnoticed. Far below, in her quarters on the north side, Mme Charcot was asleep.

Swinging on to the terrace, I moved among the dark statues, drawing low murmurs from them as I passed.

I crouched inside *Zero Orbit*, unlocked the control panel and inserted the fresh tape, slightly raising the volume.

As I left I could see on to the west terrace twenty feet below, where Lunora lay asleep under the stars on an enormous velvet bed, like a lunar princess on a purple catafalque. Her face shone in the starlight, her loose hair veiling her naked breasts. Behind her a statue stood guard, intoning, softly to itself as it pulsed to the sounds of her breathing.

Three times I visited Lunora's house after midnight, taking with me another spool of tape, another love-song from my library. On the last visit I watched her sleeping until dawn rose across the desert. I fled down the stairway and across the sand, hiding among the cold pools of shadow whenever a car moved along the beach road.

All day I waited by the telephone in my villa, hoping she would call me. In the evening I walked out to the sand reefs, climbed one of the spires and watched Lunora on the terrace after dinner. She lay on a couch before the statue, and until long after midnight it played to her, endlessly singing. Its voice was now so strong that cars would slow down several hundred yards away, the drivers searching for the source of the melodies crossing the vivid evening air.

At last I recorded the final tape, for the first time in my own voice. Briefly I described the whole sequence of imposture, and quietly asked Lunora if she would sit for me and let me design a new sculpture to replace the fraud she had bought.

I clenched the tape tightly in my hand while I walked across the lake, looking up at the rectangular outline of the terrace.

As I reached the wall, a black-suited figure put his head over the ledge and looked down at me. It was Lunora's chauffeur.

Startled, I moved away across the sand. In the moonlight the chauffeur's white face flickered bonily.

The next evening, as I knew it would, the telephone finally rang.

'Mr Milton, the statue has broken down again.' Mme Charcot's voice sounded sharp and strained. 'Miss Goalen is extremely upset. You must come and repair it. Immediately.'

I waited an hour before leaving, playing through the tape I had recorded the previous evening. This time I would be present when Lunora heard it.

Mme Charcot was standing by the glass doors. I parked in the court by the Rolls. As I walked over to her, I noticed how eerie the house sounded. All over it the statues were muttering to themselves, emitting snaps and clicks, like the disturbed occupants of a zoo settling down with difficulty after a storm. Even Mme Charcot looked worn and tense.

At the terrace she paused. 'One moment, Mr Milton. I will see if Miss Goalen is ready to receive you.' She walked quietly towards the chaise longue pulled against the statue at the end of the terrace. Lunora was stretched out awkwardly across it, her hair disarrayed. She sat up irritably as Mme Charcot approached.

'Is he here? Alice, whose car was that? Hasn't he come?'

'He is preparing his equipment,' Mme Charcot told her soothingly. 'Miss Lunora, let me dress your hair –'

'Alice, don't fuss! God, what's keeping him?' She sprang up and paced over to the statue, glowering silently out of the darkness. While Mme Charcot walked away Lunora sank on her knees before the statue, pressed her right cheek to its cold surface.

Uncontrollably she began to sob, deep spasms shaking her shoulders.

'Wait, Mr Milton!' Mme Charcot held tightly to my elbow. 'She will not want to see you for a few minutes.' She added: 'You are a better sculptor than you think, Mr Milton. You have given that statue a remarkable voice. It tells her all she needs to know.'

I broke away and ran through the darkness.

'Lunora!'

She looked around, the hair over her face matted with tears. She leaned limply against the dark trunk of the statue. I knelt down and held her hands, trying to lift her to her feet.

She wrenched away from me. 'Fix it! Hurry, what are you waiting for? Make the statue sing again!'

I was certain that she no longer recognized me. I stepped back, the spool of tape in my hand. 'What's the matter with her?' I whispered to Mme Charcot. 'The sounds don't really come from the statue, surely she realizes that?'

Mme Charcot's head lifted. 'What do you mean – not from the statue?'

I showed her the tape. 'This isn't a true sonic sculpture. The music is played off these magnetic tapes.'

A chuckle rasped briefly from Mme Charcot's throat. 'Well, put it in none the less, monsieur. She doesn't care where it comes from. She is interested in the statue, not you.'

I hesitated, watching Lunora, still hunched like a supplicant at the foot of the statue.

'You mean –?' I started to say incredulously. 'So you mean she's in love with the statue?'

Mme Charcot's eyes summed up all my naivety.

'Not with the statue,' she said. 'With *herself*.'

For a moment I stood there among the murmuring sculptures, dropped the spool on the floor and turned away.

They left Lagoon West the next day.

For a week I remained at my villa, then drove along the beach road towards the summer-house one evening after Nevers told me that they had gone.

The house was closed, the statues standing motionless in the darkness. My footsteps echoed away among the balconies and terraces, and the house reared up into the sky like a tomb. All the sculptures had been switched off, and I realized how dead and monumental non-sonic sculpture must have seemed.

Zero Orbit had also gone. I assumed that Lunora had taken it with her, so immersed in her self-love that she preferred a clouded mirror which had once told her of her beauty to no mirror at all. As she sat on some penthouse veranda in Venice or Paris, with the great statue towering into the dark sky like an extinct symbol, she would hear again the lays it had sung.

Six months later Nevers commissioned another statue from me. I went out one dusk to the sand reefs where the sonic sculptures grow. As I approached, they were creaking in the wind whenever the thermal gradients cut through them. I walked up the long slopes, listening to them mewl and whine, searching for one that would serve as the sonic core for a new statue.

Somewhere ahead in the darkness, I heard a familiar phrase, a garbled fragment of a human voice. Startled, I ran on, feeling between the dark barbs and helixes.

Then, lying in a hollow below the ridge, I found the source. Half-buried under the sand like the skeleton of an extinct bird were twenty or thirty pieces of metal, the dismembered trunk and wings of my statue. Many of the pieces had taken root again and were emitting a thin haunted sound, disconnected fragments of the testament to Lunora Goalen I had dropped on her terrace.

As I walked down the slope, the white sand poured into my footprints like a succession of occluding hourglasses. The sounds of my voice whined faintly through the metal gardens like a forgotten lover whispering over a dead harp.

1962

THE MAN ON THE 99TH FLOOR

All day Forbis had been trying to reach the 100th floor. Crouched at the foot of the short stairway behind the elevator shaft, he stared up impotently at the swinging metal door on to the roof, searching for some means of dragging himself up to it. There were eleven narrow steps, and then the empty roof deck, the high grilles of the suicide barrier and the open sky. Every three minutes an airliner went over, throwing a fleeting shadow down the steps, its jets momentarily drowning the panic which jammed his mind, and each time he made another attempt to reach the doorway.

Eleven steps. He had counted them a thousand times, in the hours since he first entered the building at ten o'clock that morning and rode the elevator up to the 95th floor. He had walked the next floor – the floors were fakes, offices windowless and unserviced, tacked on merely to give the building the cachet of a full century – then waited quietly at the bottom of the final stairway, listening to the elevator cables wind and drone, hoping to calm himself. As usual, however, his pulse started to race, within two or three minutes was up to one hundred and twenty. When he stood up and reached for the hand-rail something clogged his nerve centres, caissons settled on to the bed of his brain, rooting him to the floor like a lead colossus.

Fingering the rubber cleats on the bottom step, Forbis glanced at his wristwatch. 4.20 p.m. If he wasn't careful someone would climb the stairs up to the roof and find him there – already there were half a dozen buildings around the city where he was *persona non grata*, elevator boys warned to call the house detectives if they saw him. And there were not all that many buildings with a hundred floors. That was part of his obsession. There had to be one hundred exactly.

Why? Leaning back against the wall, Forbis managed to ask himself the question. What role was he playing out, searching the city for hundred-storey skyscrapers, then performing this obsessive ritual which invariably ended in the same way, the final peak always unscaled? Perhaps it was some sort of abstract duel between himself and the architects of these monstrous piles (dimly he remembered working in a menial job below the city streets – perhaps he was rebelling and reasserting himself, the prototype of urban ant-man trying to over-topple the totem towers of Megalopolis?)

Aligning itself on the glideway, an airliner began its final approach over the city, its six huge jets blaring. As the noise hammered across him, Forbis pulled himself to his feet and lowered his head, passively letting the sounds drive down into his mind and loosen his blocked feedbacks. Lifting his right foot, he lowered it on to the first step, clasped the rail and pulled himself up two steps.

His left leg swung freely. Relief surged through him. At last he was going to reach the door! He took another step, raised his foot to the fourth, only seven from the top, then realized that his left hand was locked to the hand-rail below. He tugged at it angrily, but the fingers were clamped together like steel bands, the thumbnail biting painfully into his index tip.

He was still trying to unclasp the hand when the aircraft had gone.

Half an hour later, as the daylight began to fade, he sat down on the bottom step, with his free right hand pulled off one of his shoes and dropped it through the railing into the elevator shaft.

Vansittart put the hypodermic away in his valise, watching Forbis thoughtfully.

'You're lucky you didn't kill anyone,' he said. 'The elevator cabin was thirty storeys down, your shoe went through the roof like a bomb.'

Forbis shrugged vaguely, letting himself relax on the couch.

The Psychology Department was almost silent, the last of the lights going out in the corridor as the staff left the medical school on their way home. 'I'm sorry, but there was no other way of attracting attention. I was fastened to the stair-rail like a dying limpet. How did you calm the manager down?'

Vansittart sat on the edge of his desk, turning away the lamp.

'It wasn't easy. Luckily Professor Bauer was still in his office and he cleared me over the phone. A week from now, though, he retires. Next time I may not be able to bluff my way through. I think we'll have to take a more direct line. The police won't be so patient with you.'

'I know. I'm afraid of that. But if I can't go on trying my brain will fuse. Didn't you get any clues at all?'

Vansittart murmured noncommittally. In fact the events had followed exactly the same pattern as on the three previous occasions. Again the attempt to reach the open roof had failed, and again there was no explanation for Forbis's compulsive drive. Vansittart had first seen him only a month earlier, wandering about blankly on the observation roof of the new administration building at the medical school. How he had gained access to the roof Vansittart had never discovered. Luckily one of the janitors had telephoned him that a man was behaving suspiciously on the roof, and Vansittart had reached him just before the suicide attempt.

At least, that was what it appeared to be. Vansittart examined the little man's placid grey features, his small shoulders and thin hands. There was something anonymous about him. He was minimal urban man, as near a nonentity as possible, without friends or family, a vague background of forgotten jobs and rooming houses. The sort of lonely, helpless man who might easily, in an unthinking act of despair, try to throw himself off a roof.

Yet there was something that puzzled Vansittart. Strictly, as a member of the university teaching staff, he should not have prescribed any treatment for Forbis and instead should have handed him over promptly to the police surgeon at the nearest station. But a curious nagging suspicion about Forbis had prevented him from doing so. Later, when he began to analyse Forbis, he found that his personality, or what there was of it, seemed remarkably well integrated, and that he had a realistic, pragmatic approach towards life which was completely unlike the over-compensated self-pity of most would-be suicides.

Nevertheless, he was driven by an insane compulsion, this apparently motiveless impulse to the 100th floor. Despite all Vansittart's probings and tranquillizers Forbis had twice set off for the down-town sector of the city, picked a skyscraper and trapped himself in his eyrie on the 99th floor, on both occasions finally being rescued by Vansittart.

Deciding to play a hunch, Vansittart asked: 'Forbis, have you ever experimented with hypnosis?'

Forbis shifted himself drowsily, then shook his head. 'Not as far as I can remember. Are you hinting that someone has given me a post-hypnotic suggestion, trying to make me throw myself off a roof?'

That was quick of you, Vansittart thought. 'Why do you say that?' he asked.

'I don't know. But who would try? And what would be the point?' He peered up at Vansittart. 'Do you think someone did?'

Vansittart nodded. 'Oh yes. There's no doubt about it.' He sat forward, swinging the lamp around for emphasis. 'Listen, Forbis, some time ago, I can't be sure how long, three months, perhaps six, someone planted a really powerful post-hypnotic command in your mind. The first part of it – "*Go up to the 100th floor*" – I've been able to uncover, but the rest is still buried. It's that half of the command which worries me. One doesn't need a morbid imagination to guess what it probably is.'

Forbis moistened his lips, shielding his eyes from the glare of the lamp. He felt too sluggish to be alarmed by what Vansittart had just said. Despite the doctor's frank admission of failure, and his deliberate but rather nervous manner, he trusted Vansittart, and was confident he would find a solution. 'It sounds insane,' he commented. 'But who would want to kill me? Can't you cancel the whole thing out, erase the command?'

'I've tried to, but without any success. I've been getting nowhere. It's still as strong as ever – stronger, in fact, almost as if it were being reinforced. Where have you been during the last week? Who have you seen?'

Forbis shrugged, sitting up on one elbow. 'No one. As far as I can remember, I've only been on the 99th floor.' He searched the air dismally, then gave up. 'You know, I can't remember a single thing, just vague outlines of cafés and bus depots, it's strange.'

'A pity. I'd try to keep an eye on you, but I can't spare the time. Bauer's retirement hadn't been expected for another year, there's a tremendous amount of reorganization to be done.' He drummed his fingers irritably on the desk. 'I noticed you've still got some cash with you. Have you had a job?'

'I think so – in the subway, perhaps. Or did I just take a train ... ?' Forbis frowned with the effort of recollection. 'I'm sorry, Doctor. Anyway, I've always heard that post-hypnotic suggestions couldn't compel you to do anything that clashed with your basic personality.'

'What is the basic personality, though? A skilful analyst can manipulate the psyche to suit the suggestion, magnify a small streak of self-destruction until it cleaves the entire personality like an axe splitting a log.'

Forbis pondered this gloomily for a few moments, then brightened slightly. 'Well, I seem to have the suggestion beaten. Whatever happens, I can't actually reach the roof, so I must have enough strength to fight it.'

Vansittart shook his head. 'As a matter of fact, you haven't. It's not you who's keeping yourself off the roof, it's *me*.'

'What do you mean?'

'I implanted another hypnotic suggestion, holding you on the 99th floor. When I uncovered the first suggestion I tried to erase it, found I wasn't even scratching the surface, so just as a precaution I inserted a second of my own. "*Get off at the 99th floor.*" How long it will hold you there I don't know, but already it's fading.

Today it took you over seven hours to call me. Next time you may get up enough steam to hit the roof. That's why I think we should take a new line, really get to the bottom of this obsession, or rather' – he smiled ruefully – 'to the top.'

Forbis sat up slowly, massaging his face. 'What do you suggest?'

'We'll let you reach the roof. I'll erase my secondary command and we'll see what happens when you step out on to the top deck. Don't worry, I'll be with you if anything goes wrong. It may seem pretty thin consolation, but frankly, Forbis, it would be so easy to kill you and get away with it that I can't understand anyone bothering to go to all this trouble. Obviously there's some deeper motive, something connected, perhaps, with the 100th floor.' Vansittart paused, watching Forbis carefully, then asked in a casual voice: 'Tell me, have you ever heard of anyone called Fowler?'

He said nothing when Forbis shook his head, but privately noted the reflex pause of unconscious recognition.

'All right?' Vansittart asked as they reached the bottom of the final stairway.

'Fine,' Forbis said quietly, catching his breath. He looked up at the rectangular opening above them, wondering how he would feel when he finally reached the roof-top. They had sneaked into the building by one of the service entrances at the rear, and then taken a freight elevator to the 80th floor.

'Let's go, then,' Vansittart walked on ahead, beckoning Forbis after him. Together they climbed up to the final doorway, and stepped out into the bright sunlight.

'Doctor ...!' Forbis exclaimed happily. He felt fresh and exhilarated, his mind clear and unburdened at last. He gazed around the small flat roof, a thousand ideas tumbling past each other in his mind like the crystal fragments of a mountain stream. Somewhere below, however, a deeper current tugged at him.

Go up to the 100th floor and ...

Around him lay the roof-tops of the city, and half a mile away, hidden by the haze, was the spire of the building he had tried to scale the previous day. He strolled about the roof, letting the cool air clear the sweat from his face. There were no suicide grilles around the balcony, but their absence caused him no anxiety.

Vansittart was watching him carefully, black valise in one hand. He nodded encouragingly, then gestured Forbis toward the balcony, eager to rest the valise on the ledge.

'Feel anything?'

'Nothing.' Forbis laughed, a brittle chuckle. 'It must have been one of those impractical jokes – "*Now let's see you get down.*" Can I look into the street?'

'Of course,' Vansittart agreed, bracing himself to seize Forbis if the little man attempted to jump. Beyond the balcony was a thousand-foot drop into a busy shopping thoroughfare.

Forbis clasped the near edge of the balcony in his palms and peered down at the lunch crowds below. Cars edged and shunted like coloured fleas, and people milled about aimlessly on the pavements. Nothing of any interest seemed to be happening.

Beside him, Vansittart frowned and glanced at his watch, wondering whether something had misfired. 'It's 12.30,' he said. 'We'll give up –'

He broke off as footsteps creaked on the stairway below. He swung around and watched the doorway, gesturing to Forbis to keep quiet.

As he turned his back the small man suddenly reached up and cut him sharply across the neck with the edge of his right hand, stunning him momentarily. When Vansittart staggered back he expertly chopped him on both sides of the throat, then sat him down and kicked him senseless with his knees.

Working swiftly, he ignored the broad shadow which reached across the roof to him from the doorway. He carefully fastened Vansittart's three jacket buttons, and then levered him up by the lapels on to his shoulder. Backing against the balcony, he slid him on to the ledge, straightening his legs one after the other. Vansittart stirred helplessly, head lolling from side to side.

And ... and ...

Behind Forbis the shadow drew nearer, reaching up the side

of the balcony, a broad neckless head between heavy shoulders.

Cutting off his pumping breath, Forbis reached out with both hands and pushed.

Ten seconds later, as horns sounded up dimly from the street below, he turned around.

'Good boy, Forbis.'

The big man's voice was flat but relaxed. Ten feet from Forbis, he watched him amiably. His face was plump and sallow, a callous mouth half-hidden by a brush moustache. He wore a bulky black overcoat, and one hand rested confidently in a deep pocket.

'Fowler!' Involuntarily, Forbis tried to move forward, for a moment attempting to reassemble his perspectives, but his feet had locked into the white surface of the roof.

Three hundred feet above, an airliner roared over. In a lucid interval provided by the noise, Forbis recognized Fowler, Vansittart's rival for the psychology professorship, remembered the long sessions of hypnosis after Fowler had picked him up in a bar three months earlier, offering to cure his chronic depression before it slid into alcoholism.

With a grasp, he remembered too the rest of the buried command. So Vansittart had been the real target, not himself! *Go up to the 100th floor and* ... His first attempt at Vansittart had been a month earlier, when Fowler had left him on the roof and then pretended to be the janitor, but Vansittart had brought two others with him. The mysterious hidden command had been the bait to lure Vansittart to the roof again. Cunningly, Fowler had known that sooner or later Vansittart would yield to the temptation.

'And ...' he said aloud.

Looking for Vansittart, in the absurd hope that he might have survived the thousand-foot fall, he started for the balcony, then tried to hold himself back as the current caught him.

'*And –?*' Fowler repeated pleasantly. His eyes, two festering points of light, made Forbis sway. 'There's still some more to come, isn't there, Forbis? You're beginning to remember it now.'

Mind draining, Forbis turned to the balcony, dry mouth sucking at the air.

'And –?' Fowler snapped, his voice harder.

... And ... and ...

Numbly, Forbis jumped up on to the balcony, and poised on the narrow ledge like a diver, the streets swaying before his eyes. Below, the horns were silent again and the traffic had resumed its flow, a knot of vehicles drawn up in the centre of a small crowd by the edge of the pavement. For a few moments he managed to resist, and then the current caught him, toppling him like a drifting spar.

Fowler stepped quietly through the doorway. Ten seconds later, the horns sounded again.

1962

THE SUBLIMINAL MAN

'The signs, Doctor! Have you seen the signs?'

Frowning with annoyance, Dr Franklin quickened his pace and hurried down the hospital steps towards the line of parked cars. Over his shoulder he caught a glimpse of a young man in ragged sandals and paint-stained jeans waving to him from the far side of the drive.

'Dr Franklin! The signs!'

Head down, Franklin swerved around an elderly couple approaching the out-patients department. His car was over a hundred yards away. Too tired to start running himself, he waited for the young man to catch him up.

'All right, Hathaway, what is it this time?' he snapped. 'I'm sick of you hanging around here all day.'

Hathaway lurched to a halt in front of him, uncut black hair like an awning over his eyes. He brushed it back with a claw-like hand and turned on a wild smile, obviously glad to see Franklin and oblivious of the latter's hostility.

'I've been trying to reach you at night, Doctor, but your wife always puts the phone down on me,' he explained without a hint of rancour, as if well-used to this kind of snub. 'And I didn't want to look for you inside the Clinic.' They were standing by a privet hedge that shielded them from the lower windows of the main administrative block, but Franklin's regular rendezvous with Hathaway and his strange messianic cries had already become the subject of amused comment.

Franklin began to say: 'I appreciate that –' but Hathaway brushed this aside. 'Forget it, Doctor, there are more important things now. They've started to build the first big signs! Over a hundred feet high, on the traffic islands outside town. They'll soon have all the approach roads covered. When they do we might as well stop thinking.'

'Your trouble is that you're thinking too much,' Franklin told him. 'You've been rambling about these signs for weeks now. Tell me, have you actually seen one signalling?'

Hathaway tore a handful of leaves from the hedge, exasperated by this irrelevancy. 'Of course I haven't, that's the whole point, Doctor.' He dropped his voice as a group of nurses walked past, watching his raffish figure out of the corners of their eyes. 'The construction gangs were out again last night, laying huge power cables. You'll see them on the way home. Everything's nearly ready now.'

'They're traffic signs,' Franklin explained patiently. 'The flyover has just been completed. Hathaway, for God's sake, relax. Try to think of Dora and the child.'

'I *am* thinking of them!' Hathaway's voice rose to a controlled scream. 'Those cables were 40,000-volt lines, Doctor, with terrific switch-gear. The trucks were loaded with enormous metal scaffolds. Tomorrow they'll start lifting them up all over the city, they'll block off half the sky! What do you think Dora will be like after six months of that? We've got to stop them, Doctor, they're trying to transistorize our brains!'

Embarrassed by Hathaway's high-pitched shouting, Franklin had momentarily lost his sense of direction. Helplessly he searched the sea of cars for his own. 'Hathaway, I can't waste any more time talking to you. Believe me, you need skilled help, these obsessions are beginning to master you.'

Hathaway started to protest, and Franklin raised his right hand firmly. 'Listen. For the last time, if you can show me one of these signs, and prove it's transmitting subliminal commands, I'll go to the police with you. But you haven't got a shred of evidence, and you know it. Subliminal advertising was banned thirty years ago, and the laws have never been repealed. Anyway, the technique was unsatisfactory, any success it had was marginal. Your idea of a huge conspiracy with all these thousands of giant signs everywhere is preposterous.'

'All right, Doctor.' Hathaway leaned against the bonnet of one of the cars. His mood seemed to switch abruptly from one level to the next. He watched Franklin amiably. 'What's the matter — lost your car?'

'All your damned shouting has confused me.' Franklin pulled out his ignition key and read the number off the tag: 'NYN 299-566-367-21 — can you see it?'

Hathaway leaned around lazily, one sandal up on the bonnet, surveying the square of a thousand or so cars facing them. 'Difficult, isn't it, when they're all identical, even the same colour? Thirty years ago there were about ten different makes, each in a dozen colours.'

Franklin spotted his car and began to walk towards it. 'Sixty years ago there were a hundred makes. What of it? The economies of standardization are obviously bought at a price.'

Hathaway drummed his palm on the roofs. 'But these cars aren't all that cheap, Doctor. In fact, comparing them on an average income basis with those of thirty years ago they're about forty per cent more expensive. With only one make being produced you'd expect a substantial reduction in price, not an increase.'

'Maybe,' Franklin said, opening his door. 'But mechanically the cars of today are far more sophisticated. They're lighter, more durable, safer to drive.'

Hathaway shook his head sceptically. 'They *bore* me. The same model, same styling, same colour, year after year. It's a sort of communism.' He rubbed a greasy finger over the windshield. 'This is a new one again, isn't it, Doctor? Where's the old one — you only had it for three months?'

'I traded it in,' Franklin told him, starting the engine. 'If you ever had any money you'd realize that it's the most economical way of owning a car. You don't keep driving the same one until it falls apart. It's the same with everything else — television sets, washing machines, refrigerators. But you aren't faced with the problem.'

Hathaway ignored the gibe, and leaned his elbow on Franklin's window. 'Not a bad idea, either, Doctor. It gives me time to think.

I'm not working a twelve-hour day to pay for a lot of things I'm too busy to use before they're obsolete.'

He waved as Franklin reversed the car out of its line, then shouted into the wake of exhaust: 'Drive with your eyes closed, Doctor!'

On the way home Franklin kept carefully to the slowest of the four-speed lanes. As usual after his discussions with Hathaway, he felt vaguely depressed. He realized that unconsciously he envied Hathaway his footloose existence. Despite the grimy cold-water apartment in the shadow and roar of the flyover, despite his nagging wife and their sick child, and the endless altercations with the landlord and the supermarket credit manager, Hathaway still retained his freedom intact. Spared any responsibilities, he could resist the smallest encroachment upon him by the rest of society, if only by generating obsessive fantasies such as his latest one about subliminal advertising.

The ability to react to stimuli, even irrationally, was a valid criterion of freedom. By contrast, what freedom Franklin possessed was peripheral, sharply demarked by the manifold responsibilities in the centre of his life – the three mortgages on his home, the mandatory rounds of cocktail parties, the private consultancy occupying most of Saturday which paid the instalments on the multitude of household gadgets, clothes and past holidays. About the only time he had to himself was driving to and from work.

But at least the roads were magnificent. Whatever other criticisms might be levelled at the present society, it certainly knew how to build roads. Eight-, ten- and twelve-lane expressways interlaced across the country, plunging from overhead causeways into the giant car parks in the centre of the cities, or dividing into the great suburban arteries with their multi-acre parking aprons around the marketing centres. Together the roadways and car parks covered more than a third of the country's entire area, and in the neighbourhood of the cities the proportion was higher. The old cities were surrounded by the vast motion sculptures of the clover-leaves and flyovers, but even so the congestion was unremitting.

The ten-mile journey to his home in fact covered over twenty-five miles and took him twice as long as it had done before the construction of the expressway, the additional miles contained within the three giant clover-leaves. New cities were springing from the motels, cafés and car marts around the highways. At the slightest hint of an intersection a shanty town of shacks and filling stations sprawled away among the forest of electric signs and route indicators.

All around him cars bulleted along, streaming towards the suburbs. Relaxed by the smooth motion of the car, Franklin edged outwards into the next speed-lane. As he accelerated from 40 to 50 m.p.h. a strident ear-jarring noise drummed out from his tyres, shaking the chassis of the car. Ostensibly an aid to lane discipline, the surface of the road was covered with a mesh of small rubber studs, spaced progressively farther apart in each of the lanes so that the tyre hum resonated exactly on 40, 50, 60 and 70 m.p.h. Driving at an intermediate speed for more than a few seconds became nervously exhausting, and soon resulted in damage to the car and tyres.

When the studs wore out they were replaced by slightly different patterns, matching those on the latest tyres, so that regular tyre changes were necessary, increasing the safety and efficiency of the expressway. It also increased the revenues of the car and tyre manufacturers. Most cars over six months old soon fell to pieces under the steady battering, but this was regarded as a desirable end, the greater turnover reducing the unit price and making more frequent model changes, as well as ridding the roads of dangerous vehicles.

A quarter of a mile ahead, at the approach to the first of the clover-leaves, the traffic stream was slowing, huge police signs signalling 'Lanes Closed Ahead' and 'Drop Speed by 10 m.p.h.'. Franklin tried to return to the previous lane, but the cars were jammed bumper to bumper. As the chassis began to shudder and vibrate, jarring his spine, he clamped his teeth and tried to restrain himself from sounding the horn. Other drivers were less self-controlled and everywhere engines were plunging and snarling, horns blaring. Road taxes were now so high, up to thirty per cent of the gross national product (by contrast, income taxes were a bare two per cent) that any delay on the expressways called for an immediate government inquiry, and the major departments of state were concerned with the administration of the road systems.

Nearer the clover-leaf the lanes had been closed to allow a gang of construction workers to erect a massive metal sign on one of the traffic islands. The palisaded area swarmed with engineers and surveyors, and Franklin assumed that this was the sign Hathaway had seen unloaded the previous night. His apartment was in one of the gimcrack buildings in the settlement that straggled away around a near-by flyover, a low-rent area inhabited by service-station personnel, waitresses and other migrant labour.

The sign was enormous, at least a hundred feet high, fitted with heavy concave grilles similar to radar bowls. Rooted in a series of concrete caissons, it reared high into the air above the approach roads, visible for miles. Franklin craned up at the grilles, tracing the power cables from the transformers up into the intricate mesh of metal coils that covered their surface. A line of red aircraft-warning beacons was already alight along the top strut, and Franklin assumed that the sign was part of the ground approach system of the city airport ten miles to the east.

Three minutes later, as he accelerated down the two-mile link of straight highway to the next clover-leaf, he saw the second of the giant signs looming up into the sky before him.

Changing down into the 40 m.p.h. lane, Franklin watched the great bulk of the second sign recede in his rear-view mirror. Although there were no graphic symbols among the wire coils covering the grilles, Hathaway's warnings still sounded in his ears. Without knowing why, he felt sure that the signs were not part of the airport approach system. Neither of them was in line with the principal air-lines. To justify the expense of siting them in the centre of the expressway – the second sign required elaborate angled buttresses to support it on the narrow island – obviously meant that their role related in some way to the traffic streams.

Two hundred yards away was a roadside auto-mart, and

Franklin abruptly remembered that he needed some cigarettes. Swinging the car down the entrance ramp, he joined the queue passing the self-service dispenser at the far end of the rank. The auto-mart was packed with cars, each of the five purchasing ranks lined with tired-looking men hunched over their wheels.

Inserting his coins (paper money was no longer in circulation, unmanageable by the automats) he took a carton from the dispenser. This was the only brand of cigarettes available – in fact there was only one brand of everything – though giant economy packs were an alternative. Moving off, he opened the dashboard locker.

Inside, still sealed in their wrappers, were three other cartons.

A strong fish-like smell pervaded the house when he reached home, steaming out from the oven in the kitchen. Sniffing it uneagerly, Franklin took off his coat and hat. His wife was crouched over the TV set in the lounge. An announcer was dictating a stream of numbers, and Judith scribbled them down on a pad, occasionally cursing under her breath. 'What a muddle!' she snapped. 'He was talking so quickly I took only a few things down.'

'Probably deliberate,' Franklin commented. 'A new panel game?'

Judith kissed him on the cheek, discreetly hiding the ashtray loaded with cigarette butts and chocolate wrappings. 'Hello, darling, sorry not to have a drink ready for you. They've started this series of Spot Bargains, they give you a selection of things on which you get a ninety per cent trade-in discount at the local stores, if you're in the right area and have the right serial numbers. It's all terribly complicated.'

'Sounds good, though. What have you got?'

Judith peered at her checklist. 'Well, as far as I can see the only thing is the infra-red barbecue spit. But we have to be there before eight o'clock tonight. It's seven thirty already.'

'Then that's out. I'm tired, angel, I need something to eat.' When Judith started to protest he added firmly: 'Look, I don't want a new infra-red barbecue spit, we've only had this one for two months. Damn it, it's not even a different model.'

'But, darling, don't you see, it makes it cheaper if you keep buying new ones. We'll have to trade ours in at the end of the year anyway, we signed the contract, and this way we save at least five pounds. These Spot Bargains aren't just a gimmick, you know. I've been glued to that set all day.' A note of irritation had crept into her voice, but Franklin stood his ground, doggedly ignoring the clock.

'Right, we lose five pounds. It's worth it.' Before she could remonstrate he said: 'Judith, please, you probably took the wrong number down anyway.' As she shrugged and went over to the bar he called: 'Make it a stiff one. I see we have health foods on the menu.'

'They're good for you, darling. You know you can't live on ordinary foods all the time. They don't contain any proteins or vitamins. You're always saying we ought to be like people in the old days and eat nothing but health foods.'

'I would, but they smell so awful.' Franklin lay back, nose in the glass of whisky, gazing at the darkened skyline outside.

A quarter of a mile away, gleaming out above the roof of the neighbourhood supermarket, were the five red beacon lights. Now and then, as the headlamps of the Spot Bargainers swung up across the face of the building, he could see the massive bulk of the sign clearly silhouetted against the evening sky.

'Judith!' He went into the kitchen and took her over to the window. 'That sign, just behind the supermarket. When did they put it up?'

'I don't know.' Judith peered at him. 'Why are you so worried, Robert? Isn't it something to do with the airport?'

Franklin stared at the dark hull of the sign. 'So everyone probably thinks.'

Carefully he poured his whisky into the sink.

After parking his car on the supermarket apron at seven o'clock the next morning, Franklin carefully emptied his pockets and stacked the coins in the dashboard locker. The supermarket was already busy with early morning shoppers and the line of thirty turnstiles clicked and slammed. Since the introduction of the '24-hour spending day' the shopping complex was never closed. The bulk of the shoppers were discount buyers, housewives contracted to make huge volume purchases of food, clothing and appliances against substantial overall price cuts, and forced to drive around all day from supermarket to supermarket, frantically trying to keep pace with their purchase schedules and grappling with the added incentives inserted to keep the schemes alive.

Many of the women had teamed up, and as Franklin walked over to the entrance a pack of them charged towards their cars, stuffing their pay slips into their bags and shouting at each other. A moment later their cars roared off in a convoy to the next marketing zone.

A large neon sign over the entrance listed the latest discount – a mere five per cent – calculated on the volume of turnover. The highest discounts, sometimes up to twenty-five per cent, were earned in the housing estates where junior white-collar workers lived. There, spending had a strong social incentive, and the desire to be the highest spender in the neighbourhood was given moral reinforcement by the system of listing all the names and their accumulating cash totals on a huge electric sign in the supermarket foyers. The higher the spender, the greater his contribution to the discounts enjoyed by others. The lowest spenders were regarded as social criminals, free-riding on the backs of others.

Luckily this system had yet to be adopted in Franklin's neighbourhood – not because the Professional men and their wives were able to exercise more discretion, but because their higher incomes allowed them to contract into more expensive discount schemes operated by the big department stores in the city.

Ten yards from the entrance Franklin paused, looking up at the huge metal sign mounted in an enclosure at the edge of the car park. Unlike the other signs and hoardings that proliferated everywhere, no attempt had been made to decorate it, or disguise the gaunt bare rectangle of riveted steel mesh. Power lines wound down its sides, and the concrete surface of the car park was crossed by a long scar where a cable had been sunk.

Franklin strolled along. Fifty feet from the sign he stopped and turned, realizing that he would be late for the hospital and needed a new carton of cigarettes. A dim but powerful humming emanated from the transformers below the sign, fading as he retraced his steps to the supermarket.

Going over to the automats in the foyer, he felt for his change, then whistled sharply when he remembered why he had deliberately emptied his pockets.

'Hathaway!' he said, loudly enough for two shoppers to stare at him. Reluctant to look directly at the sign, he watched its reflection in one of the glass door-panes, so that any subliminal message would be reversed.

Almost certainly he had received two distinct signals – 'Keep Away' and 'Buy Cigarettes'. The people who normally parked their cars along the perimeter of the apron were avoiding the area under the enclosure, the cars describing a loose semi-circle fifty feet around it.

He turned to the janitor sweeping out the foyer. 'What's that sign for?'

The man leaned on his broom, gazing dully at the sign. 'No idea,' he said. 'Must be something to do with the airport.' He had a fresh cigarette in his mouth, but his right hand reached to his hip pocket and pulled out a pack. He drummed the second cigarette absently on his thumbnail as Franklin walked away.

Everyone entering the supermarket was buying cigarettes.

Cruising quietly along the 40 m.p.h. lane, Franklin began to take a closer interest in the landscape around him. Usually he was either too tired or too preoccupied to do more than think about his driving, but now he examined the expressway methodically, scanning the roadside cafés for any smaller versions of the new signs. A host of neon displays covered the doorways and windows, but most of them seemed innocuous, and he turned his attention to the larger billboards erected along the open stretches of the expressway. Many of these were as high as four-storey houses, elaborate three-dimensional devices in which giant housewives with electric eyes and teeth jerked and postured around their ideal kitchens, neon flashes exploding from their smiles.

The areas on either side of the expressway were wasteland, continuous junkyards filled with cars and trucks, washing machines and refrigerators, all perfectly workable but jettisoned by the economic pressure of the succeeding waves of discount models. Their intact chrome hardly tarnished, the metal shells and cabinets glittered in the sunlight. Nearer the city the billboards were sufficiently close together to hide them but now and then, as he slowed to approach one of the flyovers, Franklin caught a glimpse of the huge pyramids of metal, gleaming silently like the refuse grounds of some forgotten El Dorado.

That evening Hathaway was waiting for him as he came down the hospital steps. Franklin waved him across the court, then led the way quickly to his car.

'What's the matter, Doctor?' Hathaway asked as Franklin wound up the windows and glanced around the lines of parked cars. 'Is someone after you?'

Franklin laughed sombrely. 'I don't know. I hope not, but if what you say is right, I suppose there is.'

Hathaway leaned back with a chuckle, propping one knee up on the dashboard. 'So you've seen something, Doctor, after all.'

'Well, I'm not sure yet, but there's just a chance you may be right. This morning at the Fairlawne supermarket ...' He broke off, uneasily remembering the huge black sign and the abrupt way in which he had turned back to the supermarket as he approached it, then described his encounter.

Hathaway nodded. 'I've seen the sign there. It's big, but not as big as some that are going up. They're building them everywhere now. All over the city. What are you going to do, Doctor?'

Franklin gripped the wheel tightly. Hathaway's thinly veiled amusement irritated him. 'Nothing, of course. Damn it, it may be just auto-suggestion, you've probably got me imagining –'

Hathaway sat up with a jerk. 'Don't be absurd, Doctor! If you can't believe your own senses what chance have you left?

They're invading your brain, if you don't defend yourself they'll take it over completely! We've got to act now, before we're all paralysed.'

Wearily Franklin raised one hand to restrain him. 'Just a minute. Assuming that these signs *are* going up everywhere, what would be their object? Apart from wasting the enormous amount of capital invested in all the other millions of signs and billboards, the amounts of discretionary spending power still available must be infinitesimal. Some of the present mortgage and discount schemes reach half a century ahead. A big trade war would be disastrous.'

'Quite right, Doctor,' Hathaway rejoined evenly, 'but you're forgetting one thing. What would supply that extra spending power? A big increase in production. Already they've started to raise the working day from twelve hours to fourteen. In some of the appliance plants around the city Sunday working is being introduced as a norm. Can you visualize it, Doctor – a seven-day week, everyone with at least three jobs.'

Franklin shook his head. 'People won't stand for it.'

'They will. Within the last twenty-five years the gross national product has risen by fifty per cent, but so have the average hours worked. Ultimately we'll all be working and spending twenty-four hours a day, seven days a week. No one will dare refuse. Think what a slump would mean – millions of lay-offs, people with time on their hands and nothing to spend it on. Real leisure, not just time spent buying things,' He seized Franklin by the shoulder. 'Well, Doctor, are you going to join me?'

Franklin freed himself. Half a mile away, partly hidden by the four-storey bulk of the Pathology Department, was the upper half of one of the giant signs, workmen still crawling across its girders. The airlines over the city had deliberately been routed away from the hospital, and the sign obviously had no connection with approaching aircraft.

'Isn't there a prohibition on – what did they call it – subliminal living? How can the unions accept it?'

'The fear of a slump. You know the new economic dogmas. Unless output rises by a steady inflationary five per cent the economy is stagnating. Ten years ago increased efficiency alone would raise output, but the advantages there are minimal now and only one thing is left. More work. Subliminal advertising will provide the spur.'

'What are you planning to do?'

'I can't tell you, Doctor, unless you accept equal responsibility for it.'

'That sounds rather Quixotic,' Franklin commented. 'Tilting at windmills. You won't be able to chop those things down with an axe.'

'I won't try.' Hathaway opened the door. 'Don't wait too long to make up your mind, Doctor. By then it may not be yours to make up.' With a wave he was gone.

On the way home Franklin's scepticism returned. The idea of the conspiracy was preposterous, and the economic arguments were too plausible. As usual, though, there had been a hook in the soft bait Hathaway dangled before him – Sunday working. His own consultancy had been extended into Sunday morning with his appointment as visiting factory doctor to one of the automobile plants that had started Sunday shifts. But instead of resenting this incursion into his already meagre hours of leisure he had been glad. For one frightening reason – he needed the extra income.

Looking out over the lines of scurrying cars, he noticed that at least a dozen of the great signs had been erected along the expressway. As Hathaway had said, more were going up everywhere, rearing over the supermarkets in the housing developments like rusty metal sails.

Judith was in the kitchen when he reached home, watching the TV programme on the hand-set over the cooker. Franklin climbed past a big cardboard carton, its seals still unbroken, which blocked the doorway, kissed her on the cheek as she scribbled numbers down on her pad. The pleasant odour of pot-roast chicken – or, rather a gelatine dummy of a chicken fully flavoured and free of any toxic or nutritional properties – mollified his irritation at finding her still playing the Spot Bargains.

He tapped the carton with his foot. 'What's this?'

'No idea, darling, something's always coming these days, I can't keep up with it all.' She peered through the glass door at the chicken – an economy twelve-pounder, the size of a turkey, with stylized legs and wings and an enormous breast, most of which would be discarded at the end of the meal (there were no dogs or cats these days, the crumbs from the rich man's table saw to that) – and then glanced at him pointedly.

'You look rather worried, Robert. Bad day?'

Franklin murmured noncommittally. The hours spent trying to detect false clues in the faces of the Spot Bargain announcers had sharpened Judith's perceptions. He felt a pang of sympathy for the legion of husbands similarly outmatched.

'Have you been talking to that crazy beatnik again?'

'Hathaway? As a matter of fact I have. He's not all that crazy.' He stepped backwards into the carton, almost spilling his drink. 'Well, what is this thing? As I'll be working for the next fifty Sundays to pay for it I'd like to find out.'

He searched the sides, finally located the label. '*A TV set*? Judith, do we need another one? We've already got three. Lounge, dining-room and the hand-set. What's the fourth for?'

'The guest-room, dear, don't get so excited. We can't leave a hand-set in the guest-room, it's rude. I'm trying to economize, but four TV sets is the bare minimum. All the magazines say so.'

'*And* three radios?' Franklin stared irritably at the carton. 'If we do invite a guest here how much time is he going to spend alone in his room watching television? Judith, we've got to call a halt. It's not as if these things were free, or even cheap. Anyway, television is a total waste of time. There's only one programme. It's ridiculous to have four sets.'

'Robert, there are *four* channels.'

'But only the commercials are different.' Before Judith could reply the telephone rang. Franklin lifted the kitchen receiver, listened to the gabble of noise that poured from it. At first he wondered whether this was some offbeat prestige commercial, then realized it was Hathaway in a manic swing.

'Hathaway!' he shouted back. 'Relax, for God's sake! What's the matter now?'

'– Doctor, you'll have to believe me this time. I climbed on to one of the islands with a stroboscope, they've got hundreds of high-speed shutters blasting away like machine-guns straight into people's faces and they can't see a thing, it's fantastic! The next big campaign's going to be cars and TV sets, they're trying to swing a two-month model change – can you imagine it, Doctor, a new car every two months? God Almighty, it's just –'

Franklin waited impatiently as the five-second commercial break cut in (all telephone calls were free, the length of the commercial extending with range – for long-distance calls the ratio of commercial to conversation was as high as 10:1, the participants desperately trying to get a word in edgeways between the interminable interruptions), but just before it ended he abruptly put the telephone down, then removed the receiver from the cradle.

Judith came over and took his arm. 'Robert, what's the matter? You look terribly strained.'

Franklin picked up his drink and walked through into the lounge. 'It's just Hathaway. As you say, I'm getting a little too involved with him. He's starting to prey on my mind.'

He looked at the dark outline of the sign over the supermarket, its red warning lights glowing in the night sky. Blank and nameless, like an area for ever closed-off in an insane mind, what frightened him was its total anonymity.

'Yet I'm not sure,' he muttered. 'So much of what Hathaway says makes sense. These subliminal techniques are the sort of last-ditch attempt you'd expect from an over-capitalized industrial system.'

He waited for Judith to reply, then looked up at her. She stood in the centre of the carpet, hands folded limply, her sharp, intelligent face curiously dull and blunted. He followed her gaze out over the rooftops, then with an effort turned his head and quickly switched on the TV set.

'Come on,' he said grimly. 'Let's watch television. God, we're going to need that fourth set.'

A week later Franklin began to compile his inventory. He saw nothing more of Hathaway; as he left the hospital in the evening the familiar scruffy figure was absent. When the first of the explosions sounded dimly around the city and he read of the attempts to sabotage the giant signs he automatically assumed that Hathaway was responsible, but later he heard on a newscast that the detonations had been set off by construction workers excavating foundations.

More of the signs appeared over the rooftops, isolated on the palisaded islands near the suburban shopping centres. Already there were over thirty on the ten-mile route from the hospital, standing shoulder to shoulder over the speeding cars like giant dominoes. Franklin had given up his attempt to avoid looking at them, but the slim possibility that the explosions might be Hathaway's counter-attack kept his suspicions alive.

He began his inventory after hearing the newscast, and discovered that in the previous fortnight he and Judith had traded in their

> Car (previous model 2 months old)
> 2 TV sets (4 months)
> Power mower (7 months)
> Electric cooker (5 months)
> Hair dryer (4 months)
> Refrigerator (3 months)
> 2 radios (7 months)
> Record player (5 months)
> Cocktail bar (8 months)

Half these purchases had been made by himself, but exactly when he could never recall realizing at the time. The car, for example, he had left in the garage near the hospital to be greased, that evening had signed for the new model as he sat at its wheel, accepting the saleman's assurance that the depreciation on the two-month trade-in was virtually less than the cost of the grease-job. Ten minutes later, as he sped along the expressway, he suddenly realized that he had bought a new car. Similarly, the TV sets had been replaced by identical models after developing the same irritating interference pattern (curiously, the new sets also displayed the pattern, but as the salesman assured them, this promptly vanished two days later). Not once had he actually decided of his own volition that he wanted something and then gone out to a store and bought it!

He carried the inventory around with him, adding to it as necessary, quietly and without protest analysing these new sales techniques, wondering whether total capitulation might be the only way of defeating them. As long as he kept up even a token resistance, the inflationary growth curve would show a controlled annual ten per cent climb. With that resistance removed, however, it would begin to rocket upwards out of control ...

Driving home from the hospital two months later, he saw one of the signs for the first time.

He was in the 40 m.p.h. lane, unable to keep up with the flood of new cars, and had just passed the second of the three clover-leaves when the traffic half a mile away began to slow down. Hundreds of cars had driven up on to the grass verge, and a crowd was gathering around one of the signs. Two small black figures were climbing up the metal face, and a series of grid-like patterns of light flashed on and off, illuminating the evening air. The patterns were random and broken, as if the sign was being tested for the first time.

Relieved that Hathaway's suspicions had been completely groundless, Franklin turned off on to the soft shoulder, then walked forward through the spectators as the lights stuttered in their faces. Below, behind the steel palisades around the island, was a large group of police and engineers, craning up at the men scaling the sign a hundred feet over their heads.

Suddenly Franklin stopped, the sense of relief fading instantly. Several of the police on the ground were armed with shotguns, and the two policemen climbing the sign carried submachine-guns slung over their shoulders. They were converging on a third figure, crouched by a switch-box on the penultimate tier, a bearded man in a grimy shirt, a bare knee poking through his jeans.

Hathaway!

Franklin hurried towards the island, the sign hissing and spluttering, fuses blowing by the dozen.

Then the flicker of lights cleared and steadied, blazing out continuously, and together the crowd looked up at the decks of brilliant letters. The phrases, and every combination of them possible, were entirely familiar, and Franklin knew that he had been reading them for weeks as he passed up and down the expressway.

> BUY NOW BUY NOW BUY NOW BUY NOW BUY
> NEW CAR NOW NEW CAR NOW NEW CAR NOW
> YES YES YES YES YES YES YES YES YES YES

Sirens blaring, two patrol cars swung on to the verge through the crowd and plunged across the damp grass. Police spilled from their doors, batons in their hands, and quickly began to force back the crowd. Franklin held his ground as they approached, started to say: 'Officer, I know the man –' but the policeman punched him in the chest with the flat of his hand. Winded, he stumbled back among the cars, and leaned helplessly against a fender as the police began to break the windshields, the hapless drivers protesting angrily, those farther back rushing for their vehicles.

The noise fell away when one of the submachine-guns fired a brief roaring burst, then rose in a massive gasp as Hathaway, arms outstretched, let out a cry of triumph and pain, and jumped.

'But, Robert, what does it really matter?' Judith asked as Franklin sat inertly in the lounge the next morning. 'I know it's tragic for his wife and daughter, but Hathaway was in the grip of an obsession. If he hated advertising signs so much why didn't he dynamite those we *can* see, instead of worrying so much about those we can't?'

Franklin stared at the TV screen, hoping the programme would distract him.

'Hathaway was *right*,' he said.

'Was he? Advertising is here to stay. We've no real freedom of choice, anyway. We can't spend more than we can afford, the finance companies soon clamp down.'

'Do you accept that?' Franklin went over to the window. A quarter of a mile away, in the centre of the estate, another of the signs was being erected. It was due east from them, and in the early morning light the shadows of its rectangular superstructure fell across the garden, reaching almost to the steps of the french windows at his feet. As a concession to the neighbourhood, and perhaps to allay any suspicions while it was being erected by an appeal to petty snobbery, the lower sections had been encased in mock-Tudor panelling.

Franklin stared at it, counting the half-dozen police lounging by their patrol cars as the construction gang unloaded the prefabricated grilles from a truck. He looked at the sign by the supermarket, trying to repress his memories of Hathaway and the pathetic attempts the man had made to convince Franklin and gain his help.

He was still standing there an hour later when Judith came in, putting on her hat and coat, ready to visit the supermarket.

Franklin followed her to the door. 'I'll drive you down there, Judith. I have to see about booking a new car. The next models are coming out at the end of the month. With luck we'll get one of the early deliveries.'

They walked out into the trim drive, the shadows of the signs swinging across the quiet neighbourhood as the day progressed, sweeping over the heads of the people on their way to the supermarket like the blades of enormous scythes.

1963

THE REPTILE ENCLOSURE

'They remind me of the Gadarene swine,' Mildred Pelham remarked.

Interrupting his scrutiny of the crowded beach below the cafeteria terrace, Roger Pelham glanced at his wife. 'Why do you say that?'

Mildred continued to read for a few moments, and then lowered her book. 'Well, don't they?' she asked rhetorically. 'They look like pigs.'

Pelham smiled weakly at this mild but characteristic display of misanthropy. He peered down at his own white knees protruding from his shorts and at his wife's plump arms and shoulders. 'I suppose we all do,' he temporized. However, there was little chance of Mildred's remark being overheard and resented. They were sitting at a corner table, with their backs to the hundreds of ice-cream eaters and cola-drinkers crammed elbow to elbow on the terrace. The dull hubbub of voices was overlaid by the endless commentaries broadcast over the transistor radios propped among the bottles, and by the distant sounds of the fairground behind the dunes.

A short drop below the terrace was the beach, covered by a mass of reclining figures which stretched from the water's edge up to the roadway behind the cafeteria and then away over the dunes. Not a single grain of sand was visible. Even at the tide-line, where a little slack water swilled weakly at a debris of old cigarette packets and other trash, a huddle of small children clung to the skirt of the beach, hiding the grey sand.

Gazing down at the beach again, Pelham realized that his wife's ungenerous judgment was no more than the truth. Everywhere bare haunches and shoulders jutted into the air, limbs lay in serpentine coils. Despite the sunlight and the considerable period of time they had spent on the beach, many of the people were still white-skinned, or at most a boiled pink, restlessly shifting in their little holes in a hopeless attempt to be comfortable.

Usually this spectacle of jostling, over-exposed flesh, with its unsavoury bouquet of stale suntan lotion and sweat – looking along the beach as it swept out to the distant cape, Pelham could almost see the festering corona, sustained in the air by the babble of ten thousand transistor radios, reverberating like a swarm of flies – would have sent him hurtling along the first inland highway at seventy miles an hour. But for some reason Pelham's usual private distaste for the general public had evaporated. He felt strangely exhilarated by the presence of so many people (he had calculated that he could see over 50 thousand along the five-mile stretch of beach) and found himself unable to leave the terrace, although it was now 3 o'clock and neither he nor Mildred had eaten since breakfast. Once their corner seats were surrendered they would never regain them.

To himself he mused: 'The ice-cream eaters on Echo beach . . .' He played with the empty glass in front of him. Shreds of synthetic orange pulp clung to the sides, and a fly buzzed half-heartedly from one to another. The sea was flat and calm, an opaque grey disc, but a mile away a low surface mist lay over the water like vapour on a vat.

'You look hot, Roger. Why don't you go in for a swim?'

'I may. You know, it's a curious thing, but of all the people here, not one is swimming.'

Mildred nodded in a bored way. A large passive woman, she seemed content merely to sit in the sunlight and read. Yet it was she who had first suggested that they drive out to the coast, and for once had suppressed her usual grumbles when they ran into the first heavy traffic jams and were forced to abandon the car and complete the remaining two miles on foot. Pelham had not seen her walk like that for ten years.

'It is rather strange,' she said. 'But it's not particularly warm.'

'I don't agree.' Pelham was about to continue when he suddenly stood up and looked over the rail at the beach. Halfway down the slope, parallel with the promenade, a continuous stream of people moved slowly along an informal right-of-way, shouldering past each other with fresh bottles of cola, lotion and ice-cream.

'Roger, what's the matter?'

'Nothing ... I thought I saw Sherrington.' Pelham searched the beach, the moment of recognition lost.

'You're always seeing Sherrington. That's the fourth time alone this afternoon. Do stop worrying.'

'I'm not worrying. I can't be certain, but I felt I saw him then.'

Reluctantly, Pelham sat down, edging his chair fractionally closer to the rail. Depite his mood of lethargy and vacuous boredom, an indefinable but distinct feeling of restlessness had preoccupied him all day. In some way associated with Sherrington's presence on the beach, this uneasiness had been increasing steadily. The chances of Sherrington – with whom he shared an office in the Physiology Department at the University – actually choosing this section of the beach were remote, and Pelham was not even sure why he was so convinced that Sherrington was there at all. Perhaps these illusory glimpses – all the more unlikely in view of Sherrington's black beard and high severe face, his stooped long-legged walk – were simply projections of this underlying tension and his own peculiar dependence upon Sherrington.

However, this sense of uneasiness was not confined to himself. Although Mildred seemed immune, most of the people on the beach appeared to share this mood with Pelham. As the day progressed the continuous hubbub gave way to more sporadic chatter. Occasionally the noise would fall away altogether, and the great concourse, like an immense crowd waiting for the long-delayed start of some public spectacle, would sit up and stir impatiently. To Pelham, watching carefully from his vantage point over the beach, these ripples of restless activity, as everyone swayed forward in long undulations, were plainly indicated by the metallic glimmer of the thousands of portable radios moving in an oscillating wave. Each successive spasm, recurring at roughly half-hour intervals, seemed to take the crowd slightly nearer the sea.

Directly below the concrete edge of the terrace, among the mass of reclining figures, a large family group had formed a private enclosure. To one side of this, literally within reach of Pelham, the adolescent members of the family had dug their own nest, their sprawling angular bodies, in their damp abbreviated swimming suits, entwined in and out of each other like some curious annular animal. Well within earshot, despite the continuous background of noise from the beach and the distant fair-grounds, Pelham listened to their inane talk, following the thread of the radio commentaries as they switched aimlessly from one station to the next.

'They're about to launch another satellite,' he told Mildred. 'Echo XXII.'

'Why do they bother?' Mildred's flat blue eyes surveyed the distant haze over the water. 'I should have thought there were more than enough of them flying about already.'

'Well . . .' For a moment Pelham debated whether to pursue the meagre conversational possibilities of his wife's reply. Although she was married to a lecturer in the School of Physiology, her interest in scientific matters was limited to little more than a blanket condemnation of the entire sphere of activity. His own post at the University she regarded with painful tolerance, despising the untidy office, scruffy students and meaningless laboratory equipment. Pelham had never been able to discover exactly what calling she would have respected. Before their marriage she maintained what he later realized was a polite silence on the subject of his work; after eleven years this attitude had barely changed, although the exigencies of living on his meagre salary had forced her to take an interest in the subtle, complex and infinitely wearying game of promotional snakes and ladders.

As expected, her acerbic tongue had made them few friends, but by a curious paradox Pelham felt that he had benefited from the grudging respect this had brought her. Sometimes her waspish comments, delivered at the overlong sherry parties, always in a loud voice during some conversational silence (for example, she had described the elderly occupant of the Physiology chair as 'that gerontological freak' within some five feet of the Professor's wife) delighted Pelham by their mordant accuracy, but in general there was something frightening about her pitiless lack of sympathy for the rest of the human race. Her large bland face, with its prim, rosebud mouth, reminded Pelham of the description of the Mona Lisa as looking as if she had just dined off her husband. Mildred, however, did not even smile.

'Sherrington has a rather interesting theory about the satellites,' Pelham told her. 'I'd hoped we might see him so that he could explain it again. I think you'd be amused to hear it, Mildred. He's working on IRM's at present –'

'On what?' The group of people behind them had turned up the volume of their radio and the commentary, of the final countdown at Cape Kennedy, boomed into the air over their heads.

Pelham said: 'IRM's – innate releasing mechanisms. I've described them to you before, they're inherited reflexes –' He stopped, watching his wife impatiently.

Mildred had turned on him the dead stare with which she surveyed the remainder of the people on the beach. Testily Pelham snapped: 'Mildred, I'm trying to explain Sherrington's theory about the satellites!'

Undeterred, Mildred shook her head. 'Roger, it's too noisy here, I can't possibly listen. And to Sherrington's theories less than to anyone else's.'

Almost imperceptibly, another wave of restless activity was sweeping along the beach. Perhaps in response to the final digital climax of the commentators at Cape Kennedy, people were sitting up and dusting the coarse sand from each other's backs. Pelham watched the sunlight flickering off the chromium radio sets and diamante sunglasses as the entire beach swayed and surged. The noise had fallen appreciably, letting through the sound of the wurlitzer at the funfair. Everywhere there was the same expectant stirring. To Pelham, his eyes half-closed in the glare, the beach seemed like an immense pit of seething white snakes.

Somewhere, a woman's voice shouted. Pelham sat forward, searching the rows of faces masked by sunglasses. There was a sharp edge to the air, an unpleasant and almost sinister implication of violence hidden below the orderly surface.

Gradually, however, the activity subsided. The great throng relaxed and reclined again. Greasily, the water lapped at the supine feet of the people lying by the edge of the sea. Propelled by one of the off-shore swells, a little slack air moved over the beach, carrying with it the sweet odour of sweat and suntan lotion. Averting his face, Pelham felt a spasm of nausea contract his gullet. Without doubt, he reflected, homo sapiens en masse presented a more unsavoury spectacle than almost any other species of animal. A corral of horses or steers conveyed an impression of powerful nervous grace, but this mass of articulated albino flesh sprawled on the beach resembled the diseased anatomical fantasy of a surrealist painter. Why had all these people congregated there? The weather reports that morning had not been especially propitious. Most of the announcements were devoted to the news of the imminent satellite launching, the last stage of the worldwide communications network which would now provide every square foot of the globe with a straight-line visual contact with one or other of the score of satellites in orbit. Perhaps the final sealing of this inescapable aerial canopy had prompted everyone to seek out the nearest beach and perform a symbolic act of self-exposure as a last gesture of surrender.

Uneasily, Pelham moved about in his chair, suddenly aware of the edge of the metal table cutting into his elbows. The cheap slatted seat was painfully uncomfortable, and his whole body seemed enclosed in an iron maiden of spikes and clamps. Again a curious premonition of some appalling act of violence stirred through his mind, and he looked up at the sky, almost expecting an airliner to plunge from the distant haze and disintegrate on the crowded beach in front of him.

To Mildred he remarked: 'It's remarkable how popular sun-bathing can become. It was a major social problem in Australia before the second World War.'

Mildred's eyes flickered upwards from her book. 'There was probably nothing else to do.'

'That's just the point. As long as people are prepared to spend their entire time sprawled on a beach there's little hope of ever building up any other pastimes. Sunbathing is anti-social because it's an entirely passive pursuit.' He dropped his voice when he noticed the people sitting around him glancing over their shoulders, ears drawn to his high precise diction. 'On the other hand, it does bring people together. In the nude, or the near-nude, the shop-girl and the duchess are virtually indistinguishable.'

'*Are* they?'

Pelham shrugged. 'You know what I mean. But I think the psychological role of the beach is much more interesting. The tide-line is a particularly significant area, a penumbral zone that is both of the sea and above it, forever half-immersed in the great time-womb. If you accept the sea as an image of the unconscious, then this beachward urge might be seen as an attempt to escape from the existential role of ordinary life and return to the universal time-sea –'

'Roger, please!' Mildred looked away wearily. 'You sound like Charles Sherrington.'

Pelham stared out to sea again. Below him, a radio commentator announced the position and speed of the successfully launched satellite, and its pathway around the globe. Idly, Pelham calculated that it would take some fifteen minutes to reach them, almost exactly at half past three. Of course it would not be visible from the beach, although Sherrington's recent work on the perception of infra-red radiation suggested some of the infra-red light reflected from the sun might be perceived subliminally by their retinas.

Reflecting on the opportunities this offered to a commercial or political demagogue, Pelham listened to the radio on the sand below, when a long white arm reached out and switched it off. The possessor of the arm, a plump white-skinned girl with the face of a placid madonna, her round cheeks framed by ringlets of black hair, rolled over on to her back, disengaging herself from her companions, and for a moment she and Pelham exchanged glances. He assumed that she had deliberately switched off the radio to prevent him hearing the commentary, and then realized that in fact the girl had been listening to his voice and hoped that he would resume his monologue.

Flattered, Pelham studied the girl's round serious face, and her mature but child-like figure stretched out almost as close to him, and as naked, as it would have been had they shared a bed. Her frank, adolescent but curiously tolerant expression barely changed, and Pelham turned away, unwilling to accept its implications, realizing with a pang the profound extent of his resignation to Mildred, and the now unbreachable insulation this provided against any new or real experience in his life. For ten years the thousand cautions and compromises accepted each day to make existence tolerable had steadily secreted their numbing anodynes, and what remained of his original personality, with all its possibilities, was embalmed like a specimen in a jar. Once he would have despised himself for accepting his situation so passively, but he was now beyond any real self-judgment, for no criteria were valid by which to assess himself, a state of gracelessness far more abject than that of the vulgar, stupid herd on the beach around him.

'Something's in the water.' Mildred pointed along the shore. 'Over there.'

Pelham followed her raised arm. Two hundred yards away a small crowd had gathered at the water's edge, the sluggish waves breaking at their feet as they watched some activity in the shallows. Many of the people had raised newspapers to shield their heads, and the older women in the group held their skirts between their knees.

'I can't see anything.' Pelham rubbed his chin, distracted by a bearded man on the edge of the promenade above him, a face not Sherrington's but remarkably like it. 'There seems to be no danger, anyway. Some unusual sea-fish may have been cast ashore.'

On the terrace, and below on the beach, everyone was waiting for something to happen, heads craned forward expectantly. As the radios were turned down, so that any sounds from the distant tableau might be heard, a wave of silence passed along the beach like an immense darkening cloud shutting off the sunlight. The almost complete absence of noise and movement, after the long hours of festering motion, seemed strange and uncanny, focusing an intense atmosphere of self-awareness upon the thousands of watching figures.

The group by the water's edge remained where they stood, even the small children staring placidly at whatever held the attention of their parents. For the first time a narrow section of the beach was visible, a clutter of radios and beach equipment half-buried in the sand like discarded metallic refuse. Gradually the new arrivals pressing down from the promenade occupied the empty places, a manoeuvre carried out without any reaction from the troupe by the tide-line. To Pelham they seemed like a family of penitent pilgrims who had travelled some enormous distance and were now standing beside their sacred waters, waiting patiently for its revivifying powers to work their magic.

'What *is* going on?' Pelham asked, when after several minutes there was no indication of movement from the water-side group. He noticed that they formed a straight line, following the shore, rather than an arc. 'They're not watching anything at all.'

The off-shore haze was now only five hundred yards away, obscuring the contours of the huge swells. Completely opaque, the water looked like warm oil, a few wavelets now and then dissolving into greasy bubbles as they expired limply on the sand, intermingled with bits of refuse and old cigarette cartons. Nudging the shore like this, the sea resembled an enormous pelagic beast roused from its depths and blindly groping at the sand.

'Mildred, I'm going down to the water for a moment.' Pelham stood up. 'There's something curious –' He broke off, pointing to the beach on the other side of the terrace. 'Look! There's another group. What on earth –?'

Again, as everyone watched, this second body of spectators formed by the water's edge seventy-five yards from the terrace. Altogether some two hundred people were silently assembling along the shore-line, gazing out across the sea in front of them. Pelham found himself cracking his knuckles, then clasped the rail with both hands, as much to restrain himself from joining them. Only the congestion on the beach held him back.

This time the interest of the crowd passed in a few moments, and the murmur of background noise resumed.

'Heaven knows what they're doing.' Mildred turned her back on the group. 'There are more of them over there. They must be waiting for something.'

Sure enough, half a dozen similar groups were now forming by the water's edge, at almost precise one hundred yard intervals. Pelham scanned the far ends of the bay for any signs of a motor boat. He glanced at his watch. It was nearly 3:30. 'They can't be waiting for anything,' he said, trying to control his nervousness. Below the table his feet twitched a restless tattoo, gripping for purchase on the sandy cement. 'The only thing expected is the satellite, and no one will see that anyway. There must be something in the water.' At the mention of the satellite he remembered Sherrington again. 'Mildred, don't you feel –'

Before he could continue the man behind him stood up with a curious lurch, as if hoping to reach the rail, and tipped the sharp edge of his seat into Pelham's back. For a moment, as he struggled to steady the man, Pelham was enveloped in a rancid smell of sweat and stale beer. He saw the glazed focus in the other's eyes, his rough unshaved chin and open mouth like a muzzle, pointing with a sort of impulsive appetite towards the sea.

'The satellite!' Freeing himself Pelham craned upwards at the sky. A pale impassive blue, it was clear of both aircraft and birds – although they had seen gulls twenty miles inland that morning, as if a storm had been anticipated. As the glare stung his eyes, points of retinal light began to arc and swerve across the sky in epileptic orbits. One of these, however, apparently emerging from the western horizon, was moving steadily across the edge of his field of vision, boring dimly towards him.

Around them, people began to stand up, and chairs scraped and dragged across the floor. Several bottles toppled from one of the tables and smashed on the concrete.

'Mildred!'

Below them, in a huge disorganized mêlée extending as far

as the eye could see, people were climbing slowly to their feet. The diffused murmur of the beach had given way to a more urgent, harsher sound, echoing overhead from either end of the bay. The whole beach seemed to writhe and stir with activity, the only motionless figures those of the people standing by the water. These now formed a continuous palisade along the shore, shutting off the sea. More and more people joined their ranks, and in places the line was nearly ten deep.

Everyone on the terrace was now standing. The crowds already on the beach were being driven forward by the pressure of new arrivals from the promenade, and the party below their table had been swept a further twenty yards towards the sea.

'Mildred, can you see Sherrington anywhere?' Confirming from her wristwatch that it was exactly 3:30, Pelham pulled her shoulder, trying to hold her attention. Mildred returned what was almost a vacant stare, an expression of glazed incomprehension. 'Mildred! We've got to get away from here!' Hoarsely, he shouted: 'Sherrington's convinced we can see some of the infra-red light shining from the satellites, they may form a pattern setting off IRM's laid down millions of years ago when other space vehicles were circling the earth. Mildred —!'

Helplessly, they were lifted from their seats and pressed against the rail. A huge concourse of people was moving down the beach, and soon the entire five-mile-long slope was packed with standing figures. No one was talking, and everywhere there was the same expression, self-immersed and preoccupied, like that on the faces of a crowd leaving a stadium. Behind them the great wheel of the fairground was rotating slowly, but the gondolas were empty, and Pelham looked back at the deserted funfair only a hundred yards from the multitude on the beach, its roundabouts revolving among the empty sideshows.

Quickly he helped Mildred over the edge of the rail, then jumped down on to the sand, hoping to work their way back to the promenade. As they stepped around the corner, however, the crowd advancing down the beach carried them back, tripping over the abandoned radios in the sand.

Still together, they found their footing when the pressure

behind them ceased. Steadying himself, Pelham continued: '... Sherrington thinks Cro-Magnon Man was driven frantic by panic, like the Gadarene swine – most of the bone-beds have been found under lake shores. The reflex may be too strong –' He broke off.

The noise had suddenly subsided, as the immense congregation, now packing every available square foot of the beach, stood silently facing the water. Pelham turned towards the sea, where the haze, only fifty yards away, edged in great clouds towards the beach. The forward line of the crowd, their heads bowed slightly, stared passively at the gathering billows. The surface of the water glowed with an intense luminous light, vibrant and spectral, and the air over the beach, grey by comparison, made the lines of motionless figures loom like tombstones.

Obliquely in front of Pelham, twenty yards away in the front rank, stood a tall man with a quiet, meditative expression, his beard and high temples identifying him without doubt.

'Sherrington!' Pelham started to shout. Involuntarily he looked upwards to the sky, and felt a blinding speck of light singe his retinas.

In the background the music of the funfair revolved in the empty air.

Then, with a galvanic surge, everyone on the beach began to walk forward into the water.

1963

A QUESTION OF RE-ENTRY

All day they had moved steadily upstream, occasionally pausing to raise the propeller and cut away the knots of weed, and by 3 o'clock had covered some seventy-five miles. Fifty yards away, on either side of the patrol launch, the high walls of the jungle river rose over the water, the unbroken massif of the mato grosso which swept across the Amazonas from Campos Buros to the delta of the Orinoco. Despite their progress – they had set off from the telegraph station at Tres Buritis at 7 o'clock that morning – the river showed no inclination to narrow or alter its volume. Sombre and unchanging, the forest followed its course, the aerial canopy shutting off the sunlight and cloaking the water along the banks with a black velvet sheen. Now and then the channel would widen into a flat expanse of what appeared to be stationary water, the slow oily swells which disturbed its surface transforming it into a sluggish mirror of the distant, enigmatic sky, the islands of rotten balsa logs refracted by the layers of haze like the drifting archipelagoes of a dream. Then the channel would narrow again and the cooling jungle darkness enveloped the launch.

Although for the first few hours Connolly had joined Captain Pereira at the rail, he had become bored with the endless green banks of the forest sliding past them, and since noon had remained in the cabin, pretending to study the trajectory maps. The time might pass more slowly there, but at least it was cooler and less depressing. The fan hummed and pivoted, and the clicking of the cutwater and the whispering plaint of the current past the gliding hull soothed the slight headache induced by the tepid beer he and Pereira had shared after lunch.

This first encounter with the jungle had disappointed Connolly.

His previous experience had been confined to the Dredging Project at Lake Maracaibo, where the only forests consisted of the abandoned oil rigs built out into the water. Their rusting hulks, and the huge draglines and pontoons of the dredging teams, were fauna of a man-made species. In the Amazonian jungle he had expected to see the full variety of nature in its richest and most colourful outpouring, but instead it was nothing more than a moribund tree-level swamp, unweeded and overgrown, if anything more dead than alive, an example of bad husbandry on a continental scale. The margins of the river were rarely well defined; except where enough rotting trunks had gathered to form a firm parapet, there were no formal banks, and the shallows ran off among the undergrowth for a hundred yards, irrigating huge areas of vegetation that were already drowning in moisture.

Connolly had tried to convey his disenchantment to Pereira, who now sat under the awning on the deck, placidly smoking a cheroot, partly to repay the Captain for his polite contempt for Connolly and everything his mission implied. Like all the officers of the Native Protection Missions whom Connolly had met, first in Venezuela and now in Brazil, Pereira maintained a proprietary outlook towards the jungle and its mystique, which would not be breached by any number of fresh-faced investigators in their crisp drill uniforms. Captain Pereira had not been impressed by the UN flashes on Connolly's shoulders with their orbital monogram, nor by the high-level request for assistance cabled to the Mission three weeks earlier from Brasilia. To Pereira, obviously, the office suites in the white towers at the capital were as far away as New York, London or Babylon.

Superficially, the Captain had been helpful enough, supervising the crew as they stowed Connolly's monitoring equipment aboard, checking his Smith & Wesson and exchanging a pair of defective mosquito boots. As long as Connolly had wanted to, he had conversed away amiably, pointing out this and that feature of the landscape, identifying an unusual bird or lizard on an overhead bough.

But his indifference to the real object of the mission – he had given a barely perceptible nod when Connolly described it – soon became obvious. It was this neutrality which irked Connolly, implying that Pereira spent all his time ferrying UN investigators up and down the rivers after their confounded lost space capsule like so many tourists in search of some non-existent El Dorado. Above all there was the suggestion that Connolly and the hundreds of other investigators deployed around the continent were being too persistent. When all was said and done, Pereira implied, five years had elapsed since the returning lunar spacecraft, the *Goliath* 7, had plummeted into the South American land mass, and to prolong the search indefinitely was simply bad form, even, perhaps, necrophilic. There was not the faintest chance of the pilot still being alive, so he should be decently forgotten, given a statue outside a railway station or airport car park and left to the pigeons.

Connolly would have been glad to explain the reasons for the indefinite duration of the search, the overwhelming moral reasons, apart from the political and technical ones. He would have liked to point out that the lost astronaut, Colonel Francis Spender, by accepting the immense risks of the flight to and from the Moon, was owed the absolute discharge of any assistance that could be given him. He would have liked to remind Pereira that the successful landing on the Moon, after some half-dozen fatal attempts – at least three of the luckless pilots were still orbiting the Moon in their dead ships – was the culmination of an age-old ambition with profound psychological implications for mankind, and that the failure to find the astronaut after his return might induce unassuageable feelings of guilt and inadequacy. (If the sea was a symbol of the unconscious, was space perhaps an image of unfettered time, and the inability to penetrate it a tragic exile to one of the limbos of eternity, a symbolic death in life?)

But Captain Pereira was not interested. Calmly inhaling the scented aroma of his cheroot, he sat imperturbably at the rail, surveying the fetid swamps that moved past them.

Shortly before noon, when they had covered some 40 miles, Connolly pointed to the remains of a bamboo landing stage elevated on high poles above the bank. A threadbare rope bridge trailed off among the mangroves, and through an embrasure in the forest they could see a small clearing where a clutter of abandoned adobe huts dissolved like refuse heaps in the sunlight.

'Is this one of their camps?'

Pereira shook his head. 'The Espirro tribe, closely related to the Nambikwaras. Three years ago one of them carried influenza back from the telegraph station, an epidemic broke out, turned into a form of pulmonary edema, within forty-eight hours three hundred Indians had died. The whole group disintegrated, only about fifteen of the men and their families are still alive. A great tragedy.'

They moved forward to the bridge and stood beside the tall Negro helmsman as the two other members of the crew began to shackle sections of fine wire mesh into a cage over the deck. Pereira raised his binoculars and scanned the river ahead.

'Since the Espirros vacated the area the Nambas have begun to forage down this far. We won't see any of them, but it's as well to be on the safe side.'

'Do you mean they're hostile?' Connolly asked.

'Not in a conscious sense. But the various groups which comprise the Nambikwaras are permanently feuding with each other, and this far from the settlement we might easily be involved in an opportunist attack. Once we get to the settlement we'll be all right – there's a sort of precarious equilibrium there. But even so, have your wits about you. As you'll see, they're as nervous as birds.'

'How does Ryker manage to keep out of their way? Hasn't he been here for years?'

'About twelve.' Pereira sat down on the gunwale and eased his peaked cap off his forehead. 'Ryker is something of a special case. Temperamentally he's rather explosive – I meant to warn you to handle him carefully, he might easily whip up an incident – but he seems to have manoeuvred himself into a position of authority with the tribe. In some ways he's become an umpire, arbitrating in their various feuds. How he does it I haven't discovered yet; it's quite uncharacteristic of the Indians to regard a white man in that way. However, he's useful to us, we might eventually set up a mission here. Though that's next to impossible – we tried it once and the Indians just moved 500 miles away.'

Connolly looked back at the derelict landing stage as it disappeared around a bend, barely distinguishable from the jungle, which was as dilapidated as this sole mournful artifact.

'What on earth made Ryker come out here?' He had heard something in Brasilia of this strange figure, sometime journalist and man of action, the self-proclaimed world citizen who at the age of forty-two, after a life spent venting his spleen on civilization and its gimcrack gods, had suddenly disappeared into the Amazonas and taken up residence with one of the aboriginal tribes. Most latter-day Gauguins were absconding confidence men or neurotics, but Ryker seemed to be a genuine character in his own right, the last of a race of true individualists retreating before the barbed-wire fences and regimentation of 20th-century life. But his chosen paradise seemed pretty scruffy and degenerate, Connolly reflected, when one saw it at close quarters. However, as long as the man could organize the Indians into a few search parties he would serve his purpose. 'I can't understand why Ryker should pick the Amazon basin. The South Pacific yes, but from all I've heard – and you've confirmed just now – the Indians appear to be a pretty diseased and miserable lot, hardly the noble savage.'

Captain Pereira shrugged, looking away across the oily water, his plump sallow face mottled by the lace-like shadow of the wire netting. He belched discreetly to himself, and then adjusted his holster belt. 'I don't know the South Pacific, but I should guess it's also been oversentimentalized. Ryker didn't come here for a scenic tour. I suppose the Indians are diseased and, yes, reasonably miserable. Within fifty years they'll probably have died out. But for the time being they do represent a certain form of untamed, natural existence, which after all made us what we are. The hazards facing them are immense, and they survive.' He gave Connolly a sly smile. 'But you must argue it out with Ryker.'

They lapsed into silence and sat by the rail, watching the river unfurl itself. Exhausted and collapsing, the great trees crowded the banks, the dying expiring among the living, jostling each other aside as if for a last despairing assault on the patrol boat and its passengers. For the next half an hour, until they opened their lunch packs, Connolly searched the tree-tops for the giant bifurcated parachute which should have carried the capsule to earth. Virtually impermeable to the atmosphere, it would still be visible, spreadeagled like an enormous bird over the canopy of leaves. Then, after drinking a can of Pereira's beer, he excused himself and went down to the cabin.

The two steel cases containing the monitoring equipment had been stowed under the chart table, and he pulled them out and checked that the moisture-proof seals were still intact. The chances of making visual contact with the capsule were infinitesimal, but as long as it was intact it would continue to transmit both a sonar and radio beacon, admittedly over little more than twenty miles, but sufficient to identify its whereabouts to anyone in the immediate neighbourhood. However, the entire northern half of the South Americas had been covered by successive aerial sweeps, and it seemed unlikely that the beacons were still operating. The disappearance of the capsule argued that it had sustained at least minor damage, and by now the batteries would have been corroded by the humid air.

Recently certain of the UN Space Department agencies had begun to circulate the unofficial view that Colonel Spender had failed to select the correct attitude for re-entry and that the capsule had been vaporized on its final descent, but Connolly guessed that this was merely an attempt to pacify world opinion and prepare the way for the resumption of the space programme. Not only the Lake Maracaibo Dredging Project, but his own presence on the patrol boat, indicated that the Department still believed Colonel Spender to be alive, or at least to have survived the landing. His final re-entry orbit should have brought him down into the landing zone 500 miles to the east of Trinidad, but the last radio contact before the ionization layers around the capsule severed transmission indicated that he had under-shot his trajectory and come down somewhere on the South American land-mass along a line linking Lake Maracaibo with Brasilia.

Footsteps sounded down the companionway, and Captain

Pereira lowered himself into the cabin. He tossed his hat onto the chart table and sat with his back to the fan, letting the air blow across his fading hair, carrying across to Connolly a sweet unsavoury odour of garlic and cheap pomade.

'You're a sensible man, Lieutenant. Anyone who stays up on deck is crazy. However,' – he indicated Connolly's pallid face and hands, a memento of a long winter in New York – 'in a way it's a pity you couldn't have put in some sunbathing. That metropolitan pallor will be quite a curiosity to the Indians.' He smiled agreeably, showing the yellowing teeth which made his olive complexion even darker. 'You may well be the first white man in the literal sense that the Indians have seen.'

'What about Ryker? Isn't he white?'

'Black as a berry now. Almost indistinguishable from the Indians, apart from being 7 feet tall.' He pulled over a collection of cardboard boxes at the far end of the seat and began to rummage through them. Inside was a collection of miscellaneous oddments – balls of thread and raw cotton, lumps of wax and resin, urucu paste, tobacco and seed-beads. 'These ought to assure them of your good intentions.'

Connolly watched as he fastened the boxes together. 'How many search parties will they buy? Are you sure you brought enough? I have a fifty-dollar allocation for gifts.'

'Good,' Pereira said matter-of-factly. 'We'll get some more beer. Don't worry, you can't buy these people, Lieutenant. You have to rely on their good-will; this rubbish will put them in the right frame of mind to talk.'

Connolly smiled dourly. 'I'm more keen on getting them off their hunkers and out into the bush. How are you going to organize the search parties?'

'They've already taken place.'

'What?' Connolly sat forward. 'How did that happen? But they should have waited' – he glanced at the heavy monitoring equipment – 'they can't have known what –'

Pereira silenced him with a raised hand. 'My dear Lieutenant. Relax, I was speaking figuratively. Can't you understand, these people are nomadic, they spend all their lives continually on the move. They must have covered every square foot of this forest a hundred times in the past five years. There's no need to send them out again. Your only hope is that they may have seen something and then persuade them to talk.'

Connolly considered this, as Pereira unwrapped another parcel. 'All right, but I may want to do a few patrols. I can't just sit around for three days.'

'Naturally. Don't worry, Lieutenant. If your astronaut came down anywhere within 500 miles of here they'll know about it.' He unwrapped the parcel and removed a small teak cabinet. The front panel was slotted, and lifted to reveal the face of a large ormolu table clock, its Gothic hands and numerals below a gilded belldome. Captain Pereira compared its time with his wrist-watch. 'Good. Running perfectly, it hasn't lost a second in forty-eight hours. This should put us in Ryker's good books.'

Connolly shook his head. 'Why on earth does he want a clock? I thought the man had turned his back on such things.'

Pereira packed the tooled metal face away. 'Ah, well, whenever we escape from anything we always carry a memento of it with us. Ryker collects clocks; this is the third I've bought for him. God knows what he does with them.'

The launch had changed course, and was moving in a wide circle across the river, the current whispering in a tender rippling murmur across the hull. They made their way up onto the deck, where the helmsman was unshackling several sections of the wire mesh in order to give himself an uninterrupted view of the bows. The two sailors climbed through the aperture and took up their positions fore and aft, boat-hooks at the ready.

They had entered a large bow-shaped extension of the river, where the current had overflowed the bank and produced a series of low-lying mud flats. Some two or three hundred yards wide, the water seemed to be almost motionless, seeping away through the trees which defined its margins so that the exit and inlet of the river were barely perceptible. At the inner bend of the bow, on the only firm ground, a small cantonment of huts had been built on a series of wooden palisades jutting out over the water. A narrow promontory of forest reached to either side of the cantonment, but a small area behind it had been cleared to form an open campong. On its far side were a number of wattle storage huts, a few dilapidated shacks and hovels of dried palm.

The entire area seemed deserted, but as they approached, the cutwater throwing a fine plume of white spray across the glassy swells, a few Indians appeared in the shadows below the creepers trailing over the jetty, watching them stonily. Connolly had expected to see a group of tall broad-shouldered warriors with white markings notched across their arms and cheeks, but these Indians were puny and degenerate, their pinched faces lowered beneath their squat bony skulls. They seemed undernourished and depressed, eyeing the visitors with a sort of sullen watchfulness, like pariah dogs from a gutter.

Pereira was shielding his eyes from the sun, across whose inclining path they were now moving, searching the ramshackle bungalow built of woven rattan at the far end of the jetty.

'No signs of Ryker yet. He's probably asleep or drunk.' He noticed Connolly's distasteful frown. 'Not much of a place, I'm afraid.'

As they moved towards the jetty, the wash from the launch slapping at the greasy bamboo poles and throwing a gust of foul air into their faces, Connolly looked back across the open disc of water, into which the curving wake of the launch was dissolving in a final summary of their long voyage up-river to the derelict settlement, fading into the slack brown water like a last tenuous thread linking him with the order and sanity of civilization. A strange atmosphere of emptiness hung over this inland lagoon, a flat pall of dead air that in a curious way was as menacing as any overt signs of hostility, as if the crudity and violence of all the Amazonian jungles met here in a momentary balance which some untoward movement of his own might upset, unleashing appalling forces. Away in the distance, down-shore, the great trees leaned like corpses into the glazed air, and the haze over the water embalmed the jungle and the late afternoon in an uneasy stillness.

They bumped against the jetty, rocking lightly into the palisade of poles and dislodging a couple of water-logged outriggers lashed together. The helmsman reversed the engine, waiting for the sailors to secure the lines. None of the Indians had come forward to assist them. Connolly caught a glimpse of one old simian face regarding him with a rheumy eye, riddled teeth nervously worrying a pouch-like lower lip.

He turned to Pereira, glad that the Captain would be interceding between himself and the Indians. 'Captain, I should have asked before, but – are these Indians cannibalistic?'

Pereira shook his head, steadying himself against a stanchion. 'Not at all. Don't worry about that, they'd have been extinct years ago if they were.'

'Not even – white men?' For some reason Connolly found himself placing a peculiarly indelicate emphasis upon the word 'white'.

Pereira laughed, straightening his uniform jacket. 'For God's sake, Lieutenant, no. Are you worrying that your astronaut might have been eaten by them?'

'I suppose it's a possibility.'

'I assure you, there have been no recorded cases. As a matter of interest, it's a rare practice on this continent. Much more typical of Africa – and Europe,' he added with sly humour. Pausing to smile at Connolly, he said quietly, 'Don't despise the Indians, Lieutenant. However diseased and dirty they may be, at least they are in equilibrium with their environment. And with themselves. You'll find no Christopher Columbuses or Colonel Spenders here, but no Belsens either. Perhaps one is as much a symptom of unease as the other?'

They had begun to drift down the jetty, over-running one of the outriggers, whose bow creaked and disappeared under the stern of the launch, and Pereira shouted at the helmsman: 'Ahead, Sancho! More ahead! Damn Ryker, where is the man?'

Churning out a niagara of boiling brown water, the launch moved forward, driving its shoulder into the bamboo supports, and the entire jetty sprung lightly under the impact. As the motor was cut and the lines finally secured, Connolly looked up at the jetty above his head.

Scowling down at him, an expression of bilious irritability on his heavy-jawed face, was a tall bare-chested man wearing a pair of frayed cotton shorts and a sleeve-less waistcoat of pleated raffia, his dark eyes almost hidden by a wide-brimmed straw hat. The heavy muscles of his exposed chest and arms were the colour of tropical teak, and the white scars on his lips and the fading traces of the heat ulcers which studded his shin bones provided the only lighter colouring. Standing there, arms akimbo with a sort of jaunty arrogance, he seemed to represent to Connolly that quality of untamed energy which he had so far found so conspicuously missing from the forest.

Completing his scrutiny of Connolly, the big man bellowed: 'Pereira, for God's sake, what do you think you're doing? That's my bloody outrigger you've just run down! Tell that steersman of yours to get the cataracts out of his eyes or I'll put a bullet through his backside!'

Grinning good-humouredly, Pereira pulled himself up on to the jetty. 'My dear Ryker, contain yourself. Remember your blood-pressure.' He peered down at the water-logged hulk of the derelict canoe which was now ejecting itself slowly from the river. 'Anyway, what good is a canoe to you, you're not going anywhere.'

Grudgingly, Ryker shook Pereira's hand. 'That's what you like to think, Captain. You and your confounded Mission, you want me to do all the work. Next time you may find I've gone a thousand miles up-river. And taken the Nambas with me.'

'What an epic prospect, Ryker. You'll need a Homer to celebrate it.' Pereira turned and gestured Connolly on to the jetty. The Indians were still hanging about listlessly, like guilty intruders.

Ryker eyed Connolly's uniform suspiciously. 'Who's this? Another so-called anthropologist, sniffing about for smut? I warned you last time, I will not have any more of those.'

'No, Ryker. Can't you recognize the uniform? Let me introduce Lieutenant Connolly, of that brotherhood of latter-day saints, by whose courtesy and generosity we live in peace together – the United Nations.'

'What? Don't tell me they've got a mandate here now? God

above, I suppose he'll bore my head off about cereal/protein ratios!' His ironic groan revealed a concealed reserve of acid humour.

'Relax. The Lieutenant is very charming and polite. He works for the Space Department, Reclamation Division. You know, searching for lost aircraft and the like. There's a chance you may be able to help him.' Pereira winked at Connolly and steered him forward. 'Lieutenant, the Rajah Ryker.'

'I doubt it,' Ryker said dourly. They shook hands, the corded muscles of Ryker's fingers like a trap. Despite his thick-necked stoop, Ryker was a good six to ten inches taller than Connolly. For a moment he held on to Connolly's hand, a slight trace of wariness revealed below his mask of bad temper. 'When did this plane come down?' he asked. Connolly guessed that he was already thinking of a profitable salvage operation.

'Some time ago,' Pereira said mildly. He picked up the parcel containing the cabinet clock and began to stroll after Ryker towards the bungalow at the end of the jetty. A low-eaved dwelling of woven rattan, its single room was surrounded on all sides by a veranda, the overhanging roof shading it from the sunlight. Creepers trailed across from the surrounding foliage, involving it in the background of palms and fronds, so that the house seemed a momentary formalization of the jungle.

'But the Indians might have heard something about it,' Pereira went on. 'Five years ago, as a matter of fact.'

Ryker snorted. 'My God, you've got a hope.' They went up the steps on to the veranda, where a slim-shouldered Indian youth, his eyes like moist marbles, was watching from the shadows. With a snap of irritation, Ryker cupped his hand around the youth's pate and propelled him with a backward swing down the steps. Sprawling on his knees, the youth picked himself up, eyes still fixed on Connolly, then emitted what sounded like a high-pitched nasal hoot, compounded partly of fear and partly of excitement. Connolly looked back from the doorway, and noticed that several other Indians had stepped onto the pier and were watching him with the same expression of rapt curiosity.

Pereira patted Connolly's shoulder. 'I told you they'd be impressed. Did you see that, Ryker?'

Ryker nodded curtly, as they entered his living-room pulled off his straw hat and tossed it on to a couch under the window. The room was dingy and cheerless. Crude bamboo shelves were strung around the walls, ornamented with a few primitive carvings of ivory and bamboo. A couple of rocking chairs and a card-table were in the centre of the room, dwarfed by an immense Victorian mahogany dresser standing against the rear wall. With its castellated mirrors and ornamental pediments it looked like an altar-piece stolen from a cathedral. At first glance it appeared to be leaning to one side, but then Connolly saw that its rear legs had been carefully raised from the tilting floor with a number of small wedges. In the centre of the dresser, its multiple reflections receding to infinity in a pair of small wing mirrors, was a cheap three-dollar alarm clock, ticking away loudly. An over-and-under Winchester shotgun leaned against the wall beside it.

Gesturing Pereira and Connolly into the chairs, Ryker raised the blind over the rear window. Outside was the compound, the circle of huts around its perimeter. A few Indians squatted in the shadows, spears upright between their knees.

Connolly watched Ryker moving about in front of him, aware that the man's earlier impatience had given away to a faint but noticeable edginess. Ryker glanced irritably through the window, apparently annoyed to see the gradual gathering of the Indians before their huts.

There was a sweetly unsavoury smell in the room, and over his shoulder Connolly saw that the card-table was loaded with a large bale of miniature animal skins, those of a vole or some other forest rodent. A half-hearted attempt had been made to trim the skins, and tags of clotted blood clung to their margins.

Ryker jerked the table with his foot. 'Well, here you are,' he said to Pereira. 'Twelve dozen. They took a hell of a lot of getting, I can tell you. You've brought the clock?'

Pereira nodded, still holding the parcel in his lap. He gazed distastefully at the dank scruffy skins. 'Have you got some rats in there, Ryker? These don't look much good. Perhaps we should check through them outside . . .'

'Dammit, Pereira, don't be a fool!' Ryker snapped. 'They're as good as you'll get. I had to trim half the skins myself. Let's have a look at the clock.'

'Wait a minute.' The Captain's jovial, easy-going manner had stiffened. Making the most of his temporary advantage, he reached out and touched one of the skins gingerly, shaking his head. 'Pugh . . . Do you know how much I paid for this clock, Ryker? Seventy-five dollars. That's your credit for three years. I'm not so sure. And you're not very helpful, you know. Now about this aircraft that may have come down –'

Ryker snapped his fingers. 'Forget it. Nothing did. The Nambas tell me everything.' He turned to Connolly. 'You can take it from me there's no trace of an aircraft around here. Any rescue mission would be wasting their time.'

Pereira watched Ryker critically. 'As a matter of fact it wasn't an aircraft.' He tapped Connolly's shoulder flash. 'It was a rocket capsule – with a man on board. A very important and valuable man. None other than the Moon pilot, Colonel Francis Spender.'

'Well . . .' Eyebrows raised in mock surprise, Ryker ambled to the window, stared out at a group of Indians who had advanced halfway across the compound. 'My God, what next! The Moon pilot. Do they really think he's around here? But what a place to roost.' He leaned out of the window and bellowed at the Indians, who retreated a few paces and then held their ground. 'Damn fools,' he muttered, 'this isn't a zoo.'

Pereira handed him the parcel, watching the Indians. There were more than fifty around the compound now, squatting in their doorways, a few of the younger men honing their spears. 'They are remarkably curious,' he said to Ryker, who had taken the parcel over to the dresser and was unwrapping it carefully. 'Surely they've seen a pale-skinned man before?'

'They've nothing better to do.' Ryker lifted the clock out of the cabinet with his big hands, with great care placed it beside the alarm clock, the almost inaudible motion of its pendulum lost in the metallic chatter of the latter's escapement. For a moment he gazed at the ornamental hands and numerals. Then he picked up the alarm clock and with an almost valedictory pat, like an officer dismissing a faithful if stupid minion, locked it away in the cupboard below. His former buoyancy returning, he gave Pereira a playful slap on the shoulder. 'Captain, if you want any more rat-skins just give me a shout!'

Backing away, Pereira's heel touched one of Connolly's feet, distracting Connolly from a problem he had been puzzling over since their entry into the hut. Like a concealed clue in a detective story, he was sure that he had noticed something of significance, but was unable to identify it.

'We won't worry about the skins,' Pereira said. 'What we'll do with your assistance, Ryker, is to hold a little parley with the chiefs, see whether they remember anything of this capsule.'

Ryker stared out at the Indians now standing directly below the veranda. Irritably he slammed down the blind. 'For God's sake, Pereira, they don't. Tell the Lieutenant he isn't interviewing people on Park Avenue or Piccadilly. If the Indians had seen anything I'd know.'

'Perhaps.' Pereira shrugged. 'Still, I'm under instructions to assist Lieutenant Connolly and it won't do any harm to ask.'

Connolly sat up. 'Having come this far, Captain, I feel I should do two or three forays into the bush.' To Ryker he explained: 'They've recalculated the flight path of the final trajectory, there's a chance he may have come down further along the landing zone. Here, very possibly.'

Shaking his head, Ryker slumped down on to the couch, and drove one fist angrily into the other. 'I suppose this means they'll be landing here at any time with thousands of bulldozers and flame-throwers. Dammit, Lieutenant, if you have to send a man to the Moon, why don't you do it in your own back yard?'

Pereira stood up. 'We'll be gone in a couple of days, Ryker.' He nodded judiciously at Connolly and moved towards the door.

As Connolly climbed to his feet Ryker called out suddenly: 'Lieutenant. You can tell me something I've wondered.' There was an unpleasant downward curve to his mouth, and his tone was belligerent and provocative. 'Why did they really send a man to the Moon?'

Connolly paused. He had remained silent during the conversation, not wanting to antagonize Ryker. The rudeness and complete self-immersion were pathetic rather than annoying. 'Do you mean the military and political reasons?'

'No, I don't.' Ryker stood up, arms akimbo again, measuring Connolly. 'I mean the *real* reasons, Lieutenant.'

Connolly gestured vaguely. For some reason formulating a satisfactory answer seemed more difficult than he had expected. 'Well, I suppose you could say it was the natural spirit of exploration.'

Ryker snorted derisively. 'Do you seriously believe that, Lieutenant? "The spirit of exploration!" My God! What a fantastic idea. Pereira doesn't believe that, do you, Captain?'

Before Connolly could reply Pereira took his arm. 'Come on, Lieutenant. This is no time for a metaphysical discussion.' To Ryker he added: 'It doesn't much matter what you and I believe, Ryker. A man went to the Moon and came back. He needs our help.'

Ryker frowned ruefully. 'Poor chap. He must be feeling pretty unhappy by now. Though anyone who gets as far as the Moon and is fool enough to come back deserves what he gets.'

There was a scuffle of feet on the veranda, and as they stepped out into the sunlight a couple of Indians darted away along the jetty, watching Connolly with undiminished interest.

Ryker remained in the doorway, staring listlessly at the clock, but as they were about to climb into the launch he came after them. Now and then glancing over his shoulder at the encroaching semi-circle of Indians, he gazed down at Connolly with sardonic contempt. 'Lieutenant,' he called out before they went below. 'Has it occurred to you that if he had landed, Spender might have wanted to stay on here?'

'I doubt it, Ryker,' Connolly said calmly. 'Anyway, there's little chance that Colonel Spender is still alive. What we're interested in finding is the capsule.'

Ryker was about to reply when a faint metallic buzz sounded

from the direction of his hut. He looked around sharply, waiting for it to end, and for a moment the whole tableau, composed of the men on the launch, the gaunt outcast on the edge of the jetty and the Indians behind him, was frozen in an absurdly motionless posture. The mechanism of the old alarm clock had obviously been fully wound, and the buzz sounded for thirty seconds, finally ending with a high-pitched ping.

Pereira grinned. He glanced at his watch. 'It keeps good time, Ryker.' But Ryker had stalked off back to the hut, scattering the Indians before him.

Connolly watched the group dissolve, then suddenly snapped his fingers. 'You're right, Captain. It certainly does keep good time,' he repeated as they entered the cabin.

Evidently tired by the encounter with Ryker, Pereira slumped down among Connolly's equipment and unbuttoned his tunic. 'Sorry about Ryker, but I warned you. Frankly, Lieutenant, we might as well leave now. There's nothing here. Ryker knows that. However, he's no fool, and he's quite capable of faking all sorts of evidence just to get a retainer out of you. He wouldn't mind if the bulldozers came.'

'I'm not so sure.' Connolly glanced briefly through the porthole. 'Captain, has Ryker got a radio?'

'Of course not. Why?'

'Are you certain?'

'Absolutely. It's the last thing the man would have. Anyway, there's no electrical supply here, and he has no batteries.' He noticed Connolly's intent expression. 'What's on your mind, Lieutenant?'

'You're his only contact? There are no other traders in the area?'

'None. The Indians are too dangerous, and there's nothing to trade. Why do you think Ryker has a radio?'

'He must have. Or something very similar. Captain, just now you remarked on the fact that his old alarm clock kept good time. Does it occur to you to ask *how*?'

Pereira sat up slowly. 'Lieutenant, you have a valid point.'

'Exactly. I knew there was something odd about those two

clocks when they were standing side by side. That type of alarm clock is the cheapest obtainable, notoriously inaccurate. Often they lose two or three minutes in 24 hours. But that clock was telling the right time to within ten seconds. No optical instrument would give him that degree of accuracy.'

Pereira shrugged sceptically. 'But I haven't been here for over four months. And even then he didn't check the time with me.'

'Of course not. He didn't need to. The only possible explanation for such a degree of accuracy is that he's getting a daily time fix, either on a radio or some long-range beacon.'

'Wait a moment, Lieutenant.' Pereira watched the dusk light fall across the jungle. 'It's a remarkable coincidence, but there must be an innocent explanation. Don't jump straight to the conclusion that Ryker has some instrument taken from the missing Moon capsule. Other aircraft have crashed in the forest. And what would be the point? He's not running an airline or railway system. Why should he need to know the time, the *exact* time, to within ten seconds?'

Connolly tapped the lid of his monitoring case, controlling his growing exasperation at Pereira's reluctance to treat the matter seriously, at his whole permissive attitude of lazy tolerance towards Ryker, the Indians and the forest. Obviously he unconsciously resented Connolly's sharp-eyed penetration of this private world.

'Clocks have become his idée fixe,' Pereira continued. 'Perhaps he's developed an amazing sensitivity to its mechanism. Knowing exactly the right time could be a substitute for the civilization on which he turned his back.' Thoughtfully, Pereira moistened the end of his cheroot. 'But I agree that it's strange. Perhaps a little investigation would be worthwhile after all.'

After a cool jungle night in the air-conditioned cabin, the next day Connolly began discreetly to reconnoitre the area. Pereira took ashore two bottles of whisky and a soda syphon, and was able to keep Ryker distracted while Connolly roved about the campong with his monitoring equipment. Once or twice he heard Ryker bellow jocularly at him from his window as he lolled back over the whisky. At intervals, as Ryker slept, Pereira would come out into the sun, sweating like a drowsy pig in his stained uniform, and try to drive back the Indians.

'As long as you stay within earshot of Ryker you're safe,' he told Connolly. Chopped-out pathways criss-crossed the bush at all angles, a new one added whenever one of the bands returned to the campong, irrespective of those already established. This maze extended for miles around them. 'If you get lost, don't panic but stay where you are. Sooner or later we'll come out and find you.'

Eventually giving up his attempt to monitor any of the signal beacons built into the lost capsule – both the sonar and radio meters remained at zero – Connolly tried to communicate with the Indians by sign language, but with the exception of one, the youth with the moist limpid eyes who had been hanging about on Ryker's veranda, they merely stared at him stonily. This youth Pereira identified as the son of the former witch-doctor ('Ryker's more or less usurped his role, for some reason the old boy lost the confidence of the tribe'). While the other Indians gazed at Connolly as if seeing some invisible numinous shadow, some extra-corporeal nimbus which pervaded his body, the youth was obviously aware that Connolly possessed some special talent, perhaps not dissimilar from that which his father had once practised. However, Connolly's attempts to talk to the youth were handicapped by the fact that he was suffering from a purulent ophthalmia, gonococchic in origin and extremely contagious, which made his eyes water continuously. Many of the Indians suffered from this complaint, threatened by permanent blindness, and Connolly had seen them treating their eyes with water in which a certain type of fragrant bark had been dissolved.

Ryker's casual, off-hand authority over the Indians puzzled Connolly. Slumped back in his chair against the mahogany dresser, one hand touching the ormolu clock, most of the time he and Pereira indulged in a lachrymose back-chat. Then, oblivious of any danger, Ryker would amble out into the dusty campong, push his way blurrily through the Indians and drum up a party to collect fire wood for the water still, jerking them bodily to their feet as they squatted about their huts. What interested Connolly was the Indians' reaction to this type of treatment. They seemed to be restrained, not by any belief in his strength of personality or primitive kingship, but by a grudging acceptance that for the time being at any rate, Ryker possessed the whip hand over them all. Obviously Ryker served certain useful roles for them as an intermediary with the Mission, but this alone would not explain the sources of his power. Beyond certain more or less defined limits – the perimeter of the campong – his authority was minimal.

A hint of explanation came on the second morning of their visit, when Connolly accidentally lost himself in the forest.

After breakfast Connolly sat under the awning on the deck of the patrol launch, gazing out over the brown, jelly-like surface of the river. The campong was silent. During the night the Indians had disappeared into the bush. Like lemmings they were apparently prone to these sudden irresistible urges. Occasionally the nomadic call would be strong enough to carry them 200 miles away; at other times they would set off in high spirits and then lose interest after a few miles, returning dispiritedly to the campong in small groups.

Deciding to make the most of their absence, Connolly shouldered the monitoring equipment and climbed onto the pier. A few dying fires smoked plaintively among the huts, and abandoned utensils and smashed pottery lay about in the red dust. In the distance the morning haze over the forest had lifted, and Connolly could see what appeared to be a low hill – a shallow rise no more than a hundred feet in height – which rose off the flat floor of the jungle a quarter of a mile away.

On his right, among the huts, someone moved. An old man sat alone among the refuse of pottery shards and raffia baskets, cross-legged under a small make-shift awning. Barely distinguishable from the dust, his moribund figure seemed to contain the whole futility of the Amazon forest.

Still musing on Ryker's motives for isolating himself in the jungle, Connolly made his way towards the distant rise.

Ryker's behaviour the previous evening had been curious.

Shortly after dusk, when the sunset sank into the western forest, bathing the jungle in an immense ultramarine and golden light, the day-long chatter and movement of the Indians ceased abruptly. Connolly had been glad of the silence – the endless thwacks of the rattan canes and grating of the stone mills in which they mixed the Government-issue meal had become tiresome. Pereira made several cautious visits to the edge of the campong, and each time reported that the Indians were sitting in a huge circle outside their huts, watching Ryker's bungalow. The latter was lounging on his veranda in the moonlight, chin in hand, one boot up on the rail, morosely surveying the assembled tribe.

'They've got their spears and ceremonial feathers,' Pereira whispered. 'For a moment I almost believed they were preparing an attack.'

After waiting half an hour, Connolly climbed up on to the pier, found the Indians squatting in their dark silent circle, Ryker glaring down at them. Only the witch-doctor's son made any attempt to approach Connolly, sidling tentatively through the shadows, a piece of what appeared to be blue obsidian in his hand, some talisman of his father's that had lost its potency.

Uneasily, Connolly returned to the launch. Shortly after 3 a.m. they were wakened in their bunks by a tremendous whoop, reached the deck to hear the stampede of feet through the dust, the hissing of overturned fires and cooking pots. Apparently leading the pack, Ryker, emitting a series of re-echoed 'Harooh's! disappeared into the bush. Within a minute the campong was empty.

'What game is Ryker playing?' Pereira muttered as they stood on the creaking jetty in the dusty moonlight. 'This must be the focus of his authority over the Nambas.' Baffled, they went back to their bunks.

Reaching the margins of the rise, Connolly strolled through a small orchard which had returned to nature, hearing in his mind the exultant roar of Ryker's voice as it had cleaved the midnight jungle. Idly he picked a few of the barely ripe guavas and vividly coloured cajus with their astringent delicately flavoured juice. After spitting away the pith, he searched for a way out of the orchard, but within a few minutes realized that he was lost.

A continuous mound when seen from the distance, the rise was in fact a nexus of small hillocks that formed the residue of a one-time system of ox-bow lakes, and the basins between the slopes were still treacherous with deep mire. Connolly rested his equipment at the foot of a tree. Withdrawing his pistol, he fired two shots into the air in the hope of attracting Ryker and Pereira. He sat down to await his rescue, taking the opportunity to unlatch his monitors and wipe the dials.

After ten minutes no one had appeared. Feeling slightly demoralized, and frightened that the Indians might return and find him, Connolly shouldered his equipment and set off towards the north-west, in the approximate direction of the campong. The ground rose before him. Suddenly, as he turned behind a palisade of wild magnolia trees, he stepped into an open clearing on the crest of the hill.

Squatting on their heels against the tree-trunks and among the tall grass was what seemed to be the entire tribe of the Nambikwaras. They were facing him, their expressions immobile and watchful, eyes like white beads among the sheaves. Presumably they had been sitting in the clearing, only fifty yards away, when he fired his shots, and Connolly had the uncanny feeling that they had been waiting for him to make his entrance exactly at the point he had chosen.

Hesitating, Connolly tightened his grip on the radio monitor. The Indians' faces were like burnished teak, their shoulders painted with a delicate mosaic of earth colours. Noticing the spears held among the grass, Connolly started to walk on across the clearing towards a breach in the palisade of trees.

For a dozen steps the Indians remained motionless. Then, with a chorus of yells, they leapt forward from the grass and surrounded Connolly in a jabbering pack. None of them were more than five feet tall, but their plump agile bodies buffeted him about, almost knocking him off his feet. Eventually the tumult steadied itself, and two or three of the leaders stepped from the cordon and began to scrutinize Connolly more closely, pinching and fingering him with curious positional movements of the thumb and forefinger, like connoisseurs examining some interesting taxidermic object.

Finally, with a series of high-pitched whines and grunts, the Indians moved off towards the centre of the clearing, propelling Connolly in front of them with sharp slaps on his legs and shoulders, like drovers goading on a large pig. They were all jabbering furiously to each other, some hacking at the grass with their machetes, gathering bundles of leaves in their arms.

Tripping over something in the grass, Connolly stumbled onto his knees. The catch slipped from the lid of the monitor, and as he stood up, fumbling with the heavy cabinet, the revolver slipped from his holster and was lost under his feet in the rush.

Giving way to his panic, he began to shout over the bobbing heads around him, to his surprise heard one of the Indians beside him bellow to the others. Instantly, as the refrain was taken up, the crowd stopped and re-formed its cordon around him. Gasping, Connolly steadied himself, and started to search the trampled grass for his revolver, when he realized that the Indians were now staring, not at himself, but at the exposed counters of the monitor. The six meters were swinging wildly after the stampede across the clearing, and the Indians craned forward, their machetes and spears lowered, gaping at the bobbing needles.

Then there was a roar from the edge of the clearing, and a huge wild-faced man in a straw hat, a shot-gun held like a crow-bar in his hands, stormed in among the Indians, driving them back. Dragging the monitor from his neck, Connolly felt the steadying hand of Captain Pereira take his elbow.

'Lieutenant, Lieutenant,' Pereira murmured reprovingly as they recovered the pistol and made their way back to the campong, the uproar behind them fading among the undergrowth, 'we were nearly in time to say grace.'

Later that afternoon Connolly sat back in a canvas chair on the deck of the launch. About half the Indians had returned, and were wandering about the huts in a desultory manner, kicking at the fires. Ryker, his authority re-asserted, had returned to his bungalow.

'I thought you said they weren't cannibal,' Connolly reminded Pereira.

The Captain snapped his fingers, as if thinking about something more important. 'No, they're not. Stop worrying, Lieutenant, you're not going to end up in a pot.' When Connolly demurred he swung crisply on his heel. He had sharpened up his uniform, and wore his pistol belt and Sam Browne at their regulation position, his peaked cap jutting low over his eyes. Evidently Connolly's close escape had confirmed some private suspicion. 'Look, they're not cannibal in the dietary sense of the term, as used by the Food & Agriculture Organization in its classification of aboriginal peoples. They won't stalk and hunt human game in preference for any other. But –' here the Captain stared fixedly at Connolly '– in certain circumstances, after a fertility ceremonial, for example, they will eat human flesh. Like all members of primitive communities which are small numerically, the Nambikwara never bury their dead. Instead, they eat them, as a means of conserving the loss and to perpetuate the corporeal identity of the departed. Now do you understand?'

Connolly grimaced. 'I'm glad to know now that I was about to be perpetuated.'

Pereira looked out at the campong. 'Actually they would never eat a white man, to avoid defiling the tribe.' He paused. 'At least, so I've always believed. It's strange, something seems to have ... Listen, Lieutenant,' he explained, 'I can't quite piece it together, but I'm convinced we should stay here for a few days longer. Various elements make me suspicious, I'm sure Ryker is hiding something. That mound where you were lost is a sort of sacred tumulus, the way the Indians were looking at your instrument made me certain that they'd seen something like it before – perhaps a panel with many flickering dials ... ?'

'The *Goliath 7*?' Connolly shook his head sceptically. He listened to the undertow of the river drumming dimly against the keel of the launch. 'I doubt it, Captain. I'd like to believe you, but for some reason it doesn't seem very likely.'

'I agree. Some other explanation is preferable. But what? The Indians were squatting on that hill, waiting for someone to arrive. What else could your monitor have reminded them of?'

'Ryker's clock?' Connolly suggested. 'They may regard it as a sort of ju-ju object, like a magical toy.'

'No,' Pereira said categorically. 'These Indians are highly pragmatic, they're not impressed by useless toys. For them to be deterred from killing you means that the equipment you carried possessed some very real, down-to-earth power. Look, suppose the capsule did land here and was secretly buried by Ryker, and that in some way the clocks help him to identify its whereabouts –' here Pereira shrugged hopefully '– it's just possible.'

'Hardly,' Connolly said. 'Besides, Ryker couldn't have buried the capsule himself, and if Colonel Spender had lived through re-entry Ryker would have helped him.'

'I'm not so sure,' Pereira said pensively. 'It would probably strike our friend Mr Ryker as very funny for a man to travel all the way to the Moon and back just to be killed by savages. Much too good a joke to pass over.'

'What religious beliefs do the Indians have?' Connolly asked.

'No religion in the formalized sense of a creed and dogma. They eat their dead so they don't need to invent an after-life in an attempt to re-animate them. In general they subscribe to one of the so-called cargo cults. As I said, they're very material. That's why they're so lazy. Some time in the future they expect a magic galleon or giant bird to arrive carrying an everlasting cornucopia of worldly goods, so they just sit about waiting for the great day. Ryker encourages them in this idea. It's very dangerous – in some Melanesian islands the tribes with cargo cults have degenerated completely. They lie around all day on the beaches, waiting for the WHO flying boat, or . . .' His voice trailed off.

Connolly nodded and supplied the unspoken thought. 'Or – a space capsule?'

Despite Pereira's growing if muddled conviction that something associated with the missing space-craft was to be found in the area, Connolly was still sceptical. His close escape had left him feeling curiously calm and emotionless, and he looked back on his possible death with fatalistic detachment, identifying it with the total ebb and flow of life in the Amazon forests, with its myriad unremembered deaths, and with the endless vistas of dead trees leaning across the jungle paths radiating from the campong. After only two days the jungle had begun to invest his mind with its own logic, and the possibility of the space-craft landing there seemed more and more remote. The two elements belonged to different systems of natural order, and he found it increasingly difficult to visualize them overlapping. In addition there was a deeper reason for his scepticism, underlined by Ryker's reference to the 'real' reasons for the space-flights. The implication was that the entire space programme was a symptom of some inner unconscious malaise afflicting mankind, and in particular the western technocracies, and that the space-craft and satellites had been launched because their flights satisfied certain buried compulsions and desires. By contrast, in the jungle, where the unconscious was manifest and exposed, there was no need for these insane projections, and the likelihood of the Amazonas playing any part in the success or failure of the space flight became, by a sort of psychological parallax, increasingly blurred and distant, the missing capsule itself a fragment of a huge disintegrating fantasy.

However, he agreed to Pereira's request to borrow the monitors and follow Ryker and the Indians on their midnight romp through the forest.

Once again, after dusk, the same ritual silence descended over the campong, and the Indians took up their positions in the doors of their huts. Like some morose exiled princeling, Ryker sat sprawled on his veranda, one eye on the clock through the window behind him. In the moonlight the scores of moist dark eyes never wavered as they watched him.

At last, half an hour later, Ryker galvanized his great body into life, with a series of tremendous whoops raced off across the campong, leading the stampede into the bush. Away in the distance, faintly outlined by the quarter moon, the shallow hump of the tribal tumulus rose over the black canopy of the jungle. Pereira waited until the last heel beats had subsided, then climbed onto the pier and disappeared among the shadows.

Far away Connolly could hear the faint cries of Ryker's pack as they made off through the bush, the sounds of machetes slashing at the undergrowth. An ember on the opposite side of the campong flared in the low wind, illuminating the abandoned old man, presumably the former witch doctor, whom he had seen that morning. Beside him was another slimmer figure, the limpid-eyed youth who had followed Connolly about.

A door stirred on Ryker's veranda, providing Connolly with a distant image of the white moonlit back of the river reflected in the mirrors of the mahogany dresser. Connolly watched the door jump lightly against the latch, then walked quietly across the pier to the wooden steps.

A few empty tobacco tins lay about on the shelves around the room, and a stack of empty bottles cluttered one corner behind the door. The ormolu clock had been locked away in the mahogany dresser. After testing the doors, which had been secured with a stout padlock, Connolly noticed a dog-eared paperback book lying on the dresser beside a half-empty carton of cartridges.

On a faded red ground, the small black lettering on the cover was barely decipherable, blurred by the sweat from Ryker's fingers. At first glance it appeared to be a set of logarithm tables. Each of the eighty or so pages was covered with column after column of finely printed numerals and tabular material.

Curious, Connolly carried the manual over to the doorway. The title page was more explicit.

ECHO III
CONSOLIDATED TABLES OF
CELESTIAL TRAVERSES
1965–1980

Published by the National Astronautics and Space Administration, Washington, D.C., 1965. Part XV. Longitude 40-80 West,

*Latitude 10 North-35 South (South American Sub-Continent)
Price 35ᶜ.*

His interest quickening, Connolly turned the pages. The manual fell open at the section headed: Lat. 5 South, Long, 60 West. He remembered that this was the approximate position of Campos Buros. Tabulated by year, month and day, the columns of figures listed the elevations and compass bearings for sightings of the Echo III satellite, the latest of the huge aluminium spheres which had been orbiting the earth since Echo I was launched in 1959. Rough pencil lines had been drawn through all the entries up to the year 1968. At this point the markings became individual, each minuscule entry crossed off with a small blunt stroke. The pages were grey with the blurred graphite.

Guided by this careful patchwork of cross-hatching, Connolly found the latest entry: March 17, 1978. The time and sighting were. 1-22 *a.m. Elevation* 43 *degrees WNW, Capella-Eridanus.* Below it was the entry for the next day, an hour later, its orientations differing slightly.

Ruefully shaking his head in admiration of Ryker's cleverness, Connolly looked at his watch. It was about 1.20, two minutes until the next traverse. He glanced at the sky, picking out the constellation Eridanus, from which the satellite would emerge.

So this explained Ryker's hold over the Indians! What more impressive means had a down-and-out white man of intimidating and astonishing a tribe of primitive savages? Armed with nothing more than a set of tables and a reliable clock, he could virtually pinpoint the appearance of the satellite at the first second of its visible traverse. The Indians would naturally be awed and bewildered by this phantom charioteer of the midnight sky, steadily pursuing its cosmic round, like a beacon traversing the profoundest deeps of their own minds. Any powers which Ryker cared to invest in the satellite would seem confirmed by his ability to control the time and place of its arrival.

Connolly realized now how the old alarm clock had told the correct time – by using his tables Ryker had read the exact time off the sky each night. A more accurate clock presumably freed him from the need to spend unnecessary time waiting for the satellite's arrival; he would now be able to set off for the tumulus only a few minutes beforehand.

Walking along the pier he began to search the sky. Away in the distance a low cry sounded into the midnight air, diffusing like a wraith over the jungle. Beside him, sitting on the bows of the launch, Connolly heard the helmsman grunt and point at the sky above the opposite bank. Following the up-raised arm, he quickly found the speeding dot of light. It was moving directly towards the tumulus. Steadily the satellite crossed the sky, winking intermittently as it passed behind lanes of high-altitude cirrus, the conscripted ship of the Nambikwaras' cargo cult.

It was about to disappear among the stars in the south-east when a faint shuffling sound distracted Connolly. He looked down to find the moist-eyed youth, the son of the witch doctor, standing only a few feet away from him, regarding him dolefully.

'Hello, boy,' Connolly greeted him. He pointed at the vanishing satellite. 'See the star?'

The youth made a barely perceptible nod. He hesitated for a moment, his running eyes glowing like drowned moons, then stepped forward and touched Connolly's wristwatch, tapping the dial with his horny fingernail.

Puzzled, Connolly held it up for him to inspect. The youth watched the second hand sweep around the dial, an expression of rapt and ecstatic concentration on his face. Nodding vigorously, he pointed to the sky.

Connolly grinned. 'So you understand? You've rumbled old man Ryker, have you?' He nodded encouragingly to the youth, who was tapping the watch eagerly, apparently in an effort to conjure up a second satellite. Connolly began to laugh. 'Sorry, boy.' He slapped the manual. 'What you really need is this pack of jokers.'

Connolly began to walk back to the bungalow, when the youth darted forward impulsively and blocked his way, thin legs spread in an aggressive stance. Then, with immense ceremony, he drew from behind his back a round painted object with a glass face that Connolly remembered he had seen him carrying before.

'That looks interesting.' Connolly bent down to examine the object, caught a glimpse in the thin light of a luminous instrument before the youth snatched it away.

'Wait a minute, boy. Let's have another look at that.'

After a pause the pantomime was repeated, but the youth was reluctant to allow Connolly more than the briefest inspection. Again Connolly saw a calibrated dial and a wavering indicator. Then the youth stepped forward and touched Connolly's wrist.

Quickly Connolly unstrapped the metal chain. He tossed the watch to the youth, who instantly dropped the instrument, his barter achieved, and after a delighted yodel turned and darted off among the trees.

Bending down, careful not to touch the instrument with his hands, Connolly examined the dial. The metal housing around it was badly torn and scratched, as if the instrument had been prised from some control panel with a crude implement. But the glass face and the dial beneath it were still intact. Across the centre was the legend:

LUNAR ALTIMETER
Miles: 100
GOLIATH 7
General Electric Corporation,
Schenectedy

Picking up the instrument, Connolly cradled it in his hands. The pressure seals were broken, and the gyro bath floated freely on its air cushion. Like a graceful bird the indicator needle glided up and down the scale.

The pier creaked under approaching footsteps. Connolly looked up at the perspiring figure of Captain Pereira, cap in one hand, monitor dangling from the other.

'My dear Lieutenant!' he panted. 'Wait till I tell you, what a farce, it's fantastic! Do you know what Ryker's doing? – it's so simple it seems unbelievable that no one's thought of it before.

It's nothing short of the most magnificent practical *joke*!' Gasping, he sat down on the bale of skins leaning against the gangway. 'I'll give you a clue: Narcissus.'

'Echo,' Connolly replied flatly, still staring at the instrument in his hands.

'You spotted it? Clever boy!' Pereira wiped his cap-band. 'How did you guess? It wasn't that obvious.' He took the manual Connolly handed him. 'What the –? Ah, I see, this makes it even more clear. Of course.' He slapped his knee with the manual. 'You found this in his room? I take my hat off to Ryker,' he continued as Connolly set the altimeter down on the pier and steadied it carefully. 'Let's face it, it's something of a pretty clever trick. Can you imagine it, he comes here, finds a tribe with a strong cargo cult, opens his little manual and says "Presto, the great white bird will be arriving: *NOW*!"'

Connolly nodded, then stood up, wiping his hands on a strip of rattan. When Pereira's laughter had subsided he pointed down to the glowing face of the altimeter at their feet. 'Captain, something else arrived,' he said quietly. 'Never mind Ryker and the satellite. This cargo actually landed.'

As Pereira knelt down and inspected the altimeter, whistling sharply to himself, Connolly walked over to the edge of the pier and looked out across the great back of the silent river at the giant trees which hung over the water, like forlorn mutes at some cataclysmic funeral, their thin silver voices carried away on the dead tide.

Half an hour before they set off the next morning, Connolly waited on the deck for Captain Pereira to conclude his interrogation of Ryker. The empty campong, deserted again by the Indians, basked in the heat, a single plume of smoke curling into the sky. The old witch doctor and his son had disappeared, perhaps to try their skill with a neighbouring tribe, but the loss of his watch was unregretted by Connolly. Down below, safely stowed away among his baggage, was the altimeter, carefully sterilized and sealed. On the table in front of him, no more than two feet from the pistol in his belt, lay Ryker's manual.

For some reason he did not want to see Ryker, despite his contempt for him, and when Pereira emerged from the bungalow he was relieved to see that he was alone. Connolly had decided that he would not return with the search parties when they came to find the capsule; Pereira would serve adequately as a guide.

'Well?'

The Captain smiled wanly. 'Oh, he admitted it, of course.' He sat down on the rail, and pointed to the manual. 'After all, he had no choice. Without that his existence here would be untenable.'

'He admitted that Colonel Spender landed here?'

Pereira nodded. 'Not in so many words, but effectively. The capsule is buried somewhere here – under the tumulus, I would guess. The Indians got hold of Colonel Spender, Ryker claims he could do nothing to help him.'

'That's a lie. He saved me in the bush when the Indians thought I had landed.'

With a shrug Pereira said: 'Your positions were slightly different. Besides, my impression is that Spender was dying anyway, Ryker says the parachute was badly burnt. He probably accepted a *fait accompli*, simply decided to do nothing and hush the whole thing up, incorporating the landing into the cargo cult. Very useful too. He'd been tricking the Indians with the Echo satellite, but sooner or later they would have become impatient. After the *Goliath* crashed, of course, they were prepared to go on watching the Echo and waiting for the next landing forever.' A faint smile touched his lips. 'It goes without saying that he regards the episode as something of a macabre joke. On you and the whole civilized world.'

A door slammed on the veranda, and Ryker stepped out into the sunlight. Bare-chested and hatless, he strode towards the launch.

'Connolly,' he called down, 'you've got my box of tricks there!'

Connolly reached forward and fingered the manual, the butt of his pistol tapping the table edge. He looked up at Ryker, at his big golden frame bathed in the morning light. Despite his still belligerent tone, a subtle change had come over Ryker.

The ironic gleam in his eye had gone, and the inner core of wariness and suspicion which had warped the man and exiled him from the world was now visible. Connolly realized that, curiously, their respective roles had been reversed. He remembered Pereira reminding him that the Indians were at equilibrium with their environment, accepting its constraints and never seeking to dominate the towering arbors of the forest, in a sense of externalization of their own unconscious psyches. Ryker had upset that equilibrium, and by using the Echo satellite had brought the 20th century and its psychopathic projections into the heart of the Amazonian deep, transforming the Indians into a community of superstitious and materialistic sightseers, their whole culture oriented around the mythical god of the puppet star. It was Connolly who now accepted the jungle for what it was, seeing himself and the abortive space-flight in this fresh perspective.

Pereira gestured to the helmsman, and with a muffled roar the engine started. The launch pulled lightly against its lines.

'Connolly!' Ryker's voice was shriller now, his bellicose shout overlaid by a higher note. For a moment the two men looked at each other, and in the eyes above him Connolly glimpsed the helpless isolation of Ryker, his futile attempt to identify himself with the forest.

Picking up the manual, Connolly leaned forward and tossed it through the air on to the pier. Ryker tried to catch it, then knelt down and picked it up before it slipped through the springing poles. Still kneeling, he watched as the lines were cast off and the launch surged ahead.

They moved out into the channel and plunged through the bowers of spray into the heavier swells of the open current.

As they reached a sheltering bend and the figure of Ryker faded for the last time among the creepers and sunlight, Connolly turned to Pereira. 'Captain – what actually happened to Colonel Spender? You said the Indians wouldn't eat a white man.'

'They eat their gods,' Pereira said.

1963

THE TIME-TOMBS

ONE

Usually in the evenings, while Traxel and Bridges drove off into the sand-sea, Shepley and the Old Man would wander among the gutted time-tombs, listening to them splutter faintly in the dying light as they recreated their fading personas, the deep crystal vaults flaring briefly like giant goblets.

Most of the tombs on the southern edge of the sand-sea had been stripped centuries earlier. But Shepley liked to saunter through the straggle of half-submerged pavilions, the ancient sand playing over his bare feet like wavelets on an endless beach. Alone among the flickering tombs, with the empty husks of the past ten thousand years, he could temporarily forget his nagging sense of failure.

Tonight, however, he would have to forego the walk. Traxel, who was nominally the leader of the group of tomb-robbers, had pointedly warned him at dinner that he must pay his way or leave. For three weeks Shepley had put off going with Traxel and Bridges, making a series of progressively lamer excuses, and they had begun to get impatient with him. The Old Man they would tolerate, for his vast knowledge of the sand-sea – he had combed the decaying tombs for over forty years and knew every reef and therm-pool like the palm of his hand – and because he was an institution that somehow dignified the lowly calling of tomb-robber, but Shepley had been there for only three months and had nothing to offer except his morose silences and self-hate.

'Tonight, Shepley,' Traxel told him firmly in his hard clipped voice, 'you must find a tape. We cannot support you indefinitely. Remember, we're all as eager to leave Vergil as you are.'

Shepley nodded, watching his reflection in the gold fingerbowl. Traxel sat at the head of the tilting table, his high-collared velvet jacket unbuttoned. Surrounded by the battered gold plate filched from the tombs, red wine spilling across the table from Bridges' tankard, he looked more like a Renaissance princeling than a cashiered PhD. Once Traxel had been a Professor of Semantics, and Shepley wondered what scandal had brought him to Vergil. Now, like a grave-rat, he hunted the time-tombs with Bridges, selling the tapes to the Psycho-History Museums at a dollar a foot. Shepley found it impossible to come to terms with the tall, aloof man. By contrast Bridges, who was just a thug, had a streak of blunt good humour that made him tolerable, but with Traxel he could never relax. Perhaps his coldly abrupt manner represented authority, the high-faced, stern-eyed interrogators who still pursued Shepley in his dreams.

Bridges kicked back his chair and lurched away around the table, pounding Shepley across the shoulders.

'You come with us, kid. Tonight we'll find a megatape.'

Outside, the low-hulled, camouflaged half-track waited in a saddle between two dunes. The old summer palace was sinking slowly below the desert, and the floor of the banqueting hall shelved into the white sand like the deck of a subsiding liner, going down with lights blazing from its staterooms.

'What about you, Doctor?' Traxel asked the Old Man as Bridges swung aboard the half-track and the exhaust kicked out. 'It would be a pleasure to have you along.' When the Old Man shook his head Traxel turned to Shepley. 'Well, are you coming?'

'Not tonight,' Shepley demurred hurriedly. 'I'll walk down to the tomb-beds later myself.'

'Twenty miles?' Traxel reminded him, watching reflectively. 'Very well.' He zipped up his jacket and strode away towards the half-track. As they moved off he shouted 'Shepley, I meant what I said!'

Shepley watched them disappear among the dunes. Flatly, he repeated 'He means what he says.'

The Old Man shrugged, sweeping the sand off the table. 'Traxel ... he's a difficult man. What are you going to do?' The note of reproach in his voice was mild, realizing that Shepley's motives were the same as those which had marooned himself on the lost beaches of the sand-sea four decades earlier.

Shepley snapped irritably. 'I can't go with him. After five minutes he drains me like a skull. What's the matter with Traxel? Why is he here?'

The Old Man stood up, staring out vaguely into the desert. 'I can't remember. Everyone has his own reasons. After a while the stories overlap.'

They walked out under the portico, following the grooves left by the half-track. A mile away, winding between the last of the lavalakes which marked the southern shore of the sand-sea, they could just see the vehicle vanishing into the darkness. The old tomb-beds, where Shepley and the Old Man usually walked, lay between them, the pavilions arranged in three lines along a low basaltic ridge. Occasionally a brief flare of light flickered up into the white, bone-like darkness, but most of the tombs were silent.

Shepley stopped, hands falling limply to his sides. 'The new beds are by the Lake of Newton, nearly twenty miles away. I can't follow them.'

'I shouldn't try,' the Old Man rejoined. 'There was a big sandstorm last night. The time-wardens will be out in force marking any new tombs uncovered.' He chuckled softly to himself. 'Traxel and Bridges won't find a foot of tape – they'll be lucky if they're not arrested.' He took off his white cotton hat and squinted shrewdly through the dead light, assessing the altered contours of the dunes, then guided Shepley towards the old mono-rail whose southern terminus ended by the tomb-beds. Once it had been used to transport the pavilions from the station on the northern shore of the sand-sea, and a small gyro-car still leaned against the freight platform. 'We'll go over to Pascal. Something may have come up, you never know.'

Shepley shook his head. 'Traxel took me there when I first arrived. They've all been stripped a hundred times.'

'Well, we'll have a look.' The Old Man plodded on towards the mono-rail, his dirty white suit flapping in the low breeze. Behind them the summer palace – built three centuries earlier by a business tycoon from Ceres – faded into the darkness, the rippling glass tiles in the upper spires merging into the starlight.

Propping the car against the platform, Shepley wound up the gyroscope, then helped the Old Man on to the front seat. He prised off a piece of rusting platform rail and began to punt the car away. Every fifty yards or so they stopped to clear the sand that submerged the track, but slowly they wound off among the dunes and lakes. Here and there the onion-shaped cupola of a solitary time-tomb reared up into the sky beside them, fragments of the crystal casements twinkling in the sand like minuscule stars.

Half an hour later, as they rode down the final long incline towards the Lake of Pascal, Shepley went forward to sit beside the Old Man, who emerged from his private reverie to ask pointedly, 'And you, Shepley, why are you here?'

Shepley leaned back, letting the cool air drain the sweat off his face. 'Once I tried to kill someone,' he explained tersely. 'After they cured me I found I wanted to kill myself instead.' He reached down to the hand-brake as they gathered speed. 'For ten thousand dollars I can go back on probation. Here I thought there would be a freemasonry of sorts. But then you've been kind enough, Doctor.'

'Don't worry, we'll get you a winning tape.' He leaned forward, shielding his eyes from the stellar glare, gazing down at the little cantonment of gutted time-tombs on the shore of the lake. In all there were about a dozen pavilions, their roofs holed, the group Traxel had shown to Shepley after his arrival when he demonstrated how the vaults were robbed.

'Shepley! Look, lad!'

'Where? I've seen them before, Doctor. They're stripped.'

The Old Man pushed him away. 'No, you fool. Three hundred yards to the west, by the long ridge where the big dunes have moved. Can you see them now?' He drummed a white fist on

Shepley's knee. 'You've made it, lad. You won't need to be frightened of Traxel or anyone else.'

Shepley jerked the car to a halt. As he ran ahead of the Old Man towards the escarpment he could see several of the time-tombs glowing along the sky lines, emerging briefly from the dark earth like the tents of a spectral caravan.

TWO

For ten millennia the Sea of Vergil had served as a burial ground, and the 1,500 square miles of restless sand were estimated to contain over twenty thousand tombs. All but a minute fraction had been stripped by the successive generations of tomb-robbers, and an intact spool of the 17th Dynasty could now be sold to the Psycho-History Museum at Tycho for over 3,000 dollars. For each preceding dynasty, though none older than the 12th had ever been found, there was a bonus.

There were no corpses in the time-tombs, no dusty skeletons. The cyber-architectonic ghosts which haunted them were embalmed in the metallic codes of memory tapes, three-dimensional molecular transcriptions of their living originals, stored among the dunes as a stupendous act of faith, in the hope that one day the physical re-creation of the coded personalities would be possible. After five thousand years the attempt had been reluctantly abandoned, but out of respect for the tomb-builders their pavilions were left to take their own hazard with time in the Sea of Vergil. Later the tomb-robbers had arrived, as the historians of the new epochs realized the enormous archives that lay waiting for them in this antique limbo. Despite the time-wardens, the pillaging of the tombs and the illicit traffic in dead souls continued.

'Doctor! Come on! Look at them!'

Shepley plunged wildly up to his knees in the silver-white sand, diving from one pavilion to the next like a frantic puppy.

Smiling to himself, the Old Man climbed slowly up the melting slope, submerged to his waist as the fine crystals poured away around him, feeling for spurs of firmer rock. The cupola of the nearest tomb tilted into the sky, only the top six inches of the casements visible below the overhang. He sat for a moment on the roof, watching Shepley dive about in the darkness, then peered through the casement, brushing away the sand with his hands.

The tomb was intact. Inside he could see the votive light burning over the altar, the hexagonal nave with its inlaid gold floor and drapery, the narrow chancel at the rear which held the memory store. Low tables surrounded the chancel, carrying beaten goblets and gold bowls, token offerings intended to distract any pillager who stumbled upon the tomb.

Shepley came leaping over to him. 'Let's get into them, Doctor! What are we waiting for?'

The Old Man looked out over the plain below, at the cluster of stripped tombs by the edge of the lake, at the dark ribbon of the gyro-rail winding away among the hills. The thought of the fortune that lay at his fingertips left him unmoved. For so long now he had lived among the tombs that he had begun to assume something of their ambience of immortality and timelessness, and Shepley's impatience seemed to come out of another dimension. He hated stripping the tombs. Each one robbed represented, not just the final extinction of a surviving personality, but a diminution of his own sense of eternity. Whenever a new tomb-bed emerged from the sand he felt something within himself momentarily rekindled, not hope, for he was beyond that, but a serene acceptance of the brief span of time left to him.

'Right,' he nodded. They began to cleave away the sand piled around the door, Shepley driving it down the slope where it spilled in a white foam over the darker basaltic chips. When the narrow portico was free the Old Man squatted by the timeseal. His fingers cleaned away the crystals embedded between the tabs, then played lightly over them.

Like dry sticks breaking, an ancient voice crackled

> *Orion, Betelgeuse, Altair,*
> *What twice-born star shall be my heir,*
> *Doomed again to be this scion –*

'Come on, Doctor, this is a quicker way.' Shepley put one leg up against the door and lunged against it futilely. The Old Man pushed him away. With his mouth close to the seal, he rejoined.

'Of Altair, Betelgeuse, Orion.'

As the doors accepted this and swung back he murmured:
'Don't despise the old rituals. Now, let's see.' They paused in the cool, unbreathed air, the votive light throwing a pale ruby glow over the gold drapes parting across the chancel.

The air became curiously hazy and mottled. Within a few seconds it began to vibrate with increasing rapidity, and a succession of vivid colours rippled across the surface of what appeared to be a cone of light projected from the rear of the chancel. Soon this resolved itself into a three-dimensional image of an elderly man in a blue robe.

Although the image was transparent, the brilliant electric blue of the robe revealing the inadequacies of the projection system, the intensity of the illusion was such that Shepley almost expected the man to speak to them. He was well into his seventies, with a composed, watchful face and thin grey hair, his hands resting quietly in front of him. The edge of the desk was just visible, the proximal arc of the cone enclosing part of a silver inkstand and a small metal trophy. These details, and the spectral bookshelves and paintings which formed the backdrop of the illusion, were of infinite value to the Psycho-History institutes, providing evidence of the earlier civilizations far more reliable than the funerary urns and goblets in the anteroom.

Shepley began to move forward, the definition of the persona fading slightly. A visual relay of the memory store, it would continue to play after the code had been removed, though the induction coils would soon exhaust themselves. Then the tomb would be finally extinct.

Two feet away, the wise unblinking eyes of the long dead magnate stared at him steadily, his seamed forehead like a piece of pink transparent wax. Tentatively, Shepley reached out and plunged his hand into the cone, the myriad vibration patterns racing across his wrist. For a moment he held the dead man's face in his hand, the edge of the desk and the silver inkstand dappling across his sleeve.

Then he stepped forward and walked straight through him into the darkness at the rear of the chancel.

Quickly, following Traxel's instructions, he unbolted the console containing the memory store, lifting out the three heavy drums which held the tape spools. Immediately the persona began to dim, the edge of the desk and the bookshelves vanishing as the cone contracted. Narrow bands of dead air appeared across it, one, at the level of the man's neck, decapitating him. Lower down the scanner had begun to misfire. The folded hands trembled nervously, and now and then one of his shoulders gave a slight twitch. Shepley stepped through him without looking back.

The Old Man was waiting outside. Shepley dropped the drums on to the sand. 'They're heavy,' he muttered. Brightening, he added. 'There must be over five hundred feet here, Doctor. With the bonus, and all the others as well –' He took the Old Man's arm. 'Come on, let's get into the next one.'

The Old Man disengaged himself, watching the sputtering persona in the pavilion, the blue light from the dead man's suit pulsing across the sand like a soundless lightning storm.

'Wait a minute, lad, don't run away with yourself.' As Shepley began to slide off through the sand, sending further falls down the slope, he added in a firmer voice 'And stop moving all that sand around! These tombs have been hidden for ten thousand years. Don't undo all the good work, or the wardens will find them the first time they go past.'

'Or Traxel,' Shepley said, sobering quickly. He glanced around the lake below, searching the shadows among the tombs in case anyone was watching them, waiting to seize the treasure.

THREE

The Old Man left him at the door of the next pavilion, reluctant to watch the tomb being stripped of the last vestige of its already meagre claim to immortality.

'This will be our last one tonight,' he told Shepley. 'You'll never hide all these tapes from Bridges and Traxel.'

The furnishings of the tomb differed from that of the previous one. Sombre black marble panels covered the walls, inscribed with strange gold-leaf hieroglyphs, and the inlays in the floor represented stylized astrological symbols, at once eerie and obscure. Shepley leaned against the altar, watching the cone of light reach out towards him from the chancel as the curtains parted. The predominant colours were gold and carmine, mingled with a vivid powdery copper that gradually resolved itself into the huge, harp-like head-dress of a reclining woman. She lay in the centre of what seemed to be a sphere of softly luminous gas, inclined against a massive black catafalque, from the sides of which flared two enormous heraldic wings. The woman's copper hair was swept straight back from her forehead, some five or six feet long, and merged with the plumage of the wings, giving her an impression of tremendous contained speed, like a goddess arrested in a moment of flight on a cornice of some great temple-city of the dead.

Her eyes stared forward expressionlessly at Shepley. Her arms and shoulders were bare, and the white skin, like compacted snow, had a brilliant surface sheen, the reflected light glaring against the black base of the catafalque and the long sheath-like gown that swept around her hips to the floor. Her face, like an exquisite porcelain mask, was tilted upward slightly, the half-closed eyes suggesting that the woman was asleep or dreaming. No background had been provided for the image, but the bowl of luminescence invested the persona with immense power and mystery.

Shepley heard the Old Man shuffle up behind him.

'Who is she, Doctor? A princess?'

The Old Man shook his head slowly. 'You can only guess. I

don't know. There are strange treasures in these tombs. Get on with it, we'd best be going.'

Shepley hesitated. He started to walk towards the woman on the catafalque, and then felt the enormous upward surge of her flight, the pressure of all the past centuries carried before her brought to a sudden focus in front of him, holding him back like a physical barrier.

'Doctor!' He reached the door just behind the Old Man. 'We'll leave this one, there's no hurry!'

The Old Man examined his face shrewdly in the moonlight, the brilliant colours of the persona flickering across Shepley's youthful cheeks. 'I know how you feel, lad, but remember, the woman doesn't exist, any more than a painting. You'll have to come back for her soon.'

Shepley nodded quickly. 'I know, but some other night. There's something uncanny about this tomb.' He closed the doors behind them, and immediately the huge cone of light shrank back into the chancel, sucking the woman and the catafalque into the darkness. The wind swept across the dunes, throwing a fine spray of sand on to the half-buried cupolas, sighing among the wrecked tombs.

The Old Man made his way down to the mono-rail, and waited for Shepley as he worked for the next hour, slowly covering each of the tombs.

On the Old Man's recommendation he gave Traxel only one of the canisters, containing about 500 feet of tape. As prophesied, the time-wardens had been out in force in the Sea of Newton, and two members of another gang had been caught red-handed. Bridges was in foul temper, but Traxel, as ever self-contained, seemed unworried at the wasted evening.

Straddling the desk in the tilting ballroom, he examined the drum with interest, complimenting Shepley on his initiative. 'Excellent, Shepley. I'm glad you joined us now. Do you mind telling me where you found this?'

Shepley shrugged vaguely, began to mumble something about a secret basement in one of the gutted tombs nearby, but the Old Man cut in: 'Don't broadcast it everywhere! Traxel, you shouldn't ask questions like that – he's got his own living to earn.'

Traxel smiled, sphinx-like. 'Right again, Doctor.' He tapped the smooth untarnished case. 'In mint condition, and a 15th Dynasty too.'

'Tenth!' Shepley claimed indignantly, frightened that Traxel might try to pocket the bonus. The Old Man cursed, and Traxel's eyes gleamed.

'Tenth, is it? I didn't realize there were any 10th Dynasty tombs still intact. You surprise me, Shepley. Obviously you have concealed talents.'

Luckily he seemed to assume that the Old Man had been hoarding the tape for years.

Face down in a shallow hollow at the edge of the ridge, Shepley watched the white-hulled sand-car of the time-wardens shunt through the darkness by the old cantonment. Directly below him jutted the spires of the newly discovered tomb-bed, invisible against the dark background of the ridge. The two wardens in the sand-car were more interested in the old tombs; they had spotted the gyro-car lying on its side by the mono-rail, and guessed that the gangs had been working the ruins over again. One of them stood on the running board, flicking a torch into the gutted pavilions. Crossing the mono-rail, the car moved off slowly across the lake to the north-west, a low pall of dust settling behind it.

For a few moments Shepley lay quietly in the slack darkness, watching the gullies and ravines that led into the lake, then slid down among the pavilions. Brushing away the sand to reveal a square wooden plank, he slipped below it into the portico.

As the golden image of the enchantress loomed out of the black-walled chancel to greet him, the great reptilian wings unfurling around her, he stood behind one of the columns in the nave, fascinated by her strange deathless beauty. At times her luminous face seemed almost repellent, but he had nonetheless seized on the faint possibility of her resurrection. Each night he came, stealing into the tomb where she had lain for ten thousand years, unable to bring himself to interrupt her. The long copper hair streamed behind her like an entrained time-wind, her angled body in flight between two infinitely distant universes, where archetypal beings of superhuman stature glimmered fitfully in their own self-generated light.

Two days later Bridges discovered the remainder of the drums.

'Traxel! Traxel!' he bellowed, racing across the inner courtyard from the entrance to one of the disused bunkers. He bounded into the ballroom and slammed the metal cans on to the computer which Traxel was programming. 'Take a look at these – more Tenths! The whole place is crawling with them!'

Traxel weighed the cans idly in his hands, glancing across at Shepley and the Old Man, on lookout duty by the window. 'Interesting. Where did you find them?'

Shepley jumped down from the window trestle. 'They're mine. The Doctor will confirm it. They run in sequence after the first I gave you a week ago. I was storing them.'

Bridges cut back with an oath. 'Whaddya mean, storing them? Is that your personal bunker out there? Since when?' He shoved Shepley away with a broad hand and swung round on Traxel. 'Listen, Traxel, those tapes were a fair find. I don't see any tags on them. Every time I bring something in I'm going to have this kid claim it?'

Traxel stood up, adjusting his height so that he overreached Bridges. 'Of course, you're right – technically. But we have to work together, don't we? Shepley made a mistake, we'll forgive him this time.' He handed the drums to Shepley, Bridges seething with barely controlled indignation. 'If I were you, Shepley, I'd get those cashed. Don't worry about flooding the market.' As Shepley turned away, sidestepping Bridges, he called him back. 'And there are advantages in working together, you know.'

He watched Shepley disappear to his room, then turned to survey the huge peeling map of the sand-sea that covered the facing wall.

'You'll have to strip the tombs now,' the Old Man told Shepley later. 'It's obvious you've stumbled on something, and it won't take Traxel five minutes to discover where.'

'Perhaps a little longer,' Shepley replied evenly. They stepped out of the shadow of the palace and moved away among the dunes; Bridges and Traxel were watching them from the dining-room table, their figures motionless in the light. 'The roofs are almost covered now. The next sandstorm should bury them for good.'

'Have you entered any of the other tombs?'

Shepley shook his head vigorously. 'Believe me, Doctor, I know now why the time-wardens are here. As long as there's a chance of their coming to life we're committing murder every time we rob a tomb. Even if it's only one chance in a million it may be all they bargained on. After all, we don't commit suicide because the chances of life existing anywhere are virtually nil.'

Already he had come to believe that the enchantress might suddenly resurrect herself, step down from the catafalque before his eyes. While a slender possibility existed of her returning to life he felt that he too had a valid foothold in existence, that there was a small element of certainty in what had previously seemed a random and utterly meaningless universe.

FOUR

As the first dawn light probed through the casements, Shepley turned reluctantly from the nave. He looked back briefly at the glowing persona, suppressing the slight pang of disappointment that the expected metamorphosis had not yet occurred, but relieved to have spent as much time awaiting it as possible.

He made his way down to the old cantonment, steering carefully through the shadows. As he reached the mono-rail – he now made the journey on foot, to prevent Traxel guessing that the cache lay along the route of the rail – he heard the track hum faintly in the cool air. He jumped back behind a low mound, tracing its winding pathway through the dunes.

Suddenly an engine throbbed out behind him, and Traxel's camouflaged half-track appeared over the edge of the ridge. Its front four wheels raced and spun, and the huge vehicle tipped forward and plunged down the incline among the buried tombs, its surging tracks dislodging tons of the fine sand Shepley had so laboriously pushed by hand up the slope. Immediately several of the pavilions appeared to view, the white dust cascading off their cupolas.

Half-buried in the avalanche they had set off, Traxel and Bridges leapt from the driving cab, pointing to the pavilions and shouting at each other. Shepley darted forward, and put his foot up on the mono-rail just as it began to vibrate loudly.

In the distance the gyro-car slowly approached, the Old Man punting it along, hatless and dishevelled.

He reached the tomb as Bridges was kicking the door in with a heavy boot, Traxel behind him with a bag full of wrenches.

'Hello, Shepley!' Traxel greeted him gaily. 'So this is your treasure trove.'

Shepley staggered splay-legged through the sliding sand, and brushed past Traxel as glass spattered from the window. He flung himself on Bridges and pulled the big man backwards.

'Bridges, this one's mine! Try any of the others; you can have them all!'

Bridges jerked himself to his feet, staring down angrily at Shepley. Traxel peered suspiciously at the other tombs, their porticos still flooded with sand. 'What's so interesting about this one, Shepley?' he asked sardonically. Bridges roared and slammed a boot into the casement, knocking out one of the panels. Shepley dived on to his shoulders, and Bridges snarled and flung him against the wall. Before Shepley could duck he swung a heavy left cross to Shepley's mouth, knocking him back on to the sand with a bloody face.

Traxel roared with amusement as Shepley lay there stunned, then knelt down, sympathetically examining Shepley's face in the light thrown by the expanding persona within the tomb. Bridges whooped with surprise, gaping like a startled ape at the sumptuous golden mirage of the enchantress.

'How did you find me?' Shepley muttered thickly. 'I double-tracked a dozen times.'

Traxel smiled. 'We didn't follow you, chum. We followed the rail.' He pointed down at the silver thread of the metal strip, plainly visible in the dawn light almost ten miles away. 'The gyro-car cleaned the rail. It led us straight here. Ah, hello, Doctor,' he greeted the Old Man as he climbed the slope and slumped down wearily beside Shepley. 'I take it we have you to thank for all this. Don't worry, Doctor, I shan't forget you.'

'Many thanks,' the Old Man said flatly. He helped Shepley to sit up, frowning at his split lips. 'Aren't you taking everything too seriously, Traxel? You're becoming crazed with greed. Let the boy have this tomb. There are plenty more.'

The patterns of light across the sand dimmed and broke as Bridges plunged through the persona towards the rear of the chancel. Weakly Shepley tried to stand up, but the Old Man held him back. Traxel shrugged. 'Too late, Doctor.' He looked over his shoulder at the persona, ruefully shaking his head in acknowledgment of its magnificence. 'These 10th Dynasty graves are stupendous. But there's something curious about this one.'

He was still staring at it reflectively a minute later when Bridges emerged.

'Boy, that was a crazy one, Traxel! For a second I thought it was a dud.' He handed the three canisters to Traxel, who weighed two of them in one hand against the other. Bridges added 'Kinda light, aren't they?'

Traxel began to prise them open with a wrench. 'Are you certain there are no more in there?'

'Hundred per cent. Have a look yourself.'

Two of the cans were empty, the tape spools missing. The third was only half full, a mere three-inch width of tape in its centre. Bridges bellowed in pain: 'The kid robbed us. I can't believe it!' Traxel waved him away and went over to the Old Man, who was staring in at the now flickering persona. The two men exchanged glances, then nodded slowly in confirmation. With a short laugh Traxel kicked at the can containing the half reel of tape, jerking the spool out on to the sand, where it began to unravel in the quietly moving air. Bridges protested but Traxel shook his head.

'It *is* a dud. Go and have a close look at the image.' When Bridges peered at it blankly he explained 'The woman there was dead when the matrices were recorded. She's beautiful all right – as poor Shepley here discovered – but it's all too literally skin deep. That's why there's only half a can of data. No nervous system, no musculature or internal organs – just a beautiful golden husk. This is a mortuary tomb. If you resurrected her you'd have an ice-cold corpse on your hands.'

'But why?' Bridges rasped. 'What's the point?'

Traxel gestured expansively. 'It's immortality of a kind. Perhaps she died suddenly, and this was the next best thing. When the Doctor first came here there were a lot of mortuary tombs of young children being found. If I remember he had something of a reputation for always leaving them intact. A typical piece of highbrow sentimentality – giving immortality only to the dead. Agree, Doctor?'

Before the Old Man could reply a voice shouted from below, there was a nearby roaring hiss of an ascending signal rocket and a vivid red star-shell burst over the lake below, spitting incandescent fragments over them. Traxel and Bridges leapt forwards, saw two men in a sand-car pointing up at them, and three more vehicles converging across the lake half a mile away.

'The time-wardens!' Traxel shouted. Bridges picked up the tool bag and the two men raced across the slope towards the half-track, the Old Man hobbling after them. He turned back to wait for Shepley, who was still sitting on the ground where he had fallen, watching the image inside the pavilion.

'Shepley! Come on, lad, pull yourself together! You'll get ten years!'

When Shepley made no reply he reached up to the side of the half-track as Traxel reversed it expertly out of the morraine of sand, letting Bridges swing him aboard. 'Shepley!' he called again. Traxel hesitated, then roared away as a second star-shell exploded.

* * *

Shepley tried to reach the tape, but the stampeding feet had severed it at several points, and the loose ends, which he had numbly thought of trying to reinsert into the projector, now fluttered around him in the sand. Below, he could hear the sounds of flight and pursuit, the warning crack of a rifle, engines baying and plunging, as Traxel eluded the time-wardens, but he kept his eyes fixed on the image within the tomb. Already it had begun to fragment, fading against the mounting sunlight. Getting slowly to his feet, he entered the tomb and closed the battered doors.

Still magnificent upon her bier, the enchantress lay back between the great wings. Motionless for so long, she had at last been galvanized into life, and a jerking syncopated rhythm rippled through her body. The wings shook uneasily, and a series of tremors disturbed the base of the catafalque, so that the woman's feet danced an exquisitely flickering minuet, the toes darting from side to side with untiring speed. Higher up, her wide smooth hips jostled each other in a jaunty mock tango.

He watched until only the face remained, a few disconnected traces of the wings and catafalque jerking faintly in the darkness, then made his way out of the tomb.

Outside, in the cool morning light, the time-wardens were waiting for him, hands on the hips of their white uniforms. One was holding the empty canisters, turning the fluttering strands of tape over with his foot as they drifted away.

The other took Shepley's arm and steered him down to the car.

'Traxel's gang,' he said to the driver. 'This must be a new recruit.' He glanced dourly at the blood around Shepley's mouth. 'Looks as if they've been fighting over the spoils.'

The driver pointed to the three drums. 'Stripped?'

The man carrying them nodded. 'All three. And they were 10th Dynasty.' He shackled Shepley's wrists to the dashboard. 'Too bad, son, you'll be doing ten yourself soon. It'll seem like ten thousand.'

'Unless it was a dud,' the driver rejoined, eyeing Shepley with some sympathy. 'You know, one of those freak mortuary tombs.'

Shepley straightened his bruised mouth. 'It wasn't,' he said firmly.

The driver glanced warningly at the other wardens. 'What about the tape blowing away up there?'

Shepley looked up at the tomb spluttering faintly below the ridge, its light almost gone. 'That's just the persona,' he said. 'The empty skin.'

As the engine surged forward he listened to three empty drums hit the floor behind the seat.

1963

NOW WAKES THE SEA

Again at night Mason heard the sounds of the approaching sea, the muffled thunder of breakers rolling up the near-by streets. Roused from his sleep, he ran out into the moonlight, where the white-framed houses stood like sepulchres among the washed concrete courts. Two hundred yards away the waves plunged and boiled, sluicing in and out across the pavement. Foam seethed through the picket fences, and the broken spray filled the air with the wine-sharp tang of brine.

Off-shore the deeper swells of the open sea rode across the roofs of the submerged houses, the white-caps cleft by isolated chimneys. Leaping back as the cold foam stung his feet, Mason glanced at the house where his wife lay sleeping. Each night the sea moved a few yards nearer, a hissing guillotine across the empty lawns.

For half an hour Mason watched the waves vault among the rooftops. The luminous surf cast a pale nimbus on the clouds racing overhead on the dark wind, and covered his hands with a waxy sheen.

At last the waves began to recede, and the deep bowl of illuminated water withdrew down the emptying streets, disgorging the lines of houses in the moonlight. Mason ran forwards across the expiring bubbles, but the sea shrank away from him, disappearing around the corners of the houses, sliding below the garage doors. He sprinted to the end of the road as a last glow was carried across the sky beyond the spire of the church. Exhausted, Mason returned to his bed, the sound of the dying waves filling his head as he slept.

'I saw the sea again last night,' he told his wife at breakfast.

Quietly, Miriam said: 'Richard, the nearest sea is a thousand miles away.' She watched her husband for a moment, her pale fingers straying to the coil of black hair lying against her neck. 'Go out into the drive and look. There's no sea.'

'Darling, I *saw* it.'

'Richard –!'

Mason stood up, and with slow deliberation raised his palms. 'Miriam, I felt the spray on my hands. The waves were breaking around my feet. I wasn't dreaming.'

'You must have been.' Miriam leaned against the door, as if trying to exclude the strange nightworld of her husband. With her long raven hair framing her oval face, and the scarlet dressing-gown open to reveal her slender neck and white breast, she reminded Mason of a Pre-Raphaelite heroine in an Arthurian pose. 'Richard, you must see Dr Clifton. It's beginning to frighten me.'

Mason smiled, his eyes searching the distant rooftops above the trees. 'I shouldn't worry. What's happening is really very simple. At night I hear the sounds of the sea, I go out and watch the waves in the moonlight, and then come back to bed.' He paused, a flush of fatigue on his face. Tall and slimly built, Mason was still convalescing from the illness which had kept him at home for the previous six months. 'It's curious, though,' he resumed, 'the water is remarkably luminous. I should guess its salinity is well above normal –'

'But Richard . . .' Miriam looked around helplessly, her husband's calmness exhausting her. 'The sea isn't *there*; it's only in your mind. No one else can see it.'

Mason nodded, hands lost in his pockets. 'Perhaps no one else has heard it yet.'

Leaving the breakfast-room, he went into his study. The couch on which he had slept during his illness still stood against the corner, his bookcase beside it. Mason sat down, taking a large fossil mollusc from a shelf. During the winter, when he had been confined to bed, the smooth trumpet-shaped conch, with its endless associations of ancient seas and drowned strands, had provided him with unlimited pleasure, a bottomless cornucopia of image and reverie. Cradling it reassuringly in his hands, as exquisite and ambiguous as a fragment of Greek sculpture found in a dry riverbed, he reflected that it seemed like a capsule of time, the condensation of another universe. He could almost believe that the midnight sea which haunted his sleep had been released from the shell when he had inadvertently scratched one of its helixes.

Miriam followed him into the room and briskly drew the curtains, as if aware that Mason was returning to the twilight world of his sick-bed. She took his shoulders in her hands.

'Richard, listen. Tonight, when you hear the waves, wake me and we'll go out together.'

Gently, Mason disengaged himself. 'Whether you see it or not is irrelevant, Miriam. The fact is that I see it.'

Later, walking down the street, Mason reached the point where he had stood the previous night, watching the waves break and roll towards him. The sounds of placid domestic activity came from the houses he had seen submerged. The grass on the lawns was bleached by the July heat, and sprays rotated in the bright sunlight, casting rainbows in the vivid air. Undisturbed since the rainstorms in the early spring, the long summer's dust lay between the wooden fences and water hydrants.

The street, one of a dozen suburban boulevards on the perimeter of the town, ran north-west for some three hundred yards and then joined the open square of the neighbourhood shopping centre. Mason shielded his eyes and looked out at the clock tower of the library and the church spire, identifying the protuberances which had risen from the steep swells of the open sea. All were in exactly the positions he remembered.

The road shelved slightly as it approached the shopping centre, and by a curious coincidence marked the margins of the beach which would have existed if the area had been flooded. A mile or so from the town, this shallow ridge, which formed part of the rim of a large natural basin enclosing the alluvial plain below, culminated in a small chalk outcropping. Although it was partly hidden by the intervening houses, Mason now recognized it clearly as the promontory which had reared like a citadel above the sea. The deep swells had rolled against its flanks, sending up immense plumes of spray that fell back with almost hypnotic slowness upon the receding water. At night the promontory seemed larger and more gaunt, an uneroded bastion against the sea. One evening, Mason promised himself, he would go out to the promontory and let the waves wake him as he slept on the peak.

A car moved past, the driver watching Mason curiously as he stood in the middle of the road, head raised to the air. Not wishing to appear any more eccentric than he was already considered – the solitary, abstracted husband of the beautiful but childless Mrs Mason – Mason turned into the avenue which ran along the ridge. As he approached the distant outcropping he glanced over the hedges for any signs of water-logged gardens or stranded cars. The houses had been inundated by the floodwater.

The first visions of the sea had come to Mason only three weeks earlier, but he was already convinced of their absolute validity. He recognized that after its nightly withdrawal the water failed to leave any mark on the hundreds of houses it submerged, and he felt no alarm for the drowned people who were sleeping undisturbed in the sea's immense liquid locker as he watched the luminous waves break across the roof-tops. Despite this paradox, it was his complete conviction of the sea's reality that had made him admit to Miriam that he had woken one night to the sound of waves outside the window and gone out to find the sea rolling across the neighbourhood streets and houses. At first she had merely smiled at him, accepting this illustration of his strange private world. Then, three nights later, she had woken to the sound of him latching the door on his return, bewildered by his pumping chest and perspiring face.

From then on she spent all day looking over her shoulder through the window for any signs of the sea. What worried her as much as the vision itself was Mason's complete calm in the face of this terrifying unconscious apocalypse.

Tired by his walk, Mason sat down on a low ornamental wall,

screened from the surrounding houses by the rhododendron bushes. For a few minutes he played with the dust at his feet, stirring the white grains with a branch. Although formless and passive, the dust shared something of the same evocative qualities of the fossil mollusc, radiating a curious compacted light.

In front of him, the road curved and dipped, the incline carrying it away on to the fields below. The chalk shoulder, covered by a mantle of green turf, rose into the clear sky. A metal shack had been erected on the slope, and a small group of figures moved about the entrance of a mine-shaft, adjusting a wooden hoist. Wishing that he had brought his wife's car, Mason watched the diminutive figures disappear one by one into the shaft.

The image of this elusive pantomime remained with him all day in the library, overlaying his memories of the dark waves rolling across the midnight streets. What sustained Mason was his conviction that others would soon also become aware of the sea.

When he went to bed that night he found Miriam sitting fully dressed in the armchair by the window, her face composed into an expression of calm determination.

'What are you doing?' he asked.

'Waiting.'

'For what?'

'The sea. Don't worry, simply ignore me and go to sleep. I don't mind sitting here with the light out.'

'Miriam ...' Wearily, Mason took one of her slender hands and tried to draw her from the chair. 'Darling, what on earth will this achieve?'

'Isn't it obvious?'

Mason sat down on the foot of the bed. For some reason, not wholly concerned with the wish to protect her, he wanted to keep his wife from the sea. 'Miriam, don't you understand? I might not actually *see* it, in the literal sense. It might be ...' he extemporized ... 'an hallucination, or a dream.'

Miriam shook her head, hands clasped on the arms of the chair. 'I don't think it is. Anyway, I want to find out.'

Mason lay back on the bed. 'I wonder whether you're approaching this the right way –'

Miriam sat forward. 'Richard, you're taking it all so calmly; you accept this vision as if it were a strange headache. That's what frightens me. If you were really terrified by this sea I wouldn't worry, but ...'

Half an hour later he fell asleep in the darkened room, Miriam's slim face watching him from the shadows.

Waves murmured, outside the windows the distant swish of racing foam drew him from sleep, the muffled thunder of rollers and the sounds of deep water drummed at his ears. Mason climbed out of bed, and dressed quickly as the hiss of receding water sounded up the street. In the corner, under the light reflected from the distant foam, Miriam lay asleep in the armchair, a bar of moonlight across her throat.

His bare feet soundless on the pavement, Mason ran towards the waves. He stumbled across the glistening tideline as one of the breakers struck with a guttural roar. On his knees, Mason felt the cold brilliant water, seething with animalcula, spurt across his chest and shoulders, slacken and then withdraw, sucked like a gleaming floor into the mouth of the next breaker. His wet suit clinging to him like a drowned animal, Mason stared out across the sea. In the moonlight the white houses advanced into the water like the palazzos of a spectral Venice, mausoleums on the causeways of some island necropolis. Only the church spire was still visible. The water rode in to its high tide, a further twenty yards down the street, the spray carried almost to the Masons' house.

Mason waited for an interval between two waves and then waded through the shallows to the avenue which wound towards the distant headland. By now the water had crossed the roadway, swilling over the dark lawns and slapping at the doorsteps.

Half a mile from the headland he heard the great surge and sigh of the deeper water. Out of breath, he leaned against a fence as the cold foam cut across his legs, pulling him with its undertow. Illuminated by the racing clouds, he saw the pale figure of a woman standing above the sea on a stone parapet at the cliff's edge, her black robe lifting behind her in the wind, her long hair white in the moonlight. Far below her feet, the luminous waves leapt and vaulted like acrobats.

Mason ran along the pavement, losing sight of her as the road curved and the houses intervened. The water slackened and he caught a last glimpse of the woman's icy-white profile through the spray. Turning, the tide began to ebb and fade, and the sea shrank away between the houses, draining the night of its light and motion.

As the last bubbles dissolved on the damp pavement, Mason searched the headland, but the luminous figure had gone. His damp clothes dried themselves as he walked back through the empty streets. A last tang of brine was carried away off the hedges on the midnight air.

The next morning he told Miriam: 'It *was* a dream, after all. I think the sea has gone now. Anyway, I saw nothing last night.'

'Thank heavens, Richard. Are you sure?'

'I'm certain.' Mason smiled encouragingly. 'Thanks for keeping watch over me.'

'I'll sit up tonight as well.' She held up her hand. 'I insist. I feel all right after last night, and I want to drive this thing away, once and for all.' She frowned over the coffee cups. 'It's strange, but once or twice I think I heard the sea too. It sounded very old and blind, like something waking again after millions of years.'

On his way to the library, Mason made a detour towards the chalk outcropping, and parked the car where he had seen the moonlit figure of the white-haired woman watching the sea. The sunlight fell on the pale turf, illuminating the mouth of the mine-shaft, around which the same desultory activity was taking place.

For the next fifteen minutes Mason drove in and out of the tree-lined avenues, peering over the hedges at the kitchen windows. Almost certainly she would live in one of the nearby houses, still wearing her black robe beneath a housecoat.

Later, at the library, he recognized a car he had seen on the headland. The driver, an elderly tweed-suited man, was examining the display cases of local geological finds.

'Who was that?' he asked Fellowes, the keeper of antiquities, as the car drove off. 'I've seen him on the cliffs.'

'Professor Goodhart, one of the party of paleontologists. Apparently they've uncovered an interesting bone-bed.' Fellowes gestured at the collection of femurs and jaw-bone fragments. 'With luck we may get a few pieces from them.'

Mason stared at the bones, aware of a sudden closing of the parallax within his mind.

Each night, as the sea emerged from the dark streets and the waves rolled farther towards the Masons' home, he would wake beside his sleeping wife and go out into the surging air, wading through the deep water towards the headland. There he would see the white-haired woman on the cliff's edge, her face raised above the roaring spray. Always he failed to reach her before the tide turned, and would kneel exhausted on the wet pavements as the drowned streets rose around him.

Once a police patrol car found him in its headlights, slumped against a gate-post in an open drive. On another night he forgot to close the front door when he returned. All through breakfast Miriam watched him with her old wariness, noticing the shadows which encircled his eyes like manacles.

'Richard, I think you should stop going to the library. You look worn out. It isn't that sea dream again?'

Mason shook his head, forcing a tired smile. 'No, that's finished with. Perhaps I've been over-working.'

Miriam held his hands. 'Did you fall over yesterday?' She examined Mason's palms. 'Darling, they're still *raw*! You must have grazed them only a few hours ago. Can't you remember?'

Abstracted, Mason invented some tale to satisfy her, then carried his coffee into the study and stared at the morning haze which lay across the rooftops, a soft lake of opacity that followed the same contours as the midnight sea. The mist dissolved in the sunlight, and for a moment the diminishing reality of the normal world reasserted itself, filling him with a poignant nostalgia.

Without thinking, he reached out to the fossil conch on the bookshelf, but involuntarily his hand withdrew before touching it.

Miriam stood beside him. 'Hateful thing,' she commented. 'Tell me, Richard, what do you think caused your dream?'

Mason shrugged. 'Perhaps it was a sort of memory ...' He wondered whether to tell Miriam of the waves which he still heard in his sleep, and of the white-haired woman on the cliff's edge who seemed to beckon to him. But like all women Miriam believed that there was room for only one enigma in her husband's life. By an inversion of logic he felt that his dependence on his wife's private income, and the loss of self-respect, gave him the right to withhold something of himself from her.

'Richard, what's the matter?'

In his mind the spray opened like a diaphanous fan and the enchantress of the waves turned towards him.

Waist-high, the sea pounded across the lawn in a whirlpool. Mason pulled off his jacket and flung it into the water, and then waded out into the street. Higher than ever before, the waves had at last reached his house, breaking over the doorstep, but Mason had forgotten his wife. His attention was fixed upon the headland, which was lashed by a continuous storm of spray, almost obscuring the figure standing on its crest.

As Mason pressed on, sometimes sinking to his shoulders, shoals of luminous algae swarmed in the water around him. His eyes smarted in the saline air. He reached the lower slopes of the headland almost exhausted, and fell to his knees.

High above, he could hear the spray singing as it cut through the coigns of the cliff's edge, the deep base of the breakers overlaid by the treble of the keening air. Carried by the music, Mason climbed the flank of the headland, a thousand reflections of the moon in the breaking sea. As he reached the crest, the black robe hid the woman's face, but he could see her tall erect carriage and slender hips. Suddenly, without any apparent motion of her limbs, she moved away along the parapet.

'Wait!'

His shout was lost on the air. Mason ran forwards, and the figure turned and stared back at him. Her white hair swirled around her face like a spume of silver steam and then parted to reveal a face with empty eyes and notched mouth. A hand like a bundle of white sticks clawed towards him, and the figure rose through the whirling darkness like a gigantic bird.

Unaware whether the scream came from his own mouth or from this spectre, Mason stumbled back. Before he could catch himself he tripped over the wooden railing, and in a cackle of chains and pulleys fell backwards into the shaft, the sounds of the sea booming in its hurtling darkness.

After listening to the policeman's description, Professor Goodhart shook his head.

'I'm afraid not, sergeant. We've been working on the bed all week. No one's fallen down the shaft.' One of the flimsy wooden rails was swinging loosely in the crisp air. 'But thank you for warning me. I suppose we must build a heavier railing, if this fellow is wandering around in his sleep.'

'I don't think he'll bother to come up here,' the sergeant said. 'It's quite a climb.' As an afterthought he added: 'Down at the library where he works they said you'd found a couple of skeletons in the shaft yesterday. I know it's only two days since he disappeared, but one of them couldn't possibly be his?' The sergeant shrugged. 'If there was some natural acid, say . . .'

Professor Goodhart drove his heel into the chalky turf. 'Pure calcium carbonate, about a mile thick, laid down during the Triassic Period 200 million years ago when there was a large inland sea here. The skeletons we found yesterday, a man's and a woman's, belong to two Cro-Magnon fisher people who lived on the shore just before it dried up. I wish I could oblige you – it's quite a problem to understand how these Cro-Magnon relics found their way into the bone-bed. This shaft wasn't sunk until about thirty years ago. Still, that's my problem, not yours.'

Returning to the police car, the sergeant shook his head. As they drove off he looked out at the endless stretch of placid suburban homes.

'Apparently there was an ancient sea here once. A million years ago.' He picked a crumpled flannel jacket off the back seat. 'That reminds me, I know what Mason's coat smells of – brine.'

1963

THE VENUS HUNTERS

When Dr Andrew Ward joined the Hubble Memorial Institute at Mount Vernon Observatory he never imagined that the closest of his new acquaintances would be an amateur star-gazer and spare-time prophet called Charles Kandinski, tolerantly regarded by the Observatory professionals as a madman. In fact, had either he or Professor Cameron, the Institute's Deputy Director, known just how far he was to be prepared to carry this friendship before his two-year tour at the Institute was over, Ward would certainly have left Mount Vernon the day he arrived and would never have become involved in the bizarre and curiously ironic tragedy which was to leave an ineradicable stigma upon his career.

Professor Cameron first introduced him to Kandinski. About a week after Ward came to the Hubble he and Cameron were lunching together in the Institute cafeteria.

'We'll go down to Vernon Gardens for coffee,' Cameron said when they finished dessert. 'I want to get a shampoo for Edna's roses and then we'll sit in the sun for an hour and watch the girls go by.' They strolled out through the terrace tables towards the parking lot. A mile away, beyond the conifers thinning out on the slopes above them, the three great Vernon domes gleamed like white marble against the sky. 'Incidentally, you can meet the opposition.'

'Is there another observatory at Vernon?' Ward asked as they set off along the drive in Cameron's Buick. 'What is it – an Air Force weather station?'

'Have you ever heard of Charles Kandinski?' Cameron said.

'He wrote a book called *The Landings from Outer Space*. It was published about three years ago.'

Ward shook his head doubtfully. They slowed down past the check-point at the gates and Cameron waved to the guard. 'Is that the man who claims to have seen extra-terrestrial beings? Martians or –'

'Venusians. That's Kandinski. Not only seen them,' Professor Cameron added. 'He's talked to them. Charles works at a café in Vernon Gardens. We know him fairly well.'

'He runs the other observatory?'

'Well, an old 4-inch MacDonald Refractor mounted in a bucket of cement. You probably wouldn't think much of it, but I wish we could see with our two-fifty just a tenth of what he sees.'

Ward nodded vaguely. The two observatories at which he had worked previously, Cape Town and the Milan Astrographie, had both attracted any number of cranks and charlatans eager to reveal their own final truths about the cosmos, and the prospect of meeting Kandinski interested him only slightly. 'What is he?' he asked. 'A practical joker, or just a lunatic?'

Professor Cameron propped his glasses on to his forehead and negotiated a tight hairpin. 'Neither,' he said.

Ward smiled at Cameron, idly studying his plump cherubic face with its puckish mouth and keen eyes. He knew that Cameron enjoyed a modest reputation as a wit. 'Has he ever claimed in front of you that he's seen a ... Venusian?'

'Often,' Professor Cameron said. 'Charles lectures two or three times a week about the landings to the women's societies around here and put himself completely at our disposal. I'm afraid we had to tell him he was a little too advanced for us. But wait until you meet him.'

Ward shrugged and looked out at the long curving peach terraces lying below them, gold and heavy in the August heat. They dropped a thousand feet and the road widened and joined the highway which ran from the Vernon Gardens across the desert to Santa Vera and the coast.

Vernon Gardens was the nearest town to the Observatory and most of it had been built within the last few years, evidently with an eye on the tourist trade. They passed a string of blue and pink-washed houses, a school constructed of glass bricks and an abstract Baptist chapel. Along the main thoroughfare the shops and stores were painted in bright jazzy colours, the vivid awnings and neon signs like street scenery in an experimental musical.

Professor Cameron turned off into a wide tree-lined square and parked by a cluster of fountains in the centre. He and Ward walked towards the cafés – Al's Fresco Diner, Ylla's, the Dome – which stretched down to the sidewalk. Around the square were a dozen gift-shops filled with cheap souvenirs: silverplate telescopes and models of the great Vernon dome masquerading as ink-stands and cigar-boxes, plus a juvenile omnium gatherum of miniature planetaria, space helmets and plastic 3-D star atlases.

The café to which they went was decorated in the same futuristic motifs. The chairs and tables were painted a drab aluminium grey, their limbs and panels cut in random geometric shapes. A silver rocket ship, ten feet long, its paint peeling off in rusty strips, reared up from a pedestal among the tables. Across it was painted the café's name.

'The Site Tycho.'

A large mobile had been planted in the ground by the sidewalk and dangled down over them, its vanes and struts flashing in the sun. Gingerly Professor Cameron pushed it away. 'I'll swear that damn thing is growing,' he confided to Ward. 'I must tell Charles to prune it.' He lowered himself into a chair by one of the open-air tables, put on a fresh pair of sunglasses and focused them at the long brown legs of a girl sauntering past.

Left alone for the moment, Ward looked around him and picked at a cellophane transfer of a ringed planet glued to the table-top. The Site Tycho was also used as a small science fiction exchange library. A couple of metal bookstands stood outside the café door, where a soberly dressed middle-aged man, obviously hiding behind his upturned collar, worked his way quickly through the rows of paperbacks. At another table a young man with an intent, serious face was reading a magazine. His high cerebrotonic forehead was marked across the temple by a ridge of pink tissue, which Ward wryly decided was a lobotomy scar.

'Perhaps we ought to show our landing permits,' he said to Cameron when after three or four minutes no one had appeared to serve them. 'Or at least get our pH's checked.'

Professor Cameron grinned. 'Don't worry, no customs, no surgery.' He took his eyes off the sidewalk for a moment. 'This looks like him now.'

A tall, bearded man in a short-sleeved tartan shirt and pale green slacks came out of the café towards them with two cups of coffee on a tray.

'Hello, Charles,' Cameron greeted him. 'There you are. We were beginning to think we'd lost ourselves in a time-trap.'

The tall man grunted something and put the cups down. Ward guessed that he was about 55 years old. He was well over six feet tall, with a massive sunburnt head and lean but powerfully muscled arms.

'Andrew, this is Charles Kandinski.' Cameron introduced the two men. 'Andrew's come to work for me, Charles. He photographed all those Cepheids for the Milan Conference last year.'

Kandinski nodded. His eyes examined Ward critically but showed no signs of interest.

'I've been telling him all about you, Charles,' Cameron went on, 'and how we all follow your work. No further news yet, I trust?'

Kandinski's lips parted in a slight smile. He listened politely to Cameron's banter and looked out over the square, his great seamed head raised to the sky.

'Andrew's read your book, Charles,' Cameron was saying. 'Very interested. He'd like to see the originals of those photographs. Wouldn't you, Andrew?'

'Yes, I certainly would,' Ward said.

Kandinski gazed down at him again. His expression was not so much penetrating as detached and impersonal, as if he were assessing Ward with an utter lack of bias, so complete, in fact, that it left no room for even the smallest illusion. Previously Ward had only seen this expression in the eyes of the very old. 'Good,' Kandinski said. 'At present they are in a safe deposit box at my bank, but if you are serious I will get them out.'

Just then two young women wearing wide-brimmed Rapallo hats made their way through the tables. They sat down and smiled at Kandinski. He nodded to Ward and Cameron and went over to the young women, who began to chatter to him animatedly.

'Well, he seems popular with them,' Ward commented. 'He's certainly not what I anticipated. I hope I didn't offend him over the plates. He was taking you seriously.'

'He's a little sensitive about them,' Cameron explained. 'The famous dustbin-lid flying saucers. You mustn't think I bait him, though. To tell the truth I hold Charles in great respect. When all's said and done, we're in the same racket.'

'Are we?' Ward said doubtfully. 'I haven't read his book. Does he say in so many words that he saw and spoke to a visitor from Venus?'

'Precisely. Don't you believe him?'

Ward laughed and looked through the coins in his pocket, leaving one on the table. 'I haven't tried to yet. You say the whole thing isn't a hoax?'

'Of course not.'

'How do you explain it then? Compensation-fantasy or –'

Professor Cameron smiled. 'Wait until you know Charles a little better.'

'I already know the man's messianic,' Ward said dryly. 'Let me guess the rest. He lives on yoghurt, weaves his own clothes, and stands on his head all night, reciting the Bhagavadgita backwards.'

'He doesn't,' Cameron said, still smiling at Ward. 'He happens to be a big man who suffers from barber's rash. I thought he'd have you puzzled.'

Ward pulled the transfer off the table. Some science fantast had skilfully pencilled in an imaginary topography on the planet's surface. There were canals, craters and lake systems named Verne, Wells and Bradbury. 'Where did he see this Venusian?' Ward asked, trying to keep the curiosity out of his voice.

'About twenty miles from here, out in the desert off the Santa Vera highway. He was picnicking with some friends, went off for a stroll in the sandhills and ran straight into the space-ship. His friends swear he was perfectly normal both immediately before and after the landing, and all of them saw the inscribed metallic tablet which the Venusian pilot left behind. Some sort of ultimatum, if I remember, warning mankind to abandon all its space programmes. Apparently someone up there does not like us.'

'Has he still got the tablet?' Ward asked.

'No. Unluckily it combusted spontaneously in the heat. But Charles managed to take a photograph of it.'

Ward laughed. 'I bet he did. It sounds like a beautifully organized hoax. I suppose he made a fortune out of his book?'

'About 150 dollars. He had to pay for the printing himself. Why do you think he works here? The reviews were too unfavourable. People who read science fiction apparently dislike flying saucers, and everyone else dismissed him as a lunatic.' He stood up. 'We might as well get back.'

As they left the café Cameron waved to Kandinski, who was still talking to the young women. They were leaning forward and listening with rapt attention to whatever he was saying.

'What do the people in Vernon Gardens think of him?' Ward asked as they moved away under the trees.

'Well, it's a curious thing, almost without exception those who actually know Kandinski are convinced he's sincere and that he saw an alien space craft, while at the same time realizing the absolute impossibility of the whole story.'

'"I know God exists, but I cannot *believe* in him"?'

'Exactly. Naturally, most people in Vernon think he's crazy. About three months after he met the Venusian, Charles saw another UFO chasing its tail over the town. He got the Fire Police out, alerted the Radar Command chain and even had the National Guard driving around town ringing a bell. Sure enough, there were two white blobs diving about in the clouds. Unfortunately for Charles, they were caused by the headlights of one of the asparagus farmers in the valley doing some night spraying. Charles was the first to admit it, but at 3 o'clock in the morning no one was very pleased.'

'Who is Kandinski, anyway?' Ward asked. 'Where does he come from?'

'He doesn't make a profession of seeing Venusians, if that's what you mean. He was born in Alaska, for some years taught psychology at Mexico City University. He's been just about everywhere, had a thousand different jobs. A veteran of the private evacuations. Get his book.'

Ward murmured non-committally. They entered a small arcade and stood for a moment by the first shop, an aquarium called 'The Nouvelle Vague', watching the Angel fish and Royal Brahmins swim dreamily up and down their tanks.

'It's worth reading,' Professor Cameron went on. 'Without exaggerating, it's really one of the most interesting documents I've ever come across.'

'I'm afraid I have a closed mind when it comes to interplanetary bogey-men,' Ward said.

'A pity,' Cameron rejoined. 'I find them fascinating. Straight out of the unconscious. The fish too,' he added, pointing at the tanks. He grinned whimsically at Ward and ducked away into a horticulture store halfway down the arcade.

While Professor Cameron was looking through the sprays on the hormone counter, Ward went over to a news-stand and glanced at the magazines. The proximity of the observatory had prompted a large selection of popular astronomical guides and digests, most of them with illustrations of the Mount Vernon domes on their wrappers. Among them Ward noticed a dusty, dog-eared paperback, *The Landings from Outer Space* by Charles Kandinski. On the front cover a gigantic space vehicle, at least the size of New York, tens of thousands of portholes ablaze with light, was soaring majestically across a brilliant backdrop of stars and spiral nebulae.

Ward picked up the book and turned to the end cover. Here there was a photograph of Kandinski, dressed in a dark lounge suit several sizes too small, peering stiffly into the eye-piece of his MacDonald.

Ward hesitated before finally taking out his wallet. He bought the book and slipped it into his pocket as Professor Cameron emerged from the horticulture store.

'Get your shampoo?' Ward asked.

Cameron brandished a brass insecticide gun, then slung it, buccaneer-like, under his belt. 'My disintegrator,' he said, patting the butt of the gun. 'There's a positive plague of white ants in the garden, like something out of a science fiction nightmare. I've tried to convince Edna that their real source is psychological. Remember the story "Leiningen vs the Ants"? A classic example of the forces of the Id rebelling against the Super-Ego.' He watched a girl in a black bikini and lemon-coloured sunglasses move gracefully through the arcade and added meditatively: 'You know, Andrew, like everyone else my real vocation was to be a psychiatrist. I spend so long analysing my motives I've no time left to act.'

'Kandinski's Super-Ego must be in difficulties,' Ward remarked. 'You haven't told me your explanation yet.'

'What explanation?'

'Well, what's really at the bottom of this Venusian he claims to have seen?'

'Nothing is at the bottom of it. Why?'

Ward smiled helplessly. 'You will tell me next that you really believe him.'

Professor Cameron chuckled. They reached his car and climbed in. 'Of course I do,' he said.

When, three days later, Ward borrowed Professor Cameron's car and drove down to the rail depot in Vernon Gardens to collect a case of slides which had followed him across the Atlantic, he had no intention of seeing Charles Kandinski again. He had read one or two chapters of Kandinski's book before going to sleep the previous night and dropped it in boredom. Kandinski's description of his encounter with the Venusian was not only puerile and crudely written but, most disappointing of all, completely devoid of imagination. Ward's work at the Institute was now taking up most of his time. The Annual Congress of the International

Geophysical Association was being held at Mount Vernon in little under a month, and most of the burden for organizing the three-week programme of lectures, semesters and dinners had fallen on Professor Cameron and himself.

But as he drove away from the depot past the cafés in the square he caught sight of Kandinski on the terrace of the Site Tycho. It was 3 o'clock, a time when most people in Vernon Gardens were lying asleep indoors, and Kandinski seemed to be the only person out in the sun. He was scrubbing away energetically at the abstract tables with his long hairy arms, head down so that his beard was almost touching the metal tops, like an aboriginal halfman prowling in dim bewilderment over the ruins of a futuristic city lost in an inversion of time.

On an impulse, Ward parked the car in the square and walked across to the Site Tycho, but as soon as Kandinski came over to his table he wished he had gone to another of the cafés. Kandinski had been reticent enough the previous day, but now that Cameron was absent he might well turn out to be a garrulous bore.

After serving him, Kandinski sat down on a bench by the bookshelves and stared moodily at his feet. Ward watched him quietly for five minutes, as the mobiles revolved delicately in the warm air, deciding whether to approach Kandinski. Then he stood up and went over to the rows of magazines. He picked in a desultory way through half a dozen and turned to Kandinski. 'Can you recommend any of these?'

Kandinski looked up. 'Do you read science fiction?' he asked matter-of-factly.

'Not as a rule,' Ward admitted. When Kandinski said nothing he went on: 'Perhaps I'm too sceptical, but I can't take it seriously.'

Kandinski pulled a blister on his palm. 'No one suggests you should. What you mean is that you take it too seriously.'

Accepting the rebuke with a smile at himself, Ward pulled out one of the magazines and sat down at a table next to Kandinski. On the cover was a placid suburban setting of snugly eaved houses, yew trees and children's bicycles. Spreading slowly across the roof-tops was an enormous pulpy nightmare, blocking out the sun behind it and throwing a weird phosphorescent glow over the roofs and lawns. 'You're probably right,' Ward said, showing the cover to Kandinski. 'I'd hate to want to take that seriously.'

Kandinski waved it aside. 'I have seen 11th-century illuminations of the pentateuch more sensational than any of these covers.' He pointed to the cinema theatre on the far side of the square, where the four-hour Biblical epic *Cain and Abel* was showing. Above the trees an elaborate technicolored hoarding showed Cain, wearing what appeared to be a suit of Roman armour, wrestling with an immense hydraheaded boa constrictor.

Kandinski shrugged tolerantly. 'If Michelangelo were working for MGM today would he produce anything better?'

Ward laughed. 'You may well be right. Perhaps the House of the Medicis should be re-christened "16th Century-Fox".'

Kandinski stood up and straightened the shelves. 'I saw you here with Godfrey Cameron,' he said over his shoulder. 'You're working at the Observatory?'

'At the Hubble.'

Kandinski came and sat down beside Ward. 'Cameron is a good man. A very pleasant fellow.'

'He thinks a great deal of you,' Ward volunteered, realizing that Kandinski was probably short of friends.

'You mustn't believe everything that Cameron says about me,' Kandinski said suddenly. He hesitated, apparently uncertain whether to confide further in Ward, and then took the magazine from him. 'There are better ones here. You have to exercise some discrimination.'

'It's not so much the sensationalism that puts me off,' Ward explained, 'as the psychological implications. Most of the themes in these stories come straight out of the more unpleasant reaches of the unconscious.'

Kandinski glanced sharply at Ward, a trace of amusement in his eyes. 'That sounds rather dubious and, if I may say so, second-hand. Take the best of these stories for what they are:

imaginative exercises on the theme of tomorrow.'

'You read a good deal of science fiction?' Ward asked.

Kandinski shook his head. 'Never. Not since I was a child.'

'I'm surprised,' Ward said. 'Professor Cameron told me you had written a science fiction novel.'

'Not a novel,' Kandinski corrected.

'I'd like to read it,' Ward went on. 'From what Cameron said it sounded fascinating, almost Swiftian in concept. This space-craft which arrives from Venus and the strange conversations the pilot holds with a philosopher he meets. A modern morality. Is that the subject?'

Kandinski watched Ward thoughtfully before replying. 'Loosely, yes. But, as I said, the book is not a novel. It is a factual and literal report of a Venus landing which actually took place, a diary of the most significant encounter in history since Paul saw his vision of Christ on the road to Damascus.' He lifted his huge bearded head and gazed at Ward without embarrassment. 'As a matter of interest, as Professor Cameron probably explained to you, I was the man who witnessed the landing.'

Still maintaining his pose, Ward frowned intently. 'Well, in fact Cameron did say something of the sort, but I . . .'

'But you found it difficult to believe?' Kandinski suggested ironically.

'Just a little,' Ward admitted. 'Are you seriously claiming that you did see a Venusian space-craft?'

Kandinski nodded. 'Exactly.' Then, as if aware that their conversation had reached a familiar turning he suddenly seemed to lose interest in Ward. 'Excuse me.' He nodded politely to Ward, picked up a length of hose-pipe connected to a faucet and began to spray one of the big mobiles.

Puzzled but still sceptical, Ward sat back and watched him critically, then fished in his pockets for some change. 'I must say I admire you for taking it all so calmly,' he told Kandinski as he paid him.

'What makes you think I do?'

'Well, if I'd seen, let alone spoken to a visitor from Venus I think I'd be running around in a flat spin, notifying every government and observatory in the world.'

'I did,' Kandinski said. 'As far as I could. No one was very interested.'

Ward shook his head and laughed. 'It is incredible, to put it mildly.'

'I agree with you.'

'What I mean,' Ward said, 'is that it's straight out of one of these science fiction stories of yours.'

Kandinski rubbed his lips with a scarred knuckle, obviously searching for some means of ending the conversation. 'The resemblance is misleading. They are not my stories,' he added parenthetically. 'This café is the only one which would give me work, for a perhaps obvious reason. As for the incredibility, let me say that I was and still am completely amazed. You may think I take it all calmly, but ever since the landing I have lived in a state of acute anxiety and foreboding. But short of committing some spectacular crime to draw attention to myself I don't see now how I can convince anyone.'

Ward gestured with his glasses. 'Perhaps. But I'm surprised you don't realize the very simple reasons why people refuse to take you seriously. For example, why should you be the only person to witness an event of such staggering implications? Why have *you* alone seen a Venusian?'

'A sheer accident.'

'But why should a space-craft from Venus land here?'

'What better place than near Mount Vernon Observatory?'

'I can think of any number. The UN Assembly, for one.'

Kandinski smiled lightly. 'Columbus didn't make his first contacts with the North-American Indians at the Iroquois-Sioux Tribal Conference.'

'That may be,' Ward admitted, beginning to feel impatient. 'What did this Venusian look like?'

Kandinski smiled wearily at the empty tables and picked up his hose again. 'I don't know whether you've read my book,' he said, 'but if you haven't you'll find it all there.'

'Professor Cameron mentioned that you took some photographs of the Venusian space-craft. Could I examine them?'

'Certainly,' Kandinski replied promptly. 'I'll bring them here tomorrow. You're welcome to test them in any way you wish.'

That evening Ward had dinner with the Camerons. Professor Renthall, Director of the Hubble, and his wife completed the party. The table-talk consisted almost entirely of good-humoured gossip about their colleagues retailed by Cameron and Renthall, and Ward was able to mention his conversation with Kandinski.

'At first I thought he was mad, but now I'm not so certain. There's something rather too subtle about him. The way he creates an impression of absolute integrity, but at the same time never gives you a chance to tackle him directly on any point of detail. And when you do manage to ask him outright about this Venusian his answers are far too pat. I'm convinced the whole thing is an elaborate hoax.'

Professor Renthall shook his head. 'No, it's no hoax. Don't you agree, Godfrey?'

Cameron nodded. 'Not in Andrew's sense, anyway.'

'But what other explanation is there?' Ward asked. 'We know he hasn't seen a Venusian, so he must be a fraud. Unless you think he's a lunatic. And he certainly doesn't behave like one.'

'What is a lunatic?' Professor Renthall asked rhetorically, peering into the faceted stem of his raised hock glass. 'Merely a man with more understanding than he can contain. I think Charles belongs in that category.'

'The definition doesn't explain him, sir,' Ward insisted. 'He's going to lend me his photographs and when I prove those are fakes I think I'll be able to get under his guard.'

'Poor Charles,' Edna Cameron said. 'Why shouldn't he have seen a space-ship? I think I see them every day.'

'That's just what I feel, dear,' Cameron said, patting his wife's matronly, brocaded shoulder. 'Let Charles have his Venusian if he wants to. Damn it, all it's trying to do is ban Project Apollo. An excellent idea, I have always maintained; only the professional astronomer has any business in space. After the Rainbow tests there isn't an astronomer anywhere in the world who wouldn't follow Charles Kandinski to the stake.' He turned to Renthall. 'By the way, I wonder what Charles is planning for the Congress? A Neptunian? Or perhaps a whole delegation from Proxima Centauri. We ought to fit him out with a space-suit and a pavilion – "Charles Kandinski – New Worlds for Old".'

'Santa Claus in a space-suit,' Professor Renthall mused. 'That's a new one. Send him a ticket.'

The next weekend Ward returned the twelve plates to the Site Tycho.

'Well?' Kandinski asked.

'It's difficult to say,' Ward answered. 'They're all too heavily absorbed. They could be clever montages of light brackets and turbine blades. One of them looks like a close-up of a clutch plate. There's a significant lack of any real corroborative details which you'd expect somewhere in so wide a selection.' He paused. 'On the other hand, they could be genuine.'

Kandinski said nothing, took the paper package, and went off into the café.

The interior of the Site Tycho had been designed to represent the control room of a space-ship on the surface of the Moon. Hidden fluorescent lighting glimmered through plastic wall fascia and filled the room with an eerie blue glow. Behind the bar a large mural threw the curving outline of the Moon on to an illuminated star-scape. The doors leading to the rest-rooms were circular and bulged outwards like air-locks, distinguished from each other by the symbols ♂ and ♀. The total effect was ingenious but somehow reminiscent to Ward of a twenty-fifth-century cave.

He sat down at the bar and waited while Kandinski packed the plates away carefully in an old leather briefcase.

'I've read your book,' Ward said. 'I had looked at it the last time I saw you, but I read it again thoroughly.' He waited for some comment upon this admission, but Kandinski went over to an old portable typewriter standing at the far end of the bar and began to type laboriously with one finger. 'Have you seen any more Venusians since the book was published?' Ward asked.

'None,' Kandinski said.

'Do you think you will?'

'Perhaps.' Kandinski shrugged and went on with his typing.

'What are you working on now?' Ward asked.

'A lecture I am giving on Friday evening,' Kandinski said. Two keys locked together and he flicked them back. 'Would you care to come? Eight-thirty, at the high school near the Baptist chapel.'

'If I can,' Ward said. He saw that Kandinski wanted to get rid of him. 'Thanks for letting me see the plates.' He made his way out into the sun. People were walking about through the fresh morning air, and he caught the clean scent of peach blossom carried down the slopes into the town.

Suddenly Ward felt how enclosed and insane it had been inside the Tycho, and how apposite had been his description of it as a cave, with its residential magician incanting over his photographs like a down-at-heel Merlin manipulating his set of runes. He felt annoyed with himself for becoming involved with Kandinski and allowing the potent charisma of his personality to confuse him. Obviously Kandinski played upon the instinctive sympathy for the outcast, his whole pose of integrity and conviction a device for drawing the gullible towards him.

Letting the light spray from the fountains fall across his face, Ward crossed the square towards his car.

Away in the distance 2,000 feet above, rising beyond a screen of fir trees, the three Mount Vernon domes shone together in the sun like a futuristic Taj Mahal.

Fifteen miles from Vernon Gardens the Santa Vera highway circled down from the foot of Mount Vernon into the first low scrub-covered hills which marked the southern edge of the desert. Ward looked out at the long banks of coarse sand stretching away through the haze, their outlines blurring in the afternoon heat. He glanced at the book lying on the seat beside him, open at the map printed between its end covers, and carefully checked his position, involuntarily slowing the speed of the Chevrolet as he moved nearer to the site of the Venus landings.

In the fortnight since he had returned the photographs to the Site Tycho, he had seen Kandinski only once, at the lecture delivered the previous night. Ward had deliberately stayed away from the Site Tycho, but he had seen a poster advertising the lecture and driven down to the school despite himself.

The lecture was delivered in the gymnasium before an audience of forty or fifty people, most of them women, who formed one of the innumerable local astronomical societies. Listening to the talk round him, Ward gathered that their activities principally consisted of trying to identify more than half a dozen of the constellations. Kandinski had lectured to them on several occasions and the subject of this latest instalment was his researches into the significance of the Venusian tablet he had been analysing for the last three years.

When Kandinski stepped onto the dais there was a brief round of applause. He was wearing a lounge suit of a curiously archaic cut and had washed his beard, which bushed out above his string tie so that he resembled a Mormon patriarch or the homespun saint of some fervent evangelical community.

For the benefit of any new members, he prefaced his lecture with a brief account of his meeting with the Venusian, and then turned to his analysis of the tablet. This was the familiar ultimatum warning mankind to abandon its preparations for the exploration of space, for the ostensible reason that, just as the sea was a universal image of the unconscious, so space was nothing less than an image of psychosis and death, and that if he tried to penetrate the interplanetary voids man would only plunge to earth like a demented Icarus, unable to scale the vastness of the cosmic zero. Kandinski's real motives for introducing this were all too apparent – the expected success of Project Apollo and subsequent landings on Mars and Venus would, if nothing else, conclusively expose his fantasies.

However, by the end of the lecture Ward found that his opinion of Kandinski had experienced a complete about-face.

As a lecturer Kandinski was poor, losing words, speaking in a slow ponderous style and trapping himself in long subordinate clauses, but his quiet, matter-of-fact tone and absolute conviction in the importance of what he was saying, coupled with the nature of his material, held the talk together. His analysis of the Venusian cryptograms, a succession of intricate philological theorems, was well above the heads of his audience, but what began to impress Ward, as much as the painstaking preparation which must have preceded the lecture, was Kandinski's acute nervousness in delivering it. Ward noticed that he suffered from an irritating speech impediment that made it difficult for him to pronounce 'Venusian', and he saw that Kandinski, far from basking in the limelight, was delivering the lecture only out of a deep sense of obligation to his audience and was greatly relieved when the ordeal was over.

At the end Kandinski had invited questions. These, with the exception of the chairman's, all concerned the landing of the alien space vehicle and ignored the real subject of the lecture. Kandinski answered them all carefully, taking in good part the inevitable facetious questions. Ward noted with interest the audience's curious ambivalence, simultaneously fascinated by and resentful of Kandinski's exposure of their own private fantasies, an expression of the same ambivalence which had propelled so many of the mana-personalities of history towards their inevitable Calvarys.

Just as the chairman was about to close the meeting, Ward stood up.

'Mr Kandinski. You say that this Venusian indicated that there was also life on one of the moons of Uranus. Can you tell us how he did this if there was no verbal communication between you?'

Kandinski showed no surprise at seeing Ward. 'Certainly; as I told you, he drew eight concentric circles in the sand, one for each of the planets. Around Uranus he drew five lesser orbits and marked one of these. Then he pointed to himself and to me and to a patch of lichen. From this I deduced, reasonably I maintain, that –'

'Excuse me, Mr Kandinski,' Ward interrupted. 'You say he drew five orbits around Uranus? One for each of the moons?'

Kandinski nodded. 'Yes. Five.'

'That was in 1960,' Ward went on. 'Three weeks ago Professor Pineau at Brussels discovered a sixth moon of Uranus.'

The audience looked around at Ward and began to murmur.

'Why should this Venusian have omitted one of the moons?' Ward asked, his voice ringing across the gymnasium.

Kandinski frowned and peered at Ward suspiciously. 'I didn't know there was a sixth moon ...' he began.

'Exactly!' someone called out. The audience began to titter.

'I can understand the Venusian not wishing to introduce any difficulties,' Ward said, 'but this seems a curious way of doing it.'

Kandinski appeared at a loss. Then he introduced Ward to the audience. 'Dr Ward is a professional while I am only an amateur,' he admitted. 'I am afraid I cannot explain the anomaly. Perhaps my memory is at fault. But I am sure the Venusian drew only five orbits.' He stepped down from the dais and strode out hurriedly, scowling into his beard, pursued by a few derisory hoots from the audience.

It took Ward fifteen minutes to free himself from the knot of admiring white-gloved spinsters who cornered him between two vaulting horses. When he broke away he ran out to his car and drove into Vernon Gardens, hoping to see Kandinski and apologize to him.

Five miles into the desert Ward approached a nexus of rock-cuttings and causeways which were part of an abandoned irrigation scheme. The colours of the hills were more vivid now, bright siliconic reds and yellows, crossed with sharp stabs of light from the exposed quartz veins. Following the map on the seat, he turned off the highway onto a rough track which ran along the bank of a dried-up canal. He passed a few rusting sections of picket fencing, a derelict grader half-submerged under the sand, and a collection of dilapidated metal shacks. The car bumped over the potholes at little more than ten miles an hour, throwing up clouds of hot ashy dust that swirled high into the air behind him.

Two miles along the canal the track came to an end. Ward stopped the car and waited for the dust to subside. Carrying Kandinski's book in front of him like a divining instrument, he set off on foot across the remaining three hundred yards. The contours around him were marked on the map, but the hills had shifted several hundred yards westwards since the book's publication and he found himself wandering about from one crest to another, peering into shallow depressions only as old as the last sand-storm. The entire landscape seemed haunted by strange currents and moods; the sand swirls surging down the aisles of dunes and the proximity of the horizon enclosed the whole place of stones with invisible walls.

Finally he found the ring of hills indicated and climbed a narrow saddle leading to its centre. When he scaled the thirty-foot slope he stopped abruptly.

Down on his knees in the middle of the basin with his back to Ward, the studs of his boots flashing in the sunlight, was Kandinski. There was a clutter of tiny objects on the sand around him, and at first Ward thought he was at prayer, making his oblations to the tutelary deities of Venus. Then he saw that Kandinski was slowly scraping the surface of the ground with a small trowel. A circle about 20 yards in diameter had been marked off with pegs and string into a series of wedge-shaped allotments. Every few seconds Kandinski carefully decanted a small heap of grit into one of the test-tubes mounted in a wooden rack in front of him.

Ward put away the book and walked down the slope. Kandinski looked around and then climbed to his feet. The coating of red ash on his beard gave him a fiery, prophetic look. He recognized Ward and raised the trowel in greeting.

Ward stopped at the edge of the string perimeter. 'What on earth are you doing?'

'I am collecting soil specimens.' Kandinski bent down and corked one of the tubes. He looked tired but worked away steadily.

Ward watched him finish a row. 'It's going to take you a long time to cover the whole area. I thought there weren't any gaps left in the Periodic Table.'

'The space-craft rotated at speed before it rose into the air.

This surface is abrasive enough to have scratched off a few minute filings. With luck I may find one of them.' Kandinski smiled thinly. '262. Venusium, I hope.'

Ward started to say: 'But the transuranic elements decay spontaneously . . .' and then walked over to the centre of the circle, where there was a round indentation, three feet deep and five across. The inner surface was glazed and smooth. It was shaped like an inverted cone and looked as if it had been caused by the boss of an enormous spinning top. 'This is where the space-craft landed?'

Kandinski nodded. He filled the last tube and then stowed the rack away in a canvas satchel. He came over to Ward and stared down at the hole. 'What does it look like to you? A meteor impact? Or an oil drill, perhaps?' A smile showed behind his dusty beard. 'The F-109s at the Air Force Weapons School begin their target runs across here. It might have been caused by a rogue cannon shell.'

Ward stooped down and felt the surface of the pit, running his fingers thoughtfully over the warm fused silica. 'More like a 500-pound bomb. But the cone is geometrically perfect. It's certainly unusual.'

'Unusual?' Kandinski chuckled to himself and picked up the satchel.

'Has anyone else been out here?' Ward asked as they trudged up the slope.

'Two so-called experts.' Kandinski slapped the sand off his knees. 'A geologist from Gulf-Vacuum and an Air Force ballistics officer. You'll be glad to hear that they both thought I had dug the pit myself and then fused the surface with an acetylene torch.' He peered critically at Ward. 'Why did you come out here today?'

'Idle curiosity,' Ward said. 'I had an afternoon off and I felt like a drive.'

They reached the crest of the hill and he stopped and looked down into the basin. The lines of string split the circle into a strange horological device, a huge zodiacal mandala, the dark patches in the arcs Kandinski had been working telling its stations.

'You were going to tell me why you came out here,' Kandinski said as they walked back to the car.

Ward shrugged. 'I suppose I wanted to prove something to myself. There's a problem of reconciliation.' He hesitated, and then began: 'You see, there are some things which are self-evidently false. The laws of common sense and everyday experience refute them. I know a lot of the evidence for many things we believe in is pretty thin, but I don't have to embark on a theory of knowledge to decide that the Moon isn't made of green cheese.'

'Well?' Kandinski shifted the satchel to his other shoulder.

'This Venusian you've seen,' Ward said. 'The landing, the runic tablet. I can't believe them. Every piece of evidence I've seen, all the circumstantial details, the facts given in this book . . . they're all patently false.' He turned to one of the middle chapters. 'Take this at random – "A phosphorescent green fluid pulsed through the dorsal lung-chamber of the Prime's helmet, inflating two opaque fan-like gills . . ."' Ward closed the book and shrugged helplessly. Kandinski stood a few feet away from him, the sunlight breaking across the deep lines of his face.

'Now I know what you say to my objections,' Ward went on. 'If you told a 19th century chemist that lead could be transmuted into gold he would have dismissed you as a mediaevalist. But the point is that he'd have been right to do so –'

'I understand,' Kandinski interrupted. 'But you still haven't explained why you came out here today.'

Ward stared out over the desert. High above, a stratojet was doing cuban eights into the sun, the spiral vapour trails drifting across the sky like gigantic fragments of an apocalyptic message. Looking around, he realized that Kandinski must have walked from the bus-stop on the highway. 'I'll give you a lift back,' he said.

As they drove along the canal he turned to Kandinski. 'I enjoyed your lecture last night. I apologize for trying to make you look a fool.'

Kandinski was loosening his boot-straps. He laughed unreproachfully. 'You put me in an awkward position. I could hardly have challenged you. I can't afford to subscribe to every astronomical journal. Though a sixth moon would have been big news.' As they neared Vernon Gardens he asked: 'Would you like to come in and look at the tablet analysis?'

Ward made no reply to the invitation. He drove around the square and parked under the trees, then looked up at the fountains, tapping his fingers on the windshield. Kandinski sat beside him, cogitating into his beard.

Ward watched him carefully. 'Do you think this Venusian will return?'

Kandinski nodded. 'Yes. I am sure he will.'

Later they sat together at a broad roll-top desk in the room above the Tycho. Around the wall hung white cardboard screens packed with lines of cuneiform glyphics and Kandinski's progressive breakdown of their meaning.

Ward held an enlargement of the original photograph of the Venusian tablet and listened to Kandinski's explanation.

'As you see from this,' Kandinski explained, 'in all probability there are not millions of Venusians, as every one would expect, but only three or four of them altogether. Two are circling Venus, a third Uranus and possibly a fourth is in orbit around Neptune. This solves the difficulty that puzzled you and antagonizes everyone else. Why should the Prime have approached only one person out of several hundred million and selected him on a completely random basis? Now obviously he had seen the Russian and American satellite capsules and assumed that our race, like his now, numbered no more than three or four, then concluded from the atmospheric H-bomb tests that we were in conflict and would soon destroy ourselves. This is one of the reasons why I think he will return shortly and why it is important to organize a world-wide reception for him on a governmental level.'

'Wait a minute,' Ward said. 'He must have known that the population of this planet numbered more than three or four. Even the weakest telescope would demonstrate that.'

'Of course, but he would naturally assume that the millions of inhabitants of the Earth belonged to an aboriginal sub-species, perhaps employed as work animals. After all, if he observed that despite this planet's immense resources the bulk of its population lived like animals, an alien visitor could only decide that they were considered as such.'

'But space vehicles are supposed to have been observing us since the Babylonian era, long before the development of satellite rockets. There have been thousands of recorded sightings.'

Kandinski shook his head. 'None of them has been authenticated.'

'What about the other landings that have been reported recently?' Ward asked. 'Any number of people have seen Venusians and Martians.'

'Have they?' Kandinski asked sceptically. 'I wish I could believe that. Some of the encounters reveal marvellous powers of invention, but no one can accept them as anything but fantasy.'

'The same criticism has been levelled at your space-craft,' Ward reminded him.

Kandinski seemed to lose patience. 'I *saw* it,' he explained, impotently tossing his notebook on to the desk. 'I *spoke* to the Prime!'

Ward nodded non-committally and picked up the photograph again. Kandinski stepped over to him and took it out of his hands. 'Ward,' he said carefully. 'Believe me. You must. You know I am too big a man to waste myself on a senseless charade.' His massive hands squeezed Ward's shoulders, and almost lifted him off the seat. '*Believe* me. Together we can be ready for the next landings and alert the world. I am only Charles Kandinski, a waiter at a third-rate café, but you are Dr Andrew Ward of Mount Vernon Observatory. They will listen to you. Try to realize what this may mean for mankind.'

Ward pulled himself away from Kandinski and rubbed his shoulders.

'Ward, do you believe me? Ask yourself.'

Ward looked up pensively at Kandinski towering over him, his red beard like the burning, unconsumed bush.

'I think so,' he said quietly. 'Yes, I do.'

A week later the 23rd Congress of the International Geophysical Association opened at Mount Vernon Observatory. At 3.30 P.M., in the Hoyle Library amphitheatre, Professor Renthall was to deliver the inaugural address welcoming the 92 delegates and 25 newspaper and agency reporters to the fortnight's programme of lectures and discussions.

Shortly after 11 o'clock that morning Ward and Professor Cameron completed their final arrangements and escaped down to Vernon Gardens for an hour's relaxation.

'Well,' Cameron said as they walked over to the Site Tycho, 'I've got a pretty good idea of what it must be like to run the Waldorf-Astoria.' They picked one of the sidewalk tables and sat down. 'I haven't been here for weeks,' Cameron said. 'How are you getting on with the Man in the Moon?'

'Kandinski? I hardly ever see him,' Ward said.

'I was talking to the *Time* magazine stringer about Charles,' Cameron said, cleaning his sunglasses. 'He thought he might do a piece about him.'

'Hasn't Kandinski suffered enough of that sort of thing?' Ward asked moodily.

'Perhaps he has,' Cameron agreed. 'Is he still working on his crossword puzzle? The tablet thing, whatever he calls it.'

Casually, Ward said: 'He has a theory that it should be possible to see the lunar bases. Refuelling points established there by the Venusians over the centuries.'

'Interesting,' Cameron commented.

'They're sited near Copernicus,' Ward went on. 'I know Vandone at Milan is mapping Archimedes and the Imbrium, I thought I might mention it to him at his semester tomorrow.'

Professor Cameron took off his glasses and gazed quizzically at Ward. 'My dear Andrew, what has been going on? Don't tell me you've become one of Charles' converts?'

Ward laughed and shook his head. 'Of course not. Obviously there are no lunar bases or alien space-craft. I don't for a moment believe a word Kandinski says.' He gestured helplessly. 'At the same time I admit I have become involved with him. There's something about Kandinski's personality. On the one hand I can't take him seriously –'

'Oh, I take him seriously,' Cameron cut in smoothly. 'Very seriously indeed, if not quite in the sense you mean.' Cameron turned his back on the sidewalk crowds. 'Jung's views on flying saucers are very illuminating, Andrew; they'd help you to understand Kandinski. Jung believes that civilization now stands at the conclusion of a Platonic Great Year, at the eclipse of the sign of Pisces which has dominated the Christian epoch, and that we are entering the sign of Aquarius, a period of confusion and psychic chaos. He remarks that throughout history, at all times of uncertainty and discord, cosmic space vehicles have been seen approaching Earth, and that in a few extreme cases actual meetings with their occupants are supposed to have taken place.'

As Cameron paused, Ward glanced across the tables for Kandinski, but a relief waiter served them and he assumed it was Kandinski's day off.

Cameron continued: 'Most people regard Charles Kandinski as a lunatic, but as a matter of fact he is performing one of the most important roles in the world today, the role of a prophet alerting people of this coming crisis. The real significance of his fantasies, like that of the ban-the-bomb movements, is to be found elsewhere than on the conscious plane, as an expression of the immense psychic forces stirring below the surface of rational life, like the isotactic movements of the continental tables which heralded the major geological transformations.'

Ward shook his head dubiously. 'I can accept that a man such as Freud was a prophet, but Charles Kandinski –?'

'Certainly. Far more than Freud. It's unfortunate for Kandinski, and for the writers of science fiction for that matter, that they have to perform their tasks of describing the symbols of transformation in a so-called rationalist society, where a scientific, or at least a pesudo-scientific explanation is required *a priori*. And because the true prophet never deals in what may be rationally deduced, people such as Charles are ignored or derided today.'

'It's interesting that Kandinski compared his meeting with the Venusian with Paul's conversion on the road to Damascus,' Ward said.

'He was quite right. In both encounters you see the same mechanism of blinding unconscious revelation. And you can see too that Charles feels the same overwhelming need to spread the Pauline revelation to the world. The Anti-Apollo movement is only now getting under way, but within the next decade it will recruit millions, and men such as Charles Kandinski will be the fathers of its apocalypse.'

'You make him sound like a titanic figure,' Ward remarked quietly. 'I think he's just a lonely, tired man obsessed by something he can't understand. Perhaps he simply needs a few friends to confide in.'

Slowly shaking his head, Cameron tapped the table with his glasses. 'Be warned, Andrew, you'll burn your fingers if you play with Charles' brand of fire. The mana-personalities of history have no time for personal loyalties – the founder of the Christian church made that pretty plain.'

Shortly after seven o'clock that evening Charles Kandinski mounted his bicycle and set off out of Vernon Gardens. The small room in the seedy area where he lived always depressed him on his free days from the Tycho, and as he pedalled along he ignored the shouts from his neighbours sitting out on their balconies with their crates of beer. He knew that his beard and the high, ancient bicycle with its capacious wicker basket made him a grotesque, Quixotic figure, but he felt too preoccupied to care. That morning he had heard that the French translation of *The Landings from Outer Space*, printed at his own cost, had been completely ignored by the Paris press. In addition a jobbing printer in Santa Vera was pressing him for payment for 5,000 anti-Apollo leaflets that had been distributed the previous year.

Above all had come the news on the radio that the target date of the first manned Moon flight had been advanced to 1969, and on the following day would take place the latest and most ambitious of the instrumented lunar flights. The anticipated budget for the Apollo programme (in a moment of grim humour he had calculated that it would pay for the printing of some 1,000 billion leaflets) seemed to double each year, but so far he had found little success in his attempt to alert people to the folly of venturing into space. All that day he had felt sick with frustration and anger.

At the end of the avenue he turned on to the highway which served the asparagus farms lying in the 20-mile strip between Vernon Gardens and the desert. It was a hot empty evening and few cars or trucks passed him. On either side of the road the great lemon-green terraces of asparagus lay seeping in their moist paddy beds, and occasionally a marsh-hen clacked overhead and dived out of sight.

Five miles along the road he reached the last farmhouse above the edge of the desert. He cycled on to where the road ended 200 yards ahead, dismounted and left the bicycle in a culvert. Slinging his camera over one shoulder, he walked off across the hard ground into the mouth of a small valley.

The boundary between the desert and the farm-strip was irregular. On his left, beyond the rocky slopes, he could hear a motor-reaper purring down one of the mile-long spits of fertile land running into the desert, but the barren terrain and the sense of isolation began to relax him and he forgot the irritations that had plagued him all day.

A keen naturalist, he saw a long-necked sand-crane perched on a spur of shale fifty feet from him and stopped and raised his camera. Peering through the finder he noticed that the light had faded too deeply for a photograph. Curiously, the sand-crane was clearly silhouetted against a circular glow of light which emanated from beyond a low ridge at the end of the valley. This apparently sourceless corona fitfully illuminated the darkening air, as if coming from a lighted mineshaft.

Putting away his camera, Kandinski walked forward, within a few minutes reached the ridge, and began to climb it. The face sloped steeply, and he pulled himself up by the hefts of brush and scrub, kicking away footholds in the rocky surface.

* * *

Just before he reached the crest he felt his heart surge painfully with the exertion, and he lay still for a moment, a sudden feeling of dizziness spinning in his head. He waited until the spasm subsided, shivering faintly in the cool air, an unfamiliar undertone of uneasiness in his mind. The air seemed to vibrate strangely with an intense inaudible music that pressed upon his temples. Rubbing his forehead, he lifted himself over the crest.

The ridge he had climbed was U-shaped and about 200 feet across, its open end away from him. Resting on the sandy floor in its centre was an enormous metal disc, over 100 feet in diameter and 30 feet high. It seemed to be balanced on a huge conical boss, half of which had already sunk into the sand. A fluted rim ran around the edge of the disc and separated the upper and lower curvatures, which were revolving rapidly in opposite directions, throwing off magnificent flashes of silver light.

Kandinski lay still, as his first feeling of fear retreated and his courage and presence of mind returned. The inaudible piercing music had faded, and his mind felt brilliantly clear. His eyes ran rapidly over the space-ship, and he estimated that it was over twice the size of the craft he had seen three years earlier. There were no markings or ports on the carapace, but he was certain it had not come from Venus.

Kandinski lay watching the space-craft for ten minutes, trying to decide upon his best course of action. Unfortunately he had smashed the lens of his camera. Finally, pushing himself backwards, he slid slowly down the slope. When he reached the floor he could still hear the whine of the rotors. Hiding in the pools of shadow, he made his way up the valley, and two hundred yards from the ridge he broke into a run.

He returned the way he had come, his great legs carrying him across the ruts and boulders, seized his bicycle from the culvert and pedalled rapidly towards the farmhouse.

A single light shone in an upstairs room and he pressed one hand to the bell and pounded on the screen door with the other, nearly tearing it from its hinges. Eventually a young woman appeared. She came down the stairs reluctantly, uncertain what to make of Kandinski's beard and ragged, dusty clothes.

'Telephone!' Kandinski bellowed at her, gasping wildly, as he caught back his breath.

The girl at last unlatched the door and backed away from him nervously. Kandinski lurched past her and staggered blindly around the darkened hall. 'Where is it?' he roared.

The girl switched on the lights and pointed into the sitting room. Kandinski pushed past her and rushed over to it.

Ward played with his brandy glass and discreetly loosened the collar of his dress shirt, listening to Dr MacIntyre of Greenwich Observatory, four seats away on his right, make the third of the after-dinner speeches. Ward was to speak next, and he ran through the opening phrases of his speech, glancing down occasionally to con his notes. At 34 he was the youngest member to address the Congress banquet, and by no means unimpressed by the honour. He looked at the venerable figures to his left and right at the top table, their black jackets and white shirt fronts reflected in the table silver, and saw Professor Cameron wink at him reassuringly.

He was going through his notes for the last time when a steward bent over his shoulder. 'Telephone for you, Dr Ward.'

'I can't take it now,' Ward whispered. 'Tell them to call later.'

'The caller said it was extremely urgent, Doctor. Something about some people from the Neptune arriving.'

'The Neptune?'

'I think that's a hotel in Santa Vera. Maybe the Russian delegates have turned up after all.'

Ward pushed his chair back, made his apologies and slipped away.

Professor Cameron was waiting in the alcove outside the banqueting hall when Ward stepped out of the booth. 'Anything the trouble, Andrew? It's not your father, I hope –'

'It's Kandinski,' Ward said hurriedly. 'He's out in the desert, near the farm-strip. He says he's seen another space vehicle.'

'Oh, is that all.' Cameron shook his head. 'Come on, we'd better get back. The poor fool!'

'Hold on,' Ward said. 'He's got it under observation now. It's on the ground. He told me to call General Wayne at the air base and alert the Strategic Air Command.' Ward chewed his lip. 'I don't know what to do.'

Cameron took him by the arm. 'Andrew, come on. MacIntyre's winding up.'

'What can we do, though?' Ward asked. 'He seemed all right, but then he said that he thought they were hostile. That sounds a little sinister.'

'Andrew!' Cameron snapped. 'What's the matter with you? Leave Kandinski to himself. You can't go now. It would be unpardonable rudeness.'

'I've got to help Kandinski,' Ward insisted. 'I'm sure he needs it this time.' He wrenched himself away from Cameron.

'Ward!' Professor Cameron called. 'For God's sake, come back!' He followed Ward onto the balcony and watched him run down the steps and disappear across the lawn into the darkness.

As the wheels of the car thudded over the deep ruts, Ward cut the headlights and searched the dark hills which marked the desert's edge. The warm glitter of Vernon Gardens lay behind him and only a few isolated lights shone in the darkness on either side of the road. He passed the farmhouse from which he assumed Kandinski had telephoned, then drove on slowly until he saw the bicycle Kandinski had left for him.

It took him several minutes to mount the huge machine, his feet well clear of the pedals for most of their stroke. Laboriously he covered a hundred yards, and after careering helplessly into a clump of scrub was forced to dismount and continue on foot.

Kandinski had told him that the ridge was about a mile up the valley. It was almost night and the starlight reflected off the hills lit the valley with fleeting, vivid colours. He ran on heavily, the only sounds he could hear were those of a thresher rattling like a giant metal insect half a mile behind him. Filling his lungs, he pushed on across the last hundred yards.

*   *   *

Kandinski was still lying on the edge of the ridge, watching the space-ship and waiting impatiently for Ward. Below him in the hollow the upper and lower rotor sections swung around more slowly, at about one revolution per second. The space-ship had sunk a further ten feet into the desert floor and he was now on the same level as the observation dome. A single finger of light poked out into the darkness, circling the ridge walls in jerky sweeps.

Then out of the valley behind him he saw someone stumbling along towards the ridge at a broken run. Suddenly a feeling of triumph and exhilaration came over him, and he knew that at last he had his witness.

Ward climbed up the slope to where he could see Kandinski. Twice he lost his grip and slithered downwards helplessly, tearing his hands on the gritty surface. Kandinski was lying flat on his chest, his head just above the ridge. Covered by dust, he was barely distinguishable from the slope itself.

'Are you all right?' Ward whispered. He pulled off his bow tie and ripped open his collar. When he had controlled his breathing he crawled up beside Kandinski.

'Where?' he asked.

Kandinski pointed down into the hollow.

Ward raised his head, levering himself up on his elbows. For a few seconds he peered out into the darkness, and then drew his head back.

'You see it?' Kandinski whispered. His voice was short and laboured. When Ward hesitated before replying he suddenly seized Ward's wrist in a vice-like grip. In the faint light reflected by the white dust on the ridge Ward could see plainly his bright inflamed eyes.

'Ward! Can you see it?'

The powerful fingers remained clamped to his wrist as he lay beside Kandinski and gazed down into the darkness.

Below the compartment window one of Ward's fellow passengers was being seen off by a group of friends, and the young women in bright hats and bandanas and the men in slacks and beach sandals made him feel that he was leaving a seaside resort at the end of a holiday. From the window he could see the observatory domes of Mount Vernon rising out of the trees, and he identified the white brickwork of the Hoyle Library a thousand feet below the summit. Edna Cameron had brought him to the station, but he had asked her not to come onto the platform, and she had said goodbye and driven off. Cameron himself he had seen only once, when he had collected his books from the Institute.

Trying to forget it all, Ward noted thankfully that the train would leave within five minutes. He took his bankbook out of his wallet and counted the last week's withdrawals. He winced at the largest item, 600 dollars which he had transferred to Kandinski's account to pay for the cablegrams.

Deciding to buy something to read, he left the car and walked back to the news-stand. Several of the magazines contained what could only be described as discouraging articles about himself, and he chose two or three newspapers.

Just then someone put a hand on his shoulder. He turned and saw Kandinski.

'Are you leaving?' Kandinski asked quietly. He had trimmed his beard so that only a pale vestige of the original bloom remained, revealing his high bony cheekbones. His face seemed almost fifteen years younger, thinner and more drawn, but at the same time composed, like that of a man recovering slowly from the attack of some intermittent fever.

'I'm sorry, Charles,' Ward said as they walked back to the car. 'I should have said goodbye to you but I thought I'd better not.'

Kandinski's expression was subdued but puzzled. 'Why?' he asked. 'I don't understand.'

Ward shrugged. 'I'm afraid everything here has more or less come to an end for me, Charles. I'm going back to Princeton until the spring. Freshman physics.' He smiled ruefully at himself. 'Boyle's Law, Young's Modulus, getting right back to fundamentals. Not a bad idea, perhaps.'

'But why are you leaving?' Kandinski pressed.

'Well, Cameron thought it might be tactful of me to leave. After our statement to the Secretary-General was published in

The New York Times I became very much *persona non grata* at the Hubble. The trustees were on to Professor Renthall again this morning.'

Kandinski smiled and seemed relieved. 'What does the Hubble matter?' he scoffed. 'We have more important work to do. You know, Ward, when Mrs Cameron told me just now that you were leaving I couldn't believe it.'

'I'm sorry, Charles, but it's true.'

'Ward,' Kandinski insisted. 'You can't leave. The Primes will be returning soon. We must prepare for them.'

'I know, Charles, and I wish I could stay.' They reached the car and Ward put his hand out. 'Thanks for coming to see me off.'

Kandinski held his hand tightly. 'Andrew, tell me the truth. Are you afraid of what people will think of you? Is that why you want to leave? Haven't you enough courage and faith in yourself?'

'Perhaps that's it,' Ward conceded, wishing the train would start. He reached for the rail and began to climb into the car but Kandinski held him.

'Ward, you can't drop your responsibilities like this!'

'Please, Charles,' Ward said, feeling his temper rising. He pulled his hand away but Kandinski seized him by the shoulder and almost dragged him off the car.

Ward wrenched himself away. 'Leave me alone!' he snapped fiercely. 'I saw your space-ship, didn't I?'

Kandinski watched him go, a hand picking at his vanished beard, completely perplexed.

Whistles sounded, and the train began to edge forward.

'Goodbye, Charles,' Ward called down. 'Let me know if you see anything else.'

He went into the car and took his seat. Only when the train was twenty miles from Mount Vernon did he look out of the window.

1963

END-GAME

After his trial they gave Constantin a villa, an allowance and an executioner. The villa was small and high-walled, and had obviously been used for the purpose before. The allowance was adequate to Constantin's needs – he was never permitted to go out and his meals were prepared for him by a police orderly. The executioner was his own. Most of the time they sat on the enclosed veranda overlooking the narrow stone garden, playing chess with a set of large well-worn pieces.

The executioner's name was Malek. Officially he was Constantin's supervisor, and responsible for maintaining the villa's tenuous contact with the outside world, now hidden from sight beyond the steep walls, and for taking the brief telephone call that came promptly at nine o'clock every morning. However, his real role was no secret between them. A powerful, doughy-faced man with an anonymous expression, Malek at first intensely irritated Constantin, who had been used to dealing with more subtle sets of responses. Malek followed him around the villa, never interfering – unless Constantin tried to bribe the orderly for a prohibited newspaper, when Malek merely gestured with a slight turn of one of his large hands, face registering no disapproval, but cutting off the attempt as irrevocably as a bulkhead – nor making any suggestions as to how Constantin should spend his time. Like a large bear, he sat motionlessly in the lounge in one of the faded armchairs, watching Constantin.

After a week Constantin tired of reading the old novels in the bottom shelf of the bookcase – somewhere among the grey well-thumbed pages he had hoped to find a message from one of his predecessors – and invited Malek to play chess.

The set of chipped mahogany pieces reposed on one of the empty shelves of the bookcase, the only item of decoration or recreational equipment in the villa. Apart from the books and the chess set the small six-roomed house was completely devoid of ornament. There were no curtains or picture rails, bedside tables or standard lamps, and the only electrical fittings were the lights recessed behind thick opaque bowls into the ceilings. Obviously the chess set and the row of novels had been provided deliberately, each representing one of the alternative pastimes available to the temporary tenants of the villa. Men of a phlegmatic or philosophical temperament, resigned to the inevitability of their fate, would choose to read the novels, sinking backwards into a self-anaesthetized trance as they waded through the turgid prose of those nineteenth-century romances.

On the other hand, men of a more volatile and extrovert disposition would obviously prefer to play chess, unable to resist the opportunity to exercise their Machiavellian talents for positional manoeuvre to the last. The games of chess would help to maintain their unconscious optimism and, more subtly, sublimate or divert any attempts at escape.

When Constantin suggested that they play chess Malek promptly agreed, and so they spent the next long month as the late summer turned to autumn. Constantin was glad he had chosen chess; the game brought him into immediate personal involvement with Malek, and like all condemned men he had soon developed a powerful emotional transference on to what effectively was the only person left in his life.

At present it was neither negative nor positive; but a relationship of acute dependence – already Malek's notional personality was becoming overlaid by the associations of all the anonymous but nonetheless potent figures of authority whom Constantin could remember since his earliest childhood: his own father, the priest at the seminary he had seen hanged after the revolution, the first senior commissars, the party secretaries at the ministry of foreign affairs and, ultimately, the members of the central committee themselves. Here, where the anonymous faces had crystallized into those of closely observed colleagues and rivals, the process seemed to come full circle, so that he himself was identified with those shadowy personas who had authorized his death and were now represented by Malek.

Constantin had also, of course, become dominated by another obsession, the need to know: *when*? In the weeks after the trial and sentence he had remained in a curiously euphoric state, too stunned to realize that the dimension of time still existed for him, he had already died *a posteriori*. But gradually the will to live, and his old determination and ruthlessness, which had served him so well for thirty years, reasserted themselves, and he realized that a small hope still remained to him. How long exactly in terms of time he could only guess, but if he could master Malek his survival became a real possibility.

The question remained: When?

Fortunately he could be completely frank with Malek. The first point he established immediately.

'Malek,' he asked on the tenth move one morning, when he had completed his development and was relaxing for a moment. 'Tell me, do you know – when?'

Malek looked up from the board, his large almost bovine eyes gazing blandly at Constantin. 'Yes, Mr Constantin, I know when.' His voice was deep and functional, as expressionless as a weighing machine's.

Constantin sat back reflectively. Outside the glass panes of the veranda the rain fell steadily on the solitary fir tree which had maintained a precarious purchase among the stones under the wall. A few miles to the south-west of the villa were the outskirts of the small port, one of the dismal so-called 'coastal resorts' where junior ministry men and party hacks were sent for their bi-annual holidays. The weather, however, seemed peculiarly inclement, the sun never shining through the morose clouds, and for a moment, before he checked himself, Constantin felt glad to be within the comparative warmth of the villa.

'Let me get this straight,' he said to Malek. 'You don't merely know in a general sense – for example, after receiving an instruction from so-and-so – but you know *specifically* when?'

'Exactly.' Malek moved his queen out of the game. His chess was sound but without flair or a personal style, suggesting that he had improved merely by practice – most of his opponents, Constantin realized with sardonic amusement, would have been players of a high class.

'You know the *day* and the *hour* and the *minute*,' Constantin pressed. Malek nodded slowly, most of his attention upon the game, and Constantin rested his smooth sharp chin in one hand, watching his opponent. 'It could be within the next ten seconds, or again, it might not be for ten years?'

'As you say.' Malek gestured at the board. 'Your move.'

Constantin waved this aside. 'I know, but don't let's rush it. These games are played on many levels, Malek. People who talk about three-dimensional chess obviously know nothing about the present form.' Occasionally he made these openings in the hope of loosening Malek's tongue, but conversation with him seemed to be impossible.

Abruptly he sat forward across the board, his eyes searching Malek's. 'You alone know the date, Malek, and as you have said, it might not be for ten years – or twenty. Do you think you can keep such a secret to yourself for so long?'

Malek made no attempt to answer this, and waited for Constantin to resume play. Now and then his eyes inspected the corners of the veranda, or glanced at the stone garden outside. From the kitchen came the occasional sounds of the orderly's boots scraping the floor as he lounged by the telephone on the deal table.

As he scrutinized the board Constantin wondered how he could provoke any response whatever from Malek; the man had shown no reaction at the mention of ten years, although the period was ludicrously far ahead. In all probability their real game would be a short one. The indeterminate date of the execution, which imbued the procedure with such a bizarre flavour, was not intended to add an element of torture or suspense to the condemned's last days, but simply to obscure and confuse the very fact of his exit. If a definite date were known in advance there might be a last-minute rally of sympathy, an attempt to review the sentence and perhaps apportion the blame elsewhere, and the unconscious if not conscious sense of complicity in the condemned man's crimes might well provoke an agonized reappraisal and, after the execution of the sentence, a submerged sense of guilt upon which opportunists and intriguers could play to advantage.

By means of the present system, however, all these dangers and unpleasant side-effects were obviated, the accused was removed from his place in the hierarchy when the opposition to him was at its zenith and conveniently handed over to the judiciary, and thence to one of the courts of star chamber whose proceedings were always held in camera and whose verdicts were never announced.

As far as his former colleagues were concerned, he had disappeared into the endless corridor world of the bureaucratic purgatories, his case permanently on file but never irrevocably closed. Above all, the fact of his guilt was never established and confirmed. As Constantin was aware, he himself had been convicted upon a technicality in the margins of the main indictment against him, a mere procedural device, like a bad twist in the plot of a story, designed solely to bring the investigation to a close. Although he knew the real nature of his crime, Constantin had never been formally notified of his guilt; in fact the court had gone out of its way to avoid preferring any serious charges against him whatever.

This ironic inversion of the classical Kafkaesque situation, by which, instead of admitting his guilt to a non-existent crime, he was forced to connive in a farce maintaining his innocence of offences he knew full well he had committed, was preserved in his present situation at the execution villa.

The psychological basis was more obscure but in some way far more threatening, the executioner beckoning his victim towards him with a beguiling smile, reassuring him that all was forgiven. Here he played upon, not those unconscious feelings of anxiety and guilt, but that innate conviction of individual survival, that obsessive preoccupation with personal immortality which is merely a disguised form of the universal fear of the image of one's own death. It was this assurance that all was well, and the absence of any charges of guilt or responsibility, which had made so orderly the queues into the gas chambers.

At present the paradoxical face of this diabolical device was worn by Malek, his lumpy amorphous features and neutral but ambiguous attitude making him seem less a separate personality than the personification of the apparat of the state. Perhaps the sardonic title of 'supervisor' was nearer the truth than had seemed at first sight, and that Malek's role was simply to officiate, or at the most serve as moderator, at a trial by ordeal in which Constantin was his own accused, prosecutor and judge.

However, he reflected as he examined the board, aware of Malek's bulky presence across the pieces, this would imply that they had completely misjudged his own personality, with its buoyancy and almost gallic verve and panache. He, of all people, would be the last to take his own life in an orgy of self-confessed guilt. Not for him the neurotic suicide so loved of the Slav. As long as there were a way out he would cheerfully shoulder any burden of guilt, tolerant of his own weaknesses, ready to shrug them off with a quip. This insouciance had always been his strongest ally.

His eyes searched the board, roving down the open files of the queens and bishops, as if the answer to the pressing enigma were to be found in these polished corridors.

When? His own estimate was two months. Almost certainly, (and he had no fear here that he was rationalizing) it would not be within the next two or three days, nor even the next fortnight. Haste was always unseemly, quite apart from violating the whole purpose of the exercise. Two months would see him safely into limbo, and be sufficiently long for the suspense to break him down and reveal any secret allies, sufficiently brief to fit his particular crime.

Two months? Not as long as he might have wished. As he translated his queen's bishop into play Constantin began to map out his strategy for defeating Malek. The first task, obviously, was to discover when Malek was to carry out the execution, partly to give him peace of mind, but also to allow him to adjust the context of his escape. A physical leap to freedom over the wall would be pointless. Contacts had to be established, pressure brought to bear at various sensitive points in the hierarchy, paving the way for a reconsideration of his case. All this would take time.

His thoughts were interrupted by the sharp movement of Malek's left hand across the board, followed by a guttural grunt. Surprised by the speed and economy with which Malek had moved his piece as much by the fact that he himself was in check, Constantin sat forward and examined his position with more care. He glanced with grudging respect at Malek, who had sat back as impassively as ever, the knight he had deftly taken on the edge of the table in front of him. His eyes watched Constantin with their usual untroubled calm, like those of an immensely patient governess, his great shoulders hidden within the bulky suiting. But for a moment, when he had leaned across the board, Constantin had seen the powerful extension and flexion of his shoulder musculature.

Don't look so smug, my dear Malek, Constantin said to himself with a wry smile. At least I know now that you are left-handed. Malek had taken the knight with one hand, hooking the piece between the thick knuckles of his ring and centre fingers, and then substituting his queen with a smart tap, a movement not easily performed in the centre of the crowded board. Useful though the confirmation was – Constantin had noticed Malek apparently trying to conceal his left-handedness during their meals and when opening and closing the windows – he found this sinistral aspect of Malek's personality curiously disturbing, an indication that there would be nothing predictable about his opponent, or the ensuing struggle of wits between them. Even Malek's apparent lack of sharp intelligence was belied by the astuteness of his last move.

Constantin was playing white, and had chosen the Queen's Gambit, assuming that the fluid situation invariably resulting from the opening would be to his advantage and allow him to get on with the more serious task of planning his escape. But Malek had avoided any possible errors, steadily consolidating his position, and had even managed to launch a counter-gambit, offering a knight-to-bishop exchange which would soon undermine Constantin's position if he accepted.

'A good move, Malek,' he commented. 'But perhaps a little risky in the long run.' Declining the exchange, he lamely blocked the checking queen with a pawn.

Malek stared stolidly at the board, his heavy policeman's face, with its almost square frame from one jaw angle to the other, betraying no sign of thought. His approach, Constantin reflected as he watched his opponent, would be that of the pragmatist, judging always by immediate capability rather than by any concealed intentions. As if confirming this diagnosis, Malek simply returned his queen to her former square, unwilling or unable to exploit the advantage he had gained and satisfied by the captured piece.

Bored by the lower key on to which the game had descended, and the prospect of similar games ahead, Constantin castled his king to safety. For some reason, obviously irrational, he assumed that Malek would not kill him in the middle of a game, particularly if he, Malek, were winning. He recognized that this was an unconscious reason for wanting to play chess in the first place, and had no doubt motivated the many others who had also sat with Malek on the veranda, listening to the late summer rain. Suppressing a sudden pang of fear, Constantin examined Malek's powerful hands protruding from his cuffs like two joints of meat. If Malek wanted to, he could probably kill Constantin with his bare hands.

That raised a second question, almost as fascinating as the first.

'Malek, another point.' Constantin sat back, searching in his pockets for imaginary cigarettes (none were allowed him). 'Forgive my curiosity, but I am an interested party, as it were —' He flashed Malek his brightest smile, a characteristically incisive thrust modulated by ironic self-deprecation which had been so successful with his secretaries and at ministry receptions, but the assay at humour failed to move Malek. 'Tell me, do you know ... how –?' Searching for some euphemism, he repeated: 'Do you know how you are going to ...?' and then gave up the attempt, cursing Malek to himself for lacking the social grace to rescue him from his awkwardness.

Malek's chin rose slightly, a minimal nod. He showed no signs of being bored or irritated by Constantin's laboured catechism, or of having noticed his embarrassment.

'What is it, then?' Constantin pressed, recovering himself. 'Pistol, pill or–' with a harsh laugh he pointed through the window '– do you set up a guillotine in the rain? I'd like to know.'

Malek looked down at the chess-board, his features more glutinous and dough-like than ever. Flatly, he said: 'It has been decided.'

Constantin snorted. 'What on earth does *that* mean?' he snapped belligerently. 'Is it painless?'

For once Malek smiled, a thin sneer of amusement hung fleetingly around his mouth. 'Have you ever killed anything, Mr Constantin?' he asked quietly. 'Yourself, personally, I mean.'

'Touché,' Constantin granted. He laughed deliberately, trying to dispel the tension. 'A perfect reply.' To himself he said: I mustn't let curiosity get the upper hand, the man was laughing at me.

'Of course,' he went on, 'death is always painful. I merely wondered whether, in the legal sense of the term, it would be humane. But I can see that you are a professional, Malek, and the question answers itself. A great relief, believe me. There are so many sadists about, perverts and the like –' again he watched carefully to see if the implied sneer provoked Malek '– that one can't be too grateful for a clean curtain fall. It's good to know. I can devote these last days to putting my affairs in order and coming to terms with the world. If only I knew how long there was left I could make my preparations accordingly. One can't be forever saying one's last prayers. You see my point?'

Colourlessly, Malek said: 'The Prosecutor-General advised you to make your final arrangements immediately after the trial.'

'But what does that mean?' Constantin asked, pitching his voice a calculated octave higher. 'I'm a human being, not a book-keeper's ledger that can be totted up and left to await the auditor's pleasure. I wonder if you realize, Malek, the courage this situation demands from me? It's easy for you to sit there –'

Abruptly Malek stood up, sending a shiver of terror through Constantin. With a glance at the sealed windows, he moved around the chess table towards the lounge. 'We will postpone the game,' he said. Nodding to Constantin, he went off towards the kitchen where the orderly was preparing lunch.

Constantin listened to his shoes squeaking faintly across the unpolished floor, then irritably cleared the pieces off the board and sat back with the black king in his hand. At least he had provoked Malek into leaving him. Thinking this over, he wondered whether to throw caution to the winds and begin to make life intolerable for Malek – it would be easy to pursue him around the villa, arguing hysterically and badgering him with neurotic questions. Sooner or later Malek would snap back, and might give away something of his intentions. Alternatively, Constantin could try to freeze him out, treating him with contempt as the hired killer he was, refusing to share a room or his meals with him and insisting on his rights as a former member of the central committee. The method might well be successful. Almost certainly Malek was telling the truth when he said he knew the exact day and minute of Constantin's execution. The order would have been given to him and he would have no discretion to advance or delay the date to suit himself. Malek would be reluctant to report Constantin for difficult behaviour – the reflection on himself was too obvious and his present post was not one from which he could graciously retire – and in addition not even the Police-President would be able to vary the execution date now that it had been set without convening several meetings. There was then the danger of re-opening Constantin's case. He was not without his allies, or at least those who were prepared to use him for their own advantage.

But despite these considerations, the whole business of play-acting lacked appeal for Constantin. His approach was more serpentine. Besides, if he provoked Malek, uncertainties were introduced, of which there were already far too many.

He noticed the supervisor enter the lounge and sit down quietly in one of the grey armchairs, his face, half-hidden in the shadows, turned towards Constantin. He seemed indifferent to the normal pressures of boredom and fatigue (luckily for himself, Constantin reflected – an impatient man would have pulled the trigger on the morning of the second day), and content to sit about in the armchairs, watching Constantin as the grey rain fell outside and the damp leaves gathered against the walls. The difficulties of establishing a relationship with Malek – and some sort of relationship was essential before Constantin could begin to think of escape – seemed insuperable, only the games of chess offering an opportunity.

Placing the black king on his own king's square, Constantin called out: 'Malek, I'm ready for another game, if you are.'

Malek pushed himself out of the chair with his long arms, and then took his place across the board. For a moment he scrutinized Constantin with a level glance, as if ascertaining that there would be no further outbursts of temper, and then began to set up the white pieces, apparently prepared to ignore the fact that Constantin had cleared the previous game before its completion.

He opened with a stolid Ruy Lopez, an over-analysed and uninteresting attack, but a dozen moves later, when they broke off for lunch, he had already forced Constantin to castle on the Queen's side and had established a powerful position in the centre.

As they took their lunch together at the card table behind the sofa in the lounge, Constantin reflected upon this curious element which had been introduced into his relationship with Malek. While trying to check any tendency to magnify an insignificant triviality into a major symbol, he realized that Malek's proficiency at chess, and his ability to produce powerful combinations out of pedestrian openings, was symptomatic of his concealed power over Constantin.

The drab villa in the thin autumn rain, the faded furniture and unimaginative food they were now mechanically consuming, the whole grey limbo with its slender telephone connection with the outside world were, like his chess, exact extensions of Malek's personality, yet permeated with secret passages and doors. The unexpected thrived in such an ambience. At any moment, as he shaved, the mirror might retract to reveal the flaming muzzle of a machine pistol, or the slightly bitter flavour of the soup they were drinking might be other than that of lentils.

These thoughts preoccupied him as the afternoon light began to fade in the east, the white rectangle of the garden wall illuminated against this dim backdrop like a huge tabula rasa. Excusing himself from the chess game, Constantin feigned a headache and retired to his room upstairs.

The door between his room and Malek's had been removed, and as he lay on the bed he was conscious of the supervisor sitting in his chair with his back to the window. Perhaps it was Malek's presence which prevented him from gaining any real rest, and when he rose several hours later and returned to the veranda he felt tired and possessed by a deepening sense of foreboding.

With an effort he rallied his spirits, and by concentrating his whole attention on the game was able to extract what appeared to be a drawn position. Although the game was adjourned without comment from either player, Malek seemed to concede by his manner that he had lost his advantage, lingering for a perceptible moment over the board when Constantin rose from the table.

The lesson of all this was not lost to Constantin the following day. He was fully aware that the games of chess were not only taxing his energies but providing Malek with a greater hold upon himself than he upon Malek. Although the pieces stood where they had left them the previous evening, Constantin did not suggest that they resume play. Malek made no move towards the board, apparently indifferent to whether the game was finished or not. Most of the time he sat next to Constantin by the single radiator in the lounge, occasionally going off to confer with the orderly in the kitchen. As usual the telephone rang briefly each morning, but otherwise there were no callers or visitors to the villa. To all intents it remained suspended in a perfect vacuum.

It was this unvarying nature of their daily routines which Constantin found particularly depressing. Intermittently over the next few days he played chess with Malek, invariably finding himself in a losing position, but the focus of his attention was elsewhere, upon the enigma cloaked by Malek's expressionless face. Around him a thousand invisible clocks raced onwards towards their beckoning zeros, a soundless thunder like the drumming of apocalyptic hoof-irons.

His mood of foreboding had given way to one of mounting fear, all the more terrifying because, despite Malek's real role, it seemed completely sourceless. He found himself unable to concentrate for more than a few minutes upon any task, left his meals unfinished and fidgeted helplessly by the veranda window. The slightest movement by Malek would make his nerves thrill with anguish; if the supervisor left his customary seat in the lounge to speak to the orderly Constantin would find himself almost paralysed by the tension, helplessly counting the seconds until Malek returned. Once, during one of their meals, Malek started to ask him for the salt and Constantin almost choked to death.

The ironic humour of this near-fatality reminded Constantin that almost half of his two-month sentence had elapsed. But his crude attempts to obtain a pencil from the orderly and later, failing this, to mark the letters in a page torn from one of the novels were intercepted by Malek, and he realized that short of defeating the two policemen in single-handed combat he had no means of escaping his ever more imminent fate.

Latterly he had noticed that Malek's movements and general activity around the villa seemed to have quickened. He still sat for long periods in the armchair, observing Constantin, but his formerly impassive presence was graced by gestures and inclinations of the head that seemed to reflect a heightened cerebral activity, as if he were preparing himself for some long-awaited denouement. Even the heavy musculature of his face seemed to have relaxed and grown sleeker, his sharp mobile eyes, like those of an experienced senior inspector of police, roving constantly about the rooms.

Despite his efforts, however, Constantin was unable to galvanize himself into any defensive action. He could see clearly that Malek and himself had entered a new phase in their relationship, and that at any moment their outwardly formal and polite behaviour would degenerate into a gasping ugly violence, but he was nonetheless immobilized by his own state of terror. The days passed in a blur of uneaten meals and abandoned chess games, their very identity blotting out any sense of time or progression, the watching figure of Malek always before him.

Every morning, when he woke after two or three hours of sleep to find his consciousness still intact, a discovery almost painful in its relief and poignancy, he would be immediately aware of Malek standing in the next room, then waiting discreetly in the hallway as Constantin shaved in the bathroom (also without its door) following him downstairs to breakfast, his careful reflective tread like that of a hangman descending from his gallows.

After breakfast Constantin would challenge Malek to a game of chess, but after a few moves would begin to play wildly, throwing pieces forwards to be decimated by Malek. At times the supervisor would glance curiously at Constantin, as if wondering whether his charge had lost his reason, and then continue to play his careful exact game, invariably winning or drawing. Dimly Constantin perceived that by losing to Malek he had also surrendered to him psychologically, but the games had now become simply a means of passing the unending days.

Six weeks after they had first begun to play chess, Constantin more by luck than skill succeeded in an extravagant pawn gambit and forced Malek to sacrifice both his centre and any possibility of castling. Roused from his state of numb anxiety by the temporary victory, Constantin sat forward over the board, irritably waving away the orderly who announced from the door of the lounge that he would serve lunch.

'Tell him to wait, Malek. I mustn't lose my concentration at this point, I've very nearly won the game.'

'Well . . .' Malek glanced at his watch, then over his shoulder at the orderly, who, however, had turned on his heel and returned to the kitchen. He started to stand up. 'It can wait. He's bringing the –'

'No!' Constantin snapped. 'Just give me five minutes, Malek. Damn it, one adjourns on a move, not halfway through it.'

'Very well.' Malek hesitated, after a further glance at his watch. He climbed to his feet. 'I will tell him.'

Constantin concentrated on the board, ignoring the supervisor's retreating figure, the scent of victory clearing his mind. But thirty seconds later he sat up with a start, his heart almost seizing inside his chest.

Malek had gone upstairs! Constantin distinctly remembered him saying he would tell the orderly to delay lunch, but instead he had walked straight up to his bedroom. Not only was it extremely unusual for Constantin to be left unobserved when the orderly was otherwise occupied, but the latter had still not brought in their first luncheon course.

Steadying the table, Constantin stood up, his eyes searching the open doorways in front and behind him. Almost certainly the orderly's announcement of lunch was a signal, and Malek had found a convenient pretext for going upstairs to prepare his execution weapon.

Faced at last by the nemesis he had so long dreaded, Constantin listened for the sounds of Malek's feet descending the staircase. A profound silence enclosed the villa, broken only by the fall of one of the chess pieces to the tiled floor. Outside the sun shone intermittently in the garden, illuminating the broken flagstones of the ornamental pathway and the bare face of the walls. A few stunted weeds flowered among the rubble, their pale colours blanched by the sunlight, and Constantin was suddenly filled by an overwhelming need to escape into the open air for the few last moments before he died. The east wall, lit by the sun's rays, was marked by a faint series of horizontal grooves, the remnants perhaps of a fire escape ladder, and the slender possibility of using these as hand-holds made the enclosed garden, a perfect killing ground, preferable to the frantic claustrophobic nexus of the villa.

Above him, Malek's measured tread moved across the ceiling to the head of the staircase. He paused there and then began to descend the stairs, his steps chosen with a precise and careful rhythm.

Helplessly, Constantin searched the veranda for something that would serve as a weapon. The french windows on to the garden were locked, and a slotted pinion outside secured the left-hand member of the pair to the edge of the sill. If this were raised there was a chance that the windows could be forced outwards.

Scattering the chess pieces onto the floor with a sweep of his hand, Constantin seized the board and folded it together, then stepped over to the window and drove the heavy wooden box through the bottom pane. The report of the bursting glass echoed like a gun shot through the villa. Kneeling down, he pushed his hand through the aperture and tried to lift the pinion, jerking it up and down in its rusty socket. When it failed to clear the sill he forced his head through the broken window and began to heave against it helplessly with his thin shoulders, the fragments of broken glass falling on to his neck.

Behind him a chair was kicked back, and he felt two powerful hands seize his shoulders and pull him away from the window. He struck out hysterically with the chess box, and then was flung head-first to the tiled floor.

His convalescence from this episode was to last most of the following week. For the first three days he remained in bed, recovering his physical identity, waiting for the sprained muscles of his hands and shoulders to repair themselves. When he felt sufficiently strong to leave his bed he went down to the lounge and sat at one end of the sofa, his back to the windows and the thin autumn light.

Malek still remained in attendance, and the orderly prepared his meals as before. Neither of them made any comment upon

Constantin's outburst of hysteria, or indeed betrayed any signs that it had taken place, but Constantin realized that he had crossed an important rubicon. His whole relationship with Malek had experienced a profound change. The fear of his own imminent death, and the tantalizing mystery of its precise date which had so obsessed him, had been replaced by a calm acceptance that the judicial processes inaugurated by his trial would take their course and that Malek and the orderly were merely the local agents of this distant apparat. In a sense his sentence and present tenuous existence at the villa were a microcosm of life itself, with its inherent but unfeared uncertainties, its inevitable quietus to be made on a date never known in advance. Seeing his role at the villa in this light Constantin no longer felt afraid at the prospect of his own extinction, fully aware that a change in the political wind could win him a free pardon.

In addition, he realized that Malek, far from being his executioner, a purely formal role, was in fact an intermediary between himself and the hierarchy, and in an important sense a potential ally of Constantin's. As he reformed his defence against the indictment preferred against him at the trial – he knew he had been far too willing to accept the *fait accompli* of his own guilt – he calculated the various ways in which Malek would be able to assist him. There was no doubt in his mind that he had misjudged Malek. With his sharp intelligence and commanding presence, the supervisor was very far from being a hatchet-faced killer – this original impression had been the result of some cloudiness in Constantin's perceptions, an unfortunate myopia which had cost him two precious months in his task of arranging a re-trial.

Comfortably swathed in his dressing gown, he sat at the card-table in the lounge (they had abandoned the veranda with the colder weather, and a patch of brown paper over the window reminded him of that first circle of purgatory) concentrating on the game of chess. Malek sat opposite him, hands clasped on one knee, his thumbs occasionally circling as he pondered a move. Although no less reticent than he had ever been, his manner seemed to indicate that he understood and confirmed Constantin's reappraisal of the situation. He still followed Constantin around the villa, but his attentions were noticeably more perfunctory, as if he realized that Constantin would not try again to escape.

From the start, Constantin was completely frank with Malek.

'I am convinced, Malek, that the Prosecutor-General was misdirected by the Justice Department, and that the whole basis of the trial was a false one. All but one of the indictments were never formally presented, so I had no opportunity to defend myself. You understand that, Malek? The selection of the capital penalty for one count was purely arbitrary.'

Malek nodded, moving a piece. 'So you have explained, Mr Constantin. I am afraid I do not have a legalistic turn of mind.'

'There's no need for you to,' Constantin assured him. 'The point is obvious. I hope it may be possible to appeal against the court's decision and ask for a re-trial.' Constantin gestured with a piece. 'I criticize myself for accepting the indictments so readily. In effect I made no attempt to defend myself. If only I had done so I am convinced I should have been found innocent.'

Malek murmured non-committally, and gestured towards the board. Constantin resumed play. Most of the games he consistently lost to Malek, but this no longer troubled him and, if anything, only served to reinforce the bonds between them.

Constantin had decided not to ask the supervisor to inform the Justice Department of his request for a re-trial until he had convinced Malek that his case left substantial room for doubt. A premature application would meet with an automatic negative from Malek, whatever his private sympathies. Conversely, once Malek was firmly on his side he would be prepared to risk his reputation with his seniors, and indeed his championing of Constantin's cause would be convincing proof in itself of the latter's innocence.

As Constantin soon found from his one-sided discussions with Malek, arguing over the legal technicalities of the trial, with their infinitely subtle nuances and implications, was an unprofitable method of enlisting Malek's support and he realized that he would have to do so by sheer impress of personality, by his manner, bearing and general conduct, and above all by his confidence of his innocence in the face of the penalty which might at any moment be imposed upon him. Curiously, this latter pose was not as difficult to maintain as might have been expected; Constantin already felt a surge of conviction in his eventual escape from the villa. Sooner or later Malek would recognize the authenticity of this inner confidence.

To begin with, however, the supervisor remained his usual phlegmatic self. Constantin talked away at him from morning to evening, every third word affirming the probability of his being found 'innocent', but Malek merely nodded with a faint smile and continued to play his errorless chess.

'Malek, I don't want you to think that I challenge the competence of the court to try the charges against me, or that I hold it in disrespect,' he said to the supervisor as they played their usual morning board some two weeks after the incident on the veranda. 'Far from it. But the court must make its decisions within the context of the evidence presented by the prosecutor. And even then, the greatest imponderable remains – the role of the accused. In my case I was, to all intents, not present at the trial, so my innocence is established by *force majeure*. Don't you agree, Malek?'

Malek's eyes searched the pieces on the board, his lips pursing thinly. 'I'm afraid this is above my head, Mr Constantin. Naturally I accept the authority of the court without question.'

'But so do I, Malek. I've made that plain. The real question is simply whether the verdict was justified in the light of the new circumstances I am describing.'

Malek shrugged, apparently more interested in the end-game before them. 'I recommend you to accept the verdict, Mr Constantin. For your peace of mind, you understand.'

Constantin looked away with a gesture of impatience. 'I don't agree, Malek. Besides, a great deal is at stake.' He glanced up at the windows which were drumming in the cold autumn wind. The casements were slightly loose, and the air lanced around them. The villa was poorly heated, only the single radiator in the lounge warming the three rooms downstairs. Already Constantin dreaded the winter. His hands and feet were perpetually cold and he could find no means of warming them.

'Malek, is there any chance of obtaining another heater?' he asked. 'It's none too warm in here. I have a feeling it's going to be a particularly cold winter.'

Malek looked up from the board, his bland grey eyes regarding Constantin with a flicker of curiosity, as if this last remark were one of the few he had heard from Constantin's lips which contained any overtones whatever.

'It is cold,' he agreed at last. 'I will see if I can borrow a heater. This villa is closed for most of the year.'

Constantin pestered him for news of the heater during the following week – partly because the success of his request would have symbolized Malek's first concession to him – but it failed to materialize. After one palpably lame excuse Malek merely ignored his further reminders. Outside, in the garden, the leaves whirled about the stones in a vortex of chilling air, and overhead the low clouds raced seaward. The two men in the lounge hunched over their chess-board by the radiator, hands buried in their pockets between moves.

Perhaps it was this darkening weather which made Constantin impatient of Malek's slowness in seeing the point of his argument, and he made his first suggestions that Malek should transmit a formal request for a re-trial to his superiors at the Department of Justice.

'You speak to someone on the telephone every morning, Malek,' he pointed out when Malek demurred. 'There's no difficulty involved. If you're afraid of compromising yourself – though I would have thought that a small price to pay in view of what is at stake – the orderly can pass on a message.'

'It's not feasible, Mr Constantin.' Malek seemed at last to be tiring of the subject. 'I suggest that you –'

'Malek!' Constantin stood up and paced around the lounge. 'Don't you realize that you must? You're literally my only means of contact, if you refuse I'm absolutely powerless, there's no hope of getting a reprieve!'

'The trial has already taken place, Mr Constantin,' Malek pointed out patiently.

'It was a mis-trial! Don't you understand, Malek, I accepted that I was guilty when in fact I was completely innocent!'

Malek looked up from the board, his eyebrows lifting. '*Completely* innocent, Mr Constantin?'

Constantin snapped his fingers. 'Well, virtually innocent. At least in terms of the indictment and trial.'

'But that is merely a technical difference, Mr Constantin. The Department of Justice is concerned with absolutes.'

'Quite right, Malek. I agree entirely.' Constantin nodded approvingly at the supervisor and privately noted his quizzical expression, the first time Malek had displayed a taste for irony.

He was to notice this fresh leit-motiv recurringly during the next days; whenever he raised the subject of his request for a re-trial Malek would counter with one of his deceptively naive queries, trying to establish some minor tangential point, almost as if he were leading Constantin on to a fuller admission. At first Constantin assumed that the supervisor was fishing for information about other members of the hierarchy which he wished to use for his own purposes, but the few titbits he offered were ignored by Malek, and it dawned upon him that Malek was genuinely interested in establishing the sincerity of Constantin's conviction of his own innocence.

He showed no signs, however, of being prepared to contact his superiors at the Department of Justice, and Constantin's impatience continued to mount. He now used their morning and afternoon chess sessions as an opportunity to hold forth at length on the subject of the shortcomings of the judicial system, using his own case as an illustration, and hammered away at the theme of his innocence, even hinting that Malek might find himself held responsible if by any mischance he was not granted a reprieve.

* * *

'The position I find myself in is really most extraordinary,' he told Malek almost exactly two months after his arrival at the villa. 'Everyone else is satisfied with the court's verdict, and yet I alone know that I am innocent. I feel very like someone who is about to be buried alive.'

Malek managed a thin smile across the chess pieces. 'Of course, Mr Constantin, it is possible to convince oneself of anything, given a sufficient incentive.'

'But Malek, I assure you,' Constantin insisted, ignoring the board and concentrating his whole attention upon the supervisor, 'this is no death-cell repentance. Believe me, I know. I have examined the entire case from a thousand perspectives, questioned every possible motive. There is no doubt in my mind. I may once have been prepared to accept the possibility of my guilt but I realize now that I was entirely mistaken – experience encourages us to take too great a responsibility for ourselves, when we fall short of our ideals we become critical of ourselves and ready to assume that we are at fault. How dangerous that can be, Malek, I now know. Only the truly innocent man can really understand the meaning of guilt.'

Constantin stopped and sat back, a slight weariness overtaking him in the cold room. Malek was nodding slowly, a thin and not altogether unsympathetic smile on his lips as if he understood everything Constantin had said. Then he moved a piece, and with a murmured 'excuse me' left his seat and went out of the room.

Drawing the lapels of the dressing gown around his chest, Constantin studied the board with a desultory eye. He noticed that Malek's move appeared to be the first bad one he had made in all their games together, but he felt too tired to make the most of his opportunity. His brief speech to Malek, confirming all he believed, now left nothing more to be said. From now on whatever happened was up to Malek.

'Mr Constantin.'

He turned in his chair and, to his surprise, saw the supervisor standing in the doorway, wearing his long grey overcoat.

'Malek –?' For a moment Constantin felt his heart gallop, and then controlled himself. 'Malek, you've agreed at last, you're going to take me to the Department?'

Malek shook his head, his eyes staring sombrely at Constantin. 'Not exactly. I thought we might look at the garden, Mr Constantin. A breath of fresh air, it will do you good.'

'Of course, Malek, it's kind of you.' Constantin rose a little unsteadily to his feet, and tightened the cord of his dressing gown. 'Pardon my wild hopes.' He tried to smile at Malek, but the supervisor stood by the door, hands in his overcoat pockets, his eyes lowered fractionally from Constantin's face.

They went out on to the veranda towards the french windows. Outside the cold morning air whirled in frantic circles around the small stone yard, the leaves spiralling upwards into the dark sky. To Constantin there seemed little point in going out into the garden, but Malek stood behind him, one hand on the latch.

'Malek.' Something made him turn and face the supervisor. 'You do understand what I mean, when I say I am absolutely innocent. I *know* that.'

'Of course, Mr Constantin.' The supervisor's face was relaxed and almost genial. 'I understand. When you know you are innocent, then you are guilty.'

His hand opened the veranda door on to the whirling leaves.

1963

MINUS ONE

'Where, my God, *where* is he?'

Uttered in a tone of uncontrollable frustration as he paced up and down in front of the high-gabled window behind his desk, this *cri de coeur* of Dr Mellinger, Director of Green Hill Asylum, expressed the consternation of his entire staff at the mysterious disappearance of one of their patients. In the twelve hours that had elapsed since the escape, Dr Mellinger and his subordinates had progressed from surprise and annoyance to acute exasperation, and eventually to a mood of almost euphoric disbelief. To add insult to injury, not only had the patient, James Hinton, succeeded in becoming the first ever to escape from the asylum, but he had managed to do so without leaving any clues as to his route. Thus Dr Mellinger and his staff were tantalized by the possibility that Hinton had never escaped at all and was still safely within the confines of the asylum. At all events, everyone agreed that if Hinton *had* escaped, he had literally vanished into thin air.

However, one small consolation, Dr Mellinger reminded himself as he drummed his fingers on his desk, was that Hinton's disappearance had exposed the shortcomings of the asylum's security systems, and administered a salutary jolt to his heads of departments. As this hapless group, led by the Deputy Director, Dr Normand, filed into his office for the first of the morning's emergency conferences, Dr Mellinger cast a baleful glare at each in turn, but their sleepless faces remained mutely lowered to the carpeting, as if, despairing of finding Hinton anywhere else, they now sought his hiding place in its deep ruby pile.

At least, Dr Mellinger reflected, only one patient had disappeared, a negative sentiment which assumed greater meaning in view of the outcry that would be raised from the world outside when it was discovered that a patient – obviously a homicidal lunatic – had remained at large for over twelve hours before the police were notified.

This decision not to inform the civil authorities, an error of judgement whose culpability seemed to mount as the hours passed, alone prevented Dr Mellinger from finding an immediate scapegoat – a convenient one would have been little Dr Mendelsohn of the Pathology Department, an unimportant branch of the asylum – and sacrificing him on the altar of his own indiscretion. His natural caution, and reluctance to yield an inch of ground unless compelled, had prevented Dr Mellinger from raising the general alarm during the first hours after Hinton's disappearance, when some doubt still remained whether the latter had actually left the asylum. Although the failure to find Hinton might have been interpreted as a reasonable indication that he had successfully escaped, Dr Mellinger had characteristically refused to accept such faulty logic.

By now, over twelve hours later, his miscalculation had become apparent. As the thin smirk on Dr Normand's face revealed, and as his other subordinates would soon realize, his directorship of the asylum was now at stake. Unless they found Hinton within a few hours he would be placed in an untenable position before both the civil authorities and the trustees.

However, Dr Mellinger reminded himself, it was not without the exercise of considerable guile and resource that he had become Director of Green Hill in the first place.

'Where *is* he?'

Shifting his emphasis from the first of these interrogatories to the second, as if to illustrate that the fruitless search for Hinton's whereabouts had been superseded by an examination of his total existential role in the unhappy farce of which he was the author and principal star, Dr Mellinger turned upon his three breakfastless subordinates.

'Well, have you found him? Don't sit there dozing, gentlemen! You may have had a sleepless night, but I have still to wake from the nightmare.' With this humourless shaft, Dr Mellinger flashed a mordant eye into the rhododendron-lined drive, as if hoping to catch a sudden glimpse of the vanished patient. 'Dr Redpath, your report, please.'

'The search is still continuing, Director.' Dr Redpath, the registrar of the asylum, was nominally in charge of security. 'We have examined the entire grounds, dormitory blocks, garages and outbuildings – even the patients are taking part – but every trace of Hinton has vanished. Reluctantly, I am afraid there is no alternative but to inform the police.'

'Nonsense.' Dr Mellinger took his seat behind the desk, arms outspread and eyes roving the bare top for a minuscule replica of the vanished patient. 'Don't be disheartened by your inability to discover him, Doctor. Until the search is complete we would be wasting the police's time to ask for their help.'

'Of course, Director,' Dr Normand rejoined smoothly, 'but on the other hand, as we have now proved that the missing patient is not within the boundaries of Green Hill, we can conclude, ergo, that he is outside them. In such an event is it perhaps rather a case of *us* helping the police?'

'Not at all, my dear Normand,' Dr Mellinger replied pleasantly. As he mentally elaborated his answer, he realized that he had never trusted or liked his deputy; given the first opportunity he would replace him, most conveniently with Redpath, whose blunders in the 'Hinton affair', as it could be designated, would place him for ever squarely below the Director's thumb. 'If there were any evidence of the means by which Hinton made his escape – knotted sheets or footprints in the flower-beds – we could assume that he was no longer within these walls. But no such evidence has been found. For all we know – in fact, everything points inescapably to this conclusion – the patient is still within the confines of Green Hill, indeed by rights still within his cell. 'The bars on the window were not cut, and the only way out was through the door, the keys to which remained in the possession of Dr Booth' – he indicated the third member of the trio, a slim young man with a worried expression – 'throughout the period between the last contact with Hinton and the discovery of his disappearance. Dr Booth, as the physician actually responsible for Hinton, you are quite certain you were the last person to visit him?'

Dr Booth nodded reluctantly. His celebrity at having discovered Hinton's escape had long since turned sour. 'At seven o'clock, sir, during my evening round. But the last person to *see* Hinton was the duty nurse half an hour later. However, as no treatment had been prescribed – the patient had been admitted for observation – the door was not unlocked. Shortly after nine o'clock I decided to visit the patient –'

'Why?' Dr Mellinger placed the tips of his fingers together and constructed a cathedral spire and nave. 'This is one of the strangest aspects of the case, Doctor. Why should you have chosen, almost an hour and a half later, to leave your comfortable office on the ground floor and climb three flights of stairs merely to carry out a cursory inspection which could best be left to the duty staff? Your motives puzzle me, Doctor.'

'But, Director –!' Dr Booth was almost on his feet. 'Surely you don't suspect me of colluding in Hinton's escape? I assure you –'

'Doctor, please.' Dr Mellinger raised a smooth white hand. 'Nothing could be further from my mind. Perhaps I should have said: your *unconscious* motives.'

Again the unfortunate Booth protested: 'Director, there were no unconscious motives. I admit I can't remember precisely what prompted me to see Hinton, but it was some perfectly trivial reason. I hardly knew the patient.'

Dr Mellinger bent forwards across the desk. 'That is exactly what I meant, Doctor. To be precise, you did not know Hinton at all.' Dr Mellinger gazed at the distorted reflection of himself in the silver ink-stand. 'Tell me, Dr Booth, how would you describe Hinton's appearance?'

Booth hesitated. 'Well, he was of ... medium height, if I remember, with ... yes, brown hair and a pale complexion. His eyes were – I should have to refresh my memory from the file, Director.'

Dr Mellinger nodded. He turned to Redpath. 'Could you describe him, Doctor?'

'I'm afraid not, sir. I never saw the patient.' He gestured to the Deputy Director. 'I believe Dr Normand interviewed him on admission.'

With an effort Dr Normand cast into his memory. 'It was probably my assistant. If I remember, he was a man of average build with no distinguishing features. Neither short, nor tall. Stocky, one might say.' He pursed his lips. 'Yes. Or rather, no. I'm certain it was my assistant.'

'How interesting.' Dr Mellinger had visibly revived, the gleams of ironic humour which flashed from his eyes revealed some potent inner transformation. The burden of irritations and frustrations which had plagued him for the past day seemed to have been lifted. 'Does this mean, Dr Normand, that this entire institution has been mobilized in a search for a man whom no one here could recognize even if they found him? You surprise me, my dear Normand. I was under the impression that you were a man of cool and analytical intelligence, but in your search for Hinton you are obviously employing more arcane powers.'

'But, Director! I cannot be expected to memorize the face of every patient –'

'Enough, enough!' Dr Mellinger stood up with a flourish, and resumed his circuit of the carpet. 'This is all very disturbing. Obviously the whole relationship between Green Hill and its patients must be re-examined. Our patients are not faceless ciphers, gentlemen, but the possessors of unique and vital identities. If we regard them as nonentities and fail to invest them with any personal characteristics, is it surprising that they should seem to disappear? I suggest that we put aside the next few days and dedicate them to a careful re-appraisal. Let us scrutinize all those facile assumptions we make so readily.' Impelled by this vision, Dr Mellinger stepped into the light pouring through the window, as if to expose himself to this new revelation. 'Yes, this is the task that lies before us now; from its successful conclusion will emerge a new Green Hill, a Green Hill without shadows and conspiracies, where patients and physicians stand before each other in mutual trust and responsibility.'

A pregnant silence fell at the conclusion of this homily. At last

Dr Redpath cleared his throat, reluctant to disturb Dr Mellinger's sublime communion with himself. 'And Hinton, sir?'

'Hinton? Ah, yes.' Dr Mellinger turned to face them, like a bishop about to bless his congregation. 'Let us see Hinton as an illustration of this process of self-examination, a focus of our re-appraisal.'

'So the search should continue, sir?' Redpath pressed.

'Of course.' For a moment Dr Mellinger's attention wandered. 'Yes, we must find Hinton. He is here somewhere; his essence pervades Green Hill, a vast metaphysical conundrum. Solve it, gentlemen, and you will have solved the mystery of his disappearance.'

For the next hour Dr Mellinger paced the carpet alone, now and then warming his hands at the low fire below the mantelpiece. Its few flames entwined in the chimney like the ideas playing around the periphery of his mind. At last, he felt, a means of breaking through the impasse had offered itself. He had always been certain that Hinton's miraculous disappearance represented more than a simple problem of breached security, and was a symbol of something grievously at fault with the very foundations of Green Hill.

Pursuing these thoughts, Dr Mellinger left his office and made his way down to the floor below which housed the administrative department. The offices were deserted; the entire staff of the building was taking part in the search. Occasionally the querulous cries of the patients demanding their breakfasts drifted across the warm, insulated air. Fortunately the walls were thick, and the rates charged by the asylum high enough to obviate the need for over-crowding.

Green Hill Asylum (motto, and principal attraction: 'There is a Green Hill Far, Far Away') was one of those institutions which are patronized by the wealthier members of the community and in effect serve the role of private prisons. In such places are confined all those miscreant or unfortunate relatives whose presence would otherwise be a burden or embarrassment: the importunate widows of blacksheep sons, senile maiden aunts, elderly bachelor cousins paying the price for their romantic indiscretions – in short, all those abandoned casualties of the army of privilege. As far as the patrons of Green Hill were concerned, maximum security came first, treatment, if given at all, a bad second. Dr Mellinger's patients had disappeared conveniently from the world, and as long as they remained in this distant limbo those who paid the bills were satisfied. All this made Hinton's escape particularly dangerous.

Stepping through the open doorway of Normand's office, Dr Mellinger ran his eye cursorily around the room. On the desk, hastily opened, was a slim file containing a few documents and a photograph.

For a brief moment Dr Mellinger gazed abstractedly at the file. Then, after a discreet glance into the corridor, he slipped it under his arm and retraced his steps up the empty staircase.

Outside, muted by the dark groves of rhododendrons, the sounds of search and pursuit echoed across the grounds. Opening the file on his desk, Dr Mellinger stared at the photograph, which happened to be lying upside down. Without straightening it, he studied the amorphous features. The nose was straight, the forehead and cheeks symmetrical, the ears a little oversize, but in its inverted position the face lacked any cohesive identity.

Suddenly, as he started to read the file, Dr Mellinger was filled with a deep sense of resentment. The entire subject of Hinton and the man's precarious claims to reality overwhelmed him with a profound nausea. He refused to accept that this mindless cripple with his anonymous features could have been responsible for the confusion and anxiety of the previous day. Was it possible that these few pieces of paper constituted this meagre individual's full claim to reality?

Flinching slightly from the touch of the file to his fingers, Dr Mellinger carried it across to the fireplace. Averting his face, he listened with a deepening sense of relief as the flames flared briefly and subsided.

'My dear Booth! Do come in. It's good of you to spare the time.' With this greeting Dr Mellinger ushered him to a chair beside the fire and proffered his silver cigarette case. 'There's a certain small matter I wanted to discuss, and you are almost the only person who can help me.'

'Of course, Director,' Booth assured him. 'I am greatly honoured.'

Dr Mellinger seated himself behind his desk. 'It's a very curious case, one of the most unusual I have ever come across. It concerns a patient under your care, I believe.'

'May I ask for his name, sir?'

'Hinton,' Dr Mellinger said, with a sharp glance at Booth.

'Hinton, sir?'

'You show surprise,' Dr Mellinger continued before Booth could reply. 'I find that response particularly interesting.'

'The search is still being carried on,' Booth said uncertainly as Dr Mellinger paused to digest his remarks. 'I'm afraid we've found absolutely no trace of him. Dr Normand thinks we should inform –'

'Ah, yes, Dr Normand.' The Director revived suddenly. 'I have asked him to report to me with Hinton's file as soon as he is free. Dr Booth, does it occur to you that we may be chasing the wrong hare?'

'Sir –?'

'Is it in fact *Hinton* we are after? I wonder, perhaps, whether the search for Hinton is obscuring something larger and more significant, the enigma, as I mentioned yesterday, which lies at the heart of Green Hill and to whose solution we must all now be dedicated.' Dr Mellinger savoured these reflections before continuing. 'Dr Booth, let us for a moment consider the role of Hinton, or to be more precise, the complex of overlapping and adjacent events that we identify loosely by the term "Hinton".'

'Complex, sir? You speak diagnostically?'

'No, Booth. I am now concerned with the phenomenology of Hinton, with his absolute metaphysical essence. To speak more plainly: has it occurred to you, Booth, how little we know of this elusive patient, how scanty the traces he has left of his own identity?'

'True, Director,' Booth agreed. 'I constantly reproach myself for not taking a closer interest in the patient.'

'Not at all, Doctor. I realize how busy you are. I intend to carry out a major reorganization of Green Hill, and I assure you that your tireless work here will not be forgotten. A senior administrative post would, I am sure, suit you excellently.' As Booth sat up, his interest in the conversation increasing severalfold, Dr Mellinger acknowledged his expression of thanks with a discreet nod. 'As I was saying, Doctor, you have so many patients, all wearing the same uniforms, housed in the same wards, and by and large prescribed the same treatment – is it surprising that they should lose their individual identities? If I may make a small confession,' he added with a roguish smile. 'I myself find that all the patients look alike. Why, if Dr Normand or yourself informed me that a new patient by the name of Smith or Brown had arrived, I would automatically furnish him with the standard uniform of identity at Green Hill – those same lustreless eyes and slack mouth, the same amorphous features.'

Unclasping his hands, Dr Mellinger leaned intently across his desk. 'What I am suggesting, Doctor, is that this automatic mechanism may have operated in the case of the so-called Hinton, and that you may have invested an entirely non-existent individual with the fictions of a personality.'

Dr Booth nodded slowly, 'I see, sir. You suspect that Hinton – or what we have called Hinton up to now – was perhaps a confused memory of another patient.' He hesitated doubtfully, and then noticed that Dr Mellinger's eyes were fixed upon him with hypnotic intensity.

'Dr Booth. I ask you: what actual proof have we that Hinton ever existed?'

'Well, sir, there are the . . .' Booth searched about helplessly . . . 'the records in the administrative department. And the case notes.'

Dr Mellinger shook his head with a scornful flourish. 'My dear Booth, you are speaking of mere pieces of paper. These are not proof of a man's identity. A typewriter will invent anything you choose. The only conclusive proof is his physical existence in time and space or, failing that, a distinct memory of his tangible physical presence. Can you honestly say that either of these conditions is fulfilled?'

'No, sir. I suppose I can't. Though I did speak to a patient whom I assumed to be Hinton.'

'But was he?' The Director's voice was resonant and urgent. 'Search your mind, Booth; be honest with yourself. Was it perhaps another patient to whom you spoke? What doctor ever really looks at his patients? In all probability you merely saw Hinton's name on a list and assumed that he sat before you, an intact physical existence like your own.'

There was a knock upon the door. Dr Normand stepped into the office. 'Good afternoon, Director.'

'Ah, Normand. Do come in. Dr Booth and I have been having a most instructive conversation. I really believe we have found a solution to the mystery of Hinton's disappearance.'

Dr Normand nodded cautiously. 'I am most relieved, sir. I was beginning to wonder whether we should inform the civil authorities. It is now nearly forty-eight hours since ...'

'My dear Normand, I am afraid you are rather out of touch. Our whole attitude to the Hinton case has changed radically. Dr Booth has been so helpful to me. We have been discussing the possibility that an administrative post might be found for him. You have the Hinton file?'

'Er, I regret not, sir,' Normand apologized, his eyes moving from Booth to the Director. 'I gather it's been temporarily displaced. I've instituted a thorough search and it will be brought to you as soon as possible.'

'Thank you, Normand, if you would.' Mellinger took Booth by the arm and led him to the door. 'Now, Doctor, I am most gratified by your perceptiveness. I want you to question your ward staff in the way I have questioned you. Strike through the mists of illusion and false assumption that swirl about their minds. Warn them of those illusions compounded on illusions which can assume the guise of reality. Remind them, too, that clear minds are required at Green Hill. I will be most surprised if any one of them can put her hand on her heart and swear that Hinton *really* existed.'

After Booth had made his exit, Dr Mellinger returned to his desk. For a moment he failed to notice his deputy.

'Ah, yes, Normand. I wonder where that file is? You didn't bring it?'

'No, sir. As I explained –'

'Well, never mind. But we mustn't become careless, Normand, too much is at stake. Do you realize that without that file we would know literally nothing whatever about Hinton? It would be most awkward.'

'I assure you, sir, the file –'

'Enough, Normand. Don't worry yourself.' Dr Mellinger turned a vulpine smile upon the restless Normand. 'I have the greatest respect for the efficiency of the administrative department under your leadership. I think it unlikely that they should have misplaced it. Tell me, Normand, are you sure that this file ever existed?'

'Certainly, sir,' Normand replied promptly. 'Of course, I have not actually seen it myself, but every patient at Green Hill has a complete personal file.'

'But Normand,' the Director pointed out gently, 'the patient in question is not *at* Green Hill. Whether or not this hypothetical file exists, Hinton does not.'

He stopped and waited as Normand looked up at him, his eyes narrowing.

A week later, Dr Mellinger held a final conference in his office. This was a notably more relaxed gathering; his subordinates lay back in the leather armchairs around the fire, while Dr Mellinger leaned against the desk, supervising the circulation of his best sherry.

'So, gentlemen,' he remarked in conclusion, 'we may look back on the past week as a period of unique self-discovery, a lesson for all of us to remember the true nature of our roles at Green Hill, our dedication to the task of separating reality from illusion. If our patients are haunted by chimeras, let us at least retain absolute clarity of mind, accepting the validity of any proposition only if all our senses corroborate it. Consider the example of the "Hinton affair". Here, by an accumulation of false assumptions, of illusions buttressing illusions, a vast edifice of fantasy was erected around the wholly mythical identity of one patient. This imaginary figure, who by some means we have not discovered – most probably the error of a typist in the records department – was given the name "Hinton", was subsequently furnished with a complete personal identity, a private ward, attendant nurses and doctors. Such was the grip of this substitute world, this concatenation of errors, that when it crumbled and the lack of any substance behind the shadow was discovered, the remaining vacuum was automatically interpreted as the patient's escape.'

Dr Mellinger gestured eloquently, as Normand, Redpath and Booth nodded their agreement. He walked around his desk and took his seat. 'Perhaps, gentlemen, it is fortunate that I remain aloof from the day-to-day affairs of Green Hill. I take no credit upon myself, that I alone was sufficiently detached to consider the full implications of Hinton's disappearance and realize the only possible explanation – *that Hinton had never existed!*'

'A brilliant deduction,' Redpath murmured.

'Without doubt,' echoed Booth.

'A profound insight,' agreed Normand.

There was a sharp knock on the door. With a frown, Dr Mellinger ignored it and resumed his monologue.

'Thank you, gentlemen. Without your assistance that hypothesis, that Hinton was no more than an accumulation of administrative errors, could never have been confirmed.'

The knock on the door repeated itself. A staff sister appeared breathlessly. 'Excuse me, sir. I'm sorry to interrupt you, but –'

Dr Mellinger waved away her apologies. 'Never mind. What is it?'

'A visitor, Dr Mellinger.' She paused as the Director waited impatiently. 'Mrs Hinton, to see her husband.'

For a moment there was consternation. The three men around the fire sat upright, their drinks forgotten, while Dr Mellinger remained stock-still at his desk. A total silence filled the room, only broken by the light tapping of a woman's heels in the corridor outside.

But Dr Mellinger recovered quickly. Standing up, with a grim smile at his colleagues, he said: 'To see Mr Hinton? Impossible, Hinton never existed. The woman must be suffering from terrible delusions; she requires immediate treatment. Show her in.' He turned to his colleagues. 'Gentlemen, we must do everything we can to help her.'

Minus two.

1963

THE SUDDEN AFTERNOON

What surprised Elliott was the suddenness of the attack. Judith and the children had gone down to the coast for the weekend to catch the last of the summer, leaving him alone in the house, and the three days had been a pleasant reverie of silent rooms, meals taken at random hours, and a little mild carpentry in the workshop. He spent Sunday morning reading all the reviews in the newspapers, carefully adding half a dozen titles to the list of books which he knew he would never manage to buy, let alone read. These wistful exercises, like the elaborately prepared martini before lunch, were part of the established ritual of his brief bachelor moments. He decided to take a brisk walk across Hampstead Heath after lunch, returning in time to tidy everything away before Judith arrived that evening.

Instead, a sharp attack of what first appeared to be influenza struck him just before one o'clock. A throbbing headache and a soaring temperature sent him fumbling to the medicine cabinet in the bathroom, only to find that Judith had taken the aspirin with her. Sitting on the edge of the bath, forehead in his hands, he nursed the spasm, which seemed to contract the muscles of some inner scalp, compressing his brain like fruit-pulp in a linen bag.

'Judith!' he shouted to the empty house. 'Damn!'

The pain mounted, an intense prickling that drove silver needles through his skull. Helpless for a moment, he propelled himself into the bedroom and climbed fully dressed into the bed, shielding his eyes from the weak sunlight which crossed the Heath.

After a few minutes the attack subsided slightly, leaving him with a nagging migraine and a sense of utter inertia. For the next hour he stared at the reflection of himself in the dressing-table mirror, lying like a trussed steer across the bed. Through the window he watched a small boy playing under the oaks by the edge of the park, patiently trying to catch the spiralling leaves. Twenty yards away a nondescript little man with a dark complexion sat alone on a bench, staring through the trees.

In some way this scene soothed Elliott, and the headache finally dissipated, as if charmed away by the swaying boughs and the leaping figure of the boy.

'Strange ...' he murmured to himself, still puzzled by the ferocity of the attack. Judith, however, would be sceptical; she had always accused him of being a hypochondriac. It was a pity she hadn't been there, instead of lying about on the beach at Worthing, but at least the children had been spared the spectacle of their father yelping with agony.

Reluctant to get out of bed and precipitate another attack – perhaps it was due to some virulent but short-lived virus? – Elliott lay back, the scent of his wife's skin on the pillow reminding him of his own childhood and his mother's perfumed hair. He had been brought up in India, and remembered being rowed across a river by his father, the great placid back of the Ganges turning crimson in the late afternoon light. The burnt-earth colours of the Calcutta waterfront were still vivid after an interval of thirty years.

Smiling pleasantly over this memory, and at the image of his father rowing with a rhythmic lulling motion, Elliott gazed upward at the ceiling, only distracted by the distant hoot of a car horn.

Then he sat up abruptly, staring sharply at the room around him.

'Calcutta? What the hell –?'

The memory had been completely false! He had never been to India in his life, or anywhere near the Far East. He had been born in London, and lived there all his life apart from a two-year postgraduate visit to the United States. As for his father, who had been captured by the Germans while fighting with the Eighth

Army in North Africa and spent most of the war as a POW, Elliott had seen almost nothing of him until his adolescence.

Yet the memory of being rowed across the Ganges had been extraordinarily strong. Trying to shake off the last residue of the headache, Elliott swung his feet onto the floor. The throbbing had returned slightly, but in a curious way receded as he let the image of the Calcutta waterfront fill his mind. Whatever its source, the landscape was certainly Indian, and he could see the Ganges steps, a clutter of sailing dhows and even a few meagre funeral pyres smoking on the embankment.

But what most surprised him were the emotional associations of this false memory of being rowed by his father, the sense of reassurance that came with each rhythmic motion of the dark figure, whose face was hidden by the shadows of the setting sun.

Wondering where he had collected this powerful visual impression which had somehow translated itself into a memory with unique personal undertones, Elliott left the bedroom and made his way down to the kitchen. It was now half past two, almost too late for lunch, and he stared without interest at the rows of eggs and milk bottles in the refrigerator. After lunch, he decided, he would settle down on the sofa in the lounge and read or watch television.

At the thought of the latter Elliott realized that the false memory of the Ganges was almost certainly a forgotten fragment of a film travelogue, probably one he had seen as a child. The whole sequence of the memory, with its posed shot of the boat cutting through the crimson water and the long traverse of the waterfront, was typical of the style of the travelogues made in the nineteen-forties, and he could almost see the credit titles coming up with a roll of drums.

Reassured by this, and assuming that the headache had somehow jolted loose this visual memory – the slightly blurred wartime cinema screens had often strained his eyes – Elliott began to prepare his lunch. He ignored the food Judith had left for him and hunted among the spices and pickle jars in the pantry, where he found some rice and a packet of curry powder. Judith had never mastered the intricacies of making a real curry, and Elliott's own occasional attempts had merely elicited amused smiles. Today, however, with ample time on his hands and no interference, he would succeed.

Unhurriedly Elliott began to prepare the dish, and the kitchen soon filled with steam and the savoury odours of curry powder and chutney. Outside, the thin sunlight gave way to darker clouds and the first afternoon rain. The small boy had gone, but the solitary figure under the oaks still sat on the bench, jacket collar turned up around his neck.

Delighted by the simmering brew, Elliott relaxed on his stool, and thought about his medical practice. Normally he would have been obliged to hold an evening surgery, but his locum had arranged to take over for him, much to his relief, as one of the patients had been particularly difficult – a complete neurotic, a hazard faced by every doctor, she had even threatened to report him to the general medical council for misconduct, though the allegations were so grotesque the disciplinary committee would not consider them seriously for a moment.

The curry had been strong, and a sharp pain under the sternum marked the beginning of a bout of indigestion. Cursing his bad luck, Elliott poured a glass of milk, sorry to lose the flavour of the curry.

'You're in bad shape, old sport,' he said to himself with ironic humour. 'You ought to see a doctor.'

With a sudden snap of his fingers he stood up. He had experienced his second false memory! The whole reverie about his medical practice, the locum and the woman patient were absolute fictions, unrelated to anything in his life. Professionally he was a research chemist, employed in the biochemistry department of one of the London cancer institutes, but his contacts with physicians and surgeons were virtually nil.

And yet the impression of having a medical practice, patients and all the other involvements of a busy doctor was remarkably strong and persistent – indeed, far more than a memory, a coherent area of awareness as valid as the image of the biochemistry laboratory.

With a growing sense of unease, Elliott sipped weakly at the tumbler of milk, wondering why these sourceless images, like fragments from the intelligence of some other individual, were impinging themselves on his mind. He went into the lounge and sat down with his back to the window, examining himself with as much professional detachment as he could muster. Behind him, under the trees in the park, the man on the bench sat silently in the rain, eyed at a safe distance by a wandering mongrel.

After a pause to collect himself, Elliott deliberately began to explore this second false memory. Immediately he noticed that the dyspepsia subsided, as if assuming the *persona* of the fragmented images relieved their pressure upon his mind. Concentrating, he could see a high window above a broad mahogany desk, a padded leather couch, shelves of books and framed certificates on the walls, unmistakably a doctor's consulting rooms. Leaving the room, he passed down a broad flight of carpeted stairs into a marble-floored hall. A desk stood in an alcove on the left, and a pretty red-haired receptionist looked up and smiled to him across her typewriter. Then he was outside in the street, obviously in a well-to-do quarter of the city, where Rolls-Royces and Bentleys almost outnumbered the other cars. Two hundred yards away double-decker buses crossed a familiar intersection.

'Harley Street!' Elliott snapped. As he sat up and looked around at the familiar furniture in the lounge and the drenched oaks in the park, with an effort re-establishing their reality in his mind, he had a last glimpse of the front elevation of the consulting chambers, a blurred nameplate on the cream-painted columns. Over the portico were the gilt italic numerals: *259*

'Two fifty-nine Harley Street? Now who the devil works there?' Elliott stood up and went over to the window, staring out across the Heath, then paced into the kitchen and savoured the residue of the curry aroma. Again a spasm of indigestion gripped his stomach, and he immediately focused on the image of the unknown doctor's consulting rooms. As the pain faded he had a further impression of a small middle-aged woman in a hospital ward, her left arm in a cast, and then a picture of the staff and consultants' entrance to the Middlesex Hospital, as vivid as a photograph.

Picking up the newspaper, Elliott returned to the lounge, settling himself with difficulty. The absolute clarity of the memories convinced him that they were not confused images taken from the ciné-films or elaborated by his imagination. The more he explored them the more they fixed their own reality, refusing to fade or vanish. In addition, the emotional content was too strong. The associations of the childhood river scene were reassuring but the atmosphere in the consulting rooms had been fraught with hesitation and anxiety, as if their original possessor was in the grip of a nightmare.

The headache still tugged at his temples, and Elliott went over to the cocktail cabinet and poured himself a large whisky and soda. Had he in some incredible way simultaneously become the receiver of the disembodied memories of a small Indian boy in Calcutta and a Harley Street consultant?

Glancing at the front news page, his eye caught:

INDIAN DOCTOR SOUGHT
Wife's Mystery Death

Police are continuing their search for the missing Harley Street psychiatrist, Dr Krishnamurti Singh. Scotland Yard believes he may be able to assist them in their inquiries into the death of his wife, Mrs Ramadya Singh ...

With a surge of relief, Elliott slapped the newspaper and tossed it across the room. So this explained the two imaginary memories! Earlier that morning, before the influenza attack, he had read the news item without realizing it, then during the light fever had dramatized the details. The virulent virus – a rare short-lived strain he had picked up at the laboratory – presumably acted like the hallucinogenic drugs, creating an inner image of almost photographic authenticity. Even the curry had been part of the system of fantasy.

Elliott wandered ruminatively around the lounge, listening to the rain sweep like hail across the windows. Within a few moments he knew that more of these hallucinatory memories lay below the surface of his mind, all revolving around the identity of the missing Indian doctor.

Unable to dispel them, he deliberately let himself drift off into a reverie. Perhaps the association of the funereal rain and the tiresome pain below his sternum was responsible for the gathering sense of foreboding in his mind. Formless ideas rose towards consciousness, and he stirred uneasily in his chair. Without realizing it, he found himself thinking of his wife's death, an event shrouded in pain and a peculiar dream-like violence. For a moment he was almost inside his wife's dying mind, at the bottom of an immense drowned lake, separated from the distant pinpoint of sky by enormous volumes of water that pressed upon his chest ...

In a flood of sweat, Elliott awoke from this nightmare, the whole tragic vision of his wife's death before his eyes. Judith was alive, of course, staying with her married sister at the beach-house near Worthing, but the vision of her drowning had come through with the force and urgency of a telepathic signal.

'Judith!'

Rousing himself, Elliott hurried to the telephone in the hall. Something about its psychological dimensions convinced him that he had not imagined the death scene.

The sea!

He snatched up the phone, dialling for the operator. At that very moment Judith might well be swimming alone while her sister prepared tea with the children, in sight of the beach but unaware she was in danger ...

'Operator, this is urgent,' Elliott began. 'I must talk to my wife. I think she's in some sort of danger. Can you get me Calcutta 30331.'

The operator hesitated. 'Calcutta? I'm sorry, caller, I'll transfer you to Overseas –'

'What? I don't want –' Elliott stopped. 'What number did I ask for?'

'Calcutta 30331. I'll have you transferred.'

'Wait!' Elliott steadied himself against the window. The rain beat across the glazed panes. 'My mistake. I meant Worthing 303 –'

'Are you there, caller? Worthing Three Zero Three –' Her voice waited.

Wearily Elliott lowered the telephone. 'I'll look it up,' he said thickly. 'That wasn't the number.'

He turned the pages of the memo pad, realizing that both he and Judith had known the number for years and never bothered to record it.

'Are you there, caller?' The operator's voice was sharper.

A few moments later, when he was connected to Directory Inquiries, Elliott realized that he had also forgotten his sister-in-law's name and address.

'Calcutta 30331.' Elliott repeated the number as he poured himself a drink from the whisky decanter. Pulling himself together, he recognized that the notion of a telepathic message was fatuous. Judith would be perfectly safe, on her way back to London with the children, and he had misinterpreted the vision of the dying woman. The telephone number, however, remained. The enigmatic sequence flowed off his tongue with the unconscious familiarity of long usage. A score of similar memories waited to be summoned into reality, as if a fugitive mind had taken up residence in his brain.

He picked the newspaper off the floor.

. . . Dr Krishnamurti Singh. Scotland Yard believes he may be able to assist them in their inquiries . . .

'Assist them in their inquiries' – a typical Fleet Street euphemism, part of the elaborate code built up between the newspapers and their readers. A French paper, not handicapped by the English libel laws, would be shouting 'Bluebeard! Assassin!'

Detectives are at the bedside of Mrs Ethel Burgess, the charwoman employed by Dr and Mrs Singh, who was yesterday found unconscious at the foot of the stairs . . .

Mrs Burgess! Instantly an image of the small elderly woman, with a face like a wizened apple, came before his eyes. She was lying in the hospital bed at the Middlesex, watching him with frightened reproachful glances –

The tumbler, half-filled with whisky, smashed itself on the fireplace tiles. Elliott stared at the fragments of wet glass around his feet, then sat down in the centre of the sofa with his head in his hands, trying to hold back the flood of memories. Helplessly he found himself thinking of the medical school at Calcutta. The half-familiar faces of fellow students passed in a blur. He remembered his passionate interest in developing a scientific approach to the obscurer branches of yoga and the Hindu parapsychologies, the student society he formed and its experiments in thought and body transference, brought to an end by the death of one of the students and the subsequent scandal . . .

For a moment Elliott marvelled at the coherence and convincing detail of the memories. Numbly he reminded himself that in fact he had been a chemistry student at –

Where?

With a start he realized that he had forgotten. Quickly he searched his mind, and found he could remember almost nothing of his distant past, where he was born, his parents and childhood. Instead he saw once again, this time with luminous clarity, the rowing-boat on the crimson Ganges and its dark oarsman watching him with his ambiguous smile. Then he saw another picture, of himself as a small boy, writing in a huge ledger in which all the pencilled entries had been laboriously rubbed out, sitting at a desk in a room with a low ceiling of bamboo rods over his father's warehouse by the market –

'Nonsense!' Flinging the memory from him, with all its tender associations, Elliott stood up restless, his heart racing with a sudden fever. His forehead burned with heat, his mind inventing strings of fantasies around the Dr Singh wanted by the police. He felt his pulse, then leaned into the mirror over the mantelpiece and examined his eyes, checking his pupil reflexes with expert fingers for any symptoms of concussion.

Swallowing with a dry tongue, he stared down at the physician's hands which had examined him, then decided to call his own doctor. A sedative, an hour's sleep, and he would recover.

In the falling evening light he could barely see the numerals. 'Hello, hello!' he shouted. 'Is anyone there?'

'Yes, Dr Singh,' a woman replied. 'Is that you?'

Frightened, Elliott cupped his hand over the mouthpiece. He had dialled the number from memory, but from another memory than his own. But not only had the receptionist recognized his voice – Elliott had recognized hers, and knew her name.

Experimentally he lifted the receiver, and said the name in his mind. 'Miss Tremayne –?'

'Dr Singh? Are you –'

With an effort Elliott made his voice more guttural. 'I'm sorry, I have the wrong number. What is your number?'

The girl hesitated. When she spoke the modulation and rhythm of her voice were again instantly familiar. 'This is Harley Street 30331,' she said cautiously. 'Dr Singh, the police have –'

Elliott lowered the telephone into its cradle. Wearily he sat down on the carpet in the darkness, looking up at the black rectangle of the front door. Again the headache began to drum at his temples, as he tried to ignore the memories crowding into his mind. Above him the staircase led to another world.

Half an hour later, he pulled himself to his feet. Searching for his bed, and fearing the light, he stumbled into a room and lay down. With a start he clambered upright, and found that he was lying on the table in the dining room.

He had forgotten his way around the house, and the topography of another home, apparently a single-storey apartment, had superimposed itself upon his mind. In the strange upstairs floor he found an untidy nursery full of children's toys and clothes, an unremembered frieze of childish drawings which showed tranquil skies over church steeples. When he closed the door the scene vanished like a forgotten tableau.

In the bedroom next door a portrait photograph stood on the dressing table, showing the face of a pleasant blonde-haired woman he had never seen. He gazed down at the bed in the darkness, the wardrobes and mirrors around him like the furniture of a dream.

'Ramadya, Ramadya,' he murmured, on his lips the name of the dying woman.

The telephone rang. Standing in the darkness at the top of the stairs, he listened to its sounds shrilling through the silent house. He walked down to it with leaden feet.

'Yes?' he said tersely.

'Hello, darling,' a woman's bright voice answered. In the background trains shunted and whistled. 'Hello? Is that Hampstead –'

'This is Harley Street 30331,' he said quickly. 'You have the wrong number.'

'Oh, dear, I am sorry, I thought –'

Cutting off this voice, which for a fleeting moment had drawn together the fragmented *persona* clinging to the back of his mind, he stood at the window by the front door. Through the narrow barred pane he could see that the rain had almost ended, and a light mist hung among the trees. The bedraggled figure on the bench still maintained his vigil, his face hidden in the darkness. Now and then his drenched form would glimmer in the passing lights.

For some reason a sense of extreme urgency had overtaken Elliott. He knew that there were a series of tasks to be performed, records to be made before important evidence vanished, reliable witnesses to be contacted. A hundred ignored images passed through in his mind as he searched for a pair of shoes and a jacket in the cupboard upstairs, scenes of his medical practice, a woman patient being tested by an electroencephalogram, the radiator of a Bentley car and its automobile club badges. There were glimpses of the streets near Harley Street, the residue of countless journeys to and from the consulting rooms, the entrance to the Overseas Club, a noisy seminar at one of the scientific institutes where someone was shouting at him theatrically. Then, unpleasantly, there were feelings of remorse for his wife's death, counterbalanced by the growing inner conviction that this, paradoxically, was the only way to save her, to force her to a new life. In a strange yet familiar voice he heard himself saying: 'the soul, like any soft-skinned creature, clings to whatever shell it can find. Only by cracking that shell can one force it to move to a new ...'

Attacks of vertigo came over him in waves as he descended the staircase. There was someone he must find, one man whose help might save him. He picked up the telephone and dialled, swaying giddily from side to side.

A clipped voice like polished ivory answered. 'Professor Ramachandran speaking.'

'Professor –'

'Hello? Who is that, please?'

He cleared his throat, coughing noisily into the mouthpiece. 'Professor, understand me! It was the tumour, inoperable, it was the only way to save her – metempsychosis of the somatic function as well as the psychic ...' He had launched into a semicoherent tirade, the words coming out in clotted shreds. 'Ramadya has gone over now, she is the other woman ... neither she nor any others will ever know ... Professor, will you tell her one day, and myself ... a single word –'

'Dr Singh!' The voice at the end was a shout. 'I can no longer help you! You must take the consequences of your folly! I warned you repeatedly about the danger of your experiments –'

The telephone squeaked on the floor where he dropped it. Outside the headlamps of police cars flashed by, their blue roof lights revolving like spectral beacons. As he unlatched the door and stepped out into the cold night air he had a last obsessive thought, of a fair-haired, middle-aged man with glasses who was a chemist at a cancer institute, a man with a remarkably receptive mind, its open bowl spread before him like a huge dish antenna. This man alone could help him. His name was – Elliott.

As he sat on the bench he saw the lights approaching him through the trees, like glowing aureoles in the darkness. The rain had ended and a light mist dissipated under the branches, but after the warmth indoors it was colder than he expected, and within only a few minutes in the park he began to shiver. Walking between the trees, he saw the line of police cars parked along the perimeter road two hundred yards away. Whichever way he moved, the lights seemed to draw nearer, although never coming directly toward him.

He turned, deciding to return to the house, and to his surprise saw a slim fair-haired man cross the road from the park and climb the steps to the front door. Startled, he watched this intruder disappear through the open door and close it behind him.

Then two policemen stepped from the mist on his right, their torches dazzling his eyes. He broke into a run, but a third huge figure materialized from behind a trunk and blocked his path.

'That's enough, then,' a gruff voice told him as he wrestled helplessly. 'Let's try to take it quietly.'

Lamps circled the darkness. More police ran over through the trees. An inspector with silver shoulder badges stepped up and peered into his face as a constable raised a torch.

'Dr Singh?'

For a moment he listened to the sounds of the name, which had pursued him all day, hang fleetingly on the damp air. Most of his mind seemed willing to accept the identification, but a small part, now dissolving to a minute speck, like the faint stars veiled by the mist, refused to agree, knowing that whoever he was now, he had once not been Dr Singh.

'No!' He shook his head, and with a galvanic effort managed to wrench loose one arm. He was seized at the shoulder and raised his free arm to shield himself from the lights and the pressing faces.

His glasses had fallen off and been trampled underfoot, but he could see more clearly without them. He looked at his hand. Even in the pale light the darker pigmentation was plain. His fingers were small and neat, an unfamiliar scar marking one of the knuckles.

Then he felt the small goatee beard on his chin.

Inside his mind the last island of resistance slid away into the dark unremembered past.

'Dr Krishnamurti Singh,' the inspector stated.

Among the suitcases in the doorway Judith Elliott watched the police cars drive away toward Hampstead village. Upstairs the two children romped about in the nursery.

'How horrid! I'm glad the children didn't see him arrested. He was struggling like an animal.'

Elliott paid off the taxi-driver and then closed the door. 'Who was it, by the way? No one we know, I hope?'

Judith glanced around the hall, and noticed the telephone receiver on the floor. She bent down and replaced it. 'The taxi-driver said it was some Harley Street psychiatrist. An Indian doctor. Apparently he strangled his wife in the bath. The strange thing is she was already dying of a brain tumour.'

Elliott grimaced. 'Gruesome. Perhaps he was trying to save her pain.'

'By strangling her fully conscious? A typical masculine notion, darling.'

Elliott laughed as they strolled into the lounge. 'Well, my dear, did you have a good time? How was Molly?'

'She was fine. We had a great time together. Missed you, of course. I felt a bit off-colour yesterday, got knocked over by a big wave and swallowed a lot of water.' She hesitated, looking through the window at the park. 'You know, it's rather funny, but twenty minutes ago I tried to ring you from the station and got a Harley Street number by mistake. I spoke to an Indian. He sounded rather like a doctor.'

Elliott grinned. 'Probably the same man.'

'That's what I thought. But he couldn't have got from Harley Street to Hampstead so quickly, could he? The driver said the police have been looking for him here all afternoon.'

'Maybe they've got the wrong man. Unless there are two Dr Singhs.' Elliott snapped his fingers. 'That's odd, where did I get the name? Must have read about him in the papers.'

Judith nodded, coming over to him. 'It was in this morning's.'

She took off her hat and placed it on the mantelpiece. 'Indians are strange people. I don't know why, but yesterday when I was getting over my wave I was thinking about an Indian girl I knew once. All I can remember is her name. Ramadya. I think she was drowned. She was very sweet and pretty.'

'Like you.' Elliott put his hands around her waist, but Judith pointed to the broken glass in the fireplace.

'I say, I can see I've been away.' With a laugh she put her hands on his shoulders and squeezed him, then drew away in alarm.

'Darling, where did you get this peculiar suit? For heaven's sake, look!' She squeezed his jacket, and the water poured from her fingers as from a wet sponge. 'You're soaked through! Where on earth have you been all day?'

1963

THE SCREEN GAME

Every afternoon during the summer at Ciraquito we play the screen game. After lunch today, when the arcades and café terraces were empty and everyone was lying asleep indoors, three of us drove out in Raymond Mayo's Lincoln along the road to Vermilion Sands.

The season had ended, and already the desert had begun to move in again for the summer, drifting against the yellowing shutters of the cigarette kiosks, surrounding the town with immense banks of luminous ash. Along the horizon the flat-topped mesas rose into the sky like the painted cones of a volcano jungle. The beach-houses had been empty for weeks, and abandoned sand-yachts stood in the centre of the lakes, embalmed in the opaque heat. Only the highway showed any signs of activity, the motion sculpture of concrete ribbon unfolding across the landscape.

Twenty miles from Ciraquito, where the highway forks to Red Beach and Vermilion Sands, we turned on to the remains of an old gravel track that ran away among the sand reefs. Only a year earlier this had been a well-kept private road, but the ornamental gateway lay collapsed to one side, and the guardhouse was a nesting place for scorpions and sand-rays.

Few people ever ventured far up the road. Continuous rock slides disturbed the area, and large sections of the surface had slipped away into the reefs. In addition a curious but unmistakable atmosphere of menace hung over the entire zone, marking it off from the remainder of the desert. The hanging galleries of the reefs were more convoluted and sinister, like the tortured demons of medieval cathedrals. Massive towers of obsidian reared over the roadway like stone gallows, their cornices streaked with iron-red dust. The light seemed duller, unlike the rest of the desert, occasionally flaring into a sepulchral glow as if some subterranean fire-cloud had boiled to the surface of the rocks. The surrounding peaks and spires shut out the desert plain, and the only sounds were the echoes of the engine growling among the hills and the piercing cries of the sand-rays wheeling over the open mouths of the reefs like hieratic birds.

For half a mile we followed the road as it wound like a petrified snake above the reefs, and our conversation became more sporadic and fell away entirely, resuming only when we began our descent through a shallow valley. A few abstract sculptures stood by the roadside. Once these were sonic, responding to the slipstream of a passing car with a series of warning vibratos, but now the Lincoln passed them unrecognized.

Abruptly, around a steep bend, the reefs and peaks vanished, and the wide expanse of an inland sand-lake lay before us, the great summer house of Lagoon West on its shore. Fragments of light haze hung over the dunes like untethered clouds. The tyres cut softly through the cerise sand, and soon we were overrunning what appeared to be the edge of an immense chessboard of black and white marble squares. More statues appeared, some buried to their heads, others toppled from their plinths by the drifting dunes.

Looking out at them this afternoon, I felt, not for the first time, that the whole landscape was compounded of illusion, the hulks of fabulous dreams drifting across it like derelict galleons. As we followed the road towards the lake, the huge wreck of Lagoon West passed us slowly on our left. Its terraces and balconies were deserted, and the once marble-white surface was streaked and lifeless. Staircases ended abruptly in midflight, and the floors hung like sagging marquees.

In the centre of the terrace the screens stood where we had left them the previous afternoon, their zodiacal emblems flashing like serpents. We walked across to them through the hot sunlight. For the next hour we played the screen game, pushing the screens along their intricate pathways, advancing and retreating across the smooth marble floor.

No one watched us, but once, fleetingly, I thought I saw a tall figure in a blue cape hidden in the shadows of a second-floor balcony.

'Emerelda!'

On a sudden impulse I shouted to her, but almost without moving she had vanished among the hibiscus and bougainvillaea. As her name echoed away among the dunes I knew that we had made our last attempt to lure her from the balcony.

'Paul.' Twenty yards away, Raymond and Tony had reached the car. 'Paul, we're leaving.'

Turning my back to them, I looked up at the great bleached hulk of Lagoon West leaning into the sunlight. Somewhere, along the shore of the sand-lake, music was playing faintly, echoing among the exposed quartz veins. A few isolated chords at first, the fragments hung on the afternoon air, the sustained tremolos suspended above my head like the humming of invisible insects.

As the phrases coalesced, I remembered when we had first played the screen game at Lagoon West. I remembered the last tragic battle with the jewelled insects, and I remembered Emerelda Garland ...

I first saw Emerelda Garland the previous summer, shortly after the film company arrived in Ciraquito and was invited by Charles Van Stratten to use the locations at Lagoon West. The company, Orpheus Productions, Inc. – known to the aficionados of the café terraces such as Raymond Mayo and Tony Sapphire as the 'ebb tide of the new wave' – was one of those experimental units whose output is destined for a single rapturous showing at the Cannes Film Festival, and who rely for their financial backing on the generosity of the many millionaire dilettantes who apparently feel a compulsive need to cast themselves in the role of Lorenzo de Medici.

Not that there was anything amateurish about the equipment and technical resources of Orpheus Productions. The fleet of location trucks and recording studios which descended on Ciraquito on one of those empty August afternoons looked like the entire D-Day task force, and even the more conservative estimates of the budget for *Aphrodite 80*, the film we helped to make at Lagoon West, amounted to at least twice the gross national product of a Central American republic. What was amateurish was the indifference to normal commercial restraints, and the unswerving dedication to the highest aesthetic standards.

All this, of course, was made possible by the largesse of Charles Van Stratten. To begin with, when we were first co-opted into *Aphrodite 80*, some of us were inclined to be amused by Charles's naive attempts to produce a masterpiece, but later we all realized that there was something touching about Charles's earnestness. None of us, however, was aware of the private tragedy which drove him on through the heat and dust of that summer at Lagoon West, and the grim nemesis waiting behind the canvas floats and stage props.

At the time he became the sole owner of Orpheus Productions, Charles Van Stratten had recently celebrated his fortieth birthday, but to all intents he was still a quiet and serious undergraduate. A scion of one of the world's wealthiest banking families, in his early twenties he had twice been briefly married, first to a Neapolitan countess, and then to a Hollywood starlet, but the most influential figure in Charles's life was his mother. This domineering harridan, who sat like an immense ormolu spider in her sombre Edwardian mansion on Park Avenue, surrounded by dark galleries filled with Rubens and Rembrandt, had been widowed shortly after Charles's birth, and obviously regarded Charles as providence's substitute for her husband. Cunningly manipulating a web of trust funds and residuary legacies, she ruthlessly eliminated both Charles's wives (the second committed suicide in a Venetian gondola, the first eloped with his analyst), and then herself died in circumstances of some mystery at the summer-house at Lagoon West.

Despite the immense publicity attached to the Van Stratten family, little was ever known about the old dowager's death – officially she tripped over a second-floor balcony – and Charles retired completely from the limelight of international celebrity for the next five years. Now and then he would emerge briefly at the Venice Biennale, or serve as co-sponsor of some cultural foundation, but otherwise he retreated into the vacuum left by his mother's death. Rumour had it – at least in Ciraquito – that Charles himself had been responsible for her quietus, as if revenging (how long overdue!) the tragedy of Oedipus, when the dowager, scenting the prospect of a third liaison, had descended like Jocasta upon Lagoon West and caught Charles and his paramour *in flagrante*.

Much as I liked the story, the first glimpse of Charles Van Stratten dispelled the possibility. Five years after his mother's death, Charles still behaved as if she were watching his every movement through tripod-mounted opera glasses on some distant balcony. His youthful figure was a little more portly, but his handsome aristocratic face, its strong jaw belied by an indefinable weakness around the mouth, seemed somehow daunted and indecisive, as if he lacked complete conviction in his own identity.

Shortly after the arrival in Ciraquito of Orpheus Productions, the property manager visited the cafés in the artists' quarters, canvassing for scenic designers. Like most of the painters in Ciraquito and Vermilion Sands, I was passing through one of my longer creative pauses. I had stayed on in the town after the season ended, idling away the long, empty afternoons under the awning at the Café Fresco, and was already showing symptoms of beach fatigue – irreversible boredom and inertia. The prospect of actual work seemed almost a novelty.

'*Aphrodite 80*,' Raymond Mayo explained when he returned to our table after a kerb-side discussion. 'The whole thing reeks of integrity – they want local artists to paint the flats, large abstract designs for the desert backgrounds. They'll pay a dollar per square foot.'

'That's rather mean,' I commented.

'The property manager apologized, but Van Stratten is a millionaire – money means nothing to him. If it's any consolation, Raphael and Michelangelo were paid a smaller rate for the Sistine Chapel.'

'Van Stratten has a bigger budget,' Tony Sapphire reminded

him. 'Besides, the modern painter is a more complex type, his integrity needs to be buttressed by substantial assurances. Is Paul a painter in the tradition of Leonardo and Larry Rivers, or a cut-price dauber?'

Moodily we watched the distant figure of the property manager move from café to café.

'How many square feet do they want?' I asked.

'About a million,' Raymond said.

Later that afternoon, as we turned off the Red Beach road and were waved on past the guardhouse to Lagoon West, we could hear the sonic sculptures high among the reefs echoing and hooting to the cavalcade of cars speeding over the hills. Droves of startled rays scattered in the air like clouds of exploding soot, their frantic cries lost among the spires and reefs. Preoccupied by the prospect of our vast fees – I had hastily sworn in Tony and Raymond as my assistants – we barely noticed the strange landscape we were crossing, the great gargoyles of red basalt that uncoiled themselves into the air like the spires of demented cathedrals. From the Red Beach – Vermilion Sands highway – the hills seemed permanently veiled by the sand haze, and Lagoon West, although given a brief notoriety by the death of Mrs Van Stratten, remained isolated and unknown. From the beach-houses on the southern shore of the sand-lake two miles away, the distant terraces and tiered balconies of the summer-house could just be seen across the fused sand, jutting into the cerise evening sky like a stack of dominoes. There was no access to the house along the beach. Quartz veins cut deep fissures into the surface, the reefs of ragged sandstone reared into the air like the rusting skeletons of forgotten ships.

The whole of Lagoon West was a continuous slide area. Periodically a soft boom would disturb the morning silence as one of the galleries of compacted sand, its intricate grottoes and colonnades like an inverted baroque palace, would suddenly dissolve and avalanche gently into the internal precipice below. Most years Charles Van Stratten was away in Europe, and the house was believed to be empty. The only sound the occupants of the beach villas would hear was the faint music of the sonic sculptures carried across the lake by the thermal rollers.

It was to this landscape, with its imperceptible transition between the real and the superreal, that Charles Van Stratten had brought the camera crews and location vans of Orpheus Productions, Inc. As the Lincoln joined the column of cars moving towards the summer-house, we could see the great canvas hoardings, at least two hundred yards wide and thirty feet high, which a team of construction workers was erecting among the reefs a quarter of a mile from the house. Decorated with abstract symbols, these would serve as backdrops to the action, and form a fragmentary labyrinth winding in and out of the hills and dunes.

One of the large terraces below the summer-house served as a parking lot, and we made our way through the unloading crews to where a group of men in crocodile-skin slacks and raffia shirts – then the uniform of avant-garde film men – were gathered around a heavily jowled man like a perspiring bear who was holding a stack of script boards under one arm and gesticulating wildly with the other. This was Orson Kanin, director of *Aphrodite* 80 and co-owner with Charles Van Stratten of Orpheus Productions. Sometime *enfant terrible* of the futurist cinema, but now a portly barrel-stomached fifty, Kanin had made his reputation some twenty years earlier with *Blind Orpheus*, a neo-Freudian, horror-film version of the Greek legend. According to Kanin's interpretation, Orpheus deliberately breaks the taboo and looks Eurydice in the face because he wants to be rid of her; in a famous nightmare sequence which projects his unconscious loathing, he becomes increasingly aware of something cold and strange about his resurrected wife, and finds that she is a disintegrating corpse.

As we joined the periphery of the group, a characteristic Kanin script conference was in full swing, a non-stop pantomime of dramatized incidents from the imaginary script, anecdotes, salary promises and bad puns, all delivered in a rich fruity baritone. Sitting on the balustrade beside Kanin was a handsome, youthful man with a sensitive face whom I recognized to be Charles Van Stratten. Now and then, *sotto voce*, he would interject some comment that would be noted by one of the secretaries and incorporated into Kanin's monologue.

As the conference proceeded I gathered that they would begin to shoot the film in some three weeks' time, and that it would be performed entirely without script. Kanin only seemed perturbed by the fact that no one had yet been found to play the Aphrodite of *Aphrodite* 80 but Charles Van Stratten interposed here to assure Kanin that he himself would provide the actress.

At this eyebrows were raised knowingly. 'Of course,' Raymond murmured. '*Droit de seigneur*. I wonder who the next Mrs Van Stratten is?'

But Charles Van Stratten seemed unaware of these snide undertones. Catching sight of me, he excused himself and came over to us.

'Paul Golding?' He took my hand in a soft but warm grip. We had never met but I presumed he recognized me from the photographs in the art reviews. 'Kanin told me you'd agreed to do the scenery. It's wonderfully encouraging.' He spoke in a light, pleasant voice absolutely without affectation. 'There's so much confusion here it's a relief to know that at least the scenic designs will be first-class.' Before I could demur he took my arm and began to walk away along the terrace towards the hoardings in the distance. 'Let's get some air. Kanin will keep this up for a couple of hours at least.'

Leaving Raymond and Tony, I followed him across the huge marble squares.

'Kanin keeps worrying about his leading actress,' he went on. 'Kanin always marries his latest protégé – he claims it's the only way he can make them respond fully to his direction, but I suspect there's an old-fashioned puritan lurking within the cavalier. This time he's going to be disappointed, though not by the actress, may I add. The Aphrodite I have in mind will outshine Milos's.'

'The film sounds rather ambitious,' I commented, 'but I'm sure Kanin is equal to it.'

'Of course he is. He's very nearly a genius, and that should be good enough.' He paused for a moment, hands in the pockets of his dove-grey suit, before translating himself like a chess piece along a diagonal square. 'It's a fascinating subject, you know. The title is misleading, a box-office concession. The film is really Kanin's final examination of the Orpheus legend. The whole question of the illusions which exist in any relationship to make it workable, and of the barriers we willingly accept to hide ourselves from each other. How much reality can we stand?'

We reached one of the huge hoardings that stretched away among the reefs. Jutting upwards from the spires and grottoes, it seemed to shut off half the sky, and already I felt the atmosphere of shifting illusion and reality that enclosed the whole of Lagoon West, the subtle displacement of time and space. The great hoardings seemed to be both barriers and corridors. Leading away radially from the house and breaking up the landscape, of which they revealed sudden unrelated glimpses, they introduced a curiously appealing element of uncertainty into the placid afternoon, an impression reinforced by the emptiness and enigmatic presence of the summer-house.

Returning to Kanin's conference, we followed the edge of the terrace. Here the sand had drifted over the balustrade which divided the public sector of the grounds from the private. Looking up at the lines of balconies on the south face, I noticed someone standing in the shadows below one of the awnings.

Something flickered brightly from the ground at my feet. Momentarily reflecting the full disc of the sun, like a polished node of sapphire or quartz, the light flashed among the dust, then seemed to dart sideways below the balustrade.

'My God, a scorpion!' I pointed to the insect crouching away from us, the red scythe of its tail beckoning slowly. I assumed that the thickened chitin of the headpiece was reflecting the light, and then saw that a small faceted stone had been set into the skull. As it edged forward into the light, the jewel burned in the sun like an incandescent crystal.

Charles Van Stratten stepped past me. Almost pushing me aside, he glanced towards the shuttered balconies. He feinted deftly with one foot at the scorpion, and before the insect could recover had stamped it into the dust.

'Right, Paul,' he said in a firm voice. 'I think your suggested designs are excellent. You've caught the spirit of the whole thing exactly, as I knew you would.' Buttoning his jacket he made off towards the film unit, barely pausing to scrape the damp husk of the crushed carapace from his shoe.

I caught up with him. 'That scorpion was jewelled,' I said. 'There was a diamond, or zircon, inset in the head.'

He waved impatiently and then took a pair of large sunglasses from his breast pocket. Masked, his face seemed harder and more autocratic, reminding me of our true relationship.

'An illusion, Paul,' he said. 'Some of the insects here are dangerous. You must be more careful.' His point made, he relaxed and flashed me his most winning smile.

Rejoining Tony and Raymond, I watched Charles Van Stratten walk off through the technicians and stores staff. His stride was noticeably more purposive, and he brushed aside an assistant producer without bothering to turn his head.

'Well, Paul.' Raymond greeted me expansively. 'There's no script, no star, no film in the cameras, and no one has the faintest idea what he's supposed to be doing. But there are a million square feet of murals waiting to be painted. It all seems perfectly straightforward.'

I looked back across the terrace to where we had seen the scorpion. 'I suppose it is,' I said.

Somewhere in the dust a jewel glittered brightly.

Two days later I saw another of the jewelled insects.

Suppressing my doubts about Charles Van Stratten, I was busy preparing my designs for the hoardings. Although Raymond's first estimate of a million square feet was exaggerated – less than a tenth of this would be needed – the amount of work and materials required was substantial. In effect I was about to do nothing less than repaint the entire desert.

Each morning I went out to Lagoon West and worked among the reefs, adapting the designs to the contours and colours of the terrain. Most of the time I was alone in the hot sun. After the initial frenzy of activity Orpheus Productions had lost momentum. Kanin had gone off to a film festival at Red Beach and most of the assistant producers and writers had retired to the swimming pool at the Hotel Neptune in Vermilion Sands. Those who remained behind at Lagoon West were now sitting half asleep under the coloured umbrellas erected around the mobile cocktail bar.

The only sign of movement came from Charles Van Stratten, roving tirelessly in his white suit among the reefs and sand spires. Now and then I would hear one of the sonic sculptures on the upper balconies of the summer-house change its note, and turn to see him standing beside it. His sonic profile evoked a strange, soft sequence of chords, interwoven by sharper, almost plaintive notes that drifted away across the still afternoon air towards the labyrinth of great hoardings that now surrounded the summer-house. All day he would wander among them, pacing out the perimeters and diagonals as if trying to square the circle of some private enigma, the director of a Wagnerian psychodrama that would involve us all in its cathartic unfolding.

Shortly after noon, when an intense pall of yellow light lay over the desert, dissolving the colours in its glazed mantle, I sat down on the balustrade, waiting for the meridian to pass. The sand-lake shimmered in the thermal gradients like an immense pool of sluggish wax. A few yards away something flickered in the bright sand, a familiar flare of light. Shielding my eyes, I found the source, the diminutive Promethean bearer of this brilliant corona. The spider, a Black Widow, approached on its stilted legs, a blaze of staccato signals pouring from its crown. It stopped and pivoted, revealing the large sapphire inset into its head.

More points of light flickered. Within a moment the entire terrace sparkled with jewelled light. Quickly I counted a score of the insects – turquoised scorpions, a purple mantis with a giant topaz like a tiered crown, and more than a dozen spiders, pinpoints of emerald and sapphire light lancing from their heads.

Above them, hidden in the shadows among the bougainvillaea

on her balcony, a tall white-faced figure in a blue gown looked down at me.

I stepped over the balustrade, carefully avoiding the motionless insects. Separated from the remainder of the terrace by the west wing of the summer-house, I had entered a new zone, where the bonelike pillars of the loggia, the glimmering surface of the sand-lake, and the jewelled insects enclosed me in a sudden empty limbo.

For a few moments I stood below the balcony from which the insects had emerged, still watched by this strange sybilline figure presiding over her private world. I felt that I had strayed across the margins of a dream, on to an internal landscape of the psyche projected upon the sun-filled terraces around me.

But before I could call to her, footsteps grated softly in the loggia. A dark-haired man of about fifty, with a closed, expressionless face, stood among the columns, his black suit neatly buttoned. He looked down at me with the impassive eyes of a funeral director.

The shutters withdrew upon the balcony, and the jewelled insects returned from their foray. Surrounding me, their brilliant crowns glittered with diamond hardness.

Each afternoon, as I returned from the reefs with my sketch pad, I would see the jewelled insects moving in the sunlight beside the lake, while their blue-robed mistress, the haunted Venus of Lagoon West, watched them from her balcony. Despite the frequency of her appearances, Charles Van Stratten made no attempt to explain her presence. His elaborate preparations for the filming of *Aphrodite* 80 almost complete, he became more and more preoccupied.

An outline scenario had been agreed on. To my surprise the first scene was to be played on the lake terrace, and would take the form of a shadow ballet, for which I painted a series of screens to be moved about like chess pieces. Each was about twelve feet high, a large canvas mounted on a wooden trestle, representing one of the zodiac signs. Like the protagonist of *The Cabinet of Dr Caligari*, trapped in a labyrinth of tilting walls, the Orphic hero of

Aphrodite 80 would appear searching for his lost Eurydice among the shifting time stations.

So the screen game, which we were to play tirelessly on so many occasions, made its appearance. As I completed the last of the screens and watched a group of extras perform the first movements of the game under Charles Van Stratten's directions, I began to realize the extent to which we were all supporting players in a gigantic charade of Charles's devising.

Its real object soon became apparent.

The summer-house was deserted when I drove out to Lagoon West the next weekend, an immense canopy of silence hanging over the lake and the surrounding hills. The twelve screens stood on the terrace above the beach, their vivid, heraldic designs melting into blurred pools of turquoise and carmine which bled away in horizontal layers across the air. Someone had rearranged the screens to form a narrow spiral corridor. As I straightened them, the train of a white gown disappeared with a startled flourish among the shadows within.

Guessing the probable identity of this pale and nervous intruder, I stepped quietly into the corridor. I pushed back one of the screens, a large Scorpio in royal purple, and suddenly found myself in the centre of the maze, little more than an arm's length from the strange figure I had seen on the balcony. For a moment she failed to notice me. Her exquisite white face, like a marble mask, veined by a faint shadow of violet that seemed like a delicate interior rosework, was raised to the canopy of sunlight which cut across the upper edges of the screens. She wore a long beach-robe, with a flared hood that enclosed her head like a protective bower.

One of the jewelled insects nestled on a fold above her neck. There was a curious glacé immobility about her face, investing the white skin with an almost sepulchral quality, the soft down which covered it like grave's dust.

'Who –?' Startled, she stepped back. The insects scattered at her feet, winking on the floor like a jewelled carpet. She stared at me in surprise, drawing the hood of her gown around her face like an exotic flower withdrawing into its foliage. Conscious of the protective circle of insects, she lifted her chin and composed herself.

'I'm sorry to interrupt you,' I said. 'I didn't realize there was anyone here. I'm flattered that you like the screens.'

The autocratic chin lowered fractionally, and her head, with its swirl of blue hair, emerged from the hood. '*You* painted these?' she confirmed. 'I thought they were Dr Gruber's . . .' She broke off, tired or bored by the effort of translating her thoughts into speech.

'They're for Charles Van Stratten's film,' I explained. '*Aphrodite 80*. The film about Orpheus he's making here.' I added: 'You must ask him to give you a part. You'd be a great adornment.'

'A film?' Her voice cut across mine. 'Listen. Are you sure they are for this film? It's important that I know –'

'Quite sure.' Already I was beginning to find her exhausting. Talking to her was like walking across a floor composed of blocks of varying heights, an analogy reinforced by the squares of the terrace, into which her presence had let another random dimension. 'They're going to film one of the scenes here. Of course,' I volunteered when she greeted this news with a frown, 'you're free to play with the screens. In fact, if you like, I'll paint some for you.'

'Will you?' From the speed of the response I could see that I had at last penetrated to the centre of her attention. 'Can you start today? Paint as many as you can, just like these. Don't change the designs.' She gazed around at the zodiacal symbols looming from the shadows like the murals painted in dust and blood on the walls of a Toltec funeral corridor. 'They're wonderfully alive, sometimes I think they're even more real than Dr Gruber. Though –' here she faltered '– I don't know how I'll pay you. You see, they don't give me any money.' She smiled at me like an anxious child, then brightened suddenly. She knelt down and picked one of the jewelled scorpions from the floor. 'Would you like one of these?' The flickering insect, with its brilliant ruby crown, tottered unsteadily on her white palm.

Footsteps approached, the firm rap of leather on marble. 'They may be rehearsing today,' I said. 'Why don't you watch? I'll take you on a tour of the sets.'

As I started to pull back the screens I felt the long fingers of her hand on my arm. A mood of acute agitation had come over her.

'Relax,' I said. 'I'll tell them to go away. Don't worry, they won't spoil your game.'

'No! Listen, please!' The insects scattered and darted as the outer circle of screens was pulled back. In a few seconds the whole world of illusion was dismantled and exposed to the hot sunlight.

Behind the Scorpio appeared the watchful face of the dark-suited man. A smile played like a snake on his lips.

'Ah, Miss Emerelda,' he greeted her in a purring voice. 'I think you should come indoors. The afternoon heat is intense and you tire very easily.'

The insects retreated from his black patent shoes. Looking into his eyes, I caught a glimpse of deep reserves of patience, like that of an experienced nurse used to the fractious moods and uncertainties of a chronic invalid.

'Not now,' Emerelda insisted. 'I'll come in a few moments.'

'I've just been describing the screens,' I explained.

'So I gather, Mr Golding,' he rejoined evenly. 'Miss Emerelda,' he called.

For a moment they appeared to have reached deadlock. Emerelda, the jewelled insects at her feet, stood beside me, her hand on my arm, while her guardian waited, the same thin smile on his lips. More footsteps approached. The remaining screens were pushed back and the plump, well-talcumed figure of Charles Van Stratten appeared, his urbane voice raised in greeting.

'What's this – a story conference?' he asked jocularly. He broke off when he saw Emerelda and her guardian. 'Dr Gruber? What's going – Emerelda my dear?'

Smoothly, Dr Gruber interjected. 'Good afternoon, sir. Miss Garland is about to return to her room.'

'Good, good,' Charles exclaimed. For the first time I had known him he seemed unsure of himself. He made a tentative approach to Emerelda, who was staring at him fixedly. She drew her robe around her and stepped quickly through the screens. Charles moved forwards, uncertain whether to follow her.

'Thank you, doctor,' he muttered. There was a flash of patent leather heels, and Charles and I were alone among the screens. On the floor at our feet was a single jewelled mantis. Without thinking, Charles bent down to pick it up, but the insect snapped at him. He withdrew his fingers with a wan smile, as if accepting the finality of Emerelda's departure.

Recognizing me with an effort, Charles pulled himself together. 'Well, Paul, I'm glad you and Emerelda were getting on so well. I knew you'd make an excellent job of the screens.'

We walked out into the sunlight. After a pause he said, 'That is Emerelda Garland; she's lived here since mother died. It was a tragic experience, Dr Gruber thinks she may never recover.'

'He's her doctor?'

Charles nodded. 'One of the best I could find. For some reason Emerelda feels herself responsible for mother's death. She's refused to leave here.'

I pointed to the screens. 'Do you think they help?'

'Of course. Why do you suppose we're here at all?' He lowered his voice, although Lagoon West was deserted. 'Don't tell Kanin yet, but you've just met the star of *Aphrodite 80*.'

'What?' Incredulously, I stopped. 'Emerelda? Do you mean that she's going to play –?'

'Eurydice.' Charles nodded. 'Who better?'

'But Charles, she's . . .' I searched for a discreet term.

'That's exactly the point. Believe me, Paul,' – here Charles smiled at me with an expression of surprising canniness – 'this film is not as abstract as Kanin thinks. In fact, its sole purpose is therapeutic. You see, Emerelda was once a minor film actress, I'm convinced the camera crews and sets will help to carry her back to the past, to the period before her appalling shock. It's the only way left, a sort of total psychodrama. The choice of theme, the Orpheus legend and its associations, fit the situation exactly – I see myself as a latter-day Orpheus trying to rescue my Eurydice from Dr Gruber's hell.' He smiled bleakly, as if aware of the slenderness of the analogy and its faint hopes. 'Emerelda's withdrawn completely into her private world, spends all her time inlaying these insects with her jewels. With luck the screens will lead her out into the rest of this synthetic landscape. After all, if she knows that everything around her is unreal she'll cease to fear it.'

'But can't you simply move her physically from Lagoon West?' I asked. 'Perhaps Gruber is the wrong doctor for her. I can't understand why you've kept her here all these years.'

'I haven't kept her, Paul,' he said earnestly. 'She's clung to this place and its nightmare memories. Now she even refuses to let me come near her.'

We parted and he walked away among the deserted dunes. In the background the great hoardings I had designed shut out the distant reefs and mesas. Huge blocks of colour had been sprayed on to the designs, superimposing a new landscape upon the desert. The geometric forms loomed and wavered in the haze, like the shifting symbols of a beckoning dream.

As I watched Charles disappear, I felt a sudden sense of pity for his subtle but naive determination. Wondering whether to warn him of his almost certain failure, I rubbed the raw bruises on my arm. While she started at him, Emerelda's fingers had clasped my arm with unmistakable fierceness, her sharp nails locked together like a clamp of daggers.

So, each afternoon, we began to play the screen game, moving the zodiacal emblems to and fro across the terrace. As I sat on the balustrade and watched Emerelda Garland's first tentative approaches, I wondered how far all of us were becoming ensnared by Charles Van Stratten, by the painted desert and the sculpture singing from the aerial terraces of the summer-house. Into all this Emerelda Garland had now emerged, like a beautiful but nervous wraith. First she would slip among the screens as they gathered below her balcony, and then, hidden behind the large Virgo at their centre, would move across the floor towards the lake, enclosed by the shifting pattern of screens.

Once I left my seat beside Charles and joined the game.

Gradually I manœuvred my screen, a small Sagittarius, into the centre of the maze where I found Emerelda in a narrow shifting cubicle, swaying from side to side as if entranced by the rhythm of the game, the insects scattered at her feet. When I approached she clasped my hand and ran away down a corridor, her gown falling loosely around her bare shoulders. As the screens once more reached the summer-house, she gathered her train in one hand and disappeared among the columns of the loggia.

Walking back to Charles, I found a jewelled mantis nestling like a brooch on the lapel of my jacket, its crown of amethyst melting in the fading sunlight.

'She's coming out, Paul,' Charles said. 'Already she's accepted the screens, soon she'll be able to leave them.' He frowned at the jewelled mantis on my palm. 'A present from Emerelda. Rather two-edged, I think, those stings are dangerous. Still, she's grateful to you, Paul, as I am. Now I know that only the artist can create an absolute reality. Perhaps you should paint a few more screens.'

'Gladly, Charles, if you're sure that ...'

But Charles merely nodded to himself and walked away towards the film crew.

During the next days I painted several new screens, duplicating the zodiacal emblems, so that each afternoon the game became progressively slower and more intricate, the thirty screens forming a multiple labyrinth. For a few minutes, at the climax of the game, I would find Emerelda in the dark centre with the screens jostling and tilting around her, the sculpture on the roof hooting in the narrow interval of open sky.

'Why don't you join the game?' I asked Charles. After his earlier elation he was becoming impatient. Each evening as he drove back to Ciraquito the plume of dust behind his speeding Maserati would rise progressively higher into the pale air. He had lost interest in *Aphrodite 80*. Fortunately Kanin had found that the painted desert of Lagoon West could not be reproduced by any existing colour process, and the film was now being shot from models in a rented studio at Red Beach. 'Perhaps if Emerelda saw you in the maze ...'

'No, no.' Charles shook his head categorically, then stood up and paced about. 'Paul, I'm less sure of this now.'

Unknown to him, I had painted a dozen more screens. Early that morning I had hidden them among the others on the terrace.

Three nights later, tired of conducting my courtship of Emerelda Garland within a painted maze, I drove out to Lagoon West, climbing through the darkened hills whose contorted forms reared in the swinging headlamps like the smoke clouds of some sunken hell. In the distance, beside the lake, the angular terraces of the summer-house hung in the grey opaque air, as if suspended by invisible wires from the indigo clouds which stretched like velvet towards the few faint lights along the beach two miles away.

The sculptures on the upper balconies were almost silent, and I moved past them carefully, drawing only a few muted chords from them, the faint sounds carried from one statue to the next to the roof of the summer-house and then lost on the midnight air.

From the loggia I looked down at the labyrinth of screens, and at the jewelled insects scattered across the terrace, sparkling on the dark marble like the reflection of a star field.

I found Emerelda Garland among the screens, her white face an oval halo in the shadows, almost naked in a silk gown like a veil of moonlight. She was leaning against a huge Taurus with her pale arms outstretched at her sides, like Europa supplicant before the bull, the luminous spectres of the zodiac guard surrounding her. Without moving her head, she watched me approach and take her hands. Her blue hair swirled in the dark wind as we moved through the screens and crossed the staircase into the summer-house. The expression on her face, whose porcelain planes reflected the turquoise light of her eyes, was one of almost terrifying calm, as if she were moving through some inner dreamscape of the psyche with the confidence of a sleepwalker. My arm around her waist, I guided her up the steps to her suite, realizing that I was less her lover than the architect of her fantasies. For a moment the ambiguous nature of my role, and the questionable morality of abducting a beautiful but insane woman, made me hesitate.

We had reached the inner balcony which ringed the central hall of the summer-house. Below us a large sonic-sculpture emitted a tense nervous pulse, as if roused from its midnight silence by my hesitant step.

'Wait!' I pulled Emerelda back from the next flight of stairs, rousing her from her self-hypnotic torpor. 'Up there!'

A silent figure in a dark suit stood at the rail outside the door of Emerelda's suite, the downward inclination of his head clearly perceptible.

'Oh, my God!' With both hands Emerelda clung tightly to my arm, her smooth face seized by a rictus of horror and anticipation. 'She's there ... for heaven's sake, Paul, take me –'

'It's Gruber!' I snapped. 'Dr Gruber! Emerelda!'

As we recrossed the entrance the train of Emerelda's gown drew a discordant wail from the statue. In the moonlight the insects still flickered like a carpet of diamonds. I held her shoulders, trying to revive her.

'Emerelda! We'll leave here – take you away from Lagoon West and this insane place.' I pointed to my car, parked by the beach among the dunes. 'We'll go to Vermilion Sands or Red Beach, you'll be able to forget Dr Gruber for ever.'

We hurried towards the car, Emerelda's gown gathering up the insects as we swept past them. I heard her short cry in the moonlight and she tore away from me. I stumbled among the flickering insects. From my knees I saw her disappear into the screens.

For the next ten minutes, as I watched from the darkness by the beach, the jewelled insects moved towards her across the terrace, their last light fading like a vanishing night river.

I walked back to my car, and a quiet, white-suited figure appeared among the dunes and waited for me in the cool amber air, hands deep in his jacket pockets.

'You're a better painter than you know,' Charles said when I took my seat behind the wheel. 'On the last two nights she has made the same escape from me.'

He stared reflectively from the window as we drove back to Ciraquito, the sculptures in the canyon keening behind us like banshees.

The next afternoon, as I guessed, Charles Van Stratten at last played the screen game. He arrived shortly after the game had begun, walking through the throng of extras and cameramen near the car park, hands still thrust deep into the pockets of his white suit as if his sudden appearance among the dunes the previous night and his present arrival were continuous in time. He stopped by the balustrade on the opposite side of the terrace, where I sat with Tony Sapphire and Raymond Mayo, and stared pensively at the slow shuttling movements of the game, his grey eyes hidden below their blond brows.

By now there were so many screens in the game – over forty (I had secretly added more in an attempt to save Emerelda) – that most of the movement was confined to the centre of the group, as if emphasizing the self-immolated nature of the ritual. What had begun as a pleasant divertimento, a picturesque introduction to *Aphrodite 80*, had degenerated into a macabre charade, transforming the terrace into the exercise area of a nightmare.

Discouraged or bored by the slowness of the game, one by one the extras taking part began to drop out, sitting down on the balustrade beside Charles. Eventually only Emerelda was left – in my mind I could see her gliding in and out of the nexus of corridors, protected by the zodiacal deities I had painted – and now and then one of the screens in the centre would tilt slightly.

'You've designed a wonderful trap for her, Paul,' Raymond Mayo mused. 'A cardboard asylum.'

'It was Van Stratten's suggestion. We thought they might help her.'

Somewhere, down by the beach, a sculpture had begun to play, and its plaintive voice echoed over our heads. Several of the older sculptures whose sonic cores had corroded had been broken up and left on the beach, where they had taken root again. When the heat gradients roused them to life they would emit a brief strangled music, fractured parodies of their former song.

'Paul!' Tony Sapphire pointed across the terrace. 'What's going on? There's something –'

Fifty yards from us, Charles Van Stratten had stepped over the balustrade, and now stood out on one of the black marble squares, hands loosely at his sides, like a single chess piece opposing the massed array of the screens. Everyone else had gone, and the three of us were now alone with Charles and the hidden occupant of the screens.

The harsh song of the rogue sculpture still pierced the air. Two miles away, through the haze which partly obscured the distant shore, the beach-houses jutted among the dunes, and the fused surface of the lake, in which so many objects were embedded, seams of jade and obsidian, was like a segment of embalmed time, from which the music of the sculpture was a slowly expiring leak. The heat over the vermilion surface was like molten quartz, stirring sluggishly to reveal the distant mesas and reefs.

The haze cleared and the spires of the sand reefs seemed to loom forward, their red barbs clawing towards us through the air. The light drove through the opaque surface of the lake, illuminating its fossilized veins, and the threnody of the dying sculpture lifted to a climax.

'Emerelda!'

As we stood up, roused by his shout, Charles Van Stratten was running across the terrace. 'Emerelda!'

Before we could move he began to pull back the screens, toppling them backwards on to the ground. Within a few moments the terrace was a mêlée of tearing canvas and collapsing trestles, the huge emblems flung left and right out of his path like disintegrating floats at the end of a carnival.

Only when the original nucleus of half a dozen screens was left did he pause, hands on hips.

'Emerelda!' he shouted thickly.

Raymond turned to me. 'Paul, stop him, for heaven's sake!'

Striding forward, Charles pulled back the last of the screens.

We had a sudden glimpse of Emerelda Garland retreating from the inrush of sunlight, her white gown flared around her like the broken wings of some enormous bird. Then, with an explosive flash, a brilliant vortex of light erupted from the floor at Emerelda's feet, a cloud of jewelled spiders and scorpions rose through the air and engulfed Charles Van Stratten.

Hands raised helplessly to shield his head, he raced across the terrace, the armada of jewelled insects pursuing him, spinning and diving on to his head. Just before he disappeared among the dunes by the beach, we saw him for a last terrifying moment, clawing helplessly at the jewelled helmet stitched into his face and shoulders. His voice rang out, a sustained cry on the note of the dying sculptures, lost on the stinging flight of the insects.

We found him among the sculptures, face downwards in the hot sand, the fabric of his white suit lacerated by a hundred punctures. Around him were scattered the jewels and crushed bodies of the insects he had killed, their knotted legs and mandibles like abstract ideograms, the sapphires and zircons dissolving in the light.

His swollen hands were filled with the jewels. The cloud of insects returned to the summer-house, where Dr Gruber's black-suited figure was silhouetted against the sky, poised on the white ledge like some minatory bird of nightmare. The only sounds came from the sculptures, which had picked up Charles Van Stratten's last cry and incorporated it into their own self-requiem.

'... "*She ... killed*" ...' Raymond stopped, shaking his head in amazement. 'Paul, can you hear them, the words are unmistakable.'

Stepping through the metal barbs of the sculpture, I knelt beside Charles, watching as one of the jewelled scorpions crawled from below his chin and scuttled away across the sand.

'Not him,' I said. 'What he was shouting was "*She killed – Mrs Van Stratten.*" The old dowager, his mother. That's the real clue to this fantastic menage. Last night, when we saw Gruber by the rail outside her room – I realize now that was where the old harridan was standing when Emerelda pushed her. For years Charles kept her alone with her guilt here, probably afraid that he might be incriminated if the truth emerged – perhaps he was more responsible than we imagine. What he failed to realize was that Emerelda had lived so long with her guilt that she'd confused it with the person of Charles himself. Killing him was her only release –'

I broke off to find that Raymond and Tony had gone and were already half way back to the terrace. There was the distant sound of raised voices as members of the film company approached, and whistles shrilled above the exhaust of cars.

The bulky figure of Kanin came through the dunes, flanked by a trio of assistant producers. Their incredulous faces gaped at the prostrate body. The voices of the sculptures faded for the last time, carrying with them into the depths of the fossil lake the final plaintive cry of Charles Van Stratten.

A year later, after Orpheus Productions had left Lagoon West and the scandal surrounding Charles's death had subsided, we drove out again to the summer-house. It was one of those dull featureless afternoons when the desert is without lustre, the distant hills illuminated by brief flashes of light, and the great summer-house seemed drab and lifeless. The servants and Dr Gruber had left, and the estate was beginning to run down. Sand covered long stretches of the roadway, and the dunes rolled across the open terraces, toppling the sculptures. These were silent now, and the sepulchral emptiness was only broken by the hidden presence of Emerelda Garland.

We found the screens where they had been left, and on an impulse spent the first afternoon digging them out of the sand. Those that had rotted in the sunlight we burned in a pyre on the beach, and perhaps the ascending plumes of purple and carmine smoke first brought our presence to Emerelda. The next afternoon, as we played the screen game, I was conscious of her watching us, and saw a gleam of her blue gown among the shadows.

However, although we played each afternoon throughout the summer, she never joined us, despite the new screens I painted and added to the group. Only on the night I visited Lagoon West alone did she come down, but I could hear the voices of the sculptures calling again and fled at the sight of her white face.

By some acoustic freak, the dead sculptures along the beach had revived themselves, and once again I heard the faint haunted echoes of Charles Van Stratten's last cry before he was killed by the jewelled insects. All over the deserted summer-house the low refrain was taken up by the statues, echoing through the empty galleries and across the moonlit terraces, carried away to the mouths of the sand reefs, the last dark music of the painted night.

1963

TIME OF PASSAGE

Sunlight spilled among the flowers and tombstones, turning the cemetery into a bright garden of sculpture. Like two large gaunt crows, the gravediggers leaned on their spades between the marble angels, their shadows arching across the smooth white flank of one of the recent graves.

The gilt lettering was still fresh and untarnished.

JAMES FALKMAN
1963–1901
'The End is but the Beginning'

Leisurely they began to pare back the crisp turf, then dismantled the headstone and swathed it in a canvas sheet, laying it behind the graves in the next aisle. Biddle, the older of the two, a lean man in a black waistcoat, pointed to the cemetery gates, where the first mourning party approached.

'They're here. Let's get our backs into it.'

The younger man, Biddle's son, watched the small procession winding through the graves. His nostrils scented the sweet broken earth. 'They're always early,' he murmured reflectively. 'It's a strange thing, you never see them come on time.'

A clock tolled from the chapel among the cypresses. Working swiftly, they scooped out the soft earth, piling it into a neat cone at the grave's head. A few minutes later, when the sexton arrived with the principal mourners, the polished teak of the coffin was exposed, and Biddle jumped down on to the lid and scraped away the damp earth clinging to its brass rim.

The ceremony was brief and the twenty mourners, led by

Falkman's sister, a tall white-haired woman with a narrow autocratic face, leaning on her husband's arm, soon returned to the chapel. Biddle gestured to his son. They jerked the coffin out of the ground and loaded it on to a cart, strapping it down under the harness. Then they heaped the earth back into the grave and relaid the squares of turf.

As they pushed the cart back to the chapel the sunlight shone brightly among the thinning graves.

Forty-eight hours later the coffin arrived at James Falkman's large grey-stoned house on the upper slopes of Mortmere Park. The high-walled avenue was almost deserted and few people saw the hearse enter the tree-lined drive. The blinds were drawn over the windows, and huge wreaths rested among the furniture in the hall where Falkman lay motionless in his coffin on a mahogany table. Veiled by the dim light, his square strong-jawed face seemed composed and unblemished, a short lock of hair over his forehead making his expression less severe than his sister's.

A solitary beam of sunlight, finding its way through the dark sycamores which guarded the house, slowly traversed the room as the morning progressed, and shone for a few minutes upon Falkman's open eyes. Even after the beam had moved away a faint glimmer of light still remained in the pupils, like the reflection of a star glimpsed in the bottom of a dark well.

All day, helped by two of her friends, sharp-faced women in long black coats, Falkman's sister moved quietly about the house. Her quick deft hands shook the dust from the velvet curtains in the library, wound up the miniature Louis XV clock on the study desk, and reset the great barometer on the staircase. None of the women spoke to each other, but within a few hours the house was transformed, the dark wood in the hall gleaming as the first callers were admitted.

'Mr and Mrs Montefiore . . .'

'Mr and Mrs Caldwell . . .'

'Miss Evelyn Jermyn and Miss Elizabeth . . .'

'Mr Samuel Banbury . . .'

One by one nodding in acknowledgement as they were announced, the callers trooped into the hall and paused over the coffin, examining Falkman's face with discreet interest, then passed into the dining room where they were presented with a glass of port and a tray of sweetmeats. Most of them were elderly, over-dressed in the warm spring weather, one or two obviously ill at ease in the great oak-panelled house, and all unmistakably revealed the same air of hushed expectancy.

The following morning Falkman was lifted from his coffin and carried upstairs to the bedroom overlooking the drive. The winding sheet was removed from his frail body dressed in a pair of thick woollen pyjamas. He lay quietly between the cold sheets, his grey face sightless and reposed, unaware of his sister crying softly on the high-backed chair beside him. Only when Dr Markham called and put his hand on her shoulder did she contain herself, relieved to have given way to her feelings.

Almost as if this were a signal, Falkman opened his eyes. For a moment they wavered uncertainly, the pupils weak and watery. Then he gazed up at his sister's tear-marked face, his head motionless on the pillow. As she and the doctor leaned forward Falkman smiled fleetingly, his lips parting across his teeth in an expression of immense patience and understanding. Then apparently exhausted he lapsed into a deep sleep.

After securing the blinds over the windows, his sister and the doctor stepped from the room. Below, the doors closed quietly into the drive, and the house became silent. Gradually the sounds of Falkman's breathing grew more steady and filled the bedroom, overlaid by the swaying of the dark trees outside.

So James Falkman made his arrival. For the next week he lay quietly in his bedroom, his strength increasing hourly, and managed to eat his first meals prepared by his sister. She sat in the blackwood chair, her mourning habit exchanged for a grey woollen dress, examining him critically.

'Now James, you'll have to get a better appetite than that. Your poor body is completely wasted.'

Falkman pushed away the tray and let his long slim hands fall across his chest. He smiled amiably at his sister. 'Careful, Betty, or you'll turn me into a milk pudding.'

His sister briskly straightened the eiderdown. 'If you don't like my cooking, James, you can fend for yourself.'

A faint chuckle slipped between Falkman's lips. 'Thank you for telling me, Betty, I fully intend to.'

He lay back, smiling weakly to himself as his sister stalked out with the tray. Teasing her did him almost as much good as the meals she prepared, and he felt the blood reaching down into his cold feet. His face was still grey and flaccid, and he conserved his strength carefully, only his eyes moving as he watched the ravens alighting on the window ledge.

Gradually, as his conversations with his sister became more frequent, Falkman gained sufficient strength to sit up. He began to take a fuller interest in the world around him, watching the people in the avenue through the french windows and disputing his sister's commentary on them.

'There's Sam Banbury again,' she remarked testily as a small leprechaunlike old man hobbled past. 'Off to the Swan as usual. When's he going to get a job, I'd like to know.'

'Be more charitable, Betty. Sam's a very sensible fellow. I'd rather go to the pub than have a job.'

His sister snorted sceptically, her assessment of Falkman's character apparently at variance with this statement. 'You've got one of the finest houses in Mortmere Park,' she told him. 'I think you should be more careful with people like Sam Banbury. He's not in your class, James.'

Falkman smiled patiently at his sister. 'We're all in the same class, or have you been here so long you've forgotten, Betty.'

'We all forget,' she told him soberly. 'You will too, James. It's sad, but we're in this world now, and we must concern ourselves with it. If the church can keep the memory alive for us, so much the better. As you'll find out though, the majority of folk remember nothing. Perhaps it's a good thing.'

She grudgingly admitted the first visitors, fussing about so that Falkman could barely exchange a word with them. In fact, the visits tired him, and he could do little more than pass a few formal pleasantries. Even when Sam Banbury brought him a pipe and tobacco pouch he had to muster all his energy to thank him and had none left to prevent his sister from making off with them.

Only when the Reverend Matthews called did Falkman manage to summon together his strength, for half an hour spoke earnestly to the parson, who listened with rapt attention, interjecting a few eager questions. When the Reverend left he seemed refreshed and confident, and strode down the stairs with a gay smile at Falkman's sister.

Within three weeks Falkman was out of bed, and managed to hobble downstairs and inspect the house and garden. His sister protested, dogging his slow painful footsteps with sharp reminders of his feebleness, but Falkman ignored her. He found his way to the conservatory, and leaned against one of the ornamental columns, his nervous fingers feeling the leaves of the miniature trees, the scent of flowers flushing his face. Outside, in the grounds, he examined everything around him, as if comparing it with some Elysian paradise in his mind.

He was walking back to the house when he twisted his ankle sharply in the crazy paving. Before he could cry for help he had fallen headlong across the hard stone.

'James Falkman will you never listen?' his sister protested, as she helped him across the terrace. 'I warned you to stay in bed!'

Reaching the lounge, Falkman sat down thankfully in an armchair, reassembling his stunned limbs. 'Quiet, Betty, do you mind,' he admonished his sister when his breath returned. 'I'm still here, and I'm perfectly well.'

He had stated no more than the truth. After the accident he began to recover spectacularly, his progress toward complete health accelerating without a break, as if the tumble had freed him from the lingering fatigue and discomfort of the previous weeks. His step became brisk and lively, his complexion brightened, a soft pink glow filling out his cheeks, and he moved busily around the house.

A month afterwards his sister returned to her own home, acknowledging his ability to look after himself, and her place was taken by the housekeeper. After re-establishing himself in the house, Falkman became increasingly interested in the world outside. He hired a comfortable car and chauffeur, and spent most of the winter afternoons and evenings at his club; soon he found himself the centre of a wide circle of acquaintances. He became the chairman of a number of charitable committees, where his good humour, tolerance and shrewd judgement made him well respected. He now held himself erect, his grey hair sprouting luxuriantly, here and there touched by black flecks, jaw jutting firmly from sun-tanned cheeks.

Every Sunday he attended the morning and evening services at his church, where he owned a private pew, and was somewhat saddened to see that only the older people formed the congregation. However, he himself found that the picture painted by the liturgy became increasingly detached from his own memories as the latter faded, too soon became a meaningless charade that he could accept only by an act of faith.

A few years later, when he became increasingly restless, he decided to accept the offer of a partnership in a leading firm of stockbrokers.

Many of his acquaintances at the club were also finding jobs, forsaking the placid routines of smoking room and conservatory garden. Harold Caldwell, one of his closest friends, was appointed Professor of History at the university, and Sam Banbury became manager of the Swan Hotel.

The ceremony on Falkman's first day at the stock exchange was dignified and impressive. Three junior men also joining the firm were introduced to the assembled staff by the senior partner, Mr Montefiore, and each presented with a gold watch to symbolize the years he would spend with the firm. Falkman received an embossed silver cigar case and was loudly applauded.

For the next five years Falkman threw himself wholeheartedly into his work, growing more extrovert and aggressive as his appetite for the material pleasures of life increased. He became a keen golfer; then, as the exercise strengthened his physique, played his first games of tennis. An influential member of the business community, his days passed in a pleasant round of conferences and dinner parties. He no longer attended the church, but instead spent his Sundays escorting the more attractive of his lady acquaintances to the race tracks and regattas.

He found it all the more surprising, therefore when a persistent mood of dejection began to haunt him. Although without any apparent source, this deepened slowly, and he found himself reluctant to leave his house in the evenings. He resigned from his committees and no longer visited his club. At the stock exchange he felt permanently distracted, and would stand for hours by the window, staring down at the traffic.

Finally, when his grasp of the business began to slip, Mr Montefiore suggested that he go on indefinite leave.

For a week Falkman listlessly paced around the huge empty house. Sam Banbury frequently called to see him, but Falkman's sense of grief was beyond any help. He drew the blinds over the windows and changed into a black tie and suit, sat blankly in the darkened library.

At last, when his depression had reached its lowest ebb, he went to the cemetery to collect his wife.

After the congregation had dispersed, Falkman paused outside the vestry to tip the gravedigger, Biddle, and compliment him on his young son, a cherubic three-year-old who was playing among the headstones. Then he rode back to Mortmere Park in the car following the hearse, the remainder of the cortege behind him.

'A grand turnout, James,' his sister told him approvingly. 'Twenty cars altogether, not including the private ones.'

Falkman thanked her, his eyes examining his sister with critical detachment. In the fifteen years he had known her she had coarsened perceptibly, her voice roughening and her gestures becoming broader. A distinct social gap had always separated them, a division which Falkman had accepted charitably, but it was now widening markedly. Her husband's business had recently begun to fail, and her thoughts had turned almost exclusively to the subjects of money and social prestige.

As Falkman congratulated himself on his good sense and success, a curious premonition, indistinct but nonetheless disturbing, stirred through his mind.

Like Falkman himself fifteen years earlier, his wife first lay in her coffin in the hall, the heavy wreaths transforming it into a dark olive-green bower. Behind the lowered blinds the air was dim and stifled, and with her rich red hair flaring off her forehead, and her broad cheeks and full lips, his wife seemed to Falkman like some sleeping enchantress in a magical arbour. He gripped the silver foot rail of the coffin and stared at her mindlessly, aware of his sister shepherding the guests to the port and whisky. He traced with his eyes the exquisite dips and hollows around his wife's neck and chin, the white skin sweeping smoothly to her strong shoulders. The next day, when she was carried upstairs, her presence filled the bedroom. All afternoon he sat beside her, waiting patiently for her to wake.

Shortly after five o'clock, in the few minutes of light left before the dusk descended, when the air hung motionlessly under the trees in the garden, a faint echo of life moved across her face. Her eyes cleared and then focused on the ceiling.

Breathlessly, Falkman leaned forward and took one of her cold hands. Far within, the pulse sounded faintly.

'Marion,' he whispered.

Her head inclined slightly, lips parting in a weak smile. For several moments she gazed serenely at her husband.

'Hello, Jamie.'

His wife's arrival completely rejuvenated Falkman. A devoted husband, he was soon completely immersed in their life together. As she recovered from the long illness after her arrival, Falkman entered the prime of his life. His grey hair became sleek and black, his face grew thicker, the chin firmer and stronger. He returned to the stock exchange, taking up his job with renewed interest.

He and Marion made a handsome couple. At intervals they would visit the cemetery and join in the service celebrating the arrival of another of their friends, but these became less frequent. Other parties continually visited the cemetery, thinning the ranks of graves, and large areas had reverted to open lawn as the coffins were withdrawn and the tombstones removed. The firm of undertakers near the cemetery which was responsible for notifying mourning relatives closed down and was sold. Finally, after the gravedigger, Biddle, recovered his own wife from the last of the graves the cemetery was converted into a children's playground.

The years of their marriage were Falkman's happiest. With each successive summer Marion became slimmer and more youthful, her red hair a brilliant diadem that stood out among the crowds in the street when she came to see him. They would walk home arm in arm, in the summer evening pause among the willows by the river to embrace each other like lovers.

Indeed, their happiness became such a byword among their friends that over two hundred guests attended the church ceremony celebrating the long years of their marriage. As they knelt together at the altar before the priest Marion seemed to Falkman like a demure rose.

This was the last night they were to spend together. Over the years Falkman had become less interested in his work at the stock exchange, and the arrival of older and more serious men had resulted in a series of demotions for him. Many of his friends were facing similar problems. Harold Caldwell had been forced to resign his professorship and was now a junior lecturer, taking postgraduate courses to familiarize himself with the great body of new work that had been done in the previous thirty years. Sam Banbury was a waiter at the Swan Hotel.

Marion went to live with her parents, and the Falkmans' apartment, to which they had moved some years earlier after the house was closed and sold, was let to new tenants. Falkman, whose tastes had become simpler as the years passed, took a room in a hostel for young men, but he and Marion saw each other every evening. He felt increasingly restless, half conscious that his life was moving towards an inescapable focus, and often thought of giving up his job.

Marion remonstrated with him. 'But you'll lose everything you've worked for, Jamie. All those years.'

Falkman shrugged, chewing on a stem of grass as they lay in the park during one of their lunch hours. Marion was now a salesgirl in a department store.

'Perhaps, but I resent being demoted. Even Montefiore is leaving. His grandfather has just been appointed chairman.' He rolled over and put his head in her lap. 'It's so dull in that stuffy office, with all those pious old men. I'm not satisfied with it any longer.'

Marion smiled affectionately at his naïveté and enthusiasm. Falkman was now more handsome than she had ever remembered him, his sun-tanned face almost unlined.

'It's been wonderful together, Marion,' he told her on the eve of their thirtieth anniversary. 'How lucky we've been never to have a child. Do you realize that some people even have three or four? It's absolutely tragic.'

'It comes to us all, though, Jamie,' she reminded him. 'Some people say it's a very beautiful and noble experience, having a child.'

All evening he and Marion wandered round the town together, Falkman's desire for her quickened by her increasing demureness. Since she had gone to live with her parents Marion had become almost too shy to take his hand.

Then he lost her.

Walking through the market in the town centre, they were joined by two of Marion's friends, Elizabeth and Evelyn Jermyn.

'There's Sam Banbury,' Evelyn pointed out as a firework crackled from a stall on the other side of the market. 'Playing the fool as usual.' She and her sister clucked disapprovingly. Tight-mouthed and stern, they wore dark serge coats buttoned to their necks.

Distracted by Sam, Falkman wandered off a few steps, suddenly found that the three girls had walked away. Darting through the crowd, he tried to catch up with them, briefly glimpsed Marion's red hair.

He fought his way through the stalls, almost knocking over a barrow of vegetables and shouted at Sam Banbury:

'Sam! Have you seen Marion?'

Banbury pocketed his crackers and helped him to scan the crowd. For an hour they searched. Finally Sam gave up and went home, leaving Falkman to hang about the cobbled square under the dim lights when the market closed, wandering among the tinsel and litter as the stall holders packed up for home.

'Excuse me, have you seen a girl here? A girl with red hair?'
'Please, she was here this afternoon.'
'A girl ...'
'... called ...'

Stunned, he realized that he had forgotten her name.

Shortly afterwards, Falkman gave up his job and went to live with his parents. Their small red-brick house was on the opposite side of the town; between the crowded chimney pots he could sometimes see the distant slopes of Mortmere Park. His life now began a less carefree phase, as most of his energy went into helping his mother and looking after his sister Betty. By comparison with his own house his parents' home was bleak and uncomfortable, altogether alien to everything Falkman had previously known. Although kind and respectable people, his parents' lives were circumscribed by their lack of success or education. They had no interest in music or the theatre, and Falkman found his mind beginning to dull and coarsen.

His father was openly critical of him for leaving his job, but the hostility between them gradually subsided as he more and more began to dominate Falkman, restricting his freedom and reducing his pocket money, even warning him not to play with certain of his friends. In fact, going to live with his parents had taken Falkman into an entirely new world.

By the time he began to go to school Falkman had completely forgotten his past life, his memories of Marion and the great house where they had lived surrounded by servants altogether obliterated.

During his first term at school he was in a class with the older boys, whom the teachers treated as equals, but like his parents they began to extend their influence over him as the years passed.

At times Falkman rebelled against this attempt to suppress his own personality, but at last they entirely dominated him, controlling his activities and moulding his thoughts and speech. The whole process of education, he dimly realized, was designed to prepare him for the strange twilight world of his earliest childhood. It deliberately eliminated every trace of sophistication, breaking down, with its constant repetitions and brain-splitting exercises, all his knowledge of language and mathematics, substituting for them a collection of meaningless rhymes, and chants, and out of this constructing an artificial world of total infantilism.

At last, when the process of education had reduced him almost to the stage of an inarticulate infant, his parents intervened by removing him from the school, and the final years of his life were spent at home.

'Mama, can I sleep with you?'

Mrs Falkman looked down at the serious-faced little boy who leaned his head on her pillow. Affectionately she pinched his square jaw and then touched her husband's shoulder as he stirred. Despite the years between father and son, their two bodies were almost identical, with the same broad shoulders and broad heads, the same thick hair.

'Not today, Jamie, but soon perhaps, one day.'

The child watched his mother with wide eyes, wondering why she should be crying to herself, guessing that perhaps he had touched upon one of the taboos that had exercised such a potent fascination for all the boys at school, the mystery of their ultimate destination that remained carefully shrouded by their parents and which they themselves were no longer able to grasp.

By now he was beginning to experience the first difficulties in both walking and feeding himself. He tottered about clumsily, his small piping voice tripping over his tongue. Steadily his vocabulary diminished until he knew only his mother's name. When he could no longer stand upright she would carry him in her arms, feeding him like an elderly invalid. His mind clouded, a few constants of warmth and hunger drifting through it hazily. As long as he could, he clung to his mother.

* * *

Shortly afterward, Falkman and his mother visited the lying-in hospital for several weeks. On her return Mrs Falkman remained in bed for a few days, but gradually she began to move about more freely, slowly shedding the additional weight accumulated during her confinement.

Some nine months after she returned from the hospital, a period during which she and her husband thought continually of their son, the tragedy of his approaching death, a symbol of their own imminent separation, bringing them closer together, they went away on their honeymoon.

1964